This

Rough

Ocean

Ann Swinfen

Shakenoak Press

Cover design by JD Smith www.jdsmith-design.co.uk

This

Rough

Ocean

MORE BY THIS AUTHOR

Praise for Ann Swinfen's Novels

'an absorbing and intricate tapestry of family history and private memories … warm, generous, healing and hopeful'
VICTORIA GLENDINNING

'I very much admired the pace of the story. The changes of place and time and the echoes and repetitions – things lost and found, and meetings and partings'
PENELOPE FITZGERALD

'I enjoyed this serious, scrupulous novel … a novel of character … [and] a suspense story in which present and past mysteries are gradually explained'
JESSICA MANN, *Sunday Telegraph*

'The author … has written a powerful new tale of passion and heartbreak ... What a marvellous storyteller Ann Swinfen is – she has a wonderful ear for dialogue and she brings her characters vividly to life.'
Publishing News

'Her writing …[paints] an amazingly detailed and vibrant picture of flesh and blood human beings, not only the symbols many of them have become…but real and believable and understandable.'
HELEN BROWN, *Courier and Advertiser*

'She writes with passion and the book, her fourth, is shot through with brilliant description and scholarship...[it] is a timely reminder of the harsh realities, and the daily humiliations, of the Roman occupation of First Century Israel. You can almost smell the dust and blood.'
PETER RHODES, *Express and Star*

In Memory

of

John & Anne Swynfen

All our earlier discussions were but a fight off the shore, which makes the ensuing rough ocean the more terrible.

John Swynfen, *Letter to John Crewe, 1648*

ᚼᚼᚼᚼᚼᚼᚼᚼᚼᚼᚼ

Prologue

The end must surely be near, for the army was marching on London. Death was grown so companionable that it might take its place at any man's table, sitting down like a familiar guest in peasant hut or noble mansion. Death might ride boldly up to any man's door, or slip like a thief through any man's unlatched window. A little after dusk on the last day of November, 1648, a company of troopers rode through snowfall into a meagre hamlet some two days' journey from Westminster, their horses slithering in the half-frozen bog which, even in the best of times, was no more than a strip of dirt track through the forest. Men and horses had their gaze fixed on the gleam of a cooking fire which cast an amber rag of light from the open doorway of the first hovel across this accursed path. The men imagined they could smell meat, though in truth the battered iron cookpot contained nothing more than a thin gruel seasoned with wild garlic. The horses staggered towards a dimly recalled memory of warm stables and hay, though the hamlet possessed nothing more substantial than a ramshackle shed to shelter its one donkey and a spavined, split-hoofed mare sure to die before winter was out.

A dozen cottages huddled in the clearing hacked free over many generations from this finger of the wealden forest. The soil was poor, stony and threaded through with ancient tree roots. In spring, the ploughshare skipped along the surface, leaving the land merely scratched, and the crops were as wizened as the villagers. A few scraggy sheep grazed on the small common, whose thin grass could not sustain even a solitary cow. Troops had passed this way before, as the war heaved back and forth across England, but none had troubled to halt in such a destitute place.

A woman paused at the door of the first cottage, holding the child she had just gathered up from the ground. Her hair, thinned by poverty and hunger, framed her head like a halo of dusty cobwebs. Still as a hare scenting the hounds, she froze in terror—a young woman, the bones thrusting against her gaunt cheeks, the child keening in her arms. A man came up behind her, laying his hands on her shoulders as the soldiers reined in and surveyed them. The troopers had parted company with their officers some time ago, in unpleasant circumstances, and wasted no time now.

'Bring forth all your victuals and goods,' demanded a great red-bearded fellow who rode at their head. He drew his sword and swiped off the villager's cap with the point of it. 'And don't think that you can hide from us.'

Two of the soldiers slid from their saddles and grabbed the woman, while the rest rode amongst the cottages and rounded up the small huddle of men, women and children. Not all of them came submissively. One young man slammed his fist into the face of his captor. A knife flickered, swift as an adder. The youth's scream was cut off short as blood spurted over the soldier's boots, and women began to weep hopelessly. An old crone threw herself down beside the boy with a shrill wailing cry, but the soldier kicked her aside.

The booty the troopers hauled out on to the muddy snow was a pathetic heap of household goods. They picked out a few blankets and threadbare clothes, filled their pockets with stored nuts. As they raked the useless objects aside, their anger grew. It was the red-bearded giant who set fire to the first cottage with a brand pulled from its own hearth. The flames snapped like a hungry animal devouring the frost-dry timber, and leapt quickly from cottage to cottage. In their macabre light, the soldiers went about their usual business, leaving the corpses of the men and children where they cut them down, raping the women before slitting their throats and flinging them aside into the collapsing embers of their homes.

When the troopers resumed their ride towards London, nothing remained alive in the hamlet except the old horse, which had kicked down the shed door in terror and fled into the dark, followed by the donkey. And one small boy, overlooked in the confusion, who crouched in the crimson snow beside his mother, staring into her blank unseeing eyes.

Before the soldiers took shelter for the night in a great high-rafted barn that had once belonged to an abbey grange, they had put two more villages to fire and sword. Their saddlebags held a few heavy loaves of dark barley bread and the end of a flitch of bacon, no wider than a man's palm. The third village had yielded one treasure—a four-handled flagon of ale large enough to drown the soldiers' disappointment at the worthless haul from their evening's work. As they squatted, shivering, over the fire they had built out of broken timbers from mangers and stalls, they consoled themselves with the knowledge that London lay but a short ride ahead: London, where any man with a horse and a sword and a pistol in his belt might grow rich, and damnation to all officers and men of power.

Chapter One

John Swynfen descended the icy steps from the Palace of
Westminster after the late night sitting, during which servants had
been called to bring in candles before the vote could be held. The
north-east wind cut like steel through his doublet and breeches, which
were of fine broadcloth, but sober in hue. He paused to fill his lungs,
starved in the close, smoky atmosphere of the chamber, but the London
air, as thick with foul smells as a sick man's breath, coated his throat
and lay rancid on his tongue. He shook his head to clear it after the
hours in stale company and caught himself longing for a fresh wind
clean off the moor far to the north in Staffordshire. From under his
wide-brimmed hat, he scanned the Yard and adjacent streets with a
guarded expression. The day's business in the Commons had reached a
fairly satisfactory outcome, but he could not shake off the sense of
dread that shadowed him. Today there had been no threats of physical
violence, but its presence continued to hang in the air.

'Well, Swynfen,' said Nat Fiennes, leaping down the steps
behind him and punching him cheerfully on the shoulder, 'our friends
are not lacking in resolve. A hundred and twenty-five votes to fifty-
eight, rejecting that damnable document.'

Damnable indeed. The *Grand Remonstrance*. Henry Ireton's
latest tirade of ultimatums and conditions, purporting to be on behalf of
the army, but scarcely concealing its true design. Demanding the trial
of the king and the abolition of both monarchy and House of Lords.
Dangerous and provocative demands which divided even further the
divided House of Commons.

'*Postponing* the debate, Nat,' John said cautiously, rubbing his
hands together against the cold. 'It's not been rejected yet.' Nat, merry
and debonair, was apt to leap to an optimistic conclusion without due
cause.

'Aye, but with those odds it will be rejected, never fear.'

'The odds would have been better still, if we'd voted earlier,
before the old men went off to their beds,' said John Crewe, coming
soberly down the steps behind Fiennes. He was not a young man
himself, and was mired in mud to the knees, his cloak ripped by

4

brambles and his hat a sodden wreck, for he had come straight to the House of Commons after hours of rough riding from negotiations with the king in the Isle of Wight, without pausing to change his clothes or to take bite or sup.

John pulled his cloak about his ears, which were stinging with cold as the sleet swirled around them. His chest tightened with a sickening mixture of excitement and dread at the prospect of the days which lay ahead. For these next few days would determine the fate of England. Nat was right, of course, and so was Crewe, but that could not dispel his aching sense of foreboding. He shivered, but managed to keep his voice calm and level.

'Have you heard? The latest word is that the army has encamped tonight at Hounslow,' he said. His eyes, deep-set and dark, looked bleakly through Fiennes and Crewe. 'I fear this is but the beginning of our troubles with Ireton and all his poodles. Now that they have the army at their backs, stirred up to anger like a wasps' nest poked with a stick, they'll grow more bold.'

Crewe grunted his agreement and shrugged. 'I fear you are right.'

'It will be a long session tomorrow,' said John, 'debating the terms you bring back from your discussions, Crewe. We can expect a lively time of it, so I'll bid you goodnight.'

'God be with you,' said Crewe, touching John lightly on the arm.

'And with you.'

As his friends hurried away and John started across Palace Yard, he glimpsed a woman in a blue gown, illuminated for a moment in the light from a horn lantern hung beside a house doorway. The gown was a very particular shade of blue—the blue of a cold winter's ocean, not the blue of a warm summer's sky. That particular shade of blue always awoke a foul memory in him. A memory which he had been trying to bury since he was a boy of ten. A memory he would drive from his mind now, as he had so often done before. He turned away determinedly, heading for home.

Yet it distracted him for a moment, so that when he caught a flicker of movement under the jettied storey of a nearby building, he ignored it, continuing to walk briskly, without looking behind him. His boots crunched on the frost glazing the cobbles. In places the ice had formed treacherous sheets. Here—away from Parliament and amongst the houses—the farm-smell of horse dung in the streets and the sharp metallic tang of the frost was joined by faint wisps of meals cooking: roasted beef and hot ale spiced against the insidious cold. Unlike the desolate stretches of England's war-torn countryside, London was not yet seriously short of food, but all that would change if the murderous, unruly army fell upon the capital.

It was only as he neared his rented Westminster house along the narrow St Ann's Lane, where the leaning upper storeys almost met in embrace overhead, window eyeing window, that his attention was arrested at last by the echo of other footsteps besides his own. He swore under his breath and loosened his sword in its scabbard, but took care to give no sign of drawing it or of breaking the rhythm of his stride. The footsteps drew closer, just as they had every evening for the last three days. A shadow fell across his hand as he reached out to knock on the door to rouse the servants, and he caught the flash of a blade in the pool of light cast by the pitch torch burning beside the steps.

On each of the previous nights, although he held his own dagger ready in his left hand, his right hand on the hilt of his sword, a determined assassin could probably have slipped a knife between his ribs before he had time to turn, but it had been meant merely as a warning. A warning of murder that could be executed with ease whenever his enemies—the enemies of the peace-makers in Parliament—saw fit.

Again he felt that lurch of fear.

But he sensed that tonight it was different. Even before he whirled around, drawing his sword in one swift movement, he realised that more than one man was advancing towards him out of the sleet and the dark: there were three of them. Three sturdy fellows, strangers, with swords in their hands and a discipline to their movements which did not belong to common street thieves or footpads. These men were army trained.

John drew his short dagger with his left hand, backing towards a corner which would give him some protection on his flanks and flinging a loop of his cloak around his left arm as a makeshift shield. Prevented thus from surrounding him, the men seemed content to size him up and attack at leisure. The first of them prowled forward light-footed, a squint-eyed young fellow, feinting with his blade, with a clumsiness that showed John this man's natural weapon was not the sword. A pikeman, perhaps, or a musketeer. John lunged forward, swift to envelope the unskilful stroke in the bundle of his cloak, and chopped downwards with his own sword on the other's wrist. The man yelled, dropping the sword and stumbling backwards, leaving a bloody trail in the snow. The wrist was not severed, but he would not hold a weapon again in a hurry.

John drew back again to the wall, his breath a frosty cloud before him. Under the flicker of the street torch the red stain crept outwards across the frosty cobbles. The man was moaning with pain as he wrapped his cloak around his wounded wrist, but his fellows ignored him, their eyes fixed on John. One more act of bloodshed in these mortal times, and this one could be laid to John's account. Nausea gripped his stomach. As a boy he had been well taught in sword craft and in his younger days would have made nothing of these clumsy swordsmen, even with the odds of one against three, but he had long since forsworn the use of arms except in self defence. Had he not spent this very day arguing for the laying down of arms and the embracing of peace? A man forgets such theories when his life is at stake. Drawing breath in freezing gasps, he watched a drop of blood gather at the tip of his blade and slide down, slow as a dream, to spread out on the winter ground like a fallen poppy.

The two remaining assailants hung back for a moment—another young man, with eager, predatory eyes, and an older one, calculating and deadly. They had counted on a quick fight and superior numbers, and were in no hurry to suffer injury in someone else's cause. As he kicked the fallen sword behind him into the drifted snow, John wondered how much they had been paid. And who had paid them. The wounded man had melted away into the darkness, but the other two now advanced together.

Then they were upon him in a confusion of swords, flailing in the uncertain light which hampered thrust and counter-thrust. John yelled.

'Help! To me!'

He gulped for air, his breath tight in his throat. He was in no fit state for mortal combat.

'The Watch! To me!'

Along the curve of the lane, the houses huddled silent behind closed shutters and nothing moved.

Blade rang on blade, and a shower of sparks sprang blue into the bitter air. John staggered and slid on the icy cobbles and yelped with a sudden sharp pain in the angle between his neck and his collarbone just as he drove his own blade awkwardly into the older assailant's side below the armpit. The man gave a grunt of surprise, but did not drop his weapon. From the corner of his eye, John caught the glint of the younger man's blade just in time to duck sideways as it whizzed past his ear. His attacker was caught off balance and John punched his own dagger up into his assailant's stomach with his left hand. The fellow doubled up with a screech, folding his arms instinctively around himself. A sharp downwards blow of John's sword sent the other's sword spinning off somewhere into the darkness on the far side of the street. Clutching his stomach, the man hobbled away, cursing piteously.

There remained only the older man. Two men down and a wounded adversary should have given him some chance, but John was growing weak himself, the pain from his collarbone sending tremors down his sword arm, his grip on the hilt slackened. He was gasping for breath, and his legs were uncertain beneath him. He did not like his chances against this hardened brute. Why did no one come to his aid? In this peaceful street someone within the houses must have heard the clash of swords, the screams of pain, his cry for help.

The other man drew back slightly. Then he rushed forward, as if his greater bulk behind the sword-thrust would spit John against the wall like a chicken for roasting. He had forgotten the ice underfoot. He was almost upon John when his feet slid away from under him and he crashed down on to the cobbles with a sickening crunch of breaking bone, the tip of his sword slicing through the sleeve of John's doublet.

Had his leg been broken, he could not have escaped, but, stumbling to his feet and nursing his left arm with his right hand, the last of the assailants took to his heels away down the lane in the opposite direction from where John could now see a cluster of torches approaching.

The Watch.

'You took your time,' John called.

It was the manservant Peter who opened the door to him, after he had sent the Watch running down the street after the last of his attackers.

'God help us, Master Swynfen,' the old man gasped, staring helplessly at John's drawn sword and his ripped and bloodied doublet.

'Hush, man.' John hurried along the narrow passageway. 'Keep your voice down. I don't want to frighten your mistress or the maids. Bring warm water and rags into my study and between us we'll contrive to bandage this up. It isn't as serious as it looks.'

He threw down his cloak and eased off his doublet and shirt. The gash in his shoulder was bleeding freely, but was long rather than deep. The blade must have hit a nerve, which accounted for the numbness in his hand. That was passing now, but he was dizzy with exhaustion. Peter came with water and cloths, and made a passable job of bandaging the shoulder and upper arm. Then, as John gratefully drank a glass of strong red wine, he carried off the torn clothing and brought fresh shirt and doublet.

'You fetched these without my wife seeing?'

'Aye, master. She'm with Bess, seeing the children to bed.'

Decently dressed, John made his way upstairs to find them.

'John!' Anne's face lit with a sudden glow as he came into the room where the little girls slept with the nursemaid, Bess. He bent to kiss Anne's cheek, pinned to the spot where Dorothea clutched him about the knees. Wading through the children, he took the youngest, Mary, from the nursemaid's arms and buried his face in her topknot of fair curls, fine and soft as China silk. His children all started life fair, but their hair darkened as they grew older.

'Papa!' Ralph was tugging at his elbow. 'Ned made me a boat today. He said it's certain to float but the wind might turn it over, if the pond is rough. The merchants' ships don't overturn, even on the great seas going to the Americas, do they? Why won't my boat stay steady on the pond?'

John set Mary on her fat little feet, for even her slight weight sent an arrow of pain through his shoulder. He examined the toy boat.

'It needs weight in the keel—see, here? Perhaps we can fix a piece of lead to it. We could flatten a musket ball . . .'

'Can we do it *now*?' said Ralph. 'Please, Papa?'

John saw that Anne was pressing her lips together, holding back laughter.

'No, no,' he said hastily, 'now you must go to bed. Tomorrow, if I'm not too late home from the House. Come along, boys. I'll hear your prayers before bed.'

Afterwards, John settled to spend a quiet evening with Anne, once the children were abed, seated beside a good fire in the parlour of their cramped London house. French tapestries warmed the walls, and the firelight flickered on polished and carved wood, on imported glass and silver dishes, yet it barely provided room enough for them, this small house, with six servants and five of their seven children to be accommodated. John had rented it after his election to Parliament more than three years earlier, glad of its proximity to the Palace of Westminster, but the lack of space was constricting after Swinfen Hall.

'Most members,' John had said to his wife when he was elected, 'regard their country estates as home. They visit Westminster—without their families—only when it suits them to be in London, but I'm determined to live at the heart of affairs.' He had wanted Anne and the children with him, moving them all to Westminster when he came south to take his seat. Selfish, perhaps, but he could not endure the long Parliamentary terms without them.

As the house in St Ann's Lane fell silent about them that evening and its occupants drowsed towards bed, John sat reading an army newsletter just come from Windsor. Its smudged and careless type assured the soldiers that their friends in Parliament 'do intend this day to declare and protest against the rest and rendezvous on Hounslow Heath and so on to secure those members who declare with the Army'.

'They presumed too much, in that,' he snorted, laying the paper aside and shifting in the chair to ease his shoulder.

Anne had let her embroidery fall to her lap and was staring into the fire. She looked up, startled.

'The army faction in the House,' he explained. 'They have *not* taken themselves off to Hounslow to march with the soldiers. It's not yet come to that. They hold their places in the House, hoping to defeat those of us who are working for peace.'

'You said that the vote had gone against debating the army's *Remonstrance* tonight?'

'Aye, that's but the first step. Tomorrow we debate the Treaty negotiated by the commissioners at Newport. The king has at last agreed to all the conditions we could hope for.'

'Truly?' Anne exclaimed. 'Can he be trusted?'

John shrugged. 'Judging by his past behaviour, no. But he's caught fast now. We will bind him with the law. He's God's anointed, but God doesn't sanction his tyranny. We will have peace,' he said passionately, pounding the chair with his fist, and then regretting it as pain stabbed up his arm. 'We *must* have peace, before our poor land bleeds to death, but we must have it on terms that ensure men's future, safe from the tyranny of bishop or king.'

'And what of the tyranny of the army?'

'As long as Fairfax remains in command . . . He's a good man, and honourable. But Noll Cromwell is growing too powerful and his son-in-law Ireton has all the makings of a tyrant. If they were to overthrow Fairfax . . . The army must answer to Parliament, not Parliament to the army. I will stake my life on this fight, Anne.'

She reached out and laid her hand on his sleeve. A long and slender hand, but he knew, too, that it was strong. He took it in his and raised it to his lips. He could smell the faint scent of her: the rosemary with which she rinsed her hair, the lavender laid amongst her linen, the rose-petal cream she made for chapped hands in winter.

'Don't talk of staking lives, dear heart,' she said softly. 'There have been lives enough lost already these six years past.'

He smiled at her. 'Nay, it's but a figure of speech.'

He poured himself another glass of ale from a crystal jug mounted in silver, which stood on the table beside his chair. His sword hand was steadier now. 'I forgot: John Crewe sends you his kind remembrance.'

'The commissioners have reached London, then?'

John laughed exuberantly. 'Aye, and a fine time they had of it! They got word the army was spreading a net to catch them as they journeyed from the Isle of Wight, so they broke into small parties and rode by deep country lanes and hidden ways. They outfoxed the army and reached Westminster this evening, wet and cold, but jubilant. We've chosen Nat Fiennes to speak in defence of the Treaty tomorrow. He's gone off to consult with Crewe about the terms that the commissioners have brought back with them and what points he's best to make in the debate.'

'Nat will speak well. And so would you.'

'I'm to speak at the end of the debate, the last speaker before the vote is taken.'

'Tomorrow?'

'Nay, the debate will last all tomorrow and on through Saturday. Perhaps even Monday. The future of the whole nation of England rests on what's done in Parliament these next few days.' His voice rose eagerly. 'It could mean peace at last, Anne! I truly believe we have it almost within our grasp.'

Anne smiled at him. 'So if you're to speak last in the debate, then your business is to persuade the final waverers to vote for peace?'

'Aye. I'll try my best, God willing.' He shook his head. 'There are many who'll be fearful for their lives, with the army encamped at our doors.' And was he any better than those miserable soldiers? He who had drawn blood from three men this very night on his own doorstep?

'They surely wouldn't dare to march on Westminster and the City! Our own Parliamentary army?'

'Not our army any longer, it seems,' he said grimly. 'There is talk of a *junta*.'

'A what? What is that?'

'A fine new notion from Spain.'

He smiled bitterly, and stood up, his suppressed anxiety driving him to the window, where he thrust aside the heavy curtain of Kidderminster cloth and stared out into the night. The sleet had turned to snow and was settling in a thin crust on the frosted cobbles, where the occasional street torches laid bands of golden light.

'A *junta*?' he said. 'It's the name for what happens when a secret alliance of men—officers of the army, perhaps, or political men, or both—seizes power and overthrows the lawful government. A new word for new times.'

'John?' She cleared her throat nervously. 'Are you in danger? Are we in danger?'

He came back and knelt on the red Turkey rug at her feet, taking both her hands in his. He must reassure her, but how might he do that and yet speak the truth?

'I pray that the men who were our allies and friends a few months ago,' he said gently, 'are not so far descended into villainy that they would do us any real harm. They may want to frighten us a little, to bend us to their will.'

He thought to tell her of the attack in the lane, but curbed the impulse. She would know soon enough when he undressed for bed. He wished he could spare her the knowledge, but it would be impossible to conceal. She leaned forward and rested her cheek against his.

'All the same,' she said, 'I wish the older children were here, under our eye. With Dick away at Charterhouse and now Nan at Perwicks' school, I'm fearful for them. I can only be easy in my mind when I have all the children about me.'

'Was that why you were deep in study of the fire, when you should be busy at your embroidery?'

She smiled ruefully. 'You know me too well. I've always accepted that Dick and the other boys must go away to school, but Nan . . . I miss her.'

'She's well content with the Perwicks. And the country air out at Hackney is far better for the child than these sulphurous city fogs.'

Yet the rest of the family must endure them. He seized the poker and stirred the fire. 'This sea coal gives a fine heat, but the filth of the smoke is monstrous. I'd rather one of our good Swinfen fires from the trees of our own woods.'

'So would I.' She picked up her needle and threaded it with scarlet silk. 'Truly, I do know that Nan is happy with the Perwicks. She worships their daughter Susanna.'

'The musical prodigy? You see why I think school is as fitting for our daughters as for our sons? Nan's a good little musician herself, and this admiration for the other child will spur her on. And the schooling she'll have with the Perwicks will be more than anything you could give her now at home. Think of all you do.'

He numbered his points off on his fingers, conscious they had had this argument before and that Anne was still unconvinced.

'The younger children to care for and the new babe on the way. This household to manage. Jack and Francis and Ralph to be taught their letters. And all your duties as the wife of a member of Parliament. Nan is best away at school. In this new world we're building, women will need learning as well as men.'

She reached across and ruffled his hair gently. 'But I miss her, you see. And she's but eight years old. It's young for a girl to be away from home.'

'She'll be home soon for Christmas. And that wild son of ours, too, home from school.' John shook his head at the thought of Dick, half proud and half exasperated. The boy was careless of money and heedless at his studies; he had all his mother's beauty and charm without an ounce of her thoughtful care for others or of his own hard-won self-discipline.

'The righteous Puritans haven't outlawed Christmas altogether, then?' Anne asked, looking at him slantwise.

'Now, Anne, I want to purify the church myself.'

'And so do I!' she exclaimed. 'Of course I'd be glad of an end to the bad practices in the church, and to the greed and arrogance of the bishops, just as you would! But not like the Puritans.'

She threw aside her needlework, and clasped her hands fiercely in her lap.

'Their views are so extreme, so unforgiving, they frighten me. Is theirs true Christian religion? There are those amongst these arrogant Puritans who think the Elect are themselves so *pure* that they can decide better than God himself what's best for the rest of us poor sinners! Doesn't God rejoice that we honour the day of His Son's birth? Where do the Elect find harm in that?'

'Hush. Don't speak so boldly in the hearing of others, or they'll take you for an Arminian heretic, believing in free will!' His tone was light, but he glanced towards the window in dread, as if her words might be overheard and reported.

Anne set her mouth stubbornly, but held her peace.

'I know you miss the country, Anne,' he said apologetically, 'and our country ways. A London Yuletide will be a poor substitute for the festival at home.'

London had its pleasures, but he suspected the days were often a burden to her here in the city. A rising leader of the younger men in the House, spending long hours on important committees, he had little time nowadays to give to his wife and family.

'After Cambridge and Grey's Inn, this was always my ambition—to enter Parliament. You know that. I never kept it from you.'

He knew she understood how passionate he was to serve his country, now that the very nature of England had been cast into a crucible. Church, monarchy, government—all would be changed for ever. By his own deeds, he would help to shape the future. Never had she tried to persuade him to any other course, but he knew also that she grieved for what had been lost from their lives these last years. A man's family might not take such a place of importance in his life when the greater part of his waking hours was devoted to the protection and governing of the land of England. Yet how could he withdraw into private life in times like these? It was the future of his own children at stake, as well as his country.

Anne took his hand in hers and began to trace the lines on his palm as if she could read his thoughts. The touch of her finger was soft, almost imperceptible, yet it set his blood pounding.

'I would never try to turn you from your purpose,' she said quietly. 'Never think that of me. But sometimes I feel . . . John, don't lose sight of the small, human things in life, in the midst of your great Parliamentary affairs.'

She searched his face with her wide-set dark eyes, her lips parted as if she were about to say more, then she pressed them together and released his hand.

John heard her words but only half heeded them, still caught up in his fears about the great changes afoot in the country. He could foresee terrible dangers if these changes came too fast. Already the struggle had brought years of bloody war, and now matters trembled on the brink of further disaster. And yet . . . and yet, in despite of his preoccupations, his body burned for her as her hand slipped away from his.

'If men act with care and compassion,' he said, clinging to his argument and thrusting aside the urging of his flesh, 'then at this nick of time there's hope at last for peace with honour and a way forward to a better world.'

His eyes glinted as he turned towards her in appeal.

'But Ireton and Cromwell are dangerously greedy for power, Anne. And those madmen, the Diggers—you've heard me speak of them?' His tone hardened with contempt. 'They'd seize all property and share it out in common to everyone—hard-working citizen or rascally thief alike.'

He swallowed, watching the quickened beat of the pulse in her neck, longing to reach out and caress her.

'If these radicals prevail, believe me, those men whose property is raided won't stand by helpless! No, it will mean further bloodshed.

And John Lilburne's Levellers are got into the ranks of the army and have sown dissent amongst the soldiers. *Our* soldiers.' His voice rang with angry disdain. 'Those very soldiers who were raised to uphold the right of the Parliament to govern the country against the tyranny of Charles Stuart.'

John sighed, abandoning Parliament and army and king and all.

'Come, dear heart,' he said, holding out his hand to her, 'it's time we were abed.'

She rose and as she did so, looked sharply at him.

'John! What's that lump on your shoulder? There's . . . there's blood soaking through your shirt!'

John shrugged, then regretted it.

'It's nothing, nothing but a deep scratch.'

'Dear God!' she cried, 'You've been attacked! That's a sword cut! Where did it happen?'

She reached out a hand towards his shoulder, but he caught it and kissed it.

'Just outside our door. They must have followed me from the House.'

'*They?* How many?'

'Three. But they were clumsy rogues, paid to do it, I'd wager. Truly, my love, it's nothing. A dagger in a man's left hand, not a sword. I gave them far better in return.'

'Oh, John!'

She threw her arms around him then and held him convulsively, her head on his breast, her whole body riven with sobs. He cradled her in his arms, kissing her hair, her eyelids, her cheek, salty with tears.

'It's over, beloved. There's no cause for weeping. Come to bed.'

Chapter Two

The army was marching on London. Drenched and shivering, groups of gaunt, ruthless men crouched in whatever temporary shelters they had managed to contrive for themselves on Hounslow Heath. Their Parliamentary allies had not appeared this night to share their misery, although Ireton had sent a message of encouragement to their leaders, rich in promises. To many of them, the promises sounded empty, but the prospect of London, fat London, rich London, was ample compensation.

⌘

Before dawn on the first day of December, the sleet began again. It slid down the many small panes of the window overlooking St Ann's Lane like silk skirts brushing against the glass, intimate but cold. Unable to sleep for the pain of his wound, John lay on his back staring up through the darkness into the dusty shadows of the canopy above the bed. Beyond the whisper of the sleet, beyond his wife's soft breathing, there were muffled sounds in the dark streets of Westminster. The night Watch had passed not long since, his lantern in the street outside invading the bedroom with leaping monstrous shapes. *All's well!* his cry rang out. Heedless of this hollow assurance, hurrying footsteps echoed a menace on the cobbles, a handcart rattled past. A pause, and then a group of people heading towards Palace Yard on their way to escape across the river. A child cried fretfully, and was hushed.

John flung himself restlessly on to his side. The approaching soldiers were cold, hungry, and penniless. The anger which had carried them successfully through the renewed campaigns of the summer and autumn—anger which had been directed against the king and his new Scottish allies—that anger had festered, brewing into a deep resentment towards London and Parliament. The soldiers reasoned that, if ever they were to lay hands on their arrears of pay, they would find it in the City and Westminster. They were willing to help themselves to goods in lieu of currency. Rumours of boundless pickings flowed amongst the soldiers—chests of coin in Goldsmiths' Hall, furs and plate and jewels in the homes of wealthy men, whatever their persuasion: King's men or Parliament men.

John and his fellows in the House had received fair warning of the danger. Ten days ago they had been obliged to sit for all of four hours, listening sullenly to the *Grand Remonstrance*. When the Commons had voted that first time to postpone discussion of this inflammatory document, the military delegation had openly threatened the members with violence as they left the House. Now people were fleeing London and Westminster in ever-growing panic, not merely the few remaining Royalists and the rich merchants, but ordinary citizens who feared for their lives and property if the soldiers should be set loose on the city.

How best to act, to keep safe the nation and her people? To bring peace at last after the long years of desperate and bloody warfare across the quiet shires of England? Surely, all good men must stand firm in the face of these threats from the army? Parliament *must* be persuaded to follow the path to peace. And it was in Parliament that both John's duty and his talent lay. None had been more surprised than John when, as a young man, he had discovered in himself a talent to sway men by his gift of speaking. Words flowed from him when he stood to address the House, a kind of verbal music. Thought took life as speech, effortlessly.

'The words are the man,' Crewe had once said of him, 'strong, sincere, dependable.' He had been moved but shamed on hearing it. He knew that within his most secret self he was weak, unsure, always fearing he might fail in what people expected of him. He felt like a child dressed as a man, acting a part—one of these days his disguise would be found out.

Last night, after blowing out the candle, he had gathered Anne into his arms and murmured into her hair, 'I will battle for peace, dear heart, but I will battle in my own way, I promise you. My weapon will always be man's gift of words and never the edge of the sword. Enemies may send attackers against me, but my way is not the way of violence. We must win men's hearts with words.'

Crewe also praised John's shrewd legal mind and unflinching honesty, and he hoped that the praise was merited. He tried to deserve it. Together with his talent in debate they had won him influence and many friends in the Commons, but had brought him enemies, too. Those who called themselves 'independents'. Those who courted the army for purposes of their own. And, above all, those who secretly proposed an altogether different kind of government, where power would lie in the hands of the few who had seized it by force, rather than in an honestly elected English Parliament. Which of those enemies, he wondered, lay behind last night's attack?

But would words, however eloquent, be enough to change the fate of a nation? Must there always be a blood-letting, as a physician must bleed a patient to draw off the illness? Certainly his words had not always proved effective within his own family. As recently as the spring of this year, his last encounter with his youngest brother had shown that. Richard Swynfen was seventeen then, a common soldier in the New Model Army, refusing an officer's rank for some stubborn reason of his own. He had visited them in Westminster for one night as his regiment passed through. During supper and while Anne sat with them afterwards in the parlour, Richard had been content to talk quietly of home and friends, although he had made one mention of Lilburne, praising the man's notions. He had seen Swinfen more recently than John and spoke of the bad times afflicting the countryside, with so many men away at the war.

'Fields unharvested,' he said, 'and some not even sown. Widows made amongst our own tenants. Matthew Webster's brother Thomas killed and Thomas's wife sick and two of their children dead of the plague.'

'The plague in Swinfen!'

'Nay, they caught it when they went to her family in Tamworth. Thank God, it hasn't reached Swinfen.'

Later, when Anne had gone to bed, Richard grew more outspoken.

'All this huff-puff of yours in Parliament, John—what use is it? This division in the country will never be resolved by talking.'

'Certainly it will not be resolved by killing each other.'

'Perhaps not, but at least I'm not afraid to stand and fight against the corrupt men who gather about the king only to preserve their privileges and grind down the poor. These times call for more than mealy-mouthed compromises in the name of peace.'

John felt himself flush with anger.

'How dare you!' he cried. 'There is nothing mealy-mouthed about trying to build a new world in which a parliament elected by the people holds the reins of government while the monarch is made subject to the law like the rest of us.'

'"Elected by the people"? I think not, John. Elected by a handful with land enough to be enfranchised. Why, I myself will not be able to elect a member of this wondrous parliament of yours!'

'You will have an estate, when you come of age.'

'Will I? But what of the thousands who cannot make their voices heard?'

Richard jumped to his feet and shook his fist at John.

'This country needs something more than your *moderation*!' His mouth curled scornfully. 'We must break the old pattern, build the world anew, share out more of God's gifts amongst the poor.' He drew a long shuddering breath and shouted, 'How can you live, a *gentleman*, and not hide for shame when men and women are dying for hunger and want in this poor country of ours?'

❧

Now, lying here in the icy bedroom, where his breath made a grey fog just to be discerned in the growing light, John thought of Richard's outburst. He had been infected with these radical ideas in the army, and no amount of reasoning could persuade him that fewer would suffer and fewer die if peace could brought to the country. John turned to look at his sleeping wife. She lay curled on her side with her cheek pillowed on her hand, her night-cap slightly askew. He reached across and tenderly tucked a stray dark curl behind the lace frill.

It was six weeks until the baby was due. This would be her tenth lying-in. Pregnancy had brought roundness and bloom to her cheeks and a greater fullness to her mouth. He kissed her softly, so as not to wake her, and caught again the scent of rosemary in her hair. Even when she was not pregnant, her figure had not quite that boyish slender shape it had when they were married sixteen years ago, soon after they both reached nineteen. Laced into her stays, she was still slender, though more womanly. The child-bearing had not worn her away to a shadow, like so many, nor made her gross and ugly. And they had been lucky in their children, far luckier than most. Only two of the babies had died, boys who would have been between Dick and Nan in age, had they been blessed with longer life. George, born to live just a few short months, when Dick was a year old. Then the first son to be called John, born a year after George and dead within hours. Despite the death of that newborn son, they had called the next son John also, a name the Swynfens had been giving their sons for generations back, though everyone called this young one 'Jack' to distinguish him from his father. Jack was seven now, with two younger brothers and two younger sisters. All healthy, and, God willing, the new babe would be, too.

John turned again, uneasily. He had slept badly, his brains buzzing with plans for securing an end to this bitter civil war, his shoulder throbbing with a dull heat. It would be better if they were all away from London, Anne and the children, and back home in Staffordshire, now the army was marching ever nearer, bent on seizing control of the capital. The danger was too great. He would be easier in his mind with them safely away. He would be easier, too, about the coming fight he must wage in the House against his political enemies. Yet Anne could not travel all that distance by winter roads in her present condition.

How far would Ireton and Cromwell and their cronies venture, in their desire for power? Would they use force against those who had formerly been their allies, but whom changing circumstances had driven into political opposition? Would they try to dissolve Parliament? If new elections were held, the soldiers could be used to intimidate the electors, so that they would vote only for the friends of the army. He had brushed away Anne's fears for his safety, but he did not trust Ireton. Cromwell was more cautious than his son-in-law and might have restrained him, but Cromwell lingered mysteriously in the north, under the pretext of directing the siege of Pontefract, where surely he was not needed. It was known that his commanding officer, the Lord General Fairfax, had ordered him back to London, but Cromwell had disobeyed, making clear which man was, these days, the more powerful.

Moving as quietly as he could, he slid from beneath the blankets and lowered his feet to the floor. A hiss of breath whistled between his teeth as his feet touched the freezing boards, and he picked his way across the room as if he were walking barefoot over nettles. He lifted aside the curtain at the window, which opened on to the same view as the parlour window below. The snow was scooped into the corners of jutting walls in St Ann's Lane and lay in the gaps amongst the cobbles, but the sleet, melting as it fell, was licking it away.

'John? What are you doing, standing like a pillar of ice in your nightshift? Come back to bed or put on your gown. What o'clock is it?'

'I heard the Abbey bells strike six.' He reached for his gown of ink-blue velvet and pulled it on over his nightshift, then sat on the edge of the bed.

'I think you should keep close in the house today,' he said. 'In case any rough soldiers reach Westminster.'

'But I cannot!' She struggled to sit up, groaning a little with the drag of the child within her. 'Patience Wyatt and I are to meet your sister at the New Exchange today. It was all spoken of when she and Charles dined here last week.' She regarded him critically. 'I suppose you had your mind on more important affairs.'

'I suppose I did. Nay, don't be cross with me. Send Mistress Patience with a message to Grace. You'll be safer here at home.'

'If it's safe enough in the streets for my waiting gentlewoman, then it's safe enough for me.'

'Patience is not seven and a half months gone with child,' he pointed out calmly.

'When am I not with child?' she said tartly. 'It's no great matter.'

John sighed. In company Anne was as obedient a wife as any man could wish, but in private she could be wilful. He must make allowance, he told himself wryly. For did not St Peter himself urge husbands to give 'honour unto the wife, as unto the weaker vessel', her poorer wits making her less able in understanding than a man? Whilst he was marshalling his arguments, Anne forestalled him.

'I must go, John. I've promised to accompany Grace to her tailor to bespeak the gown she will wear at Charles's next concert. Since the loss of his position at court, you know how difficult life has been for him. The concert is to be performed before Fairfax and Cromwell. If they're pleased, it could mean so much for Charles.'

'Black Tom Fairfax is not likely to be in need of a court musician,' he said, feeling the argument slipping away from him.

'Nay, but Noll Cromwell is famed for his love of music, and isn't he the man rising in power? Charles was full of the plans he's making with his brother Edward. Weren't you listening? They're going to compose a musical play, an *opera*, like those performed at the courts of Italy and France. The first ever to be staged in England! It's to be called *The Siege of Rhodes*. If Cromwell agrees to attend it, they'll be restored to their former position of honour and distinction.'

He sighed, unwilling to continue the discussion. 'Promise me, then, that you will take boat to the City. Keep away from the streets. The river will be safer.'

She leaned forward awkwardly over the hump of the baby and kissed him on the nose.

'We'll go by the river, I promise you. And I'll bring you back some new silk handkerchiefs, so that you may be as fine as the king himself.'

'Poor Charles Stuart,' said John, shaking his head. 'The man is an arrogant tyrant and slippery as a Thames eel, but I wouldn't like to be in his scarlet-heeled shoes if we fail to win the day in Parliament over this matter of the Treaty. It is our one hope for peace. Come now, will you ring for the servants to make me some hot spiced wine before I must go out into this bitter weather?'

'Aye. And I'll change the dressing on that shoulder of yours.'

John walked early to the Palace of Westminster through the sharp wind and driving sleet. At the top of the steps, Nat Fiennes and John Crewe were awaiting him, as they had agreed the previous evening, Nat more dapper than usual in a resplendent new doublet of canary yellow. He looked eager and happy. Crewe looked tired, as if he had slept as badly as John. All three withdrew into a corner to determine tactics for the day's business.

'First of all, Denzil Holles is to present the latest papers from the commissioners,' said Crewe. In the brighter morning light John detected new lines of worry on his good-natured face, which had not been there three months ago, before the mission to the king. And his hair had faded from grey to near white. 'Then we'll move to discuss the king's answers. Holles is hot for the peace on almost any terms, but he did good work in Newport, persuading the king not to be swayed by Harry Vane's sweet words. Vane claimed that His Majesty would have better terms from the army than from Parliament!'

John made a sound of muffled irritation. 'I mistrust Vane. Look how in the past he's been with the army party, for continuing the war. Then he shifts his ground and votes with us, for peace on acceptable terms. And then makes one with you on the commission to the king. Yet his closest friends are enemies to all that we're trying to achieve.'

Crewe shook his head. 'I cannot read him either. A giddy weathercock? Or a man who has sincerely changed his mind? He behaved with discretion in Newport, except for this one suggestion of his, that the army would make the king a better offer. Even Charles Stuart had the sense to give no credit to that. Is Vane really hesitating which way he will vote? Or was he sent there to spy upon us, to undermine our negotiations and report back to Cromwell and Ireton?'

'Here's John Clotworthy come to join us,' said Fiennes, waving to the man slowly climbing the steps.

Like Crewe, Clotworthy had reached London late the previous evening, and like him still looked exhausted and wan with the long negotiations and the hard ride back from the Isle of Wight. He was nearly as old as Crewe, who had been born in the last century, when Gloriana was on the throne. Clotworthy was a big man, as tall as John but much heavier built, with a neck like a prize bull and eyes that shone with all the appearance of sincerity.

He clapped John on the shoulder and remained leaning there, as if the weariness of the last days still made his bones ache. John stifled a yelp at the jab of pain in his wound.

'So, Nat,' Clotworthy boomed, 'are you preparing to lead the assault this morning?'

'Our case is good,' said Fiennes with enthusiasm. Neat and small, he had to tilt his head back to look up at Clotworthy. 'Only those who thirst for blood and revolution can deny it.'

'Before we go in,' said John, 'I want to warn you.'

Briefly he gave them an account of the previous night's attack. They looked at him in consternation.

'Who would dare do such a thing?' asked Fiennes.

John shook his head.

'I've no way of knowing, and the Watch cannot have caught up with them or they would have come back to report to me. But I think you should be on your guard. I was lucky. Next time, one of us might not be so fortunate.'

They filed into St Stephen's Chapel to take their seats on the green benches, which were beginning to fill, though not all the members would be here today. Winter weather always kept the less active members confined to their country estates, while the more nervous or cowardly, fearful of the battle which must be fought in Parliament, had stayed away from choice, or departed hastily from Westminster for the country when word of the advancing army reached them.

At last Speaker Lenthall swept in with his various clerks and attendants, and took his seat at the top end of the Commons' somewhat cramped quarters, in front of the great triple window, through which the thin winter sun shone, pale as watered ale. If all the members had chosen to attend, over five hundred of them, St Stephen's Chapel could not have held them, but no man there could recall such an event ever occurring. This morning there were about two hundred and fifty present, by John's rapid reckoning.

After the opening prayers and other formalities, Denzil Holles rose and begged leave, on behalf of the returning commissioners, to present the latest papers they bore with them from the king. His clothes hung loosely on his powerful frame as if he had lost weight in the months he had been absent. Once famous as a fiery spirit, and passionate for absolute military victory over the king and his supporters, he had been appalled and sickened by the bloody slaughter. Familiar now with the reality of war, wading through the corpses of Englishmen slain by Englishmen on the battlefield, he wanted no more of it. His only danger to John's party was that he might now be willing to accept peace on any terms, without securing the grounds which would make for a just and lasting settlement.

'The past years of war,' said Holles, his voice trembling with suppressed passion, 'have undone the ordered harmony of society and threatened the natural hierarchy, the very foundation and basis God has laid down for this sublunary world. The war policy of those members there,' he pointed a finger towards a group of the army party sitting opposite, their arms folded and thunder in their looks, 'their policy of *total revolution*, will bring great evil down upon this nation. The meanest of men, the basest and most vile, whose rightful place is in our dungeons or at the end of a hangman's rope, have got power into their hands. They have trampled upon the Crown, an institution ordained by God. They have baffled and misused this Parliament, elected by the people of the nation to protect and care for them. They have destroyed or suppressed the nobility and gentry, and laid waste their lands. They have spread rapine and famine amongst the poor. They have violated the very laws that bind together the civility of men.'

The motion was proposed that the House should consider the king's replies to the commissioners. An outcry arose from amongst the army party. They shouted and booed. Some stood upon the benches and waved their hats. Others crossed the floor and shook their fists in the faces of their enemies, but the Speaker motioned to the sergeants to restore order, and the motion was passed.

Hot on its heels, Harry Vane came late into the chamber, attracting assessing looks from both sides. He took his seat near his friends of the army party, but not too near, as if he chose to tease all the members by not showing his hand too soon. Across the intervening space of floor he studied John speculatively. Was it John's imagination, or did the look he cast at John's shoulder hold some hint of private knowledge?

Chapter Three

Not five minutes' walk away, jostled and elbowed aside at the top of Westminster Stairs, Anne wished she had yielded to John's demand that morning. It was not in John's nature to enforce obedience, but she had seen the glint of impatience in his eyes when she had insisted on persevering with her plans to meet his sister at the New Exchange and now she regretted venturing out in this crowd. Obedience did not come naturally to her. As she had grown to womanhood she had learned to curb the eagerness and independence she had enjoyed during an easy-going childhood, running wild with her brothers and avoiding her sisters' quieter pleasures of embroidery and lace-making. Much of the time she was content to live within the cage to which her sex and rank and marriage confined her, but from time to time her instinctive urge to freedom drove her to rattle the bars. Caught now in this heaving mass of frightened humanity whose very fear filled the air around her with its rank smell, she knew that John had been right. It would have been wiser to remain at home.

'Oars!' shouted Patience Wyatt, cupping her hands around her mouth. 'Eastward ho!'

Many of the families who lived in Westminster were crowding on to the river boats to be ferried across to the far side of the Thames with their bundles of clothes and household treasures hastily snatched up. For the most part they were women and children. The husbands, having deposited them in the crowd waiting on the slippery bank above the river, hastened away home to board up their shops and prepare to defend their property against the looting of the army.

'The soldiers has reached Knightsbridge,' said a woman standing beside Anne.

She was pale and distraught, clutching a child with each hand, a baby tied in a shawl on her breast. 'Raping the women and slitting the throats of them as stands in their way. We'm going to my sister in Bermondsey, but. . .' she gave a gasping sob, 'my man won't come with us, he fears for his hammers and chisels and his store of fine timber. I doubt us'll ever see him again.'

'They're our own soldiers,' Anne protested. 'I'm sure these are false rumours. They wouldn't turn on the citizens of London! Many of them are London men themselves. Of what profit would it be to set upon their own families and those of their neighbours?'

The woman fixed on her a look of scornful pity. 'A lady like you knows nothing of what yon scum will do. Them as takes to the army an't the men they was once, they'm beasts. My cousin lives near Leeds, up Yorkshire way. They was sacked first by the king's men and then Parliament's. Or was it 'tother way about? Meant naught to the soldiers—dirty, thieving rats, all o' them!'

'Mistress,' said Patience, plucking at Anne's sleeve, 'this waterman says he will take us to the City, but you must come now.'

Anne fumbled in her drawstring pocket through the placket in her overskirt and pressed a silver sixpence into the woman's hand. 'This may help with food for the children. God go with you.'

They had to make their way across the fish-reeking Thames mud, for the tide was low, the water two yards beyond the last of the steps. The weak morning light gleamed in dizzy loops across this marginal world of earth and water and mirrored sky. The waterman's boat was slippery with the mud tracked into it that morning, by the many feet which had churned up river banks already sodden with the melting snow. Patience spread handkerchiefs to protect their skirts from the filthy seat, where the mud shimmered in the low winter sun with the prismatic rainbow of a mackerel's scales. As the man pulled down river the sleet began again. Out on the water the sharp wind caught them, so that the two women huddled together, their hoods thrown up over their hats, their faces down-turned to avoid its bite. Overhead, gulls shrieked and swooped. From time to time Patience peeked out from beneath the edge of her hood at the ocean-going ships anchored in the river, the coal barges unloading fuel for London's thousands of fires, and the busy wherries scurrying across to the southern bank laden with those fleeing the city. She was but sixteen, newly come to London as Anne's waiting woman in the place of an elder sister who had returned to Staffordshire to be wed, and the sight of the Thames with its thronging life was still strange to her.

Anne wished again that she had not come. Grace's tailor in the New Exchange would entertain them with wine and sweet cakes while they fingered his stock of fabrics and debated every detail of the new gown. It would occupy an hour at the least, perhaps two. Then she had her own purchases to make. Despite the frowning disapproval of Christmas amongst the sectaries, the Swynfens still exchanged small remembrances of the Christ Child's birthday. For John she was embroidering and beading a doublet which he would consider too bright and gaudy for a man of sober tastes, but which he would wear for her sake. She was spending too long over the work, for she was an idle and impatient needlewoman. There would be no time for her to make any other gifts, so she must buy some trifles for the children from the toy shop in the Exchange. By the time all was done at the shops, the over-clouded day would be seeping away and they would have to return up river to Westminster in the dusk.

Yet after they had regained the shore and walked along the Strand to the New Exchange, the women felt somewhat reassured. The wind had dropped and the sleet, for the moment, ceased. Amongst the bustling crowds here in the City, there did not seem to be the same fear abroad as had infected Westminster. A few miles further east, a few miles further from the approaching army, the citizens were less afraid.

All the same, the effects of war had penetrated this quiet privileged place, even the finest dressmaker in the New Exchange, where Grace, with her maid Judith, was awaiting Anne.

'I'm afraid I can offer you little choice, Mistress Coleman,' said George Cutler, the master tailor, as he signalled to his boy to bring out the bolts of cloth and lay them on the long cutting table. He smoothed the material with long, clever fingers. 'Trade with Venice and the Levant has near enough come to an end, with the Dutch and the French and privateers of every nation taking advantage of our poor country's sad state. Only one ship in five has been making port unmolested, and many of our merchants have abandoned trade altogether until the war is over. I haven't been able to lay hands on any silk damask or velvet for a twelvemonth.'

Anne fingered a length of moss green velvet. It was thin, and had creased even in the bolt.

'Poor stuff, I know,' said Cutler. 'I took it because the man had nothing else, but I wouldn't recommend it.'

They turned over the small selection of cloth. The big window which gave the tailor and his journeymen light for their fine work showed up the lack of colour and quality in the goods. One crimson damask shone out amongst the dowdier fabrics, but there was no more left than would make a gown for a young child. Grace's mouth turned down with disappointment.

'There is just this,' said the tailor, as his boy lifted a small bolt of tabby silk on to the table. 'Left from before the war. You are slight of figure, Mistress Coleman, and if I pieced it with panels of white taffeta in the skirt . . . I have enough, I think.'

27

Later, seated in the Cutlers' parlour, Anne questioned him about the apparent calm they had noticed amongst the City crowds.

'In Westminster, people are closing up their homes and fleeing,' she said.

'We're far from easy in our minds,' Cutler said. 'Some are making arrangements to leave. I think we can't quite believe the army will seize the City, but if it happens, terror will surely sweep through the streets.'

He had noted Grace's requirements and was pouring out more wine as a diversion for his customers before he was obliged to tell them the calculated cost of the new gown.

'It's said the Lord Mayor sat up all night,' he added, 'trying to devise ways of raising the forty thousand pounds the army is demanding.'

'Forty thousand pounds!' Patience exclaimed. 'Why, that's a king's ransom!'

'You speak truer than you know,' said Anne. 'A nation's ransom, rather.'

Mistress Cutler came into the parlour carrying a tray with small Delft dishes of curds and cream, which she placed on the table before them. She took pewter spoons from her pocket and polished them on her apron before handing them to her husband and his customers, then withdrew quietly.

'Is John much occupied in Parliament?' Grace asked, shaking sugar over the curds from a pewter caster and dipping into her dish. She was nearly twelve years younger than her brother, and had spent some time in Westminster with Anne and John until her marriage to Charles Coleman in October two years before. Now she lived in Holborn and moved in very different company, the company of composers and musicians and singers, far from news of Westminster.

'Much occupied,' said Anne briefly, wary of speaking before the tailor. She had known him since they had first come to London, and she trusted him, but the elegant shops of the tailors in the New Exchange were hives of London gossip. Any careless remark made here would be repeated all over the City before nightfall.

She spooned up the sweet curds and cream, which were flavoured delicately with orange-water and scattered with crystallised rose petals.

'Have you seen Charles's brother of late?' she asked, sipping the fine Canary wine. 'Does he still teach music to the girls at Perwicks' school?'

Grace clapped her hand to her mouth. 'I had quite forgot!' She fumbled in her basket and brought out a small package. 'Edward gave me this two days since. He knew I was to meet you, and when he saw Nan at school on Monday, she begged him to bring it.'

Anne set down her wine glass and unfolded the packet. It was a small sampler, surprisingly not too ill made, with borders of many different coloured stitches on the ivory canvas and a motto at the centre:

GoD is My HElp

My GuiDe & freinD

Anne Swynfen

Aged 8 years ✂ 1648

'Nan wanted you to know that she spends her time well at school,' said Grace.

'A most pious sentiment,' said Anne, composing her face to severity. 'Such housewifely skills as this I could teach her at home, without the heartache of being parted from her. There needs no costly school in Hackney.' She turned away, that Grace might not see her eyes. 'I thought she was to learn French and music and the use of the globes, and even Latin and figuring.'

'I am sure she learns all these things, except perhaps the Latin. Edward says the Perwicks have very modern ideas about the teaching of girls. And Susanna Perwick is grown so famous that the most distinguished men visit the school to hear her play and sing. This must widen the girls' view of the world, surely?'

'Perhaps.' Anne finished her curds and gathered up the ribbons she had bought from Mistress Cutler for Nan's Christmas gift. 'Come, Patience, we must make our other purchases before the afternoon is quite gone.'

⇜

John's party in the Commons had achieved their first small triumph that day, having won the right to discuss the terms brought back by Crewe and the other commissioners after nearly three months of bitter and labyrinthine negotiations with Charles Stuart on the Isle of Wight. The debate opened with a number of outbursts from those members who were always the first to speak without pondering their words. Mostly they came from the war party, who shouted abuse, demanded the consideration of the *Remonstrance* in the place of the Treaty, or merely tried to score points off personal enemies in the House. One or two of the wavering sort, anxious for the safety of themselves and their property, urged the necessity of placating the advancing army.

'For,' said one, 'the army will be unforgiving towards any who urge Parliament to deal with the king. In the eyes of the common soldier, all their troubles, all the death and maiming of the last six years, can be laid at Charles Stuart's door. Any who deal with him, deal with the devil.'

When these eager members had ceased jumping to their feet and waving their hats for attention, Speaker Lenthall acknowledged the flourish of Nat Fiennes's hat and his discreetly raised eyebrow, and called on him to take the floor. The Speaker's long face was impassive as he placed his hands palm to palm and rested his chin on his finger tips, like a man deep in prayer. He affected an old-fashioned style, wearing ruff and pointed beard like one of Elizabeth's courtiers, with a pearl ear-ring dangling from his right ear like a frozen tear drop.

He was a dark and inscrutable man, who was famous for his courage in standing up to the bullying tactics of the king towards earlier Parliaments. Yet the previous year, during the troubled times when the soldiers were in a state of mutiny and Parliament voted to disband the army, Lenthall had deserted his post and taken refuge amongst the officers. Though not openly avowed at present, these inclinations of his would make him tend towards Ireton's camp, but he was judicial and fair. John could not like him, but he held him in great respect. Under Lenthall's direction, all sides would be heard in this debate and the due processes of Parliament would be observed.

Nat Fiennes rose to his feet, glanced about him and waited until the noisy jeering from the opposite benches had subsided, then he began to set out the terms the king had finally agreed. John realised Nat had laid aside his usual ebullience, and chosen to speak in a quiet and measured voice, in which he detected Crewe's guiding hand.

'His Majesty has made most of the concessions demanded by the army,' Fiennes began, 'allowing reimbursement for their arrears of pay and recognising the *de facto* structure of army command. In addition, he has agreed that *Parliament*, and not the king, should have the right to appoint the great officers of state.'

There were a few shouts of 'Hear, hear!' at this news.

He smiled wryly. 'His Majesty has not demeaned himself so far as to apologise for the war! But he has agreed to pay reparations through the sequestration of Royalist estates. He has conceded the freedom of Parliament to raise taxes and enact laws, and renewed the pledge that this present Parliament shall continue to sit until it chooses to dissolve itself for new elections.'

There was a murmur amongst the men seated on the green benches, and the leather creaked as some turned about and smiled hopefully at each other. The very air in the chamber seemed clearer.

'Better terms than our army friends would force upon this House,' Clotworthy muttered in John's ear. 'It's my belief *they* are bent upon dissolving Parliament.'

'Finally, there is the matter of religion and the abuses practised by the bishops,' Fiennes said, 'begun under the influence of Laud.'

There was a sudden stillness in the chamber. The bishops' depredations, along with the king's arbitrary taxes, had been the root cause of men's original anger and rebellion against the old state of the kingdom.

'The difference,' Fiennes continued, 'between a *moderate* episcopacy and Presbyterianism—advocated by most sitting here in this House—is a mere form of words.'

Moderate. But who could moderate the behaviour of the bishops?

'*Quis custodiet ipsos custodes?*' John murmured.

Fiennes paused, to give his next words full weight.

'His Majesty has agreed to a suspension of the episcopacy for a period of three years, after which it will be suspended *permanently* unless Parliament rules otherwise.'

Suspension?

A wave of noise rippled around the House, from those members who had not yet heard whispers of what had been agreed in the Treaty. Not long ago it would have been inconceivable that Charles would make such extraordinary concessions. Grant Parliament all the rights it demanded? Concede its right to raise taxes and appoint the officers of state? Even abolish the bishops? Surely every member must be overjoyed at this news! It cut away the grounds for further war.

'To refuse so fair an offer,' Fiennes said, 'were to betray the weakness of the Presbyterian cause, as if it would not endure the test of a three years' trial.'

Men were nodding and murmuring agreement in every part of the House, even some of those who clung about the coat-tails of the army party.

'In short,' Fiennes concluded, his voice ringing out clear and triumphant, 'His Majesty's concessions over the militia, over the appointment of officers of state, and over the Church are enough to secure religion, laws, and liberties!'

He paused again.

'Since these are the *only things* which Parliament has so often declared to be the ground of our quarrel with the Crown, nothing further is necessary to be conceded by the king. I commend this Treaty to the approval of the House.'

He sat down amidst a roar of cheering which had not been heard in that troubled House for many months.

'Peace!' said Clotworthy. 'We are sure of it.'

'I pray so,' said John, 'with all my heart.'

A few of the talkative sort attempted to interject their petty concerns into the debate, including the newly rich Edmund Harvey, babbling on about leases and tenure, almost unheard over the rising discussion along the benches, which the Speaker finally managed to suppress. The radicals seized this moment to put a motion to reject the Treaty, but they had misjudged their time. Instead, the motion to adjourn the debate on the Treaty, and resume it later, was passed by one hundred and thirty-three votes to one hundred and two. The whole body of the Commons was buzzing like a hive of bees.

As they rose from their seats to leave, John caught up with a young man from the West Country, an ally of his party, who had voted against adjourning the debate, and seized him urgently by the arm.

'What is this!,' he cried. 'I had thought you were with us, and yet you voted against adjournment.'

'Aye, but surely we might bring this matter to a successful conclusion this very day! The war party will not prevail. Why delay?'

John held him back and swung him round to confront him face to face.

'We may repudiate everything these men propose, but we must maintain their right to speak their minds.'

His voice rose as he stood firm in the crowd which was trying to push past him.

'Don't you understand? This is the very thing we are fighting for. No vote must be taken until every man who wishes to speak has done so. *Every man*. Even those whose views we find repulsive. That is the principle on which Parliament is founded.' His voice shook. 'If we suppress the right of our enemies to speak, what right have we to consider ourselves any better than a tyrannical king?'

He turned away and the younger man, abashed, scurried off. As they hastened with the rest of the Commons out of the Palace of Westminster for the brief time the Speaker had allowed them for dinner, Clotworthy took John by the elbow and he winced a little from the pain, suddenly stirred up again.

'*Heaven, Hell*, or *Purgatory*?' Clotworthy asked, naming the taverns nearest to Westminster Hall. 'Or do you go home to dine with Anne?'

32

John grinned. 'Anne is off to the New Exchange about some business of a gown for my sister. *Heaven* today, I think, don't you? In celebration of this morning's progress in the business of peace?'

'*Heaven* it shall be,' said Clotworthy, rattling the coins in his purse. 'Though the victuals in *Heaven* cost more angels than those in *Hell*, we shall dine today amongst the blessed, and at my cost.'

'Oh, very droll,' said John with a laugh, 'though 'tis not the first time I have heard that jest.'

Heaven was by far the finest of the three taverns. They sat down to crisp linen napery in a room lit by large windows. The air was pleasantly warmed with smells of good meat cooked with fresh herbs, and the serving girls were clean, a mighty difference from the greasy, sweaty wenches in *Hell*. Clotworthy continued in an expansive mood as they ate their dinner of boiled beef and cabbage, mopping up the juices with excellent freshly baked bread, free of the sweepings from the baker's floor that contaminated most of London's loaves.

'We shall have them, you know,' said Clotworthy, washing down the last of his meal with a third tankard of ale and stretching out his legs. 'I was watching their faces. And when you conclude the debate, the vote is sure to go our way.'

His big frame and somewhat bullying manner alarmed many, but John reckoned that by now he had taken Clotworthy's measure.

'I think so, too,' said John cautiously. 'But, what then? Do you suppose Cromwell and Ireton will meekly accept the decision of Parliament? By all they have been plotting and contriving these last weeks, I think not.'

'They cannot dissolve Parliament. As constituted, this Parliament can only dissolve itself.' Clotworthy waved his hand, brushing John's fears aside like gnats.

John tried to keep his sense of misgiving out of his voice. 'They may simply ignore Parliament. They have the army in their pocket. What can we do in the face of an armed mob of soldiers? Call on the London Trained Bands? We should be a laughing-stock at the least. At the worst, we should be guilty of initiating carnage on the streets of London.'

'Nay, it will never come to that. Be of good cheer, my friend. Even these men, with their lust for power, will not act against Parliament more violently and illegally than Charles Stuart himself.'

'I hope that may prove true,' said John.

Chapter Four

In the open courtyard of the New Exchange, encircled by arcades of shops, the crowds were greater than when they had first arrived, and many, it seemed, had come to seek and exchange news rather than to purchase goods. After the cost of Grace's new gown had been settled with George Cutler, and arrangements made for the first fitting, the women had taken their leave of the tailor and descended to the ground floor. During the time they had spent in his shop on the upper gallery, the mood of the citizens had shifted. Further word of the army's nearer approach had reached the City from Westminster, so that groups huddled together, talking in hushed voices. People now glanced about nervously, as if they expected the soldiers to burst in amongst the elegant galleries—the glovers and hatters, the silk merchants and Muscovy fur traders, the perfumers and goldsmiths. Some of the shopkeepers had already closed for the day, two hours before time. They were putting up shutters and bolting their shops to secure them against attack. A few, amongst them the jewellers, were packing up all their goods and removing them to safety.

'Before we return to Westminster, I must find some small Christmas gifts for the children,' said Anne, with a worried frown. 'Will you come with us, Grace?'

'Gladly. I've already knitted a red cap and gloves for young Charlie. His father,' said Grace, smiling indulgently, 'has bought him a pipe and drum.'

Young Charlie Coleman was sixteen months old.

'The pipe you may be spared a while,' said Anne dryly, 'but the drum? I'm afraid you may regret it before Twelfth Night!'

Despite her own growing sense of anxiety, Anne was determined to finish the errands she had undertaken. The children should not be deprived of Christmas remembrances because she was frightened of unruly soldiers. Such fears might, after all, be nothing but wild fancies. The army might never invade London. Trying to appear both calm and determined, she led the other women to the toy shop, which was kept by a round-faced, tidy, respectable woman who sold both English toys and others brought in by ship from France and the Low Countries.

'Ah, mistress,' said the shopkeeper, shaking her head, 'these late wars have played a merry dance with my trade. 'Tis the same with my toy flutes and poppets as 'tis with your French wines and Hollands, your dried fruits from the Mediterranean and Africa, and your spices from the Orient lands. Why, no ship is safe from the Barbary pirates or the papist freebooters, while they know our sailors and soldiers are busy a-cutting each others' throats.'

'You speak truly,' said Anne. 'Why, a few days ago I must give sixpence the ounce for peppercorns and I should never have done so in the days of peace. Before the war it was three shillings a pound.'

It was George Cutler's lament all over again. Despite the woman's apologies, the small toy shop overflowed with delights. Propped up in an open-topped barrel stood a collection of hobbyhorses, large and small, ranging from simple nags fashioned of crudely painted planks to bold steeds with finely carved heads, manes of real horse hair, and leather harness jingling with bells. A cascade of drums hung from a rope overhead and the hinged flap which was lowered to form the ware-bench was piled high with smaller toys. On one side a parade of wooden soldiers marched in formation, whilst on the other a group of dolls displayed their fashionable clothes, fine enough for the queen's own ladies and far too delicate for a child's plaything. On either side of the shop front the shopkeeper had fastened whirligigs in bright colours. In the sudden gusts of winter wind that blew across the central court of the Exchange, they spun wildly. As giddy—it seemed to Anne—as that world of politics where John spent his days, allies spun round to enemies with a careless flick of passing wind.

For Mary, a few months younger than Charlie Coleman and just able to walk by herself, Anne selected a wooden horse on wheels that could be pulled by a cord.

'Look, Patience, isn't this a cunning thing!' She drew the horse along the floor in front of the shop until it collided with a set of skittles and fell over.

'The skittles for Jack, do you think?' asked Grace, setting them upright again.

'Nay, he'll think them too childish. But Francis would like them. He's very patient and careful. He'll love to line them up and arrange them neatly. And he'll practice over and over until he can bowl them down. For Jack, I think something more manly. I'll look afterwards at the leatherworker's shop.'

'Here's a pretty thing,' said Patience, holding up a brightly painted spinning top with its toy whip. 'For Ralph?'

Anne considered. Ralph at five was clumsier than Francis had been two years ago at four. 'I can't imagine he'll contrive to make it spin, he hasn't the patience, but he'd love the whip, for playing at huntsman. Aye.' She turned to the shopkeeper. 'The horse, the top and the skittles. Have you any simple dolls? These are very beautiful, but too dainty for my rough little moppet who's only four years old.'

The woman fetched a wooden doll of the kind imported from Flanders and laid it on the counter. The doll had black painted hair and a pleasant face, somewhat astonished to find itself lying naked in a London toy shop.

'I doubt if I'll have time to fashion clothes for it,' Anne said. 'Have you no dressed ones, but not so elegant as these others?'

'I could help,' Patience said eagerly. 'For Dorothea? There are some scraps left from the gown I made for her. I could sew a gown for the doll to match Dorothea's.'

It was decided. Anne paid the woman, and Patience tucked the bundle of toys into her basket as they walked to the leatherworker's shop near the entrance to the Exchange. There remained only the two eldest boys.

'Belts for them both, I think,' said Anne, fingering the goods on display.

'Won't Dick mind having the same gift as his small brother?' asked Grace. 'At fifteen he's nearly a man.'

'Aye, your father was married at fifteen, wasn't he? But Dick's too giddy to be thought a man yet. John worries about his spendthrift ways.'

'He's a good lad,' Grace pleaded. Her eldest nephew was so close to her in age that she always championed him. 'He has such a kind and loving heart that it wins him many friends. He'll learn carefulness with money as he grows older. Better a generous nature than a mean one.'

'True!' Anne sighed and laughed all at once. As Nan was her comfort, Dick was her worry, but she too cherished his loving heart and sometimes felt John was overly strict with him, as if he ought to be ready to display a man's sobriety and wisdom simply because he was the eldest by seven years. If the other children had lived, it might not have gone so hard with him.

❧

It was the afternoon's business in the Commons to deal with the menacing approach of the army. Yesterday the Lord General Thomas

Fairfax had sent a letter to Abraham Reynardson, the Lord Mayor of London. Fairfax's letter was now read aloud to the members, though the fiery style of it was easily recognised as Ireton's and not that of the taciturn Black Tom. Nevertheless, the members were all of one mind in urging the Lord Mayor and Common Council of London to raise the forty thousand pounds demanded, and with all possible speed, to placate the officers and men. Perhaps, John thought, though with little hope, the advance on London could still be halted by the payment of this sum, before the city suffered the horror and humiliation of being looted by its own army.

Two days earlier, when the previous threatening letter from the generals had been read out in Parliament, even that rabid opponent of the army, William Prynne, had seemed paralysed with fear. Now it appeared he had found his courage again. Prynne stood up, the sole member prepared to oppose paying the arrears to the soldiers. He wore an old-fashioned close bonnet to conceal the hideously mutilated sides of his head where his ears had been cut off on the orders of Archbishop Laud, but the brands on his cheeks glowed red in the afternoon light, the letters S and L for Seditious Libeller.

'Do you call yourselves men of conscience and courage?' he shouted. 'Thus to buy off this ungovernable rabble? By their action in threatening Parliament, they have committed treason. I move they be declared rebels and traitors.'

'The notion has some appeal,' John murmured ruefully to Crewe, who was sitting with him and Clotworthy on the front bench, 'but I fear it will not serve.'

He caught the Speaker's eye and rose to his feet.

'Indeed, Mr Speaker,' he said calmly, 'my friend Master Prynne has much justice in his remarks, but the safety of the people of London is also in our hands. To declare the army rebels and traitors would certainly fill us with a sense of our own rectitude, but it would not stop the advance.'

He glanced around the chamber. Men of all parties were listening attentively.

'Moreover, the common soldiers do have a true grievance. They have not been paid for months. Many go barefoot and threadbare. They have no means to buy food or lodgings for themselves, or to travel home to their families. Their sole hope is to remain with the army. If their grievances can be settled by this payment from the City, it may be that many will choose to take themselves off home, to spend the remainder of the winter in comfort instead of sleeping in icy ditches and snow-bound fields. Let us not emulate their churlishness. Let them be paid, and no more said on the matter.'

He sat down to a splatter of applause, and Prynne's dangerous provocation to the army was overruled.

It began to grow dark in the House as the last of the light faded from the great triple-arched window behind the Speaker's chair. The members moved for candles to be brought. After the delay while the candle-sconces were filled and the candles lit, they resumed business. The members might advise the Lord Mayor to find the money for the common troops, but they still had to confront the army command.

'We must send a direct and forceful order from the House to Fairfax,' John said to Crewe, frowning. 'The Commons cannot sit in Westminster like milksops, quaking with fear and acquiescing in the invasion of London.'

'Aye.' Crewe nodded. 'We may lack teeth, but let us growl as best we may.'

As the darkness deepened in the corners of the hall where the candlelight did not reach, they argued back and forth about the terms of the order the Speaker should send to Fairfax, commanding him to halt the advance on London immediately. The members were all tired and hungry. The army party prevaricated. They had no wish to appear to be encouraging the looting of London by the soldiery. On the other hand, they must not act in any way to offend their powerful army friends. Some of the extreme members of the peace party tried to insert a clause into the order stating that the army's march was 'derogatory to the freedom of Parliament'. This was put to the vote, and the remaining exhausted members, who had not yet escaped to their lodgings, stumbled forward to the division in the dimness. By a vote of forty-four to thirty-three they agreed to delete this inflammatory clause, and the amended order was despatched to Fairfax. It was well into evening when the House rose.

Anne bade farewell to Grace and her maid at the door of the Exchange, realising as they came out into the Strand how late it had grown. The streets were nearly deserted now, a few last visitors to the shops hurrying home as darkness fell. The thought of the cold and muddy river trip back to Westminster by wherry filled her with gloom.

'I think we'll take a hackney,' said Anne uneasily. 'The streets seem safe enough for now, and the river is hateful at night.'

There was always a row of hackney carriages waiting outside the Exchange to carry home ladies and gentlemen burdened with packages. As they rattled away westwards over the cobbles, Anne peered out at the darkening streets. There were few people about anywhere, and both houses and shops were shuttered. Even the great houses fronting the river showed few signs of life. The hackney smelled of stale sweat and, curiously, of onions and rancid cheese. Through the gaps around the windows the insidious London fog crept in, a blend of brown coal smoke which caught in the throat like rotting eggs and the dark sinister vapours which rose from the river at night, when the dead boats hooked up the risen corpses of suicides. The sound of the wheels changed as they reached a stretch of unmade road between the City and Westminster. The carriage slowed. The dirt road was bogged with half-melted sleet and, light though the carriage was, the horse struggled to pull it through the mud. The two women clutched the hanging straps as they were flung from side to side, for the hackneys were built for paved streets. On rutted earth they were unstable and easily overturned. When the horse's hooves struck cobbles again in Westminster, they both relaxed with a sigh and smiled at each other as though they had outrun some pursuing peril.

Back at the house in St Ann's Lane, welcomed in by the warmth of fire and candlelight and the good smell of roasting meat turning on the spit, they were mobbed by the children.

'There were soldiers here, Mama!' said Jack, his eyes gleaming with excitement.

Anne looked up sharply at the manservant who was hanging their wet cloaks near the fire in the hallway.

'Peter? What's this tale about soldiers?'

'They were no trouble to us, Mistress Swynfen. We gave them beer and cheese and sent them off.' He gave her a meaningful look. 'They weren't seeking anyone.'

The room shimmered and dipped around her; she felt Patience take her arm and ease her into the carved chair beside the fire. *They weren't seeking anyone.* But the next group of soldiers might be looking for John, bent on violence. He had escaped assassins once, but a troop of rogue soldiers was altogether different. And without John, what could a parcel of women and children and two elderly menservants do against armed men, hardened at Naseby and Bristol and Preston?

'Is the master not home yet?' she asked, ashamed of the tremor in her voice.

'Nay, mistress. He sent word from the House that they had voted for candles. They'll sit late tonight.'

Anne frowned. John's wound should have been dressed again by now, or it would fester. When the house voted for candles the sitting could be prolonged till nine or ten o'clock. Bess, the nurse, came down the stairs with Mary and set her on her uncertain legs. Solemnly she started off across the floor towards her mother, gaining in speed as if she were running downhill, until she flung herself into the folds of Anne's skirts and clung there.

'Mama!' she cried triumphantly.

Anne picked her up and hugged her close.

'You're as warm as a toasted bannock, my pet. We should have stayed here in the house like you, and not gone adventuring out into the City in this bitter weather.' She remembered with remorse that John had not wanted her to go.

She struggled to stand, and found her legs weak. 'Nay, do not trouble, Patience,' she said impatiently, as the girl reached out a hand to support her. 'I am well enough.'

Setting Mary upon the floor, she shook out her dress, which was soaking wet six inches deep around the hem.

'Tell Hester we will sup now,' she said to Peter. 'Have the children eaten? Nay? Then they may sup with us tonight.'

This evening, John was not followed home by any menacing shadow. His relief was tempered by the thought that an assassin might instead be lurking somewhere in ambush ahead, in the caverns of darkness between the occasional torches and lanterns that careful householders placed at their doors—fewer of them now than just a week ago—but he reached home unmolested. The house was quiet. In the parlour he found Anne reading a book, which she slipped into her pocket as he stepped through the door, taking up her needlework in its place.

'Have you supped?' she asked, as he kissed her cheek.

'Nay, I have come direct from the House.' He stood with his back to the fire, warming himself and blocking its heat from the rest of the room.

Anne went off to tell the servants to bring food and drink to the parlour. When she returned, she studied his face.

'It went well, then?'

'So far. The debate has been adjourned until tomorrow, since we had the more urgent matter of the army to deal with this afternoon. That word-spouting lunatic Prynne tried to stir up trouble, but luckily failed. The Speaker has despatched an order to Fairfax to halt the army.'

'Will he obey?'

'Unlikely. Unless the Lord Mayor and Council hand over to him the forty thousand pounds he demands, but they can't possibly hope to secure that much in coin before Monday. I'm afraid that Fairfax will continue the march into London, to persuade the merchants to open their coffers the more speedily.'

John was still at his meal when there was a knock at the street door, and the manservant Peter showed John Crewe into the parlour. The older man looked worn by the day's hard debating, but his cheeks were flushed and his eyes bright. He looks, John thought, like a man on the eve of battle. Do I wear my own passions as clearly as that in my countenance?

'Mistress Swynfen,' Crewe said, bowing over her hand, 'I apologise for troubling you so late.'

'Not at all, Master Crewe. Peter, bring in some supper for our guest.'

'Nay, nay. I've eaten. But I should be glad of some of that hippocras I can smell, warming by the fire.'

'Is it still snow and sleet?' asked Anne. 'Come, sit down, Master Crewe, and I'll leave you gentlemen to discuss your affairs.'

'Nay, Mistress Swynfen,' said Crewe, staying her with a hand on her sleeve. 'I would not turn you out of your warm parlour. There's nothing you may not hear.'

When Crewe was settled in a carved chair by the fire with his tankard of spiced wine and his wet boots steaming in the heat, he regarded them both gravely. But before he could speak, there was a flurry of grey and white fur and a creature leapt on to his lap. Crewe exclaimed, as his wine splashed over his hand. Anne started up from her chair.

'Oh, I'm so sorry, Master Crewe! It's Jemima, the kitchen cat. She must have slipped in earlier, when Peter brought John's supper.'

She reached out for the cat, but Crewe shook his head, laughing.

'Is the cat named for my wife? Don't trouble. I'm fond of cats. I admire their dignity and independence. Some of our fellows in the House could learn a few lessons from them.'

The cat settled herself and began to knead Crewe's knee in its plum-coloured velvet breeches while he fondled her ears.

'I thought I'd come round,' said Crewe, 'and tell you that I have received word the army is encamped this night in Hyde Park. Of horse:

two full regiments and seventeen troops. Of foot: five full regiments and ten companies.'

'Hyde Park!' Anne's hand flew to her mouth.

John's breath caught for a moment in his chest. So near!

'Aye. Hyde Park. They'll be in no pleasant mood.'

'You speak true enough,' said John soberly. 'And their tempers will not be improved by sleeping on the muddy ground, in wet clothing, without fires or hot food.'

There rose up in his mind a vision of that huddled mass of wretched men, dirty, hungry, filled with baffled anger. The king was held prisoner now. Who else could they turn their anger on but Parliament? Yet Parliament had not the means to pay them, nor to feed them, clothe them, house them against the winter storms. It had been badly done, this creation of a permanent army. Those army commanders who had planned it, as the best means of defeating the Royalist forces, had not thought ahead, had not made provision for the maintenance and care of England's first standing army.

And now many would pay for their lack of foresight, soldiers and civilians alike. Rascals and vagabonds had flocked to the army, but there were decent poor men amongst the soldiers as well. That woman, seen last night, in the sea-green gown, jerked at his memory again. Decent poor men, as the man Edmund Watson had been, whose fate had robbed John long ago of the innocent blindness of childhood. Or Edmund's baby son, who would have grown to manhood by now. Decent poor men who thought they might provide for their families by joining the army. Men who believed, as John himself did, that it was worth the struggle if it brought a better future for their children.

'No one is sure how long they will stay at Hyde Park,' said Crewe. 'It may be that Fairfax will think that bringing the army this close will serve well enough to threaten us.'

'You know,' said John, 'I see Ireton's hand in this more than Tom Fairfax's.'

'Perhaps.' Crewe nodded. 'At the moment, their wishes march together. Fairfax wants victuals for his men, and shelter from this bitter weather. And, above all, their arrears of pay, before they turn even against him. Ireton wants to use the army to intimidate the House.'

John shifted restlessly in his chair. 'And where is Noll Cromwell? Skulking about in Yorkshire? To what purpose?'

Crewe shrugged.

Anne was sitting a little outside the light and warmth of the fire, stitching back a piece of torn Hainault lace to the cuff of one of John shirts, but now she looked up.

'Perhaps he prefers his son-in-law to carry out whatever disagreeable tasks they are plotting. Then he can come to London, his hands quite clean of any foulness. Didn't Fairfax send for him? Cromwell's *not* coming, when his commanding officer orders him to do so, argues a powerful reason. And a powerful confidence that he will not be dismissed for disobedience. Does he perhaps test his strength against the Lord General's? He courts favour amongst the soldiers and even nods and smiles at Lilburne's extreme notions. I do not like the man.'

'I've always known you for a shrewd judge of character, Mistress Anne,' said Crewe. 'And there may be reason in what you say. On the other hand, though Cromwell is decisive on the battlefield, he hesitates and prevaricates in matters of policy. I truly believe the man does not know which course to support. When the first murmurings arose about putting the king on trial, he opposed the notion. But Ireton thirsts for the king's trial and the king's death. It may be that Cromwell now desires them, too, though he may not declare it openly yet.'

'Treason,' said John grimly. 'Whatever we may think of Charles Stuart the man, as king he is the Lord's anointed. What they purpose is treason.'

On Saturday, the debate on the Treaty was resumed in Parliament, with the turn of the army party to declare their opposition to any dealings with a man as slippery and untrustworthy as Charles Stuart. They were a mixed group. Some were fanatical against the king—against monarchy itself. They spoke passionately of a Puritan Republic. The most extreme even supported the ever-increasing demands of Lilburne's Levellers, though none, even of the army's supporters, countenanced the demands of the group who had earned the contemptuous name of 'Diggers'. The members, after all, were themselves landowners and merchants. They had no plans to surrender their own property to a parcel of beggars and broken men.

Then there were those others who thought the monarchy might be allowed to continue, given certain safeguards, but not in the hands of the present king. His eldest son Charles, who was already too much his father's man, could be passed over and the Crown bestowed on one of the younger boys: James Duke of York or Henry Duke of Gloucester. This held a considerable attraction, for a boy king could be controlled by a regency.

Listening to these members now, advocating everything from a child monarchy to the radical vision of the Levellers, John wondered what would happen if the object of their hatred were indeed removed. If they no longer had Charles Stuart to blame for all their suffering and losses, what would bind them together?

It was cold in the chamber, with small, sly draughts about the feet, yet it was already stuffy, as if there was insufficient air to feed the lungs of all these ranting speakers. John would have a long wait before he could deliver his summing up of the peace party's support for the Treaty.

Even more urgent was the matter of the army. Fairfax had sent an answer to the Speaker's letter of the day before. Sir Hardress Waller had been despatched by the army officers to speak to the House in person, but the members would not admit him, so the letter was read aloud to the members by a clerk. Unfortunately, the letter said, the order had already been given for the march on London to continue, and could not now be countermanded as requested by the House. These words, it seemed, came from Fairfax himself.

'Perhaps Black Tom is not so unskilled a politician after all,' said John to Nat Fiennes. 'A bland answer, but it outfoxes us.'

For the most part, during the morning and afternoon sessions, the peace party held their fire and left the army party to speak. The debate dragged on. The air grew even more thick and stale. Men's faces shone pale and greasy in the fading light of evening and there was a constant fidgeting along the armless, backless benches. The wound in John's shoulder had begun to burn and throb with the beat of his blood. As he shifted uncomfortably, he felt the dressing pull away and the wound start to weep.

At last young Sir Harry Vane rose to speak and an expectant silence suddenly fell upon the chamber. This was the moment both sides had been awaiting with a keen sense of anticipation. Called 'young' because his father Sir Henry Vane also sat in the House, Harry was of an age with John, and they had known each other as students at Grey's Inn. He had a womanish trick of throwing back the curly tresses that hung to his shoulders, and would then stroke the finger-span of beard which ran from lower lip to chin like a thick line of brown paint.

'Gentlemen. Dear friends,' Vane said ingratiatingly, 'I can speak both as a long-standing friend of the army and also as one of the commissioners lately returned from discussions with the king. Thus I am best placed, perhaps, of any of us to judge what ought to be done in the present difficult circumstances.'

The silence grew tense, as men of all persuasions watched closely to see which way Sir Harry would jump. He looked round at them under his heavy lids and smiled a little to himself, relishing this moment of power.

'By this debate,' he continued, 'we shall soon guess who are our *friends*, and who are *enemies*.'

He paused to allow the significance of that threat to sink into the minds of his audience and ran his fine-boned fingers through those chestnut curls, curls which had undoubtedly received some assistance from his hairdresser.

'Before we make a decision in this great matter,' he said, 'let us call to mind those happy days after the *Vote of No Addresses*. Happy days indeed, when this House determined no longer to deal with the king, days when the nation was governed in great peace.'

He bowed slightly to Nat Fiennes, who was sitting crushed up against John's elbow on the crowded bench. John felt him stiffen, for it was Nat who had proposed and carried the *Vote of No Addresses* a year ago, though he had long since realised the pointlessness of a policy which simply tried to ignore the king's existence. By thus calling attention to Nat, Vane was seeking to undermine the honesty and sincerity of his speech on the previous day. There was no doubt now in the mind of any member. Vane was for the war party.

'I made one of the commissioners to the king in a last hope of securing a peaceful settlement,' he said, shaking his head sadly, 'but I soon saw that this so-called Treaty was a mistake from the outset. The king, nay monarchy itself, cannot be trusted. My friends, let us therefore return to our former resolution of making *no more addresses* to the king, but instead let us proceed to settling the government without him, and to the severe punishment of all those who have disturbed our peace and quiet.'

He paused again, his eyes moving lazily over John and Fiennes and Crewe, who sat opposite to him. An expression of delight was mirrored from face to face amongst the army party. Those who feared Harry Vane had joined the moderates and would support a peaceful settlement with the king were elated. They relished the sound of 'settling the government' and of 'punishing severely' their enemies— inside Parliament as well as out.

'By acting thus,' Sir Harry concluded, 'we shall conciliate the army and fulfil the programme of the *Remonstrance* first presented to this House twelve days ago.'

He smiled, bowed obsequiously to the Speaker, and sat down amidst the fervent applause of his relieved cronies.

'I knew he was not to be trusted,' said John flatly to Fiennes. 'He's been a poor friend since our youth.'

Before the army party could put forward more speakers to second Vane's words, Prynne jumped to his feet. For all his wordiness, he was a shrewd judge of a political moment. It was in the interest of the peace party at this juncture to delay any further debate on the Treaty. The shock of the threatened invasion of London by the army was enough to unsettle minds and panic undecided members into voting to appease the soldiers, at any cost. If the vote could be postponed until Monday, some kind of accommodation might be reached, since the City fathers had promised to meet the demand for forty thousand pounds by that day. Prynne moved for an adjournment.

'Until we are a *free* Parliament!' he shouted, glowering at the faithless Vane. 'Without a rascally army of traitors besieging this ancient House and seat of Liberty!'

There was an immediate scurry amongst the army party. For exactly the contrary reason, they wanted a decision now. Their leaders urged a quick vote, today.

Richard Norton, friend of Cromwell and Ireton, gained the floor. He shook his fist at Prynne. 'Take heed what you say against the army, for they are resolved to have a *free* Parliament to debate the king's answer, if we refuse.' The threat in his words was clear to them all. He turned to the Speaker. 'I move for candles, that the debate may be concluded this night, without further delays created by those members who have not the interests of this House and the people at heart.'

There was a hiss of indignation at these scurrilous remarks and cries of 'Shame.' Moderate members shouted that the army party was attempting to force a vote after the elderly members had gone home, who were known to support the movement for peace. The Speaker recognised the justice of this, and adjourned the House until Monday morning.

John walked home slowly through the bitter December wind. The tone of the debate—as much in what was implied as in what was said openly—disturbed him profoundly. The threat of violence against the moderates no longer seemed a remote possibility, it could be seen alive in the eyes of the war party. He must take steps to remove Anne and the children to a place of greater safety than the Westminster house. They must escape, and as quickly as possible. As he rounded the turn in the lane, he saw ahead of him a crowd of troopers and their horses clustered about one of the houses, hammering on the door. It was his own house. He began to run.

Chapter Five

A nne had promised John that she and the children would keep to the house all day on Saturday, with the army now known to be less than a mile away. There was a small walled garden behind the house, a London garden where little had been growing when they first arrived, save for a misshapen apple tree and a patch of rhubarb. The rest was weeds, rubbish, and a strong smell of cats. Anne had made a small garden of herbs for cooking and for simples, and with the manservant Peter's help had contrived a camomile seat with a rose tree in a pot to one side of it, and a honeysuckle beginning to clothe a wooden arbour above, where she would sit on summer evenings and pretend that she was once more at home in the country. This year, however, had seen more rain than any man living could remember, and she had spent little time enjoying it. News had come from all parts of the country of crops destroyed and harvests lost from the foul weather. Floods and storms had drowned both men and beasts, washed away low-lying homes, and sunk fishing boats.

Today, the garden was a bog of sodden earth, where the occasional snow of the last week lingered against the north-facing wall. There would be no chance for the children to play outdoors. The three boys, in particular, needed to run and shout. Not for the first time Anne longed for the freedom of the family properties at Swinfen, Thickbroome, Packington and Freford. If they were at home in Staffordshire, Jack and Francis could ride the quieter horses, Ralph could tumble about with the dogs, and all three could fish in Swinfen lake. In the cramped London house on this cold day, while the sleet continued to fall, they were soon quarrelling, and by dinner time Anne had already put a stop to two fights. Little Mary kept close by the nurse, Bess, but she was fretful, catching the sense of frayed tempers in the air. At four, Dorothea was an independent child, who would usually play quietly in a corner, talking to herself, but Jack and Francis had fallen over her in the midst of their brawl, and broken one of the little dishes her aunt Grace had given her. She had sobbed heartily at this, even when Peter had promised to mend it. Afterwards she twisted her fingers in Anne's skirts and followed her everywhere.

The unborn child was as fretful as the five already under foot. It twisted and kicked, till Anne felt the drag on her back increasing with every step she took. Yesterday she had worn stays, loosely fastened, but today she had donned the old comfortable gown that she wore only about the house when no visitors were expected, and had left off her stays. The baby was taking advantage of this freedom to plague her.

'Mistress?' said Patience, disentangling Dorothea and lifting her up. 'You look very tired. Won't you rest a while on your bed? Hester's making gingerbreads and the boys are going to help decorate them.'

'And me!' cried Dorothea, thumping Patience on the cheek. 'I want to make gin'erbread!'

Anne closed her eyes and nodded.

'Very well. Thank you, Patience. I think I will lie down for a time.'

She dragged herself up the stairs. Usually she bore pregnancy well, but the weeks of grey, discouraging weather, and the load of worries that John only partly shared with her, had brought on a constant sense of fatigue which she tried unsuccessfully to overcome. And all this day it had seemed as though the very city held its breath, trapped under its grim canopy of cloud. Like that moment of dread in the midst of a play, when you knew that an assassin was about to strike, everything seemed to be waiting. But this was no Bankside tragedy, where the slaughtered actors would spring to their feet to take their bows. What lurked in the wings now were sharpened swords, not wooden foils, and the blood they drew would be warm, and human, and fatal.

With a gasp at the pain in her back, she lay down on the big, carved bed that almost filled the small chamber. Already, on this dark afternoon, the room was draped in gloomy shadows. Shivering, she pulled the pieced quilt over her and spent some time restlessly turning until she could find a comfortable position. At last, she felt herself drifting into sleep and forced her eyes open. It was not her intention to sleep, just to rest a little. There was too much that needed doing about the house, after all the time she had spent preoccupied with the children's quarrels. Yet she felt dizzy and filled with some inexplicable dread.

When she was a small child, a storm had once damaged the roof of Weeford church and rain had poured down the south wall of the nave. The next Sunday, as her attention wandered during the sermon, her eye had been caught by large flakes of loosened whitewash drifting down from the wall. No one else seemed to have noticed. Small patches of bright colour began to appear. There were pictures under the thin

48

layer of wash. Anne watched, forgetting the preacher, leaning nearer as the hidden painting came to life. She reached across and picked off a fragment, which came away in a ribbon, clinging to her fingers. As more of the whitewash peeled away like ragged clothes from a beggar's nakedness—dislodged, not only by her fingers, but by the warmth and draughts caused by the crowded congregation—she saw with terror that the pictures did not depict, as she had thought at first, some kindly saint or Mary holding the Christ Child. Huge scarlet monsters with teeth as long as her father's dagger were gobbling up tiny black figures of men and women. Other people, white in their nakedness, were tumbling from a great height into an immense cauldron of flames. Then a large patch of whitewash fell away all at once and a devil with burning red eyes and scimitar claws like a hawk leaned out of the wall, ready to seize her. The church turned black and spun around her, and her ears were filled with a great confused roaring noise. She began to scream and scream, until her father wrapped her in his cloak and carried her home to Weeford Hall.

Shouting and the clatter of horses' hoofs brought her shuddering awake. Bleary and confused, she lay terrified, her heart drumming. Thick darkness surrounded her and for a few moments she had no idea where she was. She felt herself still caught up in that spinning black void, in which the violent noises made no sense, but increased her terror by their very lack of meaning. Her own screams, echoing from her memory or from her dream, still seemed to sound in her ears. Now she did not scream, but pushed herself up against the pillows and strained to make out the faint shape of the window overlooking the lane. A violent pounding on the door below was followed by more shouts and what sounded like someone kicking the door panels. Anne put her hands to her head. Her brain was swimming. Why was it so dark? At night, when the householders lit their street torches, there was always a wash of light in the bedchamber. With a groan she levered herself up from the bed and stumbled across to the window.

The street below was swarming with soldiers, mounted troopers. Some were tying their horses to the tethering rings fixed beside the front doors of gentlemen's houses here in this wealthy part of Westminster. Others were beating upon the doors with the butts of their muskets, demanding food and beds. There was not a light to be seen in any house. No one had lit the outside lanterns and torches. Anne clutched at the window transom, dizzy with confusion. Had everyone run away? Had her own household abandoned her, so that she was alone here to confront these dangerous men, with their dirty, unshaven faces, their swords and guns? She leaned forward, trying to see up the lane in the direction John would come on the way home from Parliament. Shouldn't he be home by now? Had he been waylaid? She began to tremble violently. Perhaps Parliament itself had been attacked and John himself had fallen to those very swords.

One of the men, looking up as he finished tethering his horse directly below, caught sight of her in the window.

'See, lads!' he shouted, 'some folks are at home and ready to welcome us. Hey, goody, let us in out of this stinking weather. The army has come a-visiting. We need food and drink, and what you won't give, we'll gladly take for ourselves.'

The others laughed at this fine piece of wit, and left off thumping the other doors in the street to gather around the Swynfens' house. Anne fled across the room and down the stairs, not even pausing to slip her feet into her shoes. At the bottom of the stairs she found Peter with Ned, the London manservant, each of them armed with a poker and standing uncertainly behind the front door. They had bolted it and pushed a heavy oak chest across it. Both were elderly men. Though they wore an air of determined bravery, they were no more able than she was to withstand that rabble.

'Where are the others?' she whispered. She was not sure why she whispered, when there was so much noise outside.

Ned jerked his head towards the stairs.

'Up in the attic, mistress. If the soldiers break in, Peter reckons 'tis the kitchen and cellars they'll be wanting first, and then the master's study and the parlour, for anything they can loot. Mistress Wyatt thought they'd be safest in the attic. They'll block the door.'

'Why did no one wake me?'

Ned looked confused. He was somewhat slow-witted.

Peter said, 'It happened so fast, mistress. They ha'n't been here above ten minutes. I thought you was with Mistress Wyatt.'

Just then Patience leaned over the stairs. 'Oh, Mistress Swynfen, I couldn't find you. What shall we do? Will they kill us, do you think?'

'Go back to the children and the maids,' said Anne. 'Shut yourselves in. But be ready to let us in if we come.'

Patience flew up the stairs to the attic again and Anne collapsed suddenly on to the bottom stair. The two men looked at her hopefully, glad to hand over responsibility. Her brain was still muddled with her unintended sleep. She felt sick and dizzy, and all her limbs weighed heavy. After a brief lull, the soldiers' shouting started up again outside. There was a sudden crash against the door, which shook with the impact. Anne knew that sound. The soldiers had found an axe. She must act, but her limbs refused to move. Terror had frozen her into a crouching heap at the bottom of the stairs.

'What, now, men! Is that any way to ask for meat and drink?' John's voice rose cheerfully above the noise outside. 'When I'm from home, do you seek to fright the very wits out of a few maids and a rout of small children? The eldest but seven, and my wife near her time? Nay, you'd not have your own wives and children used so. I'll gladly give you supper, but I beg you not to behave like a parcel of Dutchmen!'

Relief flooded through Anne like a warm wave. The men were laughing, some even apologising. There was a shuffling of feet on the cobbles outside.

'Come now,' said John. 'My wife will scold me a month if I let you walk in the front door with your boots all mud. Come round this passage to the kitchen and I'll fetch you ale and something to eat, then I beg you find somewhere else to sleep. We can't move in this house for falling over each other, and the youngest cries half the night with colic. There's room for the cavalry at the Mews, I'm told.'

The sound of the voices dwindled as John led the men down the side of the house towards the back door, which opened into the kitchen.

'Quick, Peter, Ned,' said Anne, regaining command of herself. 'Go and unbolt the back door for the master, and help him find food for them. Don't mention his name in front of the soldiers, and don't let them know he's a Member of Parliament. They might hold him to ransom. And give me those pokers.'

Within an hour, John had shared out the family's supper of meat stew amongst the soldiers, dispensed small ale liberally, and handed over every scrap of bread in the house. The men went away warmed, fed, and singing raucous songs, to join the other troopers in the Mews. When he had closed the back door on them and shot the bolts, he came looking for Anne. She was still crouched at the bottom of the stairs. He raised her gently to her feet and put his arms around her.

'Hush, hush, my love,' he said, for she was shaking uncontrollably with cold and fear, now the danger was averted. 'What were you going to do with these pokers? Knock out my brains?'

Anne began to sob then, clinging to him, her teeth chattering. He picked her up and carried her into the parlour, where Ned was building up the fire.

'Ned,' said John, 'go and tell the others it's safe to come down now. And ask Hester if she can find some eggs or pickled meat, so that we don't all go hungry to our beds.'

He sat down on a chair beside the fire and held his wife close in his arms.

'Hush, now,' he said again, stroking her hair. 'They meant no real harm. They were cold and soaked to the skin and hungry, enough to make any man short-tempered.'

'They took an axe to the door. If you hadn't come when you did . . . Oh, John, what is to become of us?'

❧

The weather was yet colder on Sunday, with a savage wind blowing, but John was strict in this: all the family must attend church twice every Sabbath day. Anne, still pale and shaken after the soldiers' assault on the house the previous evening, clung to her husband's arm with uncharacteristic dependence as they walked to St Margaret's. Even more than the physical support, she needed the reassurance of his solid presence next to her. At least today she would not have to wait fearfully till evening for his return from the House.

The children were more excited than upset by the army's arrival in the city.

'I would have chased away those soldiers,' Jack boasted, tilting his velvet hat rakishly over one ear, 'if Father had not come home. I would have taken Father's pistols down from the parlour wall and shot them through the window.'

Ralph nodded as he strutted along beside his brother, buttoned up in his best Sabbath day doublet of Lincoln green velvet with gold cording.

'I'd have cared for Mama,' he said, 'and then she wouldn't have been frightened and she wouldn't have cried.'

Francis was silent as they made their way through the slush and grime of the streets, but he was always the most reserved of the boys. Skipping along hand in hand with Patience, Dorothea was chattering about the Christmas festival when Dick and Nan would come home from school, for she was too young to understand the danger so narrowly escaped the night before. Bess followed behind, carrying Mary, while the rest of the servants brought up the rear—Peter and Ned, Hester the cook, and the two London maids, Tabby and Kate, who stared boldly at the occasional small groups of soldiers loitering at street corners.

Anne grew very cold during the three-hour sermon. Something seemed to have caught hold of her the previous evening, an icy chill running in the blood, that she could not shake off. She took the drowsy

Mary on her lap as much for her own warmth as for the child's comfort, while the preacher thundered against the intemperance of the army and urged a Presbyterian settlement with the king. She studied John's grave expression, but could not guess what he was thinking. He had not discussed with her yesterday's course of events in the House, and she could not decide whether he was worried or merely tired.

After the service, John's old friend and fellow moderate Samuel Gott took him aside and recounted what he had heard of the army's latest activities. There had been looting of valuables from citizens' homes and shops. Furniture and panelling had been smashed to provide wood for the soldiers' bonfires.

'Now we in London know what the rest of the country has endured from this rabble,' said Gott dourly.

'The sooner the army is disbanded, the better for the whole nation of England,' said John. 'Such men gathered together under licence as an army behave like a herd of ravening jackals. With as little concern for their victims. At home in their own counties they'd have better work for their hands, ploughing and reaping.'

'If the weather continues next year to be as foul as it has this year past,' said Gott, 'there'll be little enough ploughing and reaping, and more than enough hungry mouths crying out for bread. But it's true these men behave like beasts—some of the cavalry have been turning the churches into stables, flinging their saddles over the altar and tethering their horses amongst the pews, the floor fouled with dung. 'Tis monstrous! Have you heard the latest jest? Such is the power of this great *reformation* effected by the army that now—to the amazement of the world—it's brought not only men but even *horses* into church!'

John gave a grim bark of laughter.

In the afternoon, with dinner finished by three o'clock, John shut himself in the small dark chamber which served as his study. It was time to deal with his private papers. If all went well the next day in Parliament, the members would vote to accept the Treaty with the king and take the first steps towards peace. But would Parliament be allowed to continue governing? The war party had moved on from verbal and written threats; now the army of occupation had brought the very stench of blood and gunpowder into the streets of Westminster. John stirred up the fire in his study, and began to sort through his papers, setting aside for burning those he no longer needed. He gathered together in one pile the correspondence he had held with Crewe while he had been absent from London during the negotiations in Newport.

John himself had acted as spokesman for the commissioners here in Westminster, a go-between relaying their progress to the members, while in turn keeping Crewe informed about the mood in Parliament. Some time in the future, this correspondence might provide valuable witness to the events of the last three months. He caught sight of one of Crewe's letters:

'We shall use our utmost endeavours here,' Crewe had written, 'to bring the king nearer the Houses, and you will do good service at London in persuading the House to come nearer the king . . . No man knows what will become of religion and the Parliament if we have not peace.'

John rested his head on his folded arms and closed his eyes. His wound ached and his head throbbed from working in the light of the single candle he had carried into his study. All his muscles were tense with anxiety. For the last hour his sight had been attacked by the jagged lightning flashes which forewarned him of the onset of an acute megrim. Already the sight in his left eye was blurred; soon it would darken completely. There was no cure for these attacks, which had occurred more frequently in recent months, other than rest in a darkened room, a luxury of time he could not afford.

For a moment he felt too tired to face the struggle which still lay ahead. Well, they would know soon enough whether their endeavours in both the Isle of Wight and Westminster would indeed bring peace. For a long time it had seemed that the disputes over episcopacy and its abuses would be the immovable barrier to success. Nat's father, Lord Say and Sele, had even gone down on his knees, begging the king to accept Parliament's terms for curbing the powers of the bishops. Unless the king agreed to this condition it would mean the triumph of the war party and descent into the army's rule by force of arms. John himself was adamant that the corrupt and overweening bishops must go, but it must be brought about by legitimate means. In reply to Crewe's letter, he had written that, if the king could not be persuaded to abandon his intransigence, 'all our earlier discussions were but a fight off the shore, which makes the ensuing rough ocean the more terrible.'

This rough ocean lay now within sight.

Yet in rereading his own words, John smiled grimly at the irony: the blame for the gathering tempest could not, for once, be laid at the king's door. No, it was those gathered about Cromwell and Ireton who were bent on destroying not only the bishops and the king and the House of Lords, but the people's own elected Parliament. It was bitter enough that a man might weep.

He lifted his head and sighed at the sight of the piles of documents confronting him. He must not allow weakness to cause him to falter in these final stages. Outside the window the sound of footsteps continued, as it had done all day. And all making for the river. People passed in small groups, one or two families together, hurrying, quiet except for the crying of children or the occasional bark of a dog following, puzzled at the abandonment of its home. The very silence of the fleeing citizens made it more menacing.

When he had finished sorting his papers and determined which of them he must keep, he locked these in his writing box and stored it in the court cupboard. The rest went on the fire. For a few moments the papers lay rigid on the coals, like some early martyr enduring torment on the gridiron. Drafts of speeches before the Commons, copies of letters, private writings in which he had tried to explore and set out his own thoughts, his beliefs, his dreams of how this sorry nation might be healed. At last the thick paper began to writhe, the ink turned the reddish brown of dried blood, all those words, those desperate attempts at thought crumpled in upon themselves. The words blurred and vanished, floating in soft ashy dust up the chimney to scatter on the wind.

It was done. Nothing could bring back those lost fragments of his life. John stood gazing at the coals as they settled back to their steady, relentless burning, then shook himself impatiently. What to do with his valuables, should the next rabble of soldiers prove less persuadable than the last? They needed to be secured and concealed. Most of the family's possessions were left behind in Swinfen, but they had brought some plate to London, and Anne had her jewels. For her birthday earlier this year he had bought her a three-strand necklace of pearls that had cost as much as two years' wages for a skilled craftsman. On her marriage her father had given her matching ear-rings and necklace set with rubies and diamonds. She owned a few other valuable jewels. He was anxious not to worry her any further after last night's terror, but these things must be made safe. In the court cupboard he also had an iron-bound strong box containing coin. All these must be locked away. There was a space below the floor-boards in the bedchamber where the two boxes might be concealed.

He found Anne in the parlour, listening to Jack reading aloud a pious text for children, suitable for a Sunday. For a time John sat and listened. How different were his two eldest sons! Dick had learned to read quickly, seemingly without effort, but he was indifferent towards his studies, happier on horseback or out after pheasants with a fowling piece and a couple of setting dogs. Jack, on the other hand, progressed slowly, but took enormous pains, anxiously hoping for praise at every step along the road to learning. He was reading now with all the pompous solemnity of a prelate in the pulpit. John concealed his smile, waiting until the reading was finished and Jack made his stately way upstairs to join the other children in quiet Sabbath play.

'Have we reared a little churchman?' John asked.

Anne gave him a quick smile. 'He's always so eager for you to notice him. Have you finished with your papers?'

'As far as I may. Dear heart, I pray you, don't let what I am going to say give you cause to worry.'

'That's enough to make me worried already,' she said, her wan face belying her light-hearted tone. Their eyes met and a flash of understanding passed between them.

'I'd like you to put your jewels in the strong box with the coin,' said John. 'I'll give you a key to it, and also to my writing box. Whichever way the vote goes tomorrow, I fear Ireton and the army will act. If we lose the vote, they'll sweep ahead with their plans to put the king on trial. In that case, it may be that I'll need to absent myself from the House, for I will not countenance regicide.'

'Surely they wouldn't dare to kill the king! It would be treason. Sacrilege.'

'They'll wrap it up in the pretence of judicial process, but it will be judicial murder nonetheless.'

'So you think we may have to leave London in a hurry?'

'Aye.'

'But if you win the vote, surely there will be no need?'

'If we win the vote, they may simply continue to threaten and terrorise the members, in the hope of halting any dealings with His Majesty. No man of any party may count himself safe from his enemies. I'm not the only one to have been attacked.'

'John, why didn't you tell me this before?'

'No need to concern you too soon. Now. . .well, now, matters are coming to a head. And I believe our enemies will no longer pursue such devious means, but will show their hand at last. They don't want peace on the terms agreed with the king. Not on any terms!'

He pounded his fist on his palm in frustration.

'All the hard work of these last weeks and months has at last secured terms which are far better than *anything* we might have dreamed of a year ago. But no, they have other plans—rule by the army and its self-appointed leaders. They will set up some form of despotism. So I believe they'll attempt to dissolve Parliament by force.

It cannot be done by legitimate means, without the consent of the members.'

Anne regarded him steadily, but her face had gone white.

'And in that case we would also have to leave?'

'That would be the safest course. Tomorrow you and Patience must oversee the packing of our goods, in case we need to escape in haste, before we are trapped inside an occupied city.'

Instinctively, Anne cradled the unborn child in her womb.

'Yes,' John said. 'God knows I wouldn't wish you to travel now, not for the world.'

He thought with anguish of the child coming, and the winter weather setting in, and the rains and floods of this year, which had mired some roads thigh deep, and washed others away altogether.

'But I can't see what else to do—I fear that you and the children may be in danger, on my account. I should never have brought you here from Staffordshire. I think we must prepare for the worst. I want you packed and ready by Tuesday morning.'

'What of the servants?'

'Peter and Bess and Hester return with us to Swinfen, of course. As the other three are Londoners, it's my belief they will want to remain close to their families. We'll hire a private carriage large enough for you and Patience and the children. Hester and Bess can ride with the driver and Peter and I will go on horseback.'

'You've planned it all.'

'I have lain awake nights thinking what's best to do. Here are the keys, so you can lock away any valuables safely. It may be that we shan't need to travel all the way home to Staffordshire. If we go first to Oxford, we can seek shelter with the Harcourts, at least until you're delivered.'

'That will be two days on the road,' said Anne, threading the keys on a ribbon, and tying it around her neck, so they could lie concealed under her shift. 'I'll manage well enough. But what of Dick and Nan? Shall I send for them tomorrow? We can't leave them behind in London.'

'We'll have enough to concern us, moving you and the five younger children to safety.' John had foreseen this, and had his arguments ready. 'They'll be safe in their schools. No one will go seeking them there. It's because of your closeness to me that you may be in danger here. My house in Westminster is known. You are known. That's why we may need to move you away from here. Of course, all these plans may come to nothing, and in a week's time we shall be laughing at our fears. Or we may go no further than Oxford, while Nan and Dick spend Christmas with Grace and Charles in Holborn. One step at a time, that's how we must proceed.'

As the early dusk drew in, the entire family walked through the streets again to evening service. More soldiers were to be seen than before. Some gathered about the ale-houses, some marched in tight-knit groups like formal patrols, some who had been drinking all day shouted threats and obscenities as the family passed by. The two young maids were no longer so ready to flirt with the soldiers. Instead they clung to each other and scurried along behind Hester, with their eyes cast down.

During the service, Francis curled up on the pew with his head in his mother's lap. Anne glanced about to see whether a church warden had noticed and was bearing down upon them to rap Francis sharply on the head with his heavy rod. Happily, they were seated in a dark corner where the candlelight barely reached, and no one noticed. She laid her hand on his forehead. It was damp and burning.

Coming out of the church, Francis stumbled like a drunkard and clung to Anne's skirt. She stopped John when he turned to speak to friends and drew him aside.

'Francis is ill, John. He shouldn't be abroad in this cold wind. We must hasten home.'

John crouched down on his heels to look at the boy.

'Francis? Son, are you ill?'

Francis nodded silently and put his arms around his father's neck. With a sigh, he laid his head in the hollow under John's chin and slumped forward so that John had to catch him to stop him sliding to the ground. He stood up, cradling the child against his chest and wrapped his cloak around him.

'Come,' he said. 'We'll soon have you home and abed with a honey posset and a warm brick for your feet.'

Chapter Six

During the night, Francis grew worse, tossing endlessly and throwing off the bed clothes. His face was flushed and his eyes were bright, though he seemed hardly to recognise anyone. He had begun to cough, a dry hacking sound that made Anne hurt as she listened to it. She sat beside the bed on a joint stool, wringing out a cloth in cool water and bathing the hot little face. Around midnight, John came quietly into the boys' room and stood watching her.

'Is he no better?'

Anne shook her head mutely, not trusting herself to speak.

'If he's still ill in the morning, we'll send for a physician to bleed him.'

The thin white arm sticking out of the child's night shift lay limply on the blanket. Anne laid a protective hand on it.

'It may not come to bleeding,' she pleaded, feeling the heart clench within her. 'It did George no good.'

John pulled up another stool and sat beside her, taking her other hand in his. He stroked the back of it with his thumb.

'George was but an infant,' he said, with a doubtful air of confidence. 'Francis is a strong, hearty boy of six. It isn't the same case at all.'

Anne kept her head down, but could not take comfort from his words. She knew the death of a baby could never be the same for a man. Some children always died. A man would say that those who died so soon after birth must just be laid aside and forgotten, but she could never forget those terrible few days of watching her second son slip away, with nothing she could do to save him.

'George,' she whispered. Her mouth was dry and bitter. 'And little John, the first John, our third son.'

John put his arms around her and laid his cheek against her hair, which fell loose about her shoulders.

'I know, my love, I know.'

'And the others,' she said, her voice harsh with grief. 'You never think of the others.'

'The others?'

'You see! To you they were never children, but they were to me. The four untimely born, before Nan.'

His face looked stricken, but he rocked her silently in his arms.

'Francis is not going to die,' he said at last, though his voice lacked conviction. 'Come, now. You've watched long enough. Go and lie down for a while and I'll stay with him.'

She shook her head. 'I'll not leave him.'

'Very well, lie on the bed next to him and keep him warm. I'll bathe his face.'

He helped her onto the bed beside the child and tucked the blankets around her. She took Francis in her arms and before long her soft breathing mingled with the harsh sound of the air whistling in the child's lungs.

The frost had locked the city in silence. In this high little room under the roof beams, as the midnight turned, John could not even hear the faint disturbance of fleeing citizens which had continued all evening. His wife, his child, and this small, bleak room formed his whole world.

To you they were never children, but they were to me. The four untimely born.

What could he have said to comfort her? It was true. He should have taken more account of what the miscarriages had meant to her. Had Anne been bearing that grief all these years, and he unknowing? When does the soul enter the body? Before birth? Tired as he was, he could not remember what the church taught on this difficult question. Those children were his as well as hers, had lived and moved within her, had possessed, surely, the first flowering of a soul, and some kind of simple knowing—pleasure and pain.

And they had died. One after the other they had lived and died, like so many other children in these bitter years of war. A terrible weeping anger swept over him. How could a just God allow it to happen? All those children who had never tasted more than the first sip of life. And now Francis, his quiet, clever little boy.

John laid his forehead on the bed and let the tight chains of his control go slack. His shoulders were wrenched with dry, soundless sobs.

Do not take this one from me!

He did not know who or what he addressed. Surely not that cruel God who called upon Abraham to set the knife to his beloved son's throat as proof of his faith.

'Papa?' The whisper was so soft he thought he had imagined it.

60

'Francis?' He lifted his head. The child was gazing at him with eyes that held some dark, adult knowledge.

'Papa, am I going to die?'

'No!' He was shocked by his own fierceness. 'No, son,' he said more gently. 'I'll not let you die. I'm here to fight for you.'

The child sighed, turned over towards his mother, and slept again.

❧

In the burned-out wealden village, the snow lay untouched by man. It had drifted over the charred remains of the cottages, had moulded the huddled bodies into the hummocks of the rough woodland beyond the clearing. The horse and donkey had wandered into the forest, searching vainly for fodder, but kept returning by instinct to the village, the only place they had ever known. The mound where the boy lay beside his mother was criss-crossed with the lace of bird tracks. As yet, however, the predatory beasts of the wild had not found the dead. For a time, they lay in peace.

❧

Before the crucial matter of the Treaty could be debated on Monday, letters from the Isle of Wight reached Parliament with alarming news. The army had suddenly seized the king and moved him from the relative comfort of Carisbrooke to the grim fortress of Hurst Castle, acting illegally, without the authorisation of Parliament. The king's attendants and servants had been dismissed, and he was now surrounded by army place-men. Parliament's most valuable chess piece was now in the hands of the army.

'Once again the army acts as if it were the government of this country,' John said furiously to Crewe as they sat listening to this disastrous news. 'Where will it end?' He signalled frantically at Speaker Lenthall with his hat but was ignored.

'We must show ourselves resolute,' said Crewe. 'At our first sign of weakness the army will force this Parliament to vote for dissolution. Then they will rule the country, as the king did, without the people's elected representatives.'

'Or else they'll put in place a poodle Parliament to do their bidding.' John swore under his breath. 'Come, the clerks are calling us to vote on the motion—"that the army's latest escapade is without the knowledge or consent of this House". By God, that's true!' He sprang to his feet.

The members now turned to the real business of the day. The initial arguments centred on the exact wording of the motion which would be put to the most vital vote ever before this Parliament. Before the vote could be held, every man in the chamber must know what he was voting for or against, down to the least and smallest word. To the ordinary citizen, such quibbles probably would have seemed a waste of the members' time, but John knew that sometimes the fate of the nation could depend on a handful of words carelessly framed. The first motion proposed was:

Whether the king's answers to the Propositions of both Houses be satisfactory.

Skilled debaters in the army party tried hard and cynically to force this motion on the House. They knew that such a motion (which meant unquestioning acceptance of the king's position without imposing further safeguards) could only be acceptable to a thorough-going Royalist. But after the expulsion during recent years of some members who had openly supported the king against Parliament, and the voluntary withdrawal of others, none but secret Royalists remained in the ranks of the Commons, and certainly none of them would show their hand by voting for such a motion. The republicans hoped that, by forcing the members to vote on this form of words, they could defeat the Treaty outright.

'You're our man, John,' said Crewe, when the peace party cried out against this proposal. 'Young you may be, but you're our chosen man when it comes to the right wording for a motion or a bill.'

In his three years in the Commons, John had gained a reputation for shrewdness and subtlety in the use of Parliamentary language. As a rising man, he had been appointed to more committees than almost any other member, including the important Derby House Committee, and he regularly acted as a spokesman on behalf of the Commons to the Lords. But at this crisis, when the wrong choice of words could destroy all they had achieved so far, he hesitated.

'Nay, let us put this in the hands of one of the professional lawyers amongst us,' he pleaded.

Fiennes shook him gently by the shoulder.

'What we need is a man with a clear understanding of Parliament,' he said. 'We want no wordy lawyer's ramblings. Come, John, you know you're the one to find the way for us.'

So when a close committee of the peace party withdrew to another room to consider what should be done about this dangerously worded motion, it was John who led the discussion and who devised the appropriate form of words for a motion to replace it:

That the answers of the king to the Propositions of both Houses are a ground for the House to proceed upon for the settlement of the peace of the kingdom.

The wording was deliberately careful: 'a ground to proceed upon'. This paved the way for further negotiations with the king, and would gain the support of every member of the House who did honestly desire 'the settlement of the peace of the kingdom' on honourable terms. And it was this form of words that the Commons chose to debate. If the Commons supported this motion, it meant peace.

As the day wore on, it became clear that this would be a debate like no other ever known in Parliament. Passions burned up fiercely, and speaker after speaker rose, first on one side and then on the other. There had been violent debates before in the House—when the king had imposed ship money, when decisions had been made about the conduct of the war. But now everyone knew that on the outcome of this day's actions would depend the future of England as a constitutional monarchy, with an inherited crown and anointed king, a house of hereditary peers and a house of elected commoners. The future of the whole government of the realm hung in the balance.

Men grew hot and angry, throwing their hats on the ground in disgust. Once or twice, scuffles broke out and members had to be separated by force, swearing. One of the war party got a black eye. One of the peace party had to staunch a bloody nose on a handful of handkerchiefs passed along by his neighbours on the benches. Sometimes it seemed that a riot would develop and that the Speaker's call of 'Order!' would be lost forever in a furious brawl.

But order was restored and the speeches continued. Many spoke for peace: the Presbyterians whose principal goal was now within reach, the older men with no thirst for war and violence, men of sense and judgement, men who were sickened past bearing by the long slaughter of the last six years. As it grew dark and the violent winter wind rattled the windows, a motion for candles was carried and the members accepted that they would have a long evening of it.

On Saturday the army party had already derided and opposed the Treaty, but today there were many more of them who wanted to speak. The overt republicans knew, if this opportunity slipped through their fingers, they would not have another chance to stop all dealings with the king through the legitimate processes of Parliament. The so-called 'Independents', the war party, the allies of the army, and the radicals who wanted fundamental change in government, along with the self-serving war profiteers, all ranged themselves against the members who urged this last opportunity for peace. While John and his party believed that Parliament could so hedge the king about that he would be forced to keep to the terms agreed, their opponents were convinced, or pretended, that he would not.

'Charles Stuart,' shouted Sir Henry Mildmay, throwing his hat on the ground and stamping upon it, as if it were the king himself, 'Charles Stuart is no more to be trusted than a lion that has been caged, and is let loose again at his liberty.'

The furious arguments raged back and forth for many hours, but when at last William Prynne managed to secure Speaker Lenthall's nod, some members groaned aloud, not all of them on the benches of the war party.

'Trust Will Prynne to have his say,' John muttered to Edward Stephens, Crewe's brother-in-law, whose own speech had been mercifully short. 'What o'clock is it, do you think?'

'I heard ten strike long since,' said Crewe, on his other side. 'Best catch some sleep if you can.'

It was a poor jest, for no one could have slept through Prynne's thunderings. He was a clever and crafty lawyer, and a passionate speaker, if he could but have learned the virtue of brevity. He rehearsed, one by one, all the arguments for accepting the Treaty, down to the smallest details, and discussed and enlarged on each at length. Next, one by one, he listed the opponents' arguments, which he demolished less with the grace of a Cicero than with the brute force of a charging bull. He then proceeded to anatomise the character, antecedents, legitimacy and motives of all those who spoke against the Treaty.

'These men,' said Prynne contemptuously, with a wide flourish of his arm, 'who pretend aloud that the king's offer to grant Presbyterianism on trial for three years is the crucial issue at debate here—these men desire *no* ecclesiastical settlement at all! They come into this House with their false devotion and their pious faces, when all they desire is to seize Church lands, or to hold on to what they have already seized in the course of these bitter times, at a fairground huckster's price. Oh, yes! War breeds fine profits for unscrupulous men!'

Prynne's loss of teeth during the torture he had endured meant that he spat as he spoke. Men ducked whenever he reached a crescendo. He drew a deep breath now and glared around the chamber. He lifted his hands heavenwards and raised his voice so that it rang out in that candlelit gloom.

'Let the army do its worst. This House should respect only its own conscience and integrity!'

Prynne sat down at last, after a speech lasting three hours, amidst the relieved cheers of the peace party and the booing of their opponents, who had been bludgeoned into silence while he spoke.

'Note the Speaker, his looks,' Prynne hissed to his friends, with smirking satisfaction. 'The man is quite overcome with admiration at the cogency of my arguments.'

Speaker Lenthall was certainly overcome by the *duration* of Prynne's oration. He granted the Commons a few minutes' pause while he hurried off to refresh himself. There was an undignified scramble as the members made for the doors and the chamber pots kept in the close cupboards. Outside, at the bottom of the steps leading to Parliament, an enterprising costermonger had set up a cart from which he was selling hot pies and ale. Even the most law-abiding members were prepared to ignore the fact that the man had no licence to sell ale, since there was no time to repair to one of the celestially named inns nearby.

John bought two pies and a wooden tankard of ale and stood in Palace Yard devouring the food ravenously. It was as well that it was too dark to inspect it closely. The pies were tasty if somewhat tough, and the ale was watered, but he had eaten and drunk worse in London. The snow had ceased falling. The household fires, smoored down for the night, were no longer filling the air with their greasy smoke and sulphurous fumes. The night was frosty and clear, so that he could see the stars pulsing high in the heavens, a rare sight in London's usual fog and filth. If only, he thought, with that familiar sickening spasm of hope and dread, if only the desire for an honourable peace shone as clearly in the minds of the men now pacing and shivering in Palace Yard.

The house in St Ann's Lane was bitterly cold. In the cramped chamber occupied by the three little boys there was no hearth, so Anne told Peter to bring in a small brazier of coals, in a futile attempt to hold the winter at bay. The inside of the window glass was thickly sculpted with leaves and curling fronds of ice, so thick that, when Bess warmed a ha'penny in her hand to try to make a peephole for Ralph, the coin did no more than blur the pattern slightly. Last night they had made up a pallet for Jack and Ralph on the floor, so that Francis might have sole use of the bed they usually shared. Now, in the dead watches of the night, the two other boys were curled up together so silent in their sleep than Anne found herself holding her own breath to hear if they were breathing still.

Francis was restless, twisting this way and that until the blankets and the pieced quilt tangled his limbs. He fought against them then, coughing and moaning, but still half sleeping, half waking. The smouldering coals in the brazier gave off an ochre-yellow smoke than wound lazily about the room in the draughts from the ill-fitting window, until it settled about the beams of the ceiling, whose plaster bore the traces of other braziers which had been lit here by other tenants. Anne feared that the coal smoke would aggravate the congestion in Francis's chest, but could think of no other way to keep him warm. She had packed him about with warmed bricks wrapped in flannel, but he fretted at their hard edges and pushed them away.

He had refused food all day, except for a little broth at supper time, but he had vomited that almost at once. His eyes, dark and reproachful, had watched her as she cleaned him and fetched fresh bedding.

'I said I didn't want to eat,' he complained, 'and now see what's happened.'

'You'll grow weak if you eat nothing,' she said, keeping her voice brisk. The smell of vomit still soured the air. 'We'll try again later. Now, you must drink this infusion, and then you'll feel better. Feverfew to ease the fever, sage for the thickness in your chest, and meadowsweet to chase away your pain.'

'I don't want it!' he wailed, but submitted in the end as she spooned the bitter liquid into his mouth.

Afterwards she rubbed his chest and his aching joints with a salve made from nettles, monkshood and other warming herbs. He tried to resist as she rubbed and turned him, but he was grown as weak as an infant and soon fell into a troubled slumber.

Now, with the household all asleep around her, Anne rose stiffly from her chair beside the bed, pressing her hands into the small of her aching back. She stepped over to the window and tried to peer out through the armour of frost, but could make out nothing but one small glow where a single pitch torch burned at the end of the lane.

'Mama?'

She started and turned. Francis lay very still, his thin body barely visible beneath the bedclothes, but his eyes were wide, reflecting the light from the candle on the coffer beside the bed.

'Yes, my pet?' She sat down beside him again, and took his hand in hers under the blankets. It was cold and limp as a wet dishclout.

'Mama, am I like to die?'

He was regarding her steadily, with no expression on his face save in those eyes, darkened and enlarged with fever.

'Nay, of course not, dear heart.' She brushed back the damp hair from his forehead and kissed him lightly. 'You've nothing but a tiresome fever and cough. If you're a good boy and take my potions, you'll soon be well again.'

'I'm not afraid to die. Everyone must die, must they not?'

'Aye, but not for a long while yet. You must grow to be a great man like your father first. And marry, and have children of your own.'

'Swinfen won't be mine, though. Dick will have Swinfen.'

'Aye, Dick will have Swinfen. But we have other manors. Perhaps you'll live at Thickbroome.'

'I liked it when we lived at Thickbroome.'

He shifted restlessly, pushing away the blankets. Anne pulled them up and tucked them in again.

'Do you remember Thickbroome? You were only a little lad.'

'Aye. I remember the Black Brook, and how it roared after rain. I mislike London, Mama.'

'I too. Well, we may soon be going back to Swinfen.'

'I'd like that. Can I sit on your lap, Mama?'

She drew her chair closer to the brazier, then gathered him up in his blankets and settled him on her lap. He was silent for a long while, gazing at the changing landscapes of the fire with his head resting on her shoulder. Then he sighed and nuzzled his head against her neck.

'You mustn't be sad if I should die, Mama, for truly I'm not afraid.'

One of the Commons' clerks came and rang a handbell at the top of the steps up to the Palace of Westminster, and the members trudged wearily back to the chamber just as the Abbey clock struck two of the morning. The green benches were less crowded now, for some of the members had taken advantage of the few minutes' break to slip away home. At the time of the earlier vote, there had been three hundred and forty present. John scanned the slumped figures and reckoned that not many more than two hundred were still in their seats.

The debate dragged on with desultory speeches, but Lenthall would not allow the vote until every man who wished to speak had had his chance. Despite his attempted impartiality, it was clear to any who knew him that he wanted the motion to fail. When at last all the members had fallen silent, the window behind the Speaker's chair was turning slowly from black to grey, and the candles, renewed twice during the hours of darkness, dulled as the chamber grew a little less dark. The increasing light revealed a crowd of exhausted men wan and dishevelled from watching out the night in disputation. Some had kept themselves awake by taking a pipe of tobacco, adding to the closeness of the room and the stale, sour taste of the air. Some had loosened the strings at the necks of their shirts and unbuttoned their doublets, so that the Speaker was moved to reprimand them for their slovenliness. Some had kicked off their shoes and found their feet so swollen with sitting that they struggled to pull them on again.

When John judged that the debate had at last died from exhaustion, he caught the Speaker's eye. He had not thought he would have to wait nearly twenty-four hours before putting the final case for the peace party. This was no time for speech-making. Even his friends eyed him sullenly as he stood up, stiff with sitting on the backless bench. His head throbbed with the foul air and lack of sleep, and he could barely focus his eyes on the Speaker, who seemed to swim in a miasma of pale light and smoke. He spoke for less than five minutes, doing little more than summing up what Nat Fiennes had said four days earlier—that the concessions made by the king with regard to the bishops, to the offices of state, to the army, and to the powers and prerogatives of Parliament, met all the principal demands made by this House. He cleared his dry throat, trying to marshal the thoughts in his weary brain after two sleepless nights, one spent in tending his sick child, one in caring for his ailing nation.

'I beg of you,' he said, his voice cracked with passion, 'I plead with you, fellow members of this great House, in whose hands the fate of England rests: Reflect before you vote! A vote to reject this motion, a vote against proceeding on the basis of the Treaty to procure an honourable settlement for the peace of the kingdom, is a vote that will call down upon you infamy, and the curses of your children's children! I beg you not to take actions which will prolong the bloody war that has set neighbour against neighbour, friend against friend, brother against brother. Vote for the motion, and let us embark on the road to a just peace, with honour and integrity. I move that the motion be put to the vote.'

And it was so put. The tellers returned the verdict of the House: the Ayes were one hundred and twenty-nine, the Nays were a mere eighty-three. It was a famous victory for the peace party, since many of their number, the older men, had long before this collapsed with fatigue. The Commons had voted for good sense and an end to war. Tired as they were, the moderates broke into riotous cheers, they clapped each other upon the back, they threw their hats in the air. But the opposite party did not slink away defeated. They cursed their enemies and shouted that the business was not settled, that those voting for peace had the army still to deal with, and they should look to the safety of themselves and their families.

Lenthall imposed order on this angry pandemonium, but when he had restored quiet he made his own comment on the outcome.

'The vote of this House is duly recorded. But,' he warned, 'if you adhere to the vote, it will inevitably mean your own destruction.'

What would the army do next? That was the question on everyone's lips. The members decided that the Commons must maintain contact with the General Council of the Army. As their final action before rising, they appointed a committee to go to the royal Palace of Whitehall, which the army had seized yesterday to serve as its headquarters, 'for the keeping and preserving a good correspondence between the Parliament and the Army'.

The strength of John's party remaining in the chamber ensured that they were able to appoint four of their own to this committee. Two staunch Presbyterians were also appointed. They were more extreme against episcopacy than the moderates were, but both were friends of John's: Maynard and Colonel Birch. The radicals secured one place, Prideaux, who had spoken against the motion.

'Prideaux may be of the opposite party,' John said to Crewe, who was sagging on the bench beside him, 'but although he has many friends in the army, I think he has no wish to see the House destroyed, whatever he feels about treating with the king.'

Crewe grunted in reply. He seemed to have aged twenty years during the night and looked old and frail.

Lenthall ruled the session at an end.

'As far as I can judge,' he said, looking around at the weary men on both sides of the chamber, 'this has been the longest session ever held in the entire history of the House of Commons.'

The mid-morning winter sun surrounded his chair with a dusty halo as he rose and left the chamber. John gave his arm to Crewe as he got groaning to his feet with a snapping of his knee joints. They walked out of the House together, with Fiennes and Stephens and Clotworthy in a group behind them.

Out in the thin sunshine, John turned and smiled at his friends, suddenly revived by the cold wind and the sight of the new day.

'We have won!' he cried. 'God be praised, we have won the day and the vote is for peace!'

When John reached home late on Tuesday morning, he found it all in a bustle with the maids packing chests and bundles, their faces tear-stained. He had been gone for more than a day. The business of the House had so absorbed him that he had quite forgotten the instructions he had left with Anne on Sunday, and for a moment he wondered what could have happened in his absence. Then he remembered, greeting Anne somewhat shame-faced.

'You are busy about the packing, then?'

The look she turned on him was strained and not altogether friendly.

'Those were your orders, husband.'

'Come now,' he said, kissing her cheek, 'are you not pleased to see me? And can a man not find a bite to eat when it's Tuesday and he has had naught but scraps since Sunday?'

'And could not a man send to his wife to say that he will not be home all night, with the army roaming the streets and rumours flying through the air? I thought some terrible disaster had befallen, until John Crewe's man brought me word this morning that the House was still in session.'

'I'm sorry, Anne.' He was contrite. He had never thought of how she would worry when he had not come home the previous night. 'How is Francis? Did you send for the physician?'

'He's a little better,' she said, looking only somewhat mollified. 'My home-brewed physic has eased the fever and loosened the cough. There's no need to have him bled.'

'I'll go up and see him. Will you send me something to eat in our chamber? I must sleep or I shall fall down here where I stand.'

He started up the stairs, then called after her as she hurried towards the kitchen.

'Anne? I've asked some friends to take supper with us tonight. Crewe and Fiennes and Clotworthy. Stephens and Birch may come as well.'

She stopped and looked up at him. Her face was blank and her eyes somewhat chilly.

'As well we have food enough in the house. It's said the soldiers will eat all London out of victuals.'

He came back down the stairs and took her hands.

'I'm truly sorry to have frightened you, Anne. Don't be angry with me. And I can send to them not to come tonight, if you would prefer.'

She gripped his fingers hard.

'I was very afraid when you didn't come home.' She choked back a sob, the frozen calm of her face shattering as her eyes searched his. 'And Francis was so ill in the night. But of course your friends must sup with us. Won't you tell me whether the votes have been cast?'

'But of course!' He laughed at himself. 'It has all been so . . . And I'm half asleep with debating all night. We've won! The House has accepted the Treaty as a basis to negotiate for peace with the king.'

She hugged him briefly.

'That's wondrous news. Whatever may happen now, you know that Parliament has voted as you knew it should, as all right-thinking people want—for peace. Now, go and see Francis and I'll bring you something myself. The girls are too busy.'

'They're upset?'

'They lose their places if we leave, and they're afraid of the soldiers. I'll do what I can to find them something, but I don't know if there will be time.'

'Perhaps it's all for nothing. We've sent a committee to parley with the General Council of the Army.'

Suddenly he yawned so wide his jaw gave a cracking sound.

'Go to bed,' she said.

☙

The small house in St Ann's Lane was a warm haven that evening amidst the snow which had begun again and now fell thick, soon settling on rooftops and streets, hiding the soot-blackened walls, laying a soft blanket over the grotesque protuberances that sprouted from the huddled buildings of this stifled city, sweetening the muddy shores of the river, where a few families were still taking boat for the south bank. All was quiet in Palace Yard and in the narrow streets round about. The Swynfens' guests came in stamping their boots and shaking snow from their cloaks. Beside the roaring coal fire Peter had built up in the parlour they steamed gently as they toasted the back of their breeches and drank generous tankards of spiced wine.

The mood was uproarious. Refreshed by a few hours' sleep, all the guests were full of optimism. After the long tragedy of war, it seemed they might at last have secured an end to hatred and bloodshed.

'The people of England will thank us for this day's work!' Crewe exclaimed. 'Mark my words.'

'Our names will go down in the history of England,' Stephens said, somewhat thickly, for he had stopped off at a tavern on his way. '*We* are the men who ended the Civil War.'

'Your meeting with the Army Council, Birch,' said John, refilling the colonel's tankard, 'how did you fare?' Birch, the member for Leominster, loomed against the ceiling, his big body tight in its costly doublet.

'We fared ill,' said Birch bitterly. His voice had never lost its flat Lancashire vowels during his years as a merchant and soldier in Bristol and Herefordshire. 'Kept us kicking our heels in a royal waiting-room at Whitehall, like poor suppliants for the king's favour, then sent us away, saying they were too busy to see us.'

There were exclamations of anger from the others.

'They are become puffed up with monstrous pride,' Crewe said. 'How dare such men as Ireton and Fairfax and Ludlow behave so towards a committee of Parliament!'

'They're indeed prideful,' said John, 'but perhaps also they don't know what to do. They may have believed they would win the vote in the House. Having lost, they must devise a new strategy. Now, if you're all warmed through, come and eat.'

☙

As John and his friends sat down to supper in St Ann's Lane, a few streets away six men assembled around another table in a private chamber near the Long Gallery in Whitehall Palace. A fire had been hastily lit, but the room remained dank and chilly, abandoned since the royal family had fled London. The Lord General Fairfax, commander-in-chief of the army, was conspicuously not present. Ireton took the head of the table, and glanced around at the small group of like-minded men, appointed by the larger gathering of the army party which had met immediately after the session in the House finished.

'Very well,' he said. 'We have determined the conditions for placing a member on this list. Let us proceed through the alphabet. Ludlow? Any names amongst the A's?'

Ludlow had spread out in front of him the printed register of the members of Parliament. He studied it and shook his head. 'None amongst the A's. The B's? Aye. Birch. Boughton. Browne. Bulkeley . . .'

Ireton dipped his pen in the ink and began to write.

Chapter Seven

John started early for the Commons that cold Wednesday morning. There had been shouting in the streets during the night and he was anxious to discover what was afoot. When he kissed Anne absentmindedly at the door, she held him back by the arm.

'John, must you go to the Commons today?'

He looked at her in surprise. 'Aye. Don't worry.' He patted her cheek. 'Peter? Give me my thickest cloak. The wine velvet with the cream silk quilted lining. This winter grows more bitter with every day that passes.'

She stood watching him put on his cloak, her hands clenched together and pressed against her chest as though in pain. Her face was pinched with lack of sleep, dark smudges beneath her eyes as blue as ink.

'The soldiers . . .' she pleaded, 'and Francis so ill. Surely, now the vote is safely passed, you could stay at home for just one day?'

He buckled on his sword, half turned towards the open door.

'Keep the door barred,' he said. 'And Francis is a little better, surely? Of course I must go to the Commons, there's much still to do. The war party may try some trickery.'

Peter handed John his hat, but Anne seized it and threw it on the stairs.

'Listen to me, John!'

He turned back to her in astonishment.

'What ails you, Anne?'

'Nothing ails me! Rather ask, what ails you? Your children need you! I need you!'

Tears were pouring down her cheeks and suddenly she was shouting. She never shouted. John drew back a step.

'I have my duty, Anne. I must go to Westminster. This is no time for hysterics.'

'I am not hysterical!' she cried. 'I am begging you this once, the only time I have ever begged you, to forget your *duty* to Westminster and remember your duty to your family.'

She had seized his arm again and was shaking it, her face blotched with anger and weeping.

John withdrew his arm and picked up his hat.

'I cannot forget my duty to Westminster,' he said coldly, though his heart was pounding fast and erratically, and his breath caught in his throat. 'Calm yourself, Anne. This is not like you.'

'Perhaps I am always too calm,' she shouted. 'Ever since you came to Parliament, we have been like two ships drifting further and further apart on a rough sea. I think we have almost lost sight of each other.'

She drew a long shuddering breath and went on more quietly, although her hands were shaking.

'There was a time when we had one mind, one heart, in two bodies. Even when we were children. And when we were wed—we shared everything. I don't mean only a bed. We used to share our thoughts, we *talked* to each other.'

'Anne,' he was growing angry himself, 'we still talk. Have I not been telling you everything that is happening in Parliament?'

'Parliament!' she said drearily. 'You really do not understand what I am saying, do you?'

'No,' he answered curtly. 'I do not. Nor, I think, do you understand how your behaviour must seem, to the servants,' he nodded towards Peter, who was pressed back uncomfortably against the wall, 'and to the children, who will hear you, and the neighbours.'

'Dear God!' she cried, 'What care I for that? I am begging you, one last time, stay here with us today and let the Commons survive, if it can, without your presence.'

He shook his head and turned away.

'I cannot.'

She fled up the stairs and before Peter closed the door behind him he could hear her break into great wracking sobs.

It was an ominous start to what should be a joyful day. In truth, he realised with a sense of guilt, he wanted to go to the Commons not so much out of duty as from eagerness to triumph in yesterday's victory over the war party. Yet this strange behaviour of Anne's filled him with anger and apprehension. They almost never quarrelled, and he could not remember a time when she had ever attacked him with such passion. As he approached Palace Yard, his sense of dread deepened. He could hear shouting in the distance. There were soldiers everywhere and no sign of the London militia. Troops of the New Model Army, both cavalry and infantry, patrolled Palace Yard and blocked the entrance to the Court of Requests. John made his way round to the door of Westminster Hall and found that the hucksters and small shopkeepers who did business there had all been turned out in the snow, where they stood about in an angry crowd, complaining loudly. He could see no other members of Parliament, but a double row of armed soldiers lined the approach to the Palace of Westminster. All wore swords and carried muskets. He accosted an officer standing, apparently on duty, near the foot of the steps.

'Who are these men?' John demanded angrily. 'You have no business here, surrounding this free Parliament.'

The man stared at him insolently. 'And what's that to you, fellow? We are Colonel Rich's horse and Colonel Pride's foot. We're here carrying out the orders of the Army Council. Now get along out of here. Go home to your shopkeeping.' He raised his hand to push John in the chest. John's hand went to the dagger in his belt, but he bit down his anger.

'I am an elected member of the House of Commons,' he said coldly. 'Get out of my way, or I will summon the Sergeant-at-Arms and have you thrown in prison for interfering with the business of government.'

'Aye, sir!' shouted someone from the crowd of tradesmen. 'You tell him where to stick his musket!' Several others cheered.

'Member of Parliament, are you?' said the man with a grin, showing blackened teeth. He seemed not to care a fig for John's threats. 'Then you'd best speak to Colonel Pride. He's waiting at the top of the steps into the House.'

Colonel Pride was a bumptious, self-important little fellow, whom John had encountered once or twice before. He was a man from nowhere, though it was whispered that he had been a foundling abandoned in a basket on the steps of St Bride's church, which had bestowed on him his name. But over the years Bride had become Pride, and the man now made a pretence of being a gentleman, dressing like a fop and speaking with exaggerated care to cover his humble origins, having progressed from brewer's drayman to officer in the New Model Army. John could admire the man for making something of himself after such a sorry beginning, but he despised the affectation and hypocrisy which sought to conceal it.

Pride was indeed standing at the top of the steps, with a confused and worried-looking doorman beside him, and a group of armed troopers, with their swords drawn, standing behind. As John climbed the steps, he was seized with misgiving. He did not care for those drawn swords at Parliament's door. His steps slowed as he mounted higher. This show of military strength could mean only one thing. The army was prepared to enforce its will at sword point, in defiance of legitimate government. To make an armed attack on Parliament! Was the coterie of army officers planning to force the dissolution of Parliament? Or had they something even more dangerous in mind, the trial and execution of those who opposed them? In these lawless times, it was more than a possibility.

Cromwell believed himself to be the instrument of God. It was his contention that anything he set his hand to, if it prospered, must be the will of God, for God spoke to him directly, bidding him what to do. By this argument, if he succeeded in killing his political enemies, even members of the Commons going about their lawful business, the deed must be virtuous and providential, because he was God's chosen one. A man like Cromwell would contend that the destruction of Parliament by the sword was righteous merely because he ordered it. Against such spiritual arrogance, a man like John, who did not believe himself to be God's hand on earth, had little defence.

He found that he had stopped halfway up the stairs. Fearing to appear a coward, he ran up the remaining steps. Colonel Pride held a long sheet of paper in his hand, which flapped and struggled in the wind, so that he had to fight to hold on to it. He muttered something to the doorkeeper, who glanced at John, then slid his eyes away, as if ashamed, as he answered. Pride swept off his hat and bowed low to John.

'Sir,' he said courteously. 'Master Swynfen, Member of Parliament for Stafford?'

John looked at him stonily, but did not reply.

'Sir,' said Pride, his obsequious smile slipping a little and showing a brief flash of something satisfied and malicious in his eyes. 'I have orders to prevent you from entering this House and to place you under immediate arrest.'

Two of the armed men moved forward and seized John by the arms.

'I claim the privilege of this House,' said John levelly, although his heart was beating fast. The men were large, tough-looking rogues. 'You have no power to arrest an elected Member of Parliament without authority of this house. You are guilty of treason, colonel.'

'Take him away,' said Pride, waving his hand. He dipped his quill in the portable ink well he wore at his belt and made a mark on his paper.

Before John could be led away, Lord Grey of Groby came out to join Pride and whispered in his ear. A parliamentary clerk was sent inside. Then, at the door leading to the Commons, there was a brief commotion. Edward Stephens and John Birch, who must have arrived too early for Pride, or somehow slipped in unnoticed, were looking round the door to discover what was happening outside.

'Seize them!' cried Pride.

'Privilege! Privilege!' the two members yelled as they were grabbed by the armed soldiers. The crowd below began to shout and the mounted troopers rode forward to herd them back, away from the steps. Scuffles broke out. John saw a man struck down by a sword thrust from a trooper. Women started to scream. There was blood on the snow. Then he lost sight of the injured man as the crowd surged protectively around him. The troopers halted, but remained confronting the people, their swords held ready.

John Birch, a colonel of the army himself and no coward, broke free from the soldiers who had seized him and leaned back into the chamber.

'Do you sit there still?' he shouted to those few members who had been permitted by Pride to take their places in the House. 'Will you suffer your fellow members to be pulled out thus violently before your faces, and yet sit still? For shame!'

As John, together with Stephens and Birch, was hurried away from the steps, a loud altercation broke out behind them. Both they and their guards halted to watch. No one would expect William Prynne to accept such treatment quietly. Pride was barring his way up the stairs.

'Master Prynne, you must not go into the House.'

'I am a member of this House, sir,' Prynne shouted furiously, 'and I am going into it to discharge my duty.'

Prynne pushed up a step or two more, but Sir Hardress Waller came to Pride's assistance with more armed men and began dragging Prynne down and away towards the entrance to the Court of Requests. Prynne fought them angrily.

'This is an high breach of the privileges of Parliament,' he yelled, so that he could be heard by all around, 'and an affront to the House.'

He turned and waved his arms at the gaping bystanders. The crowd of tradesmen had not dispersed but had been swollen by many more citizens, astounded and furious at these actions taking place before the very doors of Parliament. Prynne was a popular hero, recently fêted, on his release from prison, by these same citizens dancing and cheering, and wearing festive rosemary and bay in their hats. They stared at him, thus violently arrested, in dismay. There were more angry shouts from the crowd, defying the troopers.

'Take note, you citizens of London and people of England,' Prynne cried, 'how these lawless men seek to replace one tyranny with another, the tyranny of the Stuart king with the tyranny of armed might! I am a man unarmed, going about my duties as your elected representative to this lawful Parliament. These men, being more and stronger than I, and all armed, may forcibly carry me whither they please. But stir I will not from this place of my own accord.'

At that, the soldiers put an end to it by picking him up roughly by the legs and shoulders, and carrying him off.

John and the others were hustled away, but not far. They were thrust into the open yard of the Queen's Court, which was ringed by a hundred or more soldiers with drawn swords. John was stripped of his sword and dagger, leaving him with nothing but the small pocket-knife he used to cut up his food. A few fellow members were already there, moderates and some of the more outspoken Presbyterians. Prynne was carried in amongst them, still struggling, and was dumped without ceremony on the snowy ground, where he lay a moment, regaining his breath. Birch helped him to his feet.

'Save your strength, man,' he said to the still expostulating lawyer. 'You are among none but friends here.'

Soon afterwards, the Sergeant-at-Arms hurried into the Queen's Court. He announced that Master Doddridge, who had arrived in company with Master Prynne, had informed the House what was happening. The Sergeant-at-Arms himself had been ordered by the House to come to the members here gathered, and invite them to return and take their seats. There was a surge forward amongst the prisoners, but the guards rushed to surround them tightly with a clash of their drawn swords. The low winter sun glinted on steel blade and breastplate. A surly-looking fellow dressed as a captain bowed with exaggerated courtesy to the Sergeant-at-Arms.

'I regret, sir,' he said, 'that you must inform the House that I cannot release these malefactors without orders from my superior officers.'

The Sergeant-at-Arms, looking both bewildered and afraid, departed to carry the message to the small remnant of the House.

As time passed, the prisoners roamed the confined area of the court, trying to warm their stiffening limbs, while their numbers were increased by new arrivals. Crewe greeted John ruefully.

'I suppose we should have seen this coming,' he said, 'but I hadn't thought they would act so soon.'

'What is their intention?' John asked. 'They're allowing some to enter the House. It cannot be dissolution.'

'Perhaps when they have enough of their own friends there, they will force a vote for dissolution, under the pretence of valid procedure.'

John glanced about the courtyard, puzzled.

'But there can't be above forty of us here. There would still be enough of our party left to out-vote the war party in the House.'

'Oh, we are but the distinguished few,' said Crewe wryly. 'Those that they've arrested. Our other friends are barred from the House and sent home, but they haven't been seized by force. Yet. *We* are the dangerous few. They dare not let us remain free. Look, they've even arrested old Rudyard.'

Sir Benjamin Rudyard was leaning against the wall of one of the buildings surrounding the court as John walked across to him. He looked frail and drawn, his skin bluish about the mouth, from the cold or perhaps from some more serious cause. He wiped his reddened eyes with a silk handkerchief.

'I do not weep,' he said stoutly to John. ''Tis but a rheum in the eyes, with this pestilential wind.'

'We might well all weep,' said John gravely, 'at what we see this day. The House of Commons attacked by armed men. Our elected government overthrown not by a tyrant prince but by an army recruited by Parliament itself to protect the people from the abuses of tyranny.'

'Aye, you speak truth, lad.'

'Come, sir,' said John. 'It's little enough, but there's an old mounting block over there where you may sit and rest a while.'

He led the old man to the mounting block, and then wrapped his own warm cloak around him.

'You can ill spare this,' said Rudyard.

'I shall walk up and down when I feel cold.'

John looked around at the shivering company. They were the men he expected to see here. Fiennes, who had spoken first in defence of the peace treaty. Bulkeley and Grimston from the commissioners who had negotiated with the king to secure the treaty, Clotworthy, D'Ewes, the Harleys. Those army officers who would have nothing to do with Cromwell and Ireton's seizure of power: William Waller, Edward Massey, Lionel Copley. His own fellow Stafford MP, Edward Leigh.

'I don't see Denzil Holles,' he said. 'Surely Holles is one of us they would be certain to arrest.'

Rudyard laughed aloud.

'Holles is sure to have fled before he could be arrested. The "bird" is flown once again. Some whisper of danger must have reached him. Nay, lad, you're too young to remember '29, when Holles and the other five "birds" were to be arrested by the king in the very House itself. In marches the king with his armed troopers, while out fly Holles and the others by the back door and we smuggle them aboard a waiting barge to flee down river to safety in the City.'

The old man smiled at the memory, and rubbed his bony hands together against the cold.

'Though indeed, on that occasion, Holles was all for staying, so that the king would be forced to arrest him in a struggle on the floor of the Commons, and so be shown up for a lawless tyrant who disrespected the privilege of the House. A week later, back the birds came to the House aboard a barge decorated like one of old King Harry's royal craft, and all the City and Westminster celebrating.'

'Then there was the matter of Speaker Finch, was there not?' said John. 'Was that later?'

'Aye, two months later, or thereabouts. The king ordered Speaker Finch to suspend Parliament. Now *there* was a cheeping little bird eager to do the king's bidding! When that rascal Finch tried to carry out the order, Holles pushed him back into the Speaker's chair and stood over him so that he dared not act. Holles is a big man still, but twenty years ago it would have taken a brave or a foolhardy man to resist him, and Finch was neither. Two days later, the king's men arrested nine members, including Holles, and sent them to the Tower. Sir John Eliot died there.'

'It was spoken of even in Staffordshire when I was a boy,' said John. 'We were all afire with the injustice of it. I swore then that when I grew to a man, I would defend the rights of Parliament against the king.'

'Well,' said Rudyard ironically, 'this moment in time may be your own chance of martyrdom in the Tower. I fear my old bones will not long survive imprisonment there.'

'You should not have been arrested,' said John. 'An old gentleman such as yourself. Forgive me if I speak out of turn, but you're nearly as old as my grandfather would be, had he lived till now.'

'An honest remark, if tactless,' said Rudyard. 'But I am indeed past the age for heroics. I leave that to you young men.'

John walked about the courtyard, rubbing his arms and stamping his feet against the icy chill which seeped into his boots from the churned snow. The downward drifting flakes had gathered in intensity, so that even the up-turned collar of his doublet was no defence. His shirt was soaking around his neck and shoulders, and his empty stomach ached. It was already long past mid-day, and none of the prisoners had taken food or drink since early morning, but their guards were impervious to pleas for victuals or shelter. Instead they shouted threats at the prisoners. Stephens asked quietly whether the older men, at least, might be granted some relief.

'Liars, cheats! Damned thieving bastards!' yelled one of the guards in reply, prodding Stephens none too gently with the tip of his sword. 'You've stolen our pay and pocketed it yourselves!'

'If that's the lie they've been fed,' said Nat Fiennes, 'we can expect no mercy from these men. What pay? Where do they think any money has been found? Best keep our distance from them.'

About halfway through the afternoon, Hugh Peter, the fanatical army preacher, hurried in to the Queen's Court. John turned away from the fellow in disgust. His round cheeks plump and greasy as a roasted pig, Peter bustled about with more than his usual self-important air. He was a known troublemaker, come back from the Americas, with a talent for stirring up mischief amongst the soldiers with his fiery sermons about their God-given rights and the golden future that lay ahead, did they but seize what was theirs for the taking.

'Look at him,' John said contemptuously to Crewe. 'A fine Saint he makes, with a sword by his side, like a boisterous soldier. He has decided he will have richer pickings here in England than in the savage land of the Virginias.'

But they must all swallow their pride and submit to having their names writ down on a list, Hugh Peter said, for the use of the Lord General Fairfax. When it came John's turn he repeated his name and constituency like any obedient schoolboy, although he knew that Peter recognised him and was making a great show of mishearing, and demanding the spelling of the difficult name, all to enhance his own imagined importance. He wrote down the name on his list as 'Swinton', then elaborately corrected it. As he must endure this indignity anyway, John decided to try to gain some good from it.

'Well enough, Master Peter, that you show this discourtesy to those of us who are young and able. But I am convinced that the Lord General cannot be aware that a decrepit old man like Sir Benjamin Rudyard is being kept here all day, outdoors in the storm and snow, without meat or drink, no fire to warm him, and not even a joint-stool to sit upon. 'Tis a dishonour to a man like Tom Fairfax to treat an old gentleman so, and a stain on his reputation.'

'It's not for such as you to speak of reputations,' Peter blustered, but John saw that he glanced across to where Rudyard still sat huddled on the mounting block, shaking with the cold in spite of John's cloak thrown over his own.

The rapacious agitator bustled off, but returned less than an hour later with Fairfax's order for the release of two of the prisoners. He made a great business of opening the paper and studying the names.

'Sir Benjamin Rudyard,' he read out. 'And . . . I cannot quite make out . . . ah yes, Nathaniel Fiennes.'

The prisoners murmured to each other. Rudyard they could understand, but Nat? Perhaps the whole matter was a show of strength only, and they would be released one by one, to subdue them and bring them to heel.

Nat helped the old man to his feet. He was so stiff and cold that he could barely walk.

'Give young Swynfen his cloak,' Rudyard said in a shaking voice. 'He must be as frozen as the Norway seas. I'm grateful to you, my boy. I had been dead by this, without it.'

'I don't know why I am privileged to walk away,' Nat muttered to John. 'I'll try to discover what I can, and send word to you.'

'I suspect Tom Fairfax had no hand in this seizure of our persons,' said John. 'Others are acting in his name, and he hesitates to gainsay them, for fear of mutiny in the army. But since your father is one of his oldest friends, he probably persuaded him to set you free.'

'Perhaps,' said Nat. 'I don't like to think that I am freed while the rest of you are left behind.'

'Away with you. Take that poor old man home to fire and food, and a warm bed,' said John.

He wrapped his cloak about him thankfully, for, despite moving constantly to try to keep his blood from freezing, he had rarely felt so cold in all his life, even when riding across Packington Moor through a winter's storm at home. His teeth clattered together with a noise like an ill-made loom. After the departure of Rudyard and Fiennes, the other members grew gradually more subdued as no word came of further releases. They had now been confined here for ten hours. Men had been forced to relieve themselves in corners, and the place had begun to stink. Some sat upon the ground in the snow, too exhausted to stand any longer. Some scooped handfuls of snow into their mouths, for they were parched with lack of drink. The guard of soldiers had been changed twice during the day, each new troop coming steaming out from one of the alehouses nearby, fortified with beef and beer.

Sir Robert Harley, the oldest of them now that Rudyard was gone, sat on the ground in a corner of the wall, trying to gain some shelter from the wind, for he was coughing and sneezing with a heavy cold.

'This is how our Parliamentary heroes are rewarded,' said John bitterly to Edmund Stephens, who was petulantly kicking at the snow. 'I see here William Waller, "William the Conqueror" as we used to call him, one of our most successful commanders in the early days of the war. This is the man who first suggested we should form a national army. This very army! And look at Rob Harley yonder. He'll take a fever and a flux of the lungs if he's not soon allowed indoors. The whole world knows how his lady Brilliana defended Brampton Bryan with a handful of musketeers against a besieging Royalist army. The name of Harley was admired throughout the land, and now it's come to this.'

Stephens shrugged. 'What's to be done, when we have to deal with men who think themselves Saints on earth? Even though their sainthood lie in waging war upon their friends and stealing the property of those whom, not long since, they were pleased to call their brothers. Do you suppose we are to be kept here all night? 'Tis near dark.'

As if in answer, the bustling Hugh Peter returned at that very moment, accompanied by a new group of officers.

'Gentlemen,' he said, twinkling with bonhomie, 'there are carriages awaiting you now at the Lord's stairs, to convey you to Wallingford House for the night.'

Murmurs of relief could be heard amongst the grumbling as the prisoners were herded by the armed guards, pushed and harried like a drove of beasts, along to the Lord's stairs and into a group of coaches lined up there. But it was nothing more than a stupid and cruel trick. The men settled themselves in the coaches, glad at last to be out of the snow and the wind, and off the coaches trundled, to stop a short distance further on. The doors were jerked open and they were prodded out with the points of the troopers' swords.

'Where are we?' asked Crewe. 'This is not Wallingford House.'

John peered around in the dark. The snow was falling more heavily again, but at last he made out where they were.

'I know this place,' he said. 'A fit place indeed. Gentlemen, we are come to the back door of *Hell*.'

Chapter Eight

The tavern familiarly known as *Hell* was dark, dirty, and noisy, but it did a good business amongst the clients and lawyers attending the Court of Exchequer. Like the taverns *Heaven* and *Purgatory*, it had once had another name, long forgotten by those who lived and worked about the Palace of Westminster. It was an ancient building, where men of no more than normal height must duck through doorways and under the heavy, rough-hewn oak beams that supported the low ceilings. On the ground floor there was one large room at the front where customers ate and drank. Beyond a screened passage at the back, a warren of cubby-holes provided privacy for those with secrets to discuss. The floors were strewn with filthy straw, unchanged for years, mingled with discarded chop bones, fleas, spittle, and cockroaches. Upstairs, two further storeys provided mean bedrooms, each storey jetting out further than the one below, canted over at an alarming angle and nearly pressed against the building on the opposite side of the street. In the floor of the passage behind the main room of the inn, a trapdoor opened to reveal a flight of time-worn steps, even older than the building itself, which led down to a cellar so lost in the past that men said it had been built by the Romans in the days of Londinium.

Master Duke, the inappropriately named innkeeper, stood beside the open trapdoor, wringing his hands in his greasy apron. He dared not protest against the seizure of his premises by the army, but could see only trouble for himself and his business looming ahead. He knew most of the prisoners. Since many were lawyers by training, they had often been his customers in their younger and penniless days. The poor fellow nodded and bobbed a half bow at these unwanted guests, unsure of the correct way to receive imprisoned Members of Parliament.

'Gentlemen, good evening. Welcome, ah . . . good evening to you, sir.'

With angry cries of protest, the prisoners were pushed down the steps into the windowless cellar. Lit on their way only by two candle-lanterns hung from the walls, several of them slipped on the damp stone and might have fallen to their great injury, had it not been for the press of bodies around them. When all had descended, the trapdoor dropped with a heavy thud over their heads, shutting out the noise from the tavern and the street, and with it the smell of soup, roasted meat and warm beer which the hungry men had sniffed with appreciation as they came in, despite the humble reputation of the inn.

As his eyes accustomed themselves to the poor light, John looked about to see what kind of quarters they had been given. On the soldiers' orders, clearly, Duke and his servants had removed anything which might have given comfort to the prisoners. Two wooden platforms against the walls, on which barrels normally stood, were fixed permanently in place, but the barrels, containing the solace of beer, had all been moved upstairs. The floor was bare flagstones, stained with beer but otherwise somewhat cleaner than the floor in the public room above. There was neither stool nor chair to sit upon, nor bed to lie upon. The walls glistened with running damp, and there was no fire, nor any fireplace where one might be laid.

'A Hell without hellfire, it seems,' said John to Clotworthy, who had sunk down on one of the barrel racks and was sitting with his arms crossed and his chin glumly sunk on his broad chest.

'I'm frozen to my very marrow,' said Clotworthy angrily, 'and if you don't hear my stomach growling like a lion for food, it can only be because your ears are grown deaf.'

'Or filled with the sounds of my own stomach,' said John. 'Do you suppose they intend to keep us here all night, without beds, or food, or drink? There's not so much as a piss-pot in this infernal place.'

'Aye, I've no doubt that was intentional,' said Crewe, squatting down on the floor beside Clotworthy. 'Nay, don't get up. We must take turn about to sit, for those racks will seat no more than ten of us out of the forty-two.'

'Intentional?' John echoed.

'Their desire is to humiliate us, as well as frighten us. What better way than to force us to sleep, hungry, on wet stone, and grow filthy in our own dirt?'

After perhaps an hour, the trapdoor was lifted, and the prisoners looked up hopefully as light and the smell of food drifted in. Perhaps their captors had relented. A young cornet of horse, no more than twenty, came mincing carefully down the steps, studying a piece of paper by the light of a candle in his hand. The curling feathers in his hat gave him more the look of a Royalist than one of Cromwell's men.

'I understand,' he said in a courteous tone, 'that six of you gentlemen have houses nearby: Sir Robert Harley, Master John Crewe, Master John Swynfen . . .'

'What trick is this?' John muttered.

'Perhaps they plan to move us to your six houses for the night,' said Clotworthy.

'Hush,' said Crewe.

'My orders are,' said the officer, 'to allow the six of you to go home, provided you will swear an oath to present yourselves tomorrow to the General and Council.'

John walked over and confronted him. He was taller than the officer, and took care to stand near enough to seem threatening without raising either his hand or his voice.

'I am John Swynfen, and indeed I have a house in St Ann's Lane. Will you send a message to my wife, to tell her what is afoot here?'

'You may tell her yourself, if you will swear the oath.'

'I will swear an oath indeed,' said John. 'I will swear to go home this night and I will attend the House of Commons tomorrow, as has been my duty and privilege these three years past. I will attend neither General nor Council, who have authority neither over my person nor over my responsibility to speak for the electors of Stafford in the governing of this country.'

There was a murmur of approval from behind him.

'I too,' croaked Sir Robert Harley, whose cold had almost robbed him of his voice. 'I will swear an oath to present myself at the House tomorrow morning.'

The others shouted their agreement.

'Well said.' Clotworthy clapped old Harley on the shoulder.

'This man is ill,' he said to the officer. 'You have no right to confine us in the cold and the dark. We have not eaten all day. You would not stable your horses in such a place.' Clotworthy, the great landowner, was accustomed to being obeyed, but his confident tone had no effect.

The young officer looked embarrassed, but began to climb back up the stairs, taking his candle with him.

'I have no authority to move you, nor to send for food. My orders are merely to make you this offer. If you refuse, I regret you must all stay here.'

By the time he finished speaking, his head and shoulders had risen above the level of the trapdoor. As his elegant bucket boots disappeared from sight, it was dropped back into place.

The hours dragged slowly on. It soon became clear that they were to be given no food, nor even water. The cellar was large, and must have reached away under the houses on either side of the tavern. So large was it, indeed, that the natural heat of their bodies drained away into the damp stone. Perhaps, as matters grew worse, they would huddle together for warmth like poor fugitives from one of the towns sacked during the recent years of war, but for the moment it had not come to that; they kept their dignity and their distance. John roamed about for a time, examining the cellar, more for something to occupy himself than in any hope of finding a way out. The walls were built of finely dressed stone, a construction much more skilled than the later building above, which was perhaps no more than three or four centuries old. With apologies to his fellows, he unhooked one of the lanterns and carried it into the furthest corner.

'Have you found a way of escape, Swynfen?' asked Edward Massey, following him. He was one of the youngest prisoners, younger even than John, at the age of thirty an army colonel of formidable reputation, who probably resented this restraint more than any. He had been prowling restlessly all day, first in the courtyard and now in the cellar.

'I'm afraid not. I was intrigued by this carving.' John held up the light. Where it fell upon a projecting piece of the wall, a bull's head leapt suddenly into sight as if come to life. John ran his fingers over the cut edges of the stone. It was as sharp as the day some man's hand had first carved it with skill and reverence.

'That's no idle stonemason's scratching,' said Massey. 'Look, there are letters below.'

They peered closely at the lower stone, part of which had been hacked away at some time.

'MITHR,' John read. 'Then this broken piece. Then DEO, and another break. Then AVIT. Part of a verb, but who can say what?'

'Not enough to make sense.'

'No. But the soldiers in the Roman army worshipped a god called Mithras. And I believe bulls were held to be sacred to him. Some pagan practice. I recall reading about him during my student days in Cambridge.'

'A kind of pagan altar, then?'

'Perhaps.' John shivered. 'This place is fearful enough without that. Best not to mention it.'

The heavy blocks of stone curving over his head to form the vaulted roof seemed suddenly to have sunk nearer. He felt the weight of the earth and stone and buildings above, the weight of years pressing down on him. A thin trickle of dry mortar whispered down the wall. This was how it must feel to be buried alive. His lungs struggled to draw in air.

They moved back to the main part of the cellar, and John returned the lantern to its hook.

'I cannot endure to be confined,' said Massey, slapping the indifferent wall angrily with the flat of his hand. 'If they mean to keep us imprisoned more than a few hours, I shall find some means to escape.'

'Easily said.'

Massey shrugged. 'I'd rather die escaping than rot in a dungeon.'

He went over to join other military men grouped at the foot of the steps and talking earnestly. Besides the colonels Massey and Birch, there were three generals: Sir William Waller, Sir John Clotworthy and Lionel Copley. John squatted down on the floor under the lantern, where Prynne, silent for once, was sitting on the damp stone reading his pocket Bible.

Prynne looked up. 'No secret smugglers' passage down to the river, then?' He grinned at John. When the man was neither preaching nor ranting, he wasn't a bad fellow.

John shook his head. 'All as solid built as the Tower. Here we stay until we go out through that trapdoor.'

He nodded towards the steps. Birch and Massey had climbed to the top and put their shoulders to the trap, but even with Birch's great strength they could not shift it.

'Bolted,' someone called. 'Or barrels moved on top to hold it fast.'

John's own words reminded him of Prynne's past. 'You endured long imprisonment in the Tower—how did you pass the time without losing your wits?'

'Anything that might take my mind off my plight. Prayer. Reading. Writing—when I could get paper and ink. Singing psalms.'

'Now there's an idea. Why don't you lead us in singing?'

Prynne was never unwilling to be asked.

'And you, Swynfen? Haven't I heard you have an excellent voice?'

'I sing sometimes with friends of an evening, after a good supper. Madrigals and motets. Still, the echoes of an empty stomach should lend our voices a fine resonance. Will you give us the note?'

A few of the men were trying to sleep, stretched out uncomfortably on the floor or on the barrel racks, so they sang softly.

Bless the Lord, O my soul. O Lord my God, thou art very sweet; thou art clothed with honour and majesty.

Who coverest thyself with light as with a garment: who stretches out the heavens like a curtain:

Who layeth the beams of his chambers in the waters: who maketh the clouds his chariot: who walketh upon the wings of the wind.

The stone walls cupped the music of their voices as sweetly as a wine goblet, like a great bell vibrating with the sound. One by one, other voices joined them. They were all devout men. The singing eased their hearts and the words of the psalm comforted them. The psalmist's vision of a garment of light, the wings of the wind, thrust back for a time the reality of this dark and airless prison.

He causeth the grass to grow for the cattle, and herb for the service of man: that he may bring forth food out of the earth;

And wine that maketh glad the heart of man, and oil to make his face to shine, and bread which strengtheneth man's heart.

Their voices rang out more strongly, praising the joys of life denied to them in this cold and fearful place. Bread and oil and wine, thought John. It needs little enough to make glad the heart of man. And the fir trees, the high hills, the very rocks are a refuge for man as well as beast.

O Lord, how manifold are thy works! in wisdom hast thou made them all: the earth is full of thy riches.

So is this great and wide sea, wherein are things creeping innumerable, both small and great beasts.

There go the ships: there is that leviathan, whom thou hast made to play therein.

The walls of the prison seemed to John to fade from his sight, and instead he saw the world stretching out before him in all its diversity and beauty: men and beasts, birds of the air, mountains and seas, all moving in their appointed ways, the mighty leviathan, monarch of the roughest ocean, ploughing silent and swift towards the strange new world of the Americas.

I will sing unto the Lord as long as I live: I will sing praise to my God while I have my being.

As the last words whispered and faded amongst the dark corners of their prison, all voices, singing or speaking, fell silent. A few more of the men lay down upon the ground, or crouched with their foreheads resting on their up-drawn knees, trying to sleep. Some sat together in groups. John recalled that he had his own small Bible in the pocket of his doublet. The print was difficult to read in the poor light, but Prynne was right. Best to occupy the mind, to keep it from dark thoughts. He turned over the pages. The story of Jonah in the belly of the leviathan seemed appropriate. Or of Daniel in the lion's cave.

John woke. His chin had fallen forward on his chest, painfully stretching the muscles of his neck. The icy damp of the stone floor seeped through the flesh of his thighs and stiffened the very marrow of his legs. One by one he prised his fingers from his Bible, where they had locked in a deathlike rigour, as if he gripped it to save himself from drowning in the horror of his dream. His teeth had clenched on his tongue, drawing blood that seeped warm in his mouth. The recollection of the woman hung in the air. The woman in the sea-blue gown he had seen just before he was attacked on the doorstep of his home. The woman meant nothing, but the colour of her gown preyed on his mind, unlocking those memories he had, so long and so carefully, kept hidden away.

When he was a boy of ten, he had been sent to spend a month with cousins of his grandmother, who lived in Warwickshire. His grandmother had died before ever he was born, but the Swynfens had kept up the connection with the Lisle family and John's father Richard wanted his eldest son to see a little more of the world than his native Staffordshire. In the household of Geoffrey Lisle, royal sheriff, John would meet men who held positions of power in the county of Warwick. In that year of 1623, there were already fine cracks appearing in the social fabric of England, but Richard Swynfen was not yet hostile to all those who held royal office.

John had enjoyed his visit at first, hunting and hawking with his older cousins, patiently enduring Margaret Lisle's instruction in courtly manners. Geoffrey Lisle was a busy man of affairs and considered it part of his responsibility to his young cousin to introduce him to such county duties as would one day fall to his lot. So it came about that John attended the assize over which Geoffrey presided. Afterwards, John had only a blurred recollection of the assize, except for the one case that branded itself on his memory for the rest of his life.

The man, a young fellow of about twenty called Edmund Watson, was one of Geoffrey's own tenants, living with his wife Isabel and very young baby in a one-roomed cottage which stood on swampy ground near the river. John knew the family, for he had lost his hawk and tracked it down to a willow which thrust its naked roots out from the muddy bank close beside the Watsons' cottage. Edmund had helped him catch the errant bird and afterwards John had played with the baby boy, who lay on a shawl in a patch of sun before the door. He could see that the Watsons were very poor and the roof of their cottage was falling in at one end. He was shamed by the sight of it, for he knew his own father and grandfather would not allow any of their own tenants to live so.

Now Edmund Watson was up before the assize charged with poaching a rabbit from the nearby royal warren. John understood that poaching was a terrible crime, but a magistrate might exercise some discretion and compassion in the matter. The game stolen was a rabbit, not a deer. Moreover, Edmund had taken the rabbit because his family was starving, not in order to sell it and earn coin. It lay with sheriff Geoffrey Lisle to determine the punishment—branding, perhaps, or ear-clipping.

He decreed hanging.

Geoffrey required John to attend the hanging with him, for he said that a man who held office from the king must see the king's justice carried through to full satisfaction. One day it would fall to John himself to dispense the king's justice in his own county. Edmund Watson was hanged in the grey, misty dawn following the trial. He had been permitted to speak no word at his trial. He chose to speak no word at his hanging. His hands were tied, his eyes bound with a kerchief.

Why were Edmund's eyes covered? John watched it done, gripping his hands together to hold himself in check. Was it so that the condemned man might not see his executioners? Or was it to spare the crowd the guilt of looking into the eyes of a starving man whom the king's justice had sentenced to death? There was no elaborate scaffold for this poor man's hanging, no public gibbet erected. The sheriff's officers threw a rope over the branch of a tree, ordered the blindfold man to climb onto a stool, then kicked the stool from beneath him.

John had tried to run away from the hanging, but Geoffrey kept his hand clamped on the boy's shoulder like a carpenter's vice. John closed his eyes, but he could not shut out the horror of Edmund's rasping gurgle, nor the stink as the body evacuated itself. Afterwards, Geoffrey and his fellow officials took a glass of brandy at the inn, and he forced a little of the burning liquid between John's chattering teeth.

As soon as his cousin's back was turned, John slipped between the men who crowded the small private parlour and out through the door which led to the kitchen. Sweaty women ran to and fro carrying greasy dishes piled high with some indescribable mess. To one side of the open hearth a scrofulous small boy with vacant eyes sat on a stool, endlessly turning the jack, while the meat on the spit dripped and spat, and the red flesh began to char at the edges. John ran across the flagged floor, heedless of the women he pushed aside, and out into the yard at the back of the inn. There he crouched down behind an ale barrel, retching. His stomach heaved and strained, for he had eaten nothing all day, ever since he had learned that he was sentenced to attend the hanging. Nothing came from his mouth but a dribble of yellow bile.

Before dawn the next morning, John crept out of his bedchamber with his shoes in his hands, and felt his way to the storerooms beyond the kitchen. With wild disregard of discovery, he filled a basket with venison pie, cold beef, eggs, cheese, ale and apple tarts before pulling on his shoes and letting himself out into the cold morning air. He ran through the formal gardens which surrounded the house, then along the edge of a wheat field, sodden with the morning dew. The first rays of the sun were falling across the water meadow as he came down towards the Watsons' cottage, so that the long grasses starred with shy flowers glowed with a pearly light. His shoes, stockings and breeches were soaked, his shirt clung to the sweat on his back, and his breath came in gasps, for something told him he must bring food to Isabel and the baby before they starved to death this very morning.

There was no one in the cottage. The cooking hearth was cold. He put down his basket on the earth floor and ran along the river bank, calling for Isabel. At first he paid no heed to the dark clump caught in the trailing branches of the willow, then he stopped. The gown was a curious, particular shade of blue, a blue with the green of the sea in it. John had never seen Isabel wear any other, yet it was a fine gown, too fine for a pauper girl, though stained and mended now. It must once have belonged to Margaret Lisle, and found its way from her to waiting gentlewoman, to servant, to pauper. Isabel floated amongst the yellow-green leaves of the willow, the baby held fast in her arms, and even in death she was not at rest, for her face wore a look of infinite despair.

And from that time John could never see that colour, the blue of the ocean, without tasting the bile in his mouth and remembering the circle of bitter ripples which flow outwards and outwards from the infliction of royal justice.

When his theft of food was discovered, and its purpose, he was beaten, for defying the judgement of Geoffrey Lisle. He endured it in silence. His shame was worse punishment than the beating, for he had failed in his attempt to help Isabel and her child. His greater shame—that he had not spoken out against the judgement during the trial—had remained with him lifelong. For the remainder of his time in the Lisles' household he withdrew into sullen silence. Once home again he said nothing to his parents or his grandfather, but at last, sitting on a ridge in Packington moor, the horses cropping the grass nearby, he told the story, halting and brief, to Anne.

She said nothing for long minutes, then finally took his hand.

'You cannot blame yourself,' she said hesitantly. 'It was not your fault Edmund Watson died, or his wife and babe.'

John was comforted somewhat by her small warm hand in his, but he screwed up his mouth bitterly.

'I can't forget that they were starving. Why should my cousin condemn a man to hang because he sought merely to keep his life? To feed his wife and child? I know Geoffrey Lisle acted within the law. I know it. But can the law be right? What kind of justice is that? Is that God's justice? I think not.'

'When you are a man grown, and a magistrate, you can dispense the law kindly,' she said. 'That is some kind of justice.'

'It's not enough,' he said, and fell to brooding again.

Later, at Cambridge, he launched headlong into many a heated debate, cautiously with his tutors, more wildly with his fellow students in taverns, on evenings when tongues were loosened with ale. There were many who abused him for presuming to question the rights of their families to ancient privileges of land and law, but there were also a few who agreed tentatively that England was ripe for change, certainly that something must be done to curb the powers of the king and the lords of the church. From then his way was clearly laid out before him, to Grey's Inn and Parliament.

John leaned his head back now against the rough stone of the cellar wall and closed his eyes. The memory of Edmund and Isabel had started him along the course which had brought him to this dark prison, but what had it profited the men like Edmund? Or the women like Isabel, watching their children grow grey and hollow-eyed with starvation? Were they any better in a kingdom torn and bloodied by civil war? A kingdom where land lay fallow for want of seed, and harvests rotted or burned? It seemed now that the one gift he might have given them, the gift of peace, was torn from his hands and trampled under foot.

He remembered fragments of the dream which had driven him awake, sitting in this cold prison in no better case than Edmund. A black dream, filled with confused images and terror for his family. He was a man now himself, with a wife and children to cherish. The killing of Edmund Watson had set his feet on this path, but that was long ago, a quarter of a century. Now he had his own stake in the future, those precious lives which were in danger, as he was in danger. He must somehow send word to Anne to escape from London before his enemies turned their attention to his family. Furious at his impotence, he slammed his head back against the stones of the wall, as if he could beat his way out into the light.

Anne kept to the house all day on Wednesday, thinking it safer not to venture out into the street where so many soldiers roamed about. No one came near except for tradesmen. Soon after John left for Parliament, the baker's man arrived with his basket of bread, and Anne sent Hester with threepence for three large loaves. After that the house was strangely quiet. The children seemed subdued by the continued presence of the army outside, and the servants went about their work nervously, murmuring in corners. In the afternoon Anne sat with Francis. He had been a little better in the morning, and begged to be allowed to get up, but she would not permit it. Now he lay with his eyes shut but not sleeping. His fever was so high Anne could feel the heat coming off him in waves. From time to time he moaned a little and tossed off the blankets, which she tucked firmly back again, for the attic room was bitterly cold.

Peter tapped softly at the door and put his head around it.

'Mistress Swynfen? The dairymaid has just delivered the milk. She apologised for coming so late, but there's been a great to-do, she said, and many of the streets are blocked. She had great difficulty calling at her usual houses.'

'What sort of to-do? Is she still here?'

'Nay, she wouldn't stop. Troops of horse around Parliament, she said, and foot soldiers with drawn swords standing on duty in all the roads leading there. The talk in the street is of arrests, but who's arrested, no one can say. I thought you should know. It may be the master will be late again tonight.'

'You were right to tell me. Thank you, Peter.'

'Young Master Francis, how is he?'

'Worse, I'm afraid. Come and sit with him while I fetch more of my fever medicine and make up a poultice to draw the ill humours from his head.'

The house in St Ann's Lane heard no more news of the outside world until the evening. Patience was sitting with Francis while Anne ate a hasty supper of bread, cheese and ale in the kitchen. With the household so disrupted and all the glassware and plate packed away, Anne saw no reason to maintain a pretence of normality by eating alone or with Patience in the dining parlour. Accordingly, she was in the kitchen when a knock came at the back door and Ned's nephew, young Sam Carpenter, a journeyman tailor, came in stamping the snow from his boots and shaking it off his cap into the kitchen hearth, where it set the coals spitting and steaming. His glance took in the packed cases on the floor and the cupboard doors standing ajar.

'I beg pardon, Mistress Swynfen,' he said, unable to conceal his surprise at seeing her sitting there amongst the servants at the kitchen table. He ran his fingers through his spiky red hair in an attempt to flatten it.

'We are all in a caddle here,' said Anne. 'Come to the fire and warm yourself. Have you supped?'

'Aye, thankee, but I'll take a cup of ale to steady me after running the curfew.'

'Curfew!'

'It seems the army rules London now, and they have imposed a curfew at nightfall. Our Trained Bands were sent back from Westminster to the City this morning. But I'd promised myself to come and see how my uncle was faring. And all of you,' he added courteously.

'What news?' Anne clasped her hands together anxiously. 'What has happened in Parliament, if the army has seized power in the streets? My husband hasn't been home since morning.'

He looked at her gravely, straddling the hearth with his ale mug in his hand.

'I thought you'd be sure to have heard by now. Ireton and his fellows have turned away near two hundred of the members from the House. Driven them away at the point of the sword. And seized some of them. Carried them off, no one knows where.'

He cleared his throat.

'Those who were turned away but weren't arrested—well, most of them have already fled London and gone home to their own counties. 'Tis the general belief they'll be safer there, amongst their own people. Parliament is destroyed. Everyone knows Master Swynfen is no friend of the war-mongers. Only the army's men were allowed into the House this morning. If your husband didn't come home again by noon, then he's one of those arrested and imprisoned.'

❧

Not one of the household slept that night. Anne stayed with Francis and put Jack and Ralph into her own bed. The fever was coming to a crisis and around midnight Francis became delirious.

'Go away!' he shrieked, lashing out at some monster only he could see, struggling against the bedclothes. 'Nay! Nay! I won't!'

Anne called Peter to help her hold the child so that he would not injure himself as he fought the demons. At last he slumped back, exhausted, in Anne's arms. His fair hair was darkened with sweat and plastered to his head, and his night shift was wringing wet, but he seemed a little cooler. Peter brought up a jug of warm water from the kitchen. Anne stripped the child and bathed him while Peter put dry bedding on the bed. Francis had lost weight in the last few days; his body was pathetically thin, his ribs standing out like a wrecked ship sunk in a sandbank. He lay as loose on her lap as a bundle of rags. She dressed him again in a clean night shift, wrapped him in a blanket, and cradled him in her arms.

After Peter had taken away the damp bedding to dry by the kitchen hearth, Bess peeped nervously round the door. She was a plump, kindly girl, but inexperienced. She had come to them, a scrawny thirteen-year old, just before they had come to Westminster, with little to recommend her but a natural fondness for children. Anne had had no time to search further for a woman servant before they left Staffordshire, after the death of the old family nurse two weeks earlier. Here, with no great household to run, she had taken on more care of the children herself, and Bess was learning, slowly, but in an emergency she was apt to come running to Anne, uncertain what to do. In her arms now she was carrying Mary, who sobbed fretfully, kneading a scarlet cheek with her fist.

'The babe is sickening, too, mistress,' said Bess. Her cap was gone, pulled off by the child, and her hair hung about her shoulders in a distraught tangle.

Mary held out her arms to Anne, and then, when she saw Francis occupying her rightful place on her mother's lap, she began to scream and kick with rage.

Examining the baby as best she could while Bess held her, Anne was relieved to find she was only slightly feverish. The reddened cheek and frantic rubbing convinced her what was wrong.

'I think she's teething, Bess. Go to the still-room and bring me the gallipot third from the left, on the bottom shelf. I'll rub her gums with my paste of cloves and peppermint.'

She could not trust Bess to do it herself, for the girl could not read the label. She might fill the child's mouth with an embrocation for sore muscles or a rhubarb purge.

The clove paste quietened Mary for a time, surprised and comforted by the strange taste in her mouth, but she was soon raging and screaming again, hitting out at poor Bess when she tried to comfort her. One whole side of her face was enflamed. Anne put the sleepy

96

Francis back to bed and entrusted him to Patience's care, while she took Mary down to sit by the kitchen fire, as far away from Francis as possible, that he might benefit from a healing sleep.

It was a weary while for everyone, since despite all Anne's efforts Mary screamed with pain the rest of the night, robbing the household of rest and fraying already stretched nerves. By morning all were short-tempered with fatigue. Ned had refused to go home to the City with his nephew the evening before, saying the mistress would need the two men about the house if Master Swynfen was indeed in danger. This morning, however, watching him trying to make up the fires with his shaking hands, Anne feared she could soon have another invalid to care for. Sam had promised to return as soon as he could, to help the family however he might. Anne knew she would be glad of his help, if she decided to escape from London. She had never expected she might have to make the journey home without her husband. With so many people dependent on her, she dreaded the thought of embarking on such a perilous undertaking.

As day broke and she retired to her chamber to change out of the clothes she had worn all night, she felt as if demons were pulling her brain in a dozen different directions. Should she leave or should she stay? Should she fetch Nan and Dick home from school? Would it be safe to travel all the way from Westminster, through the City, and out into the country, to fetch Nan back from Hackney? And what if the unborn babe should come early, while they were travelling home to Staffordshire? Nan, Francis and Mary had all been born before their full time. The wild country north and west of London, an area notorious for footpads and highwaymen, and in a snow-bound coach, was no place to give birth.

And still no word came from John.

The one consolation for the freezing cold in the cellar of *Hell* was the thought that in summer the stench would have been far worse. Forty-two men, confined for many hours in an airless place, some of them old and infirm, some loose in their guts with fear, took on a stink worse than a herd of animals awaiting the slaughterer's knife. As the hours of the night passed, the cellar began to reek like a midden and every breath seemed to draw in too little of the wretched air to feed the lungs. They had eventually all fallen silent, though few could sleep, and waited miserably on events. Twice during the night Master Duke had sent down a frightened servant with new candles for the lanterns, but he could not, or would not, answer the prisoners' questions.

Climbing to his feet, his breeches damp from the stone floor, John found that his injured shoulder, which had begun to mend, had stiffened in the night. As his swung his arm cautiously, trying to work some feeling back into the knotted muscles, the dressing tore from the wound with a sickening stab of pain. He leaned against the wall, dizzy, with nausea climbing in his throat. Crewe cast an anxious look at him, but he shook his head slightly, urging silence.

Clotworthy had a pocket watch, which was about as accurate as any to be had, but he could not vouch for the true time. With its Delft blue enamel laid between gold filigree, it was more a thing of ornament and vanity than an instrument of scientific accuracy. He tilted it towards the nearest lantern and tried to make it out.

'It reads ten o'clock, but that could mean anything from eight of the clock to noon.'

'Better than this, at any rate,' said Crewe with a rueful smile, holding out his pocket sundial on the flat of his palm. 'If we could but hear the Abbey bells in this infernal hole—'

Overhead, the trapdoor gave out its now familiar rasping groan as it was thrown back. Few of the prisoners even bothered to glance up, having despaired of any food or other comforts. A new, more senior officer came carefully down the steps, accompanied by a rush of fresh air.

'That's the Provost Marshal,' said Massey softly in John's ear. 'At last, someone more senior than a lackey.'

Dark-haired and sallow, his buff coat and sash showing signs of hard wear, the Provost Marshal gave a slight bow, as uncertain of the formalities in this situation as the men who regarded him resentfully.

'Gentlemen, I trust you have not spent too uncomfortable a night.'

This insulting remark was greeted with shouts of derision.

'Let us out of this filthy hole!'

'Privilege! Privilege!'

'You traitorous dog!'

'None of us has had bite or sup for more than a day. For God's sake, man, send for some breakfast!'

'There are old men here, and sick men. You've not given us so much as a crust of stale bread or a mug of water.'

The general clamour for food overwhelmed all other demands. In the end, the Provost Marshal agreed reluctantly to return to army headquarters to try to arrange for breakfast. When he had gone, the mood of the prisoners improved. Some even combed their hair. John rasped his hand along his unshaven chin. Suddenly conscious of the appearance of his fellows, he realised he must look like a filthy, half-wild brigand by now. Still, his heart lifted at the thought of food. He was growing weak with hunger. With meat in his belly, any man is twice as brave.

It must have been an hour before the Provost Marshal returned from Whitehall Palace, and as the trapdoor was lifted this time, all could hear the bells of the abbey ring out eleven o'clock.

The Provost Marshal was not accompanied by breakfast. Instead, he stood at the top of the steps and ordered the prisoners brusquely to ascend them one by one. As each man did so, his elbow was seized by a musketeer and he was hustled through the public room of the tavern to the front door. Innkeeper Duke sat forlornly amongst his empty tables, but his expression lightened considerably as he realised that his uninvited guests were being taken away. Dim as the winter sun was, and blurred with falling snow, John found himself groping and staggering across the room like a blind man, what with the long confinement in the dark cellar and the stiffness of his limbs. He clutched at the door frame for support, only to be jerked away by his guard.

'Get into the coach,' the man said, propelling him forward with a blow of his fist between the shoulder blades.

John half fell into the coach and was pulled aboard by Stephens and Copley as the door was slammed behind him. The musketeer slapped the side of the coach to signal to the driver to move on.

'Where are they taking us?' asked John. He was forced to stand, holding on to a tasselled grab-rope. All the seats were filled, and Stephens and Copley were also standing. As the coach lurched over the uneven cobbles, they fell against one another.

'To Whitehall,' said Copley, clutching John's shoulder to steady himself. 'To be interviewed by that pack of insolent traitors. Some of them were my own junior officers once.'

'I pray they give us something to eat,' said Massey, whose knees were pushed sideways against the door because of the crush. 'I swear I've never been so hungry, not even on campaign. I'll fight every man-jack of you for the first crust!'

Several groans of agreement greeted this remark.

At Whitehall Palace, once the London home of the royal family, the prisoners were marched off and confined to a very cold room, without a fire. It was an improvement on last night's prison. The walls were not running with wet. There were windows and a carpet on the floor. There were even a few chairs, although not enough for all. John walked over to a window and looked out. Until last night he had never supposed that he suffered from a fear of enclosed places, but the sense of relief he now felt came more from being out of that terrible cellar than from any hope that their fortunes had turned.

Here the prisoners were kept confined for several hours. The Provost Marshal informed them that the Army Council was too busy debating more pressing matters to turn its attention to the trivial affair of the arrested Members of Parliament. A brief diversion occurred when Thomas Gewen and Charles Vaughan were thrust through the door to join them. The prisoners crowded round them, begging for news.

'Yesterday,' said Vaughan, 'the remaining members—those allowed into the House—refused to conduct any more business until you prisoners were released. And today many who've been excluded have sent in written protests to the Speaker.'

'God be praised,' said Prynne. 'Even their cronies in the House look on appalled at what these lawless men are perpetrating.'

'Don't raise your hopes,' said Gewen. 'Fifty more were turned away from the House today, on the grounds that yesterday "they stickled for the privilege of Parliament and the restoration of the members now in hold". Then we two were arrested.'

Gewen and Vaughan had little other news, except that some members, like Holles, had fled London before they could be arrested, and many of the secluded members had retired to the country, there to lie low or else to gather local support, according to their temperaments.

John pounded his fist against the panelled wall.

'It will mean war, all to be endured again, now with those who were once friends tearing each other apart!'

The waiting continued, the room grew colder. Sir Robert Harley had lost his voice entirely and seemed to grow more ill with each passing hour.

One of the older men, Thomas Lane, had been sitting in a chair against the wall without moving for some time. His head had slumped on his shoulder in such a way that it aroused John's concern. He touched Lane on the shoulder.

'Sir? Are you unwell?'

Lane struggled to lift his head and gave a groan, then slid suddenly off the chair to the floor at John's feet. Stephens and Massey rushed forward to help John lay the man more comfortably, with someone's cloak rolled up under his head and two more spread over him against the cold.

'His breathing is light, but normal,' said John, scrambling to his feet again. 'I think he's simply fainted from lack of food and drink.'

At about six o'clock, servants at last brought in trays of victuals and set them down on a side table. They withdrew quickly before any could lift the cloths covering the trays.

'Burnt wine and biscuits!' cried Waller in disgust. 'After a day and a half of starvation. I never treated even a captured enemy thus.'

However, they fell upon the meagre food, finishing it in a few minutes. John carried a share over to Thomas Lane, who had been raised up by Crewe and now sat on the floor, leaning groggily against Crewe's shoulder.

'Take some of this, slowly now, sir,' said John. ''Tis little enough, but it will make you feel better.'

It was dark before another officer appeared, only to say insolently that the Army Council was too busy to see them today.

'You'll be told the army's terms tomorrow. You're to leave the Palace now. Follow me.'

They went shuffling out after him, dirty, stiff, hungry, even the young men bent and awkward as grandfathers. Outside stood a single coach, in which six of the oldest and most infirm were permitted to ride. The coach drove off, and a musketeer seized each of the other prisoners by the arm. They were marched off after the coach, a heavy guard of soldiers surrounding them on all sides to prevent escape. Out of the grounds of Whitehall Palace to King Street they went, the soldiers setting a fast pace, too fast for men deprived of sleep and food, whose bones ached with sitting upon wet stone and hard floors. They turned right into King Street and marched about a quarter of a mile to Charing Cross, all the way taunted and threatened by the soldiers with what fate lay in store for them.

Near Charing Cross, a small group of the prisoners was herded into an inn called the *Swan*. The rest were marched further along the Strand until they reached the *King's Head*.

'Better quarters than *Hell*, at least,' said Waller, who was walking next to John.

'Quiet, you,' said a soldier, striking him on the head with the butt of his musket.

Somehow that blow, more than all the rest of the misery and humiliation they had suffered since yesterday morning, brought home to John the real danger they faced. That a common soldier should strike a hero of the Parliamentary army with impunity could have only one meaning. General Sir William Waller and his fellows were friendless and helpless. The Tower or some other prison awaited them. And at the end of it, the hangman's noose or the executioner's axe.

Chapter Nine

'To travel from *Hell* to the *King's Head* is no great journey,' said John, 'given the present danger to the king's own head. A danger we seem likely to share.'

'Better than to travel from the *King's Head* to *Hell*,' said Crewe. His face had regained some of its rubicund hue now they were warmed at little. Someone had kindled a fire in the meagre fireplace, where they stood flexing their stiff fingers.

Six of them had been given a small room to share, on the second floor of the inn: Swynfen, Crewe, Massey, Clotworthy, Lane and Prynne. Accommodation would be much better than the previous night, though they would have to sleep three to a bed. The bedding was frayed and worn—this was a servants' room—but at least it was dry. It was a wretched chamber with a sloping ceiling, in which not one of them could stand upright. Clotworthy, with his bull-like frame, looked as though he would strike out the wall timbers if he failed to keep a watch on where he put his elbows. The inn was surrounded by a solid body of soldiers, so they had no prospect of escaping by the window, as Massey quickly ascertained. Small and slender, he had hoped to wriggle out and climb down the slope of the roof. There was scarcely room here for him to resume his restless pacing. At the door of the chamber, four more armed men were posted. Someone had taken a deal of trouble to make sure they were secure.

Care had also been taken in dividing them amongst the bed chambers. The Provost Marshal had a new list which he consulted as he ordered them to their rooms. The main feature of it, as far as John could judge, was to separate the senior army officers. All were hardened battle veterans. The maker of the list—Ireton, for sure—wanted to prevent them pooling their military skills to effect an escape. Space in the inn was limited, however, so through some oversight Massey and Clotworthy were confined in the same room.

'You may buy food from the innkeeper,' said the Provost Marshal, 'and it will be brought to your chambers. You must keep to your rooms, except when you use the privy. Do not think that is a route to escape. You'll be accompanied by an armed musketeer at all times.'

This order called forth some ribald replies from the prisoners, who were cheered at the prospect of beds and food. Shut into their chamber, John and his companions put their heads together.

'Have we the chinks for food?' asked John, pulling out his own purse.

Some had more, some less. None had set out for Parliament the previous morning with more than a handful of money.

'I put the motion,' said John, 'that we make a common purse of what we have, so we may all share equally in food and drink. None of us is carrying enough to bribe the guards to let him escape.'

The others cheerfully agreed. Crewe and Clotworthy, who knew him well, probably guessed that his motive was to provide for Prynne, whose long fight for the rights of Englishmen had beggared him. Indeed, he had no more than two sixpences and a ha'penny to add to the common purse. The guards at the door agreed to send one of the servants of the inn to deal with them. When the man came, he eyed them curiously, particularly, it seemed, Thomas Lane, who had recovered from his fainting fit and seemed determined not to yield to weakness again.

'I'll fetch your food and drink as quickly as I can, gentlemen,' said the tapman, 'but we're all of a pother in the kitchen, with thirty of you gentlemen, as I understand, and all the soldiers besides. The master has sent out for more pies to the cookhouse in the Strand, and the maids are stewing up a deal of beef and onions.'

The prisoners sat on the two beds like a row of hungry fledglings, their mouths watering, for the man had carried in on his clothes the succulent aroma of roasting onions. He was as good as his word, returning not more than half an hour later with a great tray laden with steaming dishes, and followed by a small kitchen boy carrying a flagon of ale and six pewter tankards. Once the boy was despatched downstairs again, the tapman dragged in a chest from the hall to serve as a table between the two beds and laid out the stewed beef and ale. He took care to shut the chamber door, and when the prisoners had begun to eat, with more haste than manners, he leaned over towards Lane, who was sitting at the foot of one of the beds.

'Master Lane, sir? Do you remember me?'

Lane looked up in surprise and studied the man.

'Aye, your face is somewhat familiar, but I can't bring your name to mind, nor where I knew you.'

''Tis a good many years now, sir. Twenty years ago, at least, long before all our present troubles. I used to work in your chambers at the Inner Temple, as a messenger and apprentice clerk. I wasn't above thirteen years old at the time. Jacob Waters is the name, sir. By now I'd hoped to be a lawyer's clerk myself, but it wasn't to be. In these evil times a man must make shift to earn his bread however he may.'

'Aye, of course I recall you now. Young Jacob! But you've changed, man.'

Jacob nodded, running his finger down a deep scar in his cheek.

'I got this at the siege of Bristol. And my hair has darkened. I used to have hair red as a thatch roof on fire.'

'Well, Jacob,' said Lane, shaking him by the hand, 'I hope you do well here.'

'Well enough. We've a good master, and most of the time this is one of the finest inns in Westminster or the City, as I'm sure you gentlemen know. We'll do our best for you. None of us are happy about this business. Anything I can do to help . . .'

'Two things we need,' said John. 'News of the outside world, for we've spent long hours locked in a deep cellar. And some means of sending word to our families.'

Jacob sat down on the floor and clasped his arms about his knees.

'There's a curfew imposed since nightfall,' he said, 'but tomorrow I can send the boy with letters to your families. As for news of what's happening, I've heard a great deal discussed this day, with all the coming and going in the taproom. Where to begin?'

'When we reached the Palace of Westminster yesterday morning,' said Massey, 'the London Trained Bands were nowhere to be seen. Why had they deserted their posts?'

'They did *not* desert!' Jacob said. 'They were met by the Model Army, barring their path to Westminster with drawn swords. To prevent bloodshed, Major-General Skippon turned them back to the City. Then comes word this afternoon that the Commons have voted the Trained Bands be disbanded and the army be put in charge of London.'

'It wasn't the Commons that voted this,' said Prynne angrily. 'All the good men have been turned out of the Commons. This was some cowardly rump of the lawfully elected House.'

'Beg pardon, sir. That's quite right. Folk say that yesterday no more than eighty were allowed into the House, and many of those are so angry, they've withdrawn themselves. They've vowed they won't take their places until you prisoners are released.'

'God reward them,' said Clotworthy, through a mouthful of beef and onions. 'And what has become of Noll Cromwell in all this? He should have reached London days ago, yet he comes not. I can't believe he's ignorant of this treason. Ireton may have taken charge, but he wouldn't act against Cromwell's wishes.'

'Didn't you know?' said Jacob. 'General Cromwell reached Whitehall last night. It must have been after you were cast in prison. Today he went to Parliament. He was fêted and praised by this—what did you call it, sir?' He turned to Prynne.

'A rump. An arse. The nether end of . . .'

'Aye, this "rump" of a House. Afterwards, if what I heard is right, he went back to Whitehall to meet the Army Council.'

'So that's what the Army Council was doing, while we kicked our heels, cold and hungry, at Whitehall,' said John bitterly. 'Singing the praises of Cromwell for the siege of Pontefract, which any junior captain could have commanded. I'll wager they feasted him with more than burnt wine and biscuits.'

Jacob cast puzzled glance at him, then pondered what other news he could tell them.

'It's said Cromwell sleeps in the king's bed at Whitehall Palace,' he said, with awe in his voice. 'Can he do such a thing?'

'He *can*,' said Prynne, who, even in these dire straits, was a stickler for language. 'And he *may*, for now the supreme power is in the hands of the army.'

'The army. . .' said John, who was worried for his family, 'are they misbehaving?'

Jacob pulled a face, showing what he thought of the army.

'People are terrified of what they'll do. The soldiers mock and jeer at any who show their faces in the streets. They're helping themselves to goods from men's shops, without a penny payment. They've sacked some men's houses, and not just the rich, neither. And they've no respect even for the house of God. 'Tis said they ripped out panelling and choir stalls from St Paul's Cathedral itself and made a bonfire with them, to cook their meat and warm their shanks.'

'While we lay frozen and starving in a damp cellar,' said Crewe harshly.

'And where's the Lord General all this time?' asked Massey. 'None of this bears the stamp of Fairfax's character, yet everything is being done in his name.'

'I was told by one of the servants from Whitehall Palace,' said Jacob, 'who supped here this evening, that Fairfax hasn't attended any of the meetings of the Army Council there. He's been riding about the city, arranging quartering for his soldiers, mostly in empty buildings and warehouses. To do him credit, he's tried to spare the common citizens the burden of quartering in their own houses. But we've all been ordered to hand over blankets and sheets, and mattresses and bolsters, that the men may sleep in more comfort.'

The prisoners exchanged angry glances at this, so different from their own treatment the previous night.

'I agree with you, Massey,' said John thoughtfully. 'I don't see Tom Fairfax's hand in these arrests and exclusions of the Commons. Black Tom cares for his men and cares nothing for politics, whilst Ireton cares for politics and power—he cares for the men only as an instrument to his purpose. Yet where Ireton acts, Cromwell's hand guides.'

∾

By Friday morning, Francis was clearly recovering from his illness. Anne decided to allow him out of his bed, for the chamber was bitterly cold, and Peter carried him down to the parlour, where Patience had made him up a bed of sorts by pushing two chairs together beside a good fire.

Everyone in the household was still nervous, but there had been no further trouble from the soldiers. Still no word had come from John. Anne was sure now that he must have been imprisoned. If he were free, he would have contrived to send word to her somehow, knowing she would be distraught when he had been gone for two nights. It was impossible to discover any information about the missing men. Anne had sent Ned round to the houses of John's closest friends: Crewe, Clotworthy, Fiennes, Birch, Stephens. All had vanished. None of their households knew what had become of them. Only at Fiennes's lodging was there a variation on the story. Ned was told that on Wednesday afternoon, one of Lord Say and Sele's servants had come round to Fiennes's rooms and packed up some of his belongings, but he had said nothing of Fiennes's whereabouts.

Filled with foreboding, Anne could not put off a decision much longer. John had said she might have to leave London, but he had not exactly ordered her to do so. He had warned of the danger to her and to the children, but she decided she would wait a few more days until Francis was stronger. And whatever John might say, she would not travel to Staffordshire without Dick and Nan. In this she was prepared to disobey him, despite her misgivings, for she was terrified at the thought of leaving them behind in London, with both parents gone. Who could guess what evils would befall them in the city under military occupation?

As soon as Anne had seen Francis settled in the parlour, she sent Peter to hire a hackney carriage for the day and explained to Patience what she planned to do.

'I'll leave you in charge of the household. Keep to the house, and I don't think there will be anything to fear. Perhaps the master will be home before I am.' She tried to sound cheerful, but she put no faith in her own words.

'I'll go first to Charterhouse for Dick. He can walk to the Colemans' house in Holborn from there, while I go on to Hackney to fetch Nan in the carriage, then I'll collect him on the way home. I think I'll take Peter with me. He could do little against any attack, but a man's presence alone may be some protection. Don't expect me back before supper.'

'But, mistress!' Patience looked appalled. 'There are soldiers roaming the streets everywhere. Think on the many miles from Westminster to Hackney, and the roads covered with snow and ice. It won't be safe. Please, I beg of you, don't go! Peter can fetch Dick. Surely Nan will be safe enough where she is?'

Anne shook her head. Once she had allowed herself to think of having the two eldest children safe within her sight, she could not abandon the idea. Alone, without the protection of their parents, they might be seized as pawns in this cruel game of power. Their schools could do nothing to protect them against armed soldiers. Her heart was already beating fearfully at the thought of the journey across the occupied city, but she must fetch the children home.

'And the curfew!' cried Patience. 'What of the curfew? It starts at nightfall, Sam Carpenter said, and this is the darkest time of year, with the sun setting early. You cannot be back by dark.'

'Sam made his way here safe enough after curfew,' said Anne stubbornly.

'Sam,' Patience pointed out, 'was a young man alone, on foot, who could slip into a doorway if the guard marched by. You'll be a woman great with child, an old man, a boy, and a young girl, travelling in a hackney carriage. You could as soon hide as an elephant. And suppose your hackney driver refuses to go further when night falls? You could be abandoned on the streets.'

Anne knew that everything Patience said was true, but she continued to shake her head.

'I will bring my children home,' was all she would say.

Anne and Peter started their journey shortly afterwards, loading the carriage with blankets and footwarmers containing hot coals. Peter carried a basket of food, and Anne had brought extra cloaks for the children. The driver was a man of middle age who looked reliable, although he said little, and did not climb down from his box to help with stowing their baggage. The carriage was one of the larger sort, fully enclosed and drawn by two horses. Anne had been afraid Peter would have to settle for one of the half-open carriages, in which they would have been frozen before they even reached the City.

The driver took a route by smaller streets to the west of Parliament, avoiding the army patrols, and came into King Street a little beyond the Abbey. Anne peered back through the window towards Parliament, where there was a considerable stir of infantry and troopers. Was John somewhere in there, held within the Palace of Westminster itself? As they reached Charing Cross and headed up the Strand towards the City, the horses began to trot; the road here was almost clear, from all the tramping of feet. The snow that remained was churned into a dirty slush, pocked with horse droppings and stained yellow where chamberpots had been tipped into the street. It was no longer snowing, but a fierce wind was blowing, and she was glad of the footwarmer and her heavy fur muff.

As they neared the City, the carriage was obliged to slow almost to a stop. Troops of horse clattered down the street, forcing carriages out of the way and knocking pedestrians into the filthy gutters. Usually the streets were crowded with hawkers and stalls—hot pie men, candlemakers, watercarriers, sellers of fine lace and cheap boots, knife-grinders, basket-makers, bird sellers, women with pickled eels and salted fish, men with bunches of brooms over their shoulders and faggots on their backs, milkmaids with their buckets, bakery lasses with their trays of buns, peddlers of ribbons and silks and pins and knickknacks, men shouting the value of their wares, and sturdy girls carolling their street cries. Today the only citizens on the streets scurried along, heads down. On one corner Anne saw a band of six or eight soldiers looting a clock-maker's shop, while the terrified owner, standing in the snow in his shirtsleeves, pleaded with them to spare him. Peter eyed his mistress uneasily. His cheeks were sunken and his skin frail and translucent as rubbed parchment, blotched with the dark spots of age. Anne smiled back at the old man encouragingly.

'We've nothing with us that's worth their stealing. Don't worry, Peter. I'm sure they won't trouble us.'

She had put on a simple country gown of brown kersey which usually she wore only about the house in London, in the hope she might be taken for an upper servant or the wife of a modest tradesman. She wore no jewels or lace, only a plain white kerchief pinned around her shoulders. The fur muff, however, might give her away, so she wrapped a blanket around herself, covering muff and all, as the driver turned left up Chancery Lane and so past Lincoln's Inn.

Where Chancery Lane met Holborn, the carriage came to a full stop. Peering out of the window, Anne could see a crowd of men, but not the reason why they could not drive on.

'Step out, for a moment, Peter,' she said, 'And see what's to-do. But don't get left behind!'

Peter climbed back in a few minutes later.

'There's a carriage gone into the ditch as it turned the corner, mistress,' he said, wiping his streaming nose, which had turned blue in the short time he had been outside. 'They're trying to move it, but the traces are broken and one of the horses run off. They'll be some time yet.'

'Well, pour us a sup of ale, then,' said Anne, 'to cheer us while we wait.'

It must have been the best part of an hour before they were on their way again. Chafing at the delay, Anne had begun to wish she had walked the distance to the Colemans' house and told the driver to catch her up there. By the time she was embracing Grace in her front parlour, it was past noon. She explained her plan quickly.

'Aye, of course Dick may come here until you can fetch him,' said Grace, 'but I wish you wouldn't go all the way out to Hackney. If Charles were here, he would surely go in your stead, but he's summoned to General Cromwell at Whitehall, to arrange some music for a banquet tonight.'

'General Cromwell is reigning at Whitehall Palace, is he? It seems little time since the man was but the captain of a troop of horse,' said Anne sharply. 'And I thought he was still in the north.'

Grace shrugged her shoulders. 'It's all one to me. All I know is that Charles and the babe and I will starve if he doesn't ply his trade. If you're a musician you must smile and smile, no matter what your heart is saying.'

Anne knew that Grace and Charles were half royalist, and could not blame them. Whatever Charles might think of his royal namesake as a man, he had had a good position at court. All that was now lost.

'And is there truly no word of my brother?' said Grace. 'We heard there had been arrests at the House, but we thought it would just be a few who spoke for the king. And Prynne, of course, who's never learned to curb his tongue. But not loyal and sound Parliamentmen like John.'

'John has been gone for two days and two nights now. I've had no word at all.' Twisting her fingers together, Anne whispered, 'I fear the Tower.'

Suddenly, alone with Grace, she could no longer keep up her brave pretence. She dropped into a chair and covered her face with her hands. Unable to control the terror she had been trying to hide from herself, she began to sob helplessly. Grace put her arms around her as the grief shook her bodily.

'Anne, my dear,' said Grace. 'I'm sure he'll be safe. They'll not dare to hurt Members of Parliament. Such men as John aren't small men, their names are known. They have powerful friends in London, and large bodies of supporters at home in the country.'

'It's not John alone,' Anne gasped. 'It's all our friends—Crewe, Fiennes, Stephens, Clotworthy. They've all vanished! No one knows where they are. They must be imprisoned somewhere. Or worse.'

'When Charles comes home,' said Grace firmly, 'we'll send him to find out what he can. Or he may already have heard something in Whitehall. Come, Anne, you must not give way like this. Think of the baby. Dry your eyes, and I'll tell them in the kitchen to hurry forward dinner. You must stay here and give up this idea of going to Hackney.'

'I must go!' Anne clutched at her sister-in-law's hand. 'What will happen to the children if John is in prison and I must leave London?'

'They can come to us. They'll be safe here.'

But Anne was not to be persuaded. Stubbornly, she refused all of Grace's suggestions. She would not even stay to take dinner, although she drank a little soup and ate some bread. Half an hour after she had arrived, she was on her way again. Peter and the driver had taken early dinner with the servants in the kitchen, so that Peter was more cheerful as they drove the short distance to Charterhouse.

'The driver thinks the road out into the country will be free of soldiers,' he said. 'They're mostly about the City and Westminster.'

'There's the gatehouse of the school just ahead,' said Anne. 'You may wait in the coach. I don't expect to stay long here.'

But she had miscalculated. Previously, John had brought Dick to school or fetched him home. Anne had only accompanied them once, and on that occasion had not met the Master. Arriving now, unescorted, she felt a brief spasm of unease as she confronted the handsome building, constructed like an Oxford college around a series of quadrangles, with its own chapel. It had been built some forty years earlier with a bequest from Thomas Sutton, a man from the north country who had made his money somewhat grubbily from coal and money-lending. He had squared all with his conscience, however, by endowing a hospital—a home for elderly worthies who had fallen into straitened means in their declining years. In addition a school provided for forty 'poor' scholars: not the poor of London's gutters, but the sons of professional families without large estates. Their fathers were physicians and lawyers and clergymen, the younger branches of gentry families. These 'gownboys' were entirely supported from the foundation. The school's reputation for excellence, however, had soon attracted the same number of 'townboys'—commoners whose families paid their fees.

Dick was a townboy and would go on from Charterhouse to Cambridge, like his father, or to Oxford, which John favoured for his sons. A generation ago, Dick would have been ready to move on to university now, at fifteen, as his father had done, but in the new fashion he would start university later, at seventeen or even eighteen.

Anne was ushered in through the gatehouse by a servant of the school, who peered beyond her at the hackney carriage, clearly put out that a woman on her own should pass the threshold of this male establishment. He looked about the outer court, then crooked a finger at a small boy in a gown who was crossing towards the Master's Court.

Servant and child held a hurried conversation in whispers, then the servant, a dignified man in livery, made off as fast as he could towards the Master's House. The small boy stood in front of Anne, regarding her solemnly. Clearly, he had been left to guard this dangerous female, in case she should misbehave herself.

'Are you going to keep me standing outside in the cold?' Anne asked, pleasantly enough.

The child looked horrified. He gulped and stared about, but there was no one else to ask for help.

'Well, I am afraid I am not going to wait here in the wind.'

She lifted her skirts and marched firmly towards the Master's House, following the route the servant had taken. The child, who could not have been more than eight, trotted behind her, making little mews of protest. He flung himself in front of her as she reached the door of the house.

'You cannot go in there!' He seemed terrified.

Anne took pity on him.

'Very well, I shall wait in the Chapel. Surely no one will refuse me the comfort of God's house?'

She turned and crossed through a passageway to the Chapel Court and into the Chapel itself. She was glad to sit down out of the wind, although it was almost as cold here as it was outside. At least the benches did not jolt and toss her about like the seats in the carriage. She sank to her knees and offered up a brief, formless prayer that her enterprise this day might succeed. The child had followed her in and stood on one leg halfway between her seat and the Chapel door, as if he could not decide whether he should continue to guard her or go to fetch help. Anne sat back, quietly studying the tomb of Thomas Sutton, which to her eyes resembled nothing so much as a rather flamboyant fireplace, bedecked with noble figures and a coat-of-arms, with a frieze depicting the pensioners and scholars of Charterhouse.

'Mistress Swynfen!' The Master came hurrying in to the Chapel, and the child slipped away into the shadows. A man of magnificent height, he bore down on her like an avenging fury, the black wings of his gown flapping. 'What are you doing here? 'Tis not seemly that a woman should come unaccompanied into the school.'

He was clearly very angry. Moreover, his bold stare at her pregnant shape said, *No woman in your condition should dare to do so.* She felt a rising anger herself that he should address her in such a manner, and that he should call her a *woman* in that ill-mannered way.

'A *gentleman*,' she said icily, 'would not keep the mother of one of his students standing outside in the winter's cold.'

He was not going to apologise.

'What do you want here?' he demanded.

'I've come for my son Richard. I have decided to fetch him home early for Christmas.'

Even to herself it sounded ridiculous. However, she did not dare reveal that she planned to leave London as soon as possible. The Master, she knew, was a Royalist, and his hold on his position was precarious. If John was in trouble with those who had seized power, a man such as the Master might try to curry favour by reporting her planned escape.

'Impossible. He is occupied with his lessons. We do not allow any boy to leave early at the whim of the parents.'

'This is no whim.' Anne gripped her hands together. They were shaking, but she must not let this man see any sign of weakness. 'It is our wish that he should come home now.'

'But I see no "we" here,' said the Master sarcastically. 'I see only a woman. Do you have your husband's authority for this?'

'Of course.'

'His written authority? I might consider handing the boy over to his father. Or if you had brought your husband's written authority, I might, in extraordinary circumstances, have done so. But—to a woman alone? I think not, madam.'

He turned and began to walk towards the door, his gown sweeping the dusty floor behind him.

'Wait!' Anne cried. 'At least let me see my son.'

He stopped and regarded her coldly. 'Very well. You may have five minutes' speech with him. Wait here.'

He kept her waiting another half hour before Dick tumbled into the Chapel, followed by a frowning young man also wearing an academic gown, who must be an assistant schoolmaster. Dick rushed to her and hugged her.

'The Master said you'd come to take me home, but he won't let you. Is something amiss, Mama?'

As quickly as she could, she told him what had been happening during the last week, and what she intended.

'And now I can't tell what I should do!' She hugged him again. He had grown since she had seen him last; he was taller than she, almost a man's height, but the bony wrists projecting from the sleeves of his shirt were touchingly childlike.

'Go and fetch Nan,' said Dick, firmly. 'And take her back to St Ann's Lane. I think you should go home to Swinfen, unless Father sends you word not to go. You'll all be safe there. Have no fear for me. When they let us out of here for Christmas, I'll go to Aunt Coleman and the Doctor. I can always make my own way back to Staffordshire.'

'Nay, you mustn't do that. It would be much too dangerous.'

He laughed, but would promise nothing. Anne was afraid of what he might do. He had always been a bold, adventurous boy. The thought that he might undertake the journey on his own only increased her worries. But before she could argue with him any further, the young schoolmaster sent Dick back to his lessons and seized Anne rudely by the arm to escort her briskly out of the gate, shaking and sick with anger and humiliation at her treatment. The daring spirit in which she had embarked upon this hazardous journey was seeping away. The prospect of the trip out to Hackney and the long drive back, with danger in the streets and the risk of breaking curfew, suddenly rolled over her like a dark wave. She hesitated on the threshold of the school, trying to gather her tattered courage about her.

Peter and the hackney driver were looking across the road at her expectantly. The driver had taken the opportunity to give the horses their nosebags, which he now unstrapped and stowed under his seat. He seemed anxious.

'There be a storm brewing over in the east, mistress,' he said. ''Twill be upon us before we can drive to Hackney and back.'

Anne turned and looked where he pointed towards the Thames estuary. Great black thunderclouds were building up all along the horizon. It might mean heavy rain or, cold as it was, another snow storm. She took a deep breath. She could not turn back now.

'We'd best make haste to be on our way, then,' she said. Peter handed her into the carriage and tucked the blankets around her. She was grateful for their warmth, for she had grown very chilled in the courts and chapel of the school. Her back had also begun to ache with a dull, constant pain. The drag of the baby's weight was like a tight cord pulling on her spine. She kept shifting in the seat, but no position was comfortable, and as they set off again the jolting of the carriage sent vicious jabs through her back and stomach. She turned to look out of the window, to avoid Peter's anxious glances. The strength of the anger knotted in her chest frightened her. The Master's words echoed in her head, and with his refusal to release Dick her plan for the family's escape was already slipping through her fingers.

The driver turned north along the road to Kingsland and soon they had left the city wall behind them. Despite the roughness of the road, Anne felt more relaxed. There were no more soldiers to be seen. The fresh country air rushed in at the partly open window as the carriage rattled along over the frozen mud of the country road, past hamlets clustered around parish churches and small farms tucked into south-facing slopes. This was a prosperous area, for it was London's garden, having long provided fresh milk and meat for the capital. In recent years, many of the more far-seeing farmers had been experimenting with Dutch methods of market gardening, growing vegetables intensively for sale in the stalls of London's markets at Cheapside and Leadenhall. In season, their carts rumbled along this road carrying peas and beans, onions, leeks, asparagus and spinage, even the potatoes first brought in from the Americas fifty years ago.

The farms looked well-kept and comfortable, though the present year could not have been easy for them. Incessant rain had spoiled crops and flooded low-lying land, especially a little further north in Essex, where the siege of Colchester had been burned forever into men's minds as a misery of bog and down-pouring rain. The wheat harvest had been the poorest for years. The legal size of a penny loaf had been severely reduced as a result, and the price of other foodstuffs had soared. No wonder then that the soldiers were in such a dangerous mood. They wanted pay and the spoils of looting, for back at home in the country they would find little enough income or food from the land.

Even here, now that she looked more closely, there were signs. At one of the farms, two children were swinging listlessly on a gate, a

115

boy of six or seven, a girl perhaps two years older. Their clothes were neat and clean, but their faces were pinched with hunger. Anne waved to them as the carriage drove past, but they simply gazed at her with lacklustre eyes and made no acknowledgement.

How different it had been when she and John had first brought Nan to Perwicks' school last spring! It was a balmy day, with the May all in blossom in the hedgerows. Nan kept crying out in delight at the lambs skipping in the fields, leaping straight up in the air as if they danced on springs.

'Have you forgotten the lambs at home?' Anne asked her. 'At Swinfen and Thickbroome?'

'I *think* I remember,' said Nan. 'Oh, but Mama, they're lovely! Could I have one as a pet?'

'Not in London.' Anne laughed.

'The tragedy of lambs,' said John, 'is that they must all grow into sheep. Should you want a fat, slow sheep for a pet, Nankins?'

'I shouldn't mind,' she said stoutly. 'I should love it just the same. Can I have one when we go home?'

'Home to Swinfen?' said her father. 'You shall have as many as you like, my pet. You shall have your own flock on Packington Moor.'

Anne knew that was not what Nan had in mind, but she diverted her by pointing to the birds busy nesting in the hedgerows and orchard trees. Her own heart was somewhat lightened by the beauty of Hackney, even though it ached at the thought of leaving her daughter here in the care of strangers. She comforted herself with the thought that the fresh country air up on Hackney Downs would be much better for the child's health than the smokes and fogs and filthy stench of London, especially with the summer coming on.

Now, the sharp, clean, winter air of the Downs seemed to clear her own head. She was certain there would be no trouble in bringing Nan away from the Perwicks' school. She had taken an immediate liking to Robert Perwick and his wife, who treated the girls at their school like daughters of their own. There were nearly a hundred pupils, but they knew every one by name. She had seen Mistress Perwick rush to a child who had tumbled over and carry her off herself to bathe the cut knee and comfort her with sweetmeats. Could Nan have come home from school every night, Anne would have been perfectly happy with the arrangement.

Anne herself would be treated with respect here, unlike the humiliation of her reception at Charterhouse. The Perwicks knew her as the wife of an eminent Parliamentarian. And there was the family connection through the Colemans, for the Perwicks' love of music meant that they welcomed the most distinguished musicians in Europe into their home, including Charles and Edward Coleman. As the prodigious talent of their daughter Susanna developed, the school had become more and more famous as a fount of musical achievement. It was the best school for girls anywhere in England.

They had nearly reached the school now, and the storm was still some way off. On the upper slopes of Hackney Downs, a number of the wealthier London merchants had begun to build themselves country manor houses, where they could retreat in the heat of the London summer. During the outbreak of the plague earlier in the year, more rich men had begun building here, where they and their families could live at a safe distance from infection. The Perwicks' school was one such manor house, extended with additional wings until it formed a square about a central courtyard. Although elegant, it had none of the chilly and forbidding appearance of Charterhouse.

Anne climbed down a little stiffly from the coach at the front door.

'Drive round to the kitchens,' she said to Peter, 'and beg some fresh coals for the footwarmers. I fear it will be a cold journey back. And see if they'll heat a brick or two for the driver's feet, for he'll be much colder than we will.'

A pretty maid in a lavender gown and lace cap opened the door to Anne and bobbed a curtsey. Anne explained her business. She could hear music coming from somewhere nearby.

'I'm afraid everyone is at the concert, mistress,' the maid said, nodding in the direction of the sounds. 'Will you care to join them? Or I could bring you something to refresh you in the parlour.'

There would be no chance to speak to the Perwicks until the concert ended, nor could Anne snatch Nan away in the midst of it. She would be obliged to wait until the music finished.

'I've no wish to disturb them,' she said, 'but I would dearly like to hear the music.'

The girl smiled cheerfully. 'Oh, 'twill be no disturbance. I can slip you in at the back of the room, if you'll follow me this way.'

The concert was taking place in the great hall of the original manor house, a beautiful engilded double cube room with a painted ceiling depicting the muses cavorting amongst pink clouds and cherubs garlanded with laurel and oak leaves. A considerable audience was seated on fragile gilt chairs, and Anne was able to slide in at the end of a row during the applause for a piece played on the virginals. The audience, she supposed, must consist of the Perwicks' neighbours from the surrounding great houses, unless some of the girls' parents had travelled out from London. Given the situation, with the army in occupation, this seemed unlikely, and indeed she herself had heard nothing of a concert taking place. She knew from Grace that private concerts like this were regularly held, performed mostly by the older girls, because the Perwicks believed this taught them confidence and poise. The concerts were also an opportunity to hear eleven-year-old Susanna play and sing, without putting her forward too boldly on her own, for she was a quiet and modest child.

A large group of girls now filed in at the far end of the room, led by Charles's brother, Edward Coleman, who smiled and bowed to the audience. He was grandly dressed in a doublet of wine damask with jewelled buttons, white silk breeches, and shoes with buckles of fine goldsmith's work.

'The girls will now sing a new Christmas chorale which I have composed,' he announced. 'This will be its first performance.'

The girls stood demurely, with their hands clasped in front of them and their eyes on Edward Coleman. And there, in the front row with the younger girls, was Nan. She was very like her father—tall for her age, with straight brown hair caught up with ribbons, and thoughtful, deep-set eyes. Anne felt her breath catch in her throat. Nan seemed so self-possessed and distant. Charles lifted his baton, gave a nod to a young man seated at a harpsichord, and they began.

The girls' voices were piercingly sweet and fresh. To come from the terror of occupied London and John's disappearance to this joyous music in its idyllic setting high on Hackney Down, was like coming from purgatory to paradise. Anne wanted to lay down the burdens of her aching body and her frantic worries, and simply rest in this place. The music was a physical balm; the sight and sound of the girls as they sang was healing to the very soul.

After the chorale, Edward Coleman announced that the last performance in that day's concert would be a violin solo, accompanied by himself on the harpsichord and played by Susanna Perwick. There was a murmur of anticipation amongst the audience, then a hush fell as the child came in.

She was not much taller than Nan, though she was three years older. Her looks were striking: dark curls set off a curiously pale complexion with a flush of pink in her cheeks. The most remarkable thing about her was her eyes. Large, wide-set and dark, they were bright with fierce intelligence and maturity. Yet her shy smile was that of any nervous child standing up to perform alone in front of an audience of strangers.

As the violin began its sweet song, Anne closed her eyes and felt her body, stiff with the tension of the day, soften and slacken. She did not know the music, yet it spoke to something deep inside her, gay as birdsong at first, engaged in a dance with the harpsichord, then sorrowful, as violin and harpsichord cried out to each other of partings and death. Sorrow welled up in Anne's throat as she remembered her last parting from John. Why had she left him thus, in anger, running away from him?

There was a moment's pause in the music, like an indrawn breath. And then the two instruments came together in a piercing harmony, a nocturne, a *nunc dimittis* of the old religion. Regret, acceptance, healing. But Anne crouched in her corner at the back of the room, her face turned away. Music tore down all defences, exposing all vulnerability. Inside her head she howled with grief. Would she ever see John again?

When the last notes faded away, there was complete silence in the room, as if no one was breathing, then the clapping began. Some were furtively wiping their eyes, and gazing about them as if woken, at a loss, from some potent dream.

Susanna was hurried away by her mother, and the guests were ushered into a small parlour for refreshment. The girls were nowhere to be seen. Catching sight of the long wall clock in the hallway, Anne realised how little time remained if she were to return home before the curfew. She refused the food and instead went in search of Edward Coleman, whom she found tidying the music in the great hall.

'Anne!' He hurried forward and took her by both hands. 'This is a rare pleasure. I didn't expect to see you here. Did you mark Nan in the front row of the choir? She has a sweet, true voice.'

'I knew nothing of the concert,' said Anne distractedly. 'I came to fetch Nan home. Oh, Edward, John is arrested, imprisoned perhaps, and I must take the children back to Staffordshire for safety.'

She began to tremble. If only she could resign the responsibility to Edward. It seemed suddenly too great to bear.

'Anne? When did you last eat? When is the baby due?'

He led her to a chair and forced her to sit still while he fetched wine and cakes for her, then he went in search of Mistress Perwick. Between sips of the strong burgundy, that flowed in her veins with an increase in strength and resolution, Anne explained to them the situation in Westminster and the City, news of which had not yet reached Hackney. As soon as she realised what was afoot, Mistress Perwick sent a maidservant to pack Nan's belongings and fetch her downstairs. There would be no questioning of Anne's right to claim her child here.

'I wish I could come back to Westminster with you,' said Edward, 'but I'm expected this evening at Sir Thomas Howard's levee. I'll drive with you as far as the city gate, to see you safely inside the wall, and then walk back.'

'Would you be so kind, Edward?' Anne pressed his hand. 'I confess, I'm a little worried about the journey.' She did not add that the journey across London might well be more dangerous than the country road.

Children's voices approached along the hallway, talking excitedly. Susanna came in, leading Nan by the hand. Nan ran to hug her mother. One of her hair ribbons had come untied and hung down rakishly over her ear.

'Did you hear me sing, Mama? I sing in the big choir now. Uncle Edward says I sing truly in tune, and I can read the music very well.'

'You sang beautifully, dear heart,' said Anne, 'but I'm afraid we must hurry away now, to be home before dark. See how black the sky is!'

Nan's face fell. 'But I don't want to go home!' She ran back and seized Susanna's hand again. 'I'm not to come home until Christmas, and that's a fortnight yet.' Her lip trembled, and she looked beseechingly at her mother. 'We've so much to do in school before Christmas. I'm to take part in a French play.'

'I'm sorry,' said Anne, 'but we must. Papa wants us to go home to Swinfen. We shall be able to spend Christmas with Grandfather and Grandmother.' She searched her mind for something to please Nan. 'You'll see Tray and Belle again. Remember? They were your favourite puppies.'

Huge tears began to pour down Nan's face, and she stamped her foot. 'I don't remember. I don't *remember*. I don't want to go to Swinfen. I want to stay here.' She flung herself furiously on the floor and began to sob.

Susanna knelt down and put her arms around her.

'Don't cry, Nan. It will only be for a little while. I'll write a letter to you, if you will promise to write back.'

Nan gulped and looked at her wide-eyed. Letters were very, very expensive. She had never received one in all her life.

'Do you promise me, truly?'

'Truly. I'll tell you everything that we're doing, and you must write to me about your home and your animals.'

After more persuasion, Nan grew calmer and agreed to put on her cloak. Edward, changed out of his finery, carried her to the carriage, while Anne turned to Mistress Perwick.

'Nan has been very happy here, and I can understand why. You've made a little paradise in Hackney, Mistress Perwick.'

Mistress Perwick blushed and took her hands. 'I'll pray for you and your family every day, Mistress Swinfen. Surely this madness of the army's can't continue? I'm sure your husband will return home soon, and I wish you a safe journey and a safe delivery of the new babe.'

While the Perwicks stood in the doorway to bid her farewell, Anne stooped and kissed Susanna on the cheek. 'I'm grateful for your kindness to Nan. She couldn't have a better friend.'

As Edward handed Anne into the carriage and took his seat, the first heavy drops of rain began to fall. Low grey clouds had gathered overhead, borne on by a fierce east wind. When the carriage turned out of the drive and on to the road back to London, a tongue of flame leapt towards the earth from the dense black clouds rolling in from the sea.

'A thunderstorm in December,' said Edward. 'Ominous weather for ominous times.'

The full force of the storm hit them ten minutes later, flinging the carriage sideways like a ship at sea, so that they had to clutch hold of anything firm to stop themselves being thrown in a heap on the floor. Anne sat on one seat with Nan wrapped tightly in blankets beside her, while Edward and Peter faced her from the seat opposite. Nan began to cry again, from fear and from tiredness after the excitement of the day.

'Now then,' Edward shouted over the noise of the storm, 'didn't I hear tell of a basket of food? Why don't we have a picnic to cheer ourselves?'

Anne laughed. The rain was driving into the carriage through every crack around the doors and windows. Their teeth were almost shaken from their heads by the jolting of the carriage from the ruts in the road and the buffets of the wind. They had to shout to make themselves heard. The horses, frightened by the storm, jerked nervously at the traces, trying to break into a gallop to escape the terrible thing that was looming over their heads and flashing and roaring all about them. The driver was swearing worse than a Smithfield butcher as he struggled to control them. It seemed hardly the occasion for a picnic. But Edward was right. A picnic would divert Nan's attention and give them all something to think about other than their imminent peril.

Peter opened the basket and handed out pies and bread, but pouring from the flask of ale defeated him.

'Leave it until the worst of the storm passes,' said Anne. 'It can't continue like this for long.'

She leaned forward to reach into the basket, and was thrown half on to the floor and half into Edward's lap.

'Careful!' he cried. 'Sister, you shouldn't be travelling like this, in your present condition.'

'I've no choice. Look in the basket. I'm sure Hester put in some of Nan's favourite raspberry cakes.'

Consoled by the fruit comfits, Nan curled up with her head in Anne's lap while the lightning moved away to the south. Coming past Bedlam Hospital to the city wall at last, they found Bishopsgate barred by a troop of soldiers. The driver pulled up the horses, and Edward climbed out to see what was amiss. After a few minutes, he returned with a cornet of horse.

'You see,' said Edward. 'Nothing but a child, and my sister, who's near her time, and the manservant. No spies or Royalists here.'

The cornet climbed into the carriage and poked amongst the blankets, as if he thought someone might be hidden there, then climbed down again.

'And yourself?'

'I'm returning to Hackney. I only travelled this far to see them safely inside the city wall.'

The cornet kept them waiting while he went away to consult another officer. Edward tried to shelter under the archway of the gate.

'Edward,' Anne called to him, 'you'll be like a drowned kitten before you are a quarter of the way back to Hackney, walking in this downpour. Won't you come with us? I can leave you with Charles and Grace.'

Edward shook his head, and the rain sprayed off the brim of his hat like a Catherine-wheel.

'I dare not offend my patron, Anne. We musicians are beggars these days.'

The cornet returned and said the carriage might proceed into the city. Edward waved a farewell. The carriage drove forward onto the cobbled street and Anne watched Edward disappearing into the driving rain, as he headed back up the hill to Hackney.

Chapter Ten

That first morning at the *King's Head*, after the prisoners had breakfasted on small beer, bread, and cheese, Jacob the tapman was true to his word, bringing them paper for their letters, with a supply of ink and quills. Gentlemen accustomed to writing on nothing less than the best laid linen paper from Italy seized the coarse grey stuff on which the innkeeper wrote his accounts with the eagerness of a Bankside playwright.

'I can't be spared to deliver your letters myself,' said Jacob, 'but I'll send the boy. It may take some while. He's not as sharp in his wits as some, and he can't read. He must take them one at a time, with careful directions for each, or they'll all be thrown into a caddle.'

The prisoners agreed readily to this; any communication with the outside world after two full days of silence was welcome, on whatever terms. Those confined to the other rooms in the inn had been promised the chance to send out letters as well, so it would take the child most of the day to carry them all. It was not clear whether the guards knew what was afoot, but John suspected that, with a little free beer and friendly talk, Jacob had persuaded them to look the other way.

His letter was the fourth to be despatched from their room. He had kept it short, for it would do Anne no good to hear the details of his confinement.

Wee are now held at the King's Head in the Strand, he wrote, *& are comfortable enough, but wee must buy our own food & I brought little money away with mee. I beg y^u, send mee a bundle of fresh linen that I may look & feel less of a dirty rogue. Send what else y^u please for my comfort, but noe more than I can easily carry, for if wee are mov'd again, I wou'd not wish to bee burden'd.*

He hoped that Anne would understand from these cryptic remarks that he needed money, and would send some concealed amongst the clothes.

Do not come y^{ur}self, for none is allow'd, & I wou'd not have y^u insult'd by the soldiers. I trust y^u remember that matter wee spoke of on Sunday last, & I bid y^u carry it out as swiftly as may bee. Kiss the *children from their father, & know, deare heart, that I am always y^{ur} most loving husband,*

    John Swynfen

The hours passed slowly. No fire had been lit this morning, and the room was dank and chill, the condensation from their breath steaming up the small window. Some of the prisoners spent the time in reading their Bibles. Others conferred about what representations they should make to the Army Council, if ever they were given the opportunity to present their case. Prynne, as always, was loudest of these, declaring that they must draw up a document protesting at their treatment.

'The elected Parliament has voted freely to accept the Treaty of Newport as a basis for negotiating with the king,' he said, tediously repeating yet again what they all knew. 'The imprisonment of Members of Parliament who've done no more than their duty is illegal, treasonable and contrary to the natural rights of Englishmen.'

John sat on the end of the bed nearest the window, watching the many troop movements up and down the Strand, so that he was the least surprised when Jacob, bringing in their dinner soon after the church clocks had sounded three, was full of army news gleaned in the street and the taproom.

'The army has taken over London entirely,' he said grimly, as the prisoners settled to their food. 'They've even dragged in the artillery. They've seized all the larger churches for stabling and quarters. Fairfax has issued a public proclamation, claiming that he's justified in confiscating bedding forcibly for the soldiers. They're taking it from all, even the poorest, who have barely a single blanket to cover a whole family. I didn't think Black Tom would do such a thing.'

'His soldiers always take first place with him,' said Massey. 'All other men come a long way behind.'

'And that's not the whole story,' said Jacob. 'Hewson's regiment have been ordered in to the City to seize all Parliament's money.'

They stopped eating at that, and stared at him in horror.

'They can't do that!' cried Crewe. 'The money is laid aside for the navy, for arming against foreign attack, for the repair of buildings and ports damaged in the war, for the support of widows and the poor—'

'Aye,' said John bitterly, 'it's not the soldiers alone who have a call on the public purse, but it's they alone have the swords and guns to take it by force. The treasuries have their own armed guards.' He turned to Jacob. 'Has it come to fighting, then? Have the guards defended the treasuries? Has blood been shed?'

'The guards stood firm at Haberdashers' Hall and Goldsmiths' Hall,' said Jacob. 'But at Weavers' Hall they fled or were driven away by the soldiers, who battered down the door and have been carting away the money ever since.'

'Ah,' said John, 'so that's the meaning of the procession of carts I've seen going into Whitehall Palace. I thought they were carrying victuals.'

'The army's everywhere,' said Jacob, a note of panic in his voice. 'They've the artillery drawn up at Blackfriars. From what I've heard, there are detachments in Cheapside, Paternoster Row, Lombard Street. The very heart of the City is heaving with them like a stinking, maggoty cheese.'

A little later, John Crewe received a bundle from his wife. She had little book-learning and had only managed to write a note of two lines, expressing her relief at knowing he was safe: *fore alle doe wondir qwhat is becom of you.* She sent him two clean shirts, a pair of woollen stockings and a large fruit cake, which he generously shared with his fellow prisoners.

'This puts me in mind of my student days at Cambridge,' said John, dusting cake crumbs off his doublet. 'Whenever a parcel came from home: Would it be money or would it be food? I think my mind hasn't dwelt so much on food since those days, until now.'

'It's hard for a man not to think of food in prison,' said Prynne, 'for meals mark out the hours and help the days to pass.'

Afternoon grew towards evening and the light began to drain from the sky all the more rapidly because of the gathering storm. Five of the prisoners in the room had received some acknowledgement of the letters they had sent. They became more relaxed and cheerful now that their families knew where they were. The air grew heavy with thunder, night closed in and the storm broke, but no word had come to John.

⇗

All went well enough as the hackney carriage drove down from Bishopsgate to Corn Hill and Cheapside, where the streets were now mostly empty, even of soldiers, but as they drew near St Paul's and Newgate Market, Anne could hear, even with the windows closed, that there was a noisy disturbance outside. The driver reined in the horses. Anne lowered the window and leaned out as far as she could without disturbing Nan. There seemed to be some kind of brawl further ahead in the street. The driver called out to a group of citizens standing in the doorway of a tavern watching the fight but keeping a safe distance.

'What's afoot over yonder by the market?' he asked.

A man in a greasy workman's cap stepped up to the carriage and rested his hand on the lowered window. Anne immediately sat back in the seat, retreating into the corner. He had a face brutally marked with the smallpox, and a mouthful of blackened, pointed teeth.

'A fight, that's what's afoot,' said the man, enveloping Anne in the sour smell of cheap drink and too much of it. He was addressing the driver, but his eyes were fixed on Anne, assessing her.

'Aye, a fight,' said the driver in exasperation, 'but *who* is fighting?'

'A crowd of butchers from Newgate Market who take it ill that the soldiers should help themselves to their best beef. And a crowd of soldiers who think 'tis their right to take what they please.'

The man's hand began to feel forward into the carriage, groping for Anne. She shrank back, and Nan stirred and moaned in her sleep.

'Where are you bound for?' It was a plump man in an apron, most likely the tavern-keeper, stepping forward.

'Holborn.'

'Then you'd best avoid St Paul's. It's swarming with soldiers. You must press on along Cheapside and Newgate Street, unless you want to turn back and find your way west along the river, by Thames Street and Blackfriars. I'd go by Newgate. If you move fast, they'll scarce notice you, being too much took up in their fight.'

The driver jumped down and came to the window, pushing the workman aside.

'Well, mistress, which is it to be?'

'I think we should go by Newgate,' said Anne, 'if you think you can drive past them without danger. We've no time to go wandering all over London.'

The driver climbed back up into his seat and set off again at a smart pace. Anne pulled up the window by its strap and hooked it in place. Her heart was beating painfully, yet the ruffian from the tavern had done nothing, despite his frightening appearance, save lean too close into the carriage. She had no time to think about it further, because they had drawn level with the brawl between the butchers and the soldiers. There were men battered and bloody on the ground, and several knots of struggling bodies. It was almost impossible to tell, in the near dark, which were the butchers and which the soldiers. Neither side seemed to be winning.

126

They were nearly past when someone noticed the carriage and gave a yell. Two men, soldiers by the helmets they wore, broke loose from the melee and ran towards them. Anne saw one swing his arm back. There was a crash as the small rear window of the carriage smashed. Fragments of glass flew everywhere, and a large stone, just missing Anne's head, fell between her feet. The driver whipped up the horses to a gallop, sending the carriage careering behind like a small boat in a choppy sea.

'Peter!' cried Anne. 'Are you hurt?'

Nan woke with a wail.

Peter was fingering his face. 'I don't think so, mistress. I've a graze here by my ear, but it don't seem much.'

The old man had been facing the window and might have lost an eye. Anne felt the back of her head. Her hat had fallen backward when the driver set off at speed from the tavern and now she found that there were knife-sharp bits of glass lodged in her hair. She began to pick them out, throwing them through the window. Nan was so swaddled in blankets that she was untouched, but the blankets were sprinkled over with glass like sugar on a cake. Peter and Anne were still clearing away the pieces when the carriage crossed the Fleet, mounted the hill beyond and drew up in Holborn.

Anne stopped the carriage only for a moment at the Colemans' house and sent Peter in with a message that Dick was not to be allowed to come home from Charterhouse. While he was gone she shook out the blankets and the driver helped her to wedge one of them in the broken window, for the driving rain was soaking the seat. Doctor Coleman followed Peter out into the rain and wind to beg Anne not to continue any further with her perilous journey.

'I was ill-used by a band of ruffians myself,' he said, 'on my way home from Whitehall. They knocked me about and stole my purse. I beseech you, Anne, don't carry on with this foolishness. You can spend the night here and go home to Westminster in the morning.'

Anne laid her finger on her lips.

'Hush, Charles, Nan has fallen asleep again. I must go back. There's none in charge at home but Patience Wyatt, who's little more than a child herself, with all the younger children and servants in her care. And Francis has been ill. I couldn't rest easy here.'

'It will be curfew in less than half an hour. You'll be arrested.'

'They'll not arrest a woman great with child.'

'You think not? You have more confidence in their decency than I have.'

'I thank you for your kindness, Charles, but I must go. Get in, Peter. The quicker we're on our way, the sooner we shall be there.'

As they drove away, Charles stood before the door of his house, still shaking his head at her folly.

From Holborn back down Chancery Lane and the turn right into Fleet Street and so on to the Strand. It was full dark now, and the darkest night Anne had ever seen in London, for not a single torch was lit before any citizen's door and few windows showed even the pale glow of candle-light. The only lights to be seen in the streets were the watch fires of the soldiers mounting guard at street corners. The driver kept up a brisk pace. Once or twice some of the soldiers stepped forward as if they would stop the carriage, but its air of purposefulness made them hesitate. It neither rushed past with frantic haste nor crept furtively along. The soldiers looked at each other and shrugged, then let it pass. It might have been one of the army officers' carriages going about the business of the state. Inside the carriage, Anne kept as deep in the corner as she could, in the hope that they might not be made curious by the sight of a woman travelling about the streets after curfew.

All continued well until they reached the Cross at Charing, not far past the *King's Head*, where, had she known it, John was eating his supper in silence, worried that he had still received no reply to the letter he had sent nine hours earlier. At Charing Cross a troop of cavalry was drawn up, as well as infantrymen on guard, with a grey-haired captain in command. The carriage was ordered to halt, and the captain came to the carriage and flung the door open so that Anne all but fell out. He glowered at her and at the nervous figure of Peter who, in the light of the candle lantern held by the officer, looked ill and exhausted. The captain turned to Anne with a haughty expression. Panic seized her. Imprisonment, even death, might be the penalty for breaking the curfew.

'And where do you go, mistress, at this hour of the night, against the orders of the Army Council?'

Anne cleared her throat and tried to speak, but could make no sound, as if she were trapped in some nightmare. 'We were caught by the storm and delayed,' she managed to whisper at last.

He stared at her, saying nothing.

'We'll be home in ten minutes, captain,' she pleaded. 'I need to put my little girl to bed, and I have another sick child at home.'

The man leaned into the carriage. He had not noticed Nan. His lantern, lighting up the inside of the carriage, set off glints from pieces of broken glass that Anne and Peter had overlooked in the dark.

'What's this?'

'Someone threw a stone at us by Newgate Market,' said Anne.

'Are you hurt?'

'Nay, God be thanked. But I beg you to let us continue. I'm weary to the bone, and nearly eight months gone with child.'

He lifted the lantern higher and studied her shape, then gave a grunt.

'And your name?'

Anne thought quickly. Best to be careful.

'Mistress Grace Coleman. Wife to the musician Doctor Charles Coleman.'

Safer than mentioning John's name. Surely the army had no grudge against a musician?

The captain stood back, considering. 'Very well, you may continue. And you,' he said, looking up at the driver, 'where's the station for your carriage?'

'Just beyond you here, sir, at Whitehall.'

'Very well. If you're not back here and your horses stabled within twenty minutes, I'll have my troopers after you and confiscate your horses.'

'Never doubt it, sir.'

The weary horses clopped over the cobbles past Whitehall and the Palace of Westminster, and a few minutes later came to a stop in front of the house in St Ann's Lane. The driver carried Nan into the house, followed by Peter with the blankets and the empty food basket, and the footwarmers, now cold as poverty.

Anne caught hold of the door frame to steady herself, for she could barely keep on her feet. As the driver came out again she touched his sleeve.

'I'm grateful to you, friend, for without your courage and steadiness, we could never have accomplished this.'

He pulled off his cap and smiled for the first time that day.

'We must help each other in these troubled times. I pray Master Swynfen comes home safe.'

'You *know* who I am?'

'There's not much the hackney drivers don't know, mistress. Master Swynfen is well loved. And I hope all goes well for you.'

Anne felt in her pocket with her cold fingers and pulled out a half-crown piece.

'Money is poor reward for your help, but I hope you will take this.'

'You've already paid me for the full day's hire.'

129

'Nay!' She laughed. 'Don't be so proud!' She pressed the coin into his hand, which was callused from the reins and blue with cold. 'It will buy a little extra meat and drink for your loved ones.'

'I thank you, mistress.'

He put his cap back on, climbed up on to the seat and drove swiftly away back towards Whitehall.

Patience rushed out of the door and put her arms around Anne.

'Oh, Mistress Swynfen, I've been quite frantic with worry. Come in by the fire. Hester is putting a supper for you in the parlour.'

'I must see to Nan.'

'Bess has already taken her off to bed. She's walking in her sleep.'

'And Peter?'

'Sitting in the kitchen, telling his adventures.'

'Francis, how is Francis?'

'Much better. He's done nothing all day but eat like a very soldier. He's truly better. Come.'

She tugged at Anne's arm. As soon as they were through the door she slammed it closed and shot the bolts, then sighed with relief.

'I'm glad to shut the world out this night.' She turned to look at Anne and gave a cry of distress. 'Mistress Swynfen, your face! What has happened? Your face is cut!'

Anne put her hand to her cheek where Patience pointed, and it came away sticky with blood.

'I didn't think I was hurt. The window was broken by a stone and glass flew all about the carriage. I must have been cut then and knocked it again just now, when I was getting out of the carriage.'

'I'll bring water to bathe it.'

Patience guided Anne to a chair beside the parlour fire, where she sank down gratefully, spreading out her damp skirts to the warmth.

'But first, there's a letter come.' Patience handed it to Anne. 'It was brought this morning, soon after you left, by the kitchen boy from the *King's Head* in the Strand. I couldn't get much sense from him; he was a mite simple. But I think it must be from the master.'

Anne gave a suppressed cry.

'Just after I left? Oh, that I might have seen this first, before this terrible day!'

'You're safe home now.' Patience busied herself heating a poker in the fire to plunge into the bowl of spiced wine to heat it. 'And Nan home, too. But what of Dick?'

'The Master of Charterhouse refused me leave to bring him away. He was most offensive.'

Anne slipped a sharp knife under the wax on the letter, which bore the mark of no seal. John had been wearing his seal-ring when he left home on Wednesday morning. The letter was certainly addressed in his writing, but he might have felt it safer not to seal it with his mark. She unfolded the rough sheet of paper and quickly read the few lines it contained.

'God be praised, he's safe!' She pressed her hand to her heart. A sudden sharp physical pain had stabbed her in the chest like a knife. 'He's safe! They're held now at the *King's Head*—he doesn't say where they were before. He wants clean linen.'

Patience brought a tankard of the hot wine and set it on the table beside her.

'Here. Drink this. If he can think about clean linen, all must be reasonably well.'

'He says: *Send what else y^u please for my comfort, but noe more than I can easily carry, for if wee are mov'd again, I wou'd not wish to bee burden'd.* So he doesn't expect to remain there long, I think. Nor to come home. Somehow, I must contrive to send him money, for they must pay for their own food.'

She pondered as she sipped the wine, which was heady with cloves and cinnamon. Patience had added pieces of dried apple and slices of Spanish orange which bobbed against Anne's lips like sprightly fish. The drink tasted of Christmas festivities in happier times. Hester brought in a tray of supper—lamb cutlets and pease pudding and an apple tart. Anne fell upon it, aware suddenly how hungry she was.

'I think we've work to do this night, Patience. We must sew coins into the bands of his shirts. That way, the money may have some chance of reaching him safely. I suspect the army guards will search any parcels for weapons or money.'

'It's a good thought,' said Patience. 'I'll fetch some of Master Swynfen's shirts at once and set about unpicking the sleeve bands.'

When she had left, Anne laid aside the tray and lowered herself with difficulty to her knees on the carpet before the fire. She was stiff with the long day's journey in the carriage and heavy with the child, who kicked and turned as though it too was exhausted and fretful, and wanted to sleep. But they must both of them watch out the night until the task was complete. Anne prayed, as she had prayed in the Chapel at Charterhouse, not in the words of some set prayer, but in silent yearning. John was alive. He was, for the moment at least, safe. Gratitude warmed her from within. How long he would remain safe seemed to rest on the fickle spin of fortune's wheel. She prayed for

God's protection. She prayed to hold John in her arms again, to wipe out the terrible memory of their parting.

Yet John's future, and hers, depended on the actions and fates of so many others. This army cabal, suddenly powerful, with England cowering before the swords of its soldiers—how would it act in the next few days and weeks? Would its leaders ally themselves with the most violent of the sectaries and put the king on trial? If they did, it would be nothing but a mock trial whose outcome was decided in advance.

The king would die.

Like some ancient sacrifice, the king's death would be as the sprinkling of sacred blood on his people, to bring forth a new age. Anne had no love for Charles Stuart, but she prayed for him that night. And if the king were to die, what would be the fate of those who had believed they could make peace with him? John was famed as one of the leading advocates for peace with honour. But in the eyes of Cromwell and Ireton, Anne knew, men like John would remain the hated enemy, because they spoke for tolerance and moderation, two ideas which were anathema to the fanatics who had now seized power.

John too might have to die.

When Patience returned, she found Anne still on her knees, shaking, her hands over her face.

'Come, mistress,' she said gently. 'Let me put you to bed. You're in no fit state to sit up all night at this work. I'll sew the coins into the master's shirts. Do you but find me the money and I can do it.'

Anne shook her head. Clutching hold of Patience's arm, she struggled to her feet.

'Nay. I could never forgive myself if I did not do this thing for my husband. I'll fetch the coins. Do you light more candles, so that we can see what we are about.'

She said nothing to Patience of the other part of John's message:

I trust y^u remember that matter wee spoke of on Sunday last, & I bid y^u carry it out as swiftly as may bee.

❧

On the following day about noon, John was told that a man had been sent to him with a bundle. The prisoners had been allowed a little more freedom today. Under guard they were taken down from their separate chambers to the common dining room of the inn, where they were given breakfast without having to purchase it themselves. Someone at army headquarters must have realised at last that provision must be made for the prisoners. It seemed that, in their rush to arrest their political enemies, the Army Council had not planned its strategy for more than a few hours ahead. With over forty men on their hands, many with powerful friends, they must at least make a pretence of treating their unlawfully arrested prisoners with common decency.

This new concession, the freedom to move about the inn although constantly under the eyes of the guards, had lightened John's heart. It might be that, little by little, Cromwell and his cronies were relaxing their grip. The news that a bundle had been sent to him cheered him further. Anne must, after all, have received his letter and this was her answer.

At the door of the inn stood Peter, truculently eyeing the men who barred his way with drawn swords. He was gaunt with fatigue, and seemed more bowed and shrunken than ever before.

'Peter!' John stepped forward to reach out to the man, but immediately two of the guards grabbed him by the arms. 'Is all well at home?'

'All's well, master. The mistress asked me particularly to tell you that young Francis is quite recovered, except for a slight cough, which she reckons to be nothing for concern. He'll be playing the devil with the other lads by next week.'

As an old family servant, Peter never hesitated to speak freely, and John smiled at the expression on his face.

'They've been plaguing you, have they? I remember how I hated it myself, shut up indoors in foul winter weather.'

Peter nodded, and opened his mouth to tell of the stormy journey to Hackney the day before, but shut it again just in time. Anne had warned him to say nothing about yesterday's doings, for fear the army might take too much interest in her activities.

'And my lady? She's well and . . . and safe? She received my letter?'

'Aye, and she sends you the linen you asked for. There's a letter here, too.' Peter pulled a letter from inside his jerkin, but before he could hand it to John, the officer of the guard took it from his hand.

'We'll have this read openly, lest there be any treason contained in it.'

'Treason?' said John. 'Treason? What treason could be committed by the wife of a good Parliamentman, who is occupied only about her housekeeping and the care of her seven young children? I think you see spies in shadows, sir, and conspirators in every cupboard.'

The captain looked at him stolidly. 'We shall see,' he said. 'These late years of war, some women have comported themselves more like men, withstanding sieges and galloping about the country after the armies.'

'Something you soldiers should be grateful for,' said John sharply, 'for I've heard that many lives have been saved by these same women, who've cared for the sick.'

'And some,' said the officer, ignoring him, and with a look of disgust, 'some have even donned men's clothes and gone for soldiers. 'Tis blasphemous, and contrary to God's will.'

'I'm in agreement with you there,' said John pleasantly, 'but I assure you my wife would do no such thing. Am I to be allowed my letter and my bundle, or not?'

'Hand that bundle to me,' the officer said to Peter, 'and be off with you.'

'Thank you, Peter. God be with you, and my loving blessing to all the family,' said John, as Peter was hustled away by two of the guards.

The officer carried the letter and bundle into the front parlour, which the guards were using as their quarters, and placed both on the table. Then he took the knife from his belt to lift the seal of the letter. After glancing through it, he tossed it to John.

'Now the bundle,' he said.

John untied the string, rolling it up and putting it in his pocket. In his present circumstances, even a length of string seemed a precious possession. The outer wrapping was an old pair of breeches, which he used to wear when he was out tramping around the estate at home. He had not realised that Anne had brought them to London. Perhaps she thought them only fit for rags or wrappings, but he foresaw that the time might come when he would be glad of them. Inside were three shirts, a night shift, and three pairs of stockings. He held them up so that the officer could see there was no weapon concealed amongst them, but he took care in handling them, setting them down gently on the table. All the garments, except the stockings, were unusually heavy. The officer nodded to him, and John rolled the bundle up again.

Back in the common dining room, he carried his letter to the window overlooking the Strand, where the bustle of carts carrying goods to Whitehall had continued all morning.

Deare heart, Ann had written, *My joy is so great at learning that y^u are safe, I can scarce express it. All the family is safe & well, & wee have not troubl'd again at ye house. Patience & I work'd all night*

134

to make y^ur linen ready for y^u. I am truly sorry I cou'd not send it to y^u yesterday. I have read y^ur letter with care, & will do all y^u bid me. Francis is recover'd & Mary has cut a new tooth. I pray that y^u may soon be releas'd & I beseech God to keep y^u from all ill. Y^u know that I am always, with all my heart, y^ur loving wife,

    Anne Swynfen

'You have heard from her at last, then,' said Crewe, coming over to join him by the window. 'Does she say why she didn't send word yesterday?'

'Nay. Only that she and her waiting gentlewoman have been up all night making my linen ready. Perhaps there was some to-do with the children yesterday that prevented her.'

Crewe clapped him on the shoulder. Despite his wealth and standing, he was a simple and kindly man at heart. He had known John many years, looking on him almost as another son.

'Come, look more cheerful, friend. Letting us out of our chambers is a good sign, I'm sure. They acted in haste, desperate to defy the will of Parliament to make peace with the king. Now they have us, they don't know what to do with us. I think it will all end harmlessly.'

'I pray God you are right,' said John, tucking Anne's letter into the breast of his doublet. 'But I wonder when. . . if. . . I shall ever see them again.'

Chapter Eleven

People began to venture on to the streets again in London. Even a
few of the whores were out, shivering in their thin rags as they
plied their trade in Dog and Bitch Lane, Moorfields and Saffron
Hill. For whores, too, must eat. Heavy snow was falling on Sunday,
muffling the sounds of the city, dimpling and dissolving on the sullen
grey waters of the Thames, which mirrored the colour of the cannon
lined up in Blackfriars, menacing the citizens as they went about their
Sabbath devotions. The citizens came forth from their houses timidly at
first, gazing about them with the stunned look of those who have
survived some great natural disaster. There had been looting, there had
been violence, a few women raped, a few men knifed when they tried
to resist the soldiers, but the city had not been put to fire and the sword.
This had been no Bristol or Basing House. Faces watched from
windows, peeping round shutters as the bravest dared to make their
way to church. Soon others began to follow. Fathers, having tested the
streets, came home to gather up their families and conduct them to
worship.

And there was much to be thankful for. The ministers of the
London churches, for the most part of the Presbyterian persuasion, or at
least opposed to the excesses of episcopal power, raised up prayers of
thanksgiving for the general escape of the city from destruction. They
thanked God that most of the soldiers had obeyed Fairfax's orders to
conduct themselves in a seemly manner, and hoped fervently that the
army would soon be satisfied with whatever moneys London could
raise, and move on. Of course, they would not have wished upon any
other city this army occupation that London was enduring, but they felt
that the soldiers would surely be happier elsewhere.

There was one point, however, on which the preachers of
London did not express themselves thankful. News of the
imprisonment of forty-two moderate Members of Parliament had now
spread throughout the city, at which both ministers and congregations
grew full of wrath. Apart from the extreme sectaries, who did exist in
small groups in London, the citizens in general were of the same mind
as the House of Commons which had voted early on Tuesday morning

for peace. After more than six years, the people were weary of war. They wanted no return to royal and episcopal tyranny, but no man wanted to pass his days in constant fear of the sword. The citizens of London were practical people. They desired no more than to go about the business of getting and spending, marrying and burying, eating and drinking, as any ordinary man has a right to expect. The first rumour of possible peace, back in November, had been greeted by London with bonfires and dancing in the streets. It had proved a false rumour, but the certain news of Tuesday's vote had brought the same spirit of rejoicing to men's hearts. The subsequent news, that those who had voted for peace were excluded from their seats in Parliament, and some even taken by force and imprisoned, had been received in London with a deep and furious anger.

So the preachers in their pulpits that Sunday morning had no need to persuade a reluctant audience. They poured forth in the words of their fiery sermons the hot resentment, the frustrated passion of their congregations. It was now generally known that the imprisoned members had been confined in *Hell*, which provided the theme for most of the sermons. As the snow fell heavily outside, and the faithful shivered in the unheated churches, the preachers of London compared the betrayed members to Daniel in the lion's den, and to Shadrach, Meshach and Abednego thrown into the fiery furnace. The comparison was perhaps metaphorically apt, but bore little resemblance to the real experience of the prisoners in their freezing cellar that first night of confinement. A fine anger burned up brightly, however, in the breasts of the London citizenry, on behalf of their elected members, who had been on the very point of bringing them peace.

Meanwhile, in the *Swan* and the *King's Head*, the prisoners were still uncomfortably crowded, but they were now being provided with a reasonable diet and could move about within each of the inns, although every doorway, inside and out, was heavily guarded. There had been, also, a number of approaches made, both direct and indirect, suggesting that it might be possible for them to go home, provided they agreed to swear this oath or that. But the oaths were not in accord with their sense of honour, and without exception they refused.

In the dining room of the *King's Head*, the prisoners had gathered around the long table after dinner to draft a document setting out their case and their demands for release. Prynne, of course, took a passionate lead in discussion; John, as usual, was pressed into service to express the common ideas in the best possible language.

'It shall be called *A Solemn Protestation of the Imprisoned and Secluded Members*,' said Prynne.

137

This was agreed, with grunts of approval. They set about laying down the points of law and privilege which had been flouted by the army—from the infringement of the will of Parliament to the abuse of privilege and the matter of wrongful imprisonment. Each time Prynne chose an inflammatory form of words, John attempted to modify it to language which would not so enflame the Army Council that they would toss the *Solemn Protestation* on to the fire unread. However, today his own sense of moderation and decorum were somewhat bruised and he did not check Prynne's words as much as he would once have done. He raised no objections to: 'the highest and most detestable force and breach of privilege and freedom ever offered to any Parliament of England'. Nor did he object to the demand for proceedings against the Army and its supporters as 'disturbers of the peace and settlement of the kingdom'.

Prynne tapped his teeth with the end of his quill.

'I think we may have them on a writ of *habeas corpus*,' he said.

'It's worth the attempt,' Lane agreed.

The professional lawyers amongst them huddled over their notes, conferring about legal niceties. John leaned back in his chair and stretched his arms above his head. His fingers and nails were engrained with ink.

'I doubt Ireton is in a mood to listen to the finer points of common and statute law,' he said, turning round to speak to Crewe, who was seated a little aside from the table, with his feet in the hearth, puffing at a pipe of tobacco. His Jemima knew his needs, and had sent a jar of best Virginia weed for his comfort.

Crewe blew out a long blue stream of smoke and nodded. 'Probably not. But composing this document will give them something to occupy their minds and prevent them from falling into melancholy. Let them amuse themselves.'

'Probably,' said John gloomily, 'the lawyers for the Army Council will claim the contingencies of war as the justification for their actions, though I think they've not declared martial law as yet.'

'They'll want to avoid that if they can,' said Crewe. He gave John a sharp look. 'You look tired, John.'

'It's this confinement and idleness.' John puffed out his breath in an exasperated sigh. 'I always need to be about and doing. I'm accustomed to walking every day—at home in Swinfen I walk at least ten miles a day, or ride twenty. Caged up here, I'm like a setting dog chained in his kennel when the guns are out for a day of sport. So I sleep badly by night, and I'm as cross as an ill-tempered rooster by day.'

'Swynfen! Here to us,' called William Waller. 'We plain army folk want plain words for this next passage, but Prynne and the lawyers say they will not serve. Come and negotiate between us.'

The day dragged slowly on as they hammered out the rough shape of the *Solemn Protestation*, then laid it aside to be completed the next day. During that Sabbath morning they had held a makeshift service of prayers amongst themselves, but Sir Robert Harley had pleaded with the captain on duty to send them a good preacher to take a service later in the day. To the surprise of all, a young preacher did arrive just as the day was darkening into evening. The prisoners set to with a will and moved the furniture in the inn dining room, arranging the chairs in rows. As they sat listening to the words of comfort spoken by the preacher, who urged them to faith and constancy, and as they raised their voices in singing psalms, John felt some lifting of the burden, a glimmer of hope that their imprisonment might soon end and life resume its normal course.

The next day brought more activity to lighten the wearisome time. The *Solemn Protestation* was completed to the general satisfaction. Communication with the outside world was still dependent on the whim of the particular officer on duty and it was certain sure that the officer in charge would refuse to allow them to send forth the *Solemn Protestation*. Jacob was summoned, and when the door was closed against any interference from the guards, Clotworthy drew him towards the table and the final version of the document.

'We need this document taken discreetly to the printer's office, near St Paul's,' he said, leaning over the tapman like a benign giant. Benign, at least, for the moment.

'Master Prynne will give you directions. It's too grave a responsibility to entrust to the young kitchen boy. Is there a chance you might carry it there yourself, without discovery?'

Jacob looked a little pale, but he nodded.

'In the afternoon, after dinner. I can slip out then. Near St Paul's, you say? I may hand it to someone, and then come away at once? I don't suppose I could wait for the printing of it. I should be missed.'

'Nay, nay. There will be no need to wait. There's a letter here telling the printer what to do in the publishing and distributing of it. You're a good fellow, Jacob. There are none here will forget what you have done to help us in our time of need.'

In the afternoon, soon after Jacob had been given his instructions, the prisoners received their first visitors. The earliest intimation was the sound of indignant voices outside the door of the dining room, where most of the prisoners were sitting about, reading or talking after dinner. Then the door opened and a middle-aged couple were admitted, the lady in particular looking flustered.

'My dear Mistress Packer!' Edward Stephens jumped from his chair and went to greet them. 'And you, sir! Have you come to comfort the afflicted?'

He drew them both to the fire and made a general introduction.

'Master and Mistress Packer, the parents of my son-in-law, Robert.'

Eager words greeted the visitors, for Robert Packer was another member of their own political persuasion. There was such a clamour of voices, indeed, that the Packers could not at first respond.

'What's the news about the House? Do any members still sit there?'

'Is Robert taken? Or excluded?'

'Any words of the army's plans?'

'What has happened to the king?'

'What's Black Tom about?'

'Cromwell—does he support what Ireton has done? Surely he wouldn't act so unlawfully?'

At length, the Packers were able to speak, though they had little good news to tell. Fewer and fewer members were able to attend the House. The eighty or so members allowed to take their seats last week had dwindled to about fifty—barely one in ten of the Commons—as more were barred entry and others, who refused to support the army's seizure of power, stayed away of their own will. Several votes had failed because there was no quorum. The Lords was reduced to a handful in league with the Army Council, but it was openly said that the Lords would soon be abolished altogether, and the Commons either dissolved or packed with the army's placemen. Robert had not yet attempted to take his seat, but would try later in the week, when he expected to be excluded. The Packers had no first-hand knowledge of Fairfax, Ireton or Cromwell, but rumours were flying about. It was said that Fairfax had fallen out with the other two, and was angered that so many unlawful actions had been undertaken in his name when he had neither been a party to them, nor approved of them.

'As for Cromwell and Ireton,' Master Packer shrugged and raised his eyes to heaven. 'Would Ireton have dared to lay hands on you as he did, if Cromwell had been here in London? Perhaps not. But Noll Cromwell, as indecisive as a girl with the green sickness, dallies on the road south and arrives to find all done that he might not have done, or might have done differently, had he been here. Now that it *is* done, he has spoken in favour of his son-in-law's actions. Ireton is no fool. He knows that by acting before Cromwell arrived, he forced him into the place where he wanted him. Cromwell can't now speak against Ireton, or else the whole army conspiracy would be discredited, and they would fall apart, squabbling amongst themselves.'

'Is there any word of Nat Fiennes?' John asked.

'Despatched to Oxfordshire by his father today,' said Philippa Packer. 'But, knowing we hoped to visit you, he sent a letter and these newspapers round to us by his manservant.'

She drew a packet of papers from the bodice of her dress, where she had hidden it behind the stiffened busk, to keep it safe from the searching hands of the guards. Soon after this the Packers were ordered to leave. They obeyed, promising further visits.

Philippa Packer embraced Crewe as she left.

'I'm glad to find you all so cheerful, cousin.'

'It's your presence that cheers us, dear lady,' he said. 'You have truly brought the sun into this room, to dispel our sullen gloom.'

The newspapers and Nat's letter were eagerly passed from hand to hand. The letter contained little more information than they had already gleaned from the Packers, although Nat did pass on a warning. *It is rumour'd*, he wrote, *that those who were sn^r officers during ye early days of ye Parliamentary army will soon be confined more straitly than ye rest.*

The newspapers were of every political hue, from the Leveller *Moderate* to Marchamont Nedham's *Mercurius Pragmaticus*. They reported the events of the last few days, including the imprisonment of the members, more or less accurately, but each with its own political colouring. The tone of the *Moderate* seemed somewhat ambivalent to those who knew the aspirations of the Levellers. So strong was the Leveller movement within the ranks of the army that its leaders, in particular John Lilburne, had been able to bring much influence to bear on Ireton. But it was clear that the Levellers were suspicious of the motives of the army leaders. They knew that Cromwell and Ireton would collaborate with the Levellers only so long as they either needed them or feared their power amongst the rank and file of the soldiers.

The prisoners retired to their chambers that night in the certainty that their plight was at least common knowledge on the streets of London.

'I bid you good night,' John said to his chamber companions as he blew out the candle. 'Let's pray that the morning brings us further news and more visitors.'

'Tomorrow,' rejoined Massey sleepily, 'the *Solemn Protestation* will be published. Cromwell and Ireton must make some response to our protests at last.'

❧

Despite the blizzard on Sunday morning, Anne had led her household to service in St Margaret's. It seemed as though a month had passed, not a mere week, since she had last walked here on John's arm. The children and servants followed her, very subdued, their heads bowed and their eyes averted from the army patrols. Nan, who had not been outside the house since they had arrived back from Hackney, clung to Patience's hand, and looked sick with fear. Anne walked alone, her head up. She was wearing pattens, to keep her shoes from the snow, but they made her clumsy, so that she staggered like a drunkard. In the deep snow which lay, unswept, in the streets, they did little to protect her feet. With an exclamation of annoyance, she stopped. The whole household stopped behind her, startled.

'Lend me your arm, Peter,' she said.

Steadying herself against this feeble support, she stooped and tore off the pattens, and tossed them aside into a snow drift.

'Thank you. Let us continue, children.'

Now, at least, she could walk with some dignity. As they approached the church, she was reassured to see that almost the whole congregation was gathering. Some, no doubt, had left London in the last few days. She herself planned to leave tomorrow, as John had implied she should do in his letter.

'Mistress Anne! How do you fare? Have you any word of John?'

It was Samuel Gott, who took her hand in both of his and looked at her with concern.

'Samuel! It's good to see you still walking about free.'

'I'm secluded from the House,' he said, 'but I am a small fish compared with John. They wouldn't care enough about me to imprison me. But John, any news?'

'He's held at the *King's Head* in the Strand,' she said, 'along with the others.'

'A few are at the *Swan*, I hear,' he said. 'And more than a hundred like me, perhaps two hundred or even three, barred from our seats by force. The whole business of government is in collapse. Not Parliament only, but the courts, the committees which manage the daily affairs of the nation, the commissioners of the Great Seal. Nothing can be done.'

'I hope they're pleased, then, at this wonderful state of affairs.'

Gott shook his head.

'I fear it won't teach them to restore Parliament. These men are dangerous, Anne. They won't admit they are wrong, these *Saints*.'

His lip curled in contempt.

'They will step further along this road to a dark future. The Levellers mean to have revolution and a world turned upside down. As for the army *junta*, I think they'll part company with Lilburne. They won't sacrifice their own estates and power to this great levelling down. Nay, I think we'll see a new tyranny arise, and further bloodshed.'

'They mean to put the king on trial, do they not?' Anne said softly.

'I think so. And if they do, it's certain they'll find him guilty and execute him.'

'Can they do such a thing? However much we oppose him, Charles Stuart is God's anointed.'

'When men hold absolute power,' said Gott, 'they can do whatever they please. Do you mean to stay here in Westminster?'

Anne glanced about to see whether they were overheard by any standing near. She shook her head.

'I hope to leave for Swinfen tomorrow,' she murmured. 'I'll hire the largest private coach I can find, for I've a large family to transport.'

'Alas, Anne, I've heard that every private coach is gone from London and Westminster. You must needs take the stage from Charing Cross.'

At this the tolling of the bell called them in to church. Anne hardly heard the words of the service, responding without conscious thought throughout, and mouthing the psalms. During the long sermon, although she heard the preacher call upon the Army Council to release the prisoners, she heard little else. To travel by public coach to Staffordshire with six children and four servants would be a fearful undertaking. They would need to occupy nearly the whole of a coach, and in the present circumstances that might not be possible. Yet she dared not divide their party between two coaches. They must stay together. She would send Peter or Ned out before dawn tomorrow morning to await the opening of the stage post at Charing Cross, to reserve seats for them all on the coach to Oxford. If needs must, she would bribe the clerk.

When they came out of church, they found it was snowing again. Samuel Gott came to Anne to bid her a quiet farewell.

'I'll visit John if I can, and send you word to Swinfen. I hope you find Master Richard Swynfen and Mistress Joane well.'

'Thank you,' said Anne. 'We've heard nothing from John's parents this month and more. I sent word to them yesterday of what has been happening here, but I don't know if Parliament's post is still being carried.'

'You'll probably arrive before your letter.' He kissed her hand. 'God go with you, on the journey, and with the new babe.'

Sam Carpenter arrived that afternoon, having walked out from the City to Westminster to visit his uncle and pay his respects. Anne sent Peter to bring him into the parlour. She had decided to confide in him.

'Sit down, Sam,' she said. 'I want to speak to you in confidence about my plans. Master Swynfen thinks I should move the household back to Staffordshire, and I hope to leave tomorrow.'

Sam showed no surprise. Some word of their departure must already have been spoken in the kitchen.

'We'll go by stage to Oxford, then from Oxford to Lichfield, where I should be able to hire a private coach to take us the last few miles to Swinfen.'

Sam nodded. 'Who goes with you?'

'Apart from the children and my waiting gentlewoman, all the servants who came with us from Staffordshire—Peter, Bess and Hester. I have offered to take Ned and the two girls, but they prefer to stay near their families. I won't turn them away penniless. I shall pay them each two months' board wages, and they may stay in this house as long as they need. The rent is paid until Candlemas, nearly two months yet. Now, it may be that my husband will be set free by then, and they will be welcome to stay on.'

'And if not?'

Anne clenched her hands together. She did not want to consider this possibility, but she must.

'Ned may go to you, may he not?'

'Of course. There's always room for him at my fireside.'

'I'm going to write a letter for each of the girls to take to my sister-in-law, Mistress Coleman, asking her to help them find new positions. I can do the same for Ned.'

'Perhaps that would be wise, for his pride's sake. He wouldn't wish to think himself too old for work. But I hope I can persuade him to come to my wife and me, once he's finished here.'

This was a thoughtful young man, as well as a sensible one. Anne smiled at him.

144

'You're right. I'll do it now. I hope that, after we've gone, you may be able to visit the three of them here from time to time, to see that all is well.'

'I'll be happy to do it, mistress,' said Sam. 'Could I suggest something myself?'

'Of course.'

'Let me stay here this night and help you set off on the morrow. I have a strong pair of arms, and I think you'll be needing help.'

Anne was surprised at the intensity of her gratitude. She had wracked her brains trying to think how best to move all the luggage and the children to Charing Cross. And Sam could go to buy their seats on the coach early in the morning. A strong young man, built more like a farmer than a tailor, he would not be elbowed aside by other travellers as Peter or Ned would.

'But can you stay? Won't your wife worry if you don't come home tonight?'

'I told her not to expect me until the morrow. I can't risk running the curfew too often! I planned to stop the night at a tavern somewhere along the Strand. But I can sleep in the kitchen here and make sure you're all safely aboard the coach, with no children mislaid, and still be home to open the shop by nine of the clock.'

'Sam Carpenter,' said Anne, 'you're a true gentleman. I've known noblemen who would make a poor showing beside you.'

Sam coloured and crushed his cap between his hands, but he looked pleased all the same. They discussed what was to be done the next morning, and then Sam went off to visit a friend who lived nearby, a man who owned a handcart.

'It will solve the matter of the luggage,' said Sam. 'Peter and Uncle Ned and I can push it full to Charing Cross, and then Uncle Ned and I can bring it back empty before I walk to the City.'

When he had gone, Anne fetched pen, ink and paper from John's study, to write the letters of recommendation for the London servants. As she sanded them and set them to dry, she wondered whether she would ever see the three of them again. The two girls were good workers, if a mite giddy, and she had become fond of Ned, so sturdily independent even in old age. She was sure he would not accept Sam's offer of a quiet place by the fireside.

She would need to seal the letters. Back in the study again to search for John's fob seal, which he kept on his writing table, she suddenly noticed his little shelf of books, which she had forgotten to pack. He would not forgive her if they were left behind to be looted once the house was empty. First, she carried wax and signet into the

145

parlour, where she folded and sealed her letters, addressing them on the outside to Grace at her house in Holborn. Then she took all the writing materials back to the study and unlocked John's writing box with one of the keys she had worn round her neck since he had given them to her the previous Sunday evening. There were five books. They could be fitted in to the writing box and the strong box, which she lifted out of the court cupboard and placed on the table.

One of the books was a slender volume by Boethius, *Philosphiae Consolatio*, a book John often turned to when public affairs or the horrors of war overwhelmed him with melancholy. Anne knew only a little Latin, learned when she shared her brother's lessons with his tutor when she was young. She had never attempted to read anything as difficult as the Boethius, although she knew a little about the book, written while the author was in prison, awaiting execution. Would John find solace in it now, or would his present circumstances resemble the Roman philosopher's too closely for comfort?

She held the book between her hands, caressing the ridged spine with her thumb. It was a compact duodecimo, beautifully bound in polished calf, tooled with a pattern of leaves and flowers within a geometric border, but the corners were faintly rubbed where John had carried it about in his pocket. She laid the book against her cheek. The scent of leather and thick stiff paper and printer's ink brought John to her mind with shocking clarity. She could see him bowed over the book in the uncertain light of the candle, wearing the loose velvet robe he preferred in the evening when they were alone and undisturbed by visitors. Tears welled up and began to spill over. Would they ever sit again beside the fire, in the silence without need for words? How little she had valued these things, when it seemed that the years stretched quietly ahead of them.

She brushed her eyes angrily with the back of her hand. She would ask Sam to take the book to John in the *King's Head* on his way back to the City tomorrow, and she would slip a short note inside, enough to let him know that they were safely away. And of course it would be necessary to admit that she had brought Nan home from Perwicks' school. Would he be angry with her? Probably he had too much else to concern him, to worry about where Nan was. Anne was sure she had acted wisely. If only she could have brought Dick as well. Young as he was, he would have been a support on the long journey.

The remaining books she packed in the two boxes. From the strong box she took out money enough for the servants' wages and for the journey, then she locked both and carried them upstairs to her chamber. They were heavy, but she must carry them herself, in her smaller travelling bag. It stood on the end of the bed, half packed, waiting for her night shift and toiletries to be added in the morning. The two boxes fitted on top of the clothes already folded inside, leaving just enough room for the rest to be added tomorrow. The bag was made of Turkey carpet and fastened with leather straps. She tested the weight. It was fortunate Sam was borrowing the handcart. She could rest it on the edge, but not let it out of her sight. It would have been a heavy burden to carry all the way to Charing Cross. She pushed away the thought of the later stages of the journey, when there would be no Sam to help her.

Downstairs again, she penned a short note to John. Not knowing who might see it before it reached his hands, she dared say little.

Deare heart,

I shall do as y^u bid tomorrow, for all of us, & Nan too, who is here with mee. All is well with us, & I pray God all is well with y^u. I send y^u y^{ur} Boethius his Consolatio that y^u may have wherewithal to pass ye time. I have been much help'd by Sam Carpenter, nephew to Ned, who deserves gratitude from us both. At service today I spoke to Samuel Gott, who hopes hee may be able to visit y^u. I pray y^u, if y^u may, send mee word how y^u fare.

Y^{ur} loving wife in God,
Anne Swynfen

She folded the letter and slipped it between the pages of the Boethius, which she wrapped carefully in several layers of cloth and tied with tape. It would be unforgivable if any harm came to this favourite book. Gathering up the three letters and the package, she went down the narrow passage to the kitchen, where she found Hester preparing supper with help of the London maids, all of them in tears. The two menservants were in no better state. Peter, bringing in coal from the shed outside, and Ned, rubbing the family's travelling shoes with goose grease to keep out the snow, wore expressions of misery.

'What's this?' said Anne, patting Tabby on the shoulder. 'Such tears!'

'We mislike to see you go, mistress,' the girl cried. 'We'm happy here, me and Kate. And 'tis a fearful journey you're to be making, into that wild country up north, with all them soldiers roaming about, and broken men, and footpads.'

Hester made a sound somewhere between a squeal and a sob. She was a large woman, a tribute to her own cooking, but her comfortable appearance belied her dramatic temperament. The sudden

147

flight from London might propel her at any moment into hysterics. Peter shook his head.

'Aye, 'twill be a dangerous journey, right enough,' he said gloomily. 'Miles and miles it is, to Staffordshire. And when we came to London, we travelled in a private coach and 'twas summer time. I mind it took us three days then, and that was with the roads dry and no snow and no floods. And we'd the master to look after all. Like enough we'll get no further than Reading before—'

'That's enough, Peter!' said Anne, not sure whether to laugh or cry. 'We shall miss you, all three,' she said to Tabby, 'but I've letters of recommendation here for you to take to Mistress Coleman, who'll help you find new positions. And if we return to London, I'll be happy to have you back again, any of you. You must give the cat Jemima to my sister-in-law, for we can't take her with us on the coach.'

She turned to where Peter was making up the fire, the hunch of his shoulders speaking volumes.

'And as for you, Peter, I am depending on you as the man of the party to see that everything goes smoothly for us. You'll be glad to see all your family back in Staffordshire, surely?'

Peter gave a sniff.

'And you know, Tabby, Staffordshire is not really in the north. Swinfen is barely into the south of the county of Stafford, just over the border from Warwickshire. Further north there are places like Derbyshire and Lancashire and Yorkshire. Why, there's Northumberland and even Scotland. *That's* the north!'

She laughed. Why was she giving a geography lesson to her London maid? For the girl, as for all inhabitants of the capital, civilisation ended at London's city wall.

'That's enough grieving. We must all prepare for the morrow. Is supper ready, Hester? Call the children, Kate. Let's all eat together here in the kitchen as a family for one last time.'

So they sat down together, one family about to be broken apart, as so many had been in late years, and Anne said a blessing over their final meal.

Chapter Twelve

The maid Kate woke Anne before dawn the next morning. She came awake with a start, fighting her way out of a troubled dream, unremembered yet lingering as a shadow at the back of her mind. She had been struggling to find something or someone, dragging her exhausted body through a clinging weight, like bog or snow drift. Sitting up with a groan against the bolster in the big, cold bed, she took the warmed ale and bread Kate had brought her. She scorned the interpretation of dreams, but this one had cast a sense of loss and fear over her mind. She shook her head to clear it of fantasies. Today she must show nothing but courage. All her dependants would look to her to take charge in the long and difficult journey that lay ahead, however unsure of herself she might be. Her heart jumped with sudden fear. What if the army came hunting for her family before they could escape?

'Is it snowing still?' she asked.

No idle curiosity, this. If the snow continued too heavily, the stage would not leave. The scheduled run from London to Oxford was a polite fiction maintained by the proprietors. Heavy rain, snow, flooded roads, the movement of troops, sick horses or a damaged wheel—any of these could lead to a cancellation of the coach.

Kate carried her candle across and, parting the curtains, stared out of the window, which showed as a rectangle of only slightly paler grey against the shadows on the wall. The arrow point of the candle flame reflected back from the many panes, and Kate's face, tired and forlorn, hovered ghostly behind it.

'There be a little snow, mistress, but nothing to mind. Just a light drifting.'

'Best that Sam goes to Charing Cross, then, about the places on the coach.'

'He'm gone already, this half hour. And Peter and Ned loading the baggage into the handcart.'

'Then I must be up.'

Anne drank the last of the ale, and was glad Kate had warmed it, for as she swung her legs out from under the blankets her feet touched boards as glassy cold as ice on the lake at home in Swinfen.

'I'll wear no stays for the journey,' she said. The stays had been laced less and less tightly as her pregnancy advanced, but the rigid boning even of loosened stays would be unbearable on the long coach journey, now that she was nearly eight months gone. Who was there to criticise her unseemly shape? None but a pack of women and children, and one old man. There was more at stake today than outward respectability.

'Patience has laid out my brown homespun for me to wear,' she said, 'so that I can dress myself if need be on the journey.'

The homespun was as plain a dress as any Puritan housewife's: a front-fastening bodice, easy to don, and a simple gathered skirt worn over a plain white petticoat. Before they reached Oxford, both would be spattered with mud and slush. While Anne dressed, Kate folded yesterday's fine city gown and laid it in the travelling bag on top of the writing box and strong box, which she eyed curiously.

'Is Patience awake?' Anne asked.

'Oh aye, mistress. She'm helping Bess to ready the children.'

Kate set to quickly and dressed Anne's hair in a simple style, which could be tucked into her lace cap, then packed her night shift.

Anne looked around the room. All sign of their lives here for the last three years were gone, save for a chest in which Patience had stored John's clothes. This would remain in the house, in the hope that he would soon be home. If he had not returned by the time the servants left at Candlemas, Ned had instructions to send it on to Swinfen by a reliable carrier. There was nothing more to do, except to ensure that everything was loaded on the cart, and that the food for the journey was put up in a basket. As soon as Sam returned, they could leave.

The dispirited party set out through the streets of Westminster as the sky began to grow faintly light behind the snow clouds. Kate and Tabby bade them a tearful farewell at the door, and that set the children crying. Had their father been with them, a trip back to Staffordshire to visit their grandparents would have been a grand adventure, but now even little Mary sensed there was something wrong. Dorothea was perched amongst the luggage on the handcart, with silent tears running down her cheeks, while Mary, in Bess's arms, cried heartily. Sam had rigged up a sort of harness to pull the cart from the front; old Peter and Ned had each a handle to push from behind. Jack, very conscious of his responsibilities as the eldest boy, walked between them, leaning his

150

small weight against the back of the cart and straining to take more than his share of the load.

'Well, Patience,' said Anne, 'you'll soon see your family again.'

Patience gave her a worried smile. She was leading Ralph by the hand.

'I pray so.'

Ralph gave a skip to keep up with the fast pace the adults were setting.

'Shall we be in Swinfen tonight?'

'Of course not!' Nan looked at him scornfully. 'It's *hundreds* of miles to Swinfen. We shan't be there for days and days.'

'Only four days, I hope,' said Anne. 'Two days to Oxford. Two days from Oxford to Lichfield. Then, if we don't reach Lichfield too late, Swinfen the same evening.'

'Shall we sleep at an inn?' asked Francis, slipping his hand into Anne's. His illness had left him subdued, and Anne wished she had not needed to take him so soon on this winter's journey.

'Aye,' she said, smiling down at him. 'An inn at Reading tonight, then Oxford tomorrow. The next night . . . I'm not sure where.'

Nan had been calculating in her head. 'That means we shall be home on Thursday night.'

'Or perhaps Friday.' Anne glanced over Nan's head at Patience. 'It's not so very long a journey, after all.' She said it as much to reassure herself as the others. She would not allow herself to think what would happen if any of the coaches did not run, or if the weather grew worse. They might have to spend several days at one of the inns. There was adequate money in the strong box for the moment, but not if they became stranded for a long time.

Once again she was thankful for Sam Carpenter's presence when they reached Charing Cross. Two coaches were being readied for the seven o'clock run to Reading and Oxford, one fairly new and clean looking, the other an ancient vehicle, scratched and battered, its doors half hanging from their hinges, the rack on the roof broken away, so that some of the luggage was sure to be lost at the first sharp bend in the road. An office clerk at the stage post, seeing their undistinguished party of women and children, tried to hustle them aboard the old coach, but Sam strode briskly up.

'Nay, then, none of that. We have places booked on the new coach. I've already paid extra. Don't try any of your scurvy tricks.'

Grumbling, the man ordered one of the drivers to load the Swynfens' luggage on to the top of the better coach. Anne watched till all was loaded, mistrusting the men, who had a reputation for stealing passengers' possessions. The driver held out his hand for her carpet bag, but she held it tightly.

'Not this one. We shall need it on the journey.'

'There be no room for luggage inside,' he said, seizing hold of the handle.

Again Sam intervened.

'The lady needs her bag,' he said. 'Would you have the little one fouling the coach for your other passengers?'

The driver turned away in disgust. It was clear he did not relish driving a coach full of small children. And despite Sam's best efforts to secure a whole coach for their party, they would have to share it with other passengers fleeing from the occupied city, who seemed equally displeased at the sight of their juvenile travelling companions. Peter would travel outside with the driver, along with two other men. Each of the four women in the party must needs take a child on her lap. Of the children, only Nan and Jack had seats.

With all the luggage and people stowed, Anne handed Mary to Nan and stepped down to thank Sam for his help. He brushed her grateful words aside.

'You and Master Swynfen have been more than kind to my old uncle,' he said, nodding to where Ned was attempting to reverse the handcart, 'when many would have turned him away, as too decrepit to work any longer. I pray God speed you on your journey.'

'You have the packet for my husband?'

Sam patted the breast of his coat.

'Safe in here. As soon as we've returned the cart, I'll be off home, and call at the inn on my way. You can see it from here.'

Anne spun round. She had not realised John was so near. Sam pointed down the street, to where she could make out an inn sign projecting over the road, painted with a crude representation of a crowned head.

'That's it, the *King's Head*?'

'Aye. Circled round with armed men, but nothing more than a common inn, when all's said.'

At this distance it was impossible to make out the armed men, but she glanced fearfully around the small crowd gathered about the coach station. Anyone of those lingering onlookers might be an informer, reporting to Cromwell and the Army Council on the movements of their enemies. Her breath caught in her throat in panic. Quickly, quickly—why did the coach not leave?

At last the driver blew a blast on his horn, to give warning of the coach's imminent departure.

'You must be aboard, mistress,' said Sam.

Anne climbed in and took her seat, wedged between the side of the coach and Hester's ample hips. Nan leaned across and passed Mary to her. Their good-byes to Sam and Ned were drowned by the sudden clatter of the horses' hooves on the cleared cobbles and the cacophony of creaks and groans from the leather, metal and wood of the coach as it lumbered into motion. Anne strained towards the window, watching that sign of the *King's Head* until the coach bore round to the left and headed towards Hyde Park, along the very road the soldiers had taken on their way to seize London. She let her breath escape in a long sigh of relief.

When the Oxford stage set off, John was at the window of his chamber, looking down the Strand towards Charing Cross. He knew that at least one of the coaches was bound for Oxford, but not which one, nor could he tell, at this distance, whether his family was amongst the crowd of passengers milling about in the dirty snow. So, uncertain whether or not Anne and the children were there, he sent up a prayer for all those setting out on a journey in such perilous times, under snow-heavy skies. As the last of the morning's coaches rumbled away, he felt a sudden stab of doubt. Had he done right in sending them out of London? Anne was an obedient wife. She would do as she was bid. But was he asking too much, that she travel at such a time, with no man for protection? He did not count Peter. Anne was likelier to be able to protect the old man than he was to protect her. What if the babe were to come early? Some of the other children had done so, though he could not now remember which ones. She might go into labour, there on the coach. He gripped the window frame, his forehead pressed against the chill glass. He had surely been too hasty in sending them away. These recent days he had lost his way, no longer certain of how best to act. After the initial looting and brawls, the occupying army seemed to be under stricter control. The members might not be kept imprisoned much longer, now that the Army Council had tightened its grip on all the instruments of government. Certainly they would be barred from taking their seats in Parliament, like the other members who had been secluded. But they might be allowed free from prison on some sort of bail. He chewed on his thumbnail, watching the last coach disappear from view. When would he ever see her again?

153

The prisoners had gathered in the dining room in expectation of breakfast, when Jacob came in, carrying something loosely bundled in a cloth, which he handed to John.

'The captain has examined this and says you may have it.'

Anne's note had been taken out of the book and read. It lay, somewhat crumpled by the captain's rough handling, on top of the familiar volume. He read her message quickly. So they had left, perhaps in one of those very coaches he had been watching. He stuffed the cloth in the pocket of his doublet and carried the Boethius over to the small light coming in through the window, whose glass was more than usually obscured this morning with mud and slush thrown up by the traffic in the street outside. He smiled to himself. How rightly Anne had judged in sending him this book.

'Look here!' cried Prynne.

Jacob had smuggled something else in to them, under the pretext of bringing John's packet. Prynne waved a hastily printed sheet in the air.

'The *Solemn Protestation* is printed now for all to see! They may have kept us kicking our heels in Whitehall, and not allowed us to speak, like some poor beggar from the gutter, but we have our case set out now before the world!'

The *Protestation* was passed from hand to hand as they ate their breakfast. All of them felt that, at last, they were beginning to fight back, and they were cheerfully plotting their next move, when the captain on duty that day walked in and surveyed them with no very friendly stare, his hand resting on the pommel of his sword.

'Well, we have taken your friend Major-General Richard Browne, who's been playing at fox and chickens with us this week past. Now we have him!'

'Is he coming here?' asked Waller. 'Or to the *Swan*?'

'Neither. He's taken to prison in St James's Palace, and he will not be residing in one of the state apartments, you may be sure.' The captain laughed harshly. 'He dared accuse us of trying to set up "a monstrous conception of a military anarchy". Well, Colonel Hewson was having none of that.'

He looked around at them with narrowed eyes.

'In my view, you're far too comfortably lodged here. This is no fit prison for conspirators and traitors.'

At this, Prynne leapt forward, but Massey, in one neat movement, clapped his hand over Prynne's mouth and pulled him back into the shadows until the captain had stalked out.

154

'Unhand me!' Prynne sputtered, shaking off Massey's arm. 'I was about to tell him—'

'We know what you were about to tell him, Will,' said Massey soothingly. 'It will do you no good. Can't you see, he came in here to provoke us? Don't give them that satisfaction.'

'A wise head on young shoulders,' Crewe murmured to John.

The news about Browne, imprisoned at St James's, left them downcast. They were reduced once more to their interminable waiting. Then, about halfway through the morning, two occurrences altered their mood, swinging it first one way and then the other. Thomas Lane and Henry Pelham were called out to a conference in the small private parlour belonging to the innkeeper and his family. They returned with troubled faces.

'Sir Thomas Widdrington has requested our release,' said Lane, 'on giving our word to appear when summoned by the Commons.'

The other prisoners exchanged looks.

'By the *Commons*?' John exclaimed.

This was a new tactic on the part of their gaolers. All the offers of release until now had been on condition that they agree to appear on summons by the *Army Council*. Such remnant of the Commons as now sat in the Palace of Westminster could never be regarded as the true House of Commons, but to obey their summons was not so offensive as to obey the army's command. Looked at from a certain angle, it was almost legitimate.

'Army or Commons,' said Prynne decisively, 'they have no power to order you, since your imprisonment was not legal in the first instance. You should refuse.'

Others were less sure. Lane and Pelham were two of the oldest of the prisoners. The younger men felt they had no right to urge continued imprisonment on their elders. Besides, both men were professional lawyers. Despite Prynne's arguments, if they felt they could honourably swear such an oath, that would be a decision taken with due care.

'Charles Vaughan is here under guard,' said Pelham, 'brought from the *Swan*. He has been offered the same terms, and is minded to accept, but he wanted to hear our views.'

'All three of you are lawyers,' said John slowly, 'and all three of a goodly age. Is there some meaning to be read from this?'

Pelham shook his head. 'I can't say. But it may be that we can do more good for all of us outside these walls, rather than in. We may be able to bring a case, if the law courts are still operating.'

'*Habeas corpus*,' muttered Prynne.

Pelham might be right. He was a good lawyer, and a shrewd and experienced politician. He had even served as Speaker in the Commons, during that time last year when Lenthall had deserted his post and defected to the army. The discussion ranged back and forth amongst the prisoners for nearly an hour, but in the end it was agreed by nearly all of them that Lane and Pelham should accept the offer, and urge Vaughan to do the same. Once free, they would do all they could to secure the release of the rest.

It was in a state compounded of doubt and hope that the prisoners watched their two colleagues leave, soon afterwards to be seen walking past the windows with Charles Vaughan, under armed escort.

'I hope this is not some trick,' said Crewe. 'They do not have the look of free men to me.'

However, there was little they could do other than wait upon events. The next development was not long in coming. Jacob arrived to lay out dishes for dinner, and as usual he had kept his eyes and ears open. It was clear to all that some news had pleased him greatly, for his eyes were merry and he could barely suppress his smile.

'Well, then, man, out with it!' said Crewe, smiling himself, for the man's mirth was infectious. 'What is today's tale on the street?'

At that Jacob laughed grimly.

'Thieves fallen out, over dividing the spoils of their robbery!' he cried, setting down the pile of pewter plates on the table, so that he might wipe his hands on his apron.

He had the attention of them all now. Glancing round to ensure that the door was fast closed against the hearing of the guards, he leaned over conspiratorially.

'As you know, gentlemen, none better, Ireton and his fellows could only seize London if they had the absolute support of the army, and since the debates in Putney last year, 'tis as plain as this finger before my face that, more and more, the army is turning to John Lilburne and his Levellers.'

There was some anxious stirring amongst the prisoners. Lilburne had whipped up passions in many of the people—not the poorest, but those a little above them, who wanted more political power and a greater share in the riches of the country. This idea of a 'levelling' of men was a dangerous heresy, contrary to the natural God-given hierarchy. If common men thought themselves the equals of the gentry and aristocracy, where would it end? Servants would suppose themselves the equals of their masters, and women would suppose themselves the equals of men. True, the Levellers did not themselves

156

advocate the equality of women, but you might as soon try to catch the winds in a sack as imprison such an idea once it ran about freely amongst the people. The very word, 'levelling', smacked of fearful rebellion, an overturning of civilisation.

'Anyway,' Jacob continued, 'it seems Ireton and Lilburne squabbled and fought over the words of that declaration of theirs, *The Agreement of the People*—Lilburne burning up with zeal, Ireton trying to dash cold water on it, to put out some of the fire, but until they had London in an iron grip, Ireton and Cromwell are going to speak honeyed words to Lilburne, aren't they? Now, they have London. Now, they have throttled Parliament and the courts. Now, they are not so ready to be friends with John Lilburne.'

'And?' Crewe prompted.

'And Lilburne has found them out. He's calling the officers of the Army Council "a pack of dissembling, juggling knaves". Worst of them all, he says, is that "cunningest of Machiavellians", Henry Ireton.'

Jacob dealt out the pewter plates on to the table, as if he were laying out a pack of cards to read their fortunes.

'A falling out amongst thieves, as I said, gentlemen. Who sups with the devil needs a long spoon.'

Whistling cheerfully, he left them.

'Aye,' said John thoughtfully. 'But which one is the old gentleman with the tail and horns? We are right to fear the Levellers. But if Cromwell and Ireton are grown so strong that they need no longer take account of Lilburne's influence in the army, then they are grown mighty indeed.'

Dinner came at four o'clock, but John, for one, was finding that the lack of exercise, or of any purpose to life as day followed day, left him with little appetite. He did his best to eat, however, for he thought he had read in the captain's words that morning a warning that they would soon be removed to a worse place, those of them who were not released on swearing some oath. His fears were realised in the late afternoon when the Provost Marshal, Captain Lawrence, arrived. They had not seen him since the second day of their imprisonment, when he had failed to provide them with any food in the cellar under *Hell*, and had marched them off to Whitehall for the meeting with the Army Council which never took place. His arrival was greeted by a tense silence. Those who had been reading, laid down their books. Those who had been speaking, ceased in mid-sentence.

Lawrence looked uncomfortable, perhaps aware that their feelings towards him—spokesman, willy-nilly, for the Army Council—were decidedly hostile.

'Gentlemen, I bring an order for the removal of four of your number to St James's.'

They looked at each other. Who was to be carried off to more secure confinement?

'General Sir William Waller,' said Lawrence, 'General Lionel Copley, Colonel Edward Massey, and General Sir John Clotworthy.'

Immediately an outcry arose from all those present. This was outrageous. All those imprisoned should be kept together. On what grounds were these four being singled out?

'I see no written order here,' said Waller at last. 'I warn you, sir, not one of us will stir from this place on a verbal order only.'

Lawrence tried to bluster his way out of this oversight, but in the end he yielded and went off to Whitehall to obtain the written order for the removal of the four.

'Come, John,' said Waller. 'We plain soldiers need your skills again. We must make use of this time to pen our protest, for we shall not go in silence.'

Prynne bustled forward. 'Let me. It calls for a professional lawyer. Swynfen is well enough for preparing committee reports and drafting Parliamentary Bills, but he has never practised at law—'

'Thank you, Will,' said Waller, 'but we have little enough time. All we need is something short and clear, to make our case.'

'Willingly,' said John. 'I'll do what I can.'

When Lawrence returned with the written order, the four officers came out to the door of the inn, surrounded by their friends. A small crowd of citizens had gathered, alerted by the news that something was afoot at the *King's Head*. Small tradesmen and peddlers, a woman with a basket of chickens, three or four ragged urchins, a young man in clerical dress, a milkmaid with empty buckets swinging from her yoke—they were not great folk, but their voices would carry word of this into the homes and taverns of London. By tomorrow it would be known in every corner of Westminster and the City. Standing bareheaded in the snow, as if he were in church, Waller read out in a loud clear voice the short document that had been hastily prepared.

The Protestation at the King's Head

We whose names are hereunto subscribed, being Members of the House of Commons, and free men of England, do hereby declare and protest before God, angels, and men, that the

158

General and officers of the Army, being raised by the authority of Parliament, and for defence and maintenance of the privileges thereof, have not, or ought to have any power or jurisdiction to apprehend, secure, detain, imprison, or remove our persons from place to place by any colour or authority whatsoever. And that the present imprisonment and removal of our persons is a high violation of the rights and privileges of Parliament, and of the fundamental laws of the land, and a higher usurpation and exercise of an arbitrary and unlawful power, than hath been heretofore pretended to, or attempted by this, or any King or other power whatsoever within this realm; notwithstanding which, we and every one of us do declare our readiness to submit ourselves to the legal trial of a free Parliament, for any crime or misdemeanour that can or shall be objected against us.

As Waller finished speaking, there were cheers and shouts of support from both prisoners and citizens.

'This rule of the army is worse than that of the Grand Turk or Janissaries,' shouted Prynne furiously, who for once was almost speechless with anger.

'Aye,' cried John. ''Tis worse by far than anything devised by the evil councillors of the king. This nation has fought and men have died to throw off that tyranny only to fall under a worse yoke.'

Lawrence and the armed guard he had brought with him paid them no heed. Each of the four prisoners was seized, his arms grabbed by two musketeers, and was thrust, almost thrown, into one of the two coaches. As the remaining prisoners were pushed back inside the inn by the flat of their guards' swords, the coaches vanished into the darkness.

❧

The journey to Staffordshire began uneventfully enough. The children were tired with rising so early and soon fell asleep, despite the jarring of the coach and the constant noise. It was not so easy for the women. Anne was the least burdened, with Mary, but so full-bellied was she by now that there was little enough room on her lap for the child, who squirmed even in her sleep. Before long Anne's back was aching, and her arms were grown almost numb with trying to prevent the child falling off. The unborn child, as if it felt itself crowded too, began to twist and kick, until she felt as though she was in the midst of a dog fight. The lurching movement of the coach filled her with nausea. Next to her, Hester was holding Dorothea, who kicked out from time to time in her sleep, bruising Anne's legs with her stiff little boots. Ralph, for once, was quiet, sprawled on Bess's lap, but Francis moaned against Patience's shoulder as if he were troubled again by his feverish dreams.

Although Nan and Jack had been allowed space on the seats, these were meant only to accommodate four persons on each side, so they were squashed between the adults, Nan next to Hester, and Jack next to Patience. The movement of the coach sometimes slid Jack against a hard-faced man, who threw him off with an angry exclamation each time. A gentleman, well but soberly dressed, he had perched a pair of spectacles on his nose and was reading a dull-looking book, despite the continual jostling. At first Anne apologised for the children, but the man glowered at her in such an unfriendly fashion that after a time she no longer troubled. Public travel in England with so many children was a wretched business. Charles Coleman, who had journeyed abroad to study the music of other countries, had once told her that the French and the Italians liked children. If you had a large family, you were praised and cosseted. On such a journey as this, the other passengers would be admiring and playing with the children, and eagerly talking about their own. So Charles said. She was not certain that she believed him. Wearily she leaned her head against the side of the coach. It was hardly restful, for her head bounced about like a tennis ball. It was beginning to ache.

Between half-closed lids, she studied the other passengers. On the opposite seat, next to the disagreeable man, there was a young fellow, perhaps a clerk, who sat with downcast eyes, modest as any maid. Beyond Nan, on Anne's side, sat a middle-aged couple, of the prosperous sort, most likely a City merchant and his wife escaping the looting of the army. From the way the man's eyes went constantly to a satchel on his lap, Anne—conscious all the time of the strong box near her feet—realised that he, too, was carrying a substantial amount of coin. These two spoke constantly together in whispers, as though they feared being overheard by the others in the coach. Unlike Anne, the wife had donned her finest clothes for travelling. Perhaps this journey by public coach was her first, for she would regret her soiled skirts and torn lace by the time they reached their destination. It was impossible to transpose Charles's stories of the *camaraderie* of an Italian coach journey to this stiff, mistrustful company. In such dangerous days, it was natural to be cautious with strangers, but Anne was sure that, even in the most peaceful of times, English reserve would have kept her fellow travellers walled into a tight silence, despite the physical proximity which meant their bodies rubbed and bumped together on the crowded seats.

At the first staging post the passengers climbed out of the coach while the horses were changed. The other inside passengers disappeared into the inn in search of food and drink, but the children woke up crying and bad-tempered, and all had to be found chamberpots. While Bess changed Mary's dirty clouts, Anne led her procession into the inn and asked for the privy. Already she felt tired and dirty, and they had not travelled more than eight miles. There was no time for food at the inn, once all the children had been seen to, so when the coach was once more under way, Hester pulled out the large basket which she had stored under the seat and handed out bread and cheese to their party. This appeared to annoy the man opposite even more than the children falling on top of him. He drew out of his pocket a folded copy of the *Weekly Intelligencer*, shook it out and began to read.

As the coach drew on towards Windsor, the children, revived by sleep and food, became noisy and quarrelsome. They trampled on the feet of the adults as they clambered from side to side of the coach, trying to look out of the windows. They complained of boredom and constantly asked when the coach would reach Reading.

'Madam,' said the man opposite, at last, 'can you not maintain some discipline amongst your children?'

'I'm truly sorry,' said Anne, her own nerves a-jangle, feeling some sympathy for him. 'It's very trying for them to be so confined.'

'It's very trying for *us*,' he said. 'How far do you travel?'

'Oxford.'

He heaved a dramatic sigh and retreated again behind his newspaper.

The one blessing, Anne thought, was the weather. No more than a light snow continued to fall. The sky was overcast, but the snow was not lying too thickly on the road, although it was enough to slow the coach. She had heard some of the passengers commenting on how long it had taken to reach the first stage. But the snow was no more than six inches deep, and the wind was not strong enough to cause drifts. It could have been very much worse, if a blizzard had been blowing or if a thaw had set in, turning the road to bog so that the coach could not move forward.

Even so, each delayed stage made them later and later. In summer, as long as the roads were in good repair, the express coach could reach Oxford in a day, although it was a bitterly long day of eighteen exhausted hours of travelling. In winter, only riders on urgent government business would attempt such rapid travel. The town of Reading was quite far enough for ordinary travellers to go in one day.

Darkness closed in on them. The driver pulled up long enough for the postilion to hang candle lanterns from the two corners of his footboard. On the urgent demand of the disagreeable man, he also hung one, grumbling, from a hook inside the coach, where it pitched about so violently that Anne thought they would all be set on fire.

They proceeded now at walking pace, for fear the horses should stray off the road into the ditch in the dark and overturn the coach. Despite the sixteen passengers crowded together inside, it grew bitterly cold, and Anne was worried about Peter, outside in the weather, even though she had insisted that he wrap two blankets around him. At last, as the road came over a rise, the scattered lights of a town winked into sight.

'God be thanked!' said the man opposite, 'We have reached Reading at last!' To her astonishment, he even smiled at Anne in his relief.

She smiled back. The children had been quiet for the last few hours. Perhaps she was forgiven.

The horses' hooves struck cobbles as they reached the town, though they were somewhat muffled by snow. A vast warm cave of light opened up to their right, a huge arch leading in to the courtyard of the inn. Stiff, exhausted and hungry, the passengers climbed out one by one. As if he were ashamed of his earlier behaviour, the man lifted Mary from Anne's arms and helped her out of the coach.

'I thank you, sir,' she said.

''Tis nothing, madam. I'll carry her into the inn while you gather up your brood.'

She shooed the children and servants after him, then reached into the coach for her heavy travelling bag, which she had stowed under the seat next to Hester's basket of food. As she did so, a searing pain struck her back, then rippled round her stomach like a band of iron tightened. With a gasp, she lifted the bag out of the coach. Perhaps it was no more than backache brought on by the long and uncomfortable journey. But it gripped her like the first pains of labour.

Chapter Thirteen

The inn at Reading had been a warm refuge from the cold night journey, but by morning all were scratching from the pests which colonised its bedding. As the passengers emerged into the grey dawn, they saw the two drivers arguing beside the great archway that opened from the inn courtyard on to the street beyond. From their gestures, it was clear that the subject of the dispute was the heavy layer of cloud that hung over the sky, threatening more snow. The air was still and frosty, as though it held its breath, and the stamping of the horses in the stables rang like a smith's hammer blows, iron on iron.

The ostlers led out fresh horses and began to back them into the traces of the coach in which Anne had travelled on the previous day. As they did so, she saw the driver of the other coach throw up his hands in disgust and walk back into the inn.

'See if you can discover what's to-do, Peter,' she said.

Peter accosted one of the ostlers, who shrugged and spat, and spoke a few words before joining those who were loading the passengers' luggage back on to the roof of the coach.

'The driver of the other coach refuses to set out,' said Peter, returning to the group of passengers. 'He fears a blizzard, and says his old coach won't be able to get through to Oxford. Our driver will have none of it; he thinks the storm won't break until we are nearly there, and we shan't fare so ill.'

Most of the passengers from the other coach accepted the news with resignation, and returned to the inn to wait out the storm and travel the next day, but one man, by his dress a clergyman, was perturbed.

'I must reach Oxford by this evening!' he said. 'It is of the utmost importance. I shall be obliged to join your coach.'

The man who had sat opposite Anne the previous day looked him up and down, and shook his head.

'Nay, sir, I think you will not. We are already fourteen inside and three outside. There's never room for another.'

'We shall see,' said the clergyman. 'I'm certain my business is more urgent than that of certain others.' He looked with meaning at

Anne and her forlorn party, standing shivering in the snow, before marching off to accost the driver.

'I fear we must hasten on,' said Anne. 'I have friends in Oxford. If we can but reach there . . .' She had told no one of the pains she had felt the night before, which had subsided this morning, but she was aware that they lay in wait, ready to jump out like a footpad when she least expected it. Should she go into labour in Oxford, she could send for help to the Harcourts.

'Don't worry, madam,' said her fellow passenger. 'I won't allow them to turn you off the coach. I'm afraid we did not meet on the best of terms yesterday. Will you allow me to introduce myself?' He gave a slight bow. 'My name is Doctor Matthias Hadley, fellow of Christ Church College.'

The circumstances were exceptional. Normally Anne would not have begun an acquaintance without a formal introduction by trusted friends, but these were difficult days. In time of war, the niceties of polite society can not always be maintained. The man seemed respectable. And if he would help her keep her place on the coach, his assistance was not to be scorned.

'Mistress Anne Swynfen,' she said. 'Travelling home from London with my household.'

'Swynfen?' said Doctor Hadley. 'I've heard that name before. Do you not have estates near Sutton Cheney, in Leicestershire?'

'Those are cousins of my husband's family.'

'Ah, I have it now. Near Lichfield?'

Anne nodded somewhat reluctantly. She had no wish to reveal too much.

'Then you must be the lady of John Swynfen, the Parliamentman. I have heard him speak in the House, and a fine speaker he is, indeed.'

Anne had nothing to say in reply to this, for John's eloquence had been so often praised. She was, however, astonished that the fellow of an Oxford college should have heard him speak. Their conversation was interrupted by the return of the clergyman with the driver, whose attempts to persuade Anne to remain behind in Reading with her party were brushed aside by Doctor Hadley.

'If it is absolutely essential for this gentleman,' he bowed to the clergyman, 'to reach Oxford quickly, then we shall have to make shift for him to be accommodated in the coach. I will take one of the older children on my lap, if necessary. Though I warn you,' he frowned at the other man, 'that you will have barely room to sit.'

'I couldn't ask such a thing,' said Anne, embarrassed that she had thought Doctor Hadley so disagreeable on the previous day, but he ignored her objections.

At last the coach was ready to depart. The passengers were far from comfortable, crowded together even more than on the first day of the journey, like salted herrings in a barrel, but their shared discomfort loosened tongues and even led to a certain sense of comradeship in adversity. They were not far outside the town of Reading, however, when the wind began to blow. Before long, the snow started to fall again, large flakes and palm-sized clusters, spinning through the air. The fingers of wind probed through every crack around the doors of the coach, and Anne, who was once again sitting beside the window, felt as though cold hands were slipping down the back of her neck. With difficulty, because of the confined space, she managed to pull a silk shawl out of her Turkey bag and wrap it round her shoulders, knotted it in front of Mary's chest. The additional layer was thin, but provided a little extra warmth for both of them and helped to prevent Mary sliding off her lap.

'I fear the outside passengers will be having a cold time of it,' said Doctor Hadley, regarding her over Jack's shoulder. Jack sat rigidly on the gentleman's knee, indignant at being thus treated as a child.

'Aye. Our man Peter is full old to be travelling outside in this weather.'

There was nothing to be done, however. None of the other male passengers, neither the two gentlemen nor the two of the middling sort, could be expected to take a servant's place. The merchant appeared to be dozing, while the clerk stared out of the window. The clergyman put down the book he was reading and took off his spectacles, the better to look at Anne. Now that he had won his point and found room in their carriage, he was all twinkling good will.

'If these Ranters and Levellers and Diggers and Anabaptists had their way, madam, *you* would no doubt be obliged to ride outside, our friend here would be driving the coach, and the servants would loll at their ease inside.'

Doctor Hadley frowned at him.

'That is no way to speak to a lady, sir. You forget yourself.'

'I do not say that I agree with them, Doctor Hadley. I merely state what such people believe. They would turn the world upside down.'

'*Apostles, xvii, 6,*' said Doctor Hadley. 'Even to repeat such ideas seems to me a kind of treason.'

'But perhaps . . .' the young clerk said, and then blushed deeply. It was the first time he had been heard to speak. He was sitting crushed against the farthest corner of the carriage from Anne, elbowed there by the clergyman.

'Aye, young man?' said Doctor Hadley encouragingly.

'Perhaps some of their ideas . . . Not all of them, of course, some of which are dangerous and sometimes blasphemous . . . But some of their ideas, about better provision for the poor, and protection for the weak against oppression, and . . . and perhaps a widening of the right to elect Members of Parliament . . .'

He was cried down by the clergyman and Doctor Hadley and even the merchant, who woke up to join in the general condemnation of the sectaries. Anne turned and gazed out of the window. Unlike many, she was less willing to enter into an argument about the views of the sects without being better informed of the facts. When John's youngest brother Richard, only two and a half years older than her own Dick, and now somewhere fighting in the ranks of the army, had talked with enthusiasm about Lilburne's views during his last visit to them, John had pointed out to him that if these revolutionary views were to take hold, Richard himself would lose the privileges of his own birth and inheritance.

Richard had replied scornfully. 'It's contrary to God's will that some should be born rich and some poor! When Adam was created in Eden, none were needy, none wealthy.'

'Come and tell me this again when you have lived on a labourer's hire for a year,' John had said mildly.

Later, when she was abed, Anne had heard them still quarrelling below in the parlour, with raised and angry voices. Neither had referred to it the following morning, so she had held her peace.

The two brothers had parted on somewhat strained terms.

Where would Richard be now? If he had been in one of the regiments that had now occupied London, he would surely have come to see them in St Ann's Lane. No, he must still be in the field, perhaps far in the north, ready to withstand any invasion by the Scots. He was the only member of the immediate family to have fought in the army. John's other brother, William, was newly married, his father and uncles too old and too canny. Her own elder brother was busy running his estate, and her younger brothers disinclined to join the military. Instead, the whole family looked to John to work rationally in Parliament for a peaceful outcome of the conflict.

And the reward for that was imprisonment.

She closed her eyes against a swimming headache. The men's arguing voices blurred into a distant rumble. She had slept little during the night, and felt sleep overcoming her now.

Anne woke to a sudden jolt as the coach hit a stone or a frozen rut in the road, and half slid from the seat. Her hat was askew, her mouth dry, and her neck ached from being twisted sideways. She sat up and straightened her clothes. Mary was sprawled asleep, with her mouth open. The other passengers had fallen silent. It seemed unnaturally dark. Anne peered out of the window and realised that what had been a slight shower of snow when she fell asleep had grown into a blizzard. Nothing could be seen through the window except a whirling mass of grey-white snow like porridge boiling in a pot. It pressed against the window so thickly that the coach almost seemed to be under water, and ridges of snow were building up against the coarse glass so that each window would soon wear a breastplate of snow, solid as ice.

The horses were making slow progress against the storm. They had slowed from a canter to a walk, and trudged so slowly that the coach seemed hardly to move forward, as it jolted over the frozen ground and swayed from side to side, buffeted by the wind. Anne flexed her fingers, which were stiff with the cold. She could barely feel her feet. Looking around, she saw that most of the passengers were asleep. Like her, they were no doubt tired from a night with the bed bugs. And the darkness within the coach felt like dusk, although surely it must be no more than early afternoon.

The inside of the window was misted over from the breath of those within. Anne rubbed a space clear with the side of her hand, but found she could see no better. Then suddenly the coach heaved like a ship hitting a rock, there was a shrill whinnying from the horses and a yell of fear from the driver or one of the outside passengers. The coach lurched, paused, and then crashed on to its side. All the passengers were thrown down. Anne tried to fight off the tumbled bodies piled on top of her, and at the same time to protect Mary from the crushing weight. People were screaming. A pain like a knife shot through her chest. The children sobbed and called 'Mama!'

'Don't move!' said a voice with authority. Doctor Hadley. 'We must climb out carefully, one by one. You there, by the door on the top. Can you open it?'

Anne could see nothing from where she lay, stifled and in pain, but she remembered that the plump merchant had been sitting nearest the door on her side, the clerk on the far side. She could hear someone wrestling with the door, and other voices shouting from the road. The outside passengers must have fallen further, but they probably landed softer, on the snow, and without this heap of heavy bodies pressing them down. Her chest felt so crushed, she could barely breathe.

There was a blast of icy air as someone succeeded at last in opening the far door. The handle of the nearer door, which had now become the bottom of the coach, was jammed into her ribs. She tried to shift to ease the pain and found herself nose to nose with Nan.

'Mama?' Nan whispered. 'Are we killed?'

'Nay, my poppet.' Anne tried to free an arm to reach out to her, but could not. One arm was wrapped around Mary, who was sobbing quietly, the other was trapped under Hester's considerable weight.

'Don't be afraid,' she said, trying to smile. 'The coach has overturned because of the storm. We'll have to climb out, and then the men will set all to rights. We'll just have to wait our turn.'

They had to wait a long time. The merchant climbed out quickly, but the merchant's wife fell into hysterics and refused to budge. She was a large woman, and it took all those on the outside, and Patience and the clerk on the inside, neither of them very strong, to heave her bodily out of the opening. The children were then passed out one by one, all except Mary, who was too entangled with her mother. At last Anne, Mary and Doctor Hadley were left alone inside.

'Can you move?' he asked. 'You bore most of the weight.'

'And you,' she said.

She had seen how he had braced himself to hold back the passengers on the other seat from sliding down upon Nan. She was now so stiff and numb, she could barely move. Slowly she managed to ease Mary round into Doctor Hadley's arms. The child, stunned, went without complaint, and was passed up and out through the open door. As Anne tried to scramble into an upright position, hampered by her tangled skirts and cloak, and by her ungainly body, she felt stabbing pains both in her chest and in her back.

'I think,' she gasped, 'I think I may have broke some ribs.'

The other pain was all too familiar. There was no doubting it this time. She realised that she had been aware of it ever since the coach had overturned, but had ignored it in the confusion of the accident. Wave upon wave, it was the pain of regular contractions.

Doctor Hadley was struggling to gain a foothold on what had been the side of the coach. He put his arm firmly around her waist and helped her to climb up the floor, which lay at an angle like the slope of a roof. It was a contact of unseemly intimacy, but Anne was grateful for it.

As she gripped the edge of the door frame, she suddenly remembered. 'My Turkey bag! I mustn't leave that.'

'Don't be afraid,' he murmured. 'I'll bring it with me. I've seen that you value it.'

The scramble out of the coach was difficult and painful, every movement, every breath shot through with pain. At last she was perched precariously on the top side of the coach, with Doctor Hadley supporting her from inside and the merchant and the clergyman reaching their arms up to her from below. With little care for her dignity, she let herself drop. The pain in her ribs as they caught her nearly made her faint away. Doctor Hadley, climbing out behind, helped her to a seat on some of the luggage which the driver and postilion had piled up in the snow, so the coach might more easily be righted. It was impossible to see where the road ended and the fields began, the drifting snow lay over all in a uniform white. Patience and the others had gathered the children together. They were all unhurt and, now that the initial fright was dispelled, were enjoying the excitement of the accident.

Anne pulled her hood up over her hat and huddled in her cloak, clutching the Turkey bag on her lap. It was difficult for her to breathe. Each intake of air caused a sharp pain in her chest; almost certainly she had cracked her ribs. At the same time the labour pains swelled to a peak and broke and receded, like breakers rolling on to a shore. It might be no more than a reaction to the blows from the falling bodies. Or it might be the true onset of labour. If so, it would be a race between the baby and the journey to Oxford. She closed her eyes and tried to ignore the pain.

'Mistress?'

She looked up. It was Peter, hovering over her, his kind old face screwed up with concern.

'Are you hurt?'

'A little, I think, in my ribs, Peter.' She studied him. There was a small cut on his chin. 'And you? You must have fallen a great way.'

'I didn't fall hard, mistress. I was thrown into the snow at the side of the road. This,' he touched his chin, 'came from one of the chests falling from the roof of the coach, but I was main lucky. 'Tis no more than a graze.'

Anne eased herself awkwardly round until she could see the men working on the coach. With the help of the passengers, the driver and postilion had unhitched the horses and were now struggling to heave the coach upright again. As she watched, it came up with a rattle and bounced on its leather straps. There was a faint tinkle as broken glass fell out of one of the windows.

'Do you think we'll be able to journey on?' she said.

'We must,' said Peter. 'Else how can we survive in this?'

He was right. The blizzard had not abated. Snow was piling up already on the chests and bags, on the shoulders of the shivering passengers and on the backs of the horses, whose breath poured out like smoke amongst the falling snow. There was no sign anywhere of habitation: not a house, not a cottage, not even so much as a barn or a sheepfold.

The men were now gathered around one of the coach wheels. It was still mounted on its hub, but looked somewhat misshapen. The driver had brought out a mallet and was banging on the iron wheel-rim. Then he shrugged and conferred with the postilion. Doctor Hadley came over to Anne.

'We'll be able to continue, but only slowly, because the wheel is damaged. And the road is so hidden, the postilion must walk in front to show the way. Once the luggage is reloaded and the broken window blocked up, we'll be able to get inside again, out of this infernal storm. I fear it will be long past dark before we reach Oxford. How do you feel now? Are you still in pain?'

'Nothing I can't endure,' said Anne, 'if I move with care. Tell me, are you a physician, Doctor Hadley?'

'I fear not. No, my study is mathematics and astronomy. But we'll fetch a physician to bind your ribs as soon as we reach Oxford.'

It was not her ribs that gave her most concern. If she went into the final stages of labour before the journey was over, she would have to depend for help on the other women.

At last the coach was ready, the horses backed into the traces, and the passengers, stiff with cold, climbed aboard. It was the window next to Anne which had been broken, and she realised that once again she had been fortunate not to have lacerated her face. Slowly, the coach moved off into the blizzard, at the walking pace of the man feeling his way along the road ahead, probing the snow with a long cane.

Time dragged its heels for the passengers, huddled together now with little regard for privacy or dignity. Wind and snow found their way in through the broken window. The damaged wheel caused the coach to lurch even more than usual. They had shared out what little food they had, and the merchant had produced from somewhere about his person two squat green flasks of good French brandy which they passed from hand to hand, drinking from the bottle. Even the children were permitted a small sip.

170

'It will help to keep out the cold,' said the merchant, tilting a mouthful between Francis's chattering teeth. Francis was now sitting on his lap, where he seemed surprisingly at home for a boy who was normally wary of strangers. Having done what she could to feed the children and keep them from the worst of the cold, Anne was now concentrating on her own body, willing the labour pains away. But they would not go. She closed her eyes and ground her teeth together to stop any cry from escaping.

'My dear.' A hand touched hers, and she opened her eyes to see the fat merchant's wife leaning forward. She now occupied the seat where Nan had been earlier. Recovered from the ordeal of climbing out of the fallen coach, she radiated kindness from her ample form, squat and comfortable as a round loaf. Her bright blue eyes peeped out at Anne over cheeks like fresh pippins, and her hand was soft and powdery, the rings sunk into the plump fingers.

'Aye?' said Anne.

'I think I can read the signs,' the woman whispered. 'Are you in labour?'

Anne gritted her teeth as another surge of pain engulfed her, then nodded without speaking.

'How do you come to be travelling, so near your time?'

'The baby is not due for another month. We needed to leave London.'

The woman nodded sympathetically. 'We too. We go to my brother's house in Woodstock. Our warehouse was looted and there was very little we could save. Were you attacked by the army?'

Anne smiled wanly. Why, after all, should she not tell this woman who she was and why she was fleeing from Westminster? It might be that she would need help, and the endurance of misery and accident had made comrades of them all.

'My husband is a Member of Parliament. He's arrested and imprisoned for trying to reach a peace settlement. He thought we should be safer back in Staffordshire, so I'm taking my children and household to his father's estate. If we can but reach there, we'll be safe.'

The image of Swinfen rose up before her, the rich fields and woods, the lake, above all, the rambling house. It was half timbered, with plaster and brick, three centuries old at least, the original hall house extended by wings and additional storeys as the family had grown and prospered on the land they had owned before the Conquest.

Anne felt the sting of tears beneath her eyelids, a desolate yearning for sanctuary. The house with its odd staircases, its crooked gables and elaborate Tudor chimneys, would look absurd beside some of the fine new buildings in London, designed on the classical lines of Italy. But she had loved the place since childhood. They would be safe in Swinfen, where she could lay down her burdens and become a daughter of the house again, happily yielding the lordship to her father-in-law.

The merchant's wife shook her head.

'Staffordshire? It's my opinion you'll not travel further than Oxford, my dear. How soon do you think the baby is coming?'

Anne could not suppress a small gasp as the next contraction seized her.

'Not more than an hour or two now, I fear. Do you know how long it will be till we come to Oxford?'

'We may reach it in time. If we don't, we shall tell the driver to stop, and turn the rest out into the snow. Don't be afraid. Look at your fine family about you. The new child will be as sturdy as they, I'm sure.'

'I lost two as infants,' said Anne, with a sob. Kindness was almost more than she could bear at the moment. 'After my eldest son, who's fifteen. Then four were untimely born before Nan there.' She nodded towards Nan, who was leaning against Doctor Hadley, fast asleep.

'You've never a son of fifteen!' exclaimed the woman. 'A young girl like you!'

'Ah, mistress, you flatter me,' said Anne. 'Today I feel three score at least.'

It was some comfort to talk; it diverted her mind from what was happening, beyond her control, to her body. It had grown dark outside, and the candle lamp was hanging again from the roof of the coach. At last they heard a shout from outside. The walls of Oxford were ahead. There was a lurch as the exhausted postilion climbed up to the seat at the back of the coach.

As the sound of the wheels changed, Anne drew aside the piece of canvas that had been hung over the broken window. They were passing over a ramshackle bridge.

'Magdalen Bridge,' said Dr Hadley. 'Not collapsed since I left, I see. No more than a few minutes now to Carfax.'

Through the broken parapet Anne could see the dark waters of a river reflecting back the coach lanterns. Ahead and to the right was a college with a fine tower. The horses picked up their pace, for the road had been cleared here at some time during the day, despite a later covering of snow, and they sensed a warm stable and good feed ahead

172

of them. The coach moved briskly along a wide street that curved gently to the left, past handsome buildings. As it drew to a halt finally at the Carfax crossroads, a great pealing of bells began.

'All the bells of Oxford ring out at midnight to greet you,' said Doctor Hadley, helping Anne gently down the step of the coach.

Anne nodded. At the moment neither bells nor the hour of the night interested her.

'I must reach an inn as quickly as possible,' she gasped. 'The baby is coming.'

Doctor Hadley regarded her with a bachelor's profound alarm.

'The *Mitre*. That's a respectable inn, and close by. Can you walk there?'

'Needs must,' said Anne. 'There is no other way.'

Doctor Hadley gave hasty instructions to the driver and to Peter about the luggage, then took her by the arm, carrying her Turkey bag in his other hand.

'I'll go with you,' said the merchant's wife. 'My husband will see that your family and goods come to no harm. We also stay at the *Mitre*, and he'll conduct your family there after us.'

She seized Anne's other arm, and between them they half carried her, stumbling along the snowy street. The blizzard had ceased and a moon had risen. Its light cast a strange silver luminescence over the magical city of towers, where the ringing of the bells echoed amongst the snowy spires and battlements.

At the *Mitre*, the innkeeper and his wife were soon roused, and Anne found herself hurried away through a maze of winding passages to a large room at the back of the inn. The merchant's wife, whose name she had at last discovered to be Mistress Otwood, went with her. Doctor Hadley, murmuring something about a physician, disappeared again in the direction of the street, with an air of escape. The inn-wife hastened ahead with a warming pan of coals, the kitchen boy was roused to light the fire in the chamber, and Anne allowed herself to be led, and undressed to her shift, and put to bed. It was a relief to her to surrender responsibility for herself into other hands. The contractions were coming so fast now that she knew the baby would arrive before any physician or midwife could be found, roused, and brought here.

As if at a great distance, she was aware of the sounds of her children and servants arriving, and the bustle to find them food and rooms, but her world had shrunk to this bed, the firm hand of Mistress Otwood holding hers, and the pain that women bear to atone for Eve's sins.

In sorrow shalt thou bring forth children.

Anne was not sure whether she had spoken aloud. The inn-wife was bathing her face and crying out encouragement as the agony built to a crescendo. Every time, it seemed as though her very body would be ripped apart.

'I can see the head!' exclaimed Mistress Otwood. 'Only a minute more, my dear, and a new child born to you.'

Suddenly, in an explosion of scarlet pain, the child thrust out into the world and Anne collapsed back on the bolster, her lungs heaving, as the other two women busied themselves with the baby, forgetting her. Her hair, drenched with sweat, clung stickily to her cheeks and her nails had drawn blood from her palms.

'All's well,' said the inn-wife. 'A beautiful little girl, and none the worse for coming early, for she's not much undersized.'

They wrapped the baby in a piece of blanket and gave her to Anne to hold. She was too tired to examine the child closely, but she was well formed and breathing naturally, her small wrinkled fists against her face. Yet Anne grieved. Grieved for John helpless and unknowing in prison, and for herself stranded in a strange inn, with yet another soul to care for.

The physician, a brisk bald-pated man, arrived about half an hour later and declared the baby sound and healthy. He was less happy about Anne, whose ribs were unbearably painful after the labour of bringing forth the child. The physician bound them tightly and told her she must rest and let all be done for her.

'And how is that to be?' Anne asked. 'I'm but halfway on my journey. I have a household of ten—nay, eleven—persons besides myself to convey to Lichfield.'

The physician shook his head.

'You must not travel for several weeks. Didn't your waiting gentlewoman say that you have friends in Oxford?'

'The Harcourts of Stanton Harcourt. They have a house here in town also. But I do not know if they are at home, and they aren't expecting me.'

'I'll make enquiries in the morning,' he said, 'and call on you again at noon. In the meantime, I want you to rest.'

When he had gone, Mistress Otwood laid the baby in a cradle the inn-wife had found, saying it had once belonged to her own children. Then bidding Anne goodnight, or rather good morning, she tiptoed away. Anne scarcely saw her go. The strapping around her chest made it difficult to breathe, but it eased the pain in her ribs somewhat. She tried to find a comfortable position, but, before she could do so, she fell into a heavy sleep.

Next morning the children were brought in by Patience and Bess to greet their new sister, but showed little interest. New babies were old news to them.

Nan did say, 'I'll help you all I can, Mama. I'll look after the little ones. You mustn't worry.'

Anne kissed and thanked her. It seemed she was forgiven for kidnapping her reluctant daughter from school. The inn-wife bustled in during the morning to say that Doctor Hadley had called to enquire after all the party, but would not step up to see the baby. Anne suspected a certain nervousness on his part at the prospect of venturing into a female chamber amid all the clutter of a new baby. She was deeply grateful to him, however, this stranger whom she had misjudged at first.

The physician came, true to his word, at mid-day. The baby still slept, that first exhausted sleep after birth, before hunger turns the helpless newborn into a demanding tyrant. Although he pronounced himself content with the baby, despite her early appearance in the world, he was the bearer of some bad news.

'It seems that Lady Harcourt is not in Oxfordshire,' he said. 'Or rather, Lady Waller, as she now is. The whole family is removed to her new husband's home for the winter. And the house at Stanton Harcourt is quite cut off by the blizzard. I'm afraid you must make shift to stay here, unless you wish to find other lodgings.'

But Anne was too tired to think of moving her household. There was room for them at the *Mitre*, and they would stay here until they could continue to Lichfield.

'One matter concerns me,' she said next day to Mistress Otwood, who had called to say her farewells before travelling the last miles to Woodstock. 'Since the baby was not due to arrive until we were established at home in Staffordshire, I'd intended to engage a wet nurse there. I don't suppose I shall be able to employ one in Oxford who's willing to move so far away from home.'

Mistress Otwood shook her head. 'Unlikely. You're feeding the baby yourself now?'

'Aye. I must,' said Anne. 'I've never done so before.'

'Naturally.' Any woman of sufficient means always employed a wet nurse.

Anne sighed. 'I find myself very tired. But I suppose, from Eve onwards, women have always borne this burden.'

The other woman patted her hand. 'Soon you'll be at home in your father-in-law's house and you can lay aside your cares. You will be able to rest. When your ribs have healed, I'm sure you'll feel strong and well again.'

When she had gone, Anne eased herself back on to the bolster. She clung to the thought of Swinfen Hall, its lighted windows casting golden paths across the snow, welcoming them home to peacefulness and safety. Tomorrow she would write a letter, announcing their return. Despite her worries she fell asleep smiling.

Chapter Fourteen

After the events of December twelfth—when three of their number were released and four carried off to closer confinement at St James's—a tedious week passed with little to affect the prisoners. Occasional news reached them from the outside world. Jacob passed on any gossip he gathered in taproom or street. A few informative letters arrived, despite the vigilance of their guards, and Jacob brought what newspapers he could, from the *Moderate* with its sectarian passions to the Presbyterian *Mercurius Pragmaticus*. Three more of their number were released, mockingly, one by one: Parliament's archivist and antiquarian, Sir Simonds D'Ewes, the commissioner Sir Harbottle Grimston, and Francis Drake.

On Sunday the London pulpits resounded to fierce sermons praising the prisoners' fortitude, condemning the army's purge of the members, and urging congregations to work for the release of those still imprisoned. Bold preaching, which called forth ominous threats against the clergy from the Army Council, more sure of its power and more arrogant by the day. Word on the streets was that all work of Parliament and the courts was collapsing. The citizens who had not fled London fretted under the burden of quartering and feeding the troops.

For the men who remained imprisoned, it was heartening to learn of the support of preachers and citizens, but their own situation did not improve. Apart from Prynne, who had known worse confinement in the Tower, they were unaccustomed to such restriction of their persons. All of them gentlemen of means, they were wont to command, rather than to submit to orders. Moreover, the majority of them had been reared as countrymen. London itself was distasteful to them at the best of times, with its lack of fields and open spaces, with its filthy river and choking air. To be locked in the inn, where even the most fastidious were becoming somewhat rank, was a torment.

'The one thing we may be thankful for,' John said to Crewe, 'is that it's not the summer season, with the weather hot and the air foetid. I am as fond as the next man of those who serve with me in Parliament, but I've no intimate need to know which of them snore the loudest,

177

which have the least seemly manners at table, or which fail to change their dirty linen.'

They were sitting in a corner of the dining room, which had become by now a kind of common-room for the prisoners. To occupy his hands, John had whittled a crude set of chess men from scraps of kindling, tinting half of them black with ink. They had sketched out a chess board on one of the candle tables with a bit of chalk, and now played every day. In normal times, John was skilled at chess, but he was too much distracted by his thoughts to concentrate on his moves, so that Crewe, who was more resigned to their unhappy situation, was for ever winning.

'Checkmate,' said Crewe placidly. 'You'll drive me to vanity and excess, John, if you continue to play so badly.' He began to set up the pieces again. 'I'm sure Anne and the children are safe back at Swinfen by now.'

'I've had no word.'

'Be reasonable, man. A long journey with a gaggle of children and servants! She has enough to occupy her. And even when she has time to write, how shall she send? We don't know what's afoot out there. There may be no official post any more. Or it may be reserved for the army officers and their cronies. She may have to wait weeks, until she can send a letter by a trusted friend.'

John sighed and took down his pipe from the mantelpiece. Thomas Lane had sent them a supply of tobacco two days earlier, to their great comfort. With it had come a letter, saying that their friends were striving their utmost for the prisoners' release. But apart from the three who had been recently fetched away, there was no sign that their captors were relenting.

'What day is this?' John asked.

Crewe looked up, and scratched his head.

'I've quite lost count.' He turned and called out to the room in general. 'What's the date today? Can anyone tell?'

'The nineteenth of December,' someone said.

'Nay, nay, 'tis the twentieth,' said Prynne. 'I'm keeping a record.' He tapped a packet of paper he carried with him everywhere. 'I shall write a memorial of our imprisonment from the notes I'm keeping, to lay before all the world the scurvy treatment we've received at the hands of those tyrants.'

His face flushed with enthusiasm, the branded letters showing livid on his cheeks.

'All shall know them for the devils they are, flouting the laws of the land and the privilege of Parliament!'

178

'Thank you, Will,' John called. 'I only wanted to know the date.' He grinned at Crewe and said in an undertone. 'We may mock Will, but he has maintained a sturdy courage in face of much cruelty. We should ask ourselves whether we could have endured, as he has, such torture and maiming. I fear what I might do under torture.'

He spoke the words lightly enough, but his fear was real.

'He once told me that he could endure anything,' said Crewe, 'as long as they did not cut out his tongue.'

John chuckled. 'Aye, well, he can even laugh at himself, when the mood takes him.' He rubbed his shoulder, where the dagger thrust was nearly healed, but itching.

After contemplating the board, he moved a pawn and leaned over the fire to light a spill for his pipe.

'The twentieth of December. So we've been confined for two weeks. And it's but four days till the Eve of Christ's Nativity. Do you suppose they will allow us to celebrate Christmas by attending church?'

Crewe made his move. Inattentively, John moved his bishop.

'Not they,' said Crewe. 'The "Elect"? They'd abolish Christmas. They say it's a pagan festival.'

'Maybe in some things—the Yule Log and the mistletoe and the kissing bunch. Yet they're but the trimmings. The heart of the day is the heart of our Christian faith, the birth of our Redeemer. I can't follow their arguments. I agree with the purifying of the church, ridding it of the malpractices of the bishops, with their fat lands and ill-gotten money, and their tyranny against poor Christian folk. But this Puritan desire to rob faith of all joy and all beauty, that I cannot understand.'

Crewe studied the board for some time, then moved his knight and took John's bishop.

'There's a kind of man, I think, who believes that the only true faith is a faith that hurts. If it's joyful or beautiful, it must be the work of the devil. That's why they smash the statues and the lovely old glass windows of our churches, and rip up altar cloths and vestments embroidered with love and piety.'

John nodded.

'True enough, and *that*, I would argue, is a kind of sickness. Indeed, in itself it's a kind of blasphemy, for did not God himself create the beauty of the world?'

Before Crewe could answer, the Provost Marshal entered the room, attended by his usual complement of musketeers. Everyone stopped what they were doing and eyed him warily. Captain Lawrence's appearance always heralded some significant move on the part of the Army Council.

'I have here a list of names,' said Lawrence. 'Those whose names are read out are to collect cloaks and hats and accompany me to Whitehall, to attend on the Lord General Fairfax, in his lodgings at the Palace.'

There was a mutter of annoyance at those words 'attend on', as if Fairfax were a monarch and they but poor suppliants.

'Not Fairfax's words, I'll be bound,' said Crewe. 'Why does the man permit them to use his name so?'

'Perhaps he's as powerless as we,' John suggested.

'How many names on your list?' enquired John Bulkeley.

'Sixteen,' said Lawrence, and proceeded to read them out. Crewe's name was amongst them.

John gripped his hand before he went.

'God go with you,' he said.

'And you.'

Then they were gone. Those who remained looked at each other speculatively. Were they to be the fortunate or the unfortunate ones in this division of their numbers? The sense of unease stayed with them as the day wore on. As usual, dinner was served some time between three and four o'clock, and there was speculation whether their friends would be left hungry, as they had all been on that previous summons to Whitehall. Then, in the early evening, the others came marching back.

John drew Crewe aside at once.

'Well?'

'We're set free, without conditions.' Crewe's voice was astonished.

'What happened? Did you see Fairfax?'

'As before, they kept us waiting for hours. They're little clay gods, trying to puff up their importance by practising tyranny towards others who may not strike back. There was no need to force us to wait—in that same cold room, without a fire, chairs or food. It was meant only to humiliate us.'

'And Fairfax?'

'Nay,' Crewe snorted. 'We never had a sight of Fairfax. At long last, Ireton, Rich and Whalley come out to us, all false smiles and pretended apologies.'

'Commissary Ireton again. He's everywhere.'

'Aye. So, out they come, and they say, they regret that the Lord General is sick, and cannot see us.'

'*Sick!*'

'Oh, mark my words,' said Crewe, 'he was not sick. Either he still refuses to be a part of all this, and pretends to be sick, or else he was not at Whitehall at all, and *they* merely pretended that he was, in order to keep up the myth that everything is being done in his name. Either way, I don't think we have Black Tom to blame for our imprisonment.'

'And you're truly set free? Why are you come back here?'

'We are free. They've permitted us to come and collect any belongings. I suspect, also, they wish to torment the rest of you with the thought that you've been passed over this time.' He looked at the unfinished game of chess. 'We'll have to finish that another day.'

John leaned over and scooped up the pieces, dropping them into the pocket of his doublet.

'When we meet again in happier times, my friend.'

Crewe embraced him briefly.

'I'll try to get word of your family and write to you. But I expect that you'll soon be set free. They have achieved what they desired. They've occupied London with the army. They've destroyed Parliament. They rule by decree of this so-called Army Council, which is no more than a group of unelected cronies. They've seized the king. What harm can we do them now? Our Parliamentary army is subverted, and our duty to represent the people is snatched from us. I think I shall leave London and retire to my estate, until we can decide what to do.'

John shook his head.

'I fear we shall remain powerless. Is there any word of what they intend to do to the king?'

'None. It's my belief they'll devise a mock trial before long, when they've agreed how to dress it up as justice. A man of blood, Charles Stuart. But even such a man deserves a fair trial.'

'He will not get it,' said John.

'Come, gentlemen,' Lawrence called from the door of the dining room, where he stood impatiently waiting. 'You must leave these other fellows now, and come away.'

❧

During the last few days before Christmas, two more were released, and afterwards the remaining prisoners from both inns were all gathered together at the *King's Head*. The frustration and boredom of the prisoners were now lightened by the hope that, one by one, they would all regain their freedom, except perhaps for the five officers who had been carried off to St James's.

On Christmas Eve, which was also a Sunday, they persuaded the guards to allow them a parson to conduct a service of prayers and psalms. It was not the same eager young man who had visited them before. An older man, grey-haired, gaunt and nervous, he nevertheless did his duty by them.

'And what,' John asked, as the parson packed away his surplice and bible, 'are the feelings of the London clergy? Do they support the army?'

The man cast an apprehensive glance at the door behind which the guards might be listening.

'N . . . nay.' He cleared his throat and dropped his voice to a whisper. 'We have held two meetings during this last week, and we're all of one mind. We've vowed to drive on furiously in support of the prisoners. At whatever . . . whatever cost to ourselves.'

The next day dawned slowly, the weak winter sun obscured by heavy snow clouds once again. From the Abbey and other nearby churches, the bells rang out to greet Christ's Nativity. As their iron voices reached the prisoners, they carried a message of encouragement. The inn itself, under the heavy armed guard, was permitted no Christmas festivities. No evergreens decked the rooms, no Yule Log burned in the hearth, no kissing ring hung from the smoke-darkened beams. After the pealing of the bells, the city fell silent. The streets were deserted. The itinerant street peddlers, who usually filled the air with their strange raucous cries, had stayed at home, preferring to spend the holy day with their families, even if their celebrations must needs be somewhat furtive. In the inn, the prisoners were disinclined to talk, mostly sitting and reading their Bibles or writing letters. A few retired to pray in the privacy of their chambers. About mid-day the swollen clouds began to spill forth their burden of snow, which fell in heavy, silent swathes, undisturbed today by any wind.

Everyone in the dining room heard the loud banging on the outside door, and then the familiar tones of Captain Lawrence issuing orders. When he came in, they looked at him expectantly. Whose turn would it be to go free? Or were more to join the prisoners at St James's?

'Sir Robert Harley,' said Lawrence.

'Here,' said Harley.

'And your son. Edward Harley?'

'Yes?'

'I have orders to set you free, but with conditions. You shall remain under guard in your own house here in London, not leaving there except by command of the Army Council.'

Sir Robert expostulated, but half-heartedly. The cold he had been suffering at the time of their arrest had grown steadily worse, developing into an influenza. He spent most of his time huddled over the fire in the common room, drawing harsh, rasping breaths. He had lost weight. Blue shadows ringed his sunken eyes. At night, he needed help to climb the stairs to his chamber, where he would have stayed in bed all day, but for the bitter cold which sheeted the insides of the windows with ice. After that first evening, when the innkeeper had had fires lit in their chambers, they had been deprived of this small comfort.

When the Harleys were gone, John invited Edward Leigh to a game of chess, but he declined, saying he had no head for it. Leigh, like John, was a member for Stafford. While not close friends, they had known each other and worked together for several years, as justices of the peace, members of the County Committee, and now as Members of Parliament.

'Not many of us remaining now,' said Leigh.

'Eleven,' said John, 'I've just been counting. 'With the five now in St James's, sixteen of us still imprisoned.'

'Do you think they mean to set us free?'

'Why not set us all free when Crewe and the others were released?' said John. 'I can't fathom their intentions. I suppose it's a kind of compliment, this game of cat at the mouse-hole. It seems they think us very dangerous men indeed, if they suppose they must keep us still imprisoned—helpless and unarmed as we are—when they have the whole of the New Model Army and its weapons at their backs.'

Leigh gave a rueful smile.

'Well enough that men of note such as yourself should be considered a danger, but I'm simply one of the silent mass who opposed them in Parliament. A humble colonel for a while, it's true. But I'm better known for my scholarly work than for my politics. While I could serve my country, I was happy to do so, but now I'd be glad to return to my library.'

Aye, Leigh made a sound point. John could not understand why influential leaders of men like Crewe had been released, while quiet Leigh was still here. Perhaps their enemies had merely forgotten about him.

'I'll make you a wager,' said Leigh, 'that the next of us to be set free is Will Prynne.' He jerked his head in Prynne's direction. 'He's busy drawing up some legal document or other.'

John laughed.

'I'll not take up your wager, for it's my belief too that Prynne will soon be away. Tell me, have you any word from home? How does Mistress Leigh fare? Has she the house set to rights?'

Leigh's family had not accompanied him to London, but remained behind at Rushall Hall in Staffordshire, their house which had earlier been fought over by King's men and Parliament's men, and looted by both.

'A letter came two days ago. I'd written to tell my wife that I was safe, but she hadn't received my letter when she wrote to me. By little and little she's trying to repair the damage. Did you know, they even stole the curtain rods? Over a hundred of them! I was prepared for the loss of the stock and the weapons, but the house was stripped of everything: furniture, cushions, fire irons, feather bolsters, tapestries, kitchen goods—anything they could lay hands on. Our own army, I fear, was no better than the other sort. It's a dubious blessing to inherit a manor fortified during the wars between York and Lancaster, and still as defensible as a castle today—everyone wants to take possession of it! Fortunately, I'd hidden away my books. Some of them are very ancient and precious. Mistress Swynfen is gone home, I believe?'

'Aye. They should all be safely at Swinfen with my father by this. All but our eldest boy, who's a scholar at Charterhouse.'

'I pray we'll soon be back in the country with them ourselves,' said Leigh.

The Army Council lost no time, at the start of the new year, in setting up a form of court to try the king. As such a trial had never before been held, there was much arguing about the appropriate form it should take, but by the ninth day of January the prisoners heard that the court had already begun its sessions to try the king, although Charles Stuart himself was not present. He was still held at Hurst Castle, and was to be brought to London in about a week's time.

John found the confinement at the *King's Head* slightly less irksome now that there were but eleven of them still in hold. The rooms were no longer crowded, and he shared his chamber with Prynne alone, so each had a bed to himself. This meant a better night's sleep, and with more sleep at night he felt more cheerful by day. Now, on this same ninth day of January, Prynne received the news that his case for a writ of *habeas corpus* had been allowed. He was to go free. He shook John by the hand before he left.

'I'll see what's to be done on the outside,' he said. 'I intend to publish a detailed account of the monstrous behaviour of these army tyrants. The world shall not remain in ignorance of their actions and our sufferings.'

John smiled.

'Be careful what you do, Will, or they'll thrust you back in here amongst us before you can walk a mile in the streets of London.'

But he knew his warning would never be heeded by Prynne.

More than a week after Prynne had left, a guard came in one morning to say that John had a visitor. Few visitors had appeared at the *King's Head*. The Packers, despite their promise, had not returned, perhaps concerned that over-friendliness with the prisoners might harm their son, now himself one of the secluded members. Most of the prisoners' friends and families had fled London. Others were being watched, and dared not risk coming. John hoped his visitor might be Crewe, with news that the rest were to be released, but the slight figure following the guard was not Crewe, it was his son Dick.

He stood up, astonished. How had Dick contrived to come here? Dick knelt for his blessing, then rose and embraced his father. He was not far below his father in height, although he still had a boy's angular frame and slight build. He was fairer than either of his parents, with chestnut brown hair, through which he ran his fingers nervously, holding his hat before him like a shield.

'Dick! I hadn't thought to see you. Why aren't you at school?'

He led his son to a quiet corner away from the rest.

'We had a break from school for Christmas, though the Master was as jumpy about it as a cat on a gridiron. He's a Royalist, you see, Father, so he expects at any moment to be turned out of his position. That means he's sometimes more puritan than the Puritans in his dealings with us. Anyway, the other parents came to fetch their sons away, so I took myself off to Aunt Coleman, as Mama bade me.'

'Have you heard from your mother?'

'Not a word. Not since she came and tried to steal me out from under the Master's nose. She didn't manage it, for he's a hater of the fair sex.'

John frowned. He did not like the thought of Anne going against his will by trying to fetch Dick from school, nor did he like the levity of Dick's tone.

'You would do well to show respect for the Master, Dick, whatever his political views.'

'Oh, I respect him as a scholar, but he's something of a tyrant, Father, and you always taught us to stand up against tyranny.'

Caught in my own trap, thought John wryly. Still, he would not waste these precious minutes quarrelling with the boy. He gave Dick an account of what had happened to him since his arrest.

'And as so many are let go, we hope every day that it will be our turn next.'

'Is the rest of the family away to Swinfen?' said Dick.

'Aye, more than a month ago. I've heard nothing, but in these troubled times that doesn't surprise me.'

He studied his son thoughtfully. The boy wore a faint air of defiance, as if he expected to be caught out in some misdeed. John knew that look well.

'It must be—what? — the twentieth of January now. Why are you not back in school, Dick?'

'I caught a bad rheum when I was walking from school to Holborn in the snow, and after Christmas Aunt Coleman kept me in bed with hot bricks to my feet and possets of honey and horehound to drink. It was a great change from school, I can tell you. There we shiver under one damp blanket, arise in the dark to wash under a freezing pump in the courtyard, and study for three hours before we have a breakfast of well water and dry bread. It's not how a gentleman should live, Father.'

'A gentleman should accept what befalls him and make the best of it,' said John, uncomfortably aware how pompous he sounded. 'And you're quite well again now?'

'So my aunt thinks. I'm to go back to school, but I begged leave to visit you first. She's worried for you, and so is Doctor Coleman. We have had no word but a note from Master Crewe, to say you were imprisoned here. And she thought you might have heard from Mama.'

'I'm glad Crewe wrote to her. And I'm glad to see you, Dick. It's a long walk you've had, from Holborn nearly to Charing Cross.'

'Oh, I'm strong,' said Dick cheerfully. He twisted on his stool, till his back was to the rest of the room, and spoke in a lowered voice. 'I've brought some things for you: pen and ink and paper, for Aunt knew you would be wanting to write letters. And some of her preserves. And a cheese.'

He pulled these items out of the breast of his doublet and handed them to his father.

'She's given me some provisions for school. I left them in my knapsack outside the door, so the soldiers never thought to search me.'

'Is there any news of the king?' asked John. 'Little by little we hear things, but sometimes it takes many days.'

'He was moved to London yesterday, and is to go on trial this very day,' said Dick, his voice filled with awe at the thought of it.

'We must all pray for him,' said John, 'for I fear he has not long to live.'

'And have you heard the other news?' Dick cried, his solemn tone quite gone.

'What news is that?'

'Edward Massey has escaped! One of his servants went to visit him at St James's Palace dressed as a woman. They exchanged clothes and out strolls Massey, calm as you please, a very demure serving maid. His servant then leaves dressed as a man, and of course his face is quite unknown, he's not wanted by anyone. What an adventure!' His eyes glowed. 'They say Massey has escaped to Holland.'

John broke into laughter, his first real laughter for weeks. Massey had said he would not be confined, and here he was, true to his word. He stood up and waved to catch his fellow prisoners' attention.

'Hear this, gentlemen! Edward Massey has escaped! Let's drink to him!'

There was a great cheer from the others, who crowded round, begging Dick to repeat every detail he had heard of the story.

'Now, then, Dick lad,' said John Birch. 'Why didn't you think of that? You might have come today dressed as a maid, and set your father free!'

Dick looked embarrassed. 'Indeed, sir, I did think to do it, but my aunt wouldn't lend me a gown. She feared I would be imprisoned too.'

John looked at him, torn between pride and exasperation. He could well imagine Dick carrying out such a caper, which would have landed them both in worse trouble.

'Don't think of such a thing,' he said quietly, as Dick was called away by the guard. 'These are no boys' games. Men have died for less.'

'Nay, sir. I will not, if you don't wish it.' He flushed like a girl, as if his father had humiliated him.

'Oh Dick,' said John, embracing him and trying to keep his voice steady, 'you're my dear boy. I'm not scolding you. But have a care in these perilous times.'

He stood at the window, watching as Dick walked away from the inn, and wondered why he was headed for Whitehall and not Holborn. Perhaps he had some errand for his uncle.

❧

Dick Swynfen, however, was not on an errand for his uncle. Grace Coleman had given him permission to visit his father at the *King's Head*, on the understanding that he would then return immediately to school. She had packed his knapsack with his clean linen, the school books that he had not once opened over Christmas, and a selection of the foods she had also sent to John, suspecting that the schoolboy's diet was probably little better than the prisoner's, and perhaps worse. When her back was turned, Dick had visited the larder, where he had helped himself to a loaf of bread, another piece of cheese, and as many dried figs and raisins as he could cram into his pockets and the corners of the knapsack. He was strong and healthy, now that he had shaken off the influenza that had affected him over Christmas. He had a thick cloak and a warm pair of boots. He was fifteen years old and wild to be out in the world. In his own eyes, he was a man grown. He had no intention of returning to Charterhouse. He was going to walk home to Swinfen. His notions of geography were somewhat hazy, but he knew the coach journey should take four days. He could surely walk in a week or less the distance a coach could cover in a day. Therefore, it should be possible for him to reach home before the end of February.

The fact that it was the middle of a bitter winter, that mutinous soldiers and broken men were roaming the land, worried him no more than the fact that he had only a few shillings in his purse. He intended to beg a lift with any willing carter travelling his way. He would sleep in barns or haystacks. When his food ran out, he was sure he could beg a crust and a drink from the farmhouses he would pass.

He set off at a good swinging pace. The first part of his route was familiar, more or less, because he had travelled to Windsor with his father twice since they had come to London. After that, he knew he must head north. If he kept to the main highways, they should take him where he wanted to go, and if he lost his way, he could always ask directions. The city snow was heaped in dirty piles, and the sky lowered, but there was no snow falling and little wind. Before long he grew warm with the exercise, and flung his cloak back over his shoulders. Whistling cheerfully, he followed the road to the west, leaving Whitehall and Westminster behind him.

John, believing Dick to be safely back at school and Anne, with the rest of the family, to be in the care of his father in Staffordshire, was himself more occupied with events in London. Soon after Dick's visit, he received a letter from Sir John Clotworthy, written in his familiar flamboyant hand, though upon execrable paper, and with a pen that spattered the ink like a sprinkling of black pepper over it all. It appeared to have been written in haste, from St James's Palace.

My Most Deare & Honour'd Friend,

> *Wee have rec'd Word that wee are to be mov'd this Day to Windsor & are there like to be confin'd even more scurvily that at this p^{rs}nt Place. Massey is gone, escap'd like ye bold Fellow he is, & wth our hearty goode Wishes for a Fortunate Outcome. Held here still, besides myself, are Copley, Browne, & Waller, but wee know not whether wee shall be imprison'd together or apart when wee are convey'd to Windsor. I beg y^u send Word how y^u & our Friends fare. Wee hear little, but tis suggest'd that some are free'd.*

> *In haste these p^{rs}nts, from y^r Always Deare Friend*
> *John Clotworthy*

This move to Windsor was ominous. Away from London, the prisoners were far from the possibility of rescue by their friends. Massey, in escaping, had secured freedom for himself, but had almost certainly bought it at the price of the others' more wretched imprisonment. John knew of no rooms for close confinement at St James's Palace. Probably the prisoners there had been held, like those at the *King's Head*, in ordinary chambers. Windsor, however, had been built as a fortress. Windsor possessed dungeons.

Chapter Fifteen

A nne walked carefully to the end of Broad Street, which had been cleared of snow to ease the passage of carriages. She had come out alone, resisting Patience's offers to accompany her, for she knew she would have ended by leaning upon her waiting woman's arm, and the purpose of the walk was to help her regain her strength. Almost a month had passed since that fearful night when they had reached Oxford to the tintinnabulation of the midnight bells, she not knowing whether the baby would be born in a broken coach in the midst of strangers. The strangers had proved kind, despite these suspicious times, and the *Mitre* had provided a refuge from a world of storm and disaster, but until she reached the manor of Swinfen, she would not feel entirely safe. A quiet, fragile Christmas had passed and a quiet January crept in before she had ventured out of the warm embrace of the inn.

The haunted city of Oxford still had a strange atmosphere. After several years when it had served as the seat of the king's court in exile, its people—both town and gown—wore an uneasy air. Oxford had been in Parliamentary hands for a little over two years now, but in its streets Anne felt, as she had not felt in London, the tension of divided loyalties, a sense of the great chasm that had split apart families and neighbours.

Her health had been more overset than usual by this confinement, perhaps because of the journey and her fears for John, perhaps because of her cracked ribs, which were recovering but slowly. Her supply of money, too, had been rapidly diminished in providing lodging and food for her large household at swollen wartime prices. She had hoped to resume the journey to Staffordshire at least two weeks ago, but the physician had forbidden it.

'You may think yourself strong enough, Mistress Swynfen,' he said severely, rubbing his bald pate in irritation, 'but you are not. You tire easily, merely staying quietly here at the inn. I can't answer for your condition if you undertake the journey too soon. You must think of the baby and the rest of your family. It's not a matter simply of your own desires.'

Anne had chafed under his rule, but he was a competent man and she knew he spoke the truth. So for the last three days she had been walking about the town, a little further each time, and although she was tired when she returned to the inn, she felt herself growing stronger. Today she had walked up the Turl to Broad Street, then along that fine wide avenue, as handsome as any in London. Now she turned into a narrow winding lane, which she had been told led past New College and down again to the High Street, where she planned to visit Master Clarke, the apothecary. Doctor Hadley, who had taken to calling on her, had told her that Clarke was celebrated for his preparations devised to strengthen the blood after illness.

The lane past New College was vile and shabby, the very place for cut-purses after dark. But it was afternoon now, a thin winter sun was shining, and groups of students could be seen hurrying in and out of a mean gateway, which she supposed must be the entrance to the college. Making her way past piles of rotting food and excrement, lifting her skirts to avoid the carcass of a dog, she reached the church of St-Peter-at-the-East-Gate, an ancient foundation, said to be the oldest in Oxford, first built in Saxon times, though much altered since. She looked in at the door, but did not enter. It was a fine building, larger than their own parish church at home, but without the grandeur of the London churches. It breathed a kind of ancient dignity, the very stones rapt, the windows glowing with ardour. The Puritan Elect would strip away and destroy every vestige of such beauty and colour and grace from England's places of worship.

Idly pondering this thought, she stepped out from the end of the lane and found herself, as she had been assured, in the High Street. Master Clarke's shop was a short way along the street to her right. She opened the door and set a cluster of small bells tinkling, like some dancing mummer's costume. The scents in the shop were pleasantly familiar to Anne, who kept a well-stocked stillroom herself, and had long been interested in preparing her own simples. Had she been a man, and born to the middling rank in society, she thought she might well have become an apothecary. Or she might have followed the scholar's path and become one of the new breed of men of her own rank who called themselves 'natural philosophers'. The study of the worlds terrestrial and celestial, the workings of nature and the remarkable healing properties of plants and minerals, promised greater benison to mankind than the more violent methods of the surgeons with their bleeding bowls and cutting knives. To her mind, more patients died as a result of their butcheries than recovered. In London she had purchased a few books of the new science, which she read surreptitiously, fearing that John would not approve of such studies for a woman.

She looked around the shop, breathing in the mingled perfumes: dried sage, the 'saviour' as the ancients called it, good for heating and quickening the blood; sweet cicely, *myrrhis odorata*, the poor man's myrrh, excellent for old people and a comfort to the heart; thyme, with its soothing properties, healing headaches and sore throats, rheumatic swellings and the falling sickness; and all the other herbs hanging from the beams overhead—parsley and pennyroyal, monk's hood and lavender, peppermint and feverfew, rosemary and rue, honeysuckle and camomile, sweet marjoram and pellitory—compounded with the scents of cinnamon, liquorice, cloves, wormwood, ginger, pepper, nutmeg, flowers of brimstone, orris root, oil of Spanish orange, and other aromas she could not name. Ranged on shelves along the walls, jars and phials were labelled with the names of other substances, both common and exotic—honey, mandragora, galingal, frankincense, mugwort, pearls, rhubarb, dragon's blood, dates, spikenard, asafoetida, grains of paradise, cardamom, aloe, pistachio, tansy, tamarind, serpentaria minor, and syrup of roses. On the counter, gallipots stood in rows, beside scales large and small. Everything was as clean and neat as her own stillroom, and Master Clarke proved to be quite a young man, shining and rosy, a wonderful advertisement for the quality of his cures.

'I have been recommended to you,' Anne explained, 'by Doctor Hadley of Christ Church College, 'who advised your strengthening elixir.'

'I shall be honoured, mistress, to help in any way I can. I shall need to know all you can tell me of your state of health.'

'A recent premature confinement,' said Anne, 'shortly after the overturning of a coach, in which I cracked three ribs.'

Clarke clucked his tongue sympathetically and showed her to a seat in his back room amongst the stills and alembics, the mortars, crucibles, retorts and bottles, where he questioned her closely about her present condition, her previous health, and her future plans, then listened carefully to her answers. Soon they were exchanging views on the efficacy of their own favourite ingredients. She emerged an hour later, with a phial of his recommended remedy and her basket filled with a supply of those ingredients she found most difficult to obtain in Lichfield. As she walked back along the High to the *Mitre*, through crowds of students released for the day from their lectures and eagerly making their way to the cheaper taverns, she found herself as much strengthened by the conversation as by the exercise. Within the next

few days, she would make arrangements for continuing home to
Staffordshire.

&

The coach to Lichfield stopped for the night at Warwick. The journey
from Oxford had lasted fifteen hours, along roads churned into an
unholy mire of half-melted snow and mud. All day, the rain pelted
down, sometimes turning to sleet, and towards evening to snow again.
Whenever they broke the journey to bate or change the horses, the
passengers scurried for shelter to the staging inn, but these were a mean
collection of hostelries, sunk into dirty and careless ways after years of
quartering the troops of both sides, as they marched back and forth
across the mutilated midland counties of England. If these inns had
ever possessed dishes of pewter, they had been looted long ago. Food
was served on discoloured platters of treen, ill-washed between meals,
while the thin, almost colourless ale was poured into wooden beakers,
which age and damp and proximity to fires had twisted until they
resembled galls hacked off diseased trees.

When they reached Warwick at last, long past dark, the children
tumbled into bed, too tired to eat. Anne sat up only long enough to feed
the new baby, who was still—through some strange superstitious
reluctance on her part unnamed and unchristened, known only as 'the
baby', before she stretched out on the bed next to Patience.

'Shall we truly be at home tomorrow?' Patience asked, as if she
no longer believed their journey would ever end.

'Aye,' said Anne, 'if we reach Lichfield in time to hire a carriage
to take us to Swinfen. The stage will pass along the road that edges our
estate, but there would be no use in asking to be set down there. We
should be abandoned at the side of the road with all our luggage, and
with no means of carrying it up to the Hall. Indeed, the coach will drive
directly past Blackbrook Farm, but I'm afraid I can't leave you there to
see your people. I shall need your help in Lichfield.'

'I hadn't realised we should pass Blackbrook,' said Patience,
smiling at the thought of seeing her home once more. She turned on to
her side, with a rustling of the coarse, straw-filled mattress, and soon
fell asleep.

Anne lay awake longer, imagining the comfort of a deep feather
bed again. The day's rough journey had set her sore ribs aching, and the
pain made it difficult for her to relax. Tomorrow, God willing, she
would be relieved of her cares when they reached Swinfen. The
children would no longer be fretting and tormenting each other. There

would be good, nourishing country meals of home-cured beef and ham and preserves. She would not even have the responsibility of running the household, which would be in the capable hands of her mother-in-law, Mistress Joane Swynfen. The management of accounts and the moneys she had carried from London could be handed over to John's father. She would have nothing to do but rest, and to feed the baby. Even that task would be spared her if she could find a wet nurse. There was but one matter which cast a blight over these thoughts: neither the letter to her father-in-law sent from London nor the two from Oxford, warning of her arrival, had been answered. She had no means of knowing whether they had ever reached their destination. Perhaps even now a letter might pass her by on the road, heading towards Oxford. She yawned and eased herself awkwardly into a different position. Only one more day, and she could rest.

❧

On the next day, the journey from Warwick to Lichfield passed a little more easily. The snow, while it continued to fall, was not as heavy, and the wind had dropped, so that less of the weather found its way inside the coach. When at last they drew near Weeford, the village whose church served Swinfen, it was as dark as it had been on the previous night when they had arrived in Warwick, but the road passed very close to the Wyatts' home at Blackbrook Farm, and all of the party watched eagerly out of the right hand side of the coach, looking for its lights.

'There!' cried Nan at last. 'That must be Blackbrook!'

She was right. Light showed in the parlour window and in one of the bedrooms. Patience leaned out and stared until they were past, then she sat back, glowing. Anne smiled at her. Patience had come to London hoping for adventure, but the events of the last two months had not been the kind of adventure she had been expecting.

'I can't see Weeford village,' Jack complained. 'You said Weeford was just by Patience's house.'

'Nay,' said Anne. 'You'll not be able to see it. The village is clustered down in a hollow, away from the road. And anyway, the trees would hide it. We'll be passing Swinfen soon, but the trees are too thick for us to see the Hall, even at this time of the year with all the leaves fallen. You might see a light in one of our farms or cottages.'

No one managed to pick out any lights as they passed Swinfen. However, husbandmen go early to bed, particularly in winter, when candles or even rush dips seem too costly a price for extending the day. During the last two miles to Lichfield, they gathered up their baskets and bundles, so they could disembark as quickly as possible, to go in search of a private carriage. Since the last staging post, they had been the only passengers in the coach, and Peter had been able to join the others inside, to warm himself a little.

In Lichfield, they were fortunate. While Patience and Peter oversaw the unloading of the luggage from the roof of the coach, Anne went into the Black Swan inn in the Market Square, to see if she could bespeak a carriage to convey her party back along the road to Swinfen. It was but two miles, and though it was now full dark, it was not yet half past seven by St Mary's clock. She was welcomed heartily at the inn, with many exclamations at the sight of her in Lichfield, when everyone thought her many miles away in London. Robert Verey, the innkeeper, who had been a young stable boy at Swinfen in the time of John's grandfather, promised that he himself would drive them over to the manor in the inn carriage. The luggage which could not be accommodated in the smaller vehicle could be left at the inn and sent for the next morning. While the horses were being made ready, he insisted on treating the entire party to a dish of lamb collops, while his wife whipped up a syllabub.

''Tis not how I like to make it,' she said apologetically. 'You are best to milk the cow straight into the dish of cider and sugar, but tonight the milking is long finished. And there's no time for the curd to set, so I've used a lemon to thicken it.'

'But it's excellent, Mistress Verey!' said Anne. 'And I think lemon improves the flavour.'

The two women fell into an easy exchange of receipts, but the children were too busy eating the excellent meal to speak, and as for Patience and the servants, it seemed their smiles were irrepressible. London and its dangers had faded far into the distance. Half an hour later, the journey back to Swinfen along the same road in the inn's well-sprung modern carriage was a contrast to the long uncomfortable trip from London. The horses were fresh and were, moreover, thoroughbreds of the highest quality, for Robert Verey was a man rising in society, who prided himself on his judgement in matters of horseflesh. They trotted along briskly, and were soon turning into the carriageway leading up to Swinfen Hall. Ahead and beyond the bulk of the house, looming dark above the snow-covered fields and orchards and gardens, the moon gleamed faintly on the waters of the lake.

Yet the house stood in darkness. Unlike the poorer cottagers and yeoman farmers, the Swynfen family had no need to economise on candles. It was scarcely nine o'clock. Anne knew that John's parents kept country hours, but at this time of the evening, Richard Swynfen was usually working at his rent table, bringing his estate records up to date, or seated in the parlour beside the fire with a pipe—to which he was extremely partial—and perhaps a book or newspaper. His wife, whose every hour was filled with the management of her large household, would probably still be bustling about. And the servants would not go to bed before their masters. Yet there was not a single spark of light to be seen from any window.

The innkeeper looked troubled as he drew up the carriage before the door. 'They're early abed tonight, it seems. I did hear tell something about Master Swynfen being ill, but with the winter weather and the hard times, we don't see much of folk from Swinfen and Weeford in Lichfield these days. I'll knock them up for you.'

He climbed the steps to the front door and rapped on it loudly with the butt of his whip, while the weary party of travellers clambered down from the carriage and unloaded the few pieces of luggage they had brought from Lichfield. Heartily tired of the Turkey bag, Anne looked forward to unpacking its heavy contents. Jack and Francis sat down on the steps as if they would never move from there. Dorothea was asleep in Patience's arms and Mary against Hester's shoulder. Bess was carrying the new baby, who woke and began to cry in a long keening wail that meant she would need to be fed soon. Nan and Ralph simply stood, trance like, in the midst of all the pother, getting in everyone's way, as though they had lost the ability to walk.

After Robert Verey had been knocking for several minutes, and Peter had suggested he should go round to the kitchen, the noise of someone moving on the other side of the door could just be heard.

'Who's there?' a wavering voice cried out.

''Tis Mistress Anne,' Robert shouted, 'Master John's lady, and all the children and servants, home from London. For the sake of God, open the door! We're all like to freeze out here.'

There came the groan of bolts being drawn back, and then the heavy ancient door swung slowly open, revealing old Biddy Earpe, the housekeeper, holding up a single candle, and behind her a young maid Anne had not seen before. Both looked frightened.

'Mistress Anne!' cried Biddy Earpe. 'What are you doing here? We thought you were all in London town.'

'I wrote three times to say we were coming,' said Anne. 'Did all of my letters miscarry? Did the master and mistress not expect us?'

Biddy Earpe gave her a strange, troubled look as they all filed into the great hall of the house. Two stories high, it was the heart of the original manor, and usually had a huge fire of logs burning on the hearth and candles in sconces around the walls. Tonight it loomed eerily, a cave of darkness, in which the single candle looked fragile as breath.

'Will you fare all right, Mistress Swynfen?' asked the innkeeper. He was as puzzled as she by this strange welcome, but he was anxious not to leave his horses standing and taking cold.

'Aye, of course,' she said, more heartily than she felt. 'I'm so grateful to you for all your kindness, for giving us a meal and driving us here. You must be away home. I'll send a cart in the morning to fetch the rest of the luggage.'

When he was gone, she turned to Biddy, and said briskly, 'Now, we must have more candles, Biddy, and see the children off to bed. They've eaten a good meal in Lichfield. If we weren't expected, I suppose the beds will be cold and damp. Hester, will you go with this girl to the kitchen and fill some warming pans? Patience and Bess, take the children up to their old rooms and get them ready for bed. Peter? Ah, there you are.'

Peter was leaning against the wall in a dark corner, sleeping on his feet like a horse.

'Not long now before we're all in our beds, old friend. Will you carry up the small trunk with the children's night shifts? Then I think you should sleep in the kitchen tonight. 'Twill be warmer there than in your attic.'

They all hurried to do her bidding, glad of some activity to drive away their fears about what was wrong here. Biddy opened the candle-box and handed out candlesticks. As they were lit, one by one, the hall came to life. The hearth was quite cold. Evidently no fire had been lit there for days past. A fine layer of dust covered everything. There was a smell of neglect about the place and, curiously, no smell of food cooking, yet—by some trick of the draughts within the house—the scent of roasting meat usually flowed into the hall from the kitchen and lingered here long after the food was served. As Hester and the new maid headed towards the kitchen and the others went upstairs, Anne turned to Biddy.

'Now then, Biddy, what's amiss? I come expecting a warm house, with candles and food, and my husband's parents to welcome us, and I find . . . I'm not sure what I find. Two fearful servants with a single candle in an untidy, cold house, and no sign of anyone else. Something has happened.'

Biddy began to sob, and set down her candlestick on the windowsill so that she might wipe her eyes on her apron. 'Oh, Mistress Anne, such terrible times we've had! I know the master didn't want to worry Master John, but this year's harvest was all but lost, and since then most of the beasts and winter provisions were looted by soldiers, and the stock that's left near starved, and all of the young men pressed for service in the army, with only the old men and the women to tend the land. We've scarce food enough left in the storerooms and pantry to feed us through the winter, and now with all of you come, I don't know how we shall 'scape starving. And then the master . . .'

'What of the master?' Anne cried, seized with a terrible fear. 'He's not . . . he has not . . . died?'

'As good as,' wailed Biddy. 'He's had an apoplexy. He can't speak or move. He can do naught but lie abed, and we try to dribble a little soup into him, but I can't think he'll last long.'

'When did this happen?'

'A month ago? Or was it more? Nay, I am so confused and weary myself, I can't rightly say. Before Christmas, it was.'

'But Mistress Joane? Surely she's not ill?'

Biddy sobbed harder. 'Oh, Mistress Anne, I don't know what to do. She's become quite 'mazed, I think her wits be gone. She wanders about the place, talking to herself. After the master fell ill, she's become like a child or a half-wit. Only yesterday, Margit—that's the new girl you saw just now—she found the mistress walking by the lake in nothing but her shift, in the snow, and the lake frozen round the edges. If she'd strayed on to the ice, sure as fate she'd have fallen through, and drowned or froze to death. I will say this, though, she was as biddable as a good child. Margit took her by the hand and led her back inside with no trouble at all.'

Anne sank down on to a stool and covered her face with her hands. Her whole body ached, and she felt as though someone had just laid a builder's hod of bricks on her shoulders.

Chapter Sixteen

T he next morning was deceptively lovely. The heavy clouds which
had closed in the skies for weeks had blown away; the sun lit up a
world of glinting, crystalline beauty. Anne stood at the window of
the second-best chamber, the one she and John had shared when they
were first wed, before they moved to the manor of Thickbroome. She
had stood here the morning after her wedding, a girl of nineteen on the
threshold of a new life. It was a balmy, sweet spring that year, and the
view then from this window had been green with the leaves fresh on the
trees and with thick meadow grass, already starred with flowers. She
was watching a flock of ducks on the lake, teaching their young ones to
swim and dive, when John came up behind her and put his arms around
her, burying his face in her mass of dark hair, which by day was coiled
and pinned out of sight under her lace cap, all but a few wayward curls.

'I wish you would release your beautiful hair so I could see it
always,' he said.

'That wouldn't be seemly.'

'Ah well, perhaps it's for the best. I should be jealous if any
other man beheld it by light of common day. 'Tis my secret treasure,
and I alone can cherish it by the moon's light.'

She turned then in his arms and they kissed fiercely, renewing
the turbulent pleasures of the night.

Now, on this January day, the manor lands of Swinfen stretched
out frozen hard and glittering, stiff under winter's mordant touch, down
the slope to the lake and rising again beyond towards the woods, the
trees winter black, no sign of bird or animal, the whole exquisite but
heartless. She longed then for John so bitterly, that she tried to conjure
up the warmth of his arms around her, but there was nothing but icy
cold and loneliness.

She shook her head, angry at herself. How could she be lonely, in
a house full of people? This was pure folly. Yet it was deathly silent.
The sun was up, but no one seemed to be awake. The travellers were
weary and would sleep late, but where were the servants? She could not
even hear a sound from the home farm, which was near to the house.
Biddy had said something last night about the loss of stock, but there

must be breeding stock kept to overwinter—the milch herd and the bull, the breeding ewes, some sows. And chickens—surely there must be chickens?

No maid had come to attend her, so she dressed herself in her plain travelling dress, which she could fasten without help. It was to be hoped that Mistress Joane was not yet abroad, for she would not dare to appear before her mother-in-law unless she was laced into her stays and had dressed according to her rank. Twice during the night she had fed the new baby, who was asleep now, in the cradle which had once belonged to John. Anne closed the door softly behind her and went down to the kitchen. There she found Peter, yawning and rubbing his eyes as he made up the fire from the pile of logs in the wood store. Biddy and Margit were sitting at the table, elbows amongst crusts, whispering together, but there was no sign of any food being prepared. When they saw her, the two women jumped up, looking guilty and uncertain.

Anne frowned as she looked around. The kitchen was even dirtier than the great hall had been, with splashes of spilt food on the floor, and soiled platters piled up at one end of the table. A dish of milk had been left to go sour on the dresser, where a few sleepy winter flies had found it and drowned. One paltry ham hung from the beam nearest the fire, where it benefited from any smoke that drifted up. Scarcely halfway through the winter, there should have been at least six hams hanging there, and gigots of mutton, and several sides of salted beef. If illness had struck down the elder Swynfens only during the last months, it could not explain why no more meat had been smoked or salted for winter provision, for it should have been done earlier, around Martinmas. Distracted from the dirty state of the kitchen by the lack of meat, Anne turned to Biddy.

'Why is there but one ham? Where are the rest?'

She had not meant it to sound like an accusation, but Biddy answered indignantly.

'I told you last night, Mistress Anne. The soldiers have been here, carrying off what provision they could lay hands on. That ham was still in the smokehouse, and they overlooked it.'

She spoke rudely, in a tone Mistress Joane would never have tolerated. Indeed, servants had been dismissed for less, but Anne turned away, her mind on other things.

'What about salt beef? Bacon? Dried ham? Potted mutton? Smoked gigot? Did you put up no pickled fish during the autumn?'

Without waiting for an answer, she strode through the kitchen to the back passage which led to the storerooms, the scullery and pantry, the game larder and fish room, and, at the far end, the cold, stone-lined dairy. She opened cupboards, searched the shelves and kists with growing horror. It was last night's ordeal, when her dream of welcome had turned to ashes, made more terrifying by daylight. Her mind could not accept that there was so little food. There was a barrel of coarse oatmeal and a single sack of wheat in the grain. No doubt the soldiers preferred their flour already ground. There were a few preserves—a very few—and half a dozen pots of salted and pickled meat and fish. The shelves in the fruit store still held a remnant of small withered apples, no more than three dozen. At the back of a cupboard in the dairy there was one round of cheese, covered with mould, clearly another item missed by the soldiers, who must have taken all the rest. The brewhouse was in the yard of the home farm, close to the stables. No doubt it too would have been stripped bare. Well, they must make do with well water. She went back to the kitchen.

'How many chickens?' she asked in a curt tone, concealing her own terror.

'About two dozen,' said Biddy sullenly. 'But being as it's winter, they're not laying to speak of.'

Only two dozen. No doubt the soldiers had enjoyed stewing up some of the best laying hens.

'Cows in milk?'

'Twenty, I think.'

Better, though the winter milk would be thin and scarce and poor for cheese-making, but they would have to contrive to make some. The children could drink the whey. If they could make cheese, however little and poor, it would compensate somewhat for the lack of meat.

'Rabbits,' said Anne, thinking aloud. 'Are there still rabbits in that spinney on the far side of the lake?'

'I'm sure I don't know, Mistress Anne. I ha'n't been over there these twelve months past. My legs trouble me something terrible.'

Nothing to the trouble you shall have from me, thought Anne, but she kept it to herself.

'I could go and see after breakfast, mistress,' Peter volunteered. 'I ha'n't forgotten how to set a snare for rabbits in the three years we'm been in London.'

'Aye, good, Peter.' Anne struggled for control. She must not let them guess at her dismay. The stores she had seen would feed them poorly for a month, or at the most, rationed frugally, for six weeks. 'Let's breakfast and then we shall see what we can contrive. We must think how many there are to feed. There are twelve of us come from

London: five adults, six children and a babe. In the household here, how many, Biddy?'

'The master and mistress, the two of us here, and old Josiah and his boy to look after the stock, and that's all. The day labourers are laid off for the winter—still we ha'n't but old men and boys these last years.'

No wonder the house looked so ill cared for. Only four servants to run both house and farm. Anne had never known there to be fewer than a dozen household servants, not counting the farm hands and day labourers on the land.

'No cook?'

'Old Meg died last November. Margit and I have managed as best we can,' Biddy said defiantly, but her voice shook.

Anne sank down on the bench beside the table. By daylight she could see that Biddy's shape, once as firm and plump as a bolster, had caved in upon itself. Her skin was greyish and blotched, her hands cracked about the knuckles, her hair dry as old rope.

'Oh, Biddy, I'm sure you have. I didn't understand how badly all had fared here. I'm not vexed with you, just dismayed. At least we've brought Hester home with us, who's an excellent cook. Bess will help when she's not minding the children. Go and wake Hester now, she's had long enough in her bed. Tell her we need breakfast made for all.'

'And what should she make it with?'

'There's oats a-plenty,' said Anne. 'We'll eat porridge. It's good wholesome food, enough to keep a labourer working all day, and that is what we must all do. You, girl—Margit, is it? Go and see if there are any eggs in the chicken house. Is it your job to feed them?'

The girl nodded and whispered, 'Yes, mistress.' She was a pale scrap of a creature, not much taller than Nan, with hollowed cheeks and temples. Under her gown she seemed no more than a bundle of twigs.

'Have we enough corn for them?'

'Plenty. The soldiers didn't touch it, and now there's fewer chickens . . .'

'Then give them a little extra. It may encourage them to lay better, and we'll be dependent on them this winter.'

While the women went to do her bidding, willingly or unwillingly, Anne caught up her cloak from the chest in the hall where she had laid it the previous night and went out of the front door into the frosty morning. Her hands were shaking as she fastened it around her shoulders and she strode quickly down towards the lake, to put as much distance between herself and the household as possible. Near one of the ancient oaks on the ridge above the lake she stopped. Her arms went instinctively around the great bole as far as they could reach, and she laid her forehead against the rough bark, lined and weathered like an old man's skin.

Her dream of sanctuary and rest had transformed itself into nightmare.

The household—yes, that she could try to sustain. It was in a perilous state, with starvation lurking and the threat of more raids by renegade soldiers and masterless men, yet she could manage a household, if she could but obtain food enough. The management of the land was beyond her powers. It was a man's business. She had neither experience nor training in such an enterprise. But who else was there here to undertake it? Her father-in-law stricken, John imprisoned, her own family far away. Mary Swynfen's husband Thomas Potts was not far, in Weeford, yet she felt a curious reluctance to go begging to him.

If only she were not so weary. The journey from Oxford had set her ribs aching again and she was still weakened from the latest child-bearing. Her nails gripped the oak's sturdy bark, and she remembered suddenly how she and John used to climb this tree. It had wide-spreading branches on which they could perch and imagine themselves kings of the world. She smiled wanly to herself. How pitiable to shrink from ruling one estate, when she had dreamt such imperial dreams. With a sigh cut off short, she thrust herself off the tree and straightened her back. She must return and face them all, and not allow a glimmer of her fear and helplessness to reveal itself, or they would all abandon hope. Wrapping her cloak tightly around her against the biting cold, she began to walk steadily back towards the house.

It was tempting to sit down to breakfast in the kitchen, the only warm room in the house, but Anne realised that she needed to reverse the household's slide into chaos. While Hester was preparing a breakfast of porridge, she told Peter to light a fire in the great hall and build it up well. One thing which was not in short supply was firewood, for there were extensive woods on the Swinfen estate. A fire in the hall would help to heat the whole manor house and make it feel less like a house of the dead. Once Margit had fed the chickens and brought in four precious eggs, she was set to washing the dishes and cleaning the kitchen, while Biddy wiped down the large dining table in the hall and laid it with dishes for breakfast.

She grumbled about this. 'I'm no kitchen maid, Mistress Anne, nor no housemaid neither. I'm housekeeper here.'

'We must all do what we can, Biddy,' said Anne calmly. 'Until all is set to rights. I shall roll up my sleeves and work as hard as you, that I can promise. Now tell me, when does Mistress Joane come down in the mornings?'

Biddy rolled her eyes. 'That I couldn't say. Sometimes she stays abed all day, then in the night she wanders about the house, fritting the life out of us.'

Anne swallowed hard. Illness of the mind had always unnerved her.

'Have you sent for a physician to either of them?'

'When first the master was took ill, Mistress Joane had Samuel Newboult, the apothecary, fetched from Lichfield. That was before she went queer. He came three times to bleed the master, then he said there wasn't nothing else he could do. We was to feed him as best we could. He might live and he might not, but he'll never be right again.'

Anne felt a sudden sharp grief for her father-in-law. The previous night she had been too tired to think about the full horror of his condition. Richard Swynfen had married at fifteen, and was but sixteen when John was born, which made him fifty-one now, though his wife was several years older. It was a good age, but not a great age. And people expected to live longer here in the country than in the foul air of London. When she had last seen him he was just forty-eight, and seemed in the full vigour of life. She would have to visit him later in the day, although she shrank from it.

'When the rest of us have breakfasted, you and Margit must attend to Master and Mistress Swynfen as you've been accustomed,' she said to Biddy. 'I don't want to shock them with the sight of too many of us at once, but perhaps when Mistress Joane realises that I'm here to help her, she may come back to herself.'

'It's to be hoped so,' said Biddy, though with little certainty.

'And after that, you and I will sit down together and figure how much food we have, and how best to feed everyone for the rest of the winter. I'll want to see Josiah as well, when he's finished with the beasts.'

'I'll tell him, mistress.' Biddy set out the last of the pewter dishes and went off to breakfast in the kitchen, looking a little happier than she had since they arrived.

Breakfast was not a cheerful meal. The servants were resentful, for no one should be expected to eat porridge in a gentleman's house, and the children whined about eating the grey, lumpy stuff, although they were all so hungry they ate it anyway. All except Francis, who stirred the mess in his dish and stared off into space as though he were sickening again. Bess finally managed to spoon most of it into him while he opened and closed his mouth like a fish. Patience fidgeted.

Clearly she wanted to walk over to Blackbrook Farm and visit her family, but Anne hardened her heart. There was too much to be done here. Patience would have to wait. Peter and Hester ate in the kitchen with the rest of the servants, but all knew that they breakfasted no worse than the family. When Margit came to clear away the dishes, Anne sent Patience and Bess upstairs to tidy the bedchambers and unpack the luggage that had been brought the night before.

'But keep the children away from Master and Mistress Swynfen's chambers,' she warned. 'Look out the old toys for them to play with. That should keep them occupied for the rest of the day. Apart from feeding the baby, I shall be busy with other affairs.'

She followed Margit into the kitchen. The place looked somewhat cleaner than it had earlier. Josiah and the boy were pulling on their muddy boots, ready to return to the farmyard. Josiah was almost as old as Peter, but he was a tough husbandman, hardened from years at ploughing behind the horses and scything the fields at harvest time. His skin, even in winter, was the colour of a withered walnut, and his bright blue eyes were intelligent and shrewd. Anne had rarely spoken to him in the past, save to give him 'Good Morrow', since the management of the manor was entirely in her father-in-law's hands, but if she was to organise the feeding of this large household she would need to deal with Josiah.

He paused with one boot on and the other dangling in his hand.

'You want to speak with me now, Mistress Anne?'

'Is the stock all seen to?'

'Aye, but there's a-plenty to do. I've a saddle to mend, and there be holes in the barn roof that must be patched while the weather holds fine.'

'I need you to harness up a horse and cart to fetch the rest of our luggage from Lichfield. Best do that first, then the roof. We'll speak together when that's done.'

He shook his head. 'There's more'n two days' work to the roof mending, mistress.' He seemed surprised that she should be giving him orders.

'Well, then, you must fetch the luggage and begin work on the roof. I shall come and find you when I'm ready. And take this purse. I want you to see if you can buy any meat in Lichfield. A ham or a side of bacon.'

The two labourers went out, the boy staring back over his shoulder, as if the sight of a woman directing the farm workers were some marvel.

'Come now, Biddy,' said Anne. 'I've brought paper and ink. We'll take an inventory of every last morsel of food to be found in the house. Peter, what of your rabbit snares?'

Peter, who was seated on a stool by the fire, held up a twist of wire and supple twigs. 'I'm making them now, mistress. I thought to make two dozen, then I'll get me over to the spinney and see if I can find some fresh runs.'

Anne and Biddy worked their way through all the storerooms and dairy, and as Biddy called out what was laid by, Anne wrote it down on her list. Then they donned cloaks and boots and went out to the brewhouse. It seemed to be stripped bare, but Anne had remembered something John had once told her, laughing, about how his father always kept a store of ale hidden away, in case the day labourers took to stealing, the brewhouse being somewhat difficult to guard. There was a panel in the wall, she knew, that was in fact the door to a concealed cupboard. She searched everywhere, tapping and prodding, but could not find it. Biddy stared at her all the while, clearly thinking she had taken leave of her senses. Finally, in a dark corner, the wall gave back a hollow sound. Kneeling on the floor, Anne managed to prise open the panel with her finger-nails. There, somewhat dusty, stood two huge four-handled flagons of ale. Not a whole winter's supply, but enough to cheer her household on special occasions. As they each lifted a heavy flagon out of the cupboard, Biddy looked at the usurping mistress of Swinfen with surprise and a little more respect.

When they came out of the brewhouse, Josiah and the boy were just driving up with the luggage. Anne frowned. There had been no need for the boy to go to Lichfield, he would have done nothing but sit in the cart. While there was so much work and so few hands to do it, there was no time for sitting about. She should have thought to set him to some task.

'Since I'm here, Josiah,' she said as he climbed down, 'I'll come with you now and see what we have stored in the barns and stables. Were you able to buy meat?'

He shook his head, handing her the purse.

'Folk laughed in my face, Mistress Anne. There's none has food to spare.'

She had had no real hope, but this failure heightened the cold sense of fear in her heart. She turned to Biddy. 'You and Margit can continue cleaning the hall. Be sure to strew sweet herbs on the fire when you have finished, and lay more with rose petals in dishes on the windowsills. Then you may look to the small parlour. When I come in we'll study our lists and decide how we'll manage our supplies.'

Ignoring Biddy's rebellious expression, and leaving the boy to unharness the horse from the cart, she set down the flagon of ale and followed Josiah into the barn, where the cows were accommodated on the right hand side. The other half of the barn was fenced off with hurdles to provide winter quarters for the sheep. They would stay here until the ewes dropped their lambs. In spring, when the weather allowed, they would be turned out on the meadow until shearing, then driven up to Packington Moor. The stock looked healthy, though somewhat thin.

'Have you fodder enough?' she asked.

Without answering, Josiah led her through to the adjacent hay barn, and stood in the centre of the floor, his arms folded, watching her. She sniffed. Usually the hay barn was sweet with the scent of summer fields, a haven of happy memories of warm days, stored up for winter. But there was something wrong here. A faint sour smell, elusive but detectable, troubled her.

'What's that smell?'

''Twas a terrible year here,' he said, not answering her question. 'Nothing but rain and floods all summer long.'

'In London, too. Biddy said the harvest was bad.'

'Bad isn't how I should call 'un, Mistress Anne. Disaster, that's what 'twas. We did what us could at haysel time, but there was never enough days together to dry all. Half the hay was maybe sound, but the rest is rotting. That's what you can smell. I've kept 'un separate as best I can.' He pointed to the hay piled up in two great heaps, one much smaller than the other. 'That small one is the good hay.'

'Did you build no stacks in the yard?'

'There was never the weather for 'un. 'Twas like Noah's flood. There wasn't no more hay than would fill the barn anyway, the haysel was that poor.'

Anne could never remember a time when there had not been five or six huge haystacks build out in the yard—each of them almost as big as most of the cottages on the estate—in addition to the hay ready for use here in the barn. Without hay, the remaining stock could not survive the winter. All but the breeding stock would already have been slaughtered and cured at Martinmas. That was the meat the soldiers had stolen.

As if he could read her thoughts, Josiah said, 'There be not fodder enough. Us'll need to slaughter more of the stock.'

That would provide meat for the rest of the winter, but what of next year? Anne thought of the few prime milch cows and the small flock of breeding ewes. Before he had been struck down, her father-in-law would have selected the best of the stock to be kept. The lineage of some could probably be traced back the six hundred years and more the Swynfens had held this land. She could not countenance the killing of this last handful of breeding animals.

'Nay,' she said. 'Nay, we must think of some other way.' She remembered the last of the gold she had brought with her from London.

'Perhaps we could buy hay.' It was unheard of, but worth trying.

Josiah shook his head. 'I doubt there's any would sell you hay. Everyone's in a like case. 'Tis the same as the meat.'

'Well, we shall see. The horses? Hay as well, of course, but you have oats?'

There must be oats. There was a full kist of oatmeal.

Josiah grinned cautiously.

'Troopers took what they could for their horses, but they didn't find everything. I took care to hide a good supply.'

'Good. Have we any pigs?'

'Ten sows. Isaac—that's my grandson who helps me,' he jerked his head towards the stable, where the boy could be heard leading the horse into its stall, 'Isaac gathered up plenty of acorns and beechmast for the swine. Soldiers had no use for that.'

Anne nodded. She had heard of country people eating beechmast in times of famine. It might come to that.

'Well, Josiah, it seems our chief worry for the stock is hay. I'll ride into Lichfield and see what I can do.'

He looked scandalised. This was no way for Master John's lady to behave. He spoke more frankly than he ought.

''Tis not for you to be riding about the countryside on the manor's business, mistress.'

'And who else shall do it? Master Swynfen is ill. Master John is in London. You're more use at work here. I cannot go climbing about, mending the barn roof, but I can buy hay, if there's any to be had. Though I expect I must pay far too high for it. I'll also need you to take that one sack of wheat to the mill.'

'Miller's dead and his family gone. I heard the mill needs repair anyways.'

Anne wrung her hands. 'But we must have flour! We can't survive without bread. Is there no other way to grind it?'

Josiah shrugged. 'Well . . .'

He led her to a far corner of the barn and pointed. 'There's this old quern, mistress, what they had in the old days. I've never seen one used, but I've heard tell 'tis terrible slow, hard work.'

'You'd best bring it in to the kitchen and we'll see if we can manage it.'

They began to walk back towards the house, Josiah carrying the heavy flagon. Suddenly Anne stopped. She had just realised that one member of the family was missing. Someone so quiet, she was easily overlooked. John had two younger brothers, William and Richard, the first married and moved away, the second in the army. And he had three sisters: Mary, married and living in Weeford, Grace, married and living in London, and Bridget. At twenty-one, Bridget was the youngest of the girls, but she would never marry, for she was crippled from childhood illness. She never stirred from Swinfen, but had she been here to watch over things, surely the house would not have fallen into such a terrible state.

'Josiah, where is Mistress Bridget?'

He stared at her in surprise.

'Why, she went to live with Mistress Mary, these twelve months past.'

'She's living with Mary and Thomas Pott? But why?'

It was something she would never have discussed with a farm labourer in normal times, but now she must seek information where she could.

Josiah looked uncomfortable. 'I don't know rightly how 'twas,' he said reluctantly.

That meant there had been gossip amongst the servants.

'Tell me what you know.'

'Well . . .' He avoided her eye and stared away over the fields. 'Mistress Swynfen told Mistress Bridget she would never get a husband, so she must look to make herself useful, and earn her own keep. So she's gone to Mistress Mary, who said she shouldn't go outside the family.'

'Mary Pott has taken her as a waiting gentlewoman?'

'Well . . .'

'She's taken her as a *servant*?'

Josiah shrugged.

Anne felt outrage against her mother-in-law welling up inside her, but she tried to wipe it off her face. 'I won't keep you from your roof any longer, Josiah. Tomorrow, I'll ride into Lichfield and see what may be done about hay. Leave the ale there. I'll send Margit to fetch it.'

As she walked across the muddy yard towards the back of the house, her anger made her thump her fist into the palm of her hand. Mistress Joane Swynfen had always been something of a tyrant towards her children, and she had a particular dislike of her gentle, crippled

209

daughter, as though the very sight of Bridget offended her. But to send her to be a servant! Bridget was a gentlewoman, even if she would remain dependent all her life. Mary must have taken her in out of kindness, but the situation could not be easy for either of the sisters. Provided Mary could be persuaded, Anne would bring Bridget home as soon as she could ride over to Weeford and see her sister-in-law.

৵

By early evening, Anne was weary to the very bone. At least the long and arduous journey from London had been accomplished and all her party, with their luggage, safely delivered to Swinfen. The baby, who could so easily have died at birth, was growing plump. Last night the house had dismayed her—cold, damp, and dirty as some of the wayside inns. It was still far from its normal state, but it was warmer now, and the great hall and kitchen were clean, the parlour partially tidy. Aromatic herbs and beeswax polish scented the air in the hall, mingling with the fragrance of the apple logs she had told Peter to put on the fire for the sake of their sweetness. Despite an initial air of sulky reluctance to accept her orders, the Swinfen servants were working willingly enough now that the house was beginning to come to life again. While Josiah repaired the roof of the cowbarn, she had set the boy to cutting logs with Peter, using the two-handled saw. The weather, though cold, was clear for the moment, and she wanted to be sure of an ample supply of fuel when the snow returned, as it surely must.

Fuel and food, all her attention was focused on these. Food, that was the greatest worry. The supplies in store would not be sufficient to feed the large household through the winter, but they must contrive somehow without killing any of the breeding stock. As she sat in her chamber feeding the baby, her mind whirled with plans. Before anything, they must devise a way to grind the wheat and make cheese with some of the milk. There would be no rennet at this time of year. She was sure there were herbs that could be used in its place to set the cheese, but she could not recall what they were. They could eat one meal of porridge every day, however much the children fretted. Peter had set his snares, but had caught nothing yet. This morning, in counting over the stores, she had found two strings of onions and a crock of dried peas. Hester was making a vegetable stew with some of these, to be mopped up with the remnant of bread left from the journey. In London, where every kind of food could be bought, although expensive in the late famine years, Anne had never thought so much about meals.

When the baby was laid back in her cradle, she sat before the mirror and brushed her hair, then put on a fresh lace cap, and wrapped her new silk shawl about her shoulders. It was time to confront the meeting she had been postponing with excuses all day. She must visit John's ailing parents.

She went first to Mistress Swynfen's small parlour, next to the best bedchamber, and tapped nervously on the door. In the morning and again at dinnertime she had sent Margit up to Joane Swynfen with a tray of the scarce food, but she had avoided asking whether her mother-in-law was still 'mazed', as Biddy had said. A shrinking reluctance had kept her away.

When she knocked a second time, a high voice, which she did not recognise as Mistress Swynfen's, bade her come in. She opened the door cautiously, and found Joane Swynfen sitting in a chair beside the fire staring at her with wide eyes and an odd smile. She sat with her hands clasped in her lap, tidily dressed, though in a plain gown without jewels. She rocked, very gently, back and forth in her chair.

'Good evening, Mother,' said Anne.

There was no response. She ventured nervously across the floor until she was standing directly in front of the other woman, well lit by the candles on the mantelpiece. Joane continued to smile at her in that disconcertingly vague way. She continued to rock. And, in time with the rocking, there came the faint sound of humming.

'It's Anne, Mother. John's wife. I've come back from London with the children.'

Joane giggled. 'Have you brought my breakfast?' she asked in that high, childish voice.

'It's long past breakfast. You had that this morning. It will be supper soon.'

'Where's Bunny?'

'Bunny?' Anne was confused. Did her mother-in-law have a pet rabbit?

Joane stamped her foot. 'My dog, Bunny. I want my dog. I don't know who you are. Go away. Tell them to bring me my dog.' Her face had grown suddenly red and twisted with fury. She seized a wooden cup from the table beside her chair and hurled it at Anne. Some sticky liquid flew in an arc across her skirt.

Anne started to back away towards the door. 'Supper soon,' she said soothingly. 'I'll ask them about Bunny.'

Outside the room, she closed the door and leaned on it, letting out a deep breath. She realised that she had been holding it in, suspended in horror at the sight of that imperious old woman transformed thus into a whining child. She passed a hand over her face and turned to go into the chamber next door, where Master Swynfen had lain in bed since his apoplexy. Biddy came puffing up the stairs, carrying a tray with some broth and a little of the bread broken small.

Anne opened the door for her, and they went in together. There were fewer candles here, but Peter had also built up this fire well. Richard Swynfen lay propped up on several bolsters watching them as they came in. The side of his face was dragged down, as if some beast had clawed it, distorting his mouth, which dribbled a little at the corner. His hair had gone completely grey since she had seen him last. One arm lay quite limp on the bed clothes, but the other hand seemed less affected. The fingers of this hand kept pluck, plucking at the coverlet.

Biddy sat down on a stool beside the bed and wiped the old man's mouth quite gently with a cloth, then began trying to spoon the broth rapidly between his lips. Anne could see the muscles of his throat working in desperate spasms, but all the same the broth ran down from his half-open lips. Biddy pushed a bit of the bread into his mouth after soaking it in the broth, but he gagged and retched. It was almost unbearable to watch.

'Let me,' said Anne. 'You've work to do in the kitchen. I'll help him eat and then come down to supper.'

When Biddy was gone, looking relieved, Anne set the broth and bread aside and fetched a cloth, dampened at his water jug, to wash her father-in-law's face and hands, then dried them on a towel she held before the fire to warm.

'Now, Father,' she said, 'I'm going to give you this in very small spoonfuls, with time between each for you to swallow. No need to hasten.'

Could he hear her and understand? There was no reaction on that dreadfully twisted face. She put her arm around his shoulders to support him and spooned up a bit of broth no bigger than her thumbnail. She slipped the spoon between the slack lips and then tilted it very slowly. The broth went down his throat, and did not spill on to his chest.

Ever since she had come into the room, his eyes had followed her everywhere, and unlike his wife's eyes, they were intelligent. She was sure he recognised her. She began to talk to him about the journey from London as she continued to feed him the drops of broth and then minute scraps of bread. And all the while he watched her.

The last of the broth was gone. It was cold by now, but at least he had eaten all of it. As she picked up the tray and stood looking down at him, he lifted his good hand an inch or so, and gave a kind of strangled grunt in his throat. She leaned forward and laid her hand over his.

'You mustn't worry, Father. Now I'm here, I'll see that all's well with the estate.' She hoped fervently that she spoke the truth. 'You must think only of becoming strong again. Why, you're grown quite thin! When you're a little heartier, I'll bring the children to see you.'

He made another grunt, and something that might almost have been a smile flickered in his eyes. At the door she turned.

'I'll send Peter to help you prepare for the night. And I'll visit you again tomorrow.'

As she walked down the stairs towards the enticing smells of cooking, which set her empty stomach groaning, she shook her head forlornly at her dilemma. A household gnawed by hunger. A mother-in-law perfectly sound in body, but bereft of her wits. A father-in-law paralysed and speechless, gaunt as a skeleton, but, if the expression in those eyes were anything to go by, still fiercely alive within the iron prison of his body.

Chapter Seventeen

The remaining eleven prisoners held at the *King's Head* had grown heartily tired of each other and of the inn's limited spaces. A kind of melancholy lethargy had overtaken them. It was now almost two months since that morning in December when they had been seized, and no more of them had been released since Prynne argued his way to freedom on a point of law three weeks ago. They were trapped in a glass cage, for they could see from the windows of the inn the life of London continuing around them, yet they could neither speak to the passers-by, nor hear their voices. Very few letters reached them. They suspected many were confiscated, for they could not believe they had been wholly abandoned by their families and friends.

John had received no news of his family since Dick's visit, nor any further word from Clotworthy, who must by now be imprisoned at Windsor, nor had any letter from Crewe reached him, although he was certain that his kindly older friend must have written, and was probably even now trying to secure his former companions' release. Yet how could the prisoners, in their state of ignorance, understand the world out yonder, where patrols of the New Model Army marched back and forth from Whitehall, and troopers galloped past, scattering the impotent citizens from their path?

Into this glass cage, some fragmentary news of the outside world filtered, though they saw less of Jacob these days. His friendliness towards the prisoners had been noticed by the guards, who took the precaution of rarely leaving him alone with them, and sometimes barred him altogether from the room where they generally spent their time. One day he appeared with a bruised and bloodied face; it seemed the guards had discovered his part in smuggling the *Solemn Protestation* to the printer in St Paul's churchyard.

'What's this?' John asked, indicating the man's eye, swollen almost shut and crusted with blood and puss.

Jacob shrugged.

'The captain mislikes some of the errands I have run for you gentlemen.'

'The printer?'

'Aye. But I would do it again. Can we not speak our minds freely in this fine new country of ours? My face will heal, though the country may not. I suffered worse at Bristol.'

'You must not run any risks, Jacob.'

'It may be that I won't be able to bring the newspapers any more.'

From time to time, however, he managed to whisper a few words in passing. So they knew something of the great and unprecedented events that were unfolding, in which the military *junta* had appointed themselves judge, prosecutor and jury of England's anointed king. And they knew that the king had defended himself intelligently and courageously, but to no avail, because the outcome of the trial was determined before ever it began. The king's fate was sealed, his death warrant signed, and on this very day, this thirtieth day of January, 1649, he was to die.

John stood again at the window of the common room, looking down the Strand to Charing Cross, where he had watched the coaches depart as one of them carried away Anne and the children. It was a bitterly cold morning, the road glazed with ice, the naked trees glittering with hoar frost. Crowds were flowing down the Strand, not rowdy, a quiet mass of people, their heads covered, moving relentlessly towards Whitehall Palace, where the scaffold had been erected on which, in half an hour's time, an executioner would end the life of Charles Stuart, the only king of England to have been condemned to death by a pretence of legal process. Kings of England had died violently before this day—in battle or by an assassin's hand. But never like this. John wished with all his heart that Charles could have died with honour in battle. Not like this. This hypocritical act brought shame to its perpetrators, far more than to its victim.

Drawn into this nameless crowd, the people lost their individuality, moving like a herd of beasts or a swarm of bees, compelled onwards by some kind of blind instinct. At first the crowds disappeared round the curve into Whitehall, lost from sight, but gradually the swarms began to back up, like flood water that rises too high to flow under a bridge and begins to pour back and outwards, drowning the surrounding land. Baulked of space beside the scaffold, the crowds packed into all the open area at the Cross. Boys were clambering on the roofs of coaches, the better to see; fathers hoisted their young children on to their shoulders; women stood on upturned crates, striving to look over the taller heads in front.

Then suddenly, all were still.

Although he could see no more than the backs of the back of the crowd, John knew from their stillness that the king had come out from his Palace of Whitehall, that elegant building, with its beautiful ceilings painted in the Italian style to commemorate the achievements of his father's reign. And in stepping out of the tall window, Charles Stuart stepped from the riches and splendour of his royal life on to the lonely scaffold roughly erected in haste before the Palace, a bare wooden stage prepared for the last act in the drama. The moment was frozen in the stillness of the people. John closed his eyes and offered up a prayer. When he opened them again, he saw that anonymous body of citizens sway together, as though it had uttered a deep groan, and he knew the king was dead.

છ

The execution of the king did not at first change the situation of the prisoners. Cromwell, Ireton and the Army Council were too much occupied with their affairs of state to concern themselves with the remaining men confined at the *King's Head*. Five powerful opponents, former army officers like themselves, had been safely locked up in Windsor, most of the others released on varying conditions. The military commanders, John suspected, might well have forgotten about the rest, for they were busy setting up a new government for England. Nothing so radical as a citizen democracy, nor even the partial democracy advocated by Lilburne and the Levellers, who had been cast aside now their help was no longer needed. No, this was to be a despotic republic ruled by the group of army officers who had seized power by the sword, that very *junta* he had foretold to Anne on that long-ago evening by the parlour fire. On the sixth of February they abolished the ancient upper house, the House of Lords. The following day, they abolished the Monarchy. All this under the guise of legitimacy, by passing these acts through the obedient offices of their friends, the nervous and obsequious handful of members still permitted to take their seats in the Commons.

On the fourteenth day of February, the country's new rulers created for this new Republic of England a Council of State to be the executive body, which effectively took away any last dregs of power from the dismembered House of Commons. From now on, Cromwell would rule the country as dictator and head of state, lurking behind a screen of generals and using his stooges in the Council to carry out his policies.

'According to a rumour Jacob has heard,' John said to Edward Leigh and John Birch, 'Cromwell has hinted that he would like to be regarded as the "protector" of this land. As soon set the lion to be protector of the kid, or the wolf protector of the lamb.'

He filled his pipe with a few pinches from the tobacco jar. Their supply was running short, and they each allowed themselves but one pipe a day.

Edward Leigh smiled grimly.

'I wonder how long it will be before we discover what has been gained by the killing of one tyrant in order to set up another? On his present record, little enough. Cromwell and Ireton have exercised far greater tyranny towards our elected Parliament than even Charles Stuart himself ever did.'

John nodded agreement, drawing gently on his pipe to set it alight without burning away all the tobacco in one furious burst of heat.

'A curious day to choose,' he said, 'to set up this republican Council.'

'How so?' Birch asked.

'The fourteenth of February. The feast of St Valentine. *The lyf so short, the craft so long to lerne, Th'assay so hard, so sharp the conquerynge,*' said John.

'A gardyn saw I ful of blosmy bowes
Upon a ryver, in a grene mede,
Thereas swetnesse everemore inow is,
With floures white, blewe, yelewe, and rede,
And colde welle-stremes, nothyng dede,
That swymmen ful of smale fishes lighte,
With fynnes rede and skales sylver bryghte.
On every bow the bryddes herde I synge,
With voys of aungel in here armonye . . .

'The very day when the birds choose their mates and spring whispers that it will soon make its entrance on the stage.'

Leigh laughed.

'I scarce think these hardened Puritans are aware of such a thing as St Valentine's Day. And if they were, they would condemn it as a blasphemous papist celebration.'

'It is difficult,' said John, 'to disentangle the pagan from the papist, and both from the simple country practices of our youth. I'd have no truck with the Whore of Babylon, but I cannot think the pairing of turtledoves and blackbirds is a danger to this fine new Republic of ours.' He paused, then added quietly, 'Or perhaps it is.'

'If ever I win free of this damnable place,' said Birch thoughtfully, stretching out his legs to the fire, 'I shall take myself off back to Herefordshire. Safe beyond the Malvern Hills. Ever since the days when I took Hereford and Goodrich we've been as peaceful there as fat cows in a water meadow. Nothing ever happens. Cromwell and his fellows have little interest in our backward counties along the Welsh border. There the blackbird and the turtledove may woo and nest in peace, and a man may farm his acres and breed fine horseflesh quite out of sight of these London grandees.'

He took out his own pipe, then, perhaps remembering the shortage of tobacco, put it back in his pocket.

'I think there may be some good investments to be made in land, too,' he said. 'All those properties of the Laudian bishops which are now held in trust—they'll come on to the market. Yes, I think I shall purchase more property and plough my quiet furrow. I have my eye on a manor near Weobley.'

'I should be glad to plough my own sweet acres at Swinfen,' said John. He smiled inwardly at the Bristol merchant's dreams of land-owning. 'We have land enough. I've no desire for more. Staffordshire may not be as quiet and remote as Herefordshire, but a man could do worse than plough and sow and improve his land. I have a boggy piece beside the lake that could be drained to make good grazing meadow land for my cattle.'

He drew quietly on his pipe, which was nearly burnt away. 'Aye, turtledove and blackbird may mate in peace on my land also. And if my people want to exchange love tokens on St Valentine's Day, or the maidens go out at sunrise on the first of May to wash their faces in the dew, I for one shall wink my eye and pay no heed.'

Some weeks later, perhaps because they felt secure in their impregnable fortress of power, the men who now controlled the country must have remembered the small group of prisoners still languishing at the *King's Head*. One day an extra detachment of musketeers arrived in addition to their normal guards. Half the prisoners were told to fetch their belongings, and were then marched off to Whitehall through driving rain. It had rained constantly since the death of the king, an unremitting, freezing, penetrating rain, as though the very skies wept for that unjudicial murder the country had perpetrated. One of those left behind, John watched from his accustomed window as the five taken away disappeared into the grey deluge. It must, he thought, be good to breathe the air outside this confounded inn, even if you were drenched. Leigh was gone now, and Birch also. The half dozen who were left

218

looked at each other and shrugged. They had used up all their words. John even found himself missing Prynne, who would have livened things up for them.

The next day brought rain so heavy that it was almost impossible to perceive the difference between daylight and the preceding night. About halfway through the morning, the additional soldiers arrived again, and John and the others were rounded up. John slipped his Boethius into one pocket of his doublet and his handmade chess pieces and his Bible into another. He tied up the bundle of his spare linen, and tucked his pipe amongst the clothes, hoping that somewhere he might be fortunate enough to obtain more tobacco. Coming down the stairs from his chamber, he encountered Jacob.

'So you're released at last, Master Swynfen?'

'We've been told nothing,' said John. 'It may be that they're simply moving us to another prison. Our fellows were marched off under armed guard yesterday. It didn't look much like freedom to me.'

He felt in his pocket for a coin to give Jacob, from the small store smuggled to him by Anne, and tried to press it into the man's hand, but Jacob would not take it.

'Nay, man,' said John, 'don't refuse. We've all been more grateful than we can tell for your many kindnesses.'

Jacob shook his head.

'I will not take it, sir. If you're indeed set free, then you may come back and buy me a drink, and I'll drink with you gladly, but until you're sure, best keep every penny you have. You may be going to a worse place, where you'll need money for food or blankets. I beg you, sir, keep it until you are free.'

John seized Jacob's hand and shook it warmly.

'You're a good man, Jacob. And as soon as I am free, we shall drink a bottle each of the best Canary wine that money can buy in the whole of London town. Have a care of yourself, now. In this new state of the realm, you may not be as free to bestow kindness as you have been in the past.'

With that he joined the other prisoners at the door, where the soldiers formed up in their usual fashion, a musketeer taking each prisoner firmly by the arm, while others with drawn swords surrounded them, and they were marched off down the Strand towards Whitehall Palace. They had not gone more than half a dozen paces before the rain found its way down the back of John's neck, between the brim of his hat and the collar of his cloak. Before they reached the Cross, his boots were sodden from the deep puddles in the road, and the bundle under his arm stained with the wet.

At the gates of the Palace, the party was broken up, and the prisoners were led away in different directions, without even the time to bid each other farewell. John found himself conducted around to the back premises of the Palace, into a cluster of stables and outbuildings. A farmer's cart was standing in the yard, the kind used to carry produce to market, the kind his own labourers used at Swinfen to take corn or beans to Lichfield. It was long and wide, with a shallow-sided body and a tall canvas hood stretched over hoops for a cover. Suddenly John was grabbed by two of the musketeers and heaved into the cart, cracking his head and sprawling amongst a litter of dirty straw. Dazed, he had no time to scramble up before four of the soldiers climbed into the cart behind him. They were not careful where they put their feet. One trod on his hand. Another kicked him, perhaps not accidentally, in the ribs.

John struggled to his feet, the blow on the head making him dizzy and unsteady. Two of the men immediately pushed him down again, so that he was forced to crouch on the floor, while they loaded their packs and two or three dozen wooden crates into the cart. They arranged some of the crates for seats, and laced together the flaps of the cover at the rear to keep out the rain. When their preparations were complete, one of them thrust his head between the flaps of canvas at the front of the cart and called something to the driver. With a heave and a jerk, the heavy cart got under way. John, having nothing to hold on to, tumbled sideways against the sharp edge of one of the crates. The soldiers laughed.

They were a rough and dirty set of men, the dregs of the New Model Army, into which Tom Fairfax had tried to instil discipline and pride. Certainly during the renewed fighting of the last year, the army had been obliged to conscript many unwilling men, and amongst the volunteers it had always attracted the worst sort—homeless, broken men, criminals released from prison, thieving servants turned away from employment, and men who saw in the army unlimited opportunities for violence, rape and pillage. These four had the look about them of this last sort. They kept John sitting on the floor while they lounged on their improvised seats, which must have been far from comfortable, but were at least raised from the dirt and lice mixed in with the straw on the bed of the cart.

Covertly, John studied them. A broad-shouldered man with a broken nose and wiry black hair seemed to be in charge, though he wore no distinguishing marks about his rough uniform. Another, the heaviest built of the soldiers, with hands and feet like slabs of butcher's meat, wore the vaguely unfocused look of a man weak in the wits or well into his cups. There was a small, weasel-faced youth of about eighteen, whose eyes were intent upon meeting each other across the bridge of his nose. The fourth man, the one who had kicked John so viciously, caught his eye and grinned with malicious pleasure as John sprawled at his feet.

John kept silent, assuming that he was being moved from one place of imprisonment in London to another. He had no wish to give the men the satisfaction of refusing him information. They passed a flagon of beer from hand to hand, and the youth poked at his teeth with a piece of stick. They said little to each other, merely grunting acknowledgement as the beer went round. It seemed to John that the cart had turned west as it left Whitehall Palace, but he could not guess in what direction they were now travelling. The day was so dark that even outside it had been nearly impossible to see the position of the sun. Inside the cart, under the brown canvas hood, in the dim light, there was no way of judging the points of the compass. If indeed they were heading west, it might mean he was being taken to Windsor, to join Waller, Clotworthy and the others. Why had they suddenly decided he was so dangerous that he must be imprisoned there? For, judging by the way he had been manhandled, he must still regard himself as a prisoner and not a man on his way to freedom.

After about an hour, the men opened one of the packs they had brought with them and took out food. They had pies and fresh loaves and a whole cheese which they broke apart with their dirty hands. The leader tore off the crust of a loaf and a piece of cheese, and threw them on to the floor beside John.

The vicious-looking thug jeered.

'Weren't nothing in our orders about feeding him, Tize,' he said.

The first man shrugged.

'If we hand him over dead, there's some as might ask questions, and you know it as well as I do, Ed. I don't feed him out of kindness.'

John pondered this exchange, looking at the bread and cheese lying in the straw. A beetle ran across the cheese and paused thoughtfully, waving its front legs about. It seemed interested in the smell. The men were afraid he might die if they did not feed him, so they must be travelling a great deal further than Windsor. No man would die of hunger on the way there. If a long journey lay ahead and he was not to waste away, he had better swallow his pride and eat the food they tossed him, like any beaten cur.

He picked up the bread and cheese, brushed off the beetle, and began to eat.

જ

It was many hours before the cart stopped. The men had a large supply of drink, and they became first merry and then melancholy as more of the flagons were emptied. The stench in the cart grew worse as they used a corner of it freely as a piss-pot. At first John sat with his back against the side of the cart and his hands about his knees, but the rough movement of the cart, perhaps combined with the blow he had received on the head, began to fill him with nausea. At last he lay down, as far away from the men as he could contrive, with his aching head on his bundle of clothes and curled up to protect himself in case they started kicking again.

He was woken by the sense of the cart stopping and the sound of voices. He opened his eyes cautiously. Ed and the youth also lay asleep on the floor. From the smell, one of them had vomited the last of his drink. The big man sat dozing on one of the crates, with his head bowed on his chest and his hands hanging slack between his knees. The fourth man, the one they called 'Tize', was leaning through the gap in the canvas cover at the front of the cart, talking to the driver, although John could not make out the words. Still confused and half asleep, John began to think that it might be possible to escape from his guards, if he chose his moment with care. He moved his head cautiously, so that he could examine the fixings of the canvas cover at the rear of the cart. A sharp pain stabbed through his head and he only avoided crying out by biting his lips.

The canvas flaps were still laced together. Unless all the men were to fall asleep at the same time, he would never have time to unlace them unnoticed. The cover was fastened down tightly along the sides of the cart, with no gap through which a man might slip. That left only the front, where the flaps overlapped but did not seem to be secured, perhaps so that the driver could pull them around himself for shelter. But it would be impossible to escape that way while the driver sat in his seat. At some time they would need to rest the horses and either take a meal or buy more food. If their attention were distracted, he might then be able to slip out of the rear of the cart.

What o'clock might it be? Not yet dark, but still the same half-dark it had been all day. He felt as though he might have slept two or three hours, which would make it the middle of the afternoon. It was surprising they had not rested the horses before—unless they had done so while he was asleep. They were strong beasts. He had noticed them as he had been led across the stableyard at Whitehall. The breed used by the brewers' draymen to haul the heavy carts filled with barrels of beer around the streets of London. They plodded along slow as oxen, but they were accustomed to drawing great loads all day long; this cart would be light by comparison. Perhaps his escort intended to drive on at this steady pace all day, without bating the horses at all.

Tize stepped back and the cart jerked into movement again. John closed his eyes and pretended to be asleep in case the man should make sport of him again, but Tize ignored him and sat down, yawning and belching loudly. Clearly the men took no more pleasure in this journey than he did. What could be their destination? Even at this slow pace, they might have travelled further than Windsor by now—but north, south, east or west? That was the problem. Not east, surely, or he would have smelled the sea, the scent of the Thames estuary, unless they had gone south-east into Kent. But surely he would have noticed if they had crossed London Bridge. There seemed no sense in it. Why should they move him from London? Rationally, he would have expected them to free him like Crewe and the others, or else keep him near at hand if they wanted him still in prison.

He pondered the possibilities of escape. It would be best attempted at night, because once out of the cart, he might find himself in open countryside without cover. Yet there was no chance of judging the lay of the land from inside this blind vehicle. And he would have to depend on quick concealment. After nearly two months of inactivity, he could not hope to outrun a group of hardened soldiers, unless they were so drunk they were incapable of motion. However, their plan must be to stop at some wayside tavern to sleep; even the great dray horses could not continue to draw the cart all night. Once inside the tavern, they would have him under close watch, perhaps locked up. Some time between dusk and the night's halt, then.

Pleased with this plan, he lay and awaited his chance. Perhaps he could catch up his bundle and leap from the front of the cart, pushing his way out past the driver before he realised what was happening. It was all a matter of timing his attempt carefully. He lay quietly, shamming sleep. If they thought he was asleep, they would watch him less closely.

Unfortunately, John had not allowed for the blow to his head. As he lay with eyes closed, sleep overtook him again, for the injury had made him not only dizzy but sleepy. When he woke the cart had stopped again, it was full dark, and the soldier called Ed was unlacing the cover at the back of the cart. Prodded by the boots of the men, John got to his feet with difficulty, clutching his bundle. His whole body was stiff and aching, bruised by the endless jolting of the cart and the hardness of its floor. He could barely climb down to the ground, and he realised that, even if he had been awake and seized his chance, he could not even have scrambled out of the cart before his guards caught him. His crabbed movements were humiliating, but not as humiliating as a failed attempt at escape.

He was marched into a dark and noisome tavern and put to sit in the corner furthest from the door. The youth, who was called Will, and Makey, the big slow fellow, guarded him while the others went off to demand food and lodging from the landlord. Little by little, he stretched and eased his limbs, until they came back to some kind of life, pricking and stinging as the blood flowed back into his stiffened joints. He would have to make his escape attempt tomorrow, and beforehand he must keep himself moving somehow, to avoid becoming helpless with cramp.

The company in the tavern's common room cast a few curious glances at him, then ignored him. In this dim and smoky corner the heat of the fire scarcely reached him, but the stale smells of food and the heady reek of spilt beer caused his empty stomach to rumble. Tize and Ed and the driver returned, followed by a slatternly woman whose filthy hair hung down into the bowls of greasy stew she slapped down in front of them. John still had his table knife tucked into his boot, but he left it there, out of sight of the soldiers, and ate with his fingers as they did, tearing the bread and dipping it into the stew and ripping the lumps of fatty meat apart between fingers and teeth.

They spent the night all together at the tavern in one room, the soldiers and the driver occupying the beds, John once again forced to lie on the floor. Tize locked the chamber door and put the key in his pocket, before lying down to sleep, boots and all. John's sleep during the day made it difficult for him to fall asleep now, and he lay on the boards, sticky with dust, with his head on his pack, and thought over his plans. He still had no idea where they were. He had finally humbled himself and asked, but the men had merely laughed at him. They were enjoying tormenting him; it was the only relief from the boredom of their task. They must have been instructed to keep him under close guard and deliver him up . . . somewhere.

He turned over on to his side, and cursed the discomfort of his hip-bone grinding against the floor. At least they had allowed him the same meal as they had eaten themselves. He must accept nourishment, however foul, if he was to make his bid for freedom.

Next day, they set off as before after a scratch meal of ale and bread. The rain had slackened to a surly drizzle, and today Tize decided that the rear flaps of the cover should be rolled back to give them air to breathe in the foul interior of the cart. John prayed fervently that they would be left like this, for it increased his chances of escape mightily.

All day he was quiet and obedient, in the hope of lessening their vigilance. Today they had again provided themselves with a basket full of flagons, and spent the time drinking. John passed the weary hours watching out of the back of the cart, trying to detect some sign of where they might be. The countryside was fertile and well watered, a rolling landscape, but not truly hilly. It might be almost anywhere in the middle of England. There was still a heavy cloud cover, but today there was sufficient variation in the sky for him to be able to detect where the sun lay behind those clouds, and to decide that they were travelling northwards, and perhaps a little west, for the roads were narrow and winding, and their direction changed as they travelled along.

No opportunity for escape offered itself that day or the next, though John was alert for any moment when the flaps should be unlaced and the men might fall asleep. Each day they stopped for the night at some tavern and John would promise himself that the next day he would make his attempt. The journey continued in this way until John lost track of the days. For some reason the men were not following one of the main roads across the country. They passed through no towns, only a few mean villages and hamlets of cottages so poor they seemed hardly distinguishable from the hedges. The patient dray horses plodded on at their slow but inexorable pace, although one day they did make a stop in the early afternoon to unload some of the crates at the side of the road. Across a field, John could see the tents of a regular military encampment, a method of housing the soldiers more common in these latter days of the war, when quartering was difficult to find. A group of soldiers who had been lounging under a tree, apparently waiting for them, looked curiously at John as they lifted the crates down with considerable care. Observing their caution, he wondered whether the crates contained powder and shot. Once the delivery was made, the cart did not move on at once. His guards joined the other soldiers on the verge, where they had made themselves a campfire for warmth and were cooking pieces of chicken over it, doubtless stolen from one of the neighbouring cottages. The smell of the roasting chicken made John's mouth water. He took the opportunity to walk up and down in the cart, stretching and bending to loosen the stiffness from his legs and arms. No one was keeping any kind of watch on him, but there was no need. He would not be fool enough to try to run off under the nose of an entire regiment.

At last they moved on. The men were cheerful after their good meal and the break in the boredom of the journey. The small, rat-faced one, Will, even threw him a whole loaf, nearly fresh, and a larger piece of cheese than usual. John ate sparingly, and when none of them were looking, pushed the remaining food into the centre of his bundle.

The rain had stopped, but the almost endless downpours of recent weeks, sometimes of rain, sometimes of sleet, had turned the poor road into a quagmire. The great horses strained to pull the cart through the mud. Although it had been lightened by the removal of several of the crates, it sank repeatedly into the soft surface. Then one or two of the soldiers would climb out cursing, and put planks of wood in front of the wheels, and help the horses by heaving the cart out of the mire.

As dusk began to fall, they seemed to be far from any village or crossroads or wayside inn. The countryside here was a kind of upland, not as bleak as a moor, but open and with little cover. Perhaps two hundred yards away, there were the outlying trees of a forest. Here, where the ground was high and sandy and better drained, the cart no longer became bogged down, and the four soldiers, exhausted from their efforts and bleary with the drink they had taken, were dozing—three lying on the floor, and the fourth, Will, asleep where he sat on a box, his mouth hanging open.

John had taken care to spend most of the day sitting at the back of the cart. The flaps of canvas were still unlaced, though one was no longer tied back, but had fallen down and billowed in and out in the wind. It seemed as likely a time as any to make his attempt at freedom. Wishing for a greater degree of darkness, and for trees or other cover closer to hand, he sat with one hand on the tail-board of the cart and the other holding his bundle on his knee. His heart began to thump, his breath felt constricted, as though a tight collar was pressing against his windpipe. Then, cursing himself for every kind of fool, he rolled over the back of the cart and let himself down as softly as he could into the sandy mud of the road.

There was no shout, no sound at all from the men. Crouching down low, he began to run away from the cart on the blind side, where the flap hung down, and in the direction of the wood. As he reached the rough ground of the upland, he stumbled, but escaped falling, and ran on, as hard as he could, his heart pounding with the unaccustomed effort.

He had covered about half the distance to the wood when he heard a shout. Risking a glance over his shoulder, he saw that the cart had stopped. The driver was standing up on his seat, pointing with his whip as the four soldiers tumbled out on to the road. Three of them began to run after him. The fourth—it looked like Tize—climbed up beside the driver. John lowered his head and ran on, wondering why Tize was not joining in the chase. He soon knew why. Almost at the

226

same moment, he heard a loud crack behind him and something hit the ground to his right. For a few seconds he could not place the noise, then he realised. Tize had loaded his musket and was shooting at him.

John changed his course and began to zigzag back and forth across the ground to make a more difficult target. Presumably Tize was no longer worried about whether they delivered him alive or dead. If he was killed trying to escape, that would be justification enough. He could hear the panting and shouts of the other three soldiers, but they were only gaining on him slowly. Weighed down by the beer, they were not the danger they might have been, and probably did not relish coming too close to him in case Tize missed him and shot one of them instead.

Crack! Another musket ball landed closer than the last. The man must be a very fine shot, in this poor light, aiming at a running man, with a weapon that was notoriously unreliable.

Only a hundred yards to go, and he would be in amongst the trees, where he would have some chance of eluding them and Tize would no longer be able to take aim at him. The others, he could hear, were beginning to be winded. While he had despair to drive him on, they had only the fear of what might happen to them if they lost their prisoner.

He was growing tired. The rough tussocks of grass clawed at his legs and twice he slipped in the wet slurry of cow dung, where a herd must have grazed earlier today, although he had seen no sign of farm or cottage. He seemed to have been running endlessly, the belt of trees forever unattainable, like some mockery of a dream. But his pursuers were not gaining on him, and he had heard no further shots from the cart. Either Tize thought the range impossible, or he was taking a long time to reload.

His breath came in harsh gasps and he knew he could not run much further, when he became aware that the shadow of the trees was closing over him, and underfoot the coarse grass had been replaced by a soft and treacherous quilt of leaf mould and dead twigs overlaid with last autumn's new fall of leaves. He stumbled and slowed. It would do him no good to turn his ankle in some hidden hollow or to fly headlong over a fallen branch.

In the distance he could hear the soldiers shouting, and once again the crack of the musket, but Tize must be firing now from mere bravado or fury, for within the trees and cloaked with the growing darkness, he could not possibly be seen from the road. He went on, as swiftly as he dared, but circumspectly, with no plan in his mind of where he should head. Like some frightened creature of the wild, his instinct was merely to find some dark place to hide.

At last, peering ahead through the gloom, he saw what he was seeking. Some time in the past this wood had been used by the local people for coppicing. Not thirty feet in front of him was an ancient hazel coppice, which had grown, as such coppiced trees will do, into a ring of bristling coppice-wood, like the crown for some vast giant's head. But it had been long neglected, so that the once young and pliable withies had put out sprigs of their own, which had grown into small branches, and the centre, which would have been open and bare in a managed coppice, had filled with hazel growth and scrubby brush. John pushed his way into this great tangled birds' nest of branches, to where a hollow large enough for a man still remained, arched over with the bare whippy branches. He sank gasping to his knees. As his breath quietened and his heartbeat slowed, the silence of the wood folded itself around him.

Chapter Eighteen

When Anne rode into Lichfield, she went first to see Robert Verey at the Black Swan.

'Hay?' he said, shaking his head. 'I know of none with hay to spare for selling. I had worries enough to lay in my own supply. I own a small parcel of land over at Shenstone, but it never yields me enough, even in a good year, not for my own horses and those at livery. And this last year was the worst I've ever known, even in the run of bad seasons we've had. The 'thirties were a lean time, to be sure, but since the war began, farming has grown worse with every year. What the weather doesn't destroy, the troops do, with their looting and their trampling of the crops.'

He poured two glasses of fine French wine and joined her beside the fire, where she was warming her numb fingers and toes after her cold ride.

'I bought some hay from a farm over Burntwood way,' he said thoughtfully, 'and I had to haul another load all the miles from Stafford, but that was at the end of the summer, before folk realised how bad it was going to be. The woman at Burntwood was selling up, that was why she was willing to let me buy her hay. Her husband was killed in last summer's fighting and the children were all small. She decided to sell everything and move back to her people. If someone else was selling up . . .'

He shook his head.

'None I can think of. 'Tis market day today, you'll know that. Try amongst the farmers, though I doubt you'll have any luck. I'll ask a few people who might know.'

'So there's still a market in Lichfield, despite the hard times?'

'No great show of a market. But there are some selling stock they can't feed for the winter, like you. And there's bargains to be had, for those with fodder laid in, because nobody wants to buy. Aye, any man who could think of a way to feed stock easily over the winter would soon become very rich indeed. I wish I was that man!'

Anne went out in search of hay, promising to come back in an hour or two to learn whether Robert had found anyone with a surplus.

The market was indeed a miserable affair—gaunt and hungry beasts selling for a handful of coins, gazing out from their pens at the passing crowds with lacklustre eyes; a few withered vegetables; an alewife with a small supply of earthenware flagons displayed. A stall selling farmers' sheepskin jerkins was the only one doing a brisk trade. She eyed the beasts, thinking of her need for meat, but the creatures were no more than scabby hides clinging to a brittle framework of bone. There was nothing there to feed her family.

Despite the poor state of the market, the people of Lichfield were walking about in the snow, examining what was on offer, not so much with an air of those planning to buy, as looking for company and gossip. Anne approached one of the yeoman farmers whose face she recognised as someone John had dealt with when they had lived at Thickbroome. His cousin now rented Thickbroome from the Swynfens.

'Mister Sylvester?' said Anne. 'I hope you are well.'

The man turned to her in astonishment. He was a thickset fellow with a complexion ruddy from hundreds of tiny red veins. The hair hanging down from his hat almost to his shoulders was grey and tangled, and he wore rough homespun clothes that were far from clean. He was so taken aback at being addressed by her that he simply gaped.

'You used to do business with my husband, Master John Swynfen, when we lived at Thickbroome,' said Anne, thinking he had not recognised her.

'I know who ye are,' he said. 'What d'ye want?'

His tone was rude. Anne shrank back, realising she had offended him by breaking all conventions in thus approaching him boldly in the market, but she must ignore his attitude, and those of his friends, who were staring at her in a way she did not like, if she was to achieve her purpose.

'I'm looking to buy hay,' she said, aware that she sounded conciliatory. 'I'm just home from London, and I find we are short of fodder after a bad harvest.'

'And why has your man sent you out to do men's work?'

Anne felt her face flushing. The man's manner, and the way he was eyeing her, were abominable.

'My husband is not yet returned from London,' she said with all the briskness she could muster, 'and the matter cannot wait. Now, have you any hay to sell? Or do you know any who has?'

'I heard tell Master Richard Swynfen and his wife were both took ill,' said one of the other farmers to his neighbour, but loud enough for Anne to hear.

'Aye. Both gone mad, I heard tell,' said another with a laugh.

Anne opened her mouth to protest, then clamped it shut again. It would do her no good to start an argument with these men, who had now moved to surround her. They were not exactly menacing, but there was hostility in the air.

'Well, Mister Sylvester,' she repeated. 'What do you say? I have the coin.'

For a moment greed flickered in the man's eyes, then he shook his head.

'I've none to spare, and if I had, I'd not sell it to a woman.'

And with that, he turned his back on her and walked off, followed by his friends.

After this discouraging encounter, Anne tried several other farmers in the market, some of whom she knew by sight. Though none was quite as ill-mannered as Sylvester, all were adamant that they had no hay to sell. She could not be sure whether they were speaking the truth, or whether they were prompted by the same prejudice as Sylvester, unwilling to sell to a woman. A crowd of boys had gathered, and followed at her heels. She could hear them whispering amongst themselves and even jeering at her openly. Eventually, cowed into fearfulness and shame, she returned to the inn.

Robert Verey had better news for her.

'There's one place you may be able to buy hay, but it will be expensive. Twice the usual price, I fear.'

Anne gave an exclamation of relief.

'Where? Oh, this is good news indeed!'

Robert shook his head.

''Tis too dear. But it's all a part of these strange times we live in. You'll know that the bishops' properties are held in a kind of trust, until the government decides what to do with them?'

'Aye.'

'Well, the reeve who's in charge here in Lichfield says he has more than enough hay to provide for the estate this winter, since much of the stock has already been sold. And there's the tithe hay as well. You can buy what you want, but at a scandalous price. It's my belief the extra goes into his own pocket. He's making himself a rich man out of the pickings of the job. I tried to argue the price down, but he wouldn't be stirred. He knows he holds the prize to bargain with.'

After that, the business was concluded quickly. Robert fetched the reeve for the episcopal estate into his own parlour and witnessed the transaction so that Anne should not be cheated. The reeve had a long, guileful face with eyes too closely set together, eyes which avoided Anne's. She had no wish to fill his private coffers with her coin, but swallowed her distaste and concentrated her thoughts on the Swinfen beasts. The man promised to deliver the hay to Swinfen the next day. Anne rode out of the town relieved to have secured the fodder for the beasts, but reflecting soberly that it would not be an easy matter for her to run the estate until her father-in-law recovered or John returned. Living in London, she had been accustomed to hearing news from all over England and she knew that, since the start of the war, many women had been obliged to undertake their husbands' duties. Here, in this small market town, such activities were still regarded as little better than a blasphemous overthrow of the heavenly ordained hierarchies. A woman setting herself up in man's estate would be cheated, ignored or vilified. Somehow she must contrive to retain her neighbours' respect, or circumvent their hostility, for she had to live amongst them.

It was well into the afternoon by the time she reached Swinfen, so she decided not to ride the additional miles to Weeford that day, to visit Mary and Thomas Pott. The matter of Bridget might require some delicate negotiation, for which she must allow sufficient time. Besides, this was the first occasion that she had been on horseback since the birth of the baby, and she found herself very sore and tired. The soreness of her breasts was telling her, too, that it was long past time to feed the baby. The difficulties of negotiating for the hay had driven from her mind her intention of searching out a wet nurse in Lichfield. She was torn between wanting to continue feeding the baby herself, now that she had begun, and knowing that if she was to become the gentleman manager of the estate, nursing the child would be very difficult.

She slid down from the mare in the stableyard and handed the reins the Josiah, half groaning and half laughing.

'I shall be stiff tomorrow, I fear. I'd little cause to ride in London and I've become quite weak. It's fortunate she's such a well-mannered mare.'

'Aye, she'm a good 'un, this 'un,' said Josiah, running his hand fondly down the horse's neck. 'Brandy, we call her. Sired by one of your father's stallions over at Weeford Hall. I mind when you was a bit of a girl there, you could ride anything on four legs.'

'Ah well, I thought I could. I remember taking a nasty tumble into the Black Brook once, when I rode my father's stallion Zephyr without leave. He bolted when a hare sprang across the path, and landed me right in that deep pool where we . . . where my brothers used to swim.'

'Zephyr, that was a fine stallion! He was sire to this mare's sire. Of course, the Brandreths are all away to Kent now.'

'My father thought he was best to keep watch over the estates there. The army has been a little too free in its looting of the counties near London, and with the Potts able to move into Weeford Hall . . .'

She began to move purposefully towards the house, before Josiah could engage her in a discussion of the entire stable of Brandreth horses, which he had always coveted. Even here in the stableyard she could hear the baby's frantic screams.

'I must see to the baby, Josiah, but I bring good news for you. I contrived to buy hay from the bishop's estates. It's to be delivered tomorrow.'

Leaving Josiah staring at her in disbelief, she ran for the house and the baby.

❧

When Anne went down later to the kitchen, she found Hester, Biddy and Margit sitting in a dispirited group around the stool on which Josiah had set up the quern. The open sack of wheat stood beside them on the floor, and next to the quern was a small pottery bowl holding no more than a handful of flour.

''Tis no use, mistress,' said Biddy, with what sounded like gloomy satisfaction. 'Us'll never make flour with that old thing.'

Anne stood over them, looking down at the quern. Some of the precious wheat was scattered across the stool, more of it was on the floor. She noticed that Margit's hands were red and sore, and her eyes swollen with tears.

'I tried my best, mistress,' the girl gulped, 'but 'tis so heavy and I can't rightly turn 'un and when I must put more wheat between the stones I must get the others to help me lift the top stone and then when us put 'un back the wheat it spills everywhere . . .'

She burst into tears.

Anne patted her absently on the shoulder, studying the quern more carefully than she had done before. The upper stone, the grindstone, rested on a lower stone which was slightly dished and had a shallow lip at one side. There were two holes in the grindstone—a larger one in the centre, which was bored right through it, and a smaller one offset to one side, which was about half the depth of the stone.

'I wonder,' she said, picking up some of the spilt wheat. 'Perhaps you don't need to lift the stone. Doesn't it go in here?' She dropped the grains into the central hole, then laid her palms on the grindstone and tried to turn it. The girl was right, it was deadly heavy.

233

'Then I think the flour should flow out over the lip, so you need to put a shallow dish under the edge to catch it.'

'Flow!' Biddy snorted. 'It's been all we could do to scrape that bit flour off the stone.'

'Well, I suppose you need to have more flour for it to flow.' Anne leaned over the grindstone again, struggling to make it move. It stuttered round two or three turns, and already her palms were burning.

Peter came in, empty-handed, from his rabbit snares, to find them still wrestling with the heavy stone. Anne was near tears herself by now. He looked at the quern curiously.

'My old grand-dam had one of them,' he said. 'Always ground her own flour, to save the miller's cut.'

'Do you know how to make it work?' Anne asked desperately.

He studied it. 'I wasn't more than a little lad . . . but I think there's something missing with yon. Aye, I remember. There should be a sort of a handle, nay, nothing more than a stick. See that other hole? You want a peg in that, to drive the stone round.'

He fetched a small branch from the woodpile beside the fire and snapped off a piece about nine inches long, then whittled the end till it could be wedged into the smaller hole. Anne grasped the improvised handle and found she could turn the grindstone much more easily, though it was still hard work.

'I mind,' said Peter slowly, 'that when she had 'un fairly turning, my grand-dam said 'twas the wheat itself that made 'un run smooth. She would sit there, turning and scooping in the wheat, and 'twas not so hard as you're finding, mistress.'

'Give me your stool, Margit,' said Anne, 'and pick up every last grain of that spilled wheat, for we cannot spare it.'

She sat down and tried to do at Peter had suggested. At first she struggled with the rough handle and blisters were beginning to form on the palm of her right hand before the stone suddenly, magically, began to move smoothly. She trickled wheat into the central hole from the palm of her left hand while she continued to turn with her right. The rolling grains and the natural silkiness of the flour had somehow oiled the quern so that it now turned quite easily. Her arm began to ache from the awkward movement, but she no longer had to fight the weight of the grindstone. The flour brimmed up and trickled slowly over the lip into the shallow dish Hester had placed there. Strands of hair were clinging stickily to Anne's face when she gave up her place to Biddy, who took over dubiously, but soon agreed that the wretched thing did seem to be working.

'Well,' said Anne, her voice bright with relief, 'thanks to your grand-dam, Peter, we will have fresh bread tonight!'

'Hard work for us, all the same,' she heard Biddy mutter, as she left the kitchen, but it sounded as though it was said merely for form's sake.

&

It was snowing again the next morning, but not heavily, so Anne decided she would continue with her plan of riding to Weeford, although she was aching and tender from the previous day's ride. She would not let herself give in to weakness and stay beside the fire which Peter had lit in the small parlour, though she was sorely tempted. Late the previous afternoon she had told Josiah to shift all the rotting hay on to the midden, and to wash down that part of the barn where it had been stored, lest the rot spread to the new hay.

'I don't understand why you kept it,' she said. 'It's not fit for any beast to eat.'

'It were not as rotted as this at the first. I thought us might have need of 'un,' he said defensively.

Anne shook her head. Little as she knew about farming, she knew no animal could have eaten that blackening mess.

She waited at Swinfen long enough to see the first of the haywains from the bishop's estate drive in, and fingered the hay anxiously.

'Is it good enough?' she asked Josiah.

'Aye. As good as any this year. Those meadows belonging to the bishop are on good soil, and slope away to the south. They would've made hay there early, so maybe they 'scaped the rain that caught most of us.'

Mounted again on the mare Brandy, Anne rode south to the crossroads. There the Swinfen road met Roman Watling Street, which led away west to Wales and east towards Tamworth, and beyond that to Sutton Cheney, where John's cousins lived. She nodded to a carter with a load of logs as he turned off Watling Street and headed for Lichfield, then she rode over the crossroads and south the short distance to Weeford. On the right hand lay the manor of Thickbroome where they had lived for twelve years, before John was elected to Parliament. They had leased the estate to the Sylvesters when they moved to London, but Anne looked eagerly at the familiar woods bordering the road before she turned left into the narrow lane leading down into Weeford.

This was her childhood home, for she had grown up at Weeford Hall in a large family, of whom six sisters and three brothers had survived infancy. They were married now and moved away, and when her parents had gone down into Kent, Mary and her husband had leased Weeford Hall and its manor from them. Mary Swynfen was just a year younger than her brother John, and the Swynfens and Brandreths had tumbled about like one family when they were children. The two girls had been friends since they could barely walk. Anne had been surprised and a little dismayed when Mary Swynfen married Thomas Pott nearly twenty years ago. Mary was just fifteen years old then, while Thomas was only a few months younger than her father, an old man of thirty-two. Thirty-two did not seem such a great age to Anne now, and the marriage had proved a happy one. Both John and his father had a high opinion of Thomas Pott, and Anne knew that if she needed help at Swinfen, she could rely on him, though she would not ask for it if she could manage without.

Mary embraced Anne joyfully.

'I never thought to see you here! Are you all come home? Why hasn't John ridden over with you? I'll scold him surely! And the baby . . . surely the baby was due by now? Come into the parlour and I'll ring for something to eat.'

Mary bustled about, her usual plump, energetic self, giving Anne no time to reply to her questions. A maid brought in a fine crystal flask of wine with Venetian goblets, and a plate of little currant cakes. The Potts, at least, seemed well provided for the winter. Anne, standing at the window and looking out at the familiar outline of her mother's garden, turned as the maid withdrew, and noticed she was limping. The girl looked up as she closed the door, and caught Anne's eye, but her face was carefully blank. It was Bridget.

'Now,' said Mary, urging Anne into the best seat by the fire and piling up a plate of currant cakes for her, 'tell me all. Thomas will be so vexed to miss you, but he's ridden over to Tamworth on some business or other and won't return before nightfall. *Why* are you here?'

So Anne began with the struggle between Parliament and the army, and John's part in attempting to negotiate the peace. When she came to the arrest and imprisonment of the Members of Parliament, her sister-in-law's usually merry face grew grave.

'We heard there was trouble in London, but we didn't know that John had been imprisoned. My poor brother will be half mad. He can't even bear to be confined to the house by bad weather. What will he do in this case? And have you heard from him?'

'A short note only. I managed to send him clothes and money, but he had told me to pack and leave London with the children. He feared for our safety.'

She gave a brief account of the journey to Staffordshire, the birth of the baby, and the time spent in Oxford.

'And then when we arrived at Swinfen, to find all in such disarray—your parents both ill and incapable, most of the servants gone, the house dirty and cold, and scarce any food . . .'

Mary looked uncomfortable.

'When Father fell ill, we went over to Swinfen, of course, Thomas and I, but, well, it has been difficult. My mother and I have somewhat fallen out of late. I'm afraid we quarrelled, and she sent us off. Since then the weather has been terrible . . . I didn't realise that matters had come to such a pass. My mother said some unkind things . . .'

'Perhaps her wits were already straying,' said Anne. It was the kindest assumption. 'She's become like a little child, but sometimes she has terrible rages. I find it very strange. Your father . . . I'm not sure. He's managing to take a little food now.'

'The 'pothecary said he would never recover.'

'That may be so. We must just wait on God's will.'

'As for the manor,' Mary said, 'I'll send Thomas over tomorrow. He'll soon have everything set to rights.'

Again, Anne felt that reluctance. Thomas would no doubt take over the manor and, very kindly, set her aside. She found she did not want that.

'I'd be glad to see Thomas at any time, of course, but I'm managing very well. The house is much improved, and we're contriving what we can in the way of food, though the children complain a good deal about having to eat porridge! Yesterday,' she said, trying to conceal her pride, 'I rode into Lichfield and bought enough hay to see the breeding stock through the winter.'

Mary looked shocked, and her dismay only deepened as she listened to the full story of Anne's visit to Lichfield, a story she exaggerated a little as she described the hostile reception she had received from the yeomen farmers.

'But, Anne, you must not deal with such people yourself! It's most unseemly. John would not care for it at all.'

Anne looked down at her hands. She knew very well that John would not care for it, but would he like it any better if Thomas Pott took over the running of his manor, however kindly?

'I shall have no need to deal with such people, as you say, for much of the time. I can use Josiah as an intermediary when it's suitable. Yesterday it was important that he should mend the roof of the barn to keep out the winter weather.'

Their talk turned to other family matters. Mary had only four children who had lived, the eldest, Richard, being a year older than Anne's Dick.

'I look at him,' said Mary, 'and cannot believe that I was younger than he is now when my first babe, my little Ann that I named for you, was born and died. He seems such a child.'

'Our Dick is still a wild lad, but I hope he's hard at his lessons,' said Anne, and told Mary of her unsuccessful and humiliating encounter with the Master of Charterhouse.

They had finished their wine and cakes when Anne broached the real reason for her visit.

'Bridget?' she said.

'Ah, Bridget,' said Mary, once again looking uncomfortable. 'You understand, Anne, that it was not my wish. My mother had taken the notion that Bridget . . . she thought Bridget took it for granted that she should live a gentlewoman at home. She said Bridget must not remain dependent, she was lazy . . .'

'Bridget!'

Anne thought of the many hours Bridget used to spend in kitchen and stillroom, labouring over preserves and family medicines. The hateful task of rubbing the curing hams every day with salt and saltpetre—a task which turned the hands raw and bleeding—that had always been Bridget's task, when it should have been a servant's. Who mended the family's finest silk clothes and French lace? Mistress Joane would never have trusted them to a servant. It was always Bridget who spent evening after evening in the poor candlelight, restoring them with her fine stitches. In fact, since it seemed Bridget had been here at Mary's house for more than a year, that might account for why the household supply of preserves was so low at Swinfen. It might not be entirely due to the depredations of the soldiers. Indeed, it was a wonder Mistress Joane had wanted to be rid of her, so valuable were her services. No doubt it had all been done in a moment of pique.

'I know,' said Mary. 'It was cruel and unfair. But you know how it is with my mother. She looks at Bridget and she feels guilt, and that makes her angry.'

'Why should she feel guilt?'

'Didn't you know? She wouldn't send for the physician when Bridget was ill, that time when she was a child. Perhaps he could have done nothing to help her, but I'm sure my mother half blames herself for the fact that Bridget has a twisted leg, so she can't bear to look at her.'

'But Bridget has the sweetest nature of anyone I know,' Anne protested. 'She blames no one. I can't think of anyone with a kinder heart.'

'That's true. I don't say that my mother is justified, only what I think she feels. At all events, about a year ago—aye, it was in the dull days after Christmas, a year ago—she makes up her mind that Bridget is to go into service as a gentlewoman to some upstart merchant family in Tamworth. The shame of it! The disgrace to the family! And so far away, she couldn't even have walked home to visit us. So Thomas said we had better have her here. I already had a waiting gentlewoman, as you know—Elizabeth Wyatt, cousin to your Patience. I couldn't dismiss her. Bridget must come as an upper servant. It has been very trying for us both. I know I feel it keenly. Bridget will not talk of it. Indeed, she will not talk to me at all, although I'm her sister. We didn't need another servant, and did it only out of kindness, that she might not be sent out of the family, but I think she resents it.'

And so she might, thought Anne. It was not unheard of for a youngster to spend time in the home of a relative, usually a richer relative, being tutored with the children of the family and instructed in courtly manners, but Bridget was a woman grown, and her position was clearly different.

'I would be happy,' said Anne hesitantly, 'to take her home to Swinfen with me. If you truly don't need her. She could take up her old place as a daughter of the house, and welcome.'

Mary gave her an odd look.

'You are very certain of your position to command in my parents' house,' she said sharply.

Anne recoiled as if she had been slapped, and felt the blood rising in her face. She did not think she had merited that. But perhaps Mary was still feeling ashamed because Anne had discovered the house and household at Swinfen to be in such a fearful condition, not two miles from Mary's own home.

There was an uncomfortable silence between them, which neither seemed willing to break.

'You must decide what you think best,' Anne said quietly at last. 'At the moment there's none else but myself to take charge at Swinfen. Your father is robbed of speech and movement, your mother seems to have lost her wits, at least for the time. When John returns, he will, of course, act as the eldest son must in such circumstances. In the meantime, I am only contriving to see that we all, men and beasts alike, live through the winter.'

Mary avoided her eyes, but gave a small nod.

'It seems to me that you find it difficult to have Bridget here,' Anne continued. 'Your mother, in her present state, will be quite unaware of whether Bridget is at Swinfen or here in Weeford. Why don't we ask Bridget herself what she would like to do?'

'Very well.' Mary tinkled a little silver bell, and Bridget herself knocked at the door and came in.

Before Mary could embarrass them all by addressing Bridget as a servant, Anne leapt to her feet and embraced her young sister-in-law, and told her that she would gladly take her back to Swinfen that very day, if she wished to come.

'But Mistress Pott may need my services here,' Bridget said.

Anne ground her teeth at this form of address, but, without saying anything, turned and looked at Mary.

'Of course you must go home to Swinfen, if that's what you would prefer,' said Mary. 'We only wanted to give you a home.'

With a little more skirting around the niceties, it was established that Bridget would go home with Anne, on a pillion saddle which the Potts' stableman would lend them. As if ashamed of her outburst at Anne, Mary filled a pair of saddlebags with potted beef, dried fruits, honey and cheese. Bridget took off her long apron and her servant's plain cap and donned a cloak. Apart from a small bag of linen, she left her clothes behind at Weeford Hall to be sent on.

As they rode out past the church, Bridget wrapped her arms around Anne's waist to save herself falling off.

'This mare is somewhat crowded,' she said, 'with two women and a pair of saddlebags. I don't think her back is built for such a load.'

'We haven't far to go,' said Anne. 'I'm sure she will survive as far as Swinfen. Do you mind that I came to fetch you away?'

'Anne,' said Bridget, 'you are a true friend, a Sir Galahad, a Perseus rescuing the maiden from the monster . . .'

'Oh come,' said Anne, 'Mary is become mighty proud now she has got Weeford Hall, but to call her a monster . . . !'

એ

Bridget quickly resumed her old place at home in Swinfen Hall, and took charge of the nursing of her father. She had the patience which Biddy lacked, and the time she spent feeding him and reading to him freed Anne for the many other tasks that had fallen to her lot. Anne was overwhelmed with guilty relief. With Joane Swynfen they would need to proceed more cautiously, for her moods were changeable. She might still retain her venom towards her crippled daughter, but Anne hoped secretly that Bridget might also relieve her of that distasteful duty. On the first afternoon, when she brought Bridget up to her father-in-law's room, she was sure there was a gleam of pleasure in the haunted eyes looking out of that distorted face.

'Bridget is come home, Father,' she said, unnecessarily.

They had no need of her. Bridget limped to her father's bedside and kissed him on his withered cheek. She had not seen him since his illness, and she had to turn aside to hide her tears, but soon made herself busy with the tray of food and the straightening of the bedclothes. Anne left them alone together.

The most urgent of her tasks in feeding the household was to convert some of the winter milk into cheese. Biddy made curds by setting a pan of milk by the fire and waiting for it to curdle, but the process often failed. The milk drew the hibernating flies, wood ash fell into the dish, and by the time it was sufficiently separated for the curds to be strained from the whey, it had developed an unpleasant sour taste, which not even salt and the precious pepper Anne had brought from London could disguise.

While they were riding back from Weeford, Anne had asked Bridget if she could remember the method of cheese-making without rennet.

'For,' she said, 'there will be no new suckling calf for rennet until spring, and even then I would sooner not kill any of the calves. The herd will be small enough as it is.'

'I'm sure you are right,' said Bridget, 'but I have forgot what herb the cottagers used in the old days. I can tell you who would know.'

'Who is that?'

'Old Goody Lea, who lives in that cottage the far side of Packington Moor. She's the wisest woman in these parts for herbs and old remedies.'

'Aye,' said Anne, somewhat reluctantly.

Agnes Lea was an ancient crone whose husband had built the cottage on part of Packington Moor that belonged to the Swynfens. The Leas were squatters, with no rights in the land, which Goodman Lea had claimed was common land, though it was not. John's grandfather had threatened him with the law and with eviction many years before, but the man had died, gored by a bull when he was crossing a field over

241

Freford way during a poaching expedition. He had left his wife and nine children destitute, and John's grandfather had not pursued the case.

Anne remembered that older John Swynfen, who had died a month before she was married, as a stern but just man, still wearing the full, stiff ruff of a gentleman of the great Elizabeth's day. And he was, like so many of the Swynfens, a fearless and somewhat stubborn man, with a mind and a will of his own. In January 1603, less than two years after the abortive rebellion against the Queen led by Robert Devereux, Earl of Essex—who lost his head for it—that same John Swynfen had christened his new baby son Deveroxe, a name whose significance was lost on no one. He had also been involved in some way in helping the widowed Countess of Essex, Walsingham's daughter Frances, reclaim the rights and property of her young son. That son had grown up to become Parliament's leading general at the start of the present wars—having inherited no love of the monarchy from his executed father.

Both grandfather Swynfen and Richard, his eldest son, now languishing in his bed upstairs at Swinfen, had refused to attend King James's coronation and buy their obligatory knighthoods, choosing to pay a hefty fine instead.

'There is no honour in a purchased knighthood,' old John Swynfen had said, regarding the matter as closed.

That same independence of mind and refusal to bow to tyranny was what had brought her own John to his present predicament.

As for Agnes Lea, her children were all gone now, dead or away looking for work or taken to wandering the open road, but the old woman lived on in the cottage with a few beasts and a vegetable garden. For many years she had knitted stockings to earn some pennies to buy what she could not rear or grow herself. Anne had bought stockings from the old woman when she was a girl. But since she had married into the Swynfen family she had hesitated to visit Agnes Lea, for fear of the woman's old resentment against them over the matter of the land on which her cottage stood.

The morning after her visit to Weeford Hall, Anne mentioned in the kitchen that she thought of riding out to Packington Moor to see Goody Lea. Hester and Biddy exchanged a meaning look, and the girl Margit's hand flew to her mouth, where she sat at the quern. It took so long to grind enough of the wheat for the daily bread that one of them must always be working the grindstone. Soon, she must see to the repair of the mill and the hire of a new miller.

'I shall buy some of her stockings,' Anne said briskly, 'and I want to ask her advice about cheese-making, for we must make cheese

242

or starve. Margit, make me up a basket of last night's leftovers, and a loaf of the new bread, and some of the oats in a bag.'

'There wasn't no leftovers.' Biddy was blunt, standing with her arms akimbo, and looking at Anne defiantly. 'And if there was, us'd as soon have given them to the sows as to that woman.'

'Why, Biddy, you wouldn't begrudge that poor old soul a bite of food! If times have been hard here, think how much worse it must be for her, living all alone up on the moor.'

Hester cleared her throat. Her eyes glinted with a secret excitement.

'People say she'm a witch.'

Anne spun round. This might be idle gossip, but it was dangerous gossip. The numbers of those hunted down and killed for witches had soared since she was a little girl. In recent years, the witch-finder Matthew Hopkins had brought some two or three hundred men, women and children to their deaths in East Anglia before he was accused of being a witch himself. John's colleague Sir Harbottle Grimston had sat as magistrate at the court when the first charges were brought, and had told Anne and John of the horror and panic of those times, one evening when he had come to dine in St Ann's Lane.

'If enough people believe some old woman is a witch,' he said, 'then every trouble that befalls them is laid at her door. This fellow Hopkins had all kinds of tests—pricking and swimming and examining for the devil's marks—but it always seemed to me much harder to prove any accused woman *wasn't* a witch than to prove that she was. Since Hopkins was suspected to be a fraud in the end, were all those people innocent, who died on his evidence? I was glad when it passed out of my hands and into a higher court, for the man died of consumption before it came to trial. Why, I've a mole on my leg that Hopkins would say was a devil's mark, but I've had it from birth.'

'No one would accuse you of witchcraft,' Anne said. 'You are rich, you are gently born, and you are a man. Those who are accused are poor old woman, friendless and unwanted.'

John had frowned at her, she recalled, for speaking so boldly and out of turn.

'Of course Goody Lea is no witch,' she said now, turning on Hester angrily. 'Never say such things again! She's old and bent from a hard life, and she knows how to contrive foods and medicines from the fields and hedgerows better than anyone of this neighbourhood, but that makes her a woman who should be shown respect, because of her age and her wisdom.'

She turned to the girl.

'Make up the basket anyway, Margit. Oats, bread, butter, some of those apples—though they're sadly withered—and some of the dried fruit Mistress Pott gave me. And a few eggs. And a jug of ale. Well stoppered, mind, against the jouncing on the horse's back.'

Margit went to do as she was bid, but as Hester and Biddy turned back to their cooking Anne heard them muttering about 'naught to spare'.

Anne knew very well there was naught to spare, but she had not the heart to go empty-handed to the old woman's cottage and her anger with the servants strengthened her determination.

She was still very stiff in all the muscles needed for riding, but once she was in the saddle again and had turned Brandy's head along the edge of the fields in the direction of the moor, she felt a joyous lift of the heart. It might have been the days of her girlhood again, when she had ridden over this land with John. When she was about twelve, she had taken to stealing out in her brother's clothes and meeting John not far from here. They would gallop over the moor, sometimes scattering the sheep carelessly, young and heedless as they were. John would let her fly his hawk and if they were lucky enough to take a pigeon, they would make a fire and cook it up there where the sky was wide and a kestrel or a bustard would ride the wind above their heads. One of the things John had most regretted about moving to London was giving up his hawks. They had gone to Thomas Pott. She should have asked Mary if he had them still, but Mary probably would not know.

The day was bright and clear, but very cold. As Anne cantered Brandy up over the rise of the moor, the mare's breath streamed out in great frosty clouds, and the earth rang back hard frozen beneath the snow. During the summer the grass here would be studded with wild flowers and valuable herbs of every sort, which Agnes Lea used for her simples. But in winter it was a bleak and terrible place. Packmen missing their road down into Swinfen or Weeford had been known to die up here. No more than two or three miles from the nearby villages, the place was as desolate as a mountainside in Wales or Scotland.

At last she caught sight of the cottage, which was smaller than she had remembered, huddled into a cupped dell in the sloping moor side. The colour of earth and stone, and thatched with straw cut from the wild moorland grasses, it was almost invisible in summer, but now in winter it stood out against the snow. There was a thin trickle of smoke rising from the hole in the centre of the roof, for there was no chimney. Anne slowed Brandy to a walk to cool her before she must stand waiting in the cold. And, if the truth be known, to give herself time to prepare what she would say to the old woman.

When Anne tapped hesitantly on the door, there was at first no answer, only a kind of startled waiting silence, then a cracked voice called out, 'Who be that?'

''Tis Mistress Anne Swynfen. Are you well, Goody Lea?'

There was no answer, but the door, which hung askew and scraped the earthen floor, was dragged open, and Anne found herself looking down into a pair of very bright eyes of a shifting hazel colour. Agnes Lea was smaller and more bent than she used to be, and her draggled grey hair was falling out in patches, clearly to be seen, for she wore no cap. As if some small vanity prompted her, she pulled her threadbare shawl up over her head and held it clutched under her chin. She did not move aside to let Anne enter, nor did she speak.

'I've brought you a few comforts,' Anne said, holding out her basket awkwardly. The bright glance flicked down and then up again to her face. 'Don't you remember me, Goody Lea?'

'I mind well enough who ye are,' she snapped. 'Anne Brandreth, who married that wild Swynfen boy.'

Anne smiled. It was a good many years since anyone had called John wild.

'Aye. That I did. And he was wild once, though you'd not know him now, a sober Member of Parliament.'

The old woman gave a sniff, as though she scorned such grand titles.

'Ye were wild enough yourself. I don't forget how ye galloped about the moor as though the Wild Hunt was after ye. And dressed up in boy's clothes, that your mother never wot of, I'll be bound. Well, ye'd best come in.'

Anne had to duck through the low doorway, and once inside it was a minute or two before her eyes accustomed themselves to the dim cottage. There were no windows and the only light came from the doorway and the smokehole, with a faint glow from the small fire. It was cold in the cottage, and she could see that the old woman had been wrapped in a blanket as she sat in a chair by the fire. A large tabby cat was curled up at the edge of the hearthstone; as Anne moved towards the fire, rubbing her cold hands together, it sat up and regarded her thoughtfully.

'Is that Peterkin?' she asked. 'He must be full of years by now.'

'Seventeen.' The old woman bent down and rubbed the cat behind the ears, so that he closed his eyes and rolled over contentedly.

'Let me make up the fire for you, Agnes,' said Anne, reaching out for a log from the small pile beside the hearth.

Agnes caught at her sleeve with a claw-like hand.

'Ye'll do no such thing. That store there must last me these three days. I've no forest to burn in my hearth like the great Swynfens, only the bits and pieces I find about the common.'

She slid her eyes sideways at Anne, to see how she would take this sly reference to the old dispute, but Anne would not play her game.

'I'll send the boy over with a load of logs for you,' she said. 'There's no call for you to go cold.'

She began to unpack the basket of provisions, and the old woman had the grace to look slightly ashamed. She hobbled over to a small food cupboard that hung on the wall, high out of the reach of mice, and brought down a small round of the goat's cheese she made herself. Anne poured some of the ale into a blackened pan on the hearth, and brought cloves and a stick of cinnamon out of her pocket to flavour it, then she added the log to the fire, without asking Agnes Lea's permission. The scent of the spiced ale soon filled the cottage.

'Now,' said Anne, 'here's bread and butter and hot ale, and your good cheese. A feast fit for a king.'

She spoke the words without thinking, then heard them echoing in her head. No news had reached them of the king's fate. He might still be fretting at Hurst Castle, or on trial at this very moment, or even dead. Agnes Lea fixed her with those sharp eyes as she lifted the steaming wooden beaker to her lips.

'He's dead,' she said.

Anne shivered. How had the old woman known what she was thinking? Perhaps she *was* a witch.

'I saw it,' said Agnes Lea, in a matter-of-fact tone.

'Saw it?' Anne's throat constricted and she looked at the woman with something like horror.

'Sometimes, I see things. I was dozing here at the hearthside yesterday, and I saw him lay his head on the block. 'Twas a foolish and sinful man, but those that did it will pay the like price before their days are ended.'

'Better if you don't say such things to people,' Anne cautioned nervously. 'They might think—'

'They might think I'm a witch,' the old woman interrupted. 'Well, that's a black lie. I'm a God-fearing woman, and have been all my days. I can't make my way to service now on Sundays, all that road down to Weeford, but I say my prayers on my knees as heartfelt as any Christian in this land. I'll have no truck with the devil and his evil ways. But I do see things. I have done all my life, and 'tis nothing I can either call up or put a stop to. And I've studied herbs and simples from my girlhood. I learned them from my grandmother, who was the

246

greatest wise woman these parts have ever seen. She would make a love potion sometimes for a silly girl, but nothing else of the magic sort. And I've never done even that, though there's been many who've pleaded with me to do it, and gone away angry with me when I wouldn't. All I've done is cure the sick, man and beast alike, and helped women in labour, when I was the best midwife round about.'

She bit into her bread and goat's cheese, and Anne noticed that, despite her age, she had a fine set of teeth, much better than many a row of black stumps she had seen belonging to the London gentry. The cheese was excellent, all the better for her cold ride across the moor, and it reminded her why she had come.

'I'm back from London to find Swinfen Hall poorly provided for the winter,' she said. 'Much of our store has been looted by the soldiers, and most of the meat gone. We have some eggs, and one cheese that was spared, but I need to make more cheese so the children will have good food in their stomachs to keep them through the cold weather. There's no rennet to be had, of course, at this time of year. Can you tell what herb will curdle the milk to make cheese? What do you use for your own cheese-making?'

'Lady's bedstraw,' said the old woman promptly. 'That will set your cheese as well as any rennet. Warm the milk a little at the fire—not too much, mind—and then throw in your lady's bedstraw. When it begins to curdle, ye may take out your herb, and then ye strain off the whey and put it to your press.'

'Lady's bedstraw!' said Anne. 'Thank you, Agnes. I couldn't call it to mind. But I fear we may have none dried for winter. Bridget has not been at home, and there are few herbs laid by.'

The woman got up and reached above her head to the low roof beam, which was hung all about with large bunches of dried herbs.

'I can spare ye two bunches,' she said.

'Nay, nay,' said Anne, 'you'll have need of them yourself.'

'I wouldn't offer it if I couldn't spare it,' Agnes said sharply. 'I always put extra by, in case one of my neighbours has need of some, but few visit me now. Perhaps they all take me for a witch, though that didn't stop them coming for simples before.'

'I'd take it kindly if you can spare the herbs,' said Anne. 'But don't speak of witchcraft, even in jest, for it's no jest when the hue and cry is up.'

'Oh, they'll not bother their heads with me, out here on the moor.'

'I pray God you may be right. Now, tell me, what do you lack besides firewood?'

'I'm well enough. I have my stores set by as usual. My beans did poorly this year, for the weevils had them, but all else did well.'

'You fared luckier than most, then, for the rain spoiled much at Swinfen.'

'Aye, well, 'tis bleak and bare up here on the moor, but 'twill never flood till Noah's time comes again.'

'Your hay wasn't lost?'

The old woman pursed her lips.

'Well, to be sure, the rain did flatten much of the common grass. I cut and dried what I could, but I may have to kill one of my goats before spring. 'Tis pity, for they're all in kid.'

In her determination to overwinter as much of her own stock as possible, Anne did not like the thought of even one of Agnes Lea's nannies falling victim to the lack of hay.

'I've managed to buy some hay from the bishop's lands. I'll send some with the logs, so your goat may live to bear her kid.'

The old woman smiled and nodded her thanks, but she did not humble herself. She was the same sturdy, independent and cussed woman she had been in Anne's childhood, and none the worse for it. When Anne untied Brandy from the fence to ride back to Swinfen, her basket contained two pairs of stockings knitted in fine wool to the old clock pattern, the bunches of lady's bedstraw, three small goat's cheeses for the children, and a pot of honey from Agnes Lea's bees.

'I'm very glad of the honey,' said Anne. 'We brought a little sugar from London with us, but it's costly to use. I never thought there would be any need to bring provision from the city to the country, and the children crave a little sweetness in their food. The honey will help them eat the porridge more happily. Josiah says the Swinfen bees took ill and died last summer.'

'Mayhap they knew Master Swynfen would be struck down. Bees are strange creatures. Their lives reflect the lives of their folk. Tell your Josiah or his boy to go looking in the beech copse near the stewpond, come the spring. He may be lucky and find a swarm. He'd best be sure he makes new skeps before then, and sets them to warm by the fire three days and three nights before he goes seeking.'

Anne was about to mount, when she turned and kissed the old woman on the cheek. It was an odd thing to do, she being a gentlewoman, and Agnes Lea little better than a landless peasant, but she was drawn to the old woman, as she had been when a child, however sharp her manner and strange her ways. As for the old woman, she looked startled at the kiss, then laid her gnarled hand briefly on Anne's cheek.

'Be off with ye!' she said brusquely. 'That babe of yours is crying so loud for her milk I can hear her from here.' Then she turned abruptly and went into the cottage, heaving the rotten door closed behind her.

Whether Agnes Lea had heard the baby through some magic of her own, or whether her predictions were based on sensible guesses, the child was indeed crying when Anne reached home, and so occupied was she for the rest of the day that it was not until after supper in the evening that she was able to retire to the little parlour, where Bridget and Patience sat beside the fire with their sewing. Peter had caught his first rabbit that day and Hester had made a stew for their supper. One rabbit between eighteen people was poor fare, but the meat had given flavour to the watery dish with a few pieces of vegetable floating in it. Curiously, this first hint of fresh meat had left her feeling hungrier than she had been before the meal, and the thought of food, which would not leave her, made her dizzy.

Her mind needed something else to keep it occupied. She found paper and ink and wax on the writing table, and trimmed a quill from one of the feathers thrust into an old pewter pot which had lost its handle. She lit the candle stump under the small burner in which the sealing wax was melted, and sat chewing the end of the quill and staring at the paper.

'Do you write to John?' asked Bridget.

'I can't be sure where he is,' said Anne. 'I suppose I could direct it to the *King's Head*, or to St Ann's Lane, but they may have taken him somewhere else altogether. I can't understand why he's not contrived to send me any word at all.'

She got up and paced about the room, thumping at cushions and straightening a shelf of books, before sitting down before her piece of paper again and sighing.

'I think I'll write to Samuel Gott. He was the only one of John's closest friends who wasn't imprisoned, although he was shut out of Parliament by Cromwell's armed men. I'll direct it to his lodgings in Westminster, but if he is gone down into the country, his servants will forward it to him. Surely he'll know what's afoot, and will send me word.'

'Ask him to send word even if he doesn't know what has happened,' said Bridget. 'Then at least you'll know that your letter hasn't miscarried.'

'Well thought of,' said Anne, dipping her pen at last in the ink.

Most Hon'rd & Deare Freind,

Haveing come at last to Swinfen & having noe word of my deare husband I write to y^u to knoe any word y^u may send me of him . .
.

Chapter Nineteen

The netted fragments of sky were greying towards dawn as John crawled from the tangled embrace of the hazel thicket. He squatted a moment on the floor of the wood, dusting the gold catkin dust from his clothes and taking his bearings. Over to the left, a thin wash of pink was seeping into the dull overhang of cloud, so he must be facing south, opposite the direction he sought. The cart and its army escort might be making north, but that way his own path also lay. There was nothing for him now in the south, in London or Westminster. He must withdraw, like a canny creature of the wild, to his lair, northwards into Staffordshire. He could find friends and allies there, or at the very least lie hidden on his own lands.

He turned around, so the paler sky lay on his right hand, and began to make his way cautiously north through the trees. However he might try to move silently, his passage was marked by the snapping of branches beneath his feet. Thick tangles of brier and bramble snagged his clothes as he passed, so he must continually stop and disentangle himself from their vicious thorns. Every time he stopped, he strained to hear any sound of men in the wood. Birds swooped and sang overhead, a few early butterflies, braving the late lingering winter, fanned their wings amongst the banks of nettles, and from time to time he heard the brush of an animal's body in the undergrowth, but nothing as heavy as a man. The first growth of the year, which appears before winter is gone, was breaking out amongst the layer of scrubby bushes and young trees which reached to breast height, and they held a sodden burden of the heavy rains and melting snow. Before he had been walking half an hour his clothes, his boots and his bundle were all soaking. Overhead the great branches of ancient trees cut off most of the light.

The sun was well up by the time he reached the far edge of the wood. Within the shelter of the last trees he paused to assess the ground ahead. There was no sign of the road along which they had been travelling last night. No farm or cottage lay within sight on the thin, bare ground which stretched ahead. It seemed safe enough. He stepped out into the open cautiously, fearing some shout or the sound of Tize's musket, but none came.

For the rest of the day he travelled across the upland, but his progress was not as easy as he had hoped. There were frequent patches of boggy ground, too treacherous to cross, so that over and over again he had to make detours far to east or west before he could resume his northward path. At last, as the little sun that could be seen behind gathering clouds declined towards the west, he began to look out for some shelter where he could spend the night. Without the direction of the sun to guide him, he would go astray after dusk, and the sky was too obscured for the stars to show the way once night had fallen.

Over towards the right, he noticed a thin wisp of smoke rising from a hollow where the land fell away. Where there was human habitation there might be food and help, but there might also be danger. As he neared the cottage he saw that it was a sad wreck of a place, with a few rows of what might be beans when they sprouted, and two thin chickens huddled in the unmelted snow below the wall. He was debating whether to pass by or ask for help when an old crone came out of the door. She was bent almost double with the deformities of age, and one white-walled eye showed that she was blind on her left side. The door hung open on the interior and revealed a floor that was no more than a continuation of the beaten earth of the yard. A pile of straw and rags made the bed place, and over the pitiful fire hung a dirty, rusty pot. There was little enough smell of cooking, but even so, John felt his mouth, parched and dry, begin to water.

The old woman suddenly caught sight of him and stumbled back, clutching at her throat. John spread out his hands before him placatingly.

'Fear not, goodwife, I mean you no harm.'

She stood staring at him, her toothless mouth hanging open.

'I beg of you, let me buy some dinner.'

Slowly, so as not to frighten her, he drew a silver groat out of his pocket and held it up. Her glance went from his face to the coin and back, and a certain calculating light seemed to enter her one eye.

'Food?' he asked again.

She shook her head, cupping her hand behind her ear and miming deafness. John pretended to scoop food into his mouth, then rubbed his stomach. The old woman held out her hand for the money, but John drew nearer, stepping past her into the hut. It smelled foully of age and decay, but there was something cooking in the pot. If the woman intended to eat it herself, it would not poison him, however revolting it might be. She dipped out a bowl of the mess—soup or stew—thin and watery, but hot. She held one hand out with the bowl and with the other reached for the money. John dropped the coin into her hand and tipped the bowl to his lips. It tasted of very little. Nameless roots bumped against his lips, and he scooped out with his fingers a single lump of greyish meat, run through with gristle and shrouded in yellow fat.

'I thank you, goodwife,' said John, wiping his greasy mouth on the back of his hand. He set the rough earthenware bowl on the ground beside the fire. 'Can you tell me what place this is?'

The woman stared at him, her jaw still hanging slackly, but that look of greed agleam in her eyes. She made no response. John shrugged, took up his bundle, and ducked out through the low doorway. He resumed his way northwards and, although he did not look round, he felt the woman watching him until he was out of sight.

That night he slept badly under the untidy remains of what had once been a well-kept hedge and when he resumed his journey the next morning he soon lit upon a rough track, not big enough for a road leading to a town or village, but one which bore the marks of occasional hoofs and cart wheels, and not too long since. He went warily, alert for any sound of heavier traffic or any sign this might be a route the soldiers would take, for despite a day's hard walking he had covered little distance and could hardly be out of their reach yet.

In the late afternoon he saw ahead of him a farmhouse, small but trimly kept, with three or four cattle in a meadow, where patches of grass showed through the lingering snow, and a pen where a sow lay, great-bellied with an imminent litter. He had come upon it suddenly around a bend in the track, and before he could dodge out of sight a woman in the yard, gathering her spread washing from the bushes, glanced up and saw him. At first she looked frightened, and called out to someone inside, then as John came limping up, somewhat footsore and clearly alone, she smiled at him.

'Good day, traveller,' she said.

'Good day to the mistress of the house,' said John, doffing his hat to her.

She was a buxom woman of about his own age, who stood sturdily with her feet apart, eyeing him appraisingly. Behind her, a man came out of the house and stopped. His look was more reserved. Perhaps ten years or more older than the woman, and lean, with eyes that shifted and never seemed both to look quite in the same direction. He wore a buff coat like the Parliamentary army, but had about him no appearance of a soldier. Nor, indeed, did he look like a farmer, but reminded John of those ill-nourished and sly creatures who hung about the darker alleyways of London, whose trade was that of the nip and foist, or in prosperous times a little horse-coping. He made as if to continue on his way, but the woman stayed him with a hand on his arm.

'Will you not sup with us, sir? You look weary and in need of food and rest.'

She smiled as she spoke and beckoned him towards the doorway.

'I would take it kindly,' said John, and followed her into the cottage.

It was a palace after the old woman's hovel, clean and comfortable, with pewter on the shelves and cushions on the chairs, though of rough homespun.

'Fetch a chair, William,' said the woman, laying another place at the table, where a fresh loaf and a round pat of butter showed the couple were themselves about to dine.

The man, still without a word, brought up another chair, though he never took his eyes off John. He poured small beer as his wife ladled out a rich mutton stew, thick with onions and carrots, as though war and famine had never visited these parts. John ate gratefully but silently, uncertain what to make of these people, who seemed more prosperous than the land and stock would justify.

'So, then,' said the woman, pushing her empty plate aside and resting her plump elbows on the table, 'have you travelled far?'

'Far enough,' said John. 'From London, and heading north. This track that passes your door—will it take me the right way?'

'Sure enough. And where in the north?'

'Derbyshire,' said John, who did not quite like all these questions, though they might arise from nothing more than an eagerness for news that is natural in such isolated places. The next question seemed to bear this out, for the man asked:

'What news of the war? Is the king prisoner still?'

'The king is dead,' said John. 'Beheaded in London some weeks past.'

The man nodded, as if in satisfaction, and spat accurately into the fire. 'That's a job well done. You're not a soldier yourself, then?'

John shook his head. By his dress and his unarmed state he was manifestly no soldier, so that he wondered why the man should ask. He was turning over anxiously in his mind what occupation he should claim for himself when the woman rose from her chair and began to clear the table. Over her shoulder he saw that it was growing dark.

'I must be on my way,' he said, heaving his bundle on to his shoulder. 'Will you let me pay for my supper?'

'Nay, nay,' said the woman, forestalling the man, who was clearly ready to accept. 'It would be a poor thing indeed if we could not share a meal with a traveller in these sad times.'

She turned and surveyed him, her hands on her hips.

'But there's no need for you to walk further tonight.' She smiled at him comfortably. 'There's a bed in the back room there that was our son's before he went off to the war. You take your rest there, and go your ways in the morning.'

It was hardly a room, more of a large cupboard with shelves of provisions and a small window closed by a hinged board let down with a string, but there was a low truckle bed with a straw mattress. The woman brought him blankets and closed the door softly behind her. John heard a murmur of their voices, but not the words. He sat on the edge of the bed, conscious suddenly of the weary ache in his legs and back. The small space was stifling, so he hooked up the window shutter before he flung himself down to sleep with his bundle for a pillow. As exhaustion stole over him, he thought he heard the clatter of hoofs from beyond the house, where he had noticed a small barn. He was surprised that the man should go abroad so late, but perhaps they owned other land, further away, with more flocks or herds he must attend to. That would explain the unexpected affluence of the small farm.

It was well into the night when John awoke suddenly with a jerk of the heart that brought him sitting upright, confused in the unfamiliar surroundings. He had dreamed that he was back on the cart, jolting endlessly over unknown roads. The square of the window was clear in the wall above the bed, sending a broad shaft of moonlight across the tumbled blankets to the floor. What had woken him? Then he heard it, the pounding of heavy hoofs and the rattle of a cart that was bitterly familiar. He scrambled to his feet, catching up his bundle.

He laid his ear against the crack of the door. The outer door of the house opened and he heard voices—the man of the house and Tize, disputing together, and then the woman, hushing them.

'Hold your noise,' she said, 'you'll wake him.'

'I'll see the money first,' said the man, 'before I hand him over.'

'You'll get your money when I get the prisoner,' said Tize, 'where is he?'

The man growled and spat. John could hear the hiss as it hit the fire.

'Money first.'

'How do I know it's not a trick?'

'Tall,' said the woman, 'a plum-coloured velvet cloak—a gentleman's clothes, to be sure, though he's had rough usage. Carrying a bundle, and no sword or weapon about him—and who would travel so, in these times? A broad-brimmed hat and unshaven, though not a proper beard. Is that the man you're seeking?'

'Aye, that's him.'

There was a pause and then, as though still reluctantly, the clink of coin. John waited no longer. He climbed on to the bed and forced his shoulders through the small window. At first he thought he would not manage, then he was through and lowering himself as carefully as he could to the ground outside. The cart stood before the house on the trackway, so he turned in the opposite direction, heading up towards the small meadow where he had seen the cows. The moon was full, lighting up the countryside with its bright, cold beams which robbed everything of colour. Buildings, grass, trees were all washed out to shades of bluish slate and black, with here and there a flash where the moonlight caught a reflection from puddles of snow melt. But it was clear enough for his pursuers to see him easily.

He began to run fast. No point in striving for silence now, they would open the door and find him gone at any moment. All he could hope for was to put enough distance behind him so that he could find some bolt-hole before they caught him. But everywhere was open and bare, except for a small thicket of trees crowning a mound like an ancient barrow. He made for the trees, but without hope.

Behind him there were shouts from the farmhouse and the sound of men running.

Almost at the same time he heard the report of the musket and something slammed past him and hit the ground before his feet, sending up a puff of dirt and fragments of turf. The man Tize, who had so nearly hit him across the wide stretch of upland would have no difficulty at this range, with the traitorous moon lighting him up like a player on the stage. He spurted forward, his breath sobbing in his chest, his feet uncertain on the rough grass of the meadow.

Crack! He felt as though someone had pushed his leg from under him. He stumbled and fell, sure he had put his foot in a rabbit hole. When he tried to stand up, he fell down again. His body would not obey him. He felt like one of the dummies made by the London prentice boys for Guy Fawkes Night, its legs stuffed with straw, flopping the whole ungainly body over and down on its face. He ran his hand down his leg, and it came away sticky. Curse the man! Against all the odds, he had been winged. He tried again to stand. Surely a musket ball at that distance could not do him serious harm. But something was damaged. He fell down on all fours and was trying to sit up when they caught him.

They beat him then, tossing him back and forth like a senseless Guy indeed, punching his face and his stomach until he felt his teeth loosened and he vomited all the day's food onto the grass. By then they had him down on the ground and were kicking him around like a pig's bladder in a boys' game of football.

Tize strolled up, his musket on his shoulder, and stood looking down at him. Then he spat deliberately in John's face.

'Get him back to the cart,' he said.

'I don't think he can walk,' said Ed. 'You got him in the leg, beautiful shot at that distance,' he added ingratiatingly.

Tize shrugged.

'Carry him, then. We can't waste no more time.' He turned on his heel and began to walk back towards the farm.

Makey, who was the biggest of the men, lifted John under the armpits, the other two took a leg each. Ed laid hold of the injured leg, on fire now with pain, and seemed to take particular pleasure in twisting it. His head thrumming with anguish and confusion, John retained just enough presence of mind to keep hold of his belongings.

The trek back to the farm took longer than his desperate dash, but John was only partly aware of it as he swam in and out of consciousness from the loss of blood and the beating. As they came into the circle of light cast by a lantern hanging by the farm door, John saw the couple who had taken him in with such kindness the previous evening. The man was weighing a purse in his hand. The woman stood with her plump arms crossed, watching with interest as they carried him in.

'Betrayed,' John gasped, twisting so he could look straight into the woman's eyes.

She smiled back at him complacently.

When they heaved him at last on to the floor of the cart and it moved off along the track, he turned onto his side and buried his head in his arms before a great darkness rolled over him and shut out the world.

&

Dick Swynfen lay beneath a hedge, trying not to breathe too loudly and hoping that none of the dogs he could see in the field in front of him would nose him out or betray him to the company making camp there. He had been on the road for days now, and had lost count of the time. Somewhere he had missed his way, but he persuaded himself that if he continued to head north, sooner or later he would reach Staffordshire.

At first things had gone well. Although the weather was abominable, and his clothes were soon soaked through, he had food enough, and the walking was not too strenuous. He had slept in barns when the chance offered, but no longer asked the farmers' permission. On the second day of his journey, when he had approached a farm, cheerfully hoping for a bite of food and the chance to sleep under cover that night, the farmer had turned the dogs on him, taking him for a renegade soldier or some passing, roguish tramp. He had escaped with no more than a small bite on his ankle, but he knew he had been lucky. Men had been killed by packs of half-wild farm dogs before now.

Apart from this misadventure, he was happy at first with the distance he was covering, despite the bad weather and his failure to persuade any carter to convey him a part of the way. He had escaped school, and he felt himself a man at last, embarked on a great adventure. As he walked, he sang the song with which students celebrated the start of the long summer vacation and the flight from study to haymaking:

Hang Brerewood and Carter, in Crakenthorp's garter,
Let Keckermann too bemoan us,
I'll no more be beaten for greasy Jack Seaton
Or conning of Sandersonus.

Then, at the end of a week or so, his food had run out. He regretted now the careless way he had stuffed his mouth with dried fruit whenever the whim took him. He should have parcelled it out and made it last longer. Now, whenever he passed a farm, he skulked about and raided the hen house for eggs, which he ate raw, screwing up his face in disgust, but too hungry to pass up the chance of nourishment. At one farm, a prosperous place attached to a large manor house, he had even stolen kitchen scraps from the pigs' trough. Bits of broken pie crust and half-gnawed bones and scraps of onion. But the swine had set up such an indignant squealing that he had fled from the spot and run until his breath was gone and he had to lie under a dripping hedge, sweating with terror.

He had a very small amount of money, but a sort of superstitious fear made him cling to it, as if its loss would reduce him truly to the vagabond state. From time to time he passed through a village or small market town, where he might have been able to buy food, but his few pennies would not go far, in these times of unprecedented prices. Besides, the shopkeepers would probably have driven him away at sight, for he knew he looked like the veriest beggar. His hat was broken, his clothes and person filthy, and one of his shoes was tied about with a piece of string, because the sole was half fallen off.

Now that he had made his way a little further north, he could see for himself the damage the war had wrought on the countryside. There were good fields left untended, where great weeds or unharvested crops poked up through the snow. Many of the country manors had suffered attack from one army or the other, gaping like toothless jaws where cannon balls had torn through their stonework, while cottages lay at the side of the road, burnt out and uninhabited, their blank windows staring like the eyes of the dead. He had spent a night in one, huddled in a corner where a bit of roof still gave some shelter. It had teemed with sleety rain that night, there was no whole barn or shed to be found, and the thickest of hedgerows would not have kept him dry, but he had hated the cottage. There were a few pathetic possessions still scattered about—a three-footed pot with a hole in the bottom, some filthy rags on a bed of rotten straw, and a torn baby's cap.

The cottage had kept him from the storm that night, but he had not dared to sleep, fearing the ghosts of the people who had almost certainly died at the hands of passing soldiers before their house was set afire. He found a dead chicken outside the back door, but, hungry as he was, could not bring himself to eat it. It was crawling with maggots, and its glazed eyes seemed to gaze at him sorrowfully. When the dawn came, the place seemed less terrible, and because he was exhausted, he lay down, thinking he would rest for a few minutes.

He woke with a start some time later, and his heart gave a horrible lurch. Something had brushed against his face. Shaking with terror, he pressed his eyes shut, but when it came again they flew open and he yelled in panic. Something bounded away from him, and paused at the gaping hole where the door of the cottage had been. He was still shaking, his very hands trembling as if he had the palsy, when he realised that it was a half-grown kitten. With a weak laugh, he scrambled up and went towards it, but his yell had frightened it, and it ran off into the snowy undergrowth behind the cottage.

In his knapsack he had two shrunken apples he had found still clinging to a tree he had passed the day before, so he sat down and ate one of them slowly, trying to persuade his stomach that the apple was bigger than it was. It was hours since he had drunk anything, and despite the apple his tongue cleaved to the roof of his mouth. It was one of his greatest difficulties, to find water to drink on the road. But the cottagers must have had a water supply. Searching around what had been their small plot of land, he could find no sign of a well, but a faint sound of running water led him to an ice-fringed brook, where he lay on his stomach and scooped the water into his parched mouth. It was the most delicious thing he had ever tasted. As he lay there, his hands

259

growing numb from the cold, he caught sight of a movement out of the corner of his eye. It was the kitten again. Clearly it was pining for companionship, for in spite of the fright he had given it, it gradually approached him, and at last allowed him to take it on his knee. It was a young female cat, pitifully thin, but affectionate and unafraid. Perhaps she alone had escaped the attack on the house, or perhaps she had been left behind when the family fled.

'You must have a name,' Dick said, finding the sound of his own voice strange, for he had not heard it for days. 'How do you like the name . . . Ginger? For you have patches of fur that are the very colour of the spice my mother uses in her winter cordials.'

The cat kneaded his breeches with her paws and seemed quite content with the name.

'I must warn you, however,' said Dick, 'if you come with me, you'll probably starve, as I'm like to do. If you stay here, you'll have mice and frogs to feast on, but there's little food for a cat on the road.'

He set the cat on the ground and got to his feet. She looked up at him questioningly.

'Well,' he said, 'you shall choose for yourself. If you want to join with me, you must follow.'

With that he swung his knapsack on his back and started off along the road again. He would not allow himself to look back until he reached the first bend. The cat was trotting behind, but stopped when he stopped.

'Well, then, Ginger, do you come?' he said.

At the sound of his voice, she scampered towards him, and rubbed against his ankles. With a grin he picked her up.

'Very well. I'll not oblige you to walk, for it's a long road.'

He tucked her in the front of his doublet, where her head poked out under his chin and her warmth gave him the first comfort he had felt for a long time.

Now, as he lay under the hedge a week later, he buttoned Ginger firmly out of sight inside his doublet, where she squirmed about and then settled quietly. The dogs in the field were, he feared, vicious and would probably kill her with a single snap of their great yellow teeth.

Peering out from his hiding place, he watched the curious collection of people in some puzzlement as they set up their camp. He had woken from his sleep under the thick hedge to the sound of voices and the clatter of pans hanging from three dilapidated carts with canvas tilts. At first, he thought they were a group of renegade soldiers, making off from the army with their women. The country was swarming with such groups, and he knew they should be avoided at all costs, for they had nothing to lose and all to gain from slitting your throat and stealing your every possession, down to the clothes on your back, however ragged.

Half an hour must now have passed since they had begun to make camp at the side of the road, and as he watched them he grew less sure they were soldiers. Partly, it was the way they carried themselves. They had neither the swaggering arrogance of the army, nor the furtive look of fugitives. Instead they moved with an odd grace, not only the women but the men as well. They were all dark of colouring. Then, also, there was the large number of children. Dick knew the camp followers often included children, but surely not so many in proportion to the adults. These people looked like families, not like a group of deserters thrown together by chance and followed by their whores and wives, with a few babes at the breast. They went about their tasks efficiently, each knowing what to do, down to the youngest. While the men unharnessed and fed the horses and the women skinned rabbits and cut up onions, carrots and turnips, the children went off to a nearby copse and soon came back hauling dry branches for the fires. Three of the bigger boys returned each carrying two buckets of water. They had been so quick about it, they must have known exactly where to find some stream or pond, as if they had come this way before. The boys passed quite close by the hedge, where Dick lay shaking with fear that they would find him and set about him. They were talking together, but he could not make out any of the words. At last he decided they must be speaking some foreign language. There were many bands of Huguenot refugees fleeing into England these days, but Huguenots would have been speaking French, and he had a fair knowledge of French. No, it was not French, that he was sure. He wondered if they might be Dutch spies, but dismissed the idea as fanciful. Spies would not travel so openly and in such a large group. There must be thirty of them.

The women began to cook their rabbit stew in a huge iron pot fixed over one of the fires, and turned to making some kind of flat bannocks with coarse brown flour mixed with water. They flattened the lumps of dough between their hands, as they laughed and sang together, tossing circles of the paste spinning into the air, and catching them, and slapping them down on hot stones at the side of the fire to bake. Dick crouched under the dripping hedge, feeling miserably alone as the scent of the baking bannocks and the seductive aroma of the rabbit stew floated towards him.

He was wondering how long it would be before dark, and he might have some chance of slipping past without exciting the notice of the dogs, when one of the men, taller and more thickset than the others, with grizzled hair hanging below his hat, came walking straight towards the hedge where Dick lay hidden. From the first, this man had stood out from the rest. While the others worked, he sat on the step of one of the carts, apparently giving an occasional order. He carried a slender stick like a cane, with a top elaborately carved. When he reached the hedge he stopped, not six feet from where Dick lay. Dick held his breath, and felt the sweat trickle down his back with fear. The man reached out with his stick and lifted away the branches of elder and bramble which had concealed Dick's hiding place. He regarded Dick with an expression that showed no emotion at all.

'Well, boy,' he said at last, in a curious accent, 'are you friend or foe? Do you plan to spy on us all night? Or have you the courage to show yourself?'

Dick flushed at this slight to his character, and got up stiffly, brushing dead leaves and twigs from his clothes. The man had a low, musical voice, despite his strange way of speaking, and his eyes were compelling. Dick was grateful, at least, that he spoke English.

'I am alone and you are many,' he said, with as much dignity as he could contrive. 'I couldn't tell if you meant me harm. These are strange times, and there are dangers on the road for one who travels alone. I'm no spy. I am nothing but a traveller making my way home.'

'Come and eat,' said the man simply. 'We would not leave any boy to starve when we have food.'

With that he turned his back and walked away, certain that Dick would follow.

Chapter Twenty

The soldiers had trussed John like a sheep's pelt, winding him round and about with a rope they had had off the innkeeper at the tavern where they had stopped for the night. John hardly knew what had happened from the time they threw him back into the cart until he woke the following morning to worse pain than he had ever known in his life. His injured leg was caked with dried blood, and when he tried to move it, the pain shot through his whole body, so he decided it was better to lie still and wait to see whether they would leave him in peace, or whether they were going to beat him again. His clothes were stained with vomit, and his mouth was dry as barren rock in a desert.

They had not made a very good hand at binding him. The ropes were slack enough for him to shift a little, but he was not fool enough to try to untie himself. They would only bind him the tighter once they discovered it. His arms were still wrapped around his pack, so he was roped to it, but at least they had not robbed him of his few paltry possessions. Had he been hungry, he might have tried to work free some of the stale bread and cheese hidden there, but the thought of food made his stomach rise. All he wanted was water.

He was lying in an attic room with a sloping roof, and he could hear from below the sound of voices and of much activity in the stableyard. This was a better place than the taverns they had visited before. The attic room, though small, was well swept and clean. He had some vague memory from the previous night of glimpsing a large inn built round a stableyard overlooked by balconies on two storeys, the kind of place travelling players would choose to put on their play. Beyond that, he had no idea where he was.

How much a man's perception of himself, of his very being, depends on knowing just what part he fills in the world around him. Beggar or king, waterman or innkeeper or yeoman, if he knows his position, his family, his village or town, he can be comfortable in his knowledge of his place. Stripped of his position in the world, robbed of family and friends, humiliated, beaten, betrayed and wounded, John found his sense of who he was slipping away from him. Not knowing where he was, in what village or town or county, sent him spinning down into a vortex of loss and confusion.

Only a few weeks ago he had been John Swynfen, distinguished young Member of Parliament, a man who could sway the country's rulers by the power of his words and the sweetness of his eloquence. Now he was dirty and sick, a helpless bundle, a nameless prisoner. He realised that never once, since they had set out from Whitehall Palace, had the soldiers used his name. He was 'you' or 'him'. Perhaps they did not know his name, who and what he was. To them he was no more than a job to be done, a tedious job, like delivering the ammunition to the army camps. They must deliver him somewhere, preferably intact, but if he was somewhat damaged in the process, they were indifferent, as long as they were not to lose by it.

Anne, he thought, oh beloved! I may never see you again, and we parted on such bitter terms. If I had only reached out to you that last morning, put my arms around you and held you close! He struggled against his bonds, as if reaching out his arms now he could somehow conjure her out of thin air. He fell back, biting his lip in helpless fury.

He tried to roll into a more comfortable position, but only succeeded in twisting his back. Then there came the sound of a key grating in the lock, and the door was pushed open. A young servant girl backed into the room, carrying a tray. When she turned and looked at him, she seemed startled. Probably his appearance was not calculated to inspire confidence. She set the tray down near him on the floor, and began to back away.

'Wait!' he said desperately. 'I'm tied, I cannot eat or drink. Can't you help me?'

'I was told to leave the food and lock the door again,' she said, speaking slowly and rather loud, as if he were deaf or simple.

'I don't ask you to set me free,' he said, 'but you can see I can't eat with my arms tied to my body. I beg of you, give me to drink, if nothing else.'

Cautiously, she drew nearer. She was very young, not more than twelve years old, not yet hardened with years of serving rough men with more drink than they could stomach, and evading their groping hands. Her hair was pale and soft as a brown moth's wing, her bones as fragile as a young bird's. She stopped beside the tray, which held half a loaf of bread, a small flagon of ale, and a hot meat pie, whose aroma tempted John to think perhaps he might be able to eat after all.

'My mouth is so parched, I would beg of you some water. Also, my leg is hurt and needs bathing.'

After a moment's consideration, she went out again, locking the door behind her, but she was soon back, bringing a jug of water, a basin and a cloth. She poured some of the water into the pewter tankard that was inverted over the flagon of ale, and, squatting down beside him on the floor, held it for him to drink. He drank greedily, some of the water running down his chin, but most flooding his grateful throat. He drank full three tankards before he stopped.

'I know it's none of your task,' he said humbly, 'but could you wash the dried blood off my leg, and tell me how bad is the injury?'

Again without speaking, she wetted her cloth, but first she washed his face, and as much of his hands as she could reach between the coils of rope. She worked earnestly and slowly, as if she were washing an infant brother or sister. Without lifting her eyes, she set about cleaning his leg. He tried hard not to wince, but the wound was hot and painful, and he flinched when she touched the place where the hurt was worst.

'I'm sorry,' she said. 'I'm trying not to hurt you.'

'You're doing very well. Ignore me if I recoil, it's quite involuntary.'

She gave him a quick startled look through her lashes, then turned to bathing his leg again.

'Your stocking is quite shredded away. Shall I take it off for you?'

'Can you?'

'I think so. I can free your shoe and pull off the stocking.'

She worked the stocking down behind the strands of rope, peeled it off carefully and put it aside as she eased his shoe on again. He realised that his foot had swollen. She peered closely at the injury, then leaned forward and sniffed it.

'I think it's quite clean. There's no putrefying smell.'

'Where did you learn to do that?'

She gave him a shy smile.

'I was one of fourteen children. I've often had wounds to bind. And sometimes my father would hurt himself about the farm, perhaps with the scythe at harvest time.'

'You live on a farm?'

She shook her head.

'All that was destroyed in the war. And our lord was for the king, so we were turned off our land. Then my father was killed. This hurt was done by a musket ball, wasn't it?'

'It was. How did you know that?'

'There's been much fighting in these parts. Yours is not the first wound I've cleaned, nor I don't suppose the last. The ball has passed right through the flesh of your calf, so you've been lucky. I think it should heal, but I'll bind it with what's left of your stocking.'

When she had finished dressing his leg, she helped him to eat and drink, which John did doggedly, knowing he must eat to fight off weakness. The pie was good—rich with thick gravy and tender pieces of beef and mushrooms. When he had eaten everything, and she had gathered up the tray to leave, he stopped her.

'Wait a moment. I'm grateful to you for your care. For binding my wound and for feeding me like the pelican in her piety. What's your name?'

'Martha.'

'A fitting name.'

She gave him the ghost of a smile.

'Martha or Mary? I've washed your leg, not your feet, and I've no oil for anointing. And truly I'm more Martha than Mary.'

He was startled.

'I don't cast myself in that role, though truly I am abused by mine enemies. You know your scripture.'

She shrugged.

'My eldest brother was very clever, he was to enter the church. Our lord was his patron. But both were killed fighting for the king. Now all my family is dead or scattered.'

She went to the door, then paused and said softly, 'Are you for the king? Is that why the soldiers use you so?'

'Nay, Martha, I am a Parliamentman. But I refused to countenance the killing of the king. So I am imprisoned and beaten. I believe in the middle way, the way to peace, but that's a dangerous philosophy in a time of passions so extreme. He was God's anointed, Charles Stuart, but he was arrogant and stubborn and blind to the changed times in which we live now.'

'He is dead, then, the king?'

'He is dead.'

Tears welled up in her eyes, and her shoulders slumped. John could think of no words to comfort her, but he said, 'The men who have seized the government of this land claim to act in the name of the people, but they too are corrupted by power. It will not always be so, Martha. Someday, this land must be healed. We cannot for ever tear each other apart in such hatred. '

'I pray you are right, sir.'

'Martha, tell me, where is this place? For I have no idea where we have been, or where they are taking me.'

'Why, this is Bicester, sir. 'Tis a market town in Oxfordshire.'

'I know it. So, we are heading north.'

'I must go, sir, or I shall be scolded for staying so long. Will you tell me your name?'

'My name is John. That's probably all that it's wise for you to know.'

'John. Who came to show the way.'

John shook his head.

'I cannot see my own way, Martha. Do not imagine me capable of showing the way to others.'

She was turning away and he longed to call her back again, the first person to have shown him kindness for weeks.

'Martha, wait!'

'Yes, sir?'

He hesitated.

'Will you . . . will you touch my hand, Martha? I would take yours if I could.'

She knelt down beside him, setting aside the tray, and laid her two hands over his where they were imprisoned under the rope. As she came near, he could smell her sweet clean skin. She leaned forward and kissed him lightly on the lips with her soft child's mouth. Then she scrambled to her feet, taking up the tray, and before John could speak she had slipped away, closing and locking the door behind her. John heard her swift steps descending the stairs and then suddenly a man's voice, shouting, and the crash of falling dishes and the crunch of a fist on flesh. And a girl's sharp cry, broken off.

ॐ

The journey continued later that same day. When John was pushed into the cart again, he found that more of the wooden crates had been loaded on board, so it seemed they were to deliver further supplies to the army. While he was in the cart under the eye of the four soldiers, they loosened the bonds about his arms, though not about his legs, so he was able to eat the scraps of food they threw him, which were increasingly poor and sparse. The good meal he had enjoyed at the inn must have been the gift of the innkeeper, or of the girl Martha. Now he had to survive on dry cheese rinds and ends of bread so stale he needed to soak them in the sour ale they allowed him before he could risk biting on them. The blows he had received to his face had loosened several of

267

his teeth. He had constantly to remind himself not to worry at them with his tongue, in the hope that if he let them be, they might in time sit firm in their sockets again.

The cart and its occupants continued their rambling way northwards, zigzagging across the countryside and stopping from time to time to deliver crates to camps sited at strategic crossroads, or to garrisons in towns or in manor houses seized from Royalists and now fortified against further attack. It seemed Cromwell and the generals were not yet sure whether the king's execution would provoke an uprising. John decided that the wandering route followed by the cart was an attempt to avoid detection by Royalist sympathisers, who might have attacked them and seized the military supplies for their own use.

Although Martha's care of his wound had probably saved his leg from festering, it did not heal quickly. A day or two after leaving Bicester, John developed a fever, which left him confused, so that afterwards he was never sure how long the journey had lasted. In some ways he was glad of the fever, for it sent him into a kind of half-sleep, which saved him the trouble of thinking about his plight, and helped the tedious hours pass more quickly, but it also had the effect of making him perpetually thirsty, and the soldiers would never give him enough to drink. In his more lucid moments, he noticed that his hands seemed to be withering, the skin dry and slack, the bones and sinews clearly visible. On the parts of his face not covered by stubble, the skin flaked off, making him wonder how strange he must look. Enough to frighten even a girl with as stout a heart as Martha. His head itched constantly from the lice and fleas that infested his hair, having migrated there from the straw in the bottom of the cart, and the wound on his leg continued to ooze, attracting flies. He was thankful the weather was still almost as cold as winter. In summer the insect life would have tormented him almost beyond bearing.

In the long shapeless hours lying in the cart, drifting in and out of feverish sleep, he found himself thinking constantly of Anne. Theirs had always been a marriage of minds as much as of bodies, for they had been friends long before they were lovers. When his father had first suggested to John Brandreth that a marriage between the families would be a good plan, Anne and he had smiled secretly at each other, for they had known since they were twelve years old that they would marry.

They had first seen each other as babies, carried to Weeford church every Sunday by their nursemaids, he from Swinfen Hall by carriage, she from Weeford Hall, a stone's throw from the church. They must have eyed each other even then, in their adjacent pews at the front of the church, each seeing the other as a fixed part of their shared lives of family and village and manor. No, he could not remember their first meeting. As small children, he and Anne and his sister Mary had played together, then she had gone for a while to live with relatives in Kent.

The spring when they were both nine, she had come home again, and that meeting he did remember, a memory as clear and bright as a cut jewel. He had gone down to the Swinfen lake one early morning with his fishing rod. The mist was rising from the grass, as it often did in the water meadow, so that the cows appeared to be wading up to their knees in clouds. As he neared the lake, he was indignant to see that there was someone already standing with a rod at his favourite place, a figure in breeches and a hat too large for his head, who turned and watched as he approached.

'Hey!' he shouted. 'What are you doing, poaching on our lake? Be off with you, before I set the servants on you.'

She was dressed in her brother's clothes, and she gave him an impudent smile. He glowered back, trying to appear threatening, then he snatched her rod and threw it aside. At that, she flew at him and began pummelling him with her fists. In a moment they were rolling over and over on the wet ground amongst the rushes, fighting like two lads.

'Nay, stop, stop, Anne,' he cried, for she was near to getting the better of him. 'I did but tease you. I know who you are.'

She was sitting astride him by now, her fingers twined in his hair, preparing to bang his head on the ground. Her hat had fallen off, her hair was tangled over her face, and she glowed with a mixture of anger and laughter.

'Apologise!' she demanded.

'I apologise,' he said at once. 'But it was an easy mistake. A scruffy lad, fishing where he had no right . . .'

She gave his head a small thump.

'Pax, pax, magistra! I'm sorry.' He heaved her off and sat up. 'Oh, it's good to have you home, Anne.'

She lay back amongst the rushes and gazed up through the shimmer of mist at the sky.

'I've missed all this so much. I've even missed you, John Swynfen.' She broke off the stem of a rush and began idly peeling it. 'My brother wouldn't thank you for calling his clothes scruffy.'

'Perhaps it was the wearer . . . Nay, nay! I'll have done.'

Suddenly, a look of alarm came over her face, and she tried to sit up, but thrashed about like a foundered calf.

'Oh, help me, John! I'm sinking into the marsh.'

He thought at first she was teasing him in her turn, then realised from her scared look that she was really in trouble. He lay on his stomach and reached out to her. The mud was already sucking her down, but as she struggled and he pulled, she came away from the marsh with a sucking sound and they both rolled over on to dry land.

'You owe me your life now,' he said.

That was when he first became aware of her as a separate person, when she had fought him like a boy, and he had pulled her out of the marsh. It was hard to believe, when he looked at the beautiful woman in her Westminster house, dressed in the finest Levantine silks, with jewels in her ears and clasped about her neck, that this was the same Anne who had fought him in the mud of the marsh. He had not reminded himself often enough that the two people were the same.

&

At last the day came when the fever seemed to have subsided somewhat, and he began to take more notice of his surroundings. There had been two days of late snow which lay deep on the fields which he could see out of the back of the cart. He overheard Tize and Ed talking about a final delivery to a detachment of horse stationed just north of the little town of Birmingham, and his heart leapt. A man might walk from Birmingham to Swinfen in less than a day; a man, that is, with two sound legs. Two sound legs, which John had not. Although the skin was beginning to close over his wound at last, he found when he climbed down from the cart at night that he could barely stand. The long confinement, and the ropes that tied his legs together all day long, were making him as crippled as an old man with the rheumatics. There was no danger than he might run away from his guards any more. He could barely hobble from cart to inn door and back again next morning.

But wasn't this a good omen? That they were near to Birmingham? Perhaps these men were to deliver him home, and the rigours of the journey had been meant merely as a punishment, to show the extent of the displeasure Cromwell and Ireton felt against him, for standing up so determinedly as an advocate for peace.

The army encampment where the soldiers unloaded the last of the crates was at a place called Whitehouse Common. It seemed to John that his guards, having kept him ignorant of his whereabouts for so long, were now deliberately allowing him to overhear their route as they neared his home, enough to arouse his suspicions. Given their natures and their behaviour towards him, they were more likely to be

270

tormenting him with this knowledge than holding it out as a happy promise of his journey's end. Leaving Whitehouse Common very early one morning, before dawn, they took the road that would lead past Weeford and Swinfen and so to Lichfield.

Sitting at the back of the cart, John watched the road unroll away behind them with growing excitement, which he attempted to hide. These woods, these small hills, were as familiar to him as his own fields. It was a bright morning when they passed Weeford and Thickbroome, where the Sylvesters now farmed. On the Weeford side of the road he caught sight of figures moving near the stables of the Wyatts' Blackbrook Farm, but no one turned to watch the cart passing on the road. Should he cry out? If the men of Patience's family realised he was being carrying past under their very noses, a bound prisoner, they would rush to his rescue, but Tize was sitting with that deadly musket across his knees. A man who could wing John a hundred yards away in the treacherous light of the moon could bring down any man running towards the cart in daylight. He glanced sideways at Tize and saw that the man was watching him, with a smile twitching his lips. The other soldiers might not make any connection between their prisoner and the country they were passing through, but Tize knew.

The cart passed over the crossroads and continued ahead. Unable to contain himself, John strained over the edge of the cart to catch a glimpse of the Swinfen lands as they passed. Patches of snow still lay on the ground, but the trees wore their first elusive shimmer of lime or gold or crimson, where the buds of the new leaves were forcing their way through the tough bark into the light. His heart was filled with a chaos of emotions; he longed to hold Anne in his arms again, to play with his children in the meadow beside the lake, to ride over his land and assure himself that all was in good heart, to climb the great oak in Simon's Piece and sit there as he had done as a boy, rocking gently in the wind, as if he stood on the deck of a man-of-war.

Tize leaned forward and clouted him on the side of the head with the butt of his musket.

'Don't lean out so far. Thinking of trying to run off, are you? I'll have that other leg of yours, if you do.'

John sank back and rested his forehead on his folded arms. His head throbbed with the blow, but he would not give the man the satisfaction of showing it.

Before long they were passing through Lichfield, where they stopped in the Market Square just long enough to demand food by the simple expedient of threatening the stallholders, then they were through the town and out again on the open road. For a moment John had hoped they were going to deliver him up to the magistrates in Lichfield, most of whom were old friends. Indeed, he was himself still a justice of the peace here, unless someone had thought to deprive him of that office. He cursed himself for a fool as they headed into the country. If he had simply rolled out of the cart in Lichfield, there would have been little the soldiers could have done. They were not likely to start shooting in the midst of a busy town on market day. Surely? Even if they had recaptured him—and he might have been able to seek the help of friends first—then the people of Lichfield would have known what was happening. Someone might have attempted to rescue him.

Or perhaps they would not. Would any in Lichfield recognise him in his present state? Filthy, bearded, limping, gaunt, in clothes as dirty as a tramp's, he bore little resemblance to the gentleman of Swinfen Hall, who used to ride into town to conduct manor business or county affairs with the other great men of the shire. He slumped down again, only occasionally glancing out to see how far from Lichfield they had travelled.

By mid-afternoon, they were heading along the eastern edge of Cannock Chase, and the driver was urging the great horses to a faster place. The Chase had long been the resort of outlaws and highwaymen; there was no doubting he wanted to be beyond its edge by the time night fell. Since the war had begun, this wild area had become notorious as a place of refuge for deserters and broken men of every sort. The only place of safety where the cart could stop now was Stafford, and that was some way off yet, the road in between shattered and ill-maintained during the bad years.

John sensed that the soldiers were growing nervous. Tize handed out muskets to the other three and bade them load, and light their slow matches, to be ready in case of any trouble. He himself bound John's arms again, so that he lay like an old hen trussed for the pot, only able to see one small corner of sky between the canvas flaps. Tize climbed through with his own musket to sit beside the driver. The horses, who rarely went at more than a walk, broke into a trot and then a slow canter, sending the cart, now lightened by the absence of its load of ammunition, swinging from side to side and pitching about. John bit his lip to stop himself crying out with pain as he was thrown from side to side, his wounded leg dashed against the rough framework of the cart. When he looked down, he saw that it was bleeding again.

To add to their troubles, the patch of sky showed that heavy clouds were building. If the rain came, the kind of rain that had flooded England since the king's execution, the cart might become hopelessly bogged down. If it fell as snow—and the day was cold enough—they could become snow-bound on the Chase. Many a man, native to this country and born within five miles of the Chase, had perished here.

For a time the horses kept up their canter, but the rhythm of their hooves changed as they began to tire with the long day, the hilly ground, and the fearful state of the road. They fell back to a lumbering trot. Not all the yells of the driver nor the vicious cracks of his whip could stir them up to a canter again. Though slower, the trotting pace of the horses was as uncomfortable for the passengers as the canter, for its abrupt rhythm jerked the cart violently, so that the soldiers clung on, swearing, and John rolled helplessly back and forth at their feet. Outside, it was nearly dark.

At last they heard the driver call out something. The soldiers stared at one another in alarm, but a few moments later Tize opened the canvas flap at the front of the cart and looked through.

'Stafford in sight, lads. We'll be there soon, though we won't outrun the storm.'

With that he climbed back inside, under the shelter of the hood, as the first wet snow began to fall. They heard the driver curse, and try again to hurry the horses along, but the great beasts had grown stubborn and slowed to a walk. Where John lay near the rear of the cart, the snow began to drift in on top of him, but after a while Will got up and laced the canvas together. Not, John was sure, as a kindness to him, but because the wind was whipping through the cart and making them all cold. He managed to roll on his side to ease his injured leg, and tried to rest.

It was long past dark by the time the cart finally came to a halt. For the last part of the journey the road had ascended steadily, until at last it was clear they were driving up a precipitous slope, where the horses' hooves slithered on the slippery ground. All the soldiers climbed out except Will, who was left to watch over John with his loaded musket lying ready on the floor beside him. John noticed that the slow match clipped to the side of it was still smouldering.

'Best watch your slow match,' he said, 'or you'll set straw and cart and all alight.' It was the first remark he had addressed to any of the soldiers for days.

Will jumped up in alarm and seized the musket. A small patch of straw where it had lain had already caught fire and he stamped on it, cursing.

'What's amiss?' Tize poked his head into the cart.

Will pointed to the wisps of smoke rising from the straw.

'Get him out of there,' said Tize, 'and shovel that straw out into the snow.'

They loosened the ropes around John's legs, but did not remove them, so that he fell heavily from the tailboard of the cart, and then had to shuffle his way through the snow like a hobbled horse. He saw now, with increasing apprehension, where they had arrived. The castle at Stafford had been a Royalist stronghold in the early part of the war. After it had fallen to the Parliamentary Army, the Committee for Stafford, of which young John Swynfen was a member, had ordered its destruction nearly seven years ago. The work had only been carried out in part before the Parliamentary forces had decided to make use of it themselves. It was now garrisoned by the New Model Army.

John was propelled into the guardhouse, where the soldiers on duty stared at him curiously. He could not tell whether they knew who he was—Stafford's own Member of Parliament returned to his constituency in such strange guise. His four guards, with whom he seemed to have lived a lifetime, had disappeared. The new soldiers removed the ropes from his legs and marched him away, stumbling across a courtyard and into the main castle building, then down a stone staircase to a corridor below the level of the ground.

One of the guards unhooked a ring of keys from his belt and opened a heavy studded door. In the light of the pitch torch carried by one of the men, John could see that this was a prison cell, with a bare wooden shelf to sleep on, and a narrow slit of window high in the wall, which might, in daytime, admit a little light. At one end of the wooden shelf there was a jug of water and a wooden platter with some bread and dry cheese on it. They made John sit on this bed while they untied the rest of the ropes.

'I thank you for that,' he said to the man with the keys, who regarded him sombrely as he groped about under the bed. Then John felt something clamped around his leg and heard the sound of a key turning. The men left him, taking the torch with them. Their footsteps faded away in the distance. He was alone in the darkness, in a damp cold dungeon under Stafford Castle, and he was shackled.

Chapter Twenty-One

A nne had given instructions to Biddy and Hester to scrub out all the cheese-making equipment. It had not been used since the summer, when a suckling calf had last been slaughtered for rennet and the stores of winter cheese made. The setting bowls, ladles, skimmers, rings, sieves, presses, and straining boards were now spotlessly clean and lined up in the dairy, which had also been washed throughout, walls and floors and sinks and all, for cheese-making is a delicate business. Every cheese-maker knows that dirt can spoil all the hard work quicker than winking. Anne herself had washed the fine hempen cheese clouts to her satisfaction.

At last there was enough milk to make a small batch of cheese, and their need was great. The one smoked ham, sliced as thin as paper and doled out with a miserly hand, was finished. Although Peter caught an occasional rabbit, there were few to be found. The summer floods and the winter cold had killed large numbers, and the foxes in the woods took most of those that were left. The cheese was sorely wanted, so the whole household might have some variation from the sparse diet of vegetables, porridge and bread. There was no escape from the constant pain of hunger. Most of the cheese would have to be eaten soft, or left only for a week or two to dry a little. The thin winter milk could not be expected to yield good cheese.

To Anne's relief, Agnes Lea's bunches of lady's bedstraw induced the warm fresh milk to curdle and separate. Anne, Bridget and Hester worked together on the first batch of cheese. When the milk had curdled in the setting dishes, they skimmed the wet curds off the whey and packed them into wooden hoops, which were lined with clouts and set upon the straining boards. These boards were then lifted on to wide basins to catch the whey as it drained, for no scrap of nourishment would be wasted. The whey remaining in the setting dishes they poured through colanders lined with cheese clouts. By now the whey was a thin liquid, slightly bluish in colour, but chilled in the dairy it made a good refreshing drink, and the children begged for it. Hester had baked barley bannocks that morning, and she now spread them with the

275

scrapings of curd left on the clouts in the colanders, sprinkled with a little salt.

After the children had eaten their dinner of curds and bannocks and scampered off, the women sat down at the dairy table to the same feast. Anne's sleeves were rolled above her elbows, and she was wearing an old russet gown and a white cap as plain as a maidservant. In the cool northern light of the dairy, the fine gold down on her forearms glinted, sprinkled over with a speckle of curds. She smiled to herself, imagining the disdainful looks of her elegant neighbours in Westminster if they might see her now.

'I've rinsed the lady's bedstraw in clean spring water,' she said, 'and hung it to dry. I don't know whether it will serve more than once, but I thought it worth a try.'

'We should always make cheese like this,' said Bridget in her gentle voice. 'I hate to see one of the suckling calves killed for the rennet.'

Hester was more practical. 'One calf gives plenty of rennet, and I'll be bound it sets the cheese better than the herbs.'

'Well,' said Anne, 'I know this is only a soft cheese, but I think it's very fine.'

The taste of the fresh cheese lingered on her tongue. She could have eaten far more, for like the rest of the household she was always ravenous, but this was a stolen feast and the cheeses set to dry in the hoops must feed the family in lieu of meat.

'If I can clear some of the snow from the herb garden,' said Bridget. 'I think I'll search for some sprigs of thyme and perhaps the first of the chives before we make the next batch. That way we can vary the cheeses. Later, we can wrap some in young nettle leaves.'

'In London,' said Anne, 'I tasted a cheese that had been wrapped in sage. It was somewhat strong in flavour, and a curious bright green, but a good flavour. And we can use some of these soft curds sweetened with honey, to make a pudding.'

She was full of energy and plans. So much had depended on this scheme of cheese-making; she was elated by her success. They need only survive a few more months, if they could find enough food to ward off starvation before late spring brought in the new season's bounty.

'I saw from my window this morning that they have set the plough to the land at Hill Hall,' said Bridget. 'The ground must no longer be so hard frozen. On Plough Monday, over in Weeford, everyone was saying the spring ploughing would be late this year, and so it is.'

'Did they mark Plough Monday?' said Anne. 'I was still in Oxford and saw no celebration, but perhaps the town doesn't honour such country festivals.'

'It wasn't celebrated in Weeford this year. The new minister is such a severe, uncompromising Puritan he frightens everyone.'

'Are the Turners still the tenants at Hill Hall?' Anne asked.

Bridget nodded. 'Aye, they're still there.'

Later that day, Anne opened the door of her father-in-law's estate office and went nervously in. She had never entered this room before except by invitation, and then no more than once or twice. The room smelled of tobacco and leather and gun oil, and somewhat of dog, though the dogs had now abandoned this unheated room for the kitchen. The rent table, with its row of little drawers, was covered with neat piles of paper, some of them tied in bundles with tape. There were quills, ink and wax, and under the window a great chest, a larger version of John's portable strong box. This one would take four strong men to carry it, for it was made of thick oak, bound with iron bands and secured with a lock bigger than her two hand-spans.

When Bridget had spoken of Hill Hall Farm, Anne recalled that on Lady Day the tenants would come to Swinfen Hall to pay their quarterly rents. Hill Hall was one of several large tenant farms that ringed the Swinfen manor. And as well as these and the many cottages on the estate, the family owned property in Freford and Lichfield, and—over Shropshire way—the manor of Lapley and houses in Shrewsbury. With both John's parents ill, and no word from John himself, it would fall to her to collect the rents, and she had no notion how much each tenant should pay. She searched the table and soon found the rent book, neatly set out in columns with the name of the tenant, the name of the property, and the amount. She slipped it into the capacious pocket of her apron to study later.

On the wall beside the window were two shelves of books. Richard Swynfen was not a scholar like his son, but he owned a compact library of books on country matters—hunting, hawking, agricultural oeconomy, and the breeding of cattle. Anne ran her finger along the shelves, reading the titles. Alsopp's *Compleat Husbandrie* caught her eye, and she took it down. Turning to the title page, she read that the book was: *A Compleat Husbandrie for ye Country Gentleman, Being a Most briefe & pleasaunte Treatyse, teachyng howe to Plowe, Sewe, & Harveste diverse Crops, with ye Breding and Care of ye Beastes.* It had been published in 1630, when it was on sale at the Sign of the Two Swans in St Paul's Churchyard. Below the title cavorted a smudged drawing of the goddess Ceres, smirking prettily as she poured out a cornucopia of fruits and vegetables across the bottom of the page.

Anne turned the pages thoughtfully. The book had a well-used look, as though her father-in-law made frequent reference to it. A sliver of faded silk ribbon marked a chapter on bee-keeping. There were diagrams of farm implements and drawings of distinguished bulls. At the end was a handy almanac of dates in the farming calendar. It would do no harm to borrow it. If she studied it, she might gain some insight into the mysteries that confronted her. She cast another despairing glance at the immense money chest. If there were debts owing, she must discover where the keys were kept.

A few days later, Josiah asked if he might discuss something with her. His air was so grave, she feared some of the stock might have been taken ill. She showed him in to the small parlour, where she preferred to conduct business, for she still felt like an intruder in the office. She invited Josiah to sit down, but he shook his head.

'My breeches be far too soiled, mistress,' he said, then stood, twisting his cap between his hands in silence.

'Is there trouble on the farm, Josiah?' she asked at last, as he seemed unable to make a beginning.

'Not to say trouble, exactly,' he said, relieved to be given a point at which to start. ''Tis near lambing time. Next week, I reckon.'

Anne nodded.

'Aye, of course. It must be about that time.'

'You see, mistress, I reckon us can't manage, just the boy and me. With the lambing and the spring ploughing and sowing. There always used to be six or eight of us on the farm. And Master Swynfen usually hires in the day labourers about now, and a shepherd for the lambing.'

'Oh.' Anne was startled. She should have thought of this. But she had no idea how to go about it, or how many men to hire, or what they should be paid. John used to go to Lichfield for the hiring fair, held in the spring and again at harvest time.

'Who worked here last year?' she asked cautiously.

'There was Henry Fletcher and Roland Heathe from Weeford,' said Josiah. 'That was all we could get, not near men enough. Labour's scare and costly. But Henry's nigh four score and not really able for 'un any longer. I heard he was ill before Christmas. Roland might come, but he's a weak kind of a man. Not unhandy with the beasts, though.'

'I see. Can you think on any man else?'

'I heard tell Henry's grandson Christopher is come home from the wars, but he has a holding of his own, that he rents from Master Pott. He may not want to hire himself out as well. Though the family may have need of the money.'

'How much do we pay?'

'One shilling and fourpence a day.' He saw her expression. 'I know, mistress, 'tis a terrible price. And dinner every day. And ale. And a suit of working clothes. You won't get any man for less, there's a fearful lack of working men with so many away in the army.'

Anne pondered. Two men would mean sixteen shillings a week additional wages. She had just enough coin left to pay that until Lady Day when the rents came in. And the clothes would not be a difficulty. The family kept chests of cast-off clothing for the labourers and for gifts to the poor. The problem would be feeding two extra men, farm labourers with hearty appetites from working all day in the fields.

'It's the meals, Josiah. I don't know how we can feed two more.'

He shrugged.

'We mun find the food someways. Else the work will not be done, and there'll be even less to eat come next winter.'

'You've the right of it, of course. Very well. You'd best go to Weeford this afternoon and see if you can hire Christopher Fletcher and Roland Heathe.'

'If the food be short, we can kill one of the beasts.'

'Nay!' said Anne vehemently. 'We must increase the breeding stock. I will not slaughter a single beast more unless we are all starving, and we're not reduced to that yet. With more milk soon, we can make more cheese. And the hens are laying better.'

Josiah still stood, turning his cap in his hands.

'Was there something else?'

'The shepherd, mistress. The master usually hires one in time for the lambing.'

'Aye, I remember. Then he takes the flock up to Packington Moor until autumn. Who did he hire last year?'

'Edward Weatherspoon. But he died of the consumption in January.' Josiah looked uncomfortable. 'There was a fellow come into the yard yesterday, asking for work. A strange fellow, with a strange way of speaking. He said he was a shepherd, but I don't know as we should trust 'un.'

'Not from these parts, then?'

'Nay, mistress.' He passed his hand over his face, and Anne suddenly realised how tired he looked. He had been carrying all the

279

burden of the farm work for months, and it was about to grow much heavier as spring drew on.

'I have a notion, Josiah. Suppose we hire him for a month, for the lambing. You will have him under your eye here in the farm, and the other men to help. At the end of a month, you will surely be able to judge whether he is a man for the sheep or not.'

He brightened.

'That's a grand idea, mistress. I told 'un to come back this afternoon, hoping I would have spoke to you.'

'Good. It's all settled, then. Anything else?'

'Well, mistress, should I start the ploughing?'

Anne pressed her hands to her head. How could she judge? She knew that if the ploughing were begun too soon, the soil might be so hard frozen it would rip the ploughshare from its shaft, or the plough horses might break a leg stumbling over the rock-like soil. Moreover, with all the rain there had been in the last year, the soil would be so full of water that when it did thaw completely, it would turn to bog, and then it would be impossible to put the horses on to it. And if the seed were sown too soon, the cold in the land would kill it. If it were left too late, the growing season was shortened and the harvest would be pitifully small. How could she judge?

'They've begun the ploughing at Hill Hall,' she said anxiously. 'Do you think we should start?'

'John Turner is a canny man. But I dunno . . . 'Tis not for me to say. The master always decides when us'll start.'

'Josiah, you're a far better judge of this than I am. If you think the land is ready, then you must start.'

It took some time for her to persuade him to take the responsibility for the decision, but in the end, looking worried and shaking his head, he went off, saying that he would go and feel the soil, and if it felt right, well then, he might make a start tomorrow, or soon.

When he had gone, Anne felt as exhausted as if she had climbed a hill. She had no notion how best to proceed, but there was no one else to take charge. The household here was larger than any she had run before, and the constant lack of food caused her a great deal of worry, but one household is much like another. There was satisfaction, too, in seeing the house, so cold and desolate when they arrived, thrumming again with life as it had done in the old days, when she had spent so much time here as a child. Once again the smell of baking hung in the air, the great fires of logs warmed the rooms, and the sound of children's laughter brightened the whole house.

It was another matter altogether to direct the great lands of Swinfen. Not only was there the management of the home farm. The mill must be overseen, the tenants dealt with, and the rents collected. Word would certainly have spread amongst the tenants that Master Swynfen was ill. There would be some who would use this as an excuse to absent themselves on Quarter Day. And because of the last terrible year, in which renewed fighting and stormy weather had combined to afflict farmers, there would be some who simply could not pay. In the past, Richard Swynfen had always been willing to commute some of the cash payment into kind, so that his tenants could pay in chickens or sheep or hams, but if the tenants were as hard-pressed as the manor, Anne could not accept food and leave them to starve. She would have to extend credit till next Quarter Day at Midsummer. Those who failed to appear at the Hall on Lady Day would have to be visited. John's father used to hire an agent to chase unpaid rents, such activity being beneath him as a gentleman landowner, but Anne had no idea whether anyone was still employed in this capacity. She might be obliged to ride round the tenants herself, and she shrank from the thought.

Then, as well as directing the home farm and the mill and managing the rents, if she was to act as lord of the manor, she had other responsibilities. It was the duty of the lord to undertake some of the repairs to cottages and farms, although she was not sure exactly what her obligations would be. Thomas Pott would know, of course, but she did not want to go begging like a helpless woman to her brother-in-law.

She picked up the *Compleat Husbandrie*, which she had begun to read in these last days. The early chapters were somewhat high-minded expositions of the philosophy of husbandry, interspersed with quotations from Plato's *Republic* and Vergil's *Georgics*. Now, however, she had reached a chapter on stock rearing. This year, she was determined to increase the flocks and herds, to make up the losses incurred during the war. There were so many things to take into account. How many cows or sheep could be grazed per acre? How much meadowland was needed for hay, to support how many animals over the winter? In Lincolnshire, she had read, they sometimes supplemented the winter feed for sheep with raw turnips. Such an idle fancy! Surely sheep would not eat turnips? Then there was the question of breeding the best animals, for it was not enough to breed simply for numbers. The ewes were already in lamb, and the cows in calf, but she must think ahead to next year. What would it cost to buy in a few prize animals to augment the herds, and could she judge them aright? Or would the farmers take advantage and cheat her? Should she buy the services of a prize bull?

She blushed to find herself thinking such thoughts. I am become quite as coarse as any yeoman, she told herself, yet she could not rouse herself to a true sense of shame. This was not a task she would ever have sought, but now that it was thrust upon her, she meant to show that the estate should not suffer under her guardianship.

Chickens, she thought. She could start with the chickens. A much shorter breeding cycle meant quicker returns. Besides, it was perfectly acceptable for the lady of the house to take an interest in the poultry. Already, with the increased allowance of food and the more sheltered quarters she had had Josiah build for them, the hens were laying better. Perhaps it was not too soon to select a broody hen and set her on a clutch of eggs. Her mind busy with calculations, she put her book aside, kilted up her skirts, and went out to the chicken house in search of a likely hen.

❧

Josiah hired Christopher Fletcher and Roland Heathe for general labouring, but the stranger who had come asking for work did not return that afternoon, so Anne sent Josiah to Lichfield next market day to see if he could secure the services of a shepherd. She also instructed him to call in at the posting inn to find whether any letter had arrived from John or from Samuel Gott, giving him coin enough to cover the cost of its carrying. While he was away, she supervised the boy Isaac, who was constructing a separate nesting pen for her broody hen. Being a dreamy lad, he was apt to forget what he was about. Biddy had once found him sitting in the barn with the pitchfork, gazing up at the patterns reflected off the snow on to the roof, quite forgetting to feed the cows.

When the pen was finished to her satisfaction, Ann filled the nesting box with clean straw and laid in it two eggs she had collected, which she had been keeping warm in the bosom of her dress. The small, rusty red hen was very biddable—happy as a kitten to be held and stroked. Anne set her in the nesting box, where she turned around and then settled down with every appearance of knowing what she was about. There was corn scattered on the floor and water in an old chipped dish. Everything had been done to make the hen as comfortable as might be. Now she must fulfil her part.

As Anne was crossing the yard towards the house, she saw a tall, angular figure making its way up the carriageway from the road. The man walked with great, loping strides, like one who is accustomed to making long journeys on foot. He had a smooth brown face, with many crinkles around his eyes from being out in all weathers. His hair had a reddish tint where it showed beneath a hat with a wide, drooping brim and what was surely a peacock's feather tucked into the band. Otherwise his clothes were plain, except for a glimpse of something brightly coloured between the buttons of his homespun coat, which was ornamented with curiously carved horn buttons. His knapsack looked heavy. He leaned upon a shepherd's crook as he walked, and a black and white dog followed at his heel. Anne knew at once that this must be the strange fellow Josiah had spoken of. Not only did he have the shepherd's indispensable tools of crook and dog, he carried with him an almost palpable air of foreignness.

The man stopped and swept off the hat with its ridiculously extravagant feather, and made her a bow equally extravagant.

'Tell me now, do I have the honour to be addressing the lady of the house?' said the stranger, in a low melodious voice. His English was perfect, but Anne understood why Josiah had described it as a strange way of speaking. The consonants were strong, especially the rolled letter r, while the vowels were sweetly drawled and the sentence rippled up and down like a phrase of song, till it lifted and flew off at the end. Anne knew she had heard something like it before, but could not place it.

'Aye, I'm the lady of the house, Mistress Anne Swynfen.'

'Then I'm wondering, lady, whether your man has spoken to you of me? I'm looking for work—a shepherd, as you'll have seen for yourself—and with the lambing upon us, it's questioning I am whether you could be doing with another pair of hands.'

'What's your name, and where are you from?'

'Brendan is my name, Brendan Donovan, and I'm after walking from Chester, and before that Holyhead in Wales, so.'

'You don't sound like a Welshman.'

'You'll be wanting to know my place of birth, lady—ah, 'twas a wee place in Galway, you'll never have heard tell of it.'

'You're an Irishman?'

'At your service, lady.'

He swept the ground again with his hat, raising quite a little whirlwind of chaff. The dog lay down with a resigned air, its nose upon its paws.

That was where she had heard his kind of speech before, and she realised why she could not immediately place it. About two years ago, she and John had attended dinner and a musical evening at the Colemans' house, and one of the party had been an Irish musician from Dublin, who had sung them some pretty Irish airs, but he had been a gentleman, with only the merest touch of the strange accent. It was not unpleasant, nor too difficult to understand, though this stranger's speech had something exaggerated and false about it. He did not seem quite trustworthy.

And Ireland was a terrible place of violent massacres. In the earliest days of the war, the Irish Catholics had set upon English settlers and slaughtered men, women, and even babies. Then the Protestants had turned the tables and slaughtered the Irish in their turn. John Clotworthy had great estates in Ireland, and she had heard him speak slightingly of the peasants there. Heathen barbarians and rogues to a man, he had called them. There had been talk amongst the politicians in London that the war would never be over until Ireland had been pacified.

'I'm afraid,' she said now, 'that my father-in-law will not allow you about the place if you are a Catholic.'

'And now why should I be a Catholic?' said the man merrily. 'Surely, there's many a good Protestant in Ireland.'

Anne looked at him thoughtfully. That was not quite a straight answer. However, her need for labour on the farm was great, and if the man did prove to be capable as a shepherd, it would solve one of her problems.

'Very well,' she said. 'I will hire you for one month, and we shall see how we fare, with the chance of more work afterwards, if you prove satisfactory.'

'That suits me fine, lady,' he said, with a curious gleam in his eye, almost of amusement. 'I'll be shaking your hand on the agreement.'

And to Anne's astonishment, he seized her hand and shook it as if she were a man. She was relieved he had not spit upon his palm first, as the farmers around here were wont to do. Indeed, his hand was remarkably clean for a man who was tramping rough about the country in search of work.

'You may come into the kitchen now for a bite and sup,' she said, ' and when my farm steward comes back from market, he'll show you where you may sleep and give you your duties. He expects the first lamb in the next few days.'

'In that case, lady, I'll be looking at the ewes before I take food. You'll have them penned in the barn here?'

'Yes, but—'

He was striding away from her towards the barn before she could stop him. The dog leapt instantly to its feet and padded behind, as quiet and close as a shadow. A little annoyed but amused, she followed, to find him already amongst the sheep, his crook and pack laid aside. He was crooning to the ewes in some strange words she could not understand and the ewes, who were usually restless with strangers, especially when they were so close to dropping their lambs, accepted him peacefully. He moved amongst them, running his hands over their sides, sometimes cupping his hand under a chin and lifting a ewe's face so he could look into her eyes for all the world as if she were a person.

'This one is near her time,' he said, his fingers twined in the wool of one of the ewes. 'We'll be needing to separate her out from the others. Those will be spare hurdles I'm seeing, stacked up by the door. Lady that you are, now, will you be giving me a hand to set up a pen for her?'

Anne did as she was bid, never questioning what he said, for he had an air of certainty about him. They set up the hurdles and he led the ewe into the improvised pen.

'Now, if you'll be sending someone out to me with a bucket of warm water, I'm for staying with the ewe.'

'As you wish. And I'll have them bring you some food, too.'

Later, when the family had dined, she fed the baby. Bridget, sitting with her at her needlework, expressed again her concern that the child was still unbaptised.

'She's blessedly healthy and strong, so there are no worries on that score, but it's long past time for it. You must surely do your godly duty by the babe, Anne.'

'I've decided to call her Jane,' Anne said, a defensive note in her voice, 'after my mother, though I had hoped I could wait to decide until John and I could choose a name together.'

'I'm sure John will be content with Jane,' said Bridget. 'It's a family name of ours as well. But what do you intend to do about her baptism?'

Anne stirred uncomfortably. 'I don't know. I feel her father should be here.' She did not voice her real fears. If Jane was baptised without John being present, it seemed a kind of admission that he would never be coming home. When the baby was settled back in her cradle, Anne went out to the barn through a thin drizzle, to see how the new shepherd was faring with the ewe. She had changed into a finer dress before dinner, her homespun being muddied from her earlier visit to the chickens, and she now threw a cloak around her gown to keep it from the wet.

Brendan was seated on the ground beside the ewe who was in the last stages of labour. He was stroking her head and murmuring to her. When he heard Anne's footsteps at the barn door, he spoke without looking up.

'Stop there. She's not to be frightened, and her about to drop the lamb.'

Anne stopped instantly and waited. She knew better than to speak or interfere. A few more minutes, and the lamb slithered into the world. Brendan was busy wiping its face, and giving it to the mother to feed, before he gathered up the bloody straw, stretched, and stepped over the hurdles with those long legs of his. Only then did he glance up and notice her. His expression was startled as he took in the sight of her in silk and lace, with a fur-trimmed cloak.

'Why, my lady, I took it for the servant come back for the crocks. I would never have been speaking to you like that.'

He eyed her with such knowing admiration that she clutched her cloak about her in consternation.

'I came to see how the ewe was faring.'

'All's well with her. And none others due this while. When I've made sure the lamb is feeding, I'll be coming in to the fire to warm myself.'

'Aye,' said Anne, 'you've seen where the door to the kitchen is, across the yard.'

He gave her a long, thoughtful look, and the admiration faded, to be replaced by an expression so cold and hostile that it set her heart lurching with something like fear.

She stumbled outside again and gulped the fresh air. Perhaps she had been unwise to hire this man, knowing nothing about him. No man had looked at her in that frank manner since she had married. No servant had ever dared to look at her in that manner. There was something unsettling about Brendan Donovan, more than that penetrating look in the eye. He had an air as if he knew her, stranger that he was. And that ill-assorted mixture of . . . what almost seemed to be hatred and . . . well, lust was the only honest name for it. But the man did seem to know his work. Perhaps she was misreading him entirely. In her confusion, she was relieved to see Josiah riding up the carriageway from the Lichfield road on one of the farm horses. She remembered suddenly that he might have hired another shepherd in the town, in which case she might find herself with two. But Josiah had more weighty matters on his mind.

'There's grave news from London, mistress,' he said, almost before his feet touched the ground.

Anne's hand flew to her heart.

'John?'

'Not the master. The king. He's executed at Whitehall, more than a month since. The Monarchy is abolished, and the House of Lords, and Cromwell rules in the king's place.'

'Surely all the world knew this.' The stranger was standing at the barn door watching them.

'We live very isolated here,' said Anne, not turning round. 'No one has been into Lichfield even, these three weeks past.'

'You do not seem overly grieved, lady. You're not of the king's party, then?'

'I am not.' She turned slowly to look at him, trying to guess from his expression which faction he followed. His face was bland, the eyes wide and guileless. 'But I hoped it would not come to this.' She bit back the words that almost flew from her lips: *John would have managed this better, they would not have killed the king.* But she knew it was safer to say nothing about John to one who might be . . . what? She did not know what, but the stranger seemed to be more than a mere wandering Irish shepherd.

'I had no luck in hiring a shepherd, mistress,' said Josiah, eyeing the stranger somewhat pointedly.

'Brendan Donovan is hired for a month, to see how he fares. He has birthed a lamb already.'

Josiah started for the barn, leading his horse, anxious for his ewes, but Anne laid a hand on his sleeve.

'Was there a letter?'

'I forgot.' Josiah felt in his pocket and brought out a sheet of paper, folded and sealed, and passed it to her. 'And here's the remainder of the money. I fear it's not the letter you wanted.'

Anne looked at the letter. It was addressed to Nan, and came from Susanna Perwick, true to her word. She sighed. There was at least some consolation in this. If one letter had come through all the perils from London, others might also. She turned her back on the men, forgetting them at once, and walked slowly back to the house, a dark oppression gripping her.

This killing of the king changed everything. All that John had worked for was now destroyed. No longer could the country hope for a peaceful settlement. On the one hand, John had suspected Cromwell and Ireton of plotting to set up a despotism, and now it seemed that it was accomplished. And on the other, the king's party would certainly not acknowledge defeat because of the death of Charles Stuart. The Prince of Wales lived still, and his father's party would rally around him. Indeed, there might be many more who would find it easier to support the son, now that he was free of the liability of his arrogant and untrustworthy father. Those who had remained neutral in the past might well join the young prince, who was well liked. Certainly, many men formerly on the Parliament side would no longer support Cromwell, now that he had destroyed that very Parliament. There would be more battles, more men dead, more women raped, more children orphaned, more villages burned. She pressed her hands against her stomach, as if the pain had seized her in the very guts.

Why was there no word of John? Would she ever see him again? Until this moment, she had pushed away from her mind the thought that he might be dead, refusing to believe in the possibility, but now she saw clearly that men who could kill God's anointed king would not scruple to cut the throat of a man who had opposed them over and over again, for all the world to hear, in the public forum of the Commons. John's speeches were recorded in the Commons journals, his words reported in the newspapers, his most eloquent phrases quoted at dinner tables. How could he escape their wrath?

After handing over Susanna's letter to Nan, Anne walked alone down to the lakeside, near the spot where she and John had once tussled as children at the edge of the marsh. The late afternoon sky was dark and heavy with imminent rain and the lake lay still and dull as a pewter plate. A yard or two into the reeds a solitary heron stood, angular and articulated as a puppet contrived from twigs, one scaly leg thrust down into the water as if its body grew from this stem, the other tucked into its feathers, with only the claws curled into view. Its glassy eye was fixed on her without acknowledging her presence, its thoughts withdrawn, concentrated inwards, as though it listened for its prey within the hollow of its skull. The woman standing with her shoes pressing rings of water from the mud was no more to him than the belt of willows beyond her or the boat up-turned for the winter between them. He had the air of an anchorite who, if he noticed her at all, deplored her interruption of his self-contained contemplation. Something about his solitary purposefulness reminded her of the Irish shepherd.

಄

The days, little by little, were beginning to lengthen, and the pace of work on the estate quickened. Josiah had decided that the Irishman could be trusted with the sheep, and left most of the lambing to him, with the occasional assistance of Roland Heathe, who walked over every morning from Weeford. As Josiah had warned, he was a weak sort of man, not able for heavy work, but he and Brendan established some sort of trust in each other, and lost but a single lamb, one of a pair of twins. In the meanwhile, Josiah and Christopher Fletcher set to the spring ploughing, Josiah leading the team, who were accustomed to him, and Christopher guiding the heavy plough through the rich red soil of the Swinfen fields. All the household had been cheered when Christopher had agreed to hire on, for he was a strong young man in his twenties, beside whom Josiah and Peter looked the old men they were. Christopher, too, walked over from Weeford, and went home in the evening to hoe and plant his own holding, while his young wife tended their one cow and one pig. The boy Isaac was left to the tasks about the yard, feeding the sows and the cattle, and milking, with Brendan and Roland lending a hand when they were not occupied with the sheep. The shepherd would stay on the home farm until calving and sowing and shearing were finished, then, in the warmer weather, he would drive the shorn flock of sheep up to Packington Moor and live in the bothy.

Josiah was still reluctant to take decisions about the work of the farm, so Anne received him every morning after milking, when they would sit together in the small parlour and puzzle out between them what to do. They decided which field must be left fallow, where to plant wheat, oats, barley and peas, when to move the cattle into the meadow beside the lake, and the sheep into the smaller meadow beyond, on the rising ground between the lake and the woods. On the day the cows, heavy with calf, were moved down to the meadow, Anne felt as though the worst trials of winter could at last be put behind her.

On that same day also, Brendan and Roland docked the tails of the lambs. It must be done, but Anne found she was not quite farmer enough to watch. Instead she took out paper and pen, and planned the planting of her vegetables. Nan, who had been beside herself with excitement at receiving her first letter, begged to be allowed to sit beside her at the parlour table and write a reply to Susanna, so that Anne's thoughts on onions, carrots, pompions, leeks, and lettuces were constantly being interrupted as her daughter laboriously penned an account of all that was happening at Swinfen. When Anne looked the letter over, with its blots and misspelling, she realised with a sense of guilt that she had been neglecting the children's lessons.

Hester made a hotpot of the lambs' tails, stewed with ale and onions and a few carrots stored in sand since last year, and the whole household sat down that night to the first fresh meat, apart from rabbit, that they had eaten for months.

'I'm sorry for the little lambs,' Nan said, her mouth full of stew, 'but this is very good.'

'It's stupid to be sorry for them,' said Jack. 'Brendan does it so quick, they don't feel anything. Then he tars the stumps and they run back to their dams.'

'Were you *watching*?' Nan said, aghast.

'Of course. A gentleman must know about everything on his estate.'

'You won't inherit Swinfen. It will belong to Dick.'

'I shall get an estate of my own. I'll marry a rich heiress.'

'First you'll need to find one,' said Patience.

'Anyway,' said Jack, 'tomorrow Brendan is going to make me a fishing rod, so I can fish in the lake, or up in the high pool. Brendan says now spring has come, sure the fish are just waiting to jump on to the hook.'

Anne hid her smile, for Jack had fallen into the Irishman's very way of speaking.

'You must take care, Jack, if you go fishing. There are some dangerous boggy places around the lake.'

'Of course I'll be careful, Mama. But now I am the man of the family, I must try to provide for you.'

Was this what the child believed? He had just passed his eighth birthday, he should be enjoying childhood with a light heart. Yet with both his father and his eldest brother absent, he had some reason for regarding himself as the head of the family. She was, after all, merely his mother, and a woman.

Ever since her visit to Weeford Hall to bring Bridget back to Swinfen, Anne had been uneasy about the way matters had been left with Mary, for Mary was her oldest friend and she longed not to quarrel with her. One morning, after the day's discussion with Josiah, she rode the mare over to Weeford, with a gift of some of the peppercorns she had brought home from London and a few of the rarer ingredients she had purchased from the apothecary in Oxford. Mary was wandering about her flower garden in a large straw hat, cutting early blooms for the house and passing them to a maid to carry in a basket. Anne fell in beside her, admiring the formal beds edged with box which her mother had laid out and Mary had filled with a riotous abundance of foxgloves, hollyhocks and delphiniums, which had begun to thrust their tall heads up towards the warmer rays of the sun.

'I've brought you these,' said Anne awkwardly, handing over her gifts.

Mary nodded, her face turned away, and handed the spices to the maid.

'I've come to apologise,' said Anne.

Mary flashed her a look from under the brim of her hat.

'Take the basket in, Tess,' she said, 'and these scissors. Put the flowers in water in the pantry and I will see to them later.'

The girl curtseyed and turned back to the house, while Mary headed swiftly away down the garden, with Anne following humbly at her heels. They sat down on a turf seat under an arbour, where a white climbing rose was coming into bud.

'Well?' said Mary, uncompromisingly.

Anne flushed at this brusque response, but continue gamely. 'You've always been my dearest friend, Mary, and I hope our last meeting has not marred that.'

Mary said nothing.

'I'm not certain why you are angry with me,' Anne went on, somewhat desperately. 'I am only endeavouring my best for Swinfen and the family. And you did not truly want Bridget here with you, did you? As a servant? You said it was difficult for you both. She's needed at Swinfen. She has taken over most of the nursing of your parents.'

'No doubt you are glad of her, then.'

'Yes. I am glad of her.'

'And do you still think you are fit and capable to run my father's estate? It is Thomas who should take charge.'

Anne felt a little spurt of anger.

'Mary, you know that Thomas has enough to do, managing the Weeford estate. I know that if I need help I can turn to him, and I know that his advice will be valuable, and kindly given.'

'Indeed it will.' Mary's tone was somewhat softened.

'Oh, Mary, let us be friends again!' Tears came into Anne's eyes as she threw her arms around her sister-in-law.

Mary pushed back her straw hat and Anne saw that tears were also running down her cheeks. She leaned forward and kissed Anne. 'Anne, my dear, I never wanted to quarrel with you! Of course we are friends. How could we be other than dearest friends!'

She hugged Anne and laughed.

'I've have been trying to pluck up my courage to come and apologise to you! Come inside, the sun is growing too hot. We'll have some small ale I have cooling in the dairy, and you shall tell me what you have been doing these weeks past.'

The men all being occupied with work about the manor, Anne decided next morning that she would ride to Lichfield to purchase the seeds for her vegetable garden. Roland had been set to dig it over with Isaac's help. And she had warned Brendan to have his eye on Jack at the lake after he had made the fishing rod, to ensure that the young fisherman did not fall in, carried away by his new enthusiasm.

'Sure, and does the lad not know how to swim?' said Brendan. 'Then it's the teaching of him I should have, and the other laddies.'

'Perhaps,' said Anne. 'They've been living in Westminster these three years past, with nowhere safe for them to swim. When the weather is warmer, we shall see.' She was not sure that she would trust the Irishman alone with her children. There was something calculating in this offer to teach the boys to swim.

The ride to town on Brandy was very different from the cold journey to buy hay just after her return to Swinfen. The air was full of birds and birdsong, the rich scent of freshly turned earth rose from the fields, and the leaves on the trees were unfolding like clenched hands opening out their fingers to the sun. She rode first to Hill Hall Farm to speak to Mistress Turner, where she learned that one of the chimneys had partially fallen during a winter storm. She promised to hire a stonemason from Lichfield once she had ridden round the rest of the tenant properties to see what other work there might be for him.

In Lichfield there was a reliable seedsman, William Johnson, from whom Anne had always bought her vegetable seed when she lived at Thickbroome, and she soon had the packets made up, labelled, and tied into a parcel. The lad who worked in the shop looked at her with a curious smile as he handed it to her, and she realised, with a shiver, that he was one of those who had followed her, jeering, when she had tried to do business with Sylvester and the other farmers. She was glad to leave the shop. In the street she greeted a few of the townsfolk, but their replies were reserved, even curt. One man, a yeoman farmer whose land lay to the northeast of Swinfen, turned away without a word and spat into the dust. Anne recoiled from him, shocked.

This was not a market day, so the town was quieter than usual. Despite her uneasy sense of half-hidden hostility, it was pleasant to be free of work and decisions about the farm for one morning, so she decided to stroll about the streets in the spring sunshine. It was the first time she had done so since her return from London and she found the town a bitter sight.

The third siege of Lichfield, almost three years ago, had wreaked terrible destruction. Many houses bore the scars of shelling and musket fire, and most of Beacon Street had been burnt to the ground. But worse, far worse: during those same months of siege, the plague had raged through Lichfield, spreading its inexorable, insidious terror, killing a third of the townsfolk. In the past, the town had been mercifully spared the scourge of the plague, but the two armies had brought the infection with them as they crowded into the narrow old streets. Within the space of a few years, the quiet country town of her girlhood, slumbering in its dreams of vanished mediaeval glory, had been visited with an apocalypse of war, fire, plague, and famine. Many of the people stared at her with haunted eyes, and moved with the fearful, hunched gait of those who walk amongst the dead and dying.

She went past the Minster Pool and through the cathedral close. The Royalist garrison had turned the cathedral into a fortified stronghold, and Sir William Brereton, at the head of the Parliamentary troops, had shelled it from all sides. The bishop's palace and the canons' houses, nearly demolished in the bombardment, cowered empty as skulls, the close was strewn with the debris of war, the cathedral glass shattered, the grass cratered with shell holes. The two smaller spires of the cathedral were still intact, but Royalist snipers had used the great central spire as a vantage point from which to pick off their enemies. Brereton had pounded it with his Parliamentary guns until it collapsed into the nave. When she stepped inside, the once beautiful building seemed cold and forbidding, stripped down to Puritan austerity. The altar had been moved down into the body of the nave, as empty of meaning as a tavern table, and all the embroidered cloths and vestments had disappeared. The rubble from the spire was still strewn over the chancel and nave, and stone dust had drifted everywhere. Most of the roof gaped open to the sky. When she saw a minister in stark Puritan dress hurrying towards her from the ruined choir, with a forbidding expression on his face, she slipped away and almost ran back to the Market Square.

She had left Brandy in the stable of the Black Swan, and she called in now to collect her horse and also to ask whether any letters had by chance come for Swinfen.

'There's one come yesterday,' said Robert Verey. 'I have business in Tamworth next week, and if no one from Swinfen had come to collect it, I was going to bring it and see how you were all faring.'

'Thanks to your help with buying the hay, the stock have endured the winter and are just turned out to pasture. I think we shall survive after all.'

'Excellent, excellent!' He beamed at her. 'Now, where is that letter?'

He rummaged amongst the papers on his desk.

'Here it is. That's sixpence to pay, I'm afraid, Mistress Swynfen. It has come a long journey.'

She paid it gladly, and bought a glass of ale, too, to drink while she sat and read the letter. It was from Samuel Gott.

Battle, Sussex

Deare ffreind, Mistress Swynfen

I crave y^r pardon on two counts — ye longe delay in replying to y^{rs} & ye having to sende this by public mail (I feare wee may no longer speake of royal mail) for which y^u must paye, I no longer having ye right to free passage of mail being seclud'd as a member of Parlyament. Y^r lettre missing mee in London, it follow'd mee at ye last to Sussex, where wee live verie quietly away from ye busyness of London. It therefore being difficult for mee to get worde of y^r husband. Y^e most I can lerne is this, that ye moste part of ye prisoners taken by ye army are now set free, some to a kinde of prison within theire owne houses. One is escap'd abroad, Col. Ed Massey, who has nowe declar'd for ye young king. Still held at Windsor are those that were taken there in decembre last, viz. Waller, Browne, Clotworthy, & Copley, & Sir Wm Lewis sente there afterwards, all held without trial. Of some I can get noe news, & I greive that my deare ffreind John is amongst them. He was last seen taken to Whitehall Palace with v or vi otheres, & was then put into a kind of cart. None have seene him since. I praye you, do not greive, for I beleive that if ye worst had befallen him, his many ffreinds would have worde of it. I beseeche y^u, keep up y^{ur} courage in these terrible times & I will send any further worde when I have them.

I beg y^u give my remembrance to Master & Mistress Swynfen. My wife sends y^u her lovinge regards.

Y^r constant & true ffreind,

Saml Gott

Chapter Twenty-Two

Dick had been travelling for some time now with the gypsies. For that was what they were, he had learned, these dark, secretive people with their strange language, though they called themselves the Romany people. They were kind to him, but distant. They accepted him into their company because their leader Waldo had said it was to be so, but they showed neither pleasure nor resentment. Dick was determined that he should not seem like a beggar amongst them, so he strove his hardest to make himself useful, although he soon realised that boys much younger than he found some amusement at his efforts, even if they were careful to hide it from their elders. They had such multifarious skills, these vagabond children. Any one of them above the age of four or five could catch the half-wild ponies, leap on to their backs and gallop about a meadow without either saddle or bridle. By twisting their fingers in a horse's mane and guiding it with their knees, they could perform complex manoeuvres like the riders he had once seen at a fair in London.

The women treated him like the other boys, sending him to fetch water or steal a chicken, but he usually came back empty-handed, a failure which shamed him more than the thought of stealing. Even the very small children could slip a hand under a hen and remove her eggs without causing her to stir. The only time Dick tried this, the hen set up such a squawking that he ruined the expedition for the other children, so they all had to run away and find another farm to raid. He was bigger than most of those who were counted as boys still, but he came to realise, humbly, that the boys of his own age were indeed already men by the gypsies' standards, several of them married. They could shoot a deer silently with bow and arrow, and have it gralloched and hidden away before any keeper came near. The punishment for killing a deer was death or branding or the loss of an ear, but this seemed not to concern them. Dick had hunted deer at home, for there were deer in the Swinfen forests, but he had hunted with a gun, accompanied by servants to cut up the carcass. Now he watched the business carefully, since he might need these skills once he left the gypsies.

For they were not travelling in the right direction. Waldo told Dick they were headed westward for Herefordshire, where there were a few landowners who would allow them to encamp for a while, and other manors that had been so overthrown by the war that there were good pickings amongst the game, the families who had lived there having been killed or gone away.

'There's a house called Brampton Bryan,' said Waldo, 'where we'll stay a while. It was a grand place once, and there are deer and pheasants a-plenty. But it stood for the Parliament, when all around were for the king. It held out against the siege for a long time, and my lady Brilliana defended it without her lord, who was away from home at the Parliament. She used to be kind to us, but she's dead now. Some say the siege broke her heart, and then the house was taken at last and destroyed.'

Dick knew the story. How that gallant lady, not young but as courageous as any man, had held out for months against bombardment and starvation, with her small band of loyal women and servants. And he himself knew Lady Brilliana's husband, Sir Robert Harley, and their son Edward.

'My father knows . . .' he began, then clamped his mouth shut.

Waldo nodded.

'Better not to speak of such things, eh, boy? We don't ask your business, and you don't ask ours.'

'But I do wonder,' said Dick, 'which side you favour in the war.'

Waldo laughed.

'We take no sides, we people of the road. We slip between the spaces in the lives of such people as yourself, and you never notice us. Better that way. Better to take no sides. Better to save your skin and survive.'

'But have you remained quite unscathed in all the fighting?'

'Not altogether. When we hear an army coming, we fade away into the forest. And it's not hard to hear an army coming, even when they're some miles away, when the earth itself echoes with the feet of men and horses. We haven't always been so lucky when we've stumbled on small groups of men. But mostly we've escaped unnoticed.'

There was, thought Dick, much to commend itself in such an attitude. Where had his father's idealism led, when all was said and done? Failure and prison. Now that he was in the company of the gypsies, he was gaining a taste for the open road. With a good fire and hot food in the evening, and a blanket to roll himself in when they were packed warmly together in the carts at night, he was far happier than when he had been wandering alone. The blankets—and his companions—might be somewhat verminous, and he might need to keep a sharp eye that his cat was not mauled by one of the great watch dogs, but he was safe and free from hunger. Common sense told him, however, that he must part company with his friends some day and make his way to Staffordshire.

'After you have been to Brampton Bryan,' he said to Waldo, 'where will you go then? For my road lies further east.'

'We may stay in Herefordshire till spring. We often find work there, for the crops are seasonal, and the farmers always hire extra hands. We won't go further west, for Wales is a bitter place in winter. Or we may go east, the way you want to travel. All the farms are short-handed since the war. We shall see what we shall see.'

And with that Dick had to be content.

Brampton Bryan was a wretched sight. Fire had gutted the beautiful castle after it was seized and looted, the roof had fallen in, and the windows had shattered in the heat. In the six years since the siege, good building stone had been prised from the broken walls, and plants had taken root in crevices. A rowan sprouted just inside the carved framework of the front door, and the brown skeletons of last year's weeds poked through the drifts of snow still lying on the few gables which remained intact.

Dick prowled around the house, ignoring for once the general order to the children to gather firewood. What if he were to reach home and find that Swinfen Hall was reduced to such a ruin, burnt timbers lying in the great hall, barns and stables razed to the ground, his parents' bed fallen through the floor and smashed into the parlour table? Would that be the price of his father's long struggle to do what was right? It all rose so clearly in his mind, that it seemed like a vision of what had truly happened. For a moment he was filled with blind horror. Perhaps his whole family was already slaughtered, and he was alone in the world, doomed to roam as a gypsy for the rest of his days. Suddenly this vagabond life seemed a terrible thing, a flight from his own real life of warmth and family and friends, a flight from the cruel face of war, truly, but also a flight from all he had been taught about a man's purpose in life. The gypsies had been good to him, but there was something cold about them. He was not of the same blood, nor held the same beliefs. He could never be one with them, never be altogether trusted, never be loved. He wanted to feel his mother's arms around him, as if he were a little boy again.

Because his eyes blurred for a moment with unshed tears, he did not notice where he was putting his feet, and he tripped over something sticking up from the part-melted snow. He bent to pick it up. It was a little wooden figure, a mother and child. Not a Madonna, surely, for the Harleys were as Protestant as the Swynfens. No, simply a woman, any woman, a cottager perhaps, seated and cradling her baby on her lap. It was finely carved from a pale smooth wood he could not name, but valueless to the soldiers who had destroyed Brampton Bryan and brought about the lady Brilliana's death. Not being made of precious metal or adorned in any way, it had been ignored by the looters. Dick crouched down and ran his dirty thumb over the smooth contours of the woman's mantle. It might be worthless, but it took his fancy. And it seemed like some kind of omen. He slipped it into his pocket, where he could finger it, and if he felt guilty at behaving no better than those other looters, he consoled himself that he could always return it to the Harleys when next he saw them. He patted Ginger, who was curled up in her usual place inside his shirt, and went in search of firewood. He was lucky enough to find a long piece of linen-fold panelling, only partially charred at one end. Split into smaller pieces, it would keep the cookfire going for some time this evening.

So winter ended and the snow melted, while the gypsies remained encamped in the woods near Brampton Bryan. As Waldo had foretold, the pickings were good. They ate meat two or three times a day, there was abundant firewood, and there were pheasants and partridges to be trapped in the gypsies' cunning snares. Dick knew that, as a gentleman bred, he should despise such low practices, but with every day that passed, he was thinking more like a gypsy and less like a gentleman. Why hunt game with all the noise and disturbance of men and dogs, and the habitual inaccuracy of the gun, when both deer and birds could be killed silently, and with far less trouble, by means of the arrow or the snare? The gypsies were not precisely lazy, Dick decided, but practical. Their skills were directed towards living their lives with little fruitless effort. Where the gentleman landowner despised the snaring of pheasants, the itinerant gypsy despised the ceremony and parade of the leisurely shoot. Perhaps if the gentleman were always dependent on his own skills to feed his family, he would not be so ready to condemn the methods of the gypsy. Dick remembered the poachers at home in Staffordshire, who would sometimes be brought before his father, who was a justice of the peace. He had once been taken to watch a session of the court, that he might learn what his own duties would be when he inherited the land. His father was known as a just and indeed a merciful man, but even with the most gentle interpretation, the laws against poaching were fearsome. Not even John could always spare the malefactor.

As spring began to turn the wood green, Waldo made several journeys away from the camp, sometimes staying overnight. Then one evening he called all his people together after the evening meal had been eaten. He spoke in Romany, but repeated his words in English, for Dick's benefit.

'It seems,' he said, 'that many of those who've hired us in the past are either gone away or dead or come to poverty. Last year's bad harvests mean those who remain have no coin to hire outsiders such as ourselves. They'll give work only to those of their neighbours who are reduced to beggary or become masterless men, and who're ready to work for no more than food or to pay off their debts. We can look for nothing here, so we'll return into the heart of the country, where the estates are larger and richer, and may have fared less ill from the disasters of war and weather. Our young friend here, who comes from those parts,' he pointed to Dick, 'may be some help to us in finding those farmers who are willing to take on day labourers.'

Dick smiled and nodded, but secretly he feared that he was in no position to give such help. He had been away in London for more than three years. Much would have changed in that time. Some would have lost their lands during the war, new men would have made profitable purchases when such opportunities offered. He was also certain that his own grandfather would have no dealings with the gypsies. For the first time he felt guilty that, in this carefree life he had been leading, he had given no thought to how worried his mother and his grandparents would be. By now Charterhouse must have reported his absence. His mother would believe him dead, or imprisoned like his father. He felt a mixture of relief and sadness when Waldo announced that the next day they would trap as much food as possible for their journey, then on the following morning pack up their camp and head north and eastwards, into Shropshire first, and then on to the county of Stafford.

The cell in Stafford Castle was damp and chill, the bed painfully hard, and the shackle on his leg both degrading and tormenting, but it was the lack of human contact which distressed John most. Rob a man of human company and his world is peopled with the spectres of his own feverish imaginings. He caught himself muttering aloud as he dragged his chain back and forth across the few yards of stone flags, yet the words floated without meaning in the dank air. His very thoughts flitted like may-bugs. Moments after some word or question or idea passed through his mind, it had vanished irrecoverably into grey fog. If a man cannot even follow the movements of his own mind, is he going mad?

Twice a day, a silent guard brought him food, always the same— a squat earthenware jug of water, a small loaf of bread (fresh in the morning, stale in the evening), and a lump of hard, dry cheese. He thought that if ever he left this place, he would never eat cheese again in his life. The chain allowed him movement enough to walk back and forth a short way in his cell, but not to come near either the door or the window, which was, in any case, out of reach above his head. He had made of the tattered remains of his stocking a pad to protect his wound from the chafing of the leg iron. The rough journey around Cannock Chase had opened the sore again and it was slow to heal, oozing a sticky yellow puss, streaked with blood. Surely the balance of humours in his body had been badly disturbed by his bitter time in the cart. A black melancholy settled on him.

No colour, no sound, no movement.

Within the grey stone walls of his prison, grey dust. Within the blank hollows of his mind, grey lethargy. He lay for hours staring up at the rough ceiling of his cell, trying to trace patterns in the cracks and lumps of stone, until he thought he could make out some meaning there, and then the pattern would vanish and he would cry out in pain, for he could not hold together in his mind even the simple map of the stone.

Deep underground, with nothing but that narrow slit high above his head to hint at any other world but this closeted space, he could hear no noise from outside. There were no sounds except those he made himself, or the soft footfall of rats, or the metallic rattle of cockroaches. Once, he tried to sing a psalm, as they had done in the cellar of *Hell*, but his voice emerged so harsh and broken that it frightened him and he ceased at once and never tried again.

As time passed, he even welcomed the scurry of the cockroaches across the floor, since it was a movement outside himself. He watched them attentively as they searched for any crumbs he might have dropped, then slithered back into the dusty cracks where they hid.

He could not breathe and woke often from sleep, fighting for air to fill his drowning lungs. Is this how a caught fish feels, gasping on the bank, waiting to die?

The wound in his leg had begun to fester, and a fever invaded his body. Hot in the cold cell, he tossed on the narrow shelf in half-sleep, sometimes waking on the floor amongst the straw and the rats. Into his ill-defended mind, unwelcome thoughts began to creep, like engineers cutting a mine beneath the wall of a besieged town.

God had surely abandoned him, as God had abandoned England. There was a contagion in the land itself, a festering sore, worse than any plague, a sickness of the mind.

There is no God. Fool that I was, ever to have believed in Him.

But who is this 'I', who does not believe? Do I believe in this I? Bone and sinew and blood and skin, but that is not I. Surely I must be more than this bag of rotting flesh?

In disgust, he could no longer put food into his mouth to rot there. The water was tepid and brackish and dribbled down his chin.

Slowly a boiling, furious anger began to build in him. He grew restless and could no longer sit or lie on the bed, but paced back and forth as far as the chain would allow, coming up with a jerk at one end and then back and then a jerk at the other end. Back and forth, not only by day but by night as well. He no longer wanted to sleep, for if he closed his eyes, this 'I', who might not exist except for the bag of rotting flesh, would disappear for ever. Only by staying awake and watchful could he be sure that it did not perish.

One morning the gaoler came with food and put it down on the shelf as usual. John lunged forward, grabbing the man around the throat. Taken by surprise, the gaoler went down on one knee, but in a moment had thrown John off and retreated to the door. John gave a howl like a hungry animal and flung the water jug at him. It smashed against the wall and the pieces fell musically to the floor amongst the joyous splashing of the water.

'I know who I am!' John cried, in a voice too high-pitched to be his own.

Then the man was gone and the water sank into the dust. And once again there was no colour, no sound, no movement.

For two days the light came and went in the high window slit, but no one entered his cell, and all the time John sat hunched on the floor, his head on his knees and his arms over his head, as if to ward off blows. Gradually his heartbeats slowed, his anger soaked away like the lost water.

On the third day he went as close to the door as he could reach and shouted, begging for water. Some hours later, they brought it. When he had drunk, he lay down on the shelf. Images and words swirled in his brain, but made no sense, held no structure. He knew he was descending into the hell of madness, and the fragile self would be lost for ever.

❧

And then, one day without warning, everything changed.

One of the guards arrived during the morning, about an hour after his breakfast had been brought. Normally he would not expect to see anyone for another eight hours or so.

'Fetch your belongings,' said the man, kneeling down to unlock the leg iron. 'You are to come with me.'

His manner was subtly less harsh than usual. What could it mean? John picked up his bundle, which had remained tied and serving as a pillow since he had arrived here. He had not even bothered to change his filthy, stinking clothes for the others which, however creased and musty, must be cleaner than those he was wearing. The man led the way out of the cell and back up the stairs to the open courtyard, with John limping after him. Out in the air, he screwed up his eyes against the unaccustomed light and breathed deeply. There was a scent of spring and new growth in the air, even here in the enclosed castle. He felt weak and dizzy, but struggled to gather strength for what might lie ahead.

He was not dead. This was his hand before his face, this was his cheek on which the rays of the sun fell.

'Move along,' said the guard, not unkindly. 'You mustn't keep the governor waiting.'

So he was to see the governor of the castle. If he was no longer to be held as a nameless prisoner in the dungeons, this marked a change in his fortunes, but whether for good or ill, it was difficult to judge. Since he had been told to bring his belongings, he might not be sent back there.

They entered a door on the opposite side of the courtyard and climbed a flight of wide shallow steps. John had been here before, when the Committee for Stafford had inspected the place, and had even stayed as a guest here later, when his friend Captain Henry Stone was governor. They crossed the Great Hall of the castle, then beyond it climbed more stairs and entered a small room, which the governor used as his private office. John was ushered in and told to wait.

When he had waited for perhaps half an hour—long enough to make him feel his humble status, but not long enough to allow him to contemplate the possibilities of escape—he heard the ring of booted feet on the stairs and his heart jumped painfully. The door opened, and a man entered. John recognised him, but said nothing, judging it best to guide his own behaviour by the demeanour of the governor. He clasped his hands behind his back to steady their shaking.

The man checked for the merest moment, then continued across the room to where John turned from looking out of the window, cherishing the sight of something beyond four damp stone walls. It was only by a flicker in his eyes that the governor betrayed his reaction to John's appearance.

'Good day to you, Master Swynfen,' he said, shaking John by the hand, 'the Lord be with you.'

'And with you, Colonel Danvers,' said John.

'I trust I find you well?' The governor looked embarrassed.

'As well as can be expected,' said John gravely, aware that the stench of his unwashed body and clothes must be offensive to Danvers, who was something of a dandy in his person, despite his extreme religious views, which tended to millenarianism. John's hair and beard were matted, for he had nothing to comb them with but his fingers. His torn stocking was still wrapped around his wound, which had continued to ooze after it had opened again and which gave off its own sickly stink.

'Please, sit down,' said Danvers, indicating a high-backed carved chair with a cushioned seat.

'I fear I may mark the velvet,' said John, but Danvers waved aside his comment and gave orders to the servant at the door to bring wine and food.

While they waited for this to arrive, Danvers talked inconsequentially, about the state of the castle's defences, about the spring ploughing—anything, it seemed, to fill the awkward minutes. After he had poured wine for them both, he sat back in his chair with the air of a man about to proceed to business.

'Now— ,' he said.

'Wine,' said John, interrupting him and turning the fine Venetian glass in his hand, so that the sunlight winked in the pale gold liquid, throwing a gleam over the engrained filth on his skin. 'I have not drunk wine for these . . . three months past, is it? Or would it be four? Or five? I'm not sure of the date. Not since the last evening in my own home. The seventh day of December, that would have been.'

He was physically weak, and sick; he had been shot, beaten and humiliated. His mind had trembled on the brink of disintegration. But he knew from his time in the political life of the nation that it is a wise man who takes control of the tone of a conversation from the start. He tasted the wine.

'Excellent,' he said. 'From France, of course. None of our weak English stuff. My grandfather used to say that in *his* grandfather's view, the art of wine-making was lost to us with the dissolution of the monasteries by King Harry.'

He took another sip.

'I would judge this to be from the Loire region, am I right? A very fresh, delightful wine.'

'Yes, near Amboise, I understand.' Danvers was clearly disconcerted by the direction the conversation was taking. 'I had a crate of it sent up from London.'

'And some excellent cold meats,' John continued remorselessly, eating some ham baked with a crust of mustard and Barbados sugar. 'It's good to taste something other than dry cheese. And I must temper this wine with food, must I not? For I should take care to keep a clear head, in considering whatever it is that you are going to propose.'

Danvers appeared relieved at last to find an opening.

'You are right. I have indeed a number of things to propose to you.'

'And before you do that—incidentally, this pickled beef is delicious, please convey my compliments to your cook. Yes, before you do that, perhaps you would do me the courtesy of explaining who now rules England? I have been . . . somewhat out of touch with affairs lately. A regrettable lapse on my part, I am sure you will agree.'

He calmly helped himself to more meat, and some of the fashionable cold sallat which accompanied it.

'Damn it, Swynfen!' Danvers jumped up and began to pace the room. John kept his face expressionless, but inwardly he smiled. He waited.

The governor stopped in front of him and stood with hands on hips.

'My orders are to move you to a comfortable chamber and provide all that you require, while you are given time to consider your position.'

'I am very well aware of my position,' said John.

Danvers gave an exasperated sigh.

'His Highness suggests that you might find it in your interest to abandon your previous political stance, and write a statement supporting the present government.'

John felt a shock of surprise. *His Highness*. Who did Danvers mean? Charles, Prince of Wales, was *His Royal Highness*, but perhaps, since the Monarchy had been abolished, the epithet 'royal' no longer applied? Had Cromwell come to some agreement with the prince? Surely not. Not after all his trouble in seizing London and destroying Parliament.

'His Highness?' said John cautiously.

'General Cromwell.' Danvers looked a little confused, as if he had let slip something he should not have said.

304

'General Cromwell believes you should be given time to reconsider. He has generously decided to allow you to show your support for the *de facto* government.'

'*De facto*, but not *de jure*,' John murmured, but Danvers chose not to hear him. 'He has decided that, has he? That was generous of him, certainly.'

'Most of your friends have accepted the present situation, and the need to restore the country to a state of order and stability. They have engaged with the government, and will take their seats again in Parliament.'

John gazed at him stonily. Danvers was making himself very busy about pouring out wine and helping John to more of the food, so that his face was averted. It was impossible to read his expression, but Danvers was not a subtle man, not a man to lie with the silky ease of certain politicians of his acquaintance. No, on the whole, John was suspicious of this last assertion. He was certain Danvers was lying. However, he thought it wiser not to air his suspicions. Better to accept this offer of more comfortable accommodation and await developments.

After his interview with the governor, John was conducted to a chamber on the same floor, a tower chamber which differed from the others in this part of the castle only in having a lock newly affixed to the outside of the door. A good fire was burning in the hearth, with plenty of wood to keep it stoked. There was a great carved bed, as comfortable as any at Swinfen Hall, a kist, some chairs and joint stools, a table, even a basin and jug for washing, and a towel.

The servant who had brought him to the chamber—a servant, not a soldier—asked whether there was anything else he required. John thought rapidly.

'A razor and glass,' he said, 'that I may shave. Writing materials. When I have changed my clothes, I would have the soiled ones washed and mended.'

The servant looked at John's leg. 'I'll send one of the women to dress your wound.'

An hour later, John felt as though he had undergone some kind of baptism into a new life. He was clean and shaved, and his leg had been bathed and salved with some skill by one of the women servants. She was not as gentle as the child Martha, but she knew her work, and clucked with indignation over the filth of the makeshift bandage and the state of the injury.

'I'll leave it open to the air, sir, once I've salved it,' she said, 'and look at it again tomorrow.'

She had taken away his dirty clothes for washing and mending, and he was now dressed in clothes from his bundle, which were hardly clean, for they had been wrapped around the bread and cheese which he had hidden there when he made his attempt to escape. The bread had turned as hard as a iron, and the cheese had seeped grease into the clothes, now adorned with strange, irregular patches, which the woman promised she would scrub out after she returned the clothes he had been wearing. Once he was alone, he used the razor to nick the stitches that held his remaining coins in place in his shirt bands, and knotted them in the tail of the shirt he was wearing.

After this washing of his person and sorting of his apparel, he felt suddenly overcome with exhaustion. All these past weeks he had been trying to hold himself under tight control; now that he was no longer treated to the physical abuse of a criminal, he could at last relax. His body screamed for rest, his joints hurt, his head ached. He went to the window and looked out. The room had been chosen with care. Below the window, the wall of the castle dropped sheer to the ramparts. The grass which clothed them was a bright and vigorous green, and John realised that, while he had been confined in a blind cell, spring had arrived. There was no chance of escape by way of this window. Not that he would even contemplate escape for the moment. He was too weak, too tired. Whatever game Danvers was playing with him, at the orders of the men in power, John's own aim now was to regain his health and strength. In this chess game of political recantations and imprisonment, he would play for time until he felt himself strong enough to attempt escape or face worse imprisonment again.

He saw a flutter of movement, and from a stone corbel in the wall adjacent to his window, a thrush swooped down and landed on the sill beside the open casement. It regarded him with a bright eye, knowing but unafraid.

'Unwise,' John murmured, 'for I have known men quick as a cat, who would have you, and your neck rung, before you could raise your wings.'

The bird hopped a little nearer. John backed slowly away from the window to the table where he had left the stale bread. He broke off a piece, and moving carefully back to the window, crumbled the bread and scattered it on the sill. The bird began to peck at it, seemingly unconcerned that it was so hard. John leaned his shoulder against the stone transom of the window, watching it eat, quick and efficient.

'It's a happy man,' he said, 'who has food enough to share with the dumb creatures of the field and forest.'

306

At the sound of his voice, the thrush froze, and eyed him carefully before it resumed its pecking. Soon, all the crumbs were gone. The bird hopped along the sill, leaned slightly forward and launched itself out over the void. John watched it as it swooped away and was lost to sight amongst the trees clothing the lower slopes of the castle hill.

'And happy the bird, who is free of this cage, with the liberty to move about the sky and the earth as it will.'

He felt suddenly such a longing for freedom, with this first sight of the world after his weeks in the dungeon, that he had to seize hold of the transom to avoid flinging himself out after the bird. Sweating with the wave of heat that rushed through his body, he walked unsteadily back to the table and stood gripping the edge of it. Then he took more of the bread, and crumbled it, and strewed it over the window sill in the hope that the thrush might return. After watching in vain for the bird, he went back to the table and laid out paper, ink and pen. Danvers had said that he might write to his family and friends, but where to begin? He decided in the end that it was best to spare Anne the details of his ordeal, and simply relay the facts: that he was alive and in reasonable health, and that he was in Stafford, not many miles from Swinfen. He did not flatter himself that Danvers would send the letter by private messenger. But even by the slowest of public mails, Anne should receive his letter within the week, so near at hand was she. The thought gave his heart a lift. Why, if he were released, he could walk home in a few days, provided he could survive the thieves and cut-throats of Cannock Chase.

My dearest hearte, my love, my all,

I feare y^u will thinke mee dead by all this time that has pass'd, & y^u hearing nothing of mee. Believe mee, deare hearte, had I any means of writing y^u should have hear'd tell of mee ere this. I am now held at Stafford castle, whither I was brought from London by a somewhat tardy route. Col. Danvers is governor heere, & hee has lodg'd mee in a comfortable chamber for this time, where I have meate & drinke & all things proper for my care, & physicke for a wounde I receiv'd on ye journey, but I am held faste & cannot come to y^u. I trust in God that all will bee well. I trust also that y^u & ye children are safe in my father's care by this, & that y^u may reste from all y^{ur} labour, for it is right that the woman should dwell under ye shielde of a man's arm. Since y^{ur} husband cannot bee at your side, I take comfort *knowing that my father is able to stand in his place. From my windowe I see ye ploughs about their worke in ye feilds, & in ye eye of my hearte I see ye feilds of Swinfen turned by ye plough & receiving seed for ye new seasons crop. I thank ye Lord for His manifold goodness, & pray that He keeps y^u & all our kin in His blessed care.*

I am always y^{ur} moste loving husband who lack nothing but to lie in y^{ur} armes once again, my moste beeloved.
John Swynfen

When this letter was brought to Colonel Danvers in his office, he warmed a thin knife in the flame of his candle, then with great care slid it under the seal which held the folded sheet of paper closed. The letter was addressed, not to one of Swynfen's political allies as he had hoped, but to the man's wife, at Swinfen near Lichfield. It was known that Swynfen's wife and children had slipped through the fingers of the army in those first confused days of the occupation of London, but when they had eventually turned up in Staffordshire, after an inexplicable delay on their journey, it had been decided to leave them be for the moment. As long as they kept quiet at Swinfen, they were unlikely to cause any trouble to the new government, which had more important matters to deal with. Anne Swynfen had been riding about the country in a most unseemly fashion, but it appeared that she was concerned merely with estate matters, and was not trying to rally support for her husband. However, if she knew he was so close by, she might persuade their friends to make some attempt to release him.

Danvers read quickly through the letter, and pulled a face at the tone of it. This kind of letter could be of no use to him or to his masters. It seemed he would need to wait a while before Swynfen ventured to write frankly to his political friends. With a sigh of impatience, he refolded the letter and pressed down the seal, which was still warm and soft, until it stuck to the paper. Then he balanced the letter on his fingertips until he decided what to do. It might be dangerous to send the letter. It could be kept for possible future use, or it could be destroyed. He got up and walked over to the fire, holding the letter by a corner, as if to spin it into the flames, but then he shrugged and locked it into his strong box instead. It had alerted him, however, to possible danger. It would be advisable to give Mistress Anne Swynfen good cause to remain quiet on her estate, lest she cause trouble. He opened the door and called for the captain of the guard to attend him. It was time to teach Mistress Swynfen a lesson.

At a fork in the road, the raggle-tailed procession of carts and horses and ranging dogs halted, where one road ran southeast towards Tamworth and the other south to Swinfen. Dick jumped to the ground. One of the gypsy lads handed down his knapsack with a quick grin, showing the gaps where teeth had been knocked out in some brawl. Dick walked forward along the dusty verge of the road to the leading cart, where Waldo sat high above him, the reins of his fine pair of matched dapple-greys loose in his hand.

'Thank you for your many kindnesses, Waldo,' said Dick, reaching up to shake his hand.

The gypsy took it, with a faint light of amusement in his eyes.

'I hope you have gained something by it.'

Dick regarded him seriously.

'Aye. I've come to value your people and know something of your life and your ways, but they are not my life, nor my ways. I wish I could offer you work, but my grandfather will long since have hired any day labourers he needs.'

'Don't trouble yourself, lad. We'll find work near Tamworth, or else we'll head into the fens. There's work there where they're draining the marshes, or, if the war is still putting an end to that, then there will be plenty of food to be snared in the wild country.'

'God be with you,' said Dick, though he had never heard any mention of God in all the time he had travelled with the gypsies.

'May the sun shine on you,' said Waldo, with an ironic smile, 'and good fortune go with you.'

He clucked to the horses and the cart began to move again along the eastern road. Dick turned his back on them and headed south. He had made his choice.

Chapter Twenty-Three

The fields put down to wheat shone like silk in the low-lying sun of early morning, for it had rained during the night, turning the red soil of the tilth the colour of ripe plums where it showed between the first tender green of the shoots. Anne had watched Josiah and Christopher sowing the precious seed wheat broadcast, each man carrying a satchel of seed slung from his shoulders on a leather strap. As they paced slowly up and down the fields, their arms swinging alternately in the beautiful ancient rhythm of the sower of seed, she had seen the wheat fall in great golden arcs upon the soil. Now that the young wheat was growing, it patterned the field in the painted image of those aerial arcs, sweeping across the soil like the swirls of colour on a damask brocade. But how much lovelier than damask was this fertile, this changing fabric of earth and grain, man and nature.

She knelt down at the edge of the wheat field and scanned it from the angle of a mouse. From here, the tiny stems of wheat resembled a green forest stretching away for miles, yet they were slender as grass, tender as breath, and no more than two or three inches high. It was frightening to think that the life or death of her household might depend on the survival of something so fragile. She patted the soil as she might have patted a child's head, for encouragement.

'Sure, are you praying to the wheat, lady? Best not be seen doing it, or folk will take you for a witch or a heretic, so.'

Anne sprang to her feet, her heart pounding. Brendan had a way of coming up silently behind her which constantly unnerved her. And his manner of speaking to her was intolerably familiar. She had not seen again that curiously hostile look he had given her the day he arrived, but the memory of it troubled her and she did not altogether trust him. Yet she needed him and the hard days' work he put in. She had tried to hint, without severely reprimanding, that he should not speak to her as he did, but he blithely ignored her. There was something deeply disturbing about the man. His speech, which at times was a broad peasant Irish, would at other times change utterly, so that he spoke almost like an English gentleman. And the way he eyed her, with such a knowing look: it was an expression at once intimate and assessing, ruthless yet pitying. If she permitted herself to think about it, she was frightened. They were far now from the house and the farm, alone in the early morning light. She did not like to be alone with him, so far from other people.

'I was checking the growth of the wheat,' she said, as coldly as possible, 'and feeling the warmth in the soil.'

He merely smiled at her, and did not answer her directly.

'Ach, in Ireland, 'tis the little people we're always placating indeed, hoping they'll not blight the crops because they're angry with us. A manchet of bread and a bowl of cream, we put out, for the little fellows.'

'The godly would say such practices are blasphemous,' said Anne sternly, 'but if Hester has something to spare for Robin Goodfellow, I wink my eye.'

'Have a care, nevertheless, that a little harmless kindness to the fairies be not taken for dealing with the master of darkness.'

There it was again, the seeming-false accent dissolving and slipping away. Before she could think how to answer this, he shaded his eyes with his hand, looking into the distance where the carriage drive to the house first came into sight through the trees.

'A traveller headed this way, it seems,' he said. 'A young man, and mighty footsore, I'm thinking, lady.'

She was not as tall as he, and so could not see so far over the rise in the land, but in a few moments she too saw the figure, limping a little, in clothes that looked, even at this distance, as strange and multi-coloured as a jester's. It could not be John, it was someone younger and slighter, but perhaps it might be someone with news of John. She did not know why, suddenly, she thought this might be so, after months of silence, but she ran from the fields towards the house, aware that Brendan would be standing there, unmoving, watching her with that slightly sardonic smile.

For some reason, the ragged stranger was not heading for the servants' quarters at the back of the house, like the usual beggars and travellers who passed this way. Instead he walked purposefully, despite his limp, towards the front door. Breathless and hot, she reached it almost as he did.

He was an odd figure, clad in a fool's motley of garments: a tattered buff coat which had been patched in several places with scraps of vivid cloth, scarlet, emerald, and a chequered yellow; breeches which had been made for a bigger man, folded over at the waist and held in place with a length of old cord; blue stockings, much darned; and a pair of fine bucket boots, which looked as though they might have been stolen from a Royalist cavalier. So astonishing were these clothes that they held all her attention at first, as she wondered who this extraordinary lad might be, marching up boldly to her front door. Then her eyes lifted to his face, and she started violently.

'Dick? Dick! Is it you? It cannot be!'

He was staring at her in equal bewilderment.

'Mother?' He frowned as he looked her up and down. 'You are so . . . so brown.'

He said it flatly, with an edge of such manly disapproval in his tone that she laughed merrily. He addressed her as 'Mother' only when he was out of humour with her.

'Aye, perhaps. You see, I'm turned farmer, and I'm much in the sun.' She threw her arms around him and embraced him, while he stood patiently waiting. 'But, Dick, my love, what are you doing here, and why are you dressed in those extraordinary clothes?'

'I started to walk home from London, but then I fell in with some travellers, which took me somewhat out of the way. Here I am at the last, none the worse for it. The clothes are sound and fairly clean, if odd.'

The front of his coat heaved suddenly, and a cat's head peeped out where the collar was left unbuttoned.

'A cat?' said Anne.

'A fellow traveller.' Dick grinned at her, looking more like himself. 'We're both ravenous. My companions left me just this side of Lichfield, while they headed for Tamworth. Ginger and I have had a hungry walk.'

She took him by the arm to lead him into the house, scarcely able to believe he was solid flesh, but the arm under her hand was firm and muscular. For a time there was a flurry of excitement and a good deal of rushing about by the servants and the younger children, but finally Anne sent them all off while Dick sat down in the parlour to a large meal of some pickled trout, bannocks and butter, and a tankard of ale.

'Is there no meat?' he asked, wolfing down the bannocks as though he had not eaten in days.

'Meat is scarce. When I reached home after Christmas, I found most of our winter supplies gone, looted by soldiers. We've been living these three or four months past on vegetables and cheese and eggs, and sometimes a rabbit, when we can get one. We've been close to starvation more than once, though things are a little better now. Jack caught these trout in the lake.'

'He's turned fisherman, has he? I must find my rod and lend him a hand. But why didn't you shoot a deer or two in the forest?'

'Until spring ploughing time, I had no men about the place but Peter and Josiah, and they are both too old—neither can see well enough to shoot a deer.'

'And now it's out of season. But grandfather, doesn't he shoot still? He used to be one of the best men with a gun in the whole county.'

'Dick.' She reached out and took his hand, 'your grandfather has had an apoplexy which left him unable to move or speak. He's a little better in health—Bridget nurses him, and I help when I can—but I fear he'll never shoot another deer. And I'm afraid your grandmother is ill as well. Not in her body. Her wits have become confused.'

She kept silent about Joane's violent fits. Only the day before Joane had thrown a cushion on to the fire and then rushed shrieking along the upper passage. Anne had had to call Christopher to help her wrestle the old woman back into her room, where they had put out the fire and dosed her with poppy syrup to calm her. Her mother-in-law's moods frightened her and when she could, she gladly handed over her care to Bridget. Much of the time Joane did not recognise her daughter, but when she did it provoked furious attacks. Last week Joane had scratched Bridget's cheek almost to the bone. Bridget bore these attacks with fortitude, but Anne knew that she too was afraid.

'Father hasn't come home, then?' said Dick.

'Nay.' Her grip on his hand tightened. 'I've had no news of him, save that when most of the prisoners were released, he was carried off in a cart, and no one knows where. Master Gott has tried hard to discover what has become of him, but with no success.'

'You mustn't worry, Mama. He was well enough when I saw him.'

'You've *seen* him!'

'Many weeks ago now, about the time of the king's trial. I went to visit him at the *King's Head.*'

'You must tell me everything. But I don't understand. Why aren't you at Charterhouse? Did the Master relent, and give you permission to come home? He has sent me no word. I thought you had returned to school after Christmas.'

Dick looked slightly uncomfortable.

'I didn't ask his permission. And I expect he hasn't missed me, because he would suppose you would fetch me away from my uncle's house. Of course, I learned from Aunt Coleman that you were already gone from London. It may be, also, that the Master is driven from his place. He's a known Royalist. They were saying when I was in London that any Royalists still left would lose their positions once Cromwell seized power.'

'Come,' she said. 'You've eaten everything. Walk with me while I see to my hens and chicks, and you can tell me about your father and these travelling companions of yours and why you look like a ragamuffin.'

※

Once Dick had told his tale and changed into spare clothes belonging to his father, he walked about the rest of the farmland with Anne, while she pointed out what she had done: the fields sown, the ewes and their lambs on the small meadow near the woods, the cows and their new calves in the meadow of deep, lush grass down by the lake, the sows nursing their litters in an enclosed field behind the barns, her vegetable garden laid out with some crops already planted, others awaiting her attention. She had hoped, she supposed, for praise. It was foolish of her, perhaps, to feel the need of praise from one of her family. The children, apart from Jack and Nan, hardly seemed aware that she had taken on all the duties and responsibilities of a gentleman landowner. The servants, although reluctant at first, now accepted her as the head of the household and obeyed her orders as if she were a man. Even the farm labourers, who in normal times would have looked askance at her role, had come to respect her. Yet she felt a craving for recognition that what she was doing was right, that she was exercising a proper guardianship of the land.

Dick, however, was in a strange mood, restless and critical. She should have taken advice from his uncle Thomas Pott, or written for his uncle William Swynfen to come home and take charge of the manor until his father returned. Surely the peas should have been planted where she had sown the wheat, the wheat in the field where the peas were growing. Why had she taken on an unknown Irish shepherd? Everyone knew the Irish were thieving rogues, who would happily slit your throat while you slept.

'Dick,' she said at last, exasperated, 'you tell me you've been living with a band of roving gypsies for the last months, and you think to find fault with my shepherd? Brendan Donovan is an excellent man for the sheep, and very apt for other tasks about the place. As for the crops, Josiah and I have looked carefully at the manor records for the last few years, and he mostly remembers when each field was put down to each crop. The fields have been planted according to the order of rotation for this year. The field next to the meadow where you see the

314

sheep grazing is left fallow. We'll turn out the sows and their litters there next week. Swine are useful for digging and turning the soil, as well as manuring it for next year's crop.'

He looked at her in astonishment.

'Where did you learn such things? Has Uncle Pott come to advise you?'

'Nay. I've been studying the art and practice of agriculture. It's not such a very deep study, in its essentials. All that truly worries me is the risk of bad weather, for it's been so terrible in recent years, with storms and floods. That, and the diseases of animals, which can destroy a farm. Of course, when we were at Thickbroome, I often undertook to dose the animals.'

Dick still looked glum.

'It isn't fit for a woman to manage an estate. I'm nearly a man. I should take charge.'

Anne smiled at him. So this was the root of the trouble.

'My dear, you must return to your studies. You know your father wants you to matriculate at Oxford next spring. I'm sure you have more to learn before then. Your cousin Richard Pott is working with a tutor until he goes up to Oxford. I think we should ask your uncle if you may share his studies.'

Dick had tasted a little too deeply of independence to fall in readily with this scheme. Anne allowed him some time before she put the plan into action. In the meantime, she took him riding about the estate with her, to visit the tenant farmers and the cottagers with their small-holdings. As soon as the weather permitted, she had made this her practice every few days, for she had found many of the poorer folk in desperate need. Although they had not been as severely looted by the soldiers as the Hall had been during the struggles of the previous year, yet they less to spare. The loss of one laying hen and a flitch of bacon could mean starvation to the family of a cottager. She found some of them living off thin broth, which they made by stewing again and again the same bones from long-gone legs of mutton or ham, with a handful of dried herbs and leaves to give it flavour.

She took Dick, on his third day at home, to visit the family of Matthew Webster, who lived in a cottage beyond the mill. They rode along the shore of the lake, then followed the stream where it ran out of the lake down to the mill.

'There's work to be done here,' Anne said, pointing with her riding crop at the great wheel which turned slowly with the flow of the stream. 'The grindstone needs to be balanced. I must fetch someone from Tamworth to do it, for it's a skilled task.'

315

'There will be no need until harvest.'

'Nay, it can't be left until then, for everyone will discover they need such repairs at the last minute.'

At the Websters' cottage they dismounted and tied their horses to the fence. The door was low, forcing them to duck their heads on entering, and the one small window gave so little light it was difficult to make out anything until their eyes grew accustomed to the dimness. Matthew Webster got slowly to his feet to greet them, but his leg was wrapped in bandages and Anne pressed him down into his chair again. Five small children were huddled over the fire, their eyes large and sunken in their gaunt faces, but they were well clothed, for Anne had brought them clothing on a previous visit. Now she sent Dick out to chop firewood while she dressed Matthew's leg.

'This is much healed!' she exclaimed, peeling back the bandage carefully. 'I believe we can leave off the dressing now, Matthew. I'll wash it and salve it, then I think you should go without your stocking for a few more days, and it will soon be whole again. Now, Frances, while I'm tending your father's leg, I want you to unpack those saddlebags. There's some new cheese and bread, and some of Agnes Lea's honey she has sent for you. Be careful of that jug of ale, in case the stopper has worked loose.'

The eldest girl unpacked the food eagerly, and soon the children were tearing pieces off the loaves and stuffing them in their mouths.

'Nay, nay,' said Anne, brushing off her skirts and throwing the old dressing on the fire. 'You'll make yourselves ill. Come and sit at the table and eat slowly, however hungry you are. See, I've brought milk for you, and a pie, and there are eggs for tomorrow.'

When the children were eating a little less like savage beasts, and Dick had made up the fire, Anne turned to Matthew again.

'And Margaret?' she said. 'How does she fare?'

'Much better,' said Matthew. 'The fever's nearly gone, and the lass seems much stronger. She took all of that good broth you left for her.'

'I've brought more today. I'll warm it at the fire and take it in to her.'

The cottage was partially divided by a length of old canvas nailed to a roof beam. Behind it, a wooden platform and a straw mattress provided the marriage bed, while the children slept beside the fire. Margaret Webster was sitting up, still very pale, but she smiled to see Anne. Two weeks earlier she had given birth to a son who had died within the hour. By the following day Margaret was seized with a fever and like to follow him.

'God has been good to me this time,' she said to Anne, between spoonfuls of the soup. 'He has spared me for the sake of the other children. Though when the baby died I thought I would have been glad to die also.'

'Hush,' said Anne. 'Don't say such a thing. It's an insult to God, who gave you life. You'll be well soon. I'm going to send the boy Isaac to help Matthew with the planting. His leg is near healed after that accident with the axe, and it's time he sowed his corn and vegetables. And I've set aside three good little pullets for you, so you may start a new flock.'

Tears started in the young woman's eyes, and she pressed Anne's hand against her cheek.

'The Lord was kind to the people of Swinfen when you came home to us, Mistress Anne.'

&

Ever since Anne had made her peace with Mary, she had intended to ride over again to visit the Potts, but every day her hours were so filled that when night came she seemed to have been occupied every moment, with never the time to go to Weeford. Dick went with her now, and while she took cakes and ale with Mary and her husband, he went off with his cousin Richard to admire a new pair of pistols. By the time they returned, Thomas had agreed readily to Dick's joining Richard at his lessons. The two boys had also been discussing the plan, for Dick now seemed much happier about it and Richard was eager for the company.

When they were mounted and ready to leave, Thomas stood with his hand on Brandy's neck and smiled up at Anne. His thick hair was grey now, but his blue eyes were as sharp and humorous as ever.

'I hear that you're managing Swinfen as well as any gentleman,' he said, 'and I respect you for it, Anne. But if you need aught—help, or advice, or tools—you know that I'll readily give them to you.'

She leaned down and laid her hand on his shoulder.

'I thank you, Thomas. I know that you would. And truly, if I need help, I will come to you.'

As they made their way back along the road, which had already become a dusty tunnel under the trees with the arrival of warmer weather, Dick was whistling cheerfully.

'So,' said Anne, 'you're happy now to join your cousin?'

'We plan to have some fine sport each day when our lessons are finished. I'll ride over each morning, and home in time for supper . . .'

317

'I'm sorry, Dick, but you must walk. It's less than two miles, and the horses are all needed on the farm. We can't have one of them languishing in the Potts' paddock every day.'

Dick grumbled a little at this, but he saw the fairness of it.

'If we could but hear some news of Father, then all would be well.'

'Aye,' said Anne. 'I pray every day that our hearing no news means that nothing terrible has happened. At least the rest of us are now all safely at Swinfen.'

She would never admit to her son the long hours she spent weeping, alone in her chamber at night.

During the visit to Weeford, Anne had come to an arrangement with Thomas Pott: he would send his shepherd over to Swinfen to assist with the sheep-shearing. With this additional help, the task could be completed in two days. In return, Brendan Donovan would spend two days helping to shear the Weeford Hall flock, walking home in the evening. Anne thought she had the better of the bargain, for her fleeces would be ready first, but she also knew that Thomas had suggested the plan so that he could inspect Brendan, for he had a natural distrust of Irishmen and (however much he might praise her husbandry) he wanted to assure himself that his brother-in-law's flocks were in safe hands.

The appointed day dawned and Anne went out to the meadow as soon as she had completed her morning devotions. The night before, Brendan, Christopher and Roland had built two adjacent pens in the meadow out of willow hurdles, with a kind of passageway joining them together. The unshorn sheep would be gathered into the first of these; then, as they were shorn, they would be driven along the passage to the other pen. When she arrived, she could see the three men, together with Thomas's shepherd, Zachary Fitch, already busy at herding the sheep into the first pen. Brendan's dog Niall and Zachary's dog were working the ewes up towards the temporary sheep-fold. She walked across the grass towards them, her feet marking out dark footprints in the dew. Before she was halfway there, her shoes were soaked through and her skirt was sodden a foot deep.

They greeted her abstractedly with a 'Morning, mistress'. The sheep were their usual foolish selves, making sudden darts in different directions, while the lambs leapt vertically into the air, convinced at first that it was all a game, then flying into a panic and baaing frantically for their mothers, who had become lost in the confusion.

Eventually, the sheep were all penned. They rushed to one side of the enclosure, butting up against the hurdles, so that Anne thought they would surely knock down the side and break loose again, but the hurdles were backed with heavy rocks to hold them steady. They wavered a little under the onslaught, but did not fall.

Roland caught hold of one of the older, steadier ewes and led her over to Brendan, who stood near the gap leading to the passage, which was blocked with a loose hurdle. The old ewe, after her initial resistance, seemed to remember what this was all about, and submitted patiently when Brendan gripped her head between his knees, plunged his left hand into her wool for a firm hold, and seized his shears with his right hand. The previous night, when she was visiting her hens, Anne had heard Brendan sharpening those shears. Now she watched as they slid through the heavy wool and the fleece peeled away as cleanly as an apple skin. It looked so easy a child could do it, no more difficult than removing a cloak from a man's shoulders, but the cunning of patient skill lay behind that apparent ease.

Christopher brought a ewe for Zachary and Roland bundled up Brendan's fleece, laying it on the grass outside the enclosure, while Brendan removed the loose hurdle and thrust the ewe into the passage leading to the other pen. She ran halfway along then stopped, confused, and tried to retreat. Anne slapped her on the rump until she ran on into the further enclosure, where she stopped and began to graze calmly, as if she had already forgotten what had happened.

'Thank you, lady,' Brendan called over his shoulder, already occupied in shearing the next ewe. 'Now, if you could be sending that great lad of yours up to see the ewes through the run, that would be a great help to us, so.'

Anne saw the other men exchange furtive glances, uneasy at the familiar way he addressed her, but she said calmly, 'I'll send Dick to give you all a hand. He had rather that than study his books any time. I came only to see that you have all you need. Margit will bring you ale and a cold pie by and by.'

Before she went back to the house, she picked up the fleece and examined it. It was so bulky, she could barely lift it. The wool was dense and silky, of the very best quality. She would keep about half the fleeces for spinning on the estate—many of the cottage women took in spinning and weaving for a small extra income. The cloth could be used by the household or sold on finished. The rest of the fleeces she would send to Tamworth with Josiah, to the wool merchant there who had handled the Swinfen and Weeford wool for twenty years past. As she walked down the meadow, she rubbed her hands together, working in the oil from the wool, for the natural oil from the fleeces was sovereign for softening the skin. Her hands were in dire need of it, for they had grown quite coarse. She must search her receipt book for a strong cream she could make. There was one, she remembered, using elderflowers.

At the end of the two days, Anne assessed her pile of fleeces in the barn with pride. She had plans to overwinter a larger flock this coming year, so next spring it would be even bigger. Wool was a valuable commodity, in spite of the uncertainties of foreign trade. That evening the household held a supper for the sheep-shearing, inviting the tenants as well as the day labourers with their families. While it was not such a great affair as the harvest supper, it was a merry occasion, for the shearing marked the first garnering of nature's bounty, which would occupy all the summer and autumn. After the meagre yield of the previous year, the losses to storms and floods, and the depredations of the soldiers, the whole company gathered in the scrubbed and garlanded barn could feel the confidence brought by the new season, despite the illness of the old master and mistress and the absence of Master John. Thomas and Mary Pott rode over with their eldest son to join the party, and Thomas generously proposed a toast to Anne's management of the estate. Dick and his cousin drank a mite too much ale, and were discovered, after most of the guests had gone home, fast asleep on the stack of fleeces, with an empty flagon between them.

'Leave them be,' said Thomas, when the two mothers descended on their sons in fury. 'Their aching heads will be punishment enough in the morning. Every lad must learn for himself the folly of overindulgence.'

So Thomas and Mary rode home without their son, and in the morning two green-faced boys—who had spent the entire night in the barn—refused breakfast with a shudder and spent half an hour pouring buckets of cold water over each other's sore heads in the farmyard.

᾿

Without asking Anne's permission, Brendan began to teach the three younger boys to swim, now that the weather was warmer. She only discovered what was afoot when they came in one afternoon with dripping hair and their clothes, which had been thrown aside on the shore, covered in mud.

'How dare you!' she stormed, confronting Brendan outside the barn. 'I never gave you leave! What if one of them had foundered?'

Brendan gave her a curious look.

'I had them only in the shallows, lady, holding them up one by one while they kicked and felt the water lift them, so.'

Jack had followed her out of the house and stood solidly beside Brendan.

'Brendan wouldn't let us come to harm, Mama. And I want to learn to swim. *You* couldn't teach us.'

Indeed I could, Anne thought, but held her tongue.

'Very well,' she said ungraciously, 'the lessons may continue. But I must be told every time, do you understand? Every time.'

Once again she had felt that sense of menace about Brendan, yet he seemed to be acting from nothing but good will. The next day she spent half an hour watching them in the lake, and again the next. Brendan was a good teacher and soon Jack and Francis were dog-paddling a little off shore while Ralph splashed about in the shallows, more interested in making great fountains of water than in swimming.

A day or two later she was caught up in discussions with Josiah about one of the horses who was favouring his off hind, when the boys said they were going swimming again. She let them go, but afterwards walked down to the lake. Ralph was sitting, stark naked, on the muddy bank constructing a model farm out of pebbles and twigs. Francis was solemnly swimming back and forth along the shore, keeping his chin anxiously crooked up from the water. Not far from Ralph, Brendan was standing with his arms folded, staring out across the lake. He wore nothing but his breeches, wet to the knee, and did not heed her coming. Nowhere could she see Jack. Everything about her seemed suddenly to go silent and she felt herself turn icy cold. She seized Brendan by the elbow and shook him.

'In the name of God, where's Jack?'

Brendan turned towards her slowly, his eyes blank.

'What?'

'Jack! Where's Jack?'

He turned back to the lake and pointed. More than halfway across she could just make out a small head. Jack was splashing frantically and as she watched his head dipped below the water.

'He's in trouble!'

She kicked off her shoes and ran towards the lake. She was in the water up to her thighs, her heavy skirts dragging her down, when Brendan plunged past her.

'Don't be a fool, woman,' he cried, and slipped smoothly into the water. He struck out strongly towards that broken place in the lake. He seemed to move too slowly as the fear froze Anne there in the water, her feet in the mud, weed floating about her thighs. She saw him reach the child and there was a violent churning in the water. Jack gave a shriek and she heard Brendan shouting at him.

321

Dear God, he was drowning her son. She waded further into the lake. Could she reach them in time, weighed down by her water-logged skirts? She would strip off, and be hanged what anyone might say, but it would be too late, too late.

The splashing ceased and she thought her heart had been squeezed into a hard ball by some giant hand. Then she saw that Brendan had caught Jack under the arms and begun the slow swim back.

When they reached the lake shore she was standing in her streaming clothes amongst the trodden ruins of Ralph's model, with the two younger boys gaping at her in alarm. Jack coughed and retched and collapsed on to all fours, his hair over his eyes, vomiting water over her feet. She turned on Brendan, incandescent with fury.

'May God damn you to Hell, Brendan Donovan, you tried to drown my son!'

He stood before her gasping, but still with that queer blank look in his eyes.

'No, Mama, no!' Jack croaked, tugging at the hem of her skirt. 'Brendan saved my life. I was caught in some weed and it was pulling me down. Brendan saved me!'

She narrowed her eyes, studying the shepherd, but he avoided her look and turned aside to pick up his shirt. If she had not come, would he have stood there and let Jack drown? Brendan was rubbing himself dry on his shirt and did not answer her. She did not know what to believe, but she banned all swimming unless Dick was also present. Two days later, Francis suffered a recurrence of the fever and infected throat that had struck him down in London, and all swimming came to an end.

On the last day before Dick started his lessons with his cousin, he helped Brendan herd the sheep up to Packington Moor, to save the time of one of the labourers, who were busy now with the increased milking and the endless hoeing to keep the crops free of weeds. They went up to the moor on foot, leading one of the horses loaded with Brendan's supplies for the summer—bedding, food, and cookpots. He would come down to the home farm perhaps once a fortnight to replenish his stock of food, but otherwise they would see little of him until his help was needed with hay-making.

When Dick rode back that evening, he conceded grudgingly that the Irishman seemed a decent enough shepherd, without the wild attributes of his countrymen.

'Though there's something strange about him,' Dick said.

'I know,' Anne agreed uneasily. 'Perhaps it's nothing but his foreign manner.'

Chapter Twenty-Four

As the year turned towards summer, and the floods of early spring subsided, everyone began to hope that this year, at last, the weather would be kind. The vegetables in Anne's garden grew rapidly, and the raw salads, which were a new London fashion, still regarded with suspicion by the Swinfen servants, broke the monotony of their diet. The spinage was abundant, and they ate early lettuces and the young carrots thinned out to allow the rest to grow large. Pompions and onions were beginning to fatten for winter storage. The abundant yield of fresh milk allowed the cheese-making to increase, using fresh lady's bedstraw gathered from the meadow's edge, so they were able to set some of the big round cheeses aside to age on the slatted shelves of the dairy, turning them every few days and rubbing them with salt once a week.

There were now several broody hens, kept purely for the purpose, and the flock was increased to nearly fifty. Besides her gifts of eggs and pullets to the cottagers, Anne was occupied with supervising Hester and Biddy as they tried a new method of preserving eggs in brine. The children, free at last to roam about the estate in the better weather, were growing as wild as the cottagers' children, so that Anne imposed a regime of lessons supervised by herself and Patience every morning between breakfast and mid-day, after which the older children must help with simple tasks before being released to play.

Anne herself rose every morning at four, and after half an hour of private devotions, spent four hours working at her desk or weeding her garden or walking about the home farm, before returning to conduct prayers for the whole household and to teach the children. These lessons were as much a penance for her as for the children; she had grown impatient since the days in London when she had valued sharing the lessons and taking pride in the children's progress. She blamed herself for her impatience, and tried to conceal it from the children. Dorothea was now learning to read and the boys must do their figuring and learn their globes. Anne strove valiantly to master Euclid with Nan and Jack, but she knew that she fell far short of Nan's expectations, after her time at the Perwicks' school. Dinner time came as joyful release for them all.

The baby Jane was partly weaned now. Bess was feeding her a pap of new milk and crumbled bread, and she was growing as fast as the young lambs. Freed of nursing the baby, except for one feed last thing at night and one during the day, and encouraged by the success of her farming, Anne was full of energy, striding about her demesne, or riding to the outlying farms and cottages. She watched the growth of the wheat with delight, rejoiced in the abundant blossom in the orchard, and went each morning to pick and eat a handful of young peas, pods and all. Sometimes when she found herself feeling happy, a terrible cloud of guilt overcame her. How could she possibly be content, when she did not know what had become of John? But usually the loneliness and aching she felt for him only assailed her at night in the great empty bed, when she would wrap her arms around a bolster for comfort, and muffle her sobbing in the smother of its goosedown. During the daylight hours she had blessedly little time for thinking.

A problem that had been troubling her for some time was solved with the help of Thomas Pott. Jane was unbaptised still. In earlier days, when her own eldest children were born, the christening was held on the first Sunday or saint's day after the birth, to ensure the salvation of the child's soul, in case it should die in early infancy. But such practices had been set aside with the severe reforms of the church. With so many young men away at the war, there had been no births on the manor or in the village since Anne had returned home, apart from the Webster baby. She did not know what form of baptism was now practised in Weeford. Jane must be baptised, yet still Anne delayed, as though holding the ceremony without John was proof definite that he would never return. At first she had waited because the baby was strong and healthy, and she did not want to take this momentous step without him. Then finally, as it seemed more and more likely that he would not come, she had approached the new minister at Weeford church. The former curate, Richard Pegg, had conducted her wedding to John that April day in 1632, and was married himself in the same church just three years later. But Richard Pegg had been deprived of his living by the new Puritan regime, and turned away, and a new man put in his place. The minister was a sour-faced, grim man, whose endless sermons contained no glimmer of light. When Anne spoke to him of baptising the baby, he glowered at her.

'We no longer perform such papistical rituals,' he snapped. 'All that is required is that the father of the child should bring it to church and answer for it.'

'But my husband is away,' said Anne. She suspected the minister knew exactly why, and it made him even less friendly towards her, as the wife of one of Cromwell's enemies.

'Then it may be brought by a man of your family,' the minister said.

Thomas Pott agreed to act in John's stead, and the Sunday after the sheep were moved up to the moor, Jane was duly presented at church. She beamed happily around, for she was a sweet-tempered child, but Anne had to contain her anger that this youngest child of hers was deprived of the blessing of the church, her rightful welcome into the community, and the gift of godparents, which all her other children had received.

With the sheep up on the moor, Dick at his lessons, and the hay not yet ready to cut, the early summer seemed the most peaceful time any of the household had known for a long while. There was food enough at last, a burden of anxiety lifted from all. In recent days the weather had grown hot and still and Anne feared a thunderstorm might flatten the hay before it could be cut. She was sitting one evening in her chamber beside the open casement, idly turning over the pages of a book of poetry by Edmund Spenser which she had found on the shelf in the parlour. It had been published back in the previous century, and had probably belonged to John's grandfather, that other John who had named one of his sons Deveroxe. Although she had heard of it, she had never read it—one long poem in several sections, entitled *The Faerie Queen*, an Arthurian tale of quests and chivalry, but on closer examination revealing itself as a philosophical allegory. Had she not been so tired, it might have held her attention, but she was bone weary after a day of working in her vegetable garden, turning the heavy cheeses, and riding the entire circuit around the estate, which she now did once a fortnight.

The heat, which had barely eased with the coming of nightfall, and the heavy stillness of the air which presaged thunder, kept her from sleep, despite her weariness. She laid aside her book and went to the window. Leaning on the sill, she breathed in the rich scents of the night air after a hot day, which laid their spicy taste upon her tongue. Many physicians warned against the dangerous humours lurking in night air and advocated always fastening windows close at night, but Anne felt she could not breathe this night with the casement shut. The moon was nearly at the full, and its drowned reflection swam in the lake like a disk cut from mother-of-pearl. Away beyond the woods, in the direction of Packington Moor, the sky flickered eerily with veils of lightning, but no breaking thunder eased the pressure in the air. The silence was so dense it pressed against her ears like a heavy blanket, increasing her sense of breathlessness. Then she heard some small creature shriek, followed by the bark of a fox. Amongst the shadows of the spinney, she fancied that she saw movement.

Closer to hand, much closer, there was a furtive sound. At first, she thought she was mistaken, that some sound from the home farm had been carried here on the still air, some trick or echo making it seem to come from almost beneath her window. She held her breath, listening.

This time she heard it more distinctly—a soft footstep, and a faint gasp, as if someone exhausted with running were trying to silence the sound of his breathing. John kept a pistol in this chamber, but it would take her minutes to find and load it. By then, the intruder would have gained the house or run on—where? To the farm? Or had he come from there? Who would come here, unless he sought Swinfen itself? A traveller on the way to Weeford or Lichfield or Tamworth was unlikely to come this close to the house, though he might cut a corner off his journey by walking across the further fields. Perhaps it was John himself, having evaded his captors and found his way home.

She realised suddenly that, framed against the light of the candle, she could be seen from outside. Turning her head, she blew it out and at that very moment a voice called softly.

'Anne? Is that you?'

Her heart lurched painfully. Not John's voice. But a voice she knew, a light, young voice. John's youngest brother. She leaned far out of the casement, trying to discern whether there was a more solid darkness in the shadows at the foot of the wall.

'Richard? Richard? Where are you?'

'God be thanked! For mercy's sake, sister, let me in. I never knew Swinfen locked and barred before.'

'We never had reason to bar the doors before. Come to the parlour window. Some of the servants are asleep in the kitchen, and the front door always makes such a noise.'

She saw a smaller shadow detach itself from the larger one and slip round the corner of the house. At once she fumbled for her strike-box to relight the candle, then pulled her robe over her shift and ran barefoot down the stairs to the parlour. Setting the candle down on the table, she used both hands to lift the heavy bars off the shutters and swing them inwards. Richard was already outside the window. She fumbled open one of the casements. Putting his hands on the sill, he vaulted clumsily over and collapsed on the floor at her feet. As she struggled to rebolt the shutters, she could feel his hot breath on her bare toes.

'Richard!' She knelt down beside him. 'You're hurt!'

His head was clumsily bandaged with a dirty cloth, and the seeping stain of blood was wet. He seemed in no hurry to get up off the floor, but heaved himself to a sitting position, with his arms about his legs and his chin on his knees, still breathing heavily.

'What's happened? Has there been another battle with the king's men? Where's the rest of your regiment?'

'My regiment?' He gave a harsh laugh. 'Would that be the regiment pledged to fight for freedom and an end to tyranny? Or would it be the regiment that is Cromwell's lick-spittle?'

He looked about wildly, as though he expected to see the regiment behind the door.

'Stay there,' Anne called over her shoulder, unnecessarily, running swiftly and silently to fetch water and rags and salves from her stillroom. To reach it, she had to pass through the kitchen, but the servants sleeping there on pallets did not stir, despite the thunderous heat of the night.

The cut to Richard's head was not as bad as she had feared: a sword slash above his eye, it had bled a good deal, but was not deep. She washed and dressed it, crouched on the floor beside him, while he chewed on bread and cold bacon. At last she managed to persuade him to sit on a chair at the table. His breathing had steadied and he looked less wild.

'Now, Richard,' she said, clasping her hands in her lap to steady them, 'can you tell me what's happened?'

'It's a sorry tale, and too long to tell now,' he said, 'for I fear I may be followed.'

'But *who* is following you?'

'That part of the regiment that supports King Cromwell,' he said bitterly. 'Things have come to a pretty pass when comrades in arms, who have fought side-by-side against a common enemy, fall out with each other in victory.'

He explained that when word had reached his regiment, busy keeping down the Royalists in the north, that several regiments had occupied London and were going to see that all the soldiers received their arrears of pay, there had been great rejoicing.

'For things have gone very hard with us, Anne. There have been times we've near starved, when there was no more food to be had by raiding the farms. And look at my boots!'

He held up his foot, clad in tattered remnants of leather bound together with twine.

'Some have no boots at all, nor had none all last winter, and lost their toes with frostbite, for it's hard country up there.'

Then further news had come.

'The peace voted on by Parliament was cast aside, we heard. Now, so long as we get our pay, there's many of us want peace, and a return to our homes. I know that peace is what John was working for. I don't always agree with my elder brother, who thinks he can treat me as a child, but I know he's honourable and just. If he approved the settlement, I was happy.'

He looked around.

'Is there no ale?'

Anne got up and fetched it from the court cupboard.

'Not only was the vote of Parliament cast aside by force,' he said, 'but we heard the members were driven out and imprisoned. Then we heard of the death of the king. I wept no tears, but I don't think it was honourably done.'

He drank deeply from the tankard and wiped his mouth with the back of his hand.

'All this while, we hear, Ireton is making wonderful promises to John Lilburne, and so does Cromwell, too, when he gets to London. Then Lilburne is cast aside like the Members of Parliament, and Cromwell is setting himself up like a king, to rule over the nation in solitary power, like the worst of these Stuarts.'

'You're a follower of Lilburne?' Anne asked cautiously. Richard had always been radical in his views, but she had not thought he was a Leveller.

'Of course. We're not all born the eldest sons of gentlemen, with a manor and a fortune awaiting us.' His voice was bitter.

Anne flushed.

'That's unkind and unjust. You know that John will provide for you, and will see that you're settled with a wife and land when you are come of age.'

Richard shrugged.

'Perhaps. But there are thousands of others in far worse case than I. Poor men who'll never be able to fill their bellies and cover their nakedness, nor that of their families. The Lord did not create some men

329

to starve while others are gluttons. "When Adam delved and Eve span, who was then the gentleman?"'

'But what has this to do with your present state?'

'Some of us rebelled against the actions of Cromwell and his fellows, especially when we were told we must cross the sea to fight the Irish. It's time he learned that he can't depend on the loyalty of soldiers when he cheats them.'

'You mutinied!' Anne was horrified. This meant death.

'There were plenty that thought the same, but alas, there were more who stood by that treacherous man, still hoping he'll keep his word. Fools that they are! In Burford near Oxford there's been a great mutiny, and many put to death for it. So, when things went against us in the north, I had to make a run for it.'

'You said they might pursue you here?'

'Aye, well, I was taken once, then made my escape in Stafford. They may have picked up my trail.'

As if in answer to his words, the dogs on the farm began a furious barking. Anne realised now that they had not barked earlier, when she had first heard Richard creeping about.

'You must hide!'

'I'd sooner fight them. Even if they aren't after me, they'll be after our horses. And victuals. How many men do you have?'

'Only old men and boys. The two day labourers go home to Weeford at night, the shepherd is up on the moor. I'm going to look out of the upstairs window.'

She ran upstairs, shielding the candle with her hand, and crept into the room where Dick and Jack slept, followed by Richard. The window here overlooked the carriageway leading up from the road. And there, clearly to be seen in the moonlight, was a troop of horsemen heading for the house. They carried pitch torches held high above their heads, and in the mingled shadows cast by moonlight and torchlight, the black shapes of the riders turned them into the horsemen of the Apocalypse, or the riders of the Wild Hunt that presaged death.

'What shall we do? Dear God, what shall we do?' Anne cried.

Dick and Jack had woken now, and crowded sleepily beside them at the window.

'Who are they?' said Dick.

'Soldiers,' said Anne, 'hunting for your uncle.'

'They're riding towards the wheat field,' said Jack.

In a moment, it was clear what the troopers intended. They separated, riding through the waist-high wheat, pausing to lean down and set it alight. Small patches caught fire at first, but there had been no rain for nearly a fortnight, and the wheat was dry. The fires began to spread and join up.

'My wheat!' Anne cried, turning to rush out of the room.

Richard seized her arm. 'They're trying to frighten us. What can you do? You can't put it out.'

'That wheat is what stands between us and starvation.'

'The horses!' Richard cried. 'As soon as they've torched the wheat, they'll come back for the horses. Dick, come with me. You, too, Jack. You've grown into a fine big boy. We have to get the horses away before they come back to the stable.'

'Wait!' Anne shouted, 'let me think. Richard, you must hide, but not here. If they search the house they'll find you. And we mustn't risk the children. Oh, God! The wheat!'

The flames were catching hold now, the black silhouettes of the troopers moving in front of them like some macabre puppet show. No, Richard's safety must come before the wheat.

'You're right,' she said, 'they'll come for the horses. Go up to Packington Moor. To Agnes Lea's cottage; it's hidden away. They'll never find you there. Hurry!'

Dick and Jack tumbled out of the door after him, and they were gone.

She hesitated no longer, but ran to wake Patience and the women servants, then rushed downstairs to the kitchen and shook Peter and Josiah awake. Isaac was nowhere to be seen, though his truckle bed was tumbled. He must have gone with Richard.

Anne shot the bolts on the kitchen door.

'Quick! Into the hall. Fetch the muskets and their gear and take them upstairs. Josiah at the front of the house, in the boys' room, Peter at the rear, in mine. Margit, you load for Josiah, Bess for Peter. Biddy, look to Master and Mistress Swynfen, that they don't take fright.'

She was scrambling upstairs now, hardly noticing when she stubbed her toes painfully on a step. Blurred with sleep and stumbling, they followed her.

'Hester, take all the younger children upstairs into the garret, but be ready to bring them down quickly if the troopers fire the house. Leave the baby in my chamber, I'll fetch her if needs must.'

'Bows,' said Bridget, limping up the stairs behind Anne. 'There are bows and quivers in the kist on the landing. I'm a fair shot. Patience?'

'I can shoot,' said Patience, breathless, her hair a wild roseate halo about her head, 'though I've no great talent for it.'

'In this darkness, all we can do is aim at shadows,' said Anne. 'No one is to shoot unless they shoot first. Do you hear? *No one*. We mustn't provoke them.'

They nodded their understanding, the men and maids peeling away along the corridor to their posts, while Bridget opened the kist and handed out the bows which were for sporting use rather than defence. Anne took a bow and a supply of arrows, but when she reached the boys' room she laid them aside and seized one of the muskets.

Josiah, waiting quietly by the open casement with his primed musket resting on the sill, glanced round at her.

'Can you fire a musket, mistress?'

'Aye,' said Anne grimly. 'I can fire a musket.'

She finished ramming the ball home and lit the slow match, then opened the other casement as quietly as she could. Margit was loading the two remaining muskets. She was pale with fright, but she had laid out balls, powder flasks and rags neatly on Dick's bed.

Anne leaned out of the window. From here she could not see whether Richard and the younger boys had managed to lead the horses out of the stable, but there was no sign of the troopers riding off in pursuit. It seemed as though she had been gone from here for a long time while she roused the household, but the soldiers were still at their work in the wheat field. She ground her teeth together in fury and frustration.

'They'm coming back,' Josiah murmured.

The torches had clustered together again and were moving towards the house. Anne wiped her sweaty palms on her robe and tried to hold the heavy musket steady, resting on the sill. Suddenly they were at the front door, with a heavy log pulled from the woodstack. Three or four of the men dismounted. It was difficult to see how many in the flame-lit darkness, as their shadows leapt and danced below the window. The moon which had shone earlier over the lake had been lost behind heavy clouds. There was no light of moon or stars.

With a great crash, the men swung their makeshift battering ram against the door.

'Not yet,' Anne whispered to Josiah.

''Tis a hard angle for shooting,' he said. 'Too close under us.'

'If they try to shoot at us, they'll have to step back. Then we'll have a clearer line of fire.'

The heavy oak door of Swinfen Hall had kept out intruders for several centuries. It was not going to yield easily. And the men seemed in a hurry. There was the sudden crash and tinkle of breaking glass.

Josiah's face, pale in the wash of the torches below, turned towards Anne.

'They'll be inside in a minute.'

Anne bit her lip.

'All right. We'll have to open fire.'

It was her decision. She would take the responsibility. She set the slow match to the charge and aimed at the dark mass of men below.

The crack of the first shot startled her almost as much as the soldiers. The musket crashed back into her shoulder and she staggered, try to stay on her feet. Smoke and the stench of gunpowder choked her. There was an angry yell from below. She could not have hit anyone, but the troopers were taken by surprise. The defenceless house presented a different prospect now. Josiah fired immediately after Anne, and from the window of Nan's room next door she heard the swish of an arrow. The girls could reload more quickly with arrows, but here was Margit, passing her another loaded musket. Bracing her feet firmly, Anne took aim and fired again. This time there was a cry of pain, followed at once by the crack of a shot hitting the stonework by her head. She ducked back.

'When you've loaded that musket, Margit, go and tell Peter and Bess to move to the small front room in the east wing. The men are all on this side of the house, and from the wing they'll have a clearer shot at them.'

The girl fled, her bare feet slapping on the boards. Another shot from below hit the window, sending a spray of glass shards into the room, but Anne heard the impact of her own next shot in flesh, and a scream of pain. A wild anger flooded her as she grabbed the last of the loaded muskets and fired again. Immediately afterwards she saw a flash from a window in the east wing, followed by a terrified squeal from one of the troopers' horses.

Margit was back, her hands shaking as she poured the powder into one of the muskets, spilling it amongst the broken glass.

'I'm sorry, mistress! I'm sorry!'

'Don't worry. You're doing well. Don't hurry too much.'

Anne turned to Josiah.

'You and Margit take two of the muskets to the west wing and start firing from there. I'll stay here. I can load for myself.'

She risked a look out of the window. The troopers had dropped their torches the better to load and shoot, and they burned in two heaps on either side of the door. Angry voices were arguing below, and there was a swish and then a yell of pain as an arrow found its mark. She loaded, took careful aim, and fired into the centre of the clustered dark shapes below. The musket was burning hot, and she had singed a lock of her hair on the slow match.

Then Josiah opened fire from the west wing as Peter fired again from the east. Neither ball seemed to find its mark, but the troopers, now fired on from three sides where they had hoped to surprise a house full of helpless sleepers, had had enough. Anne leaned forward and watched those on foot remounting. As the horses wheeled to head away down the drive, one rider twisted in the saddle and fired a final shot. Pain exploded in Anne's left shoulder and she fell backwards, striking her head on the corner of the bed. The dim light of the candle dipped and swayed as she clawed herself to her knees, then dragged herself upright by the post of the bed.

She ran from the room, calling the others to the kitchen, where she heaved back the bolts from the door. They came running, gentlewomen and servants alike, following her with buckets, out of the yard and down to the lake.

'We must throw water from the lake onto the fires,' Anne gasped, trying to organise them into a line, passing buckets from hand to hand, as she had seen people do when houses caught fire in London. But it was beyond hope. Their pitiful buckets were like spitting on a bonfire.

'The storm's a-coming at last, mistress,' said Josiah. 'God willing, 'twill come in time to save some of the crop.'

The thunderstorm. Of course, all day it had been threatening. Anne threw down her bucket and raised her arms to the heavens, where black clouds blotted out every trace of moon and stars. Her blood-soaked sleeve fell back as she prayed with her whole body, arguing, promising God anything, making bargains. If only he would save the wheat. The others ceased their helpless attempts and turned to stare at her. Had she cried aloud? She did not know, nor did she care. More of the fires joined together, leaping from furrow to furrow, and then, like the voice of God himself, thunder cracked once over the woods, and lightning thrust down to earth like God's finger pointing. Over the crackle of the fires there sounded a sudden rush of wind, and then a few drops of rain spattered her up-turned face.

The thunder crashed again, this time directly overhead, and the clouds opened like a heavenly flood, falling like a benison on the burning field.

It was dawn before the fire was finally extinguished. Although the storm put out most of the flames, there were pockets of embers which had to be dowsed with buckets of water from the lake. Part of the wheat

334

was saved, but a third at least was lost to the fire and to the great gashes where the troopers had ridden through it, trampling it under foot. Anne sank down amongst the charred remains of that green and hopeful forest of blades she had nurtured with such love. She covered her face with her hands and could not hold back the great cry that rose in her.

'My wheat, my precious wheat!'

And it seemed to her, kneeling there amongst the ruined crop dizzy with pain, that, in allowing this injury to befall John's land, she had somehow injured John himself.

ʠ

Richard and the other boys rode back in the middle of the morning, the younger boys still in their nightshifts. They had each ridden one horse and led two or three more, skirting round the edge of the farmland and taking refuge on the moor. Before coming back, they had visited Agnes Lea, who had given them breakfast.

Triumphant at his success in saving the horses from the troopers, Richard was dismayed when he heard of the attack on the house and saw the state of the ruined wheat. He stood appalled when he came upon Anne, still barefoot in her shift and house-gown, her face smeared with soot, her singed hair shrivelled against her cheek, her shoulder roughly bandaged, come back to survey the field again after trying to calm her household and setting them to work to keep their thoughts off the disaster.

'This is my fault,' said Richard quietly. 'I should never have come here. I'll understand if you cannot forgive me, Anne.'

She shrugged. It was difficult, still, for her to speak.

He touched her arm gently. 'When John comes home, he'll relieve you of this burden of running the estate,' he said, mistaking her altogether.

'I don't know where John is, or whether I shall ever see him again.' The bitter words caught in her throat. She had no strength to dissemble today.

He stared at her in astonishment.

'But, Anne, I thought you knew! I learned of it when I was at Stafford. John is imprisoned in Stafford Castle, not twenty miles from here.'

ʠ

'We require you to write a testament,' Danvers said.

335

But he had refused, and now he was to know the price.

They led him down the stairs and through the Great Hall, back towards the dungeons where he had wrestled with his own encroaching hell. Inside the outer door of the dungeons they turned left and descended again. Up above, in the world of light and sanity, the summer sun was warm and the clean smell of the newly washed countryside blew in over the castle walls after last night's thunderstorm. As they sank down into these nether regions of the castle, a bone-aching cold wrapped them round, so that, try as he might, John could not stop himself shivering.

There were two guards, one gripping him cruelly hard by each elbow, yet they must have known he could not escape. They thrust him ahead of them into a dark chamber, lit by a single torch flaring from a bracket on the wall. The chamber was crowded, the amber glow flickered on benches and tables, glinted off metal, caught the edge of some framework of machinery—a ratcheted wheel, straps with metal buckles.

There was a man in the room, whose shadow, cast by the torch, climbed the wall and leaned over John from the low ceiling. The man was hooded. John felt terror rising in his throat like bile, and sweat broke out on his back and trickled down to soak the waist of his breeches. There was a smell in the room—the smell of his own rank fear and the smell, soaked into the very stones, of centuries of fear, and the smell, pungent and unmistakable, of men raised to a high pitch of excitement, men watching an execution or cutting the throat of a deer or seizing a woman for rape.

The torturer stepped forward and, without a word, took John softly by the arm.

Inside his head, silent screams echoed and reverberated in the hollows of his skull.

&

Anne lay on her bed, indifferent to the sounds of the house all around her. Her clothes carried the smell of the fire, and the hands which she pressed against her eyes were scratched and filthy. The wound in her shoulder burned with pain, yet she hardly noticed it, for all she could see behind her closed lids was the blazing wheat field, the confident young shoots curling and dying in barren ash. She began to sob hopelessly as another image overlaid it. Her last parting from John. She had turned and fled from him up the stairs, leaving him with bitter words that she could never call back. John—John was in Stafford

Castle. So close. Yet this was no comfort to her. Instead she was seized by sudden overwhelming terror that knocked the breath from her lungs and wiped out her tears, as she stared into the space before her, seeing nothing but the flash of red hot iron in the darkness. She had never felt so much alone, nor known such despair that she would never see John again.

Chapter Twenty-Five

I JOHN SWYNFEN, being of sound mind, though troubled by melancholy—nay, I lie, for my mind is anything but sound—and of body sick and weakened, but not like to die, save at the hands of mine enemies, do here set down an account of my life both inward and outward, this month past. For it seems to me that I am not like to see again the wife and children I love, nor to set my foot again on the soil held by my forefathers since before the time Norman William came to these shores. I therefore put pen to paper in order that they may know that I did not choose to buy life and freedom at the price of conscience and principle. I pray that the Lord may give me the strength to write these things, for my hand shaketh like the aspen tree, and my mind is as troubled as the waters of the sea when a great wind bloweth.

In the name of the Father, and of the Son, and of the Holy Spirit, Amen.

When first I was brought to this place of confinement, being the castle close by the town of Stafford, which town sent me to speak for them in Parliament, the which I have always striven to do fairly and justly—when, I say, I was brought here in a vile kind of cart, wherein I was beaten and abused, and shot and my wound left to rot, then I was cast into a dungeon and shackled by a chain to the wall, like unto a wicked criminal. There I languished many days in a Hell and torment of mind until I was brought before the governor of this place, one Colonel Danvers, a man known to me in the past as an officer in the Parliamentary army, not over scrupulous in all his dealings, and one who will turn always towards the rising power, as the lodestone turns to the North, hoping to steer his ways through the troubled waters of these times by the strength of a greater man. So now, when Oliver Cromwell climbs to power over the men he has brought low by wickedness and cunning, this Danvers turns to him and seeks to bask in his sun while it is in the ascendant.

Acting upon his orders from those who govern him, this Danvers then moved me from my dungeon to comfortable quarters and provided me with every necessity, excepting only that one necessity without which a man may not live and call himself a man indeed, to wit,

338

freedom. For I was kept locked within the chamber like a singing bird trapped in a pretty cage for the delectation of some eastern sultan. However, the men of power misjudged me, for I would not sing.

They gave me food to eat and wine to drink, they anointed my wounds and washed my raiment, until I became, in the outward man, once more a seeming citizen of a civilised nation. But—do you say it?—this England of ours is no longer possessed of civility. A nation which imprisons its lawful representatives and murders its lawful monarch can no longer claim civility. Nay, but if these things had been done in the name of the people's good, what then? Why, so they were done, but words are one thing, actions another.

They have set up a tyranny and a despotism, they have cast aside those men who claimed to speak for the poor. For though I take John Lilburne of the Levellers to be a misguided man, and Gerrard Winstanley of the Diggers to be little better than mad, yet I know they acted from belief and kindness. What of this Ireton, this Cromwell? Even, now, what of this Fairfax, whom once I thought a good man and a just man, but who has proceeded in concert with them? These men have thrown into the dungeons at Windsor those generals who led the way before them in the war against a tyrannical king. And they have promised their soldiers, poor men who have suffered and died for them—starved, penniless and bereft of their families—promised them rewards and new freedoms, through that monstrous document the *Agreement*.

Now, so I have been told by Governor Danvers, those same soldiers who refused to cross the seas to fight the benighted Irish are turned away from the army, their only support, and their arrears of pay denied them. And some, breaking out in mutiny at their treatment, have suffered terrible punishments and even death. So this man Cromwell, under pretence of fighting the king to protect the people, robs the people of their elected Parliament, the soldiers of their due rewards, and the country of its freedom, setting himself up to rule over it with a secret coterie of men, pledged to be the instruments of his wishes.

I seem to wander from my subject, but I do not, although my mind is cast into turmoil by what I have endured.

God help me, do not let me lose my reason. My thoughts fly away and will not take shape under my hands. I will leave this writing for a time.

Once he had placed me in that better chamber, Danvers set before me temptations, like choice dishes at a banquet. He promised to convey my letters, and to deliver letters to me. During this month of promises, he

339

has had from my hand ten letters to my family and as many to friends. To none of the letters written to my family have I received an answer. My suspicion is, that none were conveyed. As for those others, I have received one reply only, but of that more anon.

These temptations were, as one might say, but the invitation to the feast. The real purpose lay elsewhere, and if I judge aright, the reason for my continued imprisonment, when others were freed long since, lies therein. For I am not a rich man like Crewe or Harley, who are set free, nor am I a general of the army, like Copley or Waller, who are kept fast, lest their old soldiers flock to them. Why then am I still held? I am but a country gentleman of moderate wealth and no military experience.

Why? God comfort me, why?

Aye, 'tis a conundrum, is it not?

My old tutors in logic and rhetoric at Cambridge would bid me set out my case by the dialectical principles of Aristotle and Tully, but my head aches too much for cogent argument. Any schoolboy, with his Aphthonius in hand, could better me. I suffer from the old trouble, when lightning seems to flash in the air before me, and my eye is veiled with darkness, when a megrim grips my head like a vice. And the wound in my leg, long neglected, will not heal cleanly, but suppurates like these evil men. I strive to find forgiveness for them, but I lack grace. I cannot. God forgive me, I cannot love mine enemies.

Why was I one of those few who were not only secluded from Parliament, but taken up and imprisoned? Why was I one of the few retained a prisoner, when so many were let go? I have thought much on this, and my conclusion is simple, but strange, in these days when so much is achieved by the sword. I was the enemy of those who pursued their own road to tyranny because I *spoke out* against them. My strength lies in *words*. (Nay, I know, this poor rambling document is hardly testimony to my skill on that score, but when I spoke in Parliament I had the power to move men and shape the fate of the nation.) *Words*, evanescent as smoke, but pregnant with so much power.

And, behold!, I am proved to have judged correctly. For next Danvers comes with the new temptation, and it is the main dish, the centrepiece of the feast, for which the other little comforts were but a prologue.

'We require you to write a testament,' says he.

Note the language:

Item: 'we require'.

Item: 'a testament'.

A 'requirement' brooks no objection or negotiation.

A 'testament' is an ominous document, smelling of legal enforcement and death.

'A testament,' says he, 'asserting your compliance with His Highness's good government established to bring this nation to order. You will make a declaration of loyalty and will praise General Cromwell for his achievements and urge on your fellow Members of Parliament and country gentry that they should submit to his rule. You will state your earnest support for his campaigns now in Ireland and planned for Scotland, to subdue the wild neighbours of this . . . nation.'

(He had nearly said 'this kingdom', but fell over the words and righted himself.)

'You will admit to your errors and crimes in the past, and beg His Highness's forgiveness. You will promise to bow to the will of him and of his government in all things.'

When he finished this speech, it seemed that the air between us buzzed, as with wasps whose nest has been broken apart. I came near to swatting out, as if I could rid myself of them. But the buzzing was inside my own troubled brain. Then a silence settled over us.

'Well?' he said.

'I am not sure,' I said, 'that I take your meaning. I have been grievously abused by the instruments of this fellow Cromwell's government. Why should that induce me to write such a document?'

'As for inducements,' said he, 'if you write this testament of apology and compliance, then His Highness will pardon you and you will be released from imprisonment. Moreover, you will be found high office in the new government, higher than you could have aspired to for many years under the old dispensation.'

Then I knew that I had judged rightly, and all that I had endured had been to this end. Because of my gift of *words*, I was a valuable piece in their game of chess. These *words* they would use to attempt the corruption of good men. So my one talent, this gift from God, would turn to poison as of the serpent.

'And if I do not write such a document?' I said, attempting to keep my voice steady, for I thought I knew what was to come next. I was full of dread. They could break my body if they chose, and I felt myself sweat with the terror of it.

He looked at me soberly. He is not an evil man by nature, I think, but he is easily led into evil by stronger men than he. I think he did not like what he had to say.

'If you do not, His Highness will be obliged to make example of you. Your estates will be sequestrated, your family dispossessed and turned out as vagabonds to wander the land. You will yourself be subjected to torture, until you understand the error of your resistance, and write the testament at the last. So you understand, there is nothing to be gained by refusing, and much to be lost.'

I thought of Prynne and his courage under torture and maiming. And I thought how he had joked about being able to endure anything but the loss of his tongue. For it is *words*, not bodies, that make men in the image of God. Let our bodies be misshapen or mutilated, yet if we retain our minds to think, and our *words* to speak, then we shall retain that spark of the divine within us. But my family, my wife, my children—what right have I under God to force them into destitution, to wander homeless over the land?

'And if I still refuse, even under torture?'

He looked at me pityingly.

'Believe me, Swynfen, I have seen men put to the torture. I think that you have not. Every man breaks in the end. Why endure that? For you *will* break. And if you refuse at the outset, and agree at the end, your family will still be dispossessed.'

He rose from his chair and walked to the door.

'I will allow you two days to ponder this. If you have not agreed in two days, then I must proceed with the other means of persuasion.'

Lord God of Hosts, give me strength in this adversity.

I passed the two days in prayer, in meditation, and in perusing Boethius's *Philosophiae Consolatio*. Previously I had found myself too distracted by my situation to concentrate my mind on his words, but now I read them in a kind of desperation, as if somewhere here I might find the answer to my dilemma. I could live, with power and riches, but shamed and bereft of honour; or I could destroy my family and myself, endure torture and death, but preserve my honour and beliefs. None would know of it but God. Should that weigh in the balance? I was a coward. I feared torture. And I feared that my family and my friends would not know why I had allowed those dearest to me to be destroyed.

A divergence, though a brief one: for those of you who know Boethius's work, the resemblance between his case and mine will be striking. Indeed, it grows closer all the while. Boethius wished to live the life of a scholar. At the end of the fifth century of Our Lord he wrote and translated many books which preserved for subsequent scholars the great works of the ancients. His works of scholarship lasted down the ages from his own time for the next thousand years, until such great men as Plato and Aristotle were rediscovered in the Greek tongue. Boethius translated the Greek philosophers into Latin, and wrote his own original works of theology, philosophy, geometry,

342

rhetoric, every branch of learning. I myself used his textbook on music while a student at university. However, Boethius was called to leave his studies and serve his country in public life, which he did selflessly and with great distinction. The ruler of Italy at the time was Theodoric, a barbarian (but Christian) king, client of the eastern Roman emperor, but who had effectively become, in those unsettled times, an independent monarch.

I see in Theodoric aspects of both *Charles Stuart* and this *Cromwell* (a man who, like Theodoric, has seized power, coming from nowhere). Theodoric was an absolute ruler, but maintained the forms of the old Roman senate (as we might say, *Parliament*), and was at first, in many ways, a just and tolerant ruler. Boethius served him loyally, and rose high, becoming consul. All changed, however, when the long-standing rift between the western empire and the east (as we might say, a *civil war*) seemed like to be healed. Theodoric was *opposed to peace*, for then he would cease to hold the absolute power he so much enjoyed, becoming again no more than a client king, answerable to the emperor. Boethius was of the *peace party* (as am I), but did not conspire against Theodoric. However, all men in politics have enemies. Boethius's enemies accused him of treason. He was imprisoned, tortured, and finally bludgeoned to death. While he awaited execution, he wrote the *Consolatio*. Theodoric's rule, which had promised so fair, ended in horrible bloodshed soon afterwards.

I do not set myself up to be a Boethius—I am a poor scholar by comparison, and had not risen so high in office as he. But like him I tried to do my duty honestly, I worked for peace, and, if God gives me strength enough, I mean to hold to my principles.

I wander again in my thoughts.

Boethius, I believe, did not condemn his family to suffering.

The two days passed.

When Danvers came to me again, I refused his demands. God help me, I do not know if he immediately put into effect the orders against my family. I was trained in the law, and I know that as long as my father lives, I am but the heir to Swinfen, he is its lord. I pray, therefore, that—unless this new government overturns all laws—they cannot sequestrate my father's property for my offences. I cling to this hope, for I can endure if others are spared.

This is arrogance. How can I believe that I will endure, when all men break in the end? God help me! God help me!

Danvers ordered that I be taken once more to the dungeons, but this time to another place, an ancient place of torture. My intention is not to dwell on what was done to me there, but to tell it in the briefest of words. At first, they bound me, arms and legs, to a chair, and left me in the dark. This seems a mild punishment, but as time passes, the pain begins. I do not know how long I was kept there; it may have been a day, it may have been two, and no food or drink. In such a length of time, a man must piss and foul himself, and this degradation is a part of the torment.

At the end I was asked, 'Would I write?'

And I refused.

Then they unbound me, and the limbs unbound are almost more of a torture than the limbs bound. They heated irons, with which they burned the soles of my feet. And I was asked, 'Would I write?'

And I refused.

Then they forced me to lie on a rack, my arms stretched above my head and bound, and my ankles bound, and they cranked it slowly, till the muscles in my shoulders cracked, and my knees and hips were strained near out of their sockets, but I do not think they racked me as far as many have been stretched. Perhaps Danvers was merciful. And I was asked, 'Would I write?'

And I refused.

Then they left me alone in the dark with my tortured flesh to think.

And I sweated with pain and my mind screamed and would not hold my thoughts together.

And after some time (I know not how long), they took me up to my comfortable chamber again, although they must half carry me up the stairs, for my legs worked but poorly and the soles of my feet burned still. Then they gave me food and drink and left me alone. I was sickened at the thought of food, but I forced myself to eat, for I knew my body needed sustenance to mend itself. Then I lay on my bed and slept, I know not how long.

The next day, or it may have been the day after, Danvers came again and reasoned with me, using all the arguments he had put forward before, but I would not be moved. And so the cycle repeated itself.

I have now visited that hellish place of torture three times, and three times have been returned to this chamber. They stay their hand from the furthest extremes of torture, I know not why. Perhaps they think that, by so doing, they will make me more fearful of what yet lies in wait.

Today, I was brought a letter, the first I have received since I was taken from London. Samuel Gott writes in reply to a letter I wrote to him a month since. I cannot fathom Danvers with certainty, but I think he chooses not to send the letters to my family, in order to torment them with worry. The letters to my friends I am sure he reads, then sends on in the hope of provoking an incautious letter in response, a trap to catch me by, or to catch the writer.

Samuel tells me of a plan he has to write a treatise *On the True Happiness of Man*, and he seeks my advice. I think he speaks in code or riddles—for how can I judge such a question in my present state?—but my mind is blurred since my last time below ground, and I cannot make him out. He also seeks guidance on how men should behave in this new state of the nation. How should we regard the courts? He wants to know if I believe them to be legitimate, since they are constituted by an illegal authority. Can the dispensers of law be regarded as lawful when the very foundation of the courts is unlawful? He also raises the matter of tithes, and their rightful recipients. These are important and useful questions, but I cannot put my mind to them. My mind slips away from my governance and wanders, as on a rough ocean. Besides, I must have a care what I write to him, for it will, of a certainty, be used against me.

The true happiness of man.

In what does it lie? Until I came to this present pass, I believed that I was blessed in that I had been chosen to serve first my home county of Stafford and then the nation of England. Is there any higher ambition for a man than to serve his fellow citizens to the summit of his ability? I know some thought me over-eager, willing to undertake more tasks than most members, sitting late on many committees, working through the night to prepare reports for the Commons and the Lords, drafting parliamentary bills. (Oh, how puffed up with pride I was, to be chosen so often for that painstaking task!) Yet I truly thought this to be a privilege, and I felt humbled as well as proud.

And what has come of it all? Those night-time, candle-lit hours? Those years of work that kept me from my family? That meant I did not watch the first steps my children took, nor hear with delight the first words they spoke? Above all, that kept me from the arms of my beloved? Dust and ashes, blown away on the wind. All gone, for nothing.

The true happiness of man.

I believe it lies in love. The love of God, and the love of a man's family. All else is vanity.

Oh, my beloved, heart of my heart, can you hear me call to you in the darkness of this night? I will strive to endure, but cannot know when my frail and treacherous body will betray me or my tormented mind disintegrate. If I could but see you again, hold you in my arms once more—

They will come for me again tomorrow.

Written by my hand, on a date I know not, in the summer of the year of our Lord one thousand six hundred and forty-nine.
    John Swynfen

Chapter Twenty-Six

Richard was eager to ride over to friends in Barton-under-Needwood. Anne considered it wiser not to enquire too closely who these friends might be, for she had heard there were radical groups in that neighbourhood more extreme even than the Levellers. She did not wish to know if they were Diggers or one of the other more fanatical sects. After the thunderstorm, two days of cloudless hot weather had dried the hay. It was not too badly laid and Anne, after consulting Josiah, had decided to begin the haymaking before they should be visited by another storm.

'I would entreat you, Richard,' she said, 'at least stay to help us get in the hay. Without it, I can't feed the stock during the winter.'

They were standing at the edge of one of the two hay meadows, just beyond the damaged field of wheat. Richard turned to look at the great charred patches.

'Of course I'll help with the hay,' he said sadly. 'Having brought upon you the loss of so much of the wheat. We've always had the custom at Swinfen that everyone helps to cut and stack the hay, gentleman and servant and labourer and all. You know that.'

'Aye,' said Anne, somewhat bitterly. 'We've long held to certain levelling practices here.'

'Let us not quarrel, sister. I'll ride up to the moor today and tell that shepherd of yours he must leave his flock to fend for themselves while he helps with the haysel. Dick says he's a strong fellow, not above thirty-five. Not quite an old man yet.'

Anne laughed, for Richard knew her own age well enough.

'Not quite. Away with you, then. Take one of the big geldings, and you may ride back two to a horse.'

After Richard had run off to the stable, his light brown hair aglint in the sun, she waded in amongst the hay, her skirts stirring up the sweet scent of it. It had always seemed to her one of the loveliest perfumes in the world, compared with which the false, contrived scents worn by the fashionable in London had always sickened her. Amongst the hay, the meadow flowers spangled the golden green with a riot of colours: the great yellow heads of goat's beard and rose pink of ragged

347

robin, the blue cornflower, meadowsweet with its creamy white like sea foam, and here and there the shy purple of meadow orchids. The sweet hay reminded her of childhood games, when she and John would slide down the growing haystacks, then scamper off laughing, before old William, Josiah's father, could catch them. He had been known to spank them both, being no respecter of rank in naughty children.

Mercifully, the hay had been untouched by the torches of the troopers. Anne sank down amongst it, her skirts billowing, and buried her faces in the fragrant stems whilst her mind flew off in speculation. Had the soldiers truly been in pursuit of the fugitive Richard? Perhaps they had merely set the field alight and attacked the house from very devilment, like so many of their kind. Or perhaps there was some thread, invisible to her at the moment, which linked the attack on Swinfen with John's imprisonment in Stafford Castle. Was she, not Richard, their intended quarry? Her injured shoulder throbbed in the hot sun. Even here there was nowhere to hide from the war.

That evening was spent preparing food for the following days, since the entire household, save for the nurse Bess and the youngest children, and the two invalids, would be out in the hay meadows from dawn to dusk. Anne and Bridget baked bread, while the other women shaped and baked raised pies to be stored in the cold dairy, and young Margit churned the butter, which would usually have been left till the next day. Dick and Jack had gone with Peter out to the barn with the farm labourers, sharpening and mending the tools. As dusk was setting in, Richard rode down with the shepherd from the moor. All went to their beds early, for the coming labour would be hard.

The weather continued hot the next day, with no relief from a breeze. Starting at the top end of the meadow, the men formed a line with their scythes and began to move forward, swinging the razor-sharp curved blades in a steady, slow rhythm that they could keep up for the whole of the day. Anne tried to avoid looking at Dick, who had never wielded a scythe before, but was determined to show himself man enough this summer to do so. A careless stroke could take off a man's foot.

The big scythes could not reach to cut the hay close to the hedge, so Anne and Patience followed along behind with their small hand-sickles, to cut the narrow strip the scythes had missed. The rest of the women raked the hay into neat piles, even Bridget with her twisted leg. She had merely looked scornful when Anne had suggested she should stay at home with Bess and the children.

'I've helped with haymaking since I was a child, Anne. I'll not play the lady today. I'll go indoors to tend my parents at dinner time, but otherwise I will work with the rest of you.' In the unshadowed sun of the hay meadow her fragile pallor warmed to a healthy glow. She wore her bark-brown hair in a single heavy plait down her back and she looked young and free from pain.

Even the younger boys helped, fetching water and ale for the thirsty. Nan was proudly wielding a rake amongst the women, much to Jack's disgust, for he was certain he was old enough to join the men and use a scythe. Here, however, Anne had stood firm in saying him nay.

It was hot, sticky, tiring work. Insects, disturbed by all their activity, rose up and stung them on every exposed bit of skin. Sharp fragments of the hay worked their way inside clothing, and clung to their arms and faces, whilst fine powdery dust and pollen settled on their hair and tickled their noses. The wound in Anne's shoulder ached with the heat and the heavy work, but she bit her lip, determined to endure it. By mid-day all the women had loosened their collars, and some looked enviously at the men, who had stripped to the waist to cool themselves. When they stopped for dinner, the boys—even Richard, who was no more than a boy, after all—ran yelling down to the stream which fed the lake and jumped in, breeches and all. Anne walked down to the edge of the stream and scooped up the cool water to pour over her burning face and neck. As she blinked through lashes starred with drops, she saw delicate gilded dragonflies dancing amongst the reeds.

Hester and Biddy fetched down the food which they had tied in cloths and hung in an elder tree, to be out of the sun and away from ants. Anne sat eating cold pie with her fingers and taking deep draughts of buttermilk, which she liked better than ale in the hot weather. While she was working, she had been pondering the news that Richard had given her three days before, that John was imprisoned in Stafford. She turned to him now, where he sat, dripping, in the shade of the hedge.

'Richard, do you think I might persuade the governor at Stafford to free John on bail?'

He finished chewing, then shook his head.

'There's been no legal process. And so there's no court to arrange bail. If a man be held illegally, how can you use the machinery of law to free him?'

'I don't know. But I received a letter from John Crewe last week. He asked whether John was yet freed, and said that William Prynne escaped imprisonment on a writ of *habeas corpus*. I don't understand the legal term, but if it served for Will, why should it not serve for John?'

'I know that no better than you,' said Richard, 'but John trained as a lawyer. Wouldn't he have used the same device, if it were possible?'

'Perhaps it's not so easy from a dungeon in Stafford Castle as from an inn in London. But when Crewe's letter came, we didn't know where John was being held. Now that we know, perhaps his friends can contrive to have him freed.'

'It's worth the attempt, but I fear I can't help. I mustn't show my face, for I'm a wanted fugitive.'

'I thought of asking Captain Henry Stone. He's long been a friend of John's, and being an army man, may know best how to proceed. Also, he was governor of Stafford himself a few years ago.'

'An army man, but where does he stand? Is he for Cromwell, or against?'

'That I don't know. But as soon as we're done haymaking, I think I shall write to him.'

The weather held fine—the hay was cut, raked and turned. By the end of the week, they were loading it into the great haywain, which lumbered back and forth between the meadows and the farmyard, where the most skilled men, Josiah and Christopher, built the haystacks.

The last load was hauled and piled loose in the haybarn not long before midnight on the eve of the Sabbath, for which all heaved a sigh of relief. In the old days, the curate would not have blamed any man overmuch if his haymaking had strayed into Sunday. The animals must be fed over the winter, and it would have seemed like a scorning of God's bountiful gifts to have risked the hay falling victim to a storm of rain. But these new Puritans directed everything by the strict rules of their interpretation of Holy Writ. When they said, 'Remember the Sabbath, to keep it holy,' they meant *no* work: no lighting of fires or cooking of food, no hauling of water or gathering of the harvest. If God sent a storm to ruin your crops, why, then, he meant you to starve. Anne wondered what was the Puritan view of a woman great with child who went into labour on the Sabbath. Would she be condemned out of hand as ungodly?

As soon as haysel was over, Richard spoke again of his plan to visit his radical friends in Barton. He believed that fugitives from the mutiny at Burford had fled there, and he was on fire to hear the full story of that uprising of Levellers and Diggers in the ranks of the army.

The church at Burford had been turned into a prison, and men had been shot in cold blood, but others had escaped. If there were plans afoot for a further uprising, he longed to be a part of it.

Anne was against his going. No good could come of it, and possibly a great deal of evil. He was not her son, however, although he was little older than Dick. He was but her brother-in-law, and she governed here by default, not through any right to authority. She had no power to forbid him. All she could do was refuse him a horse, but when it became clear that, if he could not borrow a horse, he would walk to Barton, thus exposing himself even more to danger, she conceded the point.

'You may borrow a horse for two days only,' she said grimly, 'for we'll soon begin the rest of the harvest and every horse is needed. One day to ride there and spend the night, one day to ride back. And keep to the lanes, away from the roads that the military use.'

Although he tried to argue for a longer allowance of time, she was determined in this, and he had to be content.

That same day she despatched Peter to ride over to Captain Stone's house at the village of Walsall, with a letter explaining John's present whereabouts and her hope of ransoming him or securing bail. She begged that he might send a letter of advice back with her servant.

Peter left in the early morning. By dinnertime, two men rode up to Swinfen Hall. Henry Stone had ridden over directly with Peter, eager to help. Anne took him to dine with her alone in the parlour, while she told him all she knew, omitting only the source of her information that John was in Stafford. The fewer people who knew of Richard's presence at Swinfen, the better.

Henry was a big bluff man, who tucked in heartily to his dinner, but his looks belied the shrewdness of his mind. He had worked with John on many county matters, even before the war had begun. In the army he had shown himself a brilliant officer. So high had been Sir William Brereton's opinion of Henry Stone's abilities that he had fetched him away from his position as governor of Stafford to assist in the final siege of Lichfield Cathedral. Stone was no longer serving in the army, but he had contrived to remain on good terms with some who were, and to avoid attracting the notice of those who belonged to Ireton's faction.

'You did right to come to me, Mistress Anne,' he said, when he had heard her out. He took a long draught of ale and smacked his lips. 'The product of your own brewhouse? Excellent, excellent.'

'My woman Biddy is a fine alewife. She swears it's the quality of the water in one of the springs here at Swinfen. She'll use no other.'

'She has the right of it. When you know your best tools, then you must employ them, as I am the best tool in this matter. I knew John had been taken up, but heard no more. I thought he was free again, in London, but had sent his family home.'

'Do you think we may accomplish this?' she said. 'Or am I indulging in idle fantasies, to think that we may buy John his freedom?'

'I know Harry Danvers. If the decision were his, I think we should have no trouble, provided the bribe is large enough.' He grinned at her expression. 'Oh, yes, they may call it bail money, but you'll not see it again. It will find its way into somebody's pocket. However, my guess is that Danvers takes his orders from someone higher, perhaps from Ireton or even Cromwell himself. The only way to know is to go and talk to Danvers in Stafford. A strange fellow, that Danvers. A religious fanatic but a prancing fop. Full of hot-headed schemes, yet too cowardly to carry them through. He needs to be handled with care.'

'Do you think I should come?'

'Nay, I do *not*. We'll hold your wifely pleading in reserve. That may prove useful later. Remember, many wives of the king's men have saved their estates and even their husbands' lives before this. But I wouldn't expose you to that indignity if we may succeed through my offices.'

He tapped his teeth with his thumbnail.

'He'll need bribing in gold or jewellery. Have you gold enough?'

'Very little, I fear. I've been obliged to commute many of the rents for the cottagers, and allow several of the larger tenants to run up debts. Everyone has suffered so with the bad harvests, and the losses of the war.'

'I hope they've not taken advantage of you,' he said.

'Nay, I think not. They're all families who have lived here for generations. If I cannot be merciful to them, how can I expect mercy at God's hands?'

He grunted.

'Well, then it will need to be jewels.' He studied her, sitting opposite him in her countrywoman's gown, with nothing about her neck but a plain linen neckerchief. 'Or have you been forced to sell them, in these hard times? Forgive me for my bluntness.'

'Of course. We must deal honestly with each other. I have some jewels. I see no need to wear them here. I'll fetch them.'

She ran up the stairs to her chamber, eager at the thought of being able to do something, at last, for John. At the top she collided with Bridget, and told her what Henry Stone had said.

'Then you must have my jewels also,' said Bridget quietly. 'They're not many, I being but a spinster, but you shall have them all.'

Anne hugged her.

'My dear, he's my husband. You must keep your jewels.'

Bridget shook her head.

'He's my brother. When I was a child, he never laughed or mocked at me for my lameness. He always stood between me and our mother. I must help him now if I can.'

In her chamber, Anne drew out the small jewel box which she kept hidden under the mattress—a poor enough hiding-place, she knew, if ever the house were raided. The collection was not large, for she had never dressed lavishly, but all of the pieces were valuable. The long string of pearls John had given her last year shimmered like moving water as she poured the jewels out on the coverlet. She ran it through her fingers. Its opalescent beauty always moved her and the thought of parting with it wrenched at her memories. For one last time she fastened it round her neck, where it hung to her waist, and she felt again John's hands as he caressed her neck and kissed it above the clasp. Tears started in her eyes at the thought of parting with his gift, but she brushed them aside angrily. What right had she to weep over a string of pearls, even if John had given them to her? She placed everything in a leather pouch except two rings: her marriage ring, which would never leave her finger in life, and a ring she wore on her right hand. Like her marriage ring, she wore this always, so that she hardly noticed it was there, but she turned it on her finger and kissed it now.

When John was fifteen, and on his way to Cambridge, he had travelled to London for the first time with his father, and there he had bought this curious silver ring set with a turquoise. The man he bought it from was a sailor recently returned from the New World, where he said he had bargained it off one of the savages in exchange for an axe. Anne was certain John had given much more than the price of an axe for it. When he came home that winter, he had given it to her as a Christmas gift, and they had both of them understood that this was a secret betrothal between them. This was the one jewel, apart from her plain gold wedding band, that she would not part with, for it would seem like a betrayal of John's love for her.

Bridget met her again on the landing and pressed into her hands a small collection of jewellery: three gold chains, a small strand of river pearls with matching ear-rings, and a simple amethyst and seed-pearl necklace. Anne kissed her, but made no further attempt to dissuade her.

Henry Stone looked over the jewellery spread out on the parlour table, and set a few things to one side.

'I'll not offer everything at once, but keep some back to bargain with. I'm sorry to have to deprive you of your jewels, Mistress Anne.'

She gave a dismissive wave of her hand.

'What are they but vanities, after all? I don't need them. They are nothing to me beside my husband's freedom.'

Henry returned the larger pile to the leather bag, then tied the other jewels in a silk handkerchief and stowed it in a pocket in the lining of his coat.

'I'll set off for Stafford tomorrow morning early. Don't expect any word from me too soon. It may be that Danvers will need to send to London for instructions. But believe me, I will do everything in my power to secure John for you.'

He left soon afterwards, riding away down the carriageway on a big roan stallion who sent up a great cloud of red dust from the road in his wake.

᷾

After Captain Stone had left, Anne was too restless to remain indoors. She walked down to the meadow at the lakeside to watch Isaac driving the cows up to the barn for evening milking, then she crossed over to examine the remains of her wheat crop. The undamaged part was fine and strong, ready to be cut in a few weeks, but its very quality reminded her painfully of how she had planned to use this crop. Because the wheat had been so abundant before the troopers' attack, she had thought there would be sufficient to sell a little and still provide enough for the household's needs. She had intended to use the money it raised to buy in stock for slaughtering at Martinmas, so that she could overwinter most of her own beasts, and so increase her herds. She had spent many hours calculating feed and bedding—for her skill at arithmetic had never been great—and when she had arrived at the same answers three times over she reckoned that it would be possible, provided she lost none of her hay. Now, with part of the wheat crop destroyed, all her plans were in disarray, but she was unwilling to abandon them altogether. After all, she had not brought the wild deer into her calculations. Venison from the forest could provide some of the family's meat for the winter.

She continued along the side of the wheat field, turning over these plans in her mind as a defence against her fears and hopes for Henry Stone's mission to Stafford, then went on past the barley and the oats, which were happily untouched by the soldiers. Wheat, barley and oats must be cut soon. It was fortunate that she had noticed in good time how much of the mill needed repairing. A millwright had come from Tamworth a fortnight since to rebalance and polish the grindstone, and he had oiled and tested the rest of the machinery. Tom Glastock, who used to be miller, had been impressed into the New Model Army and killed at Colchester. His wife had returned to her family at Shenstone, so the mill house now stood empty. In years past, one of Matthew Webster's tasks had been to assist Tom Glastock during the busy milling season. He had assured Anne that he understood the work. She had agreed that he could work the mill this year, with a young cousin to help him, and if he proved satisfactory, she would allow the Websters to move into the mill house and take over as millers to the estate. It would mean the daily labour at the old quern could be abandoned, to the relief of her whole household. The Websters' children had been awe-struck at this prospect. Anne had seen them just last week, beating a path through the nettles so they could peer in at the windows of the mill house.

Beyond the field of oats, on the nearside of an arm of the forest which reached around the farmland, there was an ancient stewpond. In the days of the old religion, when it was obligatory to eat fish rather than meat on Fridays and saints' days, it had been maintained and stocked as part of the home farm. With the coming of Protestantism and the gradual relaxation of this practice, care of the stewpond had lapsed, and the fish were left to their own devices. Since Dick had come home, however, he had become as enthusiastic as Jack about fishing. Together with their cousin Richard Pott they had cleared some of the dense weed at one end of the pond, so that there was room for them to cast their lines. Anne walked along the edge of the pond now, assessing the work they had done.

It was then that she heard a noise, something between a sob and a groan. She stopped and looked about fearfully. She had wandered a very long way from the house. Usually she only came this far on horseback. The noise was human. It might be a wounded soldier or one of the many tramps and vagabonds and broken men who wandered the countryside, dispossessed by the war. Then she heard another noise, like the mew of a kitten, a noise she knew well. She gathered up her skirts and ran towards it.

The woman was stretched out at the edge of the pond, as though she had crawled there to drink. The baby must have been born no more than minutes since and lay on the grass in a pool of blood between the woman's legs, still attached to the cord. The baby was crying and beating the air with its small fists, but the woman lay very still. She wore rags so thin and tattered that they could barely have given her modesty before, and now all modesty was gone as she lay sprawled where she had given birth. The blood poured out of her in a rushing stream, like a soldier fatally stabbed on the battlefield. Anne's first concern was the baby, who seemed like to drown in his mother's blood. She tore a ribbon from her sleeve and tied off the cord, then took the small knife she carried at her belt and cut it. The baby seemed lusty, but its nose was all befouled with blood, which she wiped away with a corner of her neckerchief. Then she wrapped him in the neckerchief and laid him on the clean grass while she turned to the mother.

Now that she looked at her more closely, she realised that this was a very young girl. A child—younger, probably, than Dick. And as her lifeblood poured away, she was growing pale as milk. Anne knew at once that there was no hope here. This was no natural rush of blood. When a woman bled this much in childbirth, there was only one end to it. All she could do was comfort the girl's last minutes. She dipped her handkerchief in the pond and wiped the girl's face and hands, then lifted her so that she was holding her in her arms. The girl stirred a little, and moaned.

'Is it over?' she said.

'You have a fine strong boy,' said Anne, 'and the pain is all over now.'

The girl's eyes fluttered open.

'Can I see him?'

Anne laid her down again and brought the child. Kneeling on the bloodied grass, she supported the mother and kept a protective arm around the baby, in case the girl's strength suddenly failed.

'Tell me your name,' said Anne, 'and how you came to be here.' She must discover what she might, while the girl could still speak.

'My name is Penelope,' she said obediently, like a child repeating a lesson. 'Penelope Digby. I don't know where I am.'

'This is Swinfen, near to Lichfield. I'm Anne Swynfen.'

'I thank you for your kindness, Mistress Swynfen.' The girl's voice was weak, but she was well-spoken, with a voice strangely at odds with her clothes. Her eyes closed again.

'Who is the father of the child?' Anne asked urgently. Someone would have to take the baby in charge, and she had a distaste for handing children over to the cold charity of the parish. In Richard Pegg's day it would have been done with some compassion, but she mistrusted the new minister.

'I don't know.' The voice was no more than a breath.

'You must know, for I can see you are no whore.'

The girl smiled sadly and shook her head.

'Nay. Not a whore. Though most would name me whore now.'

'Tell me.'

'The soldiers came to our house. We had a small manor in Leicestershire, near Market Bosworth. We owned the land. I'm a gentleman's daughter.'

She sighed, and her arms around the baby slackened, so that Anne tightened her grip. It seemed for a long time that the child would say nothing else, then she roused herself.

'It was early last winter, and food was scarce, you remember? The soldiers came and took everything. The servants ran away. The soldiers killed my parents and my two brothers. And then they defiled me. I don't know how many of them. After a time, my senses failed me.'

'King's men or Parliament men?' Anne asked. It seemed important.

The girl shook her head.

'I don't know. It's of no consequence. Afterwards they took me with them for their sport and kept me until I grew too great with child. They turned me away near Shrewsbury and I have been walking . . .'

Her voice had almost faded away.

'I thought, if I could but reach home, there might be friends left who would help me.'

Dear God, the child had walked fifty miles at least.

'I'll help you,' said Anne, sadly, knowing that she lied. 'What will you call your son?'

The girl answered at once, as if she had long ago decided.

'I'll call him John, after my father. He always said: It's a plain name, but a good one.'

'Aye,' said Anne, 'it's a good name.'

They sat together there beside the pond, Anne now supporting all the weight of the girl and of the baby, who had fallen asleep on his mother's breast. A blackbird was singing its evening melody in the forest behind her. When it fell silent, she realised that the girl was no longer breathing, and she held only one child in her arms.

&

Richard was gone four days, not two, and when he returned he seemed worried and secretive, but Anne did not ask about his sectarian friends. In part, she did not want to know. In part, she had too many other matters on her mind. She waited daily for word from Henry Stone, but none came. There was the burial to arrange for Penelope Digby. It was a sad affair, with none of her own people to see her to her rest, although Anne took all her household to Weeford church, and the Potts came out of kindness. More urgent still was the care of the newborn baby. Mary Pott was able to find a wet nurse at one of the cottages in Weeford. The woman could not leave her other children, so Anne took John Digby to her, riding over with the baby tied in her shawl like any peasant woman. The cottage was clean and the children healthy, but she was sad to have to leave him there. Whenever she could, she rode to Weeford to see how he was faring. She sent a letter to John's cousins at Sutton Cheney, asking if they would make enquiries in the neighbourhood of Market Harborough about the girl's family, and whether any who might be left alive would be willing to give the baby a home.

Lady Day had come and gone long since, and most of the tenants had paid their rents or come to an agreement with Anne for labour or produce in lieu of coin, but the largest of the rents remained unpaid. James Sylvester, tenant of the manor of Thickbroome, had neither come to pay his rent nor sent any message. After waiting in vain, Anne had sent him a letter, pointing out the terms of the tenancy agreed when she and John had moved to Westminster, and requiring him to pay the due rent immediately. To this letter she had received no reply. Now the next quarter day, Midsummer, was past, and six months' rent owing.

It seemed she must go herself and confront James Sylvester, though she shrank from it. At first she thought she might take one of the men with her, or Richard, so that she would not be alone in tackling Sylvester, who was a loud, bullying fellow, much like his cousin who had treated her with such rudeness in Lichfield market. But the men's labour could be ill spared at this busy season and Richard had gone off again on one of his visits, so she must perforce go alone.

Riding Brandy up the familiar drive to the manor, she was struck by an appearance of neglect. Weeds were encroaching on the roadway. The woodland was ill managed, with undergrowth crowding in below and fallen branches and uprooted trees crushing the new growth of the valuable timber. When the prospect opened out to the farmland and gardens, the same blight of poor husbandry was everywhere to be seen—the wall of a parterre crumbled and fallen away, one of the barns sagging, her pretty flower garden overgrown with bindweed and nettles. The cattle in the meadows, however, looked sleek and healthy, and there were at least twice as many of them as she had at Swinfen. There was a row of ample haystacks behind the cowbarn and a large flock of sheep grazed the higher meadow, for the Sylvesters had no pasture up on the moor.

Anne slid down from the mare and handed her over to one of the farm boys, then climbed the steps and knocked on the door. Her heart was beating fast as she waited for some sound withindoors. At last the door was opened by a slatternly maid, who showed her into the parlour and said that she would fetch Master Sylvester.

He came, after leaving her waiting there a good three-quarters of an hour. James Sylvester was something more of a gentleman than his churlish cousin, in wealth if not in manners, but his dress was that of a yeoman or working farmer, his hair—none too clean—straggled in grey locks about his shoulders, and his hands were seamed with dirt. He brought with him into the parlour, once Anne's parlour, a decided odour of pig. She was thankful that he left the door ajar.

'Well, Mistress Swynfen, and what d'ye want?'

His tone was abrupt and his face unfriendly. Anne gathered up her courage in both hands.

'I have come about the rent you owe, Master Sylvester.' She tried to speak with firmness, but it seemed to her that her voice shook a little.

He stared at her with eyes as cold and shiny as pebbles in the Black Brook. His mouth twitched slightly in a contemptuous smile and he said nothing.

She was forced to continue.

'The rent. You did not pay the rent due on Lady Day. And now Midsummer Day has come and gone. I will collect both rents now, to save you coming over to Swinfen to pay.'

He turned and spat into the empty hearth. Anne flinched.

'The rent? Nay, Mistress Swynfen, you are mistook. I owe you no rent.'

Anne felt the colour rising in her face.

'Three months' rent due last Lady Day, and now the next three months. I have the contract of tenancy here. Twenty-five pounds each quarter. Fifty pounds you owe me.'

She drew the contract out of her pocket and gripped it between both hands to try to stop their shaking. It was the most valuable rent and she needed the money badly. Sylvester did not even bother to drop his eyes to the document.

'I have no agreement with you. The contract was signed between myself and Master John Swynfen. Show me your husband, madam, and I may show you the colour of my coin.'

In a sense it was true. But during their absence in Westminster Sylvester had paid his rent without demur to old Master Swynfen. She represented John as truly as his father did.

'My husband is not here at present and my father-in-law is sick abed. Therefore I am come to collect those rents which you are obliged to deliver in person each quarter day to Swinfen Hall, which you have not done.'

Her voice sounded breathless and strange, but she was determined to hold her ground against him.

'I will not stir until you have paid what you owe.'

He narrowed his eyes and she saw a flash of something there— predatory, lustful. He took a step towards her, too close, and she backed away. He laughed then, and gave a sharp whistle. At once a hulking farm labourer stepped through the open door. He must have been standing in the hall just outside.

'Mistress Swynfen is leaving,' said Sylvester, walking out of the room and throwing the words carelessly over his shoulder. 'Show her to her horse.'

The man gripped her by the arm and marched her out of the house and down the steps, where Brandy was tied to a hitching ring. Anne did not sacrifice her dignity by struggling against his grip, but as she rode down the drive towards the high road she turned back her sleeve and saw where his fingers had marked her arm. There would be bruises later. Far worse bruised was her self-respect. She rode home in a red haze of anger and humiliation.

The picking of the peas began. Some would go to market in Lichfield, but most of them must be podded and then dried. They would provide vegetables for the winter, along with the produce from Anne's garden, for making soups and stews and pease pudding, and eking out the supply of meat. The kitchen was full of peas drying on metal trays in front of the great fire. Anne was glad to escape from the intolerable heat of the kitchen in the dog days of late July, to the cool of the dairy or the water meadow. The first of the wheat was cut, and after it was threshed Josiah took a load along past the lake to the mill, where he watched critically as Matthew Webster ground it, the great millstone turning under the force of the mill wheel. The weather had continued hot, which promised well for the harvest, but when the summer was very dry, the millstream sometimes ran a little sluggishly. This year the millpond was full after the spring rains and, with the sluice gate to control the flow, the water supply was sufficient at the moment. Josiah pronounced himself satisfied with the milling, and all the women of the house set to the baking of the Lammas loaves.

There would be no Lammastide celebration in the church and no blessing of the first bread from the new season's wheat, but, to Anne, Lammas had always seemed a most sacred festival, in its way a kind of Easter, marking the resurrection of the land, and a giving of thanks to God that His bounty had brought forth again bread for His people. She dared not draw attention to her celebrations by holding them too openly, but at dinnertime on the first day of August, the whole household sat down in the great hall, to break bread together. The table was laid with the finest of the linen napery, the Venetian glass, the silver dishes. Brendan had been sent for, to come down from the moor. Poor, childish Joane Swynfen sat beside Bridget, picking at her bread and rolling it into little pellets. In the sluggish heat of mid-summer she had become quieter, and there had been no attacks on Bridget for several weeks. Anne was most pleased that she had managed to bring Master Swynfen back to his table for the first time. Christopher and Richard between them had carried him downstairs and propped him up in his great carved chair at the head of the table. After Bridget's long months of loving care, he was beginning to be able to feed himself again with his left hand. And amongst the tortured sounds coming from his mouth, a few words could now be discerned.

Anne had said a prayer in thanks for the first wheat to be garnered, and called down a blessing on the first loaf, when there came a loud knock on the front door. Margit went to open it, and showed in Robert Verey, the innkeeper from Lichfield.

'Nay, I thank you, Mistress Swynfen,' he said, 'I'll not take dinner with you, for I have a full house to see to at home. But this letter came enclosed in one to me, in which Captain Stone bade me to bring you his letter at once, for he knows that none from your household come to Lichfield more than once a fortnight.' He glanced again at the table. 'A Lammas loaf, you say? Why, I'll try a morsel of it gladly, then be on my way.'

While he tasted of the loaf, eaten with the first of the matured cheese, Anne retired to the parlour to read Captain Stone's letter in private. It was brief. John had been moved from Stafford to Denbigh Castle, possibly during the very time when Stone himself was in Stafford kicking his heels, waiting for Danvers's answer to his proposal. After a long delay, the governor of Stafford accepted the ransom in jewels and in return gave Stone a document authorising John's release from Denbigh, on an additional recognisance of £1,000, which Henry Stone had underwritten himself. He was now setting off immediately to ride to Denbigh, but Anne must understand that matters might not go smoothly. The governor of Denbigh was not known to him. Moreover, he might not be willing to accept the authorisation from Danvers as valid. She must strive to contain herself in patience.

Anne felt a surge of anger. These petty men, these 'governors', who had climbed to power by clinging to other men's shirt-tails—they were playing a game with John's life. Where was Denbigh? Somewhere in Wales—but how far away?

When she returned to the hall, the innkeeper was about to leave.

'Stay a moment, Master Verey,' said Anne. 'Did Captain Stone give you no directions for reaching him, in the letter he sent to you? There are none in mine.'

'Nothing, save that he's going to Denbigh. I suppose he may be addressed at the nearest stage post.'

'Where is it, this place? Do the coaches run there?'

'Not by any of the regular ways. It's deep into the Welsh mountains, I believe. I suppose he would ride to Shrewsbury first, and from there into Wales, but it's dangerous country along the border, full of deserters from both armies, turned renegades. I'd not like to be travelling there myself.'

When the innkeeper had gone, Anne resumed her seat at the table. Although some of the company gave her curious looks following this interruption to their meal, she kept her own counsel.

&

This was a season which left little time for thinking about any matter other than the safe gathering in of the harvest, which proceeded apace throughout August. Everyone on the estate laboured hard for long days in the heat—cutting, stooking, loading and threshing. Anne had commuted many of the cottagers' rents to a certain number of days' work during harvest, an arrangement that suited all parties, since it meant that the harvest was garnered with good speed, and the labourers went home each with a portion of the bounty, which Anne shared with them.

Despite the troopers' destruction of part of the wheat, the yield from the rest was good, and Anne was sorry when she heard rumours that many farms in the neighbourhood, particularly over towards Hints, had been affected by a blight on their wheat and poor yields in their crops of oats. After the bad harvests during all the years of the war, and last year's famine, more would go hungry again this winter. In the breathless heat of late summer, word also reached Swinfen that the

362

plague had broken out in Tamworth. Then an entire family living in a cottage between Hints and Tamworth died of the plague within a week.

Richard had taken to riding off for a day or half a day, never saying where he was going, and abandoning his share of work in the harvest. Once, Dick had gone off with him, without a word to his mother, who had fretted with anger and worry until they came back, whistling and merry and smelling strongly of ale. Anne had given Dick such a lashing with her tongue that for once he had no impertinent answer for her and stayed meekly at home afterwards. But it was not so easy to rein in her brother-in-law. When he returned late one night at the end of August, Anne confronted him angrily.

'I've winked my eye long enough, Richard,' she said, hardly able to contain her rage. She felt her face flushing and had to clasp her hands together to prevent herself slapping him. 'I thought when you'd visited your friends at Barton, that was to be an end to it, but now you slip away two or three times a week, leaving others to do your work. We have not so many strong young men on the estate that we can spare you during harvest.'

He looked somewhat sheepish.

'I work all the harder when I'm here, Anne.'

'Perhaps. Perhaps not. But whatever it is you're plotting, it must wait until the harvest is in. I can spare neither you, nor the horse you take, until then. And I have another worry. The plague is abroad again. If you've been visiting the places where it has struck, you could carry it here. You may be careless of your own life, but I can't allow you to endanger the children and the rest of the household. Your parents are both ill, and Bridget has never been strong. Do you want to risk bringing the plague to them?'

'I hadn't thought of that,' he muttered.

'Well, think on it now. No more riding about the countryside until the harvest is in. And no visiting places which have the plague.'

'I've been to Hints a few times,' he admitted, 'but I wasn't near the cottage where they had the plague. The cottage has been burned down now, and no more cases reported. But there's another kind of sickness abroad that you should know about.'

'What is that?'

'You know old Agnes Lea, who lives up on Packington Moor, that some say is a wise woman?'

'Of course. You've known her all your life, Richard.' Anne gave an exasperated sigh. 'You know as well as I that she's wise in the way of herbs and simples. That does not make her a "wise woman" in the way I think you mean.'

'Since the crops have been blighted at Hints, folk there are openly calling her a witch. One fellow said that he asked her to cure his cow, and she said she could not, for it was dying, unless he should do thus and such, which he took to be the devil's magic. He hit her for that, and now he says she's called down her curse on him.'

'Surely he's merely a bad farmer,' she said, 'and an ill-natured brute, who seeks to lay the blame for his own failings on someone else, a woman he has injured already.'

'I think you take this too lightly, Anne. It's grown to a general complaint.'

'Then I hope you told people roundly not to be such fools.'

'I tried, but I'm a person of no great consequence. They're not likely to listen to me.'

Anne was deeply troubled at this news, although she sought to hide it from Richard. When a few people muttered that someone was a witch, it could be damaging, but not serious. When an entire community turned on an old woman, working themselves up into a fever of hatred, determined to fix on her as the cause of all their misfortunes, it became dangerous. If some of the people of Hints were resolute enough to lay a complaint of witchcraft before the magistrates, then the magistrates were obliged to make an enquiry into the matter. Agnes Lea lived solitary, an old woman without family or near neighbours to protect her. Matters could go very ill for her.

Chapter Twenty-Seven

The prison at Denbigh Castle was located in one of the three towers of the mighty gateway. The castle itself was vast, one of the monstrous fortifications built by Edward I to keep the Welsh nation in subjugation after his defeat of their princes. In occupying the site of a former Welsh stronghold, now totally destroyed, it added an arrogant English insult to the initial injury. It was plain why this place had been chosen by both Welsh and English, for it commanded the view in every direction. Such a castle could never be taken by surprise, although the stone walls bore pale gashes from the Parliamentary bombardment three years ago, which had eventually led to capitulation.

John had been able to appreciate the strategic importance of the castle when he arrived at the foot of the steep approach leading up to the gatehouse, for he reached the castle in the prolonged twilight of an early autumn evening, when the honey-gold of the setting sun lapped over the grim stone walls like lichen, lending a deceptive softness to their appearance.

His departure from Stafford had been sudden and unexpected. During one of his periods of respite in the comfortable tower chamber, when he had been about to retire for the night, one of the guards had arrived and told him to gather up his possessions, and make ready to travel. For a moment his heart had leapt, thinking they were setting him free, but then he realised that if he had been released, Danvers would probably have come to tell him so himself. Glancing around the room, he saw that a heel of bread was left on the table from his last meal. Heedless of the guard's impatience, he crumbled it on the stone windowsill, and watched the thrush swoop down at once. Tame as a lady's pet songbird, the thrush had lately consented to perch for a moment on John's finger, gripping it with cool claws delicate as straws, but tense with life. He could see the throb of its small heart now beneath the soft speckling of its breast feathers.

John was hurried down the stairs as fast as he could go—a lame halting pace, for the periods of torture had left his legs and feet in a perilous state. Outside the gate of the castle a close carriage was standing. Two soldiers seized his arms as he climbed in, and took their seats beside him. Within moments they were driving away down the steep hill into the twilight which lapped the base of the castle hill like water.

The sudden rushed departure, the hurried descent of the stairs on his maimed feet, left John weak and confused. The carriage was barely underway when faintness overcame him. When he came to his senses again they were travelling along a dark tunnel under trees, with no light to be seen from any habitation. His head swum and both sight and sound were blurred, as though he were under water or groping through fog. His hands trembled, beyond his control, and his heartbeat was irregular. Was it the aftermath of torture, or had his very body begun to betray him?

It was to be a long time before his body and his mind were to begin to come together into some kind of whole again. The journey was slow, travelling on a roundabout route: south-west first, until at Water Eaton they reached the old Roman road—still the soundest road in these parts—then westwards into Wales. Compared with the long and painful journey from London, it was relatively comfortable in the carriage and after a while John began to notice his surroundings. His guards, although hardly friendly, were not cruel and loutish like the four soldiers who had accompanied him before. They were quite willing to tell him where they were going: Denbigh Castle, amongst the mountains of Wales, where he could more easily be kept in close custody. The older man, Captain Godbarrow, a man as brown and wrinkled as an old saddle, told him this frankly, without mockery or malice. Hughes, the other soldier, younger, awkward, said little and regarded John with something akin to awe.

John wondered why the decision had been made thus suddenly to move him so far away. He asked the captain, who shrugged.

'Not my affair. But, ask me, it's because you're too well known about Stafford. Maybe the governor thought someone might be thinking of trying to carry you off.'

If this were true, the outcome had been an unhappy one, yet John felt more heartened than he had for many weeks. If Danvers feared that his friends might be planning a rescue, it meant that he was not entirely forgotten. The remoteness of Denbigh, and the impregnable nature of the castle, would make rescue a very poor proposition, but merely to know that he had not slipped for ever out of men's minds gave him greater strength and resolution.

Had the journey been made by his own choice, the first part might even have given John some pleasure. Their road lay through fertile English countryside at the height of harvest time. Between the dense green of the forests, fields of wheat, oats and barley were a rich gold in the fine late summer weather. Although in many places they passed through ruined villages and saw, standing amidst their neglected estates, houses of the gentry which had been put to the fire, yet there were signs of recovery. There were some villages where the inhabitants were working at the harvest in their strip-fields. And they saw at least two manor houses where carpenters and masons were busy repairing damage.

Yet in Shrewsbury, the streets were crowded with beggars new-made by the war—some of them injured and maimed soldiers, turned away from the army to fend for themselves, others the famine-stricken poor, who had crawled to the town in a last hope of food. They huddled in the doorways of shops, or lay stretched out at the roadside up the steep curve of the Wyle, many of them with scarce rags to cover their nakedness. Women's faces peered from beneath their shawls, faces like death's heads—their cheeks so sunken that the bones of their skulls seemed like to pierce the skin, their teeth blackened and broken, their hair, where it could be seen, fallen out in clumps and the remainder like frayed rope. Seeing the young children who clung to their skirts, John realised these old women were mostly less than thirty. As for the children—John averted his eyes, with the pity and shame of it. The children staggered on legs as thin and bent as twigs, above which bellies swollen with starvation bulged like the pigs' bladders that the London apprentices used for football. Their eyes had become the clustering home of flies.

They stayed a week at an inn in Shrewsbury. John spent much of the time at his preferred place near the window, looking out on those streets full of the destitute. The most remarkable thing about them was their silence. He thought they should have raised up their voices in lamentation, a roar against the injustice and cruelty of war, which had brought them to this state; aye, even a raging blasphemy against God Himself, who could so turn away from His children. John could not rid his mind of their faces, and in sleep he dreamt of them.

From Shrewsbury they followed the Roman road north and west into the wild northern parts of Wales. The difficulty of the country had defeated even those Roman engineers, who had laid their roads all over the Empire as straight as a builder's plumb line. For now the road began to twist and turn like a writhing snake, as if, once they were in amongst these remote mountains, the Romans themselves had become infected by some fantastical Celtic dream. The road was ill-maintained, so the horses were hard put to draw the carriage, and the progress they made was so slow that they might as soon have walked. In Shrewsbury

Captain Godbarrow had collected half a dozen musketeers from the garrison, who rode beside the carriage, with their guns at the ready, because this territory was notorious for brigands. Godbarrow and Hughes, who rode inside with John, were nervous, jumping at the sound of every crashing stone or branch snapped under the horses' hooves. It was clear they had no liking for their task, and would have preferred facing a clean-cut enemy on a battlefield to travelling in this enclosed carriage, whose very strangeness in these savage parts drew attention to itself, making it a prison and a trap for them as much as for John. If travel through these mountains was terrible in the late summer, what must it be in winter?

Occasionally they passed through vile huddles of cottages, too mean to be distinguished with the appellation of village. The houses were built of rough stones prised from the ground, unshaped by mason's chisel, piled up like any heap of rocks and plastered over with mud and dung. Their roofs were a kind of poor rush thatch bundled anyhow over the low dwellings, not skilfully cut and shaped like the straw thatch of the Midland counties, but a thatch so blackened and rotten, with time and the endless rain amongst these mountains, that it was indistinguishable from the surrounding mud. Indeed, from a few yards off, these squat hovels were almost invisible, except where a thread of smoke escaped through a hole in the roof.

The serpentine road wound its way through the mountains, following the natural crevices and valleys, but also climbing over precipitous outcrops. At night there were no inns, not even a miserable wayside tavern. They merely stopped beside the road wherever there was a semblance of shelter. Half the soldiers kept watch, while the rest tried to sleep, sitting up in the carriage with John.

It seemed impossible that the road could grow any worse, but at last they were obliged turn off the Roman road, which continued westwards, and head north on a track that was barely discernible. For four days they followed this track, in country so remote from human habitation that John began to wonder whether they could possibly still be in Britain, but instead were wandering through some deserted mountain range from the realms of legend. They passed a lake amongst the crags, sinister and silent, as though no boat had ever sailed upon its surface, as though it had never been visited by man since the dawn of Creation. At last, however, they came down into a pleasant, fertile valley, where there were a few scattered villages whose houses resembled the dwellings of men rather than of wild beasts. And so, on that evening of early autumn light, they drove up the steep approach to the castle of Denbigh, which, in all its battlemented might, was to be John's new prison.

❦

It was no worse a place than Stafford. And at first, at least, it appeared he was not to be subjected to torture. It almost seemed that his captors had forgotten why they were holding him. He was not summoned to an interview with the governor, although he did encounter the captain of the guard on the evening he arrived. A vicious, drunken brute, he looked. The demand that John should write a statement of compliance was not repeated. No one took much interest in his arrival. He was thrust into a cell in the prison tower and left, so it seemed, to rot at his leisure.

This prison cell was by no means as comfortable as his chamber at Stafford, nor was it as bad as the underground dungeon he had first occupied there. The walls were dry, there was a straw palliasse on a wooden shelf that served as a bed. And there was a window of sorts. This was not much more than an arrow slit, doubtless used in time of siege to shoot at any enemy attempting to storm the gate. Thus it was low enough for John to look through, making the place seem far less confined than that Stafford dungeon.

On his first morning, he gazed out upon a wide vista of rich farmlands in the valley below the crag on which the castle was built. Beyond, and closing in the view as far as he could see, were great mountains whose peaks, even on this warm autumn day, bore patches of snow. The prospect was both fearsome and awe-inspiring. Although he had been travelling in a carriage which had struggled through such mountains for days past, he had never been in a position to appreciate their size, whilst blundering about amongst their rocky crevasses. Now that he could see them whole and majestic, they took his breath away. Never before had he seen such mountains. He knew well the hilly country of Staffordshire, had travelled in the Cotswolds and visited the South Downs, but he understood now that those were mere wrinkles on the earth's surface, compared with these geological colossi. They were both terrible and remarkable, and he felt humbly that his knowledge of God's creation was paltry, a boy's knowledge. If ever he were set free, scant though his hope was, he would make it his business to devote less time to the petty political affairs of men, and study more widely in the book of divine riches—the diverse and various earth he had so little appreciated before.

A long monotony of days began. He had his two books, his Bible and his Boethius, from which he read every day. He had brought with him from Stafford the small supply of paper which had been in his chamber there, and on this he began to set down his thoughts, a kind of continuous meditation, which he wrote in a very small hand, hoping not to use his paper too quickly. Apart from the loneliness and the boredom, it was not, at first, a difficult time, and the damage to the soles of his feet, and to the joints of his legs, which had begun to heal during the journey into Wales, was almost repaired, although his feet retained scars and he found when he rose from bed in the morning, or from sitting too long, that his joints were painful and stiff, like those of an elderly man. The old wound, from Tize's musket ball, had healed over with a thin layer of skin, pale and glassy, and ached when he put his weight on that leg.

The most outwardly trying aspect of his new imprisonment was the captain of the guard, who had some particular hatred which he fixed upon John. There appeared to be no reason for it. The man was a total stranger. Yet he would come to John's cell from time to time, generally when he had been drinking heavily, merely in order to curse the prisoner. He call him 'king-lover' and 'boot-licker' and 'thieving rascal', and many worse, foul-mouthed names. And first John tried to explain that he was no Royalist, but he might as well have addressed his remarks to one of the great boulders protruding from the mountainside. The man was deaf to everything he said, and gripped by some strange fanatical obsession. In the end, John learned merely to sit stony-faced through these assaults, or to stand, when he was ordered to stand. He even contrived not to flinch when the man pushed his face into John's, his breath heavy with the stink of rotten teeth, and swore at him, his spittle spattering John's face. The unexpectedness of these assaults unnerved him at first, but he grew accustomed to it. There is much, he had found, that a man may grow accustomed to.

Yet he was not at ease with his own mind. His scarred and abused body was but the outer shell of a mind bruised and darkened by these months of imprisonment and torment. He looked back at the self who had walked that last morning out of his home in Westminster as at a stranger, an innocent, blind fool of a man, who believed peace could be won by reason and the goodwill of men. The innocent folly of that man had brought him to this, and at what cost? He had refused to set his hand to any document for Danvers, but for what gain? The incorruptibility of his own soul? A poor excuse for a soul, then, if it had cost his family dear. And of what value was his high-minded stance? He was no better than a pawn in Cromwell's game. If he could have

370

been turned to use, well and good; if not, he was lightly cast aside and disregarded. A worthless piece. A man easily forgotten. Diminished now, in his own eyes, to a useless scrap of detritus cast up on this remote shore. There seemed little to live for. He waited with grim patience for a final ending in death.

A change came in his circumstances after he had been in his cell at Denbigh for several weeks. He no longer attempted to keep track of the days, merely noticing the subtle changes in the season, which was moving surely through autumn now, the leaves beginning to flame red and gold in the orchards in the valley and in the forests on the lower mountain slopes.

About noon on a bright, crisp day, there was a stir of activity outside the gate as a cart was driven up. Carts arrived regularly with supplies for the garrison, but this cart had an escort of soldiers, and when it stopped a man was thrown out upon the ground, his wrists and ankles bound with chains. John's heart stirred with both pity and alarm, for he knew what that man must feel, and he feared that the chaining of another prisoner might mean the same for him.

After a good deal of noise and shouting around the gate, the soldiers heaved the man to his feet and the cart drove off. He was a man who might once have been of impressive build, but he was gaunt and hunched now. Some years older than John, he had a great mane of greying dark hair, and a short, dense, curly beard. He was so tightly chained that he could only shuffle in small steps, like a bear John had once seen led through the streets of London. Indeed, there was something altogether bear-like about him, a trapped, humiliated bear, seemingly tamed by cruel keepers, but possibly dangerous yet.

Once the prisoner and his escort had disappeared from sight inside the gate, John heard no more of them until about an hour later, when the key grated in the lock of his cell door, and it was flung open. The new prisoner, who was even larger than he had looked from the window, was pushed into the cell with John, and the door slammed shut. The two men regarded each other warily. Then the newcomer spoke, using a language that was certainly not English.

John shook his head.

'I don't understand,' he said, speaking slowly. 'Do you speak English?'

'As well as you,' said the other. 'I thought, as we are in Wales, that you would be a Welshman.'

'And you?' said John. 'Are you a Welshman?'

'One half of me is Welsh, the other half English, and the two of them always at war. I have the heart of a Welshman and the head of an Englishman, and there's a dangerous combination for you.'

He shuffled slowly across the room, his chains dragging and clanking behind him, and sat down on the bare wooden shelf opposite the one that served as John's bed.

'My name is Dafydd Williams,' he said, 'and I would shake your hand, as a fellow prisoner in this infernal place, were I not too weary to rise again.'

John smiled and crossed the room to him.

'John Swynfen,' he said, taking the man's manacled hand, 'and I'm proud to meet you, sir, though we be in like dire straits. And I must tell you that there are worse places than this, for we have light and air, and the food, though plain, is nourishing, and plentiful enough for a man who can take no more exercise than to walk ten paces in one direction, and then ten paces back again.'

'You've been here long?'

'A few weeks only. Before that I was in Stafford, and before that, London.'

'I was held in Monmouth, crowded in amongst many prisoners, but I escaped twice. Once I was free for three whole days. But after that I was chained and they brought me here. No doubt they think I'll not attempt to escape from this place.'

'It would be difficult indeed. And if you escaped, where would you go? I've pondered on this. For there are terrible mountains between here and England.'

Dafydd gave a low, rumbling laugh.

'I would have no need to escape to England. I could melt away into the Welsh hills and these English soldiers would never find me. But to escape the castle itself, that would be a challenge for any man.'

As if by mutual agreement, neither of them asked the other why he was imprisoned, or who he was in the world outside, or what enemy he had offended. They skirted around these subjects with the courtesy of well-bred dogs, each sizing the other up. When their evening meal arrived, it was brought by one of the younger guards, a pleasant lad whom John had found to be kind and thoughtful. He asked if the other prisoner's chains might be removed.

'He can't escape from here, chained or unchained, through an arrow slit a child of ten might not climb through. Nor can he break down that stout oak door. Surely he's secure enough? Don't ask the captain, though. Ask one of the other officers.'

The boy grinned. It seemed the soldiers had no more love of the captain than John had.

'I'll ask, sir. But will you not be afraid to share a cell with him, if he be unchained? He's a terrible fierce man.'

'I'll take that risk,' said John.

When the young soldier had gone, and they had begun their meal—Dafydd much hampered by his chained wrists—he inclined his head.

'I thank you for that, John Swynfen. There's not many would ask such a favour for a stranger, who might be any kind of a rogue and a murderer.'

'I think you are neither of those things,' said John.

When the boy returned to remove their dishes, he brought keys with him.

'The captain is away in the town this evening, so I asked Sergeant Conway, and he said I might unchain him. But the captain may order them back again when he learns of it.'

John noticed that the boy always spoke to him and not to Dafydd, as if the new prisoner were deaf or stupid. However, he unlocked the chains and carried them away, leaving the two men with the single smoky rush dip that John was permitted in the evening.

'I fear, as the autumn nights draw in,' said John, 'that the light of one rush dip will illuminate very little of the evening.'

'A prisoner can always sleep,' said Dafydd. 'What does that Warwickshire poet say? "Sleep—is it not?—that knits up the ravelled sleeve of care."'

John was surprised. He had not taken Dafydd Williams to be a man who read poetry.

'True,' he said, 'or a man may engage in conversation with a friend. That needs no light of rush dip or candle.'

'Only the light of the mind's illumination,' Dafydd agreed.

He seemed much restored by the food, which he had fallen upon ravenously, and much cheered by the removal of his chains. He began to pace up and down the cell, stretching his arms above his head, and bending and flexing his whole body, which had strangely the appearance of filling out as he moved about. John was reminded of a butterfly, newly emerged from its chrysalis, which patiently eases open its wings to the sunlight, and fans them gently until they fill and spread, enabling it to fly. So Dafydd spread out his great arms to embrace life again.

The two men spoke little that night. John offered Dafydd the one straw mattress to lie upon, but the other refused it, saying he had slept much harder than upon bare wood. Long before the rush dip was burnt out, he had slumped into a heavy sleep, in which he neither stirred nor made any sound.

On the following day, they ventured to tell each other a little of their histories, John beginning, sensing somehow an obligation on him as the first inhabitant of the cell. When he explained that he was one of the secluded Members of Parliament, Dafydd made a small explosive noise, but did not interrupt until John's account of how he came to be in Denbigh was at an end.

'And now I see,' said Dafydd, 'why that boy thought you shouldn't trust yourself alone with me unshackled. You—a gentleman landowner and a Member of that Parliament which would not pay its army? Should I not seize you by the neck and break it between my bare hands, like a chicken's?'

John regarded him steadily. If Dafydd so desired, he was easily capable of such a thing.

'I've done you no harm. My land is inherited from ancestors who have held it and farmed it generation upon generation. I've stolen no man's land. We have enclosed no common grazing land, nor drained any common marshes to rob the poor of fish and fowl. My tenants have always had fair treatment at my hands. When times are hard, my family has always protected them. Try me before the court of your conscience if you will, but let my people speak in my defence.'

'And what of the army's pay?'

'That's an issue which is far from simple. I've never served in the army. However, the grandees recruited and forced men into the New Model Army and promised them both pay and booty, without ever calculating the cost or reckoning where this money should be found. You know as well as I that near ten years of war have cost the country dear, trade ruined, the wool trade in especial, on which so much of the country's wealth depends.'

John stood up and walked to the window, then turned around, leaning against the wall.

'Terrible harvests have left us with food in short supply and many starving. With so many away at war, or killed, or ruined, the public moneys gathered in taxes or tithes have dwindled away—so where is the money to be found to pay the soldiers? In time, the profits from the Royalists' sequestrated estates might have been used for the purpose, but I don't know what this new government of Oliver Cromwell intends.'

'King Cromwell!' said the other, and looked as though he might spit, but restrained himself. 'If you speak of promises broken, *there* is a man could be used as a Model indeed! He has solved the problem of the army's pay in part.'

'What do you mean?'

'You don't know? I suppose, if you have been imprisoned these ten months past, there's much you don't know. Cromwell desires the utter annihilation of the wretched native Irish, and so he and the Council of State have forced the army to travel overseas to carry out his will. Many of the soldiers protested that they didn't join the army to fight the Irish but to fight the king. They refused to go. So they were turned away, unpaid and destitute. It was a great economy for the new government! There were mutinies—did you not hear of the mutinies?—months ago now.'

John shook his head.

'I was told something of the Irish matter, but it came from the mouth of the governor of Stafford, who revealed very little. Before I was taken from London, we heard that Lilburne had fallen out with Cromwell.'

Dafydd gave a laugh tinged with contempt.

'Poor little John Lilburne! He thought he had Noll Cromwell dancing to his tune, but it was all a sham. Lilburne is imprisoned again, and the promises Cromwell made—that the Leveller proposals would be enforced—are all betrayed.'

'You don't think well of Lilburne, then?' John said. 'I would have guessed you were one of his followers.'

'Nay, nay, the man is all for weak half-measures. *Some* men should have *some* more land and *some* more power, and perhaps *some* better education and *some* protection under the law. It's Winstanley has the right of it. Let the land be shared out equally amongst all men and women.'

He saw the expression on John's face and laughed.

'Aye, *and women* also. For we believe that both sexes are equal in God's eyes. Both should be given the best education they are able for. And if all hold the land in common, why, then, this land of ours is rich enough and fertile enough to feed all equally, and none shall starve.'

John saw suddenly, sharply, as if before his very eyes, the faces of the starving destitute in Shrewsbury. And he thought of the rich lands of his own estates, awaiting him, if he should ever return, at Swinfen. For all his eloquence, he was robbed of words and could find no answer to this. So he tried another tack.

'You say you would educate women. How far? For it's known that the brain of a woman is smaller than that of a man, her emotions less stable, her power of reason deficient.'

'Who has proved this?' Dafydd asked, leaning nonchalantly on the door jamb, and folding his arms. 'I have never seen it proved. I had a sister, and I never knew her less than me in intellect, or steadiness of character, or quality of reasoning.'

'A few women, perhaps,' John conceded cautiously, for in fairness to Anne . . .

'In physical courage, likewise, they can be men's equal,' said Dafydd. 'There were women who fought at the siege of Plymouth, my sister amongst them. They carried weapons, not water; they withstood the enemy, and were wounded, and died. My sister amongst them.'

There was a heavy silence in the room. A feeble protest squirmed in John's mind, and perished.

'Perhaps you have the right of it,' he said slowly. 'But I cannot see how such a world can come to pass. Such millenarian dreams, they leap ahead too fast. Step by step, that is the only way the world will change. You cannot turn it upside down in one swift motion. Too many would be hurt.'

Dafydd sat down on his bed and placed his large hands on his knees.

'Very well. You are the politician. How would you begin?'

'With the franchise,' said John promptly. 'A wider franchise would give more men some voice in shaping the nation.'

'Men only?'

'Of course.' John was impatient. 'You couldn't permit women to vote while many men cannot. Step by step, I said. In time, perhaps, but not in ours. In our grandchildren's grandchildren's day it may be that women will be enfranchised. And as for education, I've sent my own eldest daughter to school. So you see, I agree with you in part. And my own wife has a good education. She was taught by her brother's tutor. She's not perhaps as learned as Lucy, Colonel Hutchinson's wife, but she knows French and some Latin, and music. She has read the historians and philosophers. She even reads natural philosophy in secret, although she thinks I don't know.'

He turned away, for the thought of Anne was almost unbearable.

'Your wife is indeed fortunate,' said Dafydd gently. 'And others could benefit from a like education. Well, when you are restored to Parliament, you must work for all these things.'

John laughed harshly.

'I see no likelihood that I shall ever sit in Parliament again, or be able to serve the country as you suggest. Come now, you've led our talk away from how we came to be here in Denbigh. I have told you my story. What of yours?'

Dafydd shrugged.

'Simple enough. I'm a blacksmith to trade, but I always loved learning. My father sent me to a dame school as a lad, and once I could read and write, I devoured every book I could lay hands on. When I began to earn money of my own, instead of taking a wife and raising a brood of children, I spent my coin on books and paid our parish priest to teach me Latin. He was reluctant to teach such a one as I, but he was willing enough to take my money. I would dearly have loved to learn the Greek tongue as well, but our priest was no scholar, and I could find no one else to teach me.'

This was a strange man indeed, a bookish blacksmith. His trade explained the man's appearance, but the passion for knowledge was extraordinary.

'You weren't imprisoned for a love of books, surely?' said John.

'After a fashion, I suppose you might say that I was. For reading led me into the world of ideas, and when a man gets a taste of the ideas of others, he's apt to develop a few of his own. I began to search out other like-minded men, and to dispute, and discuss.'

Dafydd began to pace about from one end of the cell to the other. He stopped in front of John and laid both hands lightly on the other's shoulders.

'This has been a terrible age for war, John, but it has been a wonderful age for ideas. I've examined many sects and parties of men—Anabaptists and Quakers, and Levellers and Diggers, and some that had no more than a handful of adherents, and were unknown outside their own town. I travelled to London and heard new men preach there. I became something of a preacher myself, and fell into trouble for preaching at town crosses and on village greens, and tempting people away from church. When war came against the king, I joined the Parliamentary army, of course, for the king stood for everything I despise. And I preached in the army likewise.'

He rolled up his breeches and showed a livid scar in his thigh.

'I took a musket ball here, and was turned away from the army, sick and penniless and lame, to fend for myself as best I could. That was when I joined one of the Digger colonies in Gloucestershire, and became a kind of leader amongst them, although I didn't seek to be a leader—it's an idea which is anathema to me.'

377

John could imagine that such a man as this would become a leader, whatever his egalitarian views. Could society ever be ordered in such a way that men like Dafydd Williams would *not* rise to the top, like the cream in the milk? Surely one should never advocate a form of society—to turn the matter upside over—where men like Dafydd would be forcibly held down? These were troubling notions, which had never quite presented themselves to John in this way before. He had believed that the Diggers were fanatical, if not lunatic, sectaries. Yet Dafydd was clearly no lunatic. Hardly even fanatical, for he based his views of the good society on reason, humanity, tolerance and kindliness.

'So,' said John, 'how did it fare, this Digger colony of yours?'

'Before we could even reap our first harvest—this past July it was, when we had just begun to gather our first vegetables—a hue and cry was raised amongst the local gentry and their tenants, and all our work destroyed: cut down and put to the sword and the fire. Some of us they arrested. Some escaped, myself amongst them.'

He ran his thumb along the scar, then rolled down his breeches again.

'But I'm somewhat noticeable, being more than six feet tall, not easy of concealment. Besides, I took it ill, what they had done. I stirred up a little trouble for them, amongst the poor of that place. There were some stones thrown, some stock . . . let us say "liberated" for the common good. I fled from there into Monmouthshire, but they caught me at last, and flogged me, and stood me in the pillory. The magistrate was a just man, however. It couldn't be proved that I had laid my hand on anything, so I was neither branded, maimed, nor hanged. But they couldn't let me go free, for I was considered an inciter of riots and a destroyer of good order. So, after a cell in Monmouth, from which, as I said, I escaped twice, I'm sent here, to share a cell with a certain John Swynfen, gentleman and landowner.'

He gave a great bellow of laughter.

'A fine irony indeed,' said John. 'For both of us.'

&

The chess set which John had whittled in odd moments during his time in the *King's Head* had travelled with him in the deep pocket of his doublet ever since, but he had found no opponent, and he had never enjoyed playing against himself, for it was difficult to be even-handed when he could always predict what his own next move would be.

It emerged that Dafydd Williams was a chess player, and so John dug about in his pocket and laid out the crude pieces on the deep window embrasure. They found that two of the pawns had been lost on his journeys, but they soon made replacements from fragments of firewood left in the hearth since the previous winter. They used a half-charred stick, left in the hearth from some past fire, to sketch a chess board on Dafydd's bed, setting aside the straw palliasse he had at last been given.

'I wonder,' said Dafydd, 'whether they intend to allow us a fire? It's growing mighty chilly, with autumn moving on apace, and no shutters for that window. I thought I was like to freeze last night.'

'We should ask for blankets at least,' said John, filling in the last black square on the chess board. 'Next time we see the young lad. Now, will you draw for white?'

Chess became a passion with them, helping to pass the increasingly cold hours. John was a careful strategist, pondering each move while he calculated in his mind his opponent's possible responses, and the stages of play that would then ensue. Dafydd was a bold and erratic player, full of bravado, scarcely pausing to think before he made his move, swooping forward to advance his pieces—gallantly but often foolishly—across the board. Surprising John by his unexpected tactics, he often gained the upper hand. Their winnings were about equal.

Neither of the men was sure of the date, but it was clear that autumn was slipping by into winter. The leaves on the trees changed from the first golds and reds interspersed amongst the greens into a blaze of fiery hues, like the final flush of colour on the face of a patient dying of consumption. Then they drifted down—some fading first to tan and tawny, copper and chestnut and roan—till none were left but the persistent beech and oak. At last the prisoners procured a couple of thin blankets each, which brought with them whole colonies and nations of lice and fleas, but the insect life had more sense than to linger in such a cold place. After a few days they had migrated back to the warmer quarters occupied by the soldiers. There were, as Dafydd pointed out, certain advantages to living in a cell as cold as a dairy house.

The big blacksmith had developed a severe cough which he could not shake off, and when next they saw the young soldier—whose name they never learned—John begged him for a supply of firewood, and for a piece of canvas that they could fix over the window to keep out the wind. Once again it was Sergeant Conway who gave permission. The prisoners understood that the foul-mouthed captain had taken to his bed recently with *delirium tremens*, thus leaving the sergeant with a fair amount of freedom.

379

They had some difficulty with the canvas, for the guards were naturally reluctant to give them tools. Finally the sergeant himself came and supervised the fixing of a piece of wood above the window, to which the canvas was nailed, with another nail hammered into the wall so that the canvas could be hooked back when they wanted fresh air.

'I hope you're satisfied, sir,' the sergeant said to John with heavy sarcasm. 'These quarters have always proved acceptable to all our other guests.'

'We're grateful to you,' said John. 'I know you wouldn't wish us to die of the cold.'

He was tempted to say: For what use would we be to Cromwell then? But he bit back the words.

After some difficulties, for they had been given little kindling, they made up a good fire in the hearth, and although the smoke was inclined to blow back into the room from the huge, ancient chimney, they warmed their hands and exchanged smiles of satisfaction at another small victory. Dafydd spoiled the effect by starting to cough again, apologising as he wiped his mouth on the back of his hand. He hurriedly rubbed his hand on his breeches, but not before John had noticed blood.

Chapter Twenty-Eight

Harvest was long past before the matter of Agnes Lea came to Anne's attention again. There had been just sufficient wheat for her to sell some to a corn merchant in Lichfield and use the money to buy in a few beef cattle for slaughter at Martinmas, although not as many as she had hoped. As for the Swinfen stock, she selected for meat only the young bullocks and two of the poorest heifers, keeping the rest to increase the breeding herd. The swine were driven into the forest to fatten on fallen acorns and beechmast before some were chosen to provide the winter hams and bacon.

One afternoon in late October she had Brandy saddled, and rode up to the moor to discuss with Brendan how many ewes they would keep over the winter. She found the Irishman sitting in front of his bothy with a late dinner of barley bannocks, which he cooked on the hot stones beside his fire, eaten with the soft ewe's milk cheese that he made for himself up here on the moor. The dog Niall watched intently for any scraps that might fall to the ground. Brendan got up slowly, unfolding his long limbs from the boulder on which he had been sitting.

'This is the best seat I can be offering you, lady,' he said, 'unless you wish to sit within.'

Anne shook her head. The bothy was low and windowless, not a place where she would want to sit alone with Brendan Donovan. She accepted a wooden trencher of bannock and cheese.

'This cheese is of excellent quality, Brendan,' she said. 'I think you should make some for the winter store.'

'Is it worrying you still are, about food for the winter?' He gave a sardonic smile. 'I'm thinking house and barns are groaning indeed under the weight of what you have put by, so.'

Anne laughed.

'I shall not quickly forget what I found when we came home in January. It's become a passion with me, this storing away of food. I'm like the squirrel, who is driven to hide far more nuts than ever he can eat.'

Brendan looked grave.

'When a man has starved, and seen his family starve, he is not like to forget it either.'

'You seem to speak from experience.'

'There's been much starvation in Ireland. The land is fine and fertile in some places; in others, the soil is thin over the stone beneath, or riddled with bog. The Old English who came in Queen Elizabeth's time took much of the best land; the New English, who were sent by King James, took the rest. What should the people of Ireland do but starve?'

'I fear I know very little of the rights of it,' said Anne. 'But I hope I shall not hear that you were one of those Irish who massacred the English settlers.'

'Then you shall not hear it.' He looked at her strangely, with a flash of that angry, brooding light in his eyes that she had not seen these many months. A quiver of fear touched her skin and she shuddered.

There was an uncomfortable silence between them, broken only when Brendan gathered up the remains of the food and the trenchers and stowed them inside the bothy. He sat down again on the ground, his arms about his updrawn knees, gazing across the moor and down to where Swinfen lay. The dog sidled up and laid his head on his master's foot. Seated like this, half turned away from her and without his extravagant hat, he had almost a look of John in the set of his shoulders and the curve from spine to the vulnerable hollow at the back of his neck. His lower arms were bare where he had rolled up his sleeves, and the low autumn sun glinted on the reddish fair hairs. The muscles were tight under the skin, as though his hands were gripping each other convulsively.

'I did not think,' he said, slowly and reluctantly, 'that I should ever see an English landowner treat his people with kindness—no, with generosity. But you have taught me different, Mistress Anne.'

'I daresay you will find as many different characters amongst landowners as you will amongst any other sort,' she said. Her words sounded breathless, as though she had been running. 'Kindness, I suppose, is a sort of instinct.'

She realised that he was speaking again in that educated voice, which she took to be his true voice, for it surfaced only when his attention was concentrated elsewhere.

'Who, I wonder,' she said, speaking her thoughts aloud, 'is Brendan Donovan?'

He flashed her a bright, startled look.

'Sure, and isn't he Mistress Swynfen's hired shepherd, so?'

382

'Aye. Sure, and isn't he something other than what he pretends, so?' she said, mocking him.

'Perhaps he was something different once.'

'I think,' she said, slowly and carefully, aware that she might be risking great danger, and yet compelled by some need for honesty between them, 'I think that Brendan Donovan—if that is his name, which I doubt—I think that Brendan Donovan was once a wealthy man, and a landowner himself. I think that Brendan Donovan (or whoever he is) was well born, and educated as a gentleman, perhaps even in England at Oxford or Cambridge. I think that Brendan Donovan lost his land through no fault of his own, and carries the bitterness of that loss still.'

She saw his jaw stiffen, and then he buried his face in his hands.

'I think,' she said very softly, 'that Brendan Donovan had once a wife and children, whom he loved dearly. And I think that they, too, are lost.'

He made an inarticulate sound of grief, and twisted his body away from her.

She sighed and stood up, shaking out her skirts. She too turned away to look down over the beautiful lands of Swinfen, so much more beautiful to her now, since they had come into her care.

'Land is precious,' she said, 'but people are more precious still. I don't know why you came here, Brendan Donovan, but I do not think it was by chance. A wandering Irish shepherd, in these days when all farms are short of labour, does not make his way right across Wales and Shropshire and into Staffordshire without finding work. You came here for a purpose. I don't know why, but as long as you mean no harm to me or mine, you are welcome to stay here, as Brendan Donovan, shepherd to Mistress Anne Swynfen. It may be that you will move on, it may be that you will stay and prosper. Perhaps one day you will possess your own land again, although I know that not God Himself can bring back those you love.'

He whirled about, jumping to his feet, and seized both her hands in his, so that she was suddenly very afraid. His grip was fierce, almost cruel, yet she felt a leap in her throat that was excitement more than fear.

'If I were a superstitious man,' he said, 'I would take you for a witch. You read me too clearly. How could you divine so much about me? As for why I came, that is forgotten. I mean no harm to you or yours, not now, never again.'

He leaned forward towards her, his face barely inches from hers, and tried to take her in his arms. Her legs grew weak beneath her, and for a moment she almost yielded, but she fought free of him and pushed him away.

'You are mistaken in me,' she cried. 'I have a husband I love above all else in this world, for he is not only my lover but my dearest friend.'

He did not look chastened.

'Your husband—your lover—may never return, and the woman I loved is gone past reaching. We are both of us lonely and heart-sore.'

'Nay, for I have the hope of John's return soon. I am sorry, more sorry than I can say, for what you have lost. But you cannot have my heart, Brendan Donovan, for it is given elsewhere.'

He looked at her long and hard, as if he would penetrate deep into her soul.

'I think,' he said, 'that if there had never been a John Swynfen, that heart might not be so cold, for I can see that the body is warm.'

'The world is as it is,' she said. 'You must understand that I love John. He has been my heart's twin since we were children here on the moor.'

She clenched her fists.

'I love him!' she cried. 'Almost, I cannot bear to go on living without him. If it were not for the children . . . Can't you, can no one understand that? Oh, I rule this estate and keep my face calm and give my orders and settle disputes, but my heart cries out in rage. Rage! Do you understand? I love him. Dearer than my heart's blood. God forgive me, dearer than I love my Maker.'

Suddenly she began to weep, great wracking sobs. Never, in all the time he had been gone, had she allowed anyone to see the depth of her grief and her terror for John. Now, as if some natural disaster had been set in motion, her grief and her terror could not be contained any longer. When Brendan Donovan took her two hands in his again, she did not push him away.

'I know,' he said. 'I know. Forgive me. Christ God, forgive me! Let me be a friend to you, no more. I ask for nothing more. Friendship, after all, is one of God's greatest gifts to man. Our lovers may turn cold to us. Our friends rarely do.'

Eventually the storm subsided and Anne was able to wipe her eyes and speak calmly.

'We will not speak of this again,' she said. 'Nothing of what has been said here.'

'No,' he said. 'We will not speak of it.'

'I came here to speak to you about the sheep. We must speak of the sheep.'

'Aye,' he said, smiling a little, 'we must speak of the sheep.'

When they had spoken of the sheep, and the management of the breeding flock, and on what day Brendan would drive them down again to the home farm for the winter, Anne mounted Brandy, ready to ride down to Swinfen.

'Did you visit Agnes Lea as you came here?' Brendan asked, catching Brandy by the reins to hold her.

'Nay, I came straight here.'

'There's been trouble at her cottage. I was nearby two days ago, quite by chance, in search of some ewes which had strayed. There were three or four youths there, trying to steal her chickens, and threatening her. I chased them off, but I can't always watch over her.'

'Were they from Hints?'

'They were strangers to me, but I know very few of the people of Hints.'

'There's been trouble there. Richard warned me there were some calling her a witch, but afterwards all seemed quiet, so I thought it was forgotten.'

'I think not, for they did call her witch, and devil's whore, before they ran away.'

So it was more than simple pilfering from a defenceless old woman.

'I'll ride over there now,' said Anne, 'and see how she fares. Thank you for the warning.'

As she rode away over the moor, she knew that he watched her until she was out of sight.

When she reached Agnes's cottage, the old woman was sitting outside on a joint stool, milking one of her goats.

'Nay, don't get up,' said Anne, tying Brandy to the fence post. 'Finish your milking.'

While Agnes milked, the two women talked of the harvest, and Anne's plans for her breeding stock, and Agnes's prize brood hen.

'I must give ye some of the pullets I've had from her,' said Agnes, 'for if they prove as fruitful as she has, then they'll help to increase your flock mightily.'

'I should be glad of them,' said Anne, 'and in return I'll bring you a good store of flour and oatmeal for the winter.'

'Very well.' Agnes got stiffly to her feet. She was not too proud to accept what she could not grow herself. 'Come inside. It grows cold, these autumn evenings.'

So they went inside, and sat by the light of the fire, Agnes having moved the cat Peterkin out of one of the chairs. The old woman plied Anne with bannocks and honey, as if she were still a child. Despite her earlier meal with Brendan Donovan, Anne dared not risk Agnes's displeasure by refusing.

'I think ye have been weeping, my child,' said Agnes at last.

Anne's hand went without intention to her eyes, which were still swollen and hot.

'I'm worried for John. Captain Stone set off to fetch him home from Wales these two months past, but there's been no word. I fear one or both of them have miscarried.'

Agnes laid her knotted old hand on Anne's.

'I think not. I see young John lost and wandering amongst mountains, amongst snow, but coming home at last.'

Anne felt that hint of fear dart through her mind again. Perhaps Agnes was indeed a witch. She shivered, but spoke calmly.

'Oh, Agnes, I hope you may be right! But take a care who you speak to in such a manner, for there's danger in foretelling the future.'

Agnes shook her head.

'I don't foretell. I'm no prophetess. It's merely that sometimes I see things, as in a waking dream, nothing more.'

'There has been talk,' Anne said bluntly.

'There's always talk.'

'Do you understand what I am speaking of?'

'Aye. They're calling me a witch again, are they? Has someone's pig died?' she said scornfully. 'Or perhaps some lovelorn silly maid asked me for a love philtre, and when I told her I didn't make such things, went away angry. Has she now lost her lover to another?'

'Agnes, I think this time it's serious. There has been a blighted harvest over at Hints, and the plague also. People are afraid and angry, and they want someone to blame, someone to suffer.'

Agnes sighed and threw another log on the fire. It flared up briefly as the burning logs fell apart, and lit up her worn face. She was looking older these days, weary with so much hard living.

'What would ye have me do, child?' she said. 'I can't defend myself against whispers. If they lay a complaint with the magistrates, I shall be tried. And like most who are tried as witches, I shall be hanged or burned, innocent though I swear before God I am. If that's God's will, then nothing I can do will stay their hand. I've had a long life. Perhaps it's time it ended.'

'Do not speak so!' Anne knelt down beside the old woman and put her arms around her. 'Will you come to live at Swinfen with me?

There, we can protect you. No one would dare call you a witch if you are part of my household. You can bring your stock and all your possessions. Please, Agnes, come with me.'

The old woman laid her hand on Anne's head.

'Ye've always had a generous heart, child, sometimes too generous for your own good. But I couldn't leave here. My Nick built this cottage and brought me here as a bride. I won't leave here until I die. I couldn't breathe away from the moor, for the low valley airs are heavy. They would weigh on my heart.'

She would not be persuaded. At last, Anne untied Brandy and prepared to leave.

'I'll find out all I can, and I'll ask my shepherd to keep an eye on any who come prowling again. But I wish you would come.'

Agnes shook her head and smiled, and as Anne rode away, she was standing still at her doorway, with one of her goats grazing beside her.

∾

The field crops were harvested, the peas dried, the wheat ground into flour, the beans salted down in crocks, the cheeses made, the onions plaited into ropes, the pompions stored both fresh and dried, the stillroom supplied with fresh simples for winter coughs and colds, the herbs hung from the kitchen beams in bunches. Throughout September and October, they gathered apples from the orchard. As if in recompense for the previous year's poor crop, the old apple trees were laden with the fruit, and as fast as the pickers brought in the baskets of apples, those working in the kitchen tried to turn this abundant harvest into food that would last through winter.

The most perfect apples of the keeping sorts were laid out carefully, not touching, on slatted shelves in the apple store next to the dairy, where most of them would survive for several months. Others were peeled and cored and sliced into rings, and dried slowly before the fire, as the peas had been, until they felt like soft leather; then they were threaded on strings and hung in the larder. They would serve for pies right through until next apple picking. Anne had invested in a ten-pound loaf of sugar in Lichfield at great expense, fifteen shillings the loaf, because with sugar they could make preserves of all the autumn fruits, including apple jelly—jar upon stone jar of it, as richly red as rubies, for winter puddings and sweetening—and little dishes of apple cheese, dense and toffee-brown, firm enough to be cut into comfits. As for the present, they ate apples raw and baked and roasted and stewed

387

and stuffed and turned into pies, until no-one in the household ever wished to see an apple again.

The hedgerows and woods also yielded their autumn bounty. Anne and Patience took all the children but the two baby girls out to gather blackberries and hazelnuts. If more blackberries were popped into mouths than into baskets, Anne did not greatly mind, for this was a new excitement for her London-reared children. None but Dick had ever gone gathering the wild fruits and nuts before. They came home with stained faces and scratched hands, but presented their harvest to Bridget with great pride.

'We'll pack the nuts in crocks,' Bridget explained to the children, 'and tie them down and store them on a high shelf, for your household mouse is very partial to hazelnuts. Tomorrow you may help me make blackberry preserves. Tonight, we shall have blackberries and cream for supper.'

Anne was so occupied in managing her large household, in buying and selling at market, and preparing for the Martinmas slaughtering of beasts, that she had little time to think about Agnes Lea. She had hired a slaughterman from Lichfield, who worked quickly and skilfully, but this was never a pleasant business, and it was followed by some of the hardest work of the whole agricultural year, for everyone must turn to and help with the curing, pickling, salting, and smoking of the meat. When Richard came home with a fine stag slung over his horse, Anne was grateful for the venison, but wished that he might have chosen his time better.

The week after the slaughtering, Anne packed one saddlebag with a haunch of bacon and a jar of chitterlings and another saddlebag with apples. When Isaac had saddled Brandy for her, she rode over to Weeford, to the cottage of Liza Martin, the wet nurse who was caring for John Digby.

'He's growing well,' said Anne, looking down at the baby where he slept in his wooden cradle. Long lashes lay on the plump cheeks and his fingers curled like flower petals where they rested on the blanket. At the sound of her voice he stirred a little, but did not wake.

'Aye, mistress, he's a fine healthy boy, no doubt, for all that he came so sad into the world.'

The baby's mouth puckered and his eyelids flickered, then opened. His gaze wandered over Anne, then fixed itself on her face. The faintest shadow of a smile crinkled his cheeks and a dimple jumped and vanished again. Anne reached down and lifted him, gathering a blanket round him like a shawl.

'He'll be wet, I'm thinking,' said Liza.

Anne cupped her hand around the child's small buttocks. 'No, not at the moment.'

She carried him across to the window, where she could see him better, and he screwed up his eyes against the light. She could feel the soft flutter of his heartbeat against her breast and thought again of his child mother, as her heart stuttered and stopped, lying there on the stained grass beside the pond.

Poor little fellow, she thought, what sort of a world have we brought you into? A child of rape and death, with no family and a bloody inheritance. Would it have been better to let you die along with her?

The baby reached out for a strand of her hair which had worked loose. His movements were not yet well co-ordinated, but again and again he tried to grasp it, making little chortling noises at his own game. She could feel the energy in him, the will to gain that small victory. Perhaps he would find his own strength, make a place for himself in this new world, despite everything. What kind of world would it be by the time he came to manhood? Surely by then there would be peace of some kind, and John Digby had as much chance of making his way in it as her own children, the children of a man cast out and imprisoned.

She laid the baby gently in Liza's arms and turned to the saddlebags she had brought into the cottage.

'Look, I've brought you apples and some fresh meat from the autumn slaughtering, and a side of bacon, though it's not done salting yet.'

෨

At the end of November there was a sudden snow storm. The snow lay for no more than a day, and was gone again in the first sun, but it was a warning of a bitter winter ahead. On the day the snow fell, Anne caught sight of herself in the glass in her chamber. She rarely looked at herself now, combing her hair hastily in the morning as she walked about, then bundling it into a plain cap and never stopping to see that she was tidy. That accidental glance in the mirror stopped her short.

Looking out at her from the good piece of imported glass, in its embroidered cushion frame, was a face she did not recognise as her own. All those months ago when Dick had come home, he had said she looked brown. Now, like her other children, he was quite indifferent to her appearance. Brown her face certainly was, brown with sun and wind and weather. But more than that, her face seemed to have changed shape. Where it had once been softly curved in its contours, with an almost child-like roundness about cheeks and chin, it was now composed of flat planes and sharp angles. Her chin seemed more square, more masculine, her cheeks were slightly hollowed and her cheek bones more prominent, not as if her face were fine drawn with hunger but as if a sculptor has started with that old, soft, womanly face, and had smoothed away with his thumb the gentle curves which had given the face its former appearance. I look like a young man, she thought with surprise.

She ran her hands over her body, aware, as she had not been for months, of her own shape. Gone was the softness of constant pregnancies. Her breasts and waist and stomach were firm, her arms and legs hardened with the strengthening of her muscles. For the first time she realised how the release from child-bearing had restored her youthful body. It was as if she had become a girl again, that girl who used to ride the moors in her brother's clothes. Suddenly, gloriously, she had rediscovered her true self. She was still pondering this strange transformation later in the day when Peter rode in from a trip to Lichfield market, and asked if he might speak with her.

''Tis Goody Lea, Mistress Swynfen,' he said gravely. 'She'm taken up for a witch and lodged in Lichfield gaol. 'Twas all the talk of the market, for there's been no trials of witches this long time past.'

Anne felt a sense of shock and also of guilt, for somehow she should have prevented this.

'When was she taken there? Is she to go before the magistrates? Who are the magistrates now in Lichfield? After all these changes, are there any that we know?'

Peter looked confused by all these questions.

'She was taken yesterday,' he said slowly. 'Leastways, that's what I heard tell. No one said aught about magistrates.'

Anne was thinking rapidly as she hurried out towards the home farm. Agnes's stock must be safeguarded, or it would all be stolen as soon as it was known that she had been carried off. It did not amount to much: a flock of chickens, two or three ewes and her small herd of goats, and of course Peterkin, the cat.

'Josiah!' she called.

He was at the top of a ladder, hammering at something on the roof of the stable.

'Mistress?'

'You must go up to Goody Lea's cottage on the moor, take Isaac with you, and one of the horses with a pack-saddle and baskets. She's been carried off to Lichfield gaol. I want you to drive her stock down here, and fetch her possessions as well.'

She gave her instructions quickly, as Josiah climbed down the ladder.

'Brendan is bringing down our flock today or tomorrow. Best if you work together. And tell Isaac to saddle Brandy for me before you leave. And don't forget to bring the cat.'

Catching up her skirts, she ran inside. Finding Hester in the kitchen, she told her to make up a basket of food for Agnes Lea, then she ran upstairs to fetch her warmest cloak and a blanket from her bed.

'Anne?' said Bridget, coming to the door of her parents' chamber. 'What's to-do? Is there news of John?'

'No. Still nothing.' Anne fastened her cloak about her neck and bundled up the blanket. 'Agnes Lea is accused of witchcraft. I'm taking her some comforts in gaol. And I'm sending Josiah to bring her stock and belongings here.'

'You must take care, and so must Josiah,' said Bridget in alarm. 'If there's a crowd at Agnes's cottage . . .'

'You have the right of it. Where's Richard? He must go as well, and they'll fetch Brendan.'

'I think I saw Richard go off towards the forest with his gun this morning.'

'Why is that boy never here when he's needed?' Anne stormed. 'He's more trouble than all the children together.'

Bridget smiled.

'He's not so different from John, I think, when he was that age.'

'John has *always* been responsible,' Anne said, angrily and somewhat inaccurately.

Back in the kitchen, she peered into the basket Hester had laid ready.

'There's little enough here, Hester,' she said sharply. 'Put in some cold meat and more cheese. And heaven knows, we've more than enough apples.'

Hester glanced at her sideways and took up a knife, reluctantly it seemed, to cut slices from the ham on the dresser.

'She'm a witch, that Lea woman. You'd best have naught to do with 'un, mistress. 'Twill stain this household and all of us.'

Anne whirled about and stared at her.

'You cannot believe that, Hester. You've known Goody Lea all your life. She's nothing but a harmless old woman.'

Hester paused and pointed at Anne with the knife.

391

'Aye, I know 'un. 'Tis her that cursed my uncle's fields with the blight, over to Hints.'

Anne had forgotten that Hester had family at Hints. She drew a deep breath and spoke quietly.

'Hester, I'm truly sorry your uncle's wheat has been blighted, but you cannot lay it at Agnes's door. What has she to do with your uncle? There must be some other cause. Last year many of the crops were lost. There was no talk of witchcraft then, was there?'

'Last year, all suffered alike,' said Hester stubbornly. 'This blight, it has only touched some, and 'tis well known Agnes has a quarrel with the folk of Hints.'

'Only with the lads who come stealing her chickens,' said Anne. It was a long-standing battle.

Hester turned back to the ham.

'You should not meddle, mistress. No good will come to us if you do.'

When Anne reached Lichfield she left the horse as usual at the Black Swan in the Market Square, and made her way on foot to the gaol in Bore Street. It was a small but dreadful place, the thick walls squat and malevolent, the mean apertures, hardly windows, admitting cold slivers of grey light. The very air stank of despair and death. There, by conducting herself with unaccustomed arrogance and slipping some coins into the gaoler's hand, she gained access to Agnes's cell.

The old woman was alone in a cold, windowless room, and she looked very frightened. To Anne's eyes, she seemed much smaller and more bowed than she had up on the moor amongst her goats. For all her defiant talk, the reality of being accused of witchcraft was fearful. There was nothing at all in the cell, no bed, no chair, not even straw upon the floor. The only light came from the gaps around the ill-fitting door. The hearth, on this bitterly cold day, was unlit. Anne knelt down beside Agnes, where she crouched upon the uneven stones of the floor, and wrapped the blanket around her.

'See, I've brought you some food. When did you last eat?'

Agnes looked at her vaguely.

'I cannot call to mind.'

'You must eat now. You must keep up your strength, and we shall soon have you out of this.'

Obedient as a child, Agnes began to chew her way through the food, as though she had no idea what she was putting in her mouth.

'I've sent my men to drive your goats and ewes down to Swinfen, so we can care for them. They've taken baskets for the chickens and panniers to fetch away your goods, so no thieving lads can steal them while you're away.'

Agnes shook her head.

'I shall never leave this place alive.'

'Nay, do not talk so. You must keep up your spirits as well as your strength. A few spiteful villagers shall not have their way in this.'

'Peterkin!' said Agnes. 'What of my poor cat?'

'They'll bring him away too, if they can catch him. If they can't, I shall go up to the moor tomorrow and I shall not leave until I catch him, even if I must stay all day.'

Agnes smiled weakly.

'Cats are difficult creatures. They have strong wills and they like to stay in their own place.' She gave a suppressed sob. 'They said that Peterkin was my familiar, that he was the devil disguised. I've had him from a kitten—'twas Master Pegg the curate that gave him to me, to keep the mice away from my store of corn. My lovely Peterkin—they will kill him, and he nothing but a poor innocent creature.'

Tears began to seep from the corners of her tired eyes and trickle slowly down the furrows in her face.

'Of course he's not the devil,' said Anne. 'What fools these people are!'

'I'm no witch, child, though it may be true that some folk be. Old King James believed in witches.'

'I grant you,' said Anne, 'there may be people who meddle in things they should not. But as for the devil made manifest and working through those who are usually accused—why, if the devil is so powerful and evil, why doesn't he choose more potent instruments? People of wealth and power, instead of the poor and defenceless? I cannot believe it.' It was her reason speaking, though creeping, fearful doubts still nibbled at her mind. What if Agnes were indeed a witch?

Anne had spoken stoutly, to give Agnes courage, but she knew that the nameless terror that gripped people in a witch hunt was incapable of responding to reason. When she was sure Agnes had eaten her fill, she left the rest of the basket of food with her and went in search of the gaoler to demand a bed and a chair and a fire and another blanket. He was surly and reluctant, but another bribe persuaded him. In such cases as these, Anne knew that if the prisoner was seen to have powerful friends, it could influence not only the treatment meted out in the gaol but also the eventual conduct of the trial.

When she reached home again, the men were just coming in, driving before them the Swinfen flock of sheep as well as Agnes's stock. The chickens were making a mighty racket, taking exception to being stuffed into hampers and bounced about on a horse's back all the way down from the moor. Biddy took charge of Agnes's small store of possessions: a few clothes, some cookpots, her churn and cheese-making equipment, and her bedding, which included the one object of beauty, a pieced quilt she had made as her only marriage portion.

'Where is the cat?' Anne demanded of Josiah.

'He ran off when he saw us, mistress. We tried all we could think of, tried to tempt 'un with food, but he sat under a gorse bush and growled at us. Brendan thrust in his hands and would have grabbed 'un, but the beast lashed out and scratched 'un to the bone. Perhaps 'tis true what they say, that he's the devil.'

Anne turned on him.

'Never let me hear you speak such folly again! He's nothing but a poor frightened cat who has seen his mistress carried off by the constable and a gaggle of strange men seeming to tear apart his very home. What would you expect? It's near dark now, but I shall go up there myself directly after breakfast tomorrow.'

The sun had not yet risen above the trees beyond the lake when Anne was on her way to Agnes's cottage. She carried with her a basket for Peterkin, if she could catch him, some tempting bits of rabbit and fish, and one of Agnes's shawls, which she hoped would smell to the cat of his mistress and safety. Peterkin was sitting in the open doorway of the cottage, and glared at her balefully, but he did not immediately run away. Anne sat down at a short distance and began talking to him soothingly, telling him about Agnes. She did not believe the cat could understand her, but hoped that the sound of her voice would calm him.

After a while, she laid out a few pieces of food and stared away over the moor as if ignoring him, but she was aware when the cat crept forward and began to nibble daintily at the furthest piece of rabbit. Even when a cat is starving, it will not demean itself to admit it. It took the best part of an hour to tempt Peterkin to her. At last she had him sitting on Agnes's shawl on her lap, washing his hind leg with a casual and careless air, but as she stroked him she could hear a purr rumbling deep within. As gently as possible, she wrapped him in the shawl and stowed him in the basket. He gave one protesting yowl, but then resigned himself to being carried down to Swinfen Hall. Anne did not trust him not to run away again to the cottage, so she shut him in one of the attics, with Agnes's belongings all around him, so that he could grow accustomed to the idea. In the afternoon she rode off again to Lichfield.

In town she ascertained that Agnes was to come before the magistrates in a few days' time, the senior magistrate being Mathew

Moreton, an old man of near sixty. Moreton had been one of John's colleagues on the bench, and Anne had some hopes of persuading him to drop the case against Agnes. The other two magistrates were a greater danger: Richard Floyer, himself a man of Hints, who might take the part of his tenants, and William Jolley, who lived at Leek, but of whom she knew little else, except that he was engaged in the wool trade. That it should be necessary to call in a magistrate all the way from Leek was a fair measure of the confusion of the times. Both Henry Stone and John had been magistrates sitting in Lichfield, whose services were now lost. Michael Noble, another of John's friends, town clerk and Member of Parliament for Lichfield, had died last year. The other Member for Lichfield, Michael Biddulph, was secluded. Edward Leigh had been seized by the army, and she did not know if he was freed.

She had prepared herself for her visit to Mathew Moreton with some care, donning one of her London gowns, choosing one that was clearly of the highest quality, but not gaudy, in keeping with the sober times, and telling Patience to lace her stays as tightly as could be managed. For the first time she regretted the loss of her jewels, for an appearance of wealth and standing would help her cause. She had persuaded Bridget to dress her hair. It was one of Patience's duties, but Bridget would take more care over teasing out the tangles Anne had allowed to accumulate. When she was shown into Moreton's parlour, she was glad she had taken the trouble, for this was an elegant townhouse, far divorced from the manor of a working country estate.

She was shown at once into the parlour by a neat serving maid, while her host was fetched from his office. The room opened with wide sash windows on to a garden extensive for a house in the centre of the town, and was decorated with costly hand-tinted wallpaper. The furniture was French, and gilded, the carpets plushy underfoot, and two dozen fine wax candles in sconces around the walls were already lit, although it was still daylight outside and no one was in the room.

Mathew Moreton received her with great courtesy, expressed genuine regrets at John's continued imprisonment and his hopes that Henry Stone would succeed in his mission.

'For Stone seems quite to have disappeared,' he said. 'Some of us who are friends to both him and to John have been talking of sending out men to search for him, but we must tread very warily in these times. It must not be taken as some kind of private army.'

'I would be grateful for your help,' Anne said, at this unexpected turn in the conversation. Since Henry Stone had ridden off to Stafford, she had thought herself alone in trying to discover what had happened, uncertain whether those old friends of John's were still his friends, or whether they had accommodated themselves to the new men in power.

'Now, Mistress Swynfen,' said Moreton, 'I would like to offer you some of this new drink that is quite *à la mode* amongst the fashionable in London, I am told, brought in by some of the orient merchants. I was sent some by my cousin there, who tells me 'tis a sovereign drink in cold weather. It is made from a herb grown in China, and they call it *tay* or *chaw*.'

He poured the hot liquid from a kind of lidded jug into a deep saucer. It was the colour of amber.

'You may take it like this, or add milk and sugar. I find it best with a little milk.'

Anne let him add some milk to her saucer, then tasted it gingerly. It was not unpleasant, like a warm herbal drink, though weak. It seemed strange to put milk to it.

'What is your opinion?' Moreton asked, passing her a plate of marzipan sweetmeats.

'Quite pleasant,' said Anne, 'but I expect it will be one of these passing fashions that seize the people in London. Why should we import herbs from China, when we can grow our own?'

They talked for a time about Anne's years in London before she led him round to the subject of the charges against Agnes Lea.

'Goody Agnes has lived on our property on Packington Moor since the time of John's grandfather,' said Anne. 'I regard her as one of our people, and I know she's no witch. The complaint is foolish, and I hope you will dismiss the case out of hand.'

Moreton immediately looked serious, and slightly displeased.

'These are matters of law that are of no concern to a woman,' he said.

'I am afraid I must disagree, Master Moreton. In the absence of my husband, the incapacity of my father-in-law, and the minority of my eldest son, I am, of necessity, seigneur of the Swinfen estate. Whether I have also rights in law is another matter, which we might dispute, but whatever the rights, I have responsibilities towards my people. I cannot allow you to put Agnes Lea on trial without speaking on her behalf, and enquiring as to the nature of the complaint.'

'There is more than one,' he said reluctantly. 'Some are trivial and will not concern the court. Those of substance are, first, that she did blight the wheat crop generally at Hints, and, second, that she did cause the death of a milch cow belonging to one William Slater of Hints. These are the instances of *maleficium*. She is under examination now as to whether she did covenant with or consort with the devil. It is alleged that the devil came to her in the form of a large cat.'

'Master Moreton, I have known that cat for seventeen years. He is no more the devil than the cats we have about Swinfen to keep down the rats.'

She decided for the moment to say nothing of the fact that the cat had been the gift of the Weeford curate. If Agnes came to trial, it might be as well to have a few surprises in reserve. She did not like the sound of that word 'examination'.

'Why,' she added, 'I know that you're a lover of cats yourself. That does not make you a witch, I trust!'

Moreton flushed, whether with anger or embarrassment she could not be sure.

'Mistress Swynfen, I'm obliged by my position as justice of the peace here in Lichfield to take account of any complaints about witchcraft, and to proceed to trial if there be sufficient evidence. The preliminary hearing will be held as soon as the examination of the accused is completed. If there is held to be a case, it will proceed to a full trial shortly thereafter.'

'What do you mean by "completing the examination"? Surely you must know how long this will last?'

'There can be great variation, depending on how the accused behaves under examination.'

Anne gripped the arms of her chair as a wave of sickness came over her. She understood now what he was telling her, hidden within his legal language. Agnes was being subjected to torture. What might a weak, tired old woman not say under torture? She stood up.

'I thank you for your time, Master Moreton. I think I must visit Agnes Lea now, to see how she fares.' She saw a flash of comprehension come and go in Moreton's eyes, as he realised that she intended to investigate what was being done to Agnes.

'It is my understanding,' she said, 'that the accused may not speak to defend herself at the trial, but only to plead, guilty or not guilty. Is that right?'

'It is.'

'But her friends may speak for her? Bear witness to her good character? I may give evidence?'

'You may, but I beg you not to interfere in this matter, Mistress Swynfen. I like this business no better than you, whatever you may think. Public trials for witchcraft are very unpleasant affairs, and I would spare a lady from ever witnessing one. The evidence is likely to be obscene and fearful, and the behaviour of the common people who come to observe the trial will be gross and unseemly, for it is generally the idle sort who attend.'

'I thank you for your concern,' said Anne carefully, 'but surely these are reasons enough why I should speak for a harmless old woman who has no family left in the neighbourhood, and who must look to her landlord for support and succour?'

Anne walked directly from Mathew Moreton's house to the gaol, where her arrival caused some concern and confusion. The prisoner, it seemed, was not there. Anne refused to move from the chair where she had seated herself on arriving, and after about half an hour Agnes appeared, stumbling along between two constables. Her condition appeared to be very much worse than it had on the previous day. As soon as they were alone in the cell, Agnes sank down upon the narrow cot with a groan.

'Agnes, my dear,' said Anne, shocked at her appearance, 'what have they been doing to you? And where are your shoes?'

For the old woman's feet were naked and bleeding.

'They have been walking me,' Agnes said, in little more than a whisper. 'And they took off my shoes to do it. After ye left me yesterday, they walked me here in the gaol all night, up and down, up and down. Then this morning they took me to the town hall and questioned me.'

'Wait!' said Anne, 'before you tell me any more.'

She went to the door and called for water and bandages. They were a long time coming, but they came at last. She knelt on the dirty floor beside the old woman and bathed her bloody feet, then bound them in the clean cloths. The injuries would have fared better with salving, but she had not brought any, for she had not expected the Lichfield magistrates to break the law.

'Now,' said Anne, unpacking the basket of food. 'Tell me the rest while you eat, and then I'll make them light you a fire. Have you been without warmth all this time?'

Agnes nodded. She did not want to eat, but little by little Anne fed her scraps of bread and cold meat, as she told the rest.

'After they'd questioned me a while, they sent for a pricker. Oh, child, that an old woman should be stripped naked before men, and pins stuck in her flesh, to prove her a witch! Still, it did them no good, for I felt the pins, every one. After that, they walked me again, up and down and up and down, till I was like to fall to the ground.'

She gave a feeble smile.

'But they've not defeated me yet. I will not confess to it, for I prayed to God to give me strength to withstand them, and He has been my shield and sword.'

Anne felt herself flush with relief. The squirming little doubts she had had withered and died. Of course Agnes Lea was no witch, but had she herself needed the torturer's hand to convince her? She was shamed.

After the old woman had eaten, Anne tucked the blankets around her, and waited until a fire had been lit, with much grumbling. The gaolers were not accustomed to their prisoners having such powerful friends, and they did not quite know how to gainsay her. Once she was sure that Agnes was sleeping, Anne left the gaol to return to Mathew Moreton's house. This time she was not made so welcome, for she was kept standing in the chilly hallway, where she could hear the sound of men's voices in the parlour. She had time to work herself up into a mighty rage before she was invited to enter.

Seated around the table where she had recently drunk the exotic *tay* were three men: Moreton himself, Richard Floyer and William Jolley. The magistrates who were to try Agnes. There was a fourth man, whom she assumed to be some sort of legal clerk, who left the room as she entered. Before any of the men could speak, Anne determined she would attack.

'Gentlemen,' she said, giving them so slight a nod of the head as to be insulting, 'I have come even now from seeing Agnes Lea in the gaol. It will shock you, I am certain, to learn that illegal methods of torture have been used in questioning her.'

The men stirred uneasily and glanced at each other.

'Good day, Mistress Swynfen,' said Richard Floyer smoothly. 'I'm glad to see you in good health. You need not concern yourself with these matters. Everything is well in hand in the examination of the accused.'

Anne regarded him thoughtfully. Richard Floyer had once been married to her beloved cousin, Elizabeth Weston, who had died in childbirth at the age of twenty, the year that Anne was married. She no longer regarded him as a kinsman, although he was now married to one of the Babingtons, who were distant kin to the Swinfens.

'No, Master Floyer, everything is *not* well in hand. Everything is very ill. Everything is being carried out by unlawful means. Three illegal means of torture have been used on her.'

She counted them off on her fingers.

'She has been deprived of sleep. She has been walked. And she has been pricked. All of these practices are found to be contrary to English law.'

'How do you know that?' asked Jolley in surprise. He was a stout old man, flushed with good living and said to have made rather greater profits in his business than he should have.

'My husband,' said Anne, fixing him with a cold glance, 'is a Member of Parliament. He was also trained in the law at Grey's Inn. He takes a great interest in laws that affect the treatment of the poor and helpless. As I do.'

'Your husband *was* a Member of Parliament,' said Jolley, with a knowing smile. 'I think he is one no longer.'

'No legal action has deprived him of that position,' said Anne, whose anger was growing more icy by the moment. 'But that is not the matter in question. You—or those employed by you—have acted contrary to the law. I still have powerful friends. I think you might not care to have it known what you have done.'

She was bluffing, of course, and they might guess as much, but they might be reluctant to expose themselves to personal danger for the sake of a village witch hunt. No one knew how the new Puritan state would regard their actions. Witch hunts and torture might be in favour. They might not. A prudent man would take care to guard himself.

Mathew Moreton rose and came to her, and took both her hands in his.

'Mistress Anne, let us not quarrel over this matter. John is too old a friend of mine, as you are. I would not become your enemy. I swear to you that no more illegal methods of questioning will be used on the accused.'

'And will you bring the matter to trial quickly, so that she may be freed and allowed to come home?'

He smiled. 'You are very certain that she will be freed.'

'I am.'

'Very well. We have been discussing a date for the preliminary hearing.' He glanced at the other two men. 'I think we may fix on the twentieth day of this month.'

'May I take her home until then?'

'No, you may not.'

Anne realised she had accomplished more than she could have hoped. Had the times been normal, these men would have treated her with polite contempt, considering interference by a woman to be not only unseemly but scandalous. But in this strange new world, landowning men of wealth were less certain of their position, while women found themselves thrust into those unseemly roles, willy-nilly. Indeed, she could hardly imagine herself a mere twelvemonth ago behaving in such a brazen manner.

When she went to collect Brandy from the inn, she found a letter awaiting her, from that other John Swinfen, of Sutton Cheney, John's cousin. He wrote that, after many enquiries, he had found an aunt of Penelope Digby, living not far from Market Harborough, in Easton Magna. She had believed that all her sister's family had been killed, and had wept bitterly on hearing of her niece's sad end nearly a year later. Having dearly loved young Penelope, she was willing to take in the bastard child and rear him with her own. When Easter came, with the better weather, and the child able to be weaned, she would send for him.

Anne rode home slowly through a light shower of snow. She felt tired from her efforts at arguing with the magistrates, but glad that at least there would be some kind of future for John Digby, who was growing into such a beautiful, strong boy. A sense of melancholy settled upon her, in keeping with the lowering sky and the icy wind, thinking of that young girl's death in her arms, and the old woman, confused, frightened and alone, whose escape from the noose and the pyre depended on Anne's own uncertain strength.

Chapter Twenty-Nine

Dafydd Williams's illness grew suddenly worse. He was seized with severe headaches, and with pains in his limbs which at times left them rigid, in a kind of paralysis. In the evenings and during the night he raged with fever and delirium, crying out strangely sometimes in Welsh, sometimes in English—pleas for pity on the poor and dying, raging against injustice and cruelty. John knelt beside his bed, bathing his burning face and restraining him when he was like to hurt himself as he thrashed about.

When the fever abated a little in the morning, he would lie quiet and biddable, saying that in his unconscious ravings he had thought himself wrestling with devils.

'I fear I've taken gaol fever,' he said quietly one morning. He was lying slack on his bed, his body a vast wreck like a stricken ship under the blankets. 'There were many sick of it in Monmouth, where we were crowded together, and all the air was foetid with the stink of it.'

He seemed to doze a little, then resumed speaking as though no time had passed.

'It's strange that it's taken so long to seize hold of me, but perhaps it had a stronger fortress than usual to overcome in this great body of mine. I'm weak now, but I was a strong man once, with muscles in my arms, from beating the iron, that looked like the knotty limbs of old oak trees.'

He gave a weak laugh.

'Not the arms to hold a maid or cradle a child, but serviceable to dig and to plough.'

'You will regain your strength,' said John. 'You must use that great body of yours to fight the sickness, and you will surely overcome it.'

Another time, when he was not feverish but seemed to be wandering in some other country of the mind, he said, 'We sought to build the Kingdom of God on earth, a Christian utopia, and for that pride and blasphemy were we punished. For how could our enemies have prevailed against us, unless the hand of God Himself aided them?'

Before John could find an answer, he had slipped away into unconsciousness again.

John pleaded and argued and demanded that a physician should be sent for. Most of the guards were indifferent. The young lad promised to do what he could. After nearly a week, Sergeant Conway came himself. He stood surveying the sick man and John, who was again trying to give Dafydd relief by bathing his face, for there was little else he could do.

'You had best keep your distance from him,' said the sergeant, 'for if it is the gaol fever, it's easily caught. You'll be laid low yourself.'

'Will you send for a physician?' John said. 'You must have an army doctor in the garrison. For pity's sake, sergeant, it's little enough to do for a fellow creature.'

The sergeant grunted, and left without giving any undertaking, but the next day the army physician did come. He examined the patient and shook his head.

'You see this rash on his body? The clusters like ripe mulberries? And the swellings in the groin and armpits? It's the gaol fever, right enough. There's little I can do except bleed him, to relieve the excess of the choleric humour in the body. I'll require your assistance to hold the bleeding bowl.'

So John held the bowl, with its bite out of the rim to accommodate the patient's arm, while the physician rolled up Dafydd's shirt sleeve, selected a vein, and cut into it with a quick neat movement. At least he seemed skilled at his business. The red blood spurted out, splashing John but not the physician, who had moved aside with the swiftness of long practice. When about a pint of blood had flowed into the bowl, the physician stopped the flow with pressure from his thumb.

'Set that bowl aside now and place your thumb here while I bind him up.'

John did as he was told. It brought back to him painful memories of his little son George being bled thus, and all to no avail, though they had called in the best physician in the county.

'I'll visit him again tomorrow, to see how he fares.'

He lifted one of Dafydd's eyelids by the lashes and peered into his eye. He shrugged.

'I have no great hopes for him.'

As he was about to leave the cell, he turned back.

'You're John Swynfen, are you not?'

Surprised, John agreed that he was.

'I once heard you speak in Parliament, when I attended a debate there. We're come to a pretty pass, are we not? That you should languish a prisoner in Denbigh. Though I understand not for much longer.'

'You've heard some news?' John took a step forward and laid his hand on the man's arm to stay him.

'Only that the governor received a letter from the governor of Stafford. A Captain Stone was on his way here with a document securing your release. Since then, nothing further has been heard of the man.'

With that he left, carrying his bag of instruments and the bowl of Dafydd's blood with him.

This unexpected news made John so restless he could not keep still, but paced about the room. Could the man have been sent to say this merely to torment him? Yet he had an honest face, and had spoken as though the news were nothing very remarkable. And the mention of Henry Stone's name gave the tale credibility. How could this man—or the governor of Denbigh, for that matter—have known of John's friendship with Stone? But if Danvers had sent his letter to the governor here at the same time as Stone set out on his journey, why had Stone not reached Denbigh by now? John thought of the terrible countryside he had travelled through on the way into Wales, and shuddered. What if Henry Stone should not survive the journey? It would be an end to both of them.

His thoughts of himself and his own concerns were interrupted by a cry from Dafydd, who was writhing about on his mattress, and, even as John hurried over to him, rolled over and crashed to the floor. It was almost more than John could do, on his own, to raise the big man back on to his bed. Had Dafydd been still in his prime, he would not had succeeded, but the blacksmith had grown thin before ever he came to Denbigh, and since the fever had struck him down he had visibly wasted away. Now he was like the skeleton of a great tree, stripped of living growth but clinging to life by the last dregs of willpower.

On the following day, the physician came to them again, as he had promised, and pronounced Dafydd to be somewhat better. John could see little sign of it himself, weary with sitting up all night again while his companion raved. It seemed that the physician came only when Dafydd was at his least feverish and most calm. John's own mind was fevered with thoughts of his possible release and with concern at Henry Stone's disappearance. Was there indeed a chance that he might go free, when he had given up all hope for the future? He felt ill himself, and had difficulty eating his dinner when it was brought, but set it down to lack of sleep.

He had persuaded the physician to prescribe broth for Dafydd, for he could not stomach meat. The blacksmith was awake and fully conscious now, though too weak to hold a spoon. John ladled soup into him in the intervals of eating his own meal.

'So you're like to leave me,' said Dafydd, between mouthfuls.

John turned to him, astonished, for he thought the other had been unconscious when the physician had spoken to him the previous day.

'You heard?'

'Aye. I heard. I was half awake. I could hear you speaking, though whether I could have spoken in my turn is another matter.'

He swallowed another spoonful with difficulty.

'You think your friend has gone astray?'

'I fear so. If he was travelling alone . . . Perhaps he was set upon and robbed.'

'Certainly likely. But if the governor knows you are meant to be freed, why doesn't he release you?'

'You know such people as well as I. If they don't receive the proper document, nothing on earth will move them.'

'John, will you look at my right boot?'

Thinking his companion was raving again, John picked up the right boot and held it out to him.

'Nay, I'm as weak as a newborn rabbit. You'll see that there's an extra inner sole to the boot?'

John peered into the boot, whose smell was none too pleasant. There was indeed an extra layer of thin leather fitted into the sole of the boot.

'Pull it up. It's glued in place, but only lightly.'

John did as he was told. Beneath this inner sole, the heel of the boot was hollowed out, and concealed inside was a purse.

'Take it out.'

John pulled the purse out, and it jingled faintly.

'There's little enough in it, but I want you to take it. However you escape from here, with or without your friend, you'll have need of money to help you on your way. It's all I have to give you, a few silver shillings and some pennies, but take it, in remembrance of a wild sectary who wished you well.'

'I cannot take it, Dafydd. You will need it yourself.'

'I shall not leave this place alive, as well you know. Be honest, man. I'm sick unto death and all I can do is wait in patience for God's summons. It was kind of you to fetch the physician to me, but he can do no more than delay me a little on the road.'

John tried again to refuse the money, but Dafydd became so agitated that he thought it best to comply. He took off his own boots; inside one, folded and grubby, was a sheet of paper, written small. With a stab of remembrance, he read the words:

I, JOHN SWYNFEN, being of sound mind, though troubled by melancholy—nay, I lie, for my mind is anything but sound— and of body sick and weakened, but not like to die, save at the hands of mine enemies . . .

He hesitated, thinking he would toss the wretched document on the fire, then replaced it. It marked, after all, a stage on this unknowable journey he had been compelled to take. Under Dafydd's instructions, he set to, hollowing out the heel of his other boot with the point of his knife, to make a hiding place for the purse, then cutting down the false sole of Dafydd's boot to fit inside his own smaller one. He tried walking about the cell in his modified boot and found that, if he gave it his attention, the right boot did weigh a little heavier than the left, yet he soon ceased to be aware of it.

Dafydd sank back on his bed, exhausted by the effort of forcing his will on John, but it seemed he had not finished.

'You told me of the way you came here when you were brought by the soldiers from Stafford. That's not the shortest way, and I don't know why they came by that route.'

'I know they wanted to stay on the Roman road as long as possible, for they said it was the easier for the coach.'

'Aye, perhaps. But a man on foot or horseback would not come by Cerrig-y-Druidion. Nay, to make your way home you should go up the valley here, south-eastwards into the mountains, not south-west. You'll pass through a place called Ruthin, and so up along the river Clwyd. The tracks are very poor and broken, not easy for a carriage, I grant you.'

His voice grew fainter, and John saw that he had fallen asleep again. He did not wake even when the guard came to take away their dirty plates and to bring the rush dip. About half an hour later Dafydd stirred.

'By Ruthin I said, did I not?'

It was as though he did not know he had been asleep.

'And up the Clwyd. You must skirt the mountain of Llantysilio on the west side, and then you'll meet your Roman road once again. By the time you reach Llangollen you'll be nearly out of the mountains, and the road takes you south and east to Shrewsbury.'

'I shall never remember these strange Welsh names,' said John. 'What was that last one? Clan Gothlen? I never heard of such a place. I'm sure we didn't pass through there on our journey here.'

Dafydd gave a weak laugh, a mere mockery of his usual bellow.

'Your English soldiers probably called it "Lan Gollen", but no Welshman will understand you if you ask for directions to such a place. Come now, see if you can speak it like a Welshman.'

John repeated the name after him until he was satisfied.

'Llangollen,' said Dafydd. 'That is your goal. After that it will be easy.'

'You seem very certain I'll be making the journey.'

'The physician said you were to be released, did he not? Ah, we've not many more hours together, John, my friend, for we shall both be going on our journeys.'

'Before you came here,' said John, sitting down on the floor beside Dafydd's bed and tucking the rough blanket around him, 'I had given up all hope of leaving this place. Worse than that, I no longer cared what became of me. Despair is a sin against God, but I confess I had sunk deep into despair.'

'You do not seem to me a despairing man.'

'In the past, perhaps not. Then, I thought I saw my way clear. When I was young, and ignorant, and prideful. The world changed for me when I was taken prisoner. In my despair, aye, and in my hatred, my path was lost, the lamp before my feet darkened.'

'But now it is lit again?' Dafydd lifted his head with an effort and studied John's face.

'You lit it for me,' said John simply.

'Then my time has not been in vain.'

Dafydd said no more that night. On the following day John could no longer deceive himself that his companion would recover. Dafydd spent most of the day sleeping, his breath ragged and painful, the fever sometimes sending his whole body into violent convulsions, so that he half woke and stared about him unseeing. He took no food, only water, which he called for whenever he woke. The sickly smell of death was in the room. John felt it drawing near, a malign presence, though not as that emblematic figure of a skeleton bearing a scythe. No, it hovered like a dark intangible shape, just glimpsed from the corner of his eye; sometimes it seemed a great dark bird, like a monstrous crow, sometimes a man clad in black armour, whose eyes burned within the shadow of his helmet like fire.

He must be growing feverish, that was the source of these nightmare visions, but whether he was truly ill, or merely shared in

407

Dafydd's sufferings, he did not know. He spent much of his time on his knees, praying for his friend's soul, and for a painless and quiet end to his torment. When night came, he could not sleep, but kept watch beside his friend's bed.

It must have been near midnight when Dafydd woke and asked quietly for water.

'I feel most wonderfully restored,' he said, when he had drunk. 'The pain in my limbs is gone and the fevered imaginings. I am ready, I think, to go forward to my Maker.'

John found he was weeping like a woman, and was glad of the dark, that he might wipe away his tears unseen.

'The fever is broken,' he said, 'and you will recover now.'

'Nay. My body is telling me that this is enough. *Nunc dimittis.* They had the right of it in some things, the priests of the old religion, in ministering the last rites to the dying. It would be a kind of loosening of the final bonds, would it not? As when a ship sets sail, and the ropes that held it to the shore are cast off into the water, and then are hauled in, hand over hand, to make the vessel trim for her voyage into the unknown, over the unfathomable rough ocean. We need that kind of release.'

He sighed deeply. 'Yet I have loved life. Birdsong and falling water, and the joy of a day's hard labour well done. Is it dark, John?'

'Deepest midnight.'

'Fasten back the curtain, that we may see if the moon be out.'

John pulled back the piece of canvas and hooked it behind the nail.

'A sliver of a moon,' he said, 'no bigger than the paring of a child's thumbnail. But such stars! It must be a frosty night, for the stars are pulsing, blue and silver and gold, so near you could reach out your hand and touch them.'

He heard a sound behind him and turned to see Dafydd trying to stand up.

'Help me, will you? I would see the moon and the stars one last time.'

Leaning heavily on John, who held him firmly round the back, with his shoulder serving as a crutch, Dafydd stumbled to the window. The stars were more numerous than John had ever seen them before, a multitude of the heavenly host, the veritable signature of the Creator writ across the heavens.

When Dafydd began to shiver, John led him gently back to bed, and covered him with all their blankets, although he continued to shake, as if with the palsy. John felt his hands. They were as icy as a mountain stream in winter.

'I hope,' Dafydd whispered, 'that you may find yourself a better chess partner than I.'

'I could never find one who taught me more,' said John, 'for I have played the chess game of life too much with my head, too little with my heart. I have learned better now, I hope.'

'Remember. Land for every man and woman,' said Dafydd faintly, 'that none may starve.'

He said no more.

⁊

For many days, John knew nothing of what was happening around him, for he had fallen ill of the same gaol fever that had afflicted Dafydd. He did not even see them come to take away the body of his dead friend, nor did he know where he was buried or whether it was done with decency and respect. The fever had entered him like an evil spirit, tormenting him both body and soul. Pain gripped his head like a vice, and licked along his back and limbs with the fierceness of flame. There was no one to tend him, as he had tended Dafydd, but one of the guards must have kept the fire up, and he remembered, as if half dreaming, that a woman had come from time to time, perhaps a woman from the kitchens, and given him broth. He bore the physical mark of it afterwards, for she had fed it to him too hot, and it had scalded his palate. As the fever gradually began to loosen its grip, the blister in his mouth troubled him inordinately, out of all proportion compared with the far worse storm he had weathered.

Weathered it he had, although he could not guess why the strong blacksmith had been struck fatally, while he—younger, indeed, but less hardy—had survived. It had left him pitifully weak, and the memories of the nightmares which had afflicted him haunted his waking hours. The fever had brought hallucinations, of monstrous shapes pursuing him along narrow, dark passages, of his beloved Anne crying out to him for help. He had seen her drowning in the boggy depths of a marsh, stretching out her arms to him, but he could not reach her. Their fingertips almost touched, and he tried to call to her, but nothing but an animal-like grunt would come from his throat, as she was slowly sucked down out of his sight.

Afterwards, as he lay on his bed, convalescing from the fever and thinking of this dream which had visited him repeatedly, he wondered whether it had its seed in that long ago time in childhood, when he had pulled Anne from the marsh, or whether it was true, as some believed, that dreams foretold the future. Was Anne in danger? If the dream was a foretelling, then surely it would not be an exact picture, but rather a metaphor for the truth. Perhaps Anne was falling into a trap, was caught about with some snare from which she could not escape without his help. He did not know what to believe. Once, he would have laughed at such ideas, but in his weakened state, he felt any horror might be true.

By the time he was fit to take notice of his surroundings again, he saw from the window that it was full winter. The snow had descended from the mountains into the valley, so that the little town of Denbigh and the farms in the river valley were no more than humps in the white blanket which lay over the land. A few trackways were beaten through the snow, and supplies continued to arrive for the garrison from time to time, though less frequently than before. John could not judge whether this was due to the difficulties of transport during winter, or whether the garrison in the castle had been reduced, for none were likely to make war here in north Wales in such conditions. Besides, according to what Dafydd had told him about Cromwell's plans to put down the Irish, and the difficulties of retaining men for the campaign overseas, it might have become necessary to move some of the soldiers from garrison duty to active service.

He returned again to that lonely condition in which he had passed his time before Dafydd had come to share his cell, and he realised how much the philosopher blacksmith had changed his imprisonment. Having had that companionship for a short time, he missed it all the more bitterly now that he was alone again. He had still no idea of the date. It might have been a bitter late November, or near Christmastide, or even the beginning of the new year, when one of the guards arrived unexpectedly to summon him to a meeting with the governor. John went to gather up his clothes and books, thinking he was to be moved again.

'Nay, leave all that be,' said the soldier. 'He'll not keep you above half an hour, I'll be bound.'

The governor received John in his office, as Danvers had done, but the contrast between the two rooms was immense. Where Danvers's room had thick Turkey carpets and tapestries on the walls and comfortable cushioned chairs, this room was spare and uncarpeted, the furniture old and good but ferociously uncomfortable. The man, too, was a contrast to the elegant Danvers. He was a thickset, squat man, dressed in buff coat and light body armour, with a plain, unadorned sword at his belt. His lobster-tailed helmet lay on a chest

410

next to the table that served as his desk, and his brow bore a permanent weal where the edge of that helmet pressed into the flesh. This was a professional soldier, whose clothes and surroundings spoke of a hard, perhaps ruthless nature.

The governor left him standing.

'I understand that you have been ill,' he said at last, after he had kept John waiting while he read and signed papers before him on the table.

'I have had the gaol fever,' said John, 'that killed my fellow prisoner.'

The man grunted, but expressed no regret.

'Are you recovered?'

'If you mean: Is the fever gone?—then, yes. But I am much weakened by it.'

'I'm confronted by a difficult situation,' said the governor. 'I received word some weeks ago from Colonel Danvers that a—', he consulted a paper, 'a Captain Stone would be arriving with a document authorising your release into his custody on recognisance of one thousand pounds. This is after you wife paid bail for you at Stafford, with jewellery to the value of . . . two thousand, four hundred pounds.'

John barely stopped himself from gasping aloud. Anne must have handed over everything of value that she owned.

'However,' the governor continued, 'this Captain Stone has never appeared. The road from Stafford is, of course, long and dangerous, but he should have arrived by now. Until I received this document of authorisation, I was unwilling to take it upon myself to release you.'

'But if you received a letter from Colonel Danvers—'

'Do not interrupt. The letter was a personal one, not an official document, bearing the proper seals and authorisations.'

He shuffled the papers in front of him.

'This has now arrived.'

He held up a document written on parchment, from which a red seal dangled on a ribbon.

'It came here in rather curious circumstances. It seems that your friend Stone was attacked, beaten and robbed, shortly after passing through the town of Llangollen. Fortunately for him, he was found in a ditch by a farmer on his way into the town, who carried him to an inn and left him there. When he had recovered sufficiently from his injuries—I understand he suffered a severe blow to the head—he produced this document from some hidden pocket within his clothes.

No doubt the robbers could have taken it had they wished, but they were interested only in stealing his money and his horse.'

'How badly hurt is he? Will he recover?'

The governor held up his hand to silence John. He would tell this story in his own way and no other.

'Stone begged the innkeeper to send the document on to Denbigh with a reliable man. He himself was not fit to ride further. There was great difficulty in finding someone who was willing to make the journey, since the footpads and broken men have been growing ever more dangerous in the mountains. Finally, a troop of horse being sent up here to the garrison agreed to bring it with them, and so it reached me at last only yesterday. I understand that Stone was to be carried by slow stages home in a carriage, once further funds had reached him. However, he sent a letter to me with this document, begging me to release you in any case.'

'Thank you.'

'I have not said that I will do it. There is a further problem. I can spare no men to escort you. We are short of troops here as it is. If you go, you must go alone. I don't need to tell you of the risks, travelling alone, in winter, in wartime, in this mountain country which is the haunt, even in peace, of men little better than beasts.'

'If I'm given the choice, then I will go.'

The governor looked him up and down with a cold eye.

'You do not seem to me to be very robust. I know little about you, or why you are here in custody, but I believe you are not a soldier.'

'No.'

'I would not be too sanguine that even a soldier could make such a journey. However, as I have the authorisation and you are willing to take the risk, then I will give orders for you to be provided for. I cannot concern myself with the details. It will fall to the captain of the guard.'

John felt a sinking at his heart. If indeed it fell to the captain of the guard, then he would be ill provided, unless the governor gave specific instructions. Better to risk offending him and say something.

'You will provide me with a horse and supplies for the journey?'

'Settle it with the captain of the guard.' The governor was irritated. 'I have told you, I have no time to look into matters of detail.'

࿐

Whether the governor gave his orders at once to the captain of the guard, John had no way of knowing, but while he waited for his

412

release, the weather grew worse. For three days it snowed without ceasing, and on the fourth, when he looked down on the town of Denbigh, even the usual faint tracks had disappeared. Worse than this, his fever had flared up once again. He was constantly thirsty, and his head ached abominably, so that he could barely think. This feverishness was aggravated by worries that there were other matters he should have raised with the governor. He could have asked if he might send a letter in the next military post that went out. In a letter to his father, he could have asked for a coach and an escort of friends to be sent out to meet him, at least as far as Shrewsbury, perhaps to Llangollen, thus reducing the danger of attack. In his present feeble state, he would do well if he was able to ride even as far as Llangollen in this weather. Dafydd had said that, following the way he advised up the Clwyd valley, it would be about thirty-five miles, instead of something like fifty following the other road to the west, by Cerrig-y-Druidion.

While he waited, he made what preparations he could. He folded up his spare clothes and his books, and wrapped them in both of Dafydd's blankets, which had remained on his bed, together with Dafydd's cloak, which had also been left behind. If he was to make a journey in bitter winter weather, he would need anything he could carry to keep out the cold. He had flint and tinder, but it would be difficult to make a fire in such conditions. Dafydd had not told him whether there were in the Clwyd valley any towns where he might hope to find an inn, or even a mean wayside tavern. From what he had seen on the outward journey, most of this part of Wales was thinly inhabited, no more than scattered farms and cottages, where the people would be unlikely to take in an unknown traveller. There was one place he had mentioned, Ruthin, but John did not know whether it was town or village. For the most part, he would need to fend for himself until he reached Llangollen. He felt saddened, recalling the name, and smiled ruefully at the remembrance of Dafydd's care that he should pronounce the place like a true Welshman.

After several days, the captain of the guard paid him a visit. John had not seen the man for weeks, not since before Dafydd's illness. It might be that the fellow had been keeping his distance, not wanting to become infected with the gaol fever. Or there might have been some more private reason. In any case, the man's appearance was shockingly altered. His clothes were dirty and the stink of his person, which had always heralded his entrance, was more foul than ever. He walked unsteadily, although it was morning, and he could surely not have drunk many bottles yet. His eyes were bloodshot and they roamed feverishly about the room, then fixed themselves on John with a kind of manic intensity.

'So, where's your cell mate, the vile blacksmith, the ungodly preacher and leader of mutiny and riot?'

John stared at him. Surely he must know that Dafydd was dead?

The captain staggered up to him and caught hold of the front of his doublet.

'We know how to deal with people like you, you and that Anabaptist sectary. Hang 'em all, that's what I say. Hang 'em, and cut 'em down, and put 'em to the fire. That'll soon start 'em singing another tune.'

The captain let go of John so suddenly that he stumbled backwards as the man began to roam the cell.

'Any other dirty little sectaries hiding in here? Or maybe you keep a whore under the bed, eh?'

He got down on all fours to look under John's bed. John, raising his eyes, saw two of the guards standing just outside the open door. As they caught his eye, they blanked out all expression from their faces, but not quite quickly enough. He had caught there a mixture of embarrassment, amusement, and fear. Did the governor know that the captain of the guard had fallen into this state? And what would it mean for those 'details' of his release, with which the governor refused to concern himself?

After this performance, the captain staggered to his feet and headed towards the door. He would be gone in a moment, with John left waiting still to hear when he would be released.

'Captain,' he said, with as much politeness as he could muster, 'I understand from the governor that you are to arrange my release.'

The captain stopped in the doorway and rotated slowly, as though he was standing in the crow's nest of a ship in a high gale.

'Released? Aye, he's going to release you, you filthy scum. Be ready this evening.'

With that he slammed the door, and John heard the key turn in the lock. The man was going mad with the drink, that much was clear, or perhaps he was simply going mad. But if John were released from the castle and sent out in the evening, with a winter's night coming on, it would be an ill-omened start to his journey. He paced about the cell, along the same path he felt he had worn into the very stones of the floor. When he lifted the canvas and looked out of the window, he could see more snow clouds building up over the mountains.

They came for him at last as it was growing dusk. He had eaten every scrap of food they had brought him, although it tasted like sawdust in his mouth. His heart was beating painfully as he slung his pack on his back with a kind of harness he had contrived out of a length of cord he had persuaded the young guard to bring him. At the last minute he snatched up one of the blankets off his bed and wrapped it around his shoulders like an extra cloak.

Three guards, commanded by Sergeant Conway, led him from the prison tower and out to the great gate of the castle. The soldiers of the watch drew back the huge bolts and swung open the gate. An icy wind rushed in, carrying flurries of snow with it. John looked around. Neither within the gatehouse, nor outside, nor in the vast central court of the castle, was there any sign of a horse. He turned to the sergeant.

'Where is my mount?' he asked.

The sergeant shifted his feet uncomfortably and avoided his eye.

'The captain said you were not to be given a horse. There are none to be spared.'

John drew a deep breath.

'The governor wishes me to be given a mount and supplies of food. Look out yonder!' He gestured towards the desolate landscape of snow-covered mountains, looming against the darkening sky.

'If you drive me out into that, on foot and without food, you are driving me to certain death. The governor has received authorisation for my release, not for my death by starvation or freezing on a mountainside. Where is my supply of food?'

Gone was any submissiveness. John knew that if he did not act with authority now, he would be conniving in his own destruction.

'I received no orders about a supply of food,' said the sergeant, but he said it with uncertainty.

'I will not move from here—nay, I will go now and report you to the governor if you do not give the order for it yourself. You know that the captain is as mad as the fools in Bedlam.'

The sergeant muttered something to one of the soldiers, who ran off in the direction of the kitchens. It would mean an even greater delay and an even later start to his journey, but John knew he must contain himself in patience. When the man returned, with a saddlebag containing food, he examined it.

'Not sufficient,' he said grimly. 'I need dried fruit and more cheese. And salted bacon and another loaf and butter sealed in a wooden box.'

And he would not stir until these things were brought. John realised that he could not force the sergeant to give him a horse, if he had received a definite order from the captain forbidding it. Somehow he must make his way on foot at first. He would see what fate would bring. Perhaps he could steal a horse.

What kind of man am I become, that I should think of taking to horse-stealing? he thought. A man who will die, driven out to walk through these mountains in winter, that is what I am become.

Finally they brought him the food he demanded and—somewhat sheepish now—they contrived to fasten the saddlebag to the pack he wore already on his back. The weight bore down on his weakened frame, not yet recovered from the effects of his illness, but he hitched it up with a shrug of his shoulders and found, if he leaned forward against the weight, he could balance it better.

'I thank you for this much at least,' he said to the sergeant. 'And I hope that sending me forth without horse or protection into a winter night amongst these Welsh mountains does not trouble your sleep or your conscience.'

The sergeant reddened.

'God go with you, sir. It's not my wish that you should be driven out thus.'

John turned away and started down the steep descent to the little town. Behind him he heard the castle gate crash shut, and then the sound of the bolts drawn into place on the far side. Now he was no longer a prisoner shut in, but a man shut out of all human habitation, at the mercy of whatever God and nature might inflict on him.

Chapter Thirty

'Thomas,' said Anne, 'I would ask a favour of you.' It was the Sunday following her visit to Mathew Moreton, and as usual she had conducted all the able-bodied members of her household to church in Weeford. They sat through a grim sermon from the new minister, whose chief delight lay in predicting the horrible end of all those not of the Elect.

'And what sort of choice is that,' Anne had said once to Bridget, 'in the moral life? If you are one of the Elect, then surely you may live your life in the delightful knowledge that heavenly bliss awaits you at the end of it, whatever you do. Whereas, if you are not of these *soi disant* Saints, nothing you can do on this earth will save you, so you might as well sin as much as you choose.'

Bridget had been appalled, protesting about obedience and faith, but Anne, who had been moved more by a mischievous impulse to shock than by any expectation of a theological disputation, had patted her hand absently and changed the subject.

Today she had scarcely listened to the sermon, having more urgent matters on her mind, which must be dealt with here and now, if one of the innocent were not to suffer a terrible death at the hands of the wicked. Yet even distracted as she was, she sensed some disturbance in the air, an awareness that eyes were directed at her. Hostility breathed around her. The pews for Swinfen Hall and Weeford Hall occupied the two foremost positions in the church, so that she was directly under the gaze of the minister, but she was more conscious of an intensity of attention which gathered about her from further back in the church, where the yeomen sat with their families, and beyond, where servants and lesser folk had their appointed place. As the Swinfen party emerged from church, her neighbours turned their steps away from her. When Anne spoke to John Digby's wet nurse, admiring how rosy and plump he had grown, the woman avoided her eyes and stood tongue-tied.

After the service, Anne and Bridget sent the rest of the family home and stayed on at Weeford Hall, where they partook of a cold dinner with Mary and Thomas Pott (for none must cook on the

Sabbath). Pride had prevented her asking for Thomas's help for herself, but she was not too proud to ask for it when Agnes Lea's life was at stake.

'I'll gladly help you in any way I can, Anne,' said Thomas, doubtless thinking that she needed his assistance with the estate accounts or the marketing of some stock. He drew happily on his pipe, which he had lit with some difficulty, for the tobacco was damp. Fortunate, Anne thought, that the minister could not see him, for surely a pleasure such as a pipe of tobacco must be banned on Sundays.

'It's the matter of Agnes Lea.'

'Oh,' said Thomas, his countenance grave. 'I've heard,' he said slowly, 'that you have been interfering with the examination of the supposed witch.'

Mary was staring first at Thomas, then at Anne, a look of horror on her usually placid face. 'Anne, you must not think of it! How could you shame us so? Witchcraft! You must give over this dangerous folly at once! It's embarrassment enough since you came home, the way you have pretended to a man's place, but this . . .'

It was there again, that naked resentment in Mary's eyes, which she had not glimpsed for weeks now. Perhaps it had merely slumbered.

'Thomas!' Anne cried in exasperation, 'Agnes Lea is no witch! How can you think it? You're an educated man of good sense. Surely you don't believe these foolish villagers at Hints who are trying to blame her for the disease in their wheat?'

'It seems unfounded,' he conceded. 'I've been sent one of the London newspapers which makes room in its pages to report the state of the countryside, as well as the achievements of the army in Ireland. It appears the blight has been widespread this year, and has afflicted particularly those lands that were flooded so badly in the spring. For myself, I found a patch of it in one corner of a field which dips low. And, certainly, that corner was flooded.'

'It didn't spread to the rest of the field?'

'Nay, because I took care to have that part of the crop dug up and carried off to be burnt. A man who keeps a close watch on his crops can sometimes forestall such trouble.'

'That's excellent news! I don't mean merely for your own crop, though I congratulate you on your swift action. Rather, it shows that the cause of the blight was the weather, and its spread was due to bad husbandry.'

'What was the favour you wanted to ask?' Thomas said cautiously.

'In part, you've conferred it already, for you've shown that one of the charges against Agnes is certainly groundless. The favour is this: will you accompany me to the trial, and stand with me in her defence?'

Thomas exchanged a glance with Mary, and both looked worried.

'It's better to leave these matters to the magistrates, Anne,' said Thomas. 'They know their business. They can weigh the evidence and decide if the case is good.'

Mary was more passionate.

'You must not interfere, Anne! It's far too dangerous. You know well how the taint of one witch can infect all those who have to do with her.'

Bridget kept silence. She had already warned Anne of the dangers, but knew she could not be persuaded.

'But if they don't *have* all the evidence?' Anne cried. 'Surely it's God's will that we should defend the innocent? You're a just man, Thomas. You could not stand by and allow an old woman to burn or hang just because you did not tell what you know. I ask you to do no more than support me and tell the truth, not to perjure yourself.'

Her brother-in-law looked uncomfortable, but she would not spare him. Eventually, when they were about to leave, he agreed to escort her to the trial, and to stand up in court and say what he knew about the causes of the blight.

'I hope also,' said Anne cunningly, once she had secured his agreement, 'that you will let it be known widely throughout Weeford and Hints and Shenstone that you intend to speak in Agnes's defence. The folk hereabouts will take little account of the fact that I intend to speak for her, but once it's known that Thomas Pott of Weeford Hall refutes this charge of witchcraft, I think the crowd that's baying after her like a pack of hounds may begin to dwindle away. *That* was the favour I came to ask. Your news about the blight is additional proof of their willingness to blame another for the result of their own neglect.'

'What is the other charge? You said the blight was only part of the charge.'

'Some fellow called William Slater complains that he sought her help to cure his sick cow. She said she couldn't help, that the cow would die unless he himself did certain things—I don't know what. He struck her, and the cow died. He swears she cursed his cow. But she had already said that the cow was dying, *before* he struck her—'

'Aye, aye. I take your drift. I don't know this Slater, but I'll make enquiries.'

'Thomas, you're a true friend!

Anne was delighted, despite Thomas's reluctance. Her own somewhat dubious position, in daring to intervene in the trial, would be entirely altered if Thomas were at her side.

'Surely . . .' said Bridget quietly.

'Aye, Bridget?' Thomas said.

'Well, surely, the character of the accused must count for something? Agnes Lea has never hurt anyone, and she's helped many with her cures and good counsel.'

'The danger is,' said Thomas, 'that her very knowledge of cures condemns her in some people's eyes. Nor will they like that she lives alone up in that strange wild place, where no one else would choose to dwell, save a few shepherds with their flocks in summer. Have you not observed? Those who are accused of witchcraft are usually old, poor, friendless women, with no one to defend them. Their very existence, alone and uncared for, and their poverty, are a reproach to us all, that we do not show more concern for them. So our guilt becomes twisted into accusation, in order that we may rid ourselves of this mote in our eye.'

Anne looked at him thoughtfully.

'That's a wise observation, Thomas.'

The time until Agnes's preliminary trial passed all too swiftly, for now that Thomas was prepared to stand beside her, Anne wanted news of his support to spread as widely as possible. Had there been more time, more people would have heard of Master Pott's intervention, and that would have benefited her plans. Yet for Agnes's sake, the trial could not come soon enough, that she might be set free from her wretched prison. Early in the morning of the twentieth of December, Thomas rode to Swinfen, and then joined Anne in the carriage to drive on to Lichfield. Anne had chosen to travel by carriage for several reasons. The winter had truly descended upon the land in the last few days, and the journey would be more comfortable by carriage. Then, if Agnes were freed, she could be carried home more easily, for she was too old and frail to ride pillion. Above all, Anne was well aware how much more valuable their defence of the old woman would be if they were to drive up to the court in the grandeur of a carriage and four. The whole of the previous day had been devoted by Josiah and Isaac to grooming the horses, washing down the carriage, and polishing all the leather and brass. Josiah now drove them to Lichfield smartly clad in the livery which used to adorn the Swynfens' young coachman, who had been impressed for army service four years before.

The bitter weather had brought an additional benefit: the crowd of the curious and the idle hanging about the court was smaller than it would have been on a fine summer's day. Word of Thomas's support had also affected the composition of the crowd. Most were townspeople from Lichfield, very few were the villagers from Hints who had first stirred up the trouble. William Slater was there, with a group of his friends about him, but Anne recognised only a dozen or so others from Hints village as she entered the court on Thomas's arm, with her head held high, bestowing gracious smiles on those who were known to her. Inwardly, she mocked herself, for she thought she must resemble Queen Henrietta Maria, parading through the state rooms at Whitehall, condescendingly acknowledging the obsequious bows of courtiers. There were no obsequious bows here, however. Her smiles were returned with unfriendly stares and she was followed into the courtroom by audible jeers. For the first time since she had taken up Agnes's cause, Anne began to be afraid.

She had never attended a law court before, and found it intimidating, even though she was not here as a prisoner. How much more frightening it would be for the accused, standing in the dock, a little bent old woman, with all this malice and venom, and the full rigour of the law, directed against her.

From her discussion with Thomas as they rode to Lichfield in the carriage, Anne understood that all legal process in the country was currently in a state of confusion since the execution of the king. Many who had held office were now turned out, some had not been replaced, some new men's appointments were not recognised. Since the overthrow of the bishops, there had been disputes about who should hear the cases which formerly had come before the bishops' courts. Witchcraft, as a form of blasphemy and heresy, would once have been tried before the bishop of Lichfield. Uncertain of the correct course of action to take in this case, the three magistrates had called an assize. They entered now in the sombre majesty of their robes, and took their seats at the raised bench.

The crowd fell silent in awe of the magistrates, then a faint hum rose up amongst them, like a swarm of bees clustering about the branch of a tree, hot and angry. Anne strained to see what was afoot. From a door at the back of the courtroom, near the platform where the magistrates were shuffling their papers and murmuring together, two constables led in the tiny figure of Agnes Lea. Her wrists were bound together and her feet, still bloodied and bereft of shoes, were shackled with heavy iron chains, so that with each step she must jerk the weight of chain forward. It made her movements curiously unnatural, puppet-like. Her sparse grey hair hung over her face and shoulders in a tangled mat, through which she peered with the terrified eyes of a trapped animal. To any who did not know her, she was the very image of a loathed and outcast witch.

Some in the crowd furtively crossed themselves, with the unconscious response of the old religion. With an instinct even older, some gave the sign of the horned fingers to ward off evil spirits. Some had carried into court twigs of rowan or hazel, which they pointed towards Agnes. On all the faces in that crowd, Anne could read nothing but horror and disgust, which seemed to throb in the very air of the room. How could she turn the minds of this fevered mob with her cool evidence and rational arguments? When already the mob was hostile to Anne herself? In the minds of these people there needed no trial to decide the fate of Agnes Lea. Their desire was already wholly bent on seeing her hang.

The accusations against Agnes Lea were read out by the clerk of the court, and Anne was relieved that they were confined to the two she knew of, for she was afraid that some other complaint might have been made. While the clerk was speaking, the magistrate Mathew Moreton caught her eye briefly, and seemed disconcerted that she had carried out her intention of coming to the trial. It was clear that she was the only woman of any standing here. The courtroom was filled almost entirely with men, apart from a few rough women from the worst parts of the town. A group of the town's whores lingered near the door, not so much for the sake of the trial, but rather to tout for business when the men came away afterwards in a high state of excitement, for there was nothing like the prospect of a hanging or burning to whet men's appetites for the pleasures of the flesh.

The first charge, of blighting the crops at Hints, took a deal of time to read out, with its list of complainants and details of the fields affected and the damage done. When the clerk resumed his seat, Mathew Moreton called on the complainants of the first charge to enlarge on their grievances. Although seven had been named in the charge, it was discovered that only three of them were present, the others having failed to appear in court. Moreton therefore ordered that those other four sections of the complaint should be struck out.

Of the three men who were then called upon to speak, the first was a big red-faced man with a blustering manner, by name Edward Goodens, who launched upon a long tirade of grievances—against the bad harvests of the last ten years, against the damage the troops had done to his land, against the taxes imposed first by the king's government and now by the republican government, against the incessant rains and floods of the spring, which had near drowned his best fields. At this, Thomas smiled at Anne. He was busy writing notes in a small pocket-book. Finally Moreton raised his hand to stay the flow of recriminations.

'I am sure many of those present have every sympathy with you, Edward Goodens, but these are the misfortunes that have afflicted us all. What is your complaint against the accused, Agnes Lea?'

The man looked confused for a moment at thus having his river of words halted.

'Well, as to that, your honour, it must have been the witch blighted my wheat, because she blighted everyone else's wheat.'

'But do you have any evidence that she did so?' said Richard Floyer.

'Well, last spring she said as how one of my boys had stole a hen of hers, and she come seeking 'un back. I soon sent 'un packing. But stands to reason she'd try to get her revenge on me, don't it?'

'And had your boy stolen her hen?'

The man shuffled his feet.

'He may have done. How am I to know? I can't be counting my fowl every day, now, can I?'

'Was she heard to utter a curse against you or your wheat?' said Moreton.

'She said as how I should take my belt to the boy for his own good.'

There was a ripple of laughter in the court. And from somewhere came a shout: 'Aye, and so ye should. They boys o' yourn bin robbing my orchard these five years past!'

'Edward Goodens,' said Moreton patiently, 'this is no evidence of *maleficium* by the accused. You may stand down.'

The other two villagers from Hints who had come to complain about their wheat were both small, nervous-looking men. When they saw their leader dismissed from the field, they took fright. Both mumbled vague accusations against Agnes, but could not, on oath, recall any specific instance of her ill-wishing them, or being seen to prepare magical charms against them. The three magistrates listened with a mixture of contempt and boredom. Finally Moreton asked whether anyone else in court wished to speak on the matter of the wheat. Thomas Pott rose, and a ripple of expectancy ran over the court. A shaft of sunlight falling through a high window lit upon his grey hair, turning it a glinting silver.

'Master Thomas Pott, of Weeford Hall. Gentleman,' the clerk announced, and then administered the oath.

Thomas read aloud the item from the London newspaper on the causes of the blight. He then produced a letter from a friend in Northamptonshire about problems in that county, where fields had been flooded in spring. He explained how his own field had suffered the beginnings of the blight, and the measures he had taken to prevent its spreading. He then read out the list of fields mentioned by the men from Hints, and pointed out that every one of them was low-lying, and had been flooded for several weeks in the spring of the year.

Moreton, Floyer, and Jolley all looked much relieved at this logical explanation of the blight, presented by a gentleman landowner like themselves who had personal experience of the problem. When Thomas had finished his testimony, Moreton consulted the other two magistrates, then turned to the clerk.

'The accusation of blighting the crops should be struck from the register. We find no case to answer here.'

'Before I resume my seat,' said Thomas mildly, 'I should like to say something further about the prisoner, Agnes Lea.'

Moreton nodded to him to continue.

'Agnes Lea,' said Thomas, 'has been a resident in the parish of Weeford since her birth in the year of our Lord, 1576. She came from a poor but respectable family in the village, her father being apprentice and then assistant to the blacksmith, later becoming blacksmith in the village himself. Agnes married Nick Lea in 1596, and they went to live on Packington Moor, where Nick built a one-roomed cottage and established a small-holding, also hiring himself out as a day labourer to various farms in the area. Nick Lea was in dispute with my wife's grandfather about possession of the land, but after Nick's death at a young age, leaving his wife to fend for herself as best she could, the family dropped the case, and ever since have regarded Agnes Lea as one of their people. She bore nine children, five of whom lived past childhood, but these have all moved away in search of work, so that she no longer enjoys the protection of a family.'

The court had grown quiet. Most probably knew Agnes's story, but set out thus in Thomas's calm, level voice, it had a grim familiarity about it—the loss of the husband, the dead children, the desperate struggle to scrape sustenance from poor soil, the bitter poverty.

'In all those years, Agnes Lea has never, to my knowledge, or that of any other respectable citizen of the parish, done any harm to any person. She is known as a woman of a sharp tongue but a kind heart.

Gentlemen, I would ask you to take this into consideration when reaching your verdict.'

Thomas stepped down, and returned to his seat next to Anne.

'Thank you,' she whispered.

'I spoke naught but the truth. There is still the other charge, however. I thought it best to speak for her character before that was considered.'

The clerk now read out in full the second charge, that Agnes Lea did charm, enchant or bewitch a valuable milch cow belonging to William Slater and, in connivance with the devil, did cause it to swell up grossly until it died most horribly. Anne watched William Slater closely as he stepped forward to take the oath and state his case. He looked a cunning man, a far greater threat than the bumbling Edward Goodens. His manner towards the magistrates was a nice blend of obsequiousness and candour. He had sought the help of Agnes Lea, when his cow fell sick, but she had refused to help him and the cow had died. He had always believed her to be a good woman, a wise woman, until that moment, just as Master Pott had said.

Dangerous, thought Anne. He twists Thomas's words, insinuating that he said Agnes is a wise woman, with the clear inference that she is a witch. Nor does he mention that he struck her.

'And did the prisoner offer you no help?' asked Richard Floyer.

This too, was a dangerous question, for if Agnes had given Slater some potion for the cow, and it had then died, it could be argued that she had poisoned it. Now that she saw what kind of man Slater was, Anne understood why Agnes might have been reluctant to help him. He looked like a man who would be ready to lash out at others, a man whose malice would be quickly aroused and slowly, if ever, appeased.

Slater hesitated before answering the question.

'Remember,' said Moreton, 'that you are under oath.'

Perhaps Slater feared divine retribution if he committed perjury even more than he desired to harm Agnes. He muttered something under his breath. Jolley, who was even more advanced in years than Moreton, cupped his hand behind his ear.

'What was that?'

'She told me some foolishness about walking the cow, and that otherwise it would die.'

Walking the cow, thought Anne in triumph. *Now, surely, all will be well, for he has admitted it!*

This seemed to be the whole of Slater's case. The magistrates dismissed him and conferred amongst themselves, then Moreton turned to the people filling the room and asked if anyone had anything to add.

People looked one to another. Anne sensed that there was not much sympathy for Slater. Thomas had told her that he was disliked by his neighbours for his meanness and his neglect of his beasts, but he had thought it unwise to mention this in his own statement, for it was no more than hearsay.

Anne gripped the book she was holding on her lap and fought a rising sense of panic. When she had learned from Thomas how Slater's cow had died, she had consulted her beloved *Compleat Husbandrie*. She thought she knew the cause of the cow's death. But dare she, a gentlewoman, stand up and speak in court? Mathew Moreton's glance brushed lightly across her as he looked about to see if anyone would speak, but it did not linger. Perhaps it was that careless dismissal that propelled her to her feet.

'I wish to say something,' she said.

There was an audible gasp from the crowd, and an angry murmuring. Aware that her hands were shaking, she stepped forward to the clerk and reached out her right hand for the Bible, still holding the *Compleat Husbandrie* in her left. The clerk, dismayed, went to the bench for directions.

'Administer the oath,' said Moreton coldly.

When she had sworn, Anne took her place before the magistrates.

'I have two things to say,' Anne began, trying to keep her voice steady and calm. 'First, I know Agnes Lea to be a good, God-fearing woman. And I would ask you to consider this. If she be, as accused, in league with the devil and possessed of great powers, why does she not call upon him to relieve her from her state of poverty and wretchedness? If she can transform herself into other creatures, as witches are said to do, why does she not become a bird, and fly away from this place? But I see only a poor old woman, half fainting, injured, and so tired she may barely stand, for this court is too cruel even to provide her with a chair. As I would hope they would do for any other old woman. For their own grandmothers, perhaps.'

The magistrates all three regarded her with expressions in which astonishment at her audacity was mingled with a certain amount of shame.

'But I am sure the folly of this trial will soon be done with,' said Anne, 'and then Agnes Lea will be acquitted and may receive the kindness she deserves.'

She drew a deep breath.

'My second point is this. It is well known that William Slater has had illness and death amongst his kine before. It is also well known that

426

the meadow where they are set to graze contains a great deal of clover. Gentlemen, I do not believe William Slater's cow was bewitched. I believe it was merely suffering from the bloat, which, had he been a more careful farmer, he could have avoided. And which, had he followed Agnes Lea's advice, he could have cured without the need for any magic potions or enchantments. He would thereby have saved himself the loss of a good milch cow, and would have saved this court the loss of much time and the people of Lichfield the loss of a working day.'

There was a low laugh from somewhere at the back of the courtroom, but it was quickly drowned in angry mutters. Moreton signed to one of the constables to suppress the disturbance.

I must be careful, Anne thought. *I am becoming too sharp with them.*

'I would like to read to you a receipt from a well-known manual on farming, which we use in Swinfen, and which treats of this condition in cows, as follows.'

She opened the place she had marked in the book with a length of ribbon, and read aloud.

'A reciept for a Cow that is hov'd or
swell'd by eating Clover.
Take a quart of Milk from a sound Cow & give the disorder'd
Beast one quart of it warm; walk her about slowly at first & by
degrees bring her to a pretty quick trot. This easy remedy
generally perfects a cure & has been seldom known to fail. NB.
The Cow must not be fed with Clover again soon. Three pints of
Milk may be given to a Bullock.'

There was a rustle of interest from the crowd. Perhaps this trial would do some good, if a few more people learned how to treat the bloat. Anne could hear from behind her a general whispering, but could not make out what was being said. She kept her eyes on the magistrates.

'I have tried this remedy myself,' she said, 'when one of our cows strayed into the hay meadow where there was an area of clover. The remedy does indeed effect a cure. I suppose this must relate to the cow's four-chambered stomach, and the gradual movement of the milk within the stomachs in dispelling the wind. You must ask William Slater whether Agnes Lea also recommended that he give his cow milk, as well as walking her, but perhaps he felt he could not spare it.'

Someone snickered again in the crowd, but was silenced when Moreton frowned at him.

'Is that all, Mistress Swynfen?'

'Aye, Master Moreton.' Anne paused. Should she try to put the case for reason? 'I believe we see here a matter where the new science provides solutions to problems which foolish people in the past attributed to black enchantments. For the blight on the wheat is a phenomenon noticed all over England, a disease provoked by the bad floods of this last spring and preventable with proper husbandry, while the cow was not the first to have died of the bloat, which can be cured with a small amount of care, and perhaps a rather larger amount of effort, for the farmer may need to devote some time to his beast to make her well again. Neither of these sad occurrences, neither the blight nor the death of the cow, it is clear, are in any way due to Agnes Lea.'

Anne walked back to her seat with her heart pounding and her knees shaking. She had gambled her reputation to save Agnes Lea. Please God, those three men tricked out in their robes would recognise common sense when it was laid before them.

'William Slater,' said Moreton, 'did Agnes Lea bid you give the cow milk to drink before walking her, and after a time to take her to a pretty quick trot?'

Slater twisted his hat in his hand as one of the constables pushed him before the bench. He mumbled something, his eyes upon the floor.

'What was that?' said Floyer. 'You must speak so all may hear. Remember that you are still under oath.'

'I said, she may have said some such, but any man could tell 'twas nothing but foolishness. What man ever heard tell of milk being medicine for a dying cow?'

'So indeed,' said Moreton slowly, 'she gave you the very remedy that Mistress Swynfen has read aloud to this court. A remedy taken from a printed work of animal husbandry.'

The magistrates withdrew to consider their verdict. Thomas gave Anne a curious look.

'I remember you as a headstrong child,' he said, 'but I thought you'd reformed long since and become a good, biddable wife. I fear John may find you much changed when he returns.'

'When John returns,' said Anne, 'I shall be happy to be a good, biddable wife again, like many women who have been obliged to do men's work in these tumultuous times.' Though as she spoke, she wondered if she lied.

The magistrates returned in a short while. Indeed, Anne suspected they had only stayed away long enough to maintain their reputation for careful consideration of the evidence, and perhaps to take a sup of wine. When the clerk had called the courtroom to order, Mathew Moreton, as presiding magistrate, gave their verdict.

'The complaints are held to be without substance. The accused is acquitted.'

The verdict was greeted with a sudden burst of sound, but it was not clear whether the crowd was pleased or disappointed. On the one hand, there had not been much support for the complainants from Hints, but on the other they had been robbed both of the thrill of seeing a witch executed and of the sense of righteousness felt by good citizens when evil was rooted out.

Anne and Thomas rushed immediately to Agnes, but she had already collapsed and would have fallen to the floor save for the quick action of one of the town constables, who caught her in a clumsy embrace. He was glad enough to hand her over, as though the accusation of witchcraft alone was enough to contaminate her.

Before they left, Mathew Moreton approached them. Anne thought he was going to chide her for speaking openly in court, but instead he ignored her and thanked Thomas for helping the magistrates avoid an unjust outcome in the case.

'I also have news for you,' he said, looking pointedly over Anne's shoulder and speaking solely to Thomas. 'We have heard at last what is become of Henry Stone. He was attacked on his journey and left for dead, but fortunately rescued by a good Samaritan, who carried him to an inn, where he has been making a slow recovery from an injury to the head. After some considerable time he was able to send the document for Swynfen's release on its way to Denbigh, and has been informed in return that Swynfen is to make his own way home.'

'And John himself?' Anne burst out, flushed at his rudeness, but unable to contain her anxiety. 'Is there any news of John?'

Moreton continued to turn his face from her, but answered her question. 'Not directly. Stone received word that Swynfen was to be released, but no one has heard of him since. Stone himself was too badly hurt to go after him and is travelling back slowly by coach, having sent this letter ahead. I'm sure all will be well. Swynfen is out of their filthy prison, and will journey home as quickly as he may.'

'Thank you,' said Anne, looking down and speaking softly, that she might not embarrass him further. 'I'm so grateful for your kindness. I wish, though, that he need not travel through the mountains of Wales in winter.'

Cold kindness indeed, and Moreton's manner warned her of what she might expect in future from her neighbours. She dared not let her mind dwell on his news of John, for fear that once again it would all come to nothing.

It took some time to force their way through the crowd and into the carriage, but at last they reached it, and eased the old woman on to the seat, recovered from her faint but still confused and shaken. Thomas had climbed into the carriage to help Agnes, but as he reached out his hand to Anne, the crowd suddenly surged forward around her. Men were spitting and cursing her. A woman struck her on the cheek. Suddenly a hail of stones and horse dung fell upon her, so that she stumbled against the carriage step and fell to her knees. Terrified, she crossed her arms over her head to protect herself, as someone kicked her in the ribs. Then Thomas managed to seize her below the elbows and drag her into the carriage, slamming the door behind her. Before she could sit, Josiah had whipped up the horses and broken through the howling crowd.

Agnes stared about her in confusion.

'Is it over, child?'

'It is over, Agnes,' said Anne, leaning forward to kiss the withered cheek. 'We are going home to Swinfen now.'

She sank back on to the seat, but she was shaking so that her teeth rattled, and her palms were clammy with sweat.

It was dark by the time they reached home, and Thomas decided to spend the night at Swinfen. Anne gave Agnes into the care of Biddy, that she might be washed and fed and given clean clothes, free of the prison taint. She climbed wearily to her own chamber, where she shed her clothes, muddied and torn and tainted also with the stench of that hostile crowd. She washed herself all over, but could not rid herself of the shock of the attack on her person. Later that evening, she found Biddy and Agnes in the kitchen together, sitting by the fire. Hester had taken herself off to bed, muttered about evil women. Anne had released Peterkin from his garret and Agnes was cradling him on her lap. He had abandoned his restless prowling now that his mistress was here, and he opened one sleepy eye at Anne with a look that seemed to say that he forgave her. She was determined to keep both of them at Swinfen until winter was past. The memory of the trial would surely disappear from men's minds by the spring, once the hard work began at the start of the new farming year. Before that time she did not trust Edward Goodens and William Slater not to harm Agnes if she were left alone up on the moor.

While she had been occupied with the trial, the children, under the guidance of Patience and Bridget, had been making their preparations for Christmas. Richard and Dick had hauled in the trunk of a fallen beech tree to serve as the Yule log, and had placed it ready beside the hall fireplace. Nan was carefully stringing holly berries on threads, and weaving garlands of ivy and pine, while Bridget bloodied her hands making a complicated kissing ring of holly, mistletoe and ivy. Anne went to admire their work amongst a litter of branches and berries in the hall, where she found Jack was demanding that Dick should allow him to climb the ladder and help to fasten up the garlands, and Francis had just prevented Mary from eating a handful of holly berries. Quietly absorbed, Ralph and Dorothea were fashioning scraps of raw pastry into miniature Christmas pies.

The baby Jane sat on the floor by Patience's chair, hindering her from the difficult task of weaving together a large garland for the main door of the house. When she saw her mother, she pulled herself upright by clutching Patience's skirt, then wobbled three or four steps towards Anne, before sitting down suddenly at her mother's feet.

'My clever poppet!' Anne cried, bending down to lift her up. 'Walking already, and you barely a year old.'

She held her youngest daughter close, remembering last Christmas, stranded at the Mitre in Oxford, where, apart from the good meal they were served by the inn, the festivity was marked only by the toys she had bought at the New Exchange on that visit with Grace. It seemed far longer than a year ago, nearer half a lifetime. She had never completed the embroidered doublet for John. Sudden sadness came over her that he had never seen this child, did not even know that he had another daughter. Jane patted her face, then held it firmly between her two plump palms and kissed her mother on the nose. Anne kissed her back. I have so much to be thankful for, she thought. And surely John will come home to me soon. A just God cannot deny these children their father.

The next morning, Anne asked Thomas to ride up to Packington Moor with her to look at Agnes's cottage, before he went home to Weeford.

'I'd like your counsel on how I might make the cottage more comfortable for her,' Anne said. 'I know you've done much to improve the cottages on your land.'

It was a bright, cold morning, the grass sparkling in sheathes of ice, and the trees draped in the frozen lace of hoar-frost. Since their journey to the trial, Anne felt happier in Thomas's company, and no longer suspected that he wanted to oust her from her guardianship of

431

Swinfen. She could ask him for help now, if she should need it, and not feel that she was somehow failing.

As they neared the cottage, Thomas pointed ahead. There was a drift of smoke rising from the shrubby trees behind which the cottage stood.

'I fear there may be a squatter in the squatters' cottage,' he said.

Angrily, Anne urged Brandy into a canter, until, rounding the stand of trees, she came on the full sight of what had happened. Agnes's cottage, so lovingly and illegally erected by Nick Lea more than half a century before, was gone. The rough stone walls of Agnes's home were torn down and scattered, the thatch and wooden beams reduced to ashes and charred ends of timber, still smouldering amongst the frosted grass, her fence broken, her chicken house smashed, her winter vegetables ripped from the ground and trampled.

'Oh, Thomas,' Anne cried, in anger and guilt, 'I should have been able to prevent this. I should have foreseen it.'

'Anne,' he said, riding over until he was close enough to reach across and lay his hand on her arm, 'you cannot take the whole burden of the world upon your shoulders. The men of Hints are no better and no worse than those in any other village in England. But there will always be a few rotten ones, just as, when you pick the apples from the tree, a few are already rotten at the core, although they grew on the same branch, with the same sun and rain to nourish them. And men of that kind will always find a way to do such evil as this.'

John huddled into the hollowed base of a great oak tree, which formed a sort of shallow cave, and watched the snow sweep down like folds of cloth, piling up outside his temporary refuge until he wondered whether he might be trapped here. It no longer seemed to matter. He was lost in this wilderness of tumbled mountains and thick forests, unable, in the unending snowstorms, to make out which direction was south and which north. Day only differed from night in the faint, bluish light which took the place of impenetrable dark, but so deep was the layer of cloud above the earth, so constant the falling snow, that he could not distinguish where the sun rose or where it set.

His store of food was nearly gone. He had been reduced to eating snow for water. The soles of his boots were worn into great holes. He had padded them from within with pieces roughly hacked off one of his blankets with his knife. Although these protected his feet a little from the sharp stones of the mountain tracks, they soon grew sodden from the snow, so that his feet were as wet as if he walked barefoot. The lower parts of his stockings having worn away, he had ripped the lace from his shirt cuffs and wrapped it around his feet. For a time he had worried about his feet, fearing they were beginning to rot like the hoofs of an ill-kept horse, but now he no longer cared.

With numb fingers he prised off his left boot, where a pulpy mass of paper had disintegrated into blots and scraps of words: *freedom . . . power . . . wife and children . . . I would not sing . . . a just man . . . write . . . temptations . . . words . . . God help me . . .* He prodded the lumps flat and pulled on the boot again. One of the fragments clung to his fingers and he scraped it off. *The true happiness of man.*

He was so tired. He had slept a little during the darkness, but had woken to the sound of a snow-laden branch cracking and crashing to the ground. That faint blue-grey light enabled him to see a short way beyond his refuge, but there was nothing in this matted forest of great trees and thick undergrowth to indicate which way he should take. The forest tracks he had been following for the last weeks led nowhere. Finally he decided they were not the paths of men but of wild beasts, for there was neither habitation nor any other sign of human life along their length. Perhaps there were no men in these mountains. Lost and without food, he could not live much longer.

For the first part of his journey, he had followed Dafydd's directions, working his way up the valley, going south into the mountains and following the river Clwyd upstream. It was grim travelling even then, for the snow was falling when he left Denbigh, and a bitter north wind blew at his back. It was when he was nearing the top of the valley that his journey had taken a different turn, for he had spied a band of mounted men on the track some distance away but coming up fast behind him, who did not look like regular army troopers. He withdrew into the edge of the forest, which here lay quite close to the track, and hid himself within a thicket of broom.

It was wise, he found, to have done so. For as the men drew near, he saw that they were a desperate group of thievish cut-throats, heavily armed. Crouched behind the concealing bushes, John waited for them to pass, but a mocking fate had decreed they would make camp just below his hiding-place. He watched them hobble their horses and build a great fire to cook a deer—no doubt unlawfully killed—which one of them carried slung across his horse's rump. While the meat cooked, skewered on green sticks over the fire, they passed around great jugs of earthenware which must have contained a particularly potent brew, for by the time the venison was cooked they were so drunken and clumsy that one of them scorched his hand in grabbing for his share of their

433

dinner. John was too far away to catch their words, though it was evident from their swaggering manner that they were violent braggarts. He was near enough, however, to smell the roast venison, and he lay with his mouth watering, for he had eaten nothing but stale bread, dry cheese and raisins for several days.

Despite the poached deer, despite the pieces of old army uniform worn by some, declaring them to be deserters, the outlaws seemed unconcerned about halting at the side of the road, in full view from both directions along the valley. Either they were recklessly confident of their own safety, or they knew themselves a match for any army patrol that might ride along the road. When it became clear that they proposed to stay where they were for the night, John withdrew stealthily into the woods, moving as carefully and quietly as if he were himself stalking a deer, though perhaps his caution was wasted, for by now the men were stupefied with food and drink. That night he nibbled a dry crust before rolling himself in his blankets and lying down under some bushes to sleep. He hoped that by morning the men would be gone.

When he crept down to the bank overlooking the road the next morning, he found that the men were still there, some asleep, some awake and quarrelling. They gave no sign of moving, so he decided that he would have to continue his journey by working his way through the woods, keeping parallel with the road but out of sight. Once the outlaws had overtaken him, he could climb down to the road and make his way onwards by the easier route.

For the next two days, it seemed as though the outlaws were playing some kind of game with him. He was sure they had not noticed him there above them in the woods, but they moved along the road at an amble, their horses keeping pace with his slow and difficult scramble through the undergrowth and around thick stands of ancient trees. The valley had grown very narrow, and he was forced nearer to them as the road wound into the mountains, which were closing in on both sides.

On the third day, John, who had started early and was ahead of the outlaws, came over a shoulder of the mountains and saw a small village ahead, nestled in a curve at the top of the valley where track, river and squat cottages jostled for space on the narrow ribbon of land. He was kneeling, looking down over the village and wondering whether he should seek help there, when he heard the jingle of harness and saw the outlaws come into sight below, riding now at a canter, some with pistols in their hands, some with drawn swords.

It all happened so quickly that John seemed to hold his breath throughout. The outlaws broke into a gallop, riding up and around the cottages as though this was a manoeuvre they had perfected through practice. Any person out in the open, man, woman or child, they cut down or shot at once, despite pleas for mercy, many of the villagers falling on their knees and praying, young children standing and staring open-mouthed. All about the cottages the white snow was daubed with spreading patches of crimson, which steamed in the icy air. Then the outlaws rounded up the villagers who had taken refuge in their homes. Like a herd of beasts at slaughter time, they were swiftly massacred. Except for some of the women.

There was one young woman who fought them. Tall, amongst these small dark Welshmen, she had a beautiful wild bush of black hair which one of the outlaws used to drag her to one side, away from the killing. She fought like a wild animal, biting the man's hand, scratching his face, and struggling until he managed to force her to the ground. For a moment she seemed to go limp, but John, who was watching in horror, saw her hand creep towards the knife sticking out of the outlaw's belt. With a sudden twist she pulled it free and thrust it upwards into his stomach. As he fell, she threw him off and scrambled to her feet. The outlaw was beyond help, but as two more ran towards her, she raised the knife in both hands and plunged it into her own breast.

John turned away, retching. When he was able to look back, he saw that the men had piled up a pathetic collection of possessions looted from the village, and were setting the cottages on fire. As soon as these were well alight, they bundled up their booty and rode off laughing, leaving their comrade's body lying amongst the miserable villagers.

After the assault on the village, John was determined to follow another route. As long as he clung to the road the outlaws were following, he was in danger of being taken by them. They seemed in no hurry to go elsewhere, and perhaps intended to spend the rest of the winter in the valley, living off what they could seize from the neighbouring cottages and farms. The only way to escape them was to find another way through the mountains to Llangollen. And so the following day he had turned his back on the nearest thing to a road in this remote country, and made his way deeper into the mountains, thinking that if he travelled south for a time and then turned east, he must come, sooner or later, to a road that would take him to the town, or a friendly village where the people would direct him.

John, however, was a stranger to mountain country. His plan might have served amongst the gentler hills of Staffordshire. Here, amid the mountains of Berwyn, he was hopelessly confused within a day. Then the blizzards began, and he lost all sense of where he was, and where he should direct his steps. Now as he lay partly sheltered by the hollowed oak tree, he knew that his strength had nearly given out. If he remained here, then the outcome was certain. With his food gone in a few days, he would die in this nameless forest. If he struggled on, he could more easily choose the wrong way than the right one, for in all this dense, deserted country, all ways but one would lead him to death.

He spent the rest of the day unable to decide whether to stay and give himself up to the creeping tiredness which was overtaking him, or whether to try to summon up the very last of his feeble strength and walk for one more day, in the hope of finding some sign of human life. For the last week he had felt the gaol fever seizing hold of him again, and as that snow-laden day drew towards evening, he began to slip into the twilight of the soul which he had known after Dafydd's death at Denbigh. The memory of the outlaws' murderous assault on the village haunted him, however much he struggled to force the images from his mind. Over and over again he saw, as in an horrific vision that was neither dream nor living sight, the killings, the burning of the poor cottages. And above all, the death of the young woman with black hair, who had taken her own life rather than fall into their hands.

As he twisted and turned in the agony of his fever, he thought his head must burst with the pain that crushed the very brain within his skull. And as the darkness deepened, shutting out all sight of the snow which fell, and fell, and fell, silent and unceasing, it seemed that the girl with the dark hair leaned over him, the knife in her hand. And he tried to cry out to her to kill him and free him from the pain. And as her face drew near his, it was Anne's face, though it was lost in the wiry bush of that strange dark hair, so different from Anne's soft tresses. And the girl plunged the knife into her own breast and fell, as slowly and silently as the snow, until she lay at his feet. And when he reached out to touch her, there came a roaring in his ears like the sea whipped up by a mighty storm. And when he touched her, it was not the girl, but the big blacksmith, lying waxy and cold, his hands folded upon his breast, his eyes open and staring blankly at John.

Chapter Thirty-One

The festival of Christmas 1649 was observed somewhat furtively at Swinfen lest their rebellion against the new Puritan strictures might be reported to the powers in the land. Anne had become recklessly defiant since her intervention in the witch trial. She would dare all in defence of her family, her household, and her dependants, yet there were other things also which must be defended. Without pausing to reason out such matters, she knew in her heart that the simple beliefs and customs of the countryside would wither under the fiery breath of the Puritan dragon, and if they did, the spirit of the people would turn to ashes. She saw no hurt to the Christ Child in the burning of a Yule log and the hanging of a kissing ring to celebrate his birth. He had brought light to the world, and was this not symbolised by the Yule fire? And he had brought love to mankind, love woven into the kissing ring itself. What matter if the log and the ring had their origin in more ancient times? Should we not treasure what is good, and only cast out what is bad?

To Anne the story of the poor couple from Nazareth, with their fragile infant son endangered by Herod's wrath, brought humanity and warmth to her faith. Mother and father and child. The simplest peasant could understand them as well as the greatest scholar or king. Yet this new fierce religion of the Elect seemed to have cast aside the human heart of Christianity and turned its face instead to the cruel and wrathful Jehovah of the Old Testament. They spoke of punishment and hellfire more readily than kindness and love. Love, she had come to realise, was the foundation of all her belief, in life and in morals. And so she celebrated Christmas with her people, her household and tenants, in joy and love. If punishment should follow on its heels, she was ready to confront it, though the attack from the crowd after the trial had terrified her.

The final celebrations of the season were held on Twelfth Night, when they ate the traditional great cake which Hester had baked, with its bean for the king, pea for the queen, clove for the knave and rag for the slut. Grumbling a little still, Hester had accepted that Agnes was now part of the family, though Anne had seen her once or twice make the sign of the horns behind Agnes's back. The whole household gathered in the great hall that morning, to partake of ale from the best Venetian goblets and to eat the fruit cake from plates of silver: the rich Christmas cake stuffed with hazelnuts and apricots, figs and walnuts and dried cherries, crystallised peel of lemons and oranges, and sweetened and scented with honey and nutmeg and cinnamon and allspice and cloves. The cake was cut into pieces, then each piece was wrapped in a napkin and placed on a tray. When all had chosen their pieces, they broke them open amid much laughter, to see what part they should play for the day. Irish Brendan was king and young Margit queen, at which she blushed and stammered, not knowing which way to look. The clove fell to Ralph, who declared boldly that he would much rather be knave than king, for knaves might do as they pleased.

'Well said!' cried Richard, tossing him up in the air. 'Let us all be knaves!'

'Have a care,' said Bess, 'he has just eaten that monstrous big piece of cake.'

'But who shall be the slut?' said Nan. 'Not I.'

Then Dick picked the bit of cloth out of his cake.

'I am the slut. Can I be the slut? I thought it must be a maid.'

Richard seized one of the aprons from the back of a chair and tied it around Dick's waist, and placed a dish clout on his head for a cap.

'A very fine slut indeed,' he said, 'if somewhat rough of countenance. Now, Brendan.' He advanced on Brendan with a cushion in his hand. 'As king you are obliged to wear a cushion as a crown for the rest of the day.'

Brendan accepted his crown gravely, seated on Master Swynfen's great carved chair, where the kissing ring winked above his head, spinning slowly in the draught from the Yule fire. He was still wearing the cushion much later when they went out all together to the orchard as it was growing dark, the adults carrying wisps of straw.

'What is this strange pagan rite we are to practice now, lady?' he asked Anne.

'Nay, it's no such thing. We're going to burn the moss off the orchard trees. This is the best time of year to do it, when the trees are dormant, and no harm can come to them. It keeps the moss from taking the goodness from the fruit.'

'I never heard of such a thing.'

'We've always done it at Swinfen.'

It was the custom for the lord of the manor to set light to the moss on the first tree, an ancient apple tree whose great limbs were bowed by the years but which still bore an ample crop each autumn. Everyone stood silent at the edge of the orchard. At first, Anne could not understand why they waited, and then she realised that they all looked her as the lord, with the right of first fire. She took out her strike-light and lit her wisp of straw, then touched the frost-dry moss with it.

The fire lay amongst the curled moss for a moment, no more than a winking spark, then glowing ribbons shot forth from it, licking up and down the trunk and along the branches, wrapping the whole tree in a cloak of fire.

'You'll destroy the tree!' cried Brendan.

Anne shook her head, running from tree to tree with her straw, and the others followed her. Soon every tree was alight, and Anne paused alone at the far side of the orchard, gasping and elated. The orchard was on fire! The very trees seemed to dance, their flaming limbs outlined against the black dark of the winter sky. This might be no pagan rite, but she felt like a priestess baptised and reborn by fire.

It was as well that Swinfen lay at a distance from both village and town while these dangerous practices were taking place. Since her defence of Agnes Lea, Anne knew herself to be vulnerable, for she had drawn attention by stepping outside the role to which her birth and station assigned her. From the time she had returned to Swinfen, she had defied the proprieties and scandalised many. How innocent now seemed that first act, of riding alone into Lichfield and attempting to buy hay in the market! Yet that had offended many of her neighbours. While some had accepted that the absence of their menfolk during the war forced upon wives and widows many of the tasks that would be regarded as unseemly in time of peace, Anne's readiness to assume the direction of the estate, and even to propose new schemes, went beyond what was acceptable. For was not Thomas Pott at hand? And men enough of her own blood, though far away in Kent? The Sylvesters still refused to pay the rent for Thickbroome, and Anne knew that she had no recourse but to go to law. She doubted whether she could win her case, for too many of her own rank now looked at her askance. Even Mary had grown cold again, and Thomas seemed uncomfortable in her company.

By the time she stood up in the Lichfield courthouse, she was already marked out. Since that day, she had been treated with reserve and even hostility by her wealthier neighbours, though the poor turned to her more than ever. It was fortunate that the severe winter weather meant that she had little contact with society outside her own domain at

Swinfen, except for the weekly visit to the church at Weeford. There she was forced to endure several sermons in which the Puritan minister ranted against scandalous women, sermons unmistakably directed at her, sitting prominently in the Swinfen Hall pew at the front of the church. In her heart she rebelled. It might be justice to call a whore a scandalous woman. She did not think it right that a woman who defended an innocent in a court of law should be so described. However, she dared not show, by word or even expression, that she raged against the minister's words, even when he raised his finger and pointed at her, there in front of all the congregation. In the new state of the nation, such a man as this had unknown powers, and for the sake of her family she dared not defy or offend him.

After church, when by custom friends and neighbours gathered to exchange courtesies and news, the congregation avoided her, the women whisking aside their skirts when she passed, as if she might contaminate them, the men staring through her with haughty insolence, as though she had vanished for ever from the sight of decent people. She had not ventured again into Lichfield, for fear she might be pelted with worse than stones and horse dung.

Late in January, the weather turned so severe that it was impossible to take the household to Weeford for services on Sundays, for they were snowbound. Anne greeted the snowdrifts with relief, for they spared her the weekly public humiliation. Instead, on Sundays she extended the normal daily prayers that she conducted for her household to an hour and a half of Bible readings, prayers, and psalms. Brendan attended these, as he attended the daily prayers, like any obedient servant, although Anne still suspected that he belonged to the Romish faith. Yet she had no intention of betraying him.

Despite the fact that this winter there was an abundance of food and fuel, after her year of hard work and careful provision, Anne found herself a prey to melancholy as January drew towards February. As soon as the weather improved in the spring, Dick would leave for Oxford. He was eager to go. For him it was a chance to escape the restraints of home and embark on a new and freer life, but Anne recognised it as the first parting of many from her children. One by one they would leave, the girls to marriage, the boys to the universities and the inns of court, perhaps for the younger ones to a career as a merchant in London, where they might earn their own fortunes. None would be like Bridget, crippled and unmarriageable, and so destined to remain at home for life.

Anne was grateful with all her heart to have Bridget at home, for she could not have nursed the two older Swynfens as Bridget did, while she carried the whole burden of managing the estate as well. Joane Swynfen seemed lost forever in her twilight, childish world, but along with so much else she had forgotten her old dislike of her crippled daughter, and now depended on her totally. There had been no violent attacks now for many weeks. Bridget had discovered that, although her mother's mind had lost its adult reason, her fingers, strangely, still retained their skill. She found Joane silks and pattern books and set her embroidering again, and from her needle flowed riots of flowers and fruit and meticulously rendered geometric designs, better even than any work she had done when she was in her right mind.

'It's as if,' Anne said to Bridget one day, 'all her mind has drained into her fingertips. For while she has the mind of a child, this is no child's work.'

She held up an embroidered bed-hanging stiff with the crowded images of strange entwined beasts and foliage, which reminded her of carvings around an ancient church door.

Old Master Swynfen had gained a little more movement, a little more speech. To listen to him striving to put together words into a coherent utterance drove Anne into an agony of pity and impatience. It would take him whole minutes to form a single sentence. Yet she knew that he was still there, locked inside the prison of his body. He enjoyed listening to Bridget read to him, and sometimes Nan took a turn. She had grown into a thoughtful girl, rising ten now, and the only one of the family apart from Bridget who seemed able to interpret her grandfather's wishes before he could grunt out those distorted words.

After her sad discovery of Agnes's ruined cottage, Anne had decided to keep this news from the old woman, who, since the trial, had become frail and helpless, even handing over the care of her beloved goats to Brendan. He referred to them as 'those accursed devil's spawn', but took great trouble with them, and insisted that only he and Agnes knew the correct way to make goat's cheese. He would bring it to Agnes for her to sample, and they would engage in long discussions about the methods of cheese-making from the milk of goats and ewes, which both swore to be superior to the cheese made from mere cows' milk.

Apart from this, Agnes sat all day in her chair in a corner of the kitchen, with the elderly Peterkin on her lap, who seemed at last to have abandoned ratting for the quiet, unstirring life of the aged. Anne was apprehensive for Agnes. All her fighting spirit had drained away from her. It was as though what she had told Anne many months ago was true, that she could not breathe away from the moor. Anne had promised herself that she would have Agnes's cottage rebuilt in the spring, but in her heart she feared that the old woman would finally fade away before spring ever came.

Anne herself had taken to spending a good deal of her time alone in her chamber reading. She had always disliked the dead heart of winter, the long bitter nights and overcast days, when it seemed that sunlight and warmth would never return to the earth. In London there had been many diversions to help her forget this misery—plays, concerts, dinners with friends, and gatherings at the house in St Ann's Lane with John's political colleagues. Last winter she had been so occupied, every waking minute, in ensuring her household avoided starvation, that it had left no opening for this melancholic mood to seize hold of her.

Now that her household was safely provided for, she seemed to have lost her bearings. In the mornings she could scare drag herself from her bed, although at night she lay awake for hours, listening to the silence in the room. Jane now shared a room with Mary and Dorothea. Without the soft sound of her breathing in the cradle, the air in Anne's room was as uninhabited as the grave.

To tell truth, she knew well enough the real source of the melancholy. The days and weeks had passed since Mathew Moreton had passed on the news of John's release from Denbigh, yet there had been no further word of him. Henry Stone had eventually reached home in late January, travelling by easy stages in a coach, for he was still weak from his injuries. When he arrived in Walsall, he wrote to tell her all that he knew, but in substance it was no more than she had already learned from Moreton. Paradoxically, it seemed almost better when she had known that John was imprisoned, first at Stafford and then at Denbigh. Now he had vanished. Sitting in her chamber and looking out across the frozen lake, at a landscape so lost beneath snow that field blended with forest, Anne thought with dread how much worse the winter must be in the Welsh mountains. Little by little she was abandoning hope that she would ever see John again.

Lying curled up in the hollow oak, like some poor beast which has found a quiet place to nurse its injuries, John gradually became aware of light. He did not wake so much as swim back to the surface of consciousness from a great darkness that had overcome him with fever and hallucinations. He felt light-headed now, slightly dizzy, but for the moment the fever had abated.

Where could the light be coming from? He was aware of it before he opened his eyes, confused at first about where he was, and why something sharp was pressing into his back. Gradually, he opened his eyes and saw, no more than a foot from his face, a rough surface of pale grey wood. Then he remembered the oak tree which had partially spilt apart at the base, the outer bark curling protectively around the edge of the opening like an arboreal lip, the inside of the hollow space walled with the vulnerable naked wood of the tree's heart. It was a protuberance of this wood that was causing the pain in his back.

His limbs had become locked into a death-like rigour, so that he had to unfold them one by one, like the legs on a collapsible gaming-table. When at last the shooting spasms in his joints allowed him to crawl on all fours outside the tree, he saw that the snow had finally stopped falling. The heavens were still clouded, but the brightness of one area of the sky indicated where the sun stood. The east lay on his right hand.

Would he have remained in the tree, gone to earth like a dying animal, if the snow had not ceased and a faint sun appeared? He did not choose to ask himself. Outside the tree he took deep breaths of the sharp air, then scooped handfuls of the snow into his mouth, where they melted into thin trickles of water. It did not satisfy his thirst, but his mouth felt a little less like a sawyer's pit. He shook the dead leaves off his cloak and brushed down his breeches. During the time he had sheltered in the tree, his boots and feet had dried, but the leather of his boots had hardened and cracked, and already he could feel the snow soaking the blanket linings. He rummaged in his bundle for a few of the last raisins, and ate them one by one, chewing each as if it were a piece of meat, to fool his aching stomach into believing that he was feeding it. He retrieved his hat from the tree. It was a sorry wreck, like some bit of flotsam in a London gutter, but it would warm his head a little. His simple preparations complete, he hoisted his pack on his back and started off, heading towards the morning sun. The old wound in his leg began to ache as the blood flowed through it again, so that he found himself treading tenderly, like a lamed horse.

After he had been walking for about two hours, not following any track but setting his course purely by the direction of the sun, he began to feel that the ground was sloping downwards in front of him. It might be no more than a gully between two peaks, or some small upland valley, but he allowed a small flame of hope to kindle in his mind that he might have reached the eastern edge of the mountains, where they began to fall away into the border country between Wales and England. Had he felt stronger, he would have tried to climb a tree to see if he could make out the ground ahead, but he knew that in his present state he would never manage it, so he continued, planting one foot doggedly in front of the other with care, for if he turned an ankle or fell amongst twisted roots and fallen branches concealed by the snow, he would never be able to escape from the forest.

From time to time he scooped up more snow for water, but he allowed himself nothing more to eat until the sun was directly overhead. The clouds had begun to clear, and the sunlight danced off the frozen crust of the snow, like candlelight off some crisp confectionery of spun sugar, adding to his sense of unreality. For he felt as though he were moving through a dream landscape, beautiful but menacing, which might at any moment turn to nightmare. He was dizzy with hunger and the lingering effects of his fever, so that when he found a small stream which was partially free of ice, he lay down and drank from it out of simple gratitude, not seeing at once that it might have some other significance. After his first drink of true water for days, he ate his very last heel of stale bread, which he dipped in the stream to soften. It was rash, perhaps, to eat it, but he reasoned that it would swell in his stomach with all the water he had drunk, and thus give him an illusion of having eaten well.

It was only as he was slowly chewing the last precious fragment of bread that he realised how the stream might be of use to him. Most streams, he reasoned, unless they disappear underground or into bog, will flow downhill to join a river. And rivers flow down into valleys. As this stream was flowing eastwards, there was a chance that it might be flowing down towards the river that Dafydd had told him ran through Llangollen. He decided to follow it, at least for as long as it seemed to be running eastwards.

By the time dusk fell, the stream had grown to twice the width and it was certain that the land was falling away towards a valley. John had been able to drink cold, pure water whenever he wanted all day, and he felt the better for it, even though he now had nothing left to eat but a handful of raisins and a bit of cheese smaller than the palm of his hand. He slept that night under a bush, and before he slept he prayed simply that it would not begin to snow again. For he felt that, if he could be spared another snow storm, he might survive to reach some village or farm.

The next day dawned clear but very cold, his breath steaming before his face. There was ice dangling in his straggled beard and sugaring his eyebrows, and when he went to drink at the stream he was forced to break a fresh covering of ice with a stone. He was so light-headed now from hunger that he no longer made his way by rational thought, choosing his direction by the sun, but merely clung to the stream, like Theseus clinging to the thread that would lead him out of the labyrinth of death. This became more difficult as the stream leapt down steeper ground now, over rapids and waterfalls, with a strange muffled roaring sound beneath its casing of ice, as if the nearer it came to its union with some greater river, the more headlong became its downward rush.

Sometime during the afternoon, with his shadow jumping ahead of him, John reached a bank tumbling down into a narrow valley through which ran the river his stream was seeking. And the stream, broken free from the mountains and the ice, flung itself over the bank in a final waterfall to join the river. A well-trodden track ran below him alongside the river, and ahead, just before it rounded a bend, there was a cottage, from which smoke was rising. It was a miserable hovel, like those he had seen when first he had been brought into Wales, but the fire was a sign of human company as welcoming as trumpeters proclaiming the Lord Mayor's feast in London. John slithered down the snowy bank and began to stumble along the track towards it, weaving as erratically as a drunkard.

He had almost reached it, was just wondering whether he should shout halloo to warn the inhabitants of his arrival, when he heard the pounding of horses' hooves behind him. After all that unfathomable time lost in the mountains, suddenly he was surrounded by people on all sides! He turned and looked over his shoulder. At first, he thought his fever had returned, and the waking nightmares, for he thought he saw the selfsame band of outlaws riding towards him. After all his suffering, they would slay him in the end. Fate had been mocking him, tormenting him with the terrors and privations of his escape, only to hand him over to these brigands at last.

John sank to his knees beside the road. He had no strength to endure any longer. Before he covered his face with his hands, in order to offer up his soul to God, he saw that, although it was the same group of men, they were less than half in number, and several wore bloody bandages. It made little difference. He was armed with nothing more than the knife with which he cut his food, and he was as weak as a three-year-old child.

It seemed the inhabitants of the cottage had heard the horsemen also, for the door was suddenly thrown open. Then John felt himself clouted on the head, and heard, at the same moment, the explosion of a gun. He was dragged some distance by one of the horsemen, then the man let him go, and he rolled away into the snow-filled ditch at the side of the road. As he felt himself slipping into darkness, there seemed to

445

be a battle taking place above him on the road, followed by the sound of horses galloping away. Someone rolled him over. People were talking in words he could not understand, then he felt himself lifted gently and carried into a place that was warm and dim.

John was never sure afterwards how long it was before he woke and found himself bedded down on a straw mattress in the cottage, for he discovered that his rescuers spoke no English. There were two of them: a huge, raw-boned old woman and a young man of about twenty, who was probably her grandson and who was even bigger, so tall he had to stoop except in the very centre of the cottage. Their size, so much larger than most Welshmen, perplexed John. He had read tales of giants who had lived on in the Welsh mountains long after most of their kind had been driven out by the present native inhabitants, long before the Romans came, but he had always taken them to be the fantastical imaginings of poets. Now he was not so sure. As well as being so immense, the old woman and her grandson were both ugly: she with misshapen features and the warts and protuberances of age, he with the round face, hanging mouth and squinting eyes of the simpleton.

Grateful as he was for his rescue from the brigands, John was afraid of the pair at first. It was the woman who had wielded the gun, for he saw her later cleaning and reloading it, no doubt in preparation for any further attack. This gun was an ancient arquebus, at least a hundred years old, and John was somewhat nervous it might explode of itself when the old crone propped it up in a corner near the fire. He decided that it must have been the boy who had carried him to the cottage, for although he was simple-minded, he seemed able to speak a few words, and could undertake easy tasks like chopping wood and making up the fire, or churning milk. The hovel was as squalid inside as John had suspected, and the pair were far from clean. The bed (which he shared with a large dog of wolfish appearance) was hopping with fleas and lice, an affliction he had been spared since the day the infested blankets had been brought to the cell in Denbigh.

After a time, however, he began to see that these people, rough and dirty as they looked, were truly kind. When he had recovered a little they gave him broth to eat. The boy squatted on the ground beside the bed, watching him with that vacuous look while he ate. It made John nervous, but when he had finished and made to put the empty bowl aside, the boy seized it, saying something it his strange language, and brought John more of the broth, with a chunk of excellent fresh bread, only slightly marred by bits of grit in the coarse-ground corn. When John thanked him and gave a nervous smile, the boy beamed

446

broadly and gave a little dance on his big clumsy feet, before settling down to watch him again.

By the next day, John could feel strength beginning to seep back into his body, and when the old woman made him a dish of buttered eggs, he fell on it as ravenously as the wolf-like dog would have done. He was perplexed how to speak to these people and show his gratitude for their kindness, for all he could do was to nod and smile, and say 'Thank you' in English again and again. It seemed that they understood, for they said something in Welsh that he understood to mean: 'You're welcome. Please, it's our pleasure.'

The woman gave him goat's milk to drink, which had a strong odour, but seemed to satisfy his shrunken stomach. The boy began to present him with gifts, little treasures which he must have found over a long period, and which he kept in a broken dish balanced on the beam above the door. At first it was pretty coloured stones, then one day a scallop shell, of pure white until you held it to the light, when it shone faintly rose. The boy held it up to show off this magical property. John was unsure whether he was supposed to admire it or to keep it, but when he tried to give it back, the boy shook his head and pressed it back into John's hand, folding his fingers over it. Where could such a thing have come from, to this poor dwelling so far from the sea? It might have been the treasure of some pilgrim of the old faith who had journeyed long ago to Santiago di Compostela, but how had it ended here?

John spent a week recovering in the cottage, gradually getting up for a little longer each day, moving stiffly about the confined space, and at last, when he was sure there was no one on the road, venturing outside. The weather continued very cold, but no more snow had fallen. Could he but have known where he was, he would have been content, for now that he was stronger, he felt that he could walk the rest of the way into England. He tried asking the old woman, 'Llangollen?', pointing ahead eastwards along the road. As first she seemed confused, then she shook her head.

'Llangollen,' she said, or he thought she said, pointing to the west.

He must be pronouncing it wrongly. Llangollen could not lie to the west. The next day, he tried again, but the woman was adamant. Llangollen, she was surely telling him, lay to the west. Somehow he must have come around it through the mountains. He tried again, asking, 'Shrewsbury?' She looked blank. 'Oswestry?' Still this meant nothing. Then she seized his arm and began to gabble in Welsh, with many gestures, her hands waving back and forth along the road, her tongue making the clop-clop noise of horses' hooves. John clutched his head between his hands. Since he had left Denbigh, he seemed to be living in a fantastical world out of some old knightly tale, to have strayed into strange territories inhabited by grotesque creatures, where he was robbed of speech. All the while he tried to speak to the old woman, the boy shuffled round them, bobbing his head, laughing, and clapping his hands.

Yet, in the end, the old woman's attempts to explain fell into place. She must, after all, have been as frustrated as he. On the eighth or ninth day after he had been taken in by the strange couple, John heard the sound of a horse on the road. At once he leapt up, and took a step towards the loaded gun. If the brigands were returning, he did not want to depend on the old woman's shooting skills again. But she laid her hand on his arm and shook her head, smiling happily. A few minutes later, the cottage door opened and a man entered. He was as small and wizened as the woman was large and gross, but he greeted her like an old friend, taking off his hat to her and nodding to the boy. He looked with suspicion at John. At once the woman launched into an explanation and he relaxed.

'So, you are a traveller fallen amongst thieves, is it?' he said.

'You speak English!'

'English and Irish as well as my mother tongue, which is the language of Wales. Mother Bronwen is telling me you want to travel on, but she cannot make out where you are going.'

'Lichfield, in Staffordshire,' said John, feeling his face flush with relief. 'I asked for Llangollen and Shrewsbury and Oswestry, but she didn't seem to understand.'

The man gave him an odd look.

'But why would you want to go to Llangollen? That's further back into Wales.'

'I must have come by another way and missed it. I came from Denbigh through the mountains.'

The man gave a low whistle. 'You came over Llantysilio, in the midst of this winter? I would not have said any man could do that and live.'

'I think,' said John soberly, 'if these good people had not found me, I should not have lived.'

'Aye, they're kind folk, though many might call them strange. I don't know what will become of the boy when the grandmother dies.'

'Can you direct me which way to go?'

'I can do better,' said the man, 'I'm a carter to trade. If you are not in great haste, I can carry you to Birmingham. That's as close as I go to Lichfield on this journey.'

'I can walk with ease from Birmingham,' said John, near overcome with relief. He held out his hand. 'John Swynfen,' he said.

'Dewi Morgan,' said the man, shaking his hand and sketching a comic little bow. 'Glad to be of service.' Then he turned to the old woman Bronwen, and explained their exchange to her in Welsh.

Dewi stayed the night in the cottage, sleeping in a chair beside the fire, and the two of them set off next morning early, for, as Dewi said, the outlaws were still troubling the area, but they rose late from their sleep and he wanted to be on the road before they stirred. As Dewi gathered up the reins, John leaned down from the seat beside him and handed Bronwen one of his precious shillings, which he had taken from its hiding place in his boot. She peered at it with her watery eyes, looking puzzled, then she smelled it, shook her head, and handed it back to John.

'They've little use for money in these parts,' said Dewi, who was watching in amusement.

'I have nothing else to give her,' said John.

He pressed the shilling into her hand, and folded her fingers around it as the boy had done. She smiled at him, and nodded, as if she understood. Then as Dewi clicked his tongue at his horse, the boy came running from the house with his strange lop-sided gait, and held out one last treasure for John. It was the bright feather from the tail of some fine cockerel, and it gleamed with rainbow colours in the early light.

John smiled and laid his hand gently on the boy's rough head.

'Tell him,' he said to Dewi, 'that I will keep it always, and always I shall remember the kindness shown me by two strangers in Wales.'

Dewi translated and then they were on their way, rounding the corner almost at once and losing sight of the cottage, which John no longer thought of as a miserable hovel. Desperately poor, yes, but a place where more goodness might be found than in the palace of a king. He remembered Dafydd and his words: 'Land for every man and woman, that none may starve.'

❧

The carter's journey back into England went slowly, for the roads were burdened with snow and the old horse proceeded at his own leisurely pace, down through Oswestry to Shrewsbury, and then south and east towards Warwickshire. John spent much of the time sleeping amongst the bales of Welsh wool, which seemed as soft as goosedown compared with the hard sleeping he had known for months past. When he was not sleeping, he sat beside the carter on the seat at the front of the cart, grateful for his thick cloak against the north wind, dirty and torn though it now was, and even more grateful for the two fleeces Dewi unpacked for them to wrap around themselves. For much of the time they sat in companionable silence, each man occupied with his own thoughts, but from time to time Dewi would launch upon a long monologue, describing the places they were passing, along a route he had followed for thirty years, and commenting on the harm they had suffered in the war. But he was accustomed to travelling alone, and it seemed to John that he addressed his remarks to his horse more than his companion.

At last, after many days, they came east out of Birmingham, on the way to Tamworth. Dewi halted the cart on the road near a great oak tree, and said that this was the nearest he came to Lichfield. He screwed up his eyes, looking into the north as John climbed down from the cart and lifted the tattered remains of his bundle after him.

'I fear there's more snow coming,' said Dewi. 'I don't like the look of that great cloud looming over there. How far is your home from here?'

'About three or four hours' walk. I hope I may reached it before nightfall.'

John followed Dewi's glance to the north and gave a rueful laugh.

'It seems that whenever I must go afoot, I bring down snow storms about my ears.'

'Come with me to Tamworth instead,' said Dewi. 'And we'll try to find another carter who may take you with him nearer to your home.'

John looked from the black cloud to Dewi and back again. It was hard to confront the long walk and the coming storm, but now that he was so near, he was impatient to head for Swinfen. He shook his head.

'I thank you for all your help, my friend, but I'll be on my way. I haven't seen my family this year and more, and I cannot turn away now.'

The two men shook hands. Then Dewi stirred up his horse on the road to the town; John shouldered his pack and headed northwest towards Swinfen.

At first he made good progress, but the snow that Dewi had foreseen soon began to fall. The wind grew stronger, whirling the flakes in a blinding curtain, so that, in whatever direction John turned, the surrounding countryside was blotted out. Still, this was fairly familiar territory for him, although when he did come this way, it was on horseback, which gives a man a very different view of hill and wood than when he goes afoot. The road, already hidden in drifting snow, disappeared in the blizzard. He knew he had missed his way after he had been walking two hours and had not come across the village of Hints. When he felt himself beginning to climb, he realised he must have strayed on to Packington Moor. The moor was no place to be walking in a blizzard, but on the far side of the moor lay Swinfen. Reason told him that if he continued to put one foot in front of the other, he must, in time, come home.

Putting one foot in front of another was not such an easy matter. Dewi had given him some pieces of sacking to wrap around the broken remains of his boots, which had served to keep his feet warm while he sat in the cart. Now, however, the snow began to cling to the sacking like dough to a baker's fingers. Before long, each foot was encased in a monstrous boot of freezing snow, growing heavier by the minute. He could not unwrap the sacking, for his boots would finally fall apart, and he would be left barefoot. His survival, barefoot on the moor in February, would be doomed. All he could do was to stop from time to time and prise the armour of snow from his feet, but each time this grew more difficult. He had no gloves, and must keep his hands as warm as he could by burying them in his pockets. As soon as he tried to free his feet from the snow, his fingers stiffened and turned blue with the cold. The wretched object on his head, which was all that was left of his hat, barely kept the snow out of his hair; it could not prevent snow slipping down the back of his neck, where it mingled with his effortful sweat to soak his shirt and doublet. Icicles had formed in his beard and rang together like bells of glass.

With the struggle of climbing the moor into the teeth of the storm and burdened by packed snow, the muscles of his legs began to throb with pain. He realised that the days in the cart, which he thought had restored a little of his strength, had merely deceived him into thinking he was well again. Every few yards, his calf muscles went into spasms of cramp which left him gasping, bent over and rubbing his legs to try to force them to function again. The weird sense of unreality which had haunted his gaol fever crept back into his mind, magnified by the confusion of the endless snow. Faces peered out at him from amongst the flakes, leering and then vanishing. He thought he could hear the howling of the wolves which had once lived here. A wind-twisted tree looming up in his path reached out gigantic arms to clutch at him, so that he gave a cry like a frightened animal and stumbled into a run to escape from it. In his haste he tripped over something buried beneath

451

the snow and was flung forward on his knees, where he stayed, sobs rising in his throat, as he cried out against a God who had inflicted such punishment on him.

At length he rose to his feet again and dragged himself onwards, but he knew, now, that he did not have the strength to cross the moor and reach Swinfen. In one final twist to the cruel game Fortune had played with him, he saw she would bring him so close to home and allow him to die here. Then, as the curtain of snow wavered aside for a moment, he caught a glimpse of a projecting rock face ahead of him. Suddenly all his desires were narrowed down to reaching the place and crawling beneath it to find some shelter from the storm. It leaned forward at an angle from a slight rise in the ground, with a space below it into which he crept. He would rest here for a while. Perhaps the snow would abate, or the wind drop, and he could continue on his way. He curled on his side, and laid his head on his bundle. He was quite unaware when sleep overtook him.

❦

In the afternoon at Swinfen Hall, most of the household were gathered in the kitchen, for despite large fires the rest of the house ached with a bitter winter chill. In the kitchen, however, the large cavernous space was cheerfully lit both by hearth and by candles on tables and in sconces. Margit was wiping dry the last of the pewter plates from dinner and storing them in their places on the rack of the dresser. The older boys, along with Richard, were tying fishing flies at one end of the huge old scrubbed table, which was dented and scored with knife marks from generations of cutting bread. At the other end, the younger children were helping Hester make tarts for supper from circles of pastry and blackberry preserves. Rather more of the preserve had found its way into sticky mouths than on to the pastry. The baby Jane was confined to a triangular frame on wheels in which she trundled about the floor, knocking into everyone's shins. Bridget was listening to Nan reading, while she mended a chemise, and Patience was tracing out a pattern for Joane's next piece of embroidery. Near the fire, Agnes and Biddy dozed in their chairs, and the men were mending harness nearby. Dick's kitten Ginger, now a full-grown cat, was stretched out beside the hearth, with a wary eye on Peterkin, who had quietly asserted his rule amongst the cats and dogs of the house.

Indeed, almost all the household was here. The two eldest Swynfens were asleep upstairs and Brendan had gone out to check his sheep before nightfall. Anne's sense of duty had taken her off to the

452

estate office to figure her accounts, which were woefully behindhand because of her recent mood of lethargy and depression. After she had sat staring at the columns of numbers for an hour without lifting her pen, the office proved too chilly in spite of her good intentions, and she came in carrying the account book, ink and quill, in the hope of claiming a little space on the table in the warmth and companionship of the kitchen. As she did so, the door at the end of the passageway slammed open, allowing a blast of wintry air to bend the candle flames and stir up the ashes on the hearth into a dancing flurry. Brendan came in, still in his snowy boots, but before Hester could chide him, he took off his hat and shook out the snow, and said:

'The hurdles are broken down, and someone left the barn door part ajar. Some of the ewes have escaped.'

The boys glanced furtively at each other. They had gone out before dinner to fetch their fishing gear. Had they failed to latch the door? That was five hours since. If the ewes had escaped then, they could be far away by now.

'They'll likely not have strayed far,' said Josiah, toasting his feet by the fire. 'They'll have wandered down to the meadow, the silly creatures.'

'Do you think I am such a fool as not to look there already?' Brendan flared out at him. 'I've been searching this half hour. I found some tracks in the snow, under the lee of a hedge, heading towards the moor, but there's so much snow falling that any further tracks were long vanished.'

'You'll not be thinking of going after them?' said Biddy. ''Tis wild out there, and far worse up on the moor.'

'There's a dozen of the best ewes gone,' said Brendan grimly. 'And most are near their time.' He looked across the room at Anne, who was standing just inside the doorway from the hall. 'You'll recall we put the ram to them early this year, planning for earlier lambing and bigger lambs for market.'

Anne did recall. They had debated it long and hard. The risk lay in the chance of bad weather at early lambing time, and nothing could be worse than this.

'What do you want to do?' she asked.

'Take out a search party,' he said. 'Up to the part of the moor they know. I need the youngest and strongest: Master Richard and Master Dick, and Isaac. We'll make two parties and take a horse each, in case we need to carry any home.'

'Isaac has a bad cold,' said Anne. 'I don't think he should go.'

'Then I'll go alone, and the other two can go together.'

453

'Wait!' Anne set down her load amongst the discarded fishing tackle. 'I'll put on warmer clothes and come with you. They're my ewes and my responsibility. Richard, Dick, run quickly and dress as warmly as you can.'

They went off at once. It would be a bleak undertaking, but they never questioned the need for it.

'It's not a task for a woman,' said Brendan, still speaking to her across the whole length of the big room.

'I am as strong as any here. Let's waste no more time discussing it.'

Within half an hour they were on their way, past the lake and the cultivated land and heading towards the moor. Brendan insisted that Anne should stay with him, where, as he said bluntly, he could have her under his eye. He sent the two boys off to the left, along the edge of the forest, towards the Freford end of the moor. With Anne riding one of the big geldings, and his dog at his heels, Brendan strode up the slope to the moor, heading in the direction of the flock's summer feeding grounds.

Despite her bold words, Anne was more than a little afraid once they were outside in the blizzard. Her hat blew off at once, to be retrieved by Brendan. She pulled the hood of her cloak over it and tied it down, but the wind whipped her cloak away from her body, and she had to clutch it around her with one hand, needing the other for the reins. As they climbed above the shelter of the forest, the wind redoubled in fury, and the snow fell so thick Anne was blinded, and hardly knew how to guide the horse. Brendan, who was walking a little ahead, turned round to check that she was still following, then, as though he could read her thoughts, he took hold of the reins near the bridle and led the horse.

It was impossible to speak, for the wind ripped their words from their mouths and bore them away screaming, but they signalled to each other by gesturing. Anne thought she saw a sheep, but it was only a rock. Then the dog Niall nosed up something from under a snow-laden gorse bush. A hare rose up on its hind legs and stared at them, its nose working, then leapt away across the snow. The shepherd whistled to the dog to stop him chasing the hare, and he came back reluctantly. Brendan shouted something to Anne, but she shook her head and cupped her hand behind her ear to show she could not hear. He came close to her stirrup and she leaned down, as he laid his arm along the back of her saddle and put his mouth close to her ear.

'I said, 'tis a common belief that hares are witches' familiars, so. I'll not let the dog hurt it, lest 'tis one of Agnes's. We would not want to call down bad luck indeed, now would we?'

Anne made a face at him and he laughed. She saw that, incredibly, he was enjoying this wild trek across the moor through the blizzard, and she thought: So am I. For some reason, I feel suddenly hopeful. Perhaps we'll find the ewes alive in spite of all.

When they reached the ruins of Agnes's cottage, Brendan made her halt and dismount. They sat in the lee of one of the fallen walls, where there was a little shelter from the falling snow, and the noise of the wind was lessened.

'Here,' he said, pulling a flask out of his pocket, 'drink some of this, it will warm you.'

Anne took a drink, then choked and sputtered.

'What is it?'

'We of Ireland and Scotland call it *uisge beatha*. The water of life. I always keep a small store for times like these. It will give you heart to carry on.'

'It will make me so drunk, I suppose I'll forget that we're on Packington Moor in a blizzard.' But she consented to swallow one more mouthful.

As Brendan began to get up, she stopped him.

'Before we go on,' Anne said, 'and as we may die of the cold up here, I would have you tell me one thing, Brendan Donovan.'

'And what is that?' he asked, sinking back beside her.

'You've never told me why you came here, for what purpose. Do you trust me enough to tell me now?'

He shivered, and huddled deeper into his cloak, and did not at first answer. When he did, his words surprised her.

'You know a man called Sir John Clotworthy.'

'He was one of my husband's colleagues in the House of Commons. They both belonged to the moderate party.'

'Moderate, is it? And do you know him well?'

'Not very well. John knows him better than I. Why do you ask?'

'It was John Clotworthy cheated my family out of their estates. We were considerable landowners in Antrim. Fair land of Antrim, on the sweet shores of Lough Neagh. Clotworthy made some fraudulent deal under the new settlements, and we lost everything—land and stock and goods and home and all. My father died of despair.'

His voice was flat, all emotion drained from it.

'My mother lives with my dowerless sisters in a labourer's cottage—she who was one of the greatest ladies of Antrim. My two

455

brothers were killed fighting in the war. My wife and two children were put to the sword by English soldiers. I must needs hire myself out as a shepherd to provide for the women of the family who are left.'

Anne, bereft of words, touched his arm. After a silence, she spoke hesitantly.

'Alas, Brendan, these are terrible times we live in. I know nothing about John Clotworthy's affairs in Ireland. But what has this to do with me?'

'I came to England sworn to avenge my family on him. I would kill him if I could, or harm him in any way I might. I prayed to God to guide my hand. Aye, God forgive me, I prayed that. Then, to my disgust, I learn that Cromwell is there before me, and has shut Clotworthy up in Windsor Castle, where I may no more come at him than he may gain his freedom.'

He gave a bitter laugh.

''Tis a mockery, is it not? He is imprisoned because he is so *moderate*, and that serves to protect him from the consequences of his cruel deeds.'

'But—'

'In Dublin I had spent time discovering more about my enemy. Who were his friends? John Swynfen, John Crewe, Denzil Holles, Nathaniel Fiennes and others. So, when I had made my way to London, I thought: I will take my vengeance on his friends, until such time as I can lay my hands on him.'

He paused and looked at her intently, and took her hand.

'I think, perhaps, I was mad then.'

Anne felt her heart jerk against her ribs.

'And so you came to Swinfen.'

He nodded.

'And so I came to Swinfen. And here I found, not John Swynfen—himself a prisoner—but his wife and children. And by all I can learn, John Swynfen is a good man, who would not steal another's land.'

'You are right. He would not.'

'And I hired myself to Anne Swynfen, plotting how I might hurt her—kill her, perhaps, and her children, one by one.'

Anne shivered and tried to pull her hand away, but he would not let it go.

'That time at the lake,' she said, choking on the words, 'would you have left Jack to drown?'

There was a silence, then Brendan drew a long shuddering breath.

'I do not know. God help me, I do not know. But you came, and I woke from my madness, and Jack did not drown.'

He was silent again, until Anne thought he had no more to say. Then he shook himself and turned towards her.

'I found that this Anne Swynfen, who struggled to save her manor from the fate of so many in this war, was not the woman I had imagined in those vengeful dreams of mine back in Ireland. She loved and cared for all alike—her family and servants, her labourers and tenants, down to the least lamb or silly hen. She even cared for her Irish shepherd, him with his deceitful ways and murderous heart.'

Anne shook her head. She could not speak, her heart pounding like a trapped hare in her throat.

'And her Irish shepherd found his own frozen soul beginning to warm a little, in the midst of all this kindness. Until he realised his wickedness and folly, and swore to himself and to God, that he would lay aside his sinful plan, and try to go forth and live again. For 'tis not so bad a fate for a man, to be Anne Swynfen's Irish shepherd.'

There was silence between them. Then he pulled her to her feet.

'Come, we'll turn into figures of ice ourselves, indeed, sitting here in the ruins of Agnes's home. Let us go once more in search of those feckless ewes.'

He helped her to mount, untied the horse, and whistled up the dog. Anne was too stunned by his revelations to speak, until at last she said:

'Where are you headed?'

'I'm making for the place they call the Devil's Dressing Room. I think they'll not have gone further than that. Then we'll work our way round to my bothy. All of that was their grazing ground in the summer.'

They found that the wind had abated a little while they were sheltering, but the snow continued to fall inexorably. The dog ranged ahead of them and to either side, seeking the sheep, but after the hare he flushed out no living thing. It was only as they came near that ill-omened part of the moor called the Devil's Dressing Room, where few people cared to venture, that the dog ran ahead and disappeared from sight. They could hear him whining, somewhere a little to their right.

'Run ahead,' said Anne to Brendan, who was still plodding along at the horse's head. 'I can follow the sounds, but I'll not press the horse too hard. It's treacherous ground around here.'

A few minutes later she came up with them. The dog, wagging his tail with pleasure, was digging in a drift, throwing the snow up in a great arc behind him. Brendan was on his knees, digging more carefully with his hands. Anne slid from the horse's back and ran over to them.

'Is it the ewes? Have you found them?'

At that moment Brendan stayed his hand and gave her a startled glance. She looked down at the hole he was digging. A piece of cloth protruded from it.

'I fear we've found some poor wandering beggar,' he said. 'What fool would come up here alone? I think you should stay back, mistress, for I think he's dead.'

Anne shook her head angrily and knelt down beside him.

'We must try,' she said.

Brendan shooed the dog off, and together they dug away the snow that covered the body. It was a pitiful sight. The man lay curled like a dying dog, his ragged clothes barely covering his skeletal frame.

'Poor soul!' Anne cried out in pity. 'Look at his boots. Nothing but canvas wrapped around scraps of leather.'

Brendan was burrowing away near the man's head.

'This cloak was a good one once,' he said. 'He probably had it off a Royalist soldier on a battlefield full of the dead.'

He lifted a corner of the wine-coloured velvet, lined with pale quilted silk, dirty and stained. Anne's hand flew to her lips. Then she crawled forward and began to dig frantically to clear the man's head and shoulders of snow. At last, pale as the very snow, all the blood drained from her face, she sat back and looked at Brendan across the body.

'It is John. And you have your wish, Brendan Donovan, for he is dead.'

An expression of horror came into his eyes, then he reached out and heaved John free of the clinging snow, until he held him across his knees. He felt for a pulse in John's wrist and under his ear, then pressed his own ear close to John's lips.

'He's cold as ice and deathly still, but his heart is beating faintly. Help me to rub him warm.'

So they knelt on either side of John and pummelled and rubbed his limbs and his chest until their arms ached and their hands throbbed.

'Stop your weeping, woman,' Brendan said brutally. 'You'll do him no good by that, nor yourself either.'

'And why should I not weep?' she shouted at him. 'My beloved is come home like a starving ghost and is like to die. Why should I not weep?'

'He will not die,' said Brendan between his teeth.

And at that moment, whether roused by their shouting or their efforts to warm him, John opened his eyes. His glance was unfocused and confused, and his lids dropped again over his eyes, but it gave them hope.

'We must get him across the horse,' said Brendan, 'so we can take him to the bothy. He cannot sit astride, we'll have to lay him across like a shot deer. Help me lift him.'

With some difficulty, stumbling around in the snow, they managed to lift John onto the horse, although they were so tired Anne thought for a moment that they would not have the strength to do it, wasted away though he was. He hung there, head dangling down on one side of the horse, legs on the other. Anne found the bundle where his head had rested.

'There's a blanket here.'

'Put it over him.' Brendan was taking off his cloak and spreading it over John.

'What good will it do if you freeze to death?' she asked.

'I shall keep warm enough walking.'

She unfastened her own cloak and tucked that around John.

Brendan opened his mouth to object, then closed it again.

As if the heavens had emptied their final burden of snow, the storm began to ease, although now night had crept up on them and it was growing dark. But Brendan swore he could see in the dark to find his way to the bothy. Anne placed more faith in the dog, who ran ahead and then back to them, certain of its way. At last the bothy showed as a more solid darkness against the darkening sky. As they approached, the dog began to yelp excitedly.

'What now?' said Brendan. 'Do you suppose those boys are here?'

It was the sheep, all twelve of them, huddled against the door of the bothy and watching their arrival with pathetic foolish eyes. Anne gave an incredulous laugh.

'So they came straight here. They must have been here all the time.'

And it came to her with a cold sense of shock, that if they had come here first, instead of going up the other side of the moor, they would never have found John. They lifted him down and carried him in to Brendan's straw mattress at the back of the bothy. The sheep tried to crowd in behind them, and Anne batted them away with her hands.

'Nay, let them come in,' said Brendan. 'It's small, but there's room enough for all. Their body heat will help to warm the place.'

There was a store of firewood beside the hearth, and he soon had a fire going, while Anne continued to rub John's frozen limbs. His flesh felt clammy and chill, like dead meat stored in the cold outhouse at Swinfen. Once Brendan was satisfied that the fire had caught, he helped her rub John, and he pummelled his chest, as if his beating hands could force the heart within to beat more strongly. The bothy began to heat up, and to smell strongly of wet, greasy sheep, and at last John moved again and groaned.

'Pass me my flask,' said Brendan.

Anne reached across to where he had left it warming by the fire and gave it to him. John's eyes opened again, and this time he looked directly at her.

'Anne? Is it you?'

She smiled at him, though she was near weeping again.

'You're home, dear heart, or nearly. You're safe now.'

'Lift him up,' said Brendan, so she slid her arm under John's shoulders and raised him to a sitting position. Brendan forced a little of the *uisge beatha* between John's lips. Like Anne, he coughed and choked, but then he drank again and seemed glad of it.

'I must go for help,' said Brendan. 'We need warm food for him to eat, and thick dry clothes for him to wear. Keep the fire as high as you can. If you can warm him through, I think he'll live. I've seen this happen with fishermen in Ireland. They may be pulled from the sea all but frozen to death, but if they can be warmed quickly enough, they recover.'

'Take the horse.'

'Aye, I shall be quicker then. Give him a sip of the *uisge beatha* from time to time, but not too much, not until he has eaten.'

'It would make him drunk as a lord,' said Anne merrily.

'I was thinking it might prove too much for the weakness of his heart,' he said dryly.

'I think you will find,' she said, 'that he has as stout a heart as any man living.'

Brendan Donovan stood looking down at them.

'Aye, I can see that. And I think his wife has a heart to match it.'

He ducked under the low lintel, and pushed the door closed. A moment later she heard him riding away.

'Who was that?' John asked, in a weak voice.

'That?' said Anne. 'That was my Irish shepherd.'

She built up the fire and the sheep settled down, huddled together in one corner of the bothy, not altogether trusting the strange creature on their shepherd's bed and watching Anne with their vacuous amber eyes. Despite the warmth of the fire, John continued to shiver. None of Brendan's bedding had been left here for the winter, so there was nothing to cover him with but the threadbare blanket and the two cloaks. Two cloaks! Anne realised that Brendan had ridden off without his. She comforted herself with the thought that he would soon be in Swinfen. John shivered again.

'Do you not feel warm at all?' she asked anxiously.

'I feel cold deep inside,' he said. 'And I'm so filthy and louse-ridden, I could not ask you to lie beside me.'

She gave a little cry.

'Oh, my beloved, my dearest one! I don't care how louse-ridden you are! What foolish talk!'

She lay down beside him on Brendan's rough, prickling mattress, and put her arms around him. He caressed her cheek, as he had always loved to do.

'*Heureux qui, comme Ulysse, a fait un beau voyage,*' he said. 'I thought I should never see you again.'

'And I,' she said. 'You had vanished into darkness.'

He laid his head on her breast and sighed.

'I am growing warm at last.'

They lay in silence, each warming the other.

'Do you remember,' said Anne, 'when we were children, we used to ride up here, to the bothy? It was strictly forbidden.'

'Aye. It was here I first kissed you. Very clumsily, as I recall. We must have been ten years old.'

'Eleven.'

'You slapped me.'

'Of course.' She gave one of those rich, warm laughs he had missed so much. 'Think what our parents would have done, had they known! I would have been beaten, for sure. And sent away again to my aunt in Kent.'

'I think I'm better skilled at it now.'

He kissed her long and soft. They were too tired for passion, but both craved kindness.

'When we are very old,' said Anne, 'old and bent and grey, I want you to bring me up here once more, that we may remember this.'

'I promise you that,' he said, kissing her again.

'Oh, John,' she said, burying her face in his matted hair, 'thank God it is over!'

'Over?' he said, smiling secretly. 'Oh, my love, it is only just beginning.'

461

Envoi

Samuel Pepys, Diary, 10 November, 1662

'By and by came in great Mr. Swinfen, the parliament-man.'

Historical Note

This Rough Ocean is a work of fiction, not of history, but it is based on the real experiences of John Swynfen (1613-1694) and Anne Swynfen (1613-90) during the period from December 1648 to February 1650. John was indeed imprisoned after Pride's Purge, because, as a Moderate, he believed in constitutional monarchy and the rights and power of Parliament, especially the elected Commons (although the electorate was then much smaller than it is now). However he was opposed to the killing of the king by the extremist republicans, which led to his falling-out with Cromwell and Ireton. Eventually he would go on to become one of the founders of what became the Whig (or Liberal) Party. During John's absence it fell to Anne, as to many women in the Civil War period, to run the family's large estates in Staffordshire. From the tone of their letters, it seems to have been a love match, and the marriage lasted for fifty-eight years, from the time when they were both nineteen until her death, four years before her husband.

There are many gaps in the historical record, but where the facts are known, I have retained them. For example, John's political allies are known, his parliamentary career is a matter of public record, the family lived at Thickbroome in their early married life and in St. Ann's Lane, Westminster, in the 1640s. Parish records for the period are chaotic, so that the dates when some of the Swynfens' children were born are conjectural. John's younger brother Richard was in trouble after the Restoration for his dissenting views, so I have used this to shape his character. John's eldest son Dick's happy-go-lucky nature is revealed in the letters he wrote home while a student at Oxford (usually asking for money). The tone and spelling of the letters in the text are based on actual surviving family letters

A quirk in the spelling of the family name: the place-name always seems to have been spelled 'Swinfen' and the family name usually has the 'i'. John in fact appears in his baptismal record as 'John Swinfen'. At some point in his adult life he took to spelling it 'Swynfen'. His wife was baptised 'Ann Brandreth', so on marriage she became 'Ann Swinfen', my exact namesake. However, her name also changed later to 'Anne'. Our shared name has always drawn me to her, together with her courage and her strong family feeling – she cared not only for her own large family but also for most of her grandchildren. One of the grandsons, Dr Samuel Swynfen, was godfather to Dr Samuel Johnson.

Another oddity: the strange practice of burning the moss off the orchard trees is actually recorded. Late in life, John was visited by a gentleman who was making a survey of the county of Staffordshire, and described this odd Swinfen custom to him. Was it a gentle leg-pull? His sense of humour was noted by Pepys amongst others.

Sadly, the original Swinfen Hall, where Anne and John lived, was pulled down when it was replaced by the present Georgian manor house in the mid-eighteenth century. This was designed and built by local builder Benjamin Wyatt of Blackbrook Farm by Weeford, founder of the distinguished dynasty of architects and artists. Swinfen Hall was their first major building.

The *Envoi* to this story is one of several mentions of John in Pepys's *Diary* (together with one reference to his eldest son). Pepys had reason to be grateful to John, for when Pepys was accused in Parliament of being a crypto-Catholic, it was John who came to his defence and had the accusation thrown out.

It was only one of many kindnesses to friends and colleagues, who sought his help and advice throughout his life. Based on what I have learned about them both, I felt compelled to write Anne and John's story.

The Author

Ann Swinfen spent her childhood partly in England and partly on the east coast of America. She was educated at Somerville College, Oxford, where she read Classics and Mathematics and married a fellow undergraduate, the historian David Swinfen. While bringing up their five children and studying for a postgraduate MSc in Mathematics and a BA and PhD in English Literature, she had a variety of jobs, including university lecturer, translator, freelance journalist and software designer. She served for nine years on the governing council of the Open University and for five years worked as a manager and editor in the technical author division of an international computer company, but gave up her full-time job to concentrate on her writing, while continuing part-time university teaching. In 1995 she founded Dundee Book Events, a voluntary organisation promoting books and authors to the general public.

Her first three novels, *The Anniversary*, *The Travellers*, and *A Running Tide*, all with a contemporary setting but also an historical resonance, were published by Random House, with translations into Dutch and German. *The Testament of Mariam* marks something of a departure. Set in the first century, it recounts, from an unusual perspective, one of the most famous and yet ambiguous stories in human history. At the same time it explores life under a foreign occupying force, in lands still torn by conflict to this day. Her second historical novel, *Flood*, is set in the fenlands of East Anglia during the seventeenth century, where the local people fought desperately to save their land from greedy and unscrupulous speculators.

Currently she is working on a late sixteenth century series, featuring a young Marrano physician who is recruited as a code-breaker and spy in Walsingham's secret service. The first book in the series is *The Secret World of Christoval Alvarez*, the second is *The Enterprise of England*, the third is *The Portuguese Affair* and the fourth is *Bartholomew Fair*.

This Rough Ocean is based on the real-life experiences of the Swinfen family during the 1640s, at the time of the English Civil War.

She now lives in Broughty Ferry, on the northeast coast of Scotland, with her husband, formerly vice-principal of the University of Dundee, a cocker spaniel, and a rescue kitten.

www.annswinfen.com

CPSIA information can be obtained
at www.ICGtesting.com
Printed in the USA
LVOW08s0014201217
560334LV00009B/667/P

9 780992 822897